THE AUTHOR

YVES BEAUCHEMIN was born in Noranda, Quebec, in 1941. After receiving his *licence ès lettres* in French and art history at the University of Montreal in 1965, he taught literature at the Collège Garneau and Laval University, then worked as an editor in a Montreal publishing firm while beginning to contribute essays and stories to magazines and newspapers. In 1969 he accepted a position as a researcher at Radio-Quebec.

Beauchemin's first novel, *The Bamboozled* (1974), won the Prix France-Québec, his second novel, *The Alley Cat* (1981), became the all-time best-selling novel in Quebec literature and has been translated into fifteen languages, and his third novel, *Juliette* (1989), won the Prix Jean Giono.

In his fiction Beauchemin is a detached but caring observer of the contemporary world around him. The panoramic canvases of his novels capture the teeming life of the streets, reflecting their author's appreciation of such great nineteenth-century writers as Balzac and Dickens, Dostoevsky and Gogol.

Yves Beauchemin resides in Longueuil, Quebec.

THE ALLEY CAT

YVES BEAUCHEMIN

TRANSLATED BY

SHEILA FISCHMAN

AFTERWORD BY

KENNETH RADU

The following dedication appeared in the original translated edition: *To Viviane*

This New Canadian Library edition 2008.

Library and Archives Canada Cataloguing in Publication

Beauchemin, Yves, 1941-
[Le matou. English]
The alley cat / Yves Beauchemin ; translated by Sheila Fischman ; with an afterword by Kenneth Radu.

(New Canadian library)
Translation of: Le matou.
Originally publ.: 1986.
ISBN 978-0-7710-9361-6

I. Fischman, Sheila II. Title. III. Title: Le matou. English. IV. Series.

PS8553.E172M3813 2008 C843.'54 C2008-900796-4

We acknowledge the financial support of the Government of Canada through the Book Publishing Industry Development Program and that of the Government of Ontario through the Ontario Media Development Corporation's Ontario Book Initiative. We further acknowledge the support of the Canada Council for the Arts and the Ontario Arts Council for our publishing program.

Typeset in Garamond by M&S, Toronto
Printed and bound in the United States of America

McClelland & Stewart Ltd.
75 Sherbourne Street
Toronto, Ontario
M5A 2P9
www.mcclelland.com/NCL

2 3 4 5 14 13 12 11

D'un coup de scalpel il ouvrit l'animal. – Vous voyez? murmura le docteur après avoir tripoté les viscères. Ce n'est qu'un matou.

– Oui, bien sûr. Du moins en apparence, répondit le patient avec un fin sourire.

– Alexeï Dangoulov, L'obus

Cependant, l'allocation familiale ne devient payable ou ne cesse de l'être qu'à compter du mois qui suit l'événement donnant droit à l'allocation ou y mettant fin.

Ainsi, le mois de la naissance de l'enfant n'est pas payable tandis que le mois de son décès est payable.

– Régie des rentes du Québec Service des allocations familiales Formule H-100

He sliced the animal open with a scalpel. "You see," the doctor murmured, after he had rummaged in the viscera, "it's just an alley cat."

"Of course," replied the patient, smiling shrewdly. "Outwardly, in any case."

– *Alexeï Dangoulov,* The Shell

The family allowance becomes payable, or ceases to be payable, only in the month following the event that grants or terminates eligibility.

Accordingly, the child's month of birth is not payable, while the month of his decease is payable.

– Quebec Pension Board, Department of Family Allowances, Form H-100

ONE

One April morning around eight o'clock, Médéric Duchêne was walking briskly past postal station "C" at the corner of Ste-Catherine and Plessis Streets when one of the bronze quotation marks from the inscription at the top of the old building fell onto his skull. There was a crack like an egg being broken against a dish, and Duchêne crumpled to the sidewalk, blinking oddly.

Florent Boissonneault, a young man of twenty-six with a twinkle in his eye, saw the accident. Without wasting a moment, he loosened the victim's belt, unbuttoned his collar, and ran to a phone to call the police. A gawking crowd was already pressing around the injured man, who was losing a great deal of blood. This didn't disturb him in the least, as it happens, for he was reliving a childhood fishing trip on the Assumption River.

Florent came back and tried to disperse the crowd. One man stood out. Old, tall and skinny, he wore a black frock coat, and his chin was shaped like a pair of buttocks. From the beginning he had been observing Florent with admiration.

"A young man who knows what to do and how to do without getting his shirt steamed up," he said aloud in an odd accent. "A national resource, indeed."

Florent, busy answering the policeman's questions, didn't hear the man. He left a few minutes later – his car was parked two blocks away – and soon he was at Musipop, the record distribution company where he'd been a salesman for three years.

"Late as usual," observed Mr. Spufferbug, raising his bald head, which reflected the neon lights in an unattractive glare.

Florent shrugged, winked at his colleague Slipskin, and performed the day's tasks with his usual gusto.

When he came to work the next morning, Mademoiselle Relique, Musipop's ancient secretary, handed him a beribboned package that reeked of musk. He tore it open, then stood there, speechless for a moment. A huge bronze M lay gleaming in a blue-velvet-lined box.

"What joker gave you this?" he asked the secretary.

"No joker, – it was the janitor," she replied dryly. "It came at seven this morning."

Two days later Florent received a second package, equally fragrant. This one contained an N.

"It's an old fellow with a goatee," Mademoiselle Relique told him disapprovingly. "First he laughed in the janitor's face, then he gave him a bottle of wine. I wouldn't taste it if the Blessed Virgin herself asked me to."

When the third package arrived, containing an O and a scrap of paper on which someone had scrawled: "Be patient, there's a message," the secretaries started chattering mysteriously. At this point Florent had to leave for a three-day trip to Lac Saint-Jean. When he returned, R, L and E were waiting in a stack on his desk, and Mademoiselle Relique was complaining that musk gave her migraines.

"What am I supposed to do with this alphabet soup?" Florent wondered.

"Sell it to an antique dealer," Slipskin suggested, then gave him the address of his father's store.

Two days passed. When his benefactor's generosity showed no signs of abating, Florent resolved to get to the bottom of things and take delivery of the next package himself. Rising at dawn, he waited at his desk with a cup of coffee.

At twenty past six, he heard a car stop in front of Musipop. Leaping from his chair, he ran to open the door and found himself face-to-face with a bedraggled cripple, his gaunt face hidden by a bushy beard, who stared at him dully, mouth agape.

"Monn . . . Monnsoor Boosonalt," he spluttered, holding out a package, as the car started up with a roar.

Florent peered at him briefly, then went back to his office. The cripple set the parcel on the floor and limped out into the middle of the street, turning his head this way and that, completely bewildered.

"Nothing to it!" said Elise, after looking at the bronze letters her husband had just brought home. "There aren't *that* many combinations: Nelson Room 330."

She gave him an amused look that reflected her modest satisfaction at having solved a simple problem. Florent was pacing the kitchen and chewing his nails.

"That's it! The Hotel Nelson, of course, on Place Jacques-Cartier. Room 330 – or 303."

He ruffled his hair and sighed heavily.

"Probably some old fag getting off on sending me hundred-dollar love letters. Bronze isn't cheap! And he won't leave me in peace till he gets a close-up of my fist."

"Cool it, Florent, he'll get tired eventually."

Len Slipskin disagreed when Florent told him, the next morning, of his discovery. Slipskin held that it's unnatural if a man doesn't grab a chance to earn a few easy bucks. Though he was timid because of a slight lisp, he cheerfully followed this maxim.

"I'll come along if you're afraid he'll give you a rough time."

Florent refused. It would have been cowardly not to turn up alone. The oddness of the situation had made him curiously giddy, as if he'd had too much coffee or hard rock.

And so, after lunch at La Blanche Ermine on St-Hubert Street, a *crêperie* he'd taken a shine to (for Florent was something of a gourmet, with highly elaborate theories on the fine art of dining), he got in his car and drove to the Hotel Nelson.

At this time of day the place was unusually quiet. Two employees were carrying metal tables out to the terrace for the customers who came there in fine weather. Despite his apprehension, Florent took in the warm atmosphere of the old hotel lobby, with its dark woodwork, soft lighting, and period photographs.

"Room 330?" said the desk clerk, a fat boy with a chubby face and yellow suspenders. "No such number."

"Three-oh-three, then."

On hearing this number, the clerk ran his hand through his hair, stunned, like a small-town first communicant dazzled by Grace.

"That's . . . that's Monsieur Ratablavasky's room. He never sees anyone. Is he . . . is he expecting you?"

Florent nodded. The clerk telephoned to check, then came back to the desk.

"Take the stairs at the back to the third floor, and turn left."

And he watched Florent move away as if by levitation.

With a heavy heart Florent began to climb the small white marble staircase that he'd used on many occasions before he was married – and twice since – when fate sent his way a pretty girl with an urge to know him better.

With its threadbare carpets, loose doorknobs, and old sofas scattered along the corridors, the Hotel Nelson had the untidy look of a family boardinghouse. The atmosphere was charming, free and easy – an invitation to folly, to love, to tiny betrayals.

When he was on the third floor, Florent went to room 303 and knocked twice.

"Come in," said a muffled voice.

Florent turned the knob and found himself in a large room filled with a golden half-light. The walls were covered with huge oil paintings, nineteenth-century bucolic scenes. Heavily carved tables, immense sideboards, massive armchairs covered in crimson velvet cluttered the huge room without overwhelming it. An elderly man in a black dressing gown and old slippers, holding a newspaper, slowly rose from an armchair and came to greet him.

"I know you think I'm a variety of lunatic," he launched in, not bothering to introduce himself, "but duty impels me to make you at your ease, so we can talk together comfortably, like two serious people, like – how do you say – good-willing men?"

Florent stared at him, dumbfounded.

"I'm not offering you to drink," the man added with a good-natured smile. "You'll be suspectful of drugs, isn't it? That's normal. Please be so good as to follow me."

Florent was rather pleasantly surprised. He'd been expecting a kind of elegant maniac. But before him stood a distinguished individual, apparently quite lucid despite his odd appearance. There was just one shocking detail: the unpleasant odor that seemed to emanate from his slippers.

Egon Ratablavasky had walked to the other end of the room. He pushed aside a drapery and showed his visitor into a sitting room as large as the first room, but much brighter. Huge pots of ferns stood everywhere, and the air was filled with a strong medicinal smell.

It must cost a fortune to live here, Florent thought. I didn't know they rented suites.

"Do let me apologize for the aroma," said the old man, offering Florent a chair from which he had removed several small pots filled with muddy earth, "but my darling plants require a special fertilizer that's somewhat . . . difficult on the nose."

Then he sat down, crossing his legs briskly and gracefully.

Florent found his accent quite amazing. He'd never before heard *r*'s rolled so strangely, sounding like a contented cat.

"I do thank you for coming," the other man continued, with a smile. "It proves you have imagination and that I've made no mistaking about you. So let me tell you without any more ado that I'm not a sexual bazaar (forgive my frankness!) or anything of that sort. And I suggest that you take a good deep breath. Go on now, breathe deeply, in spite of the smell from these plants. Trust will enter your veins along with the wondrous oxygen. I know. I'm not a young man and fate has graced my person with an appearance that is – how do you say – original. I have peculiar ideas about almost everything – but by St. Vladimir's Cross, I vomit on those that are an offense to honesty!"

"What do you want from me?" interrupted Florent, who loathed idle chitchat.

"I've brought you to this sitting room to give you some interesting news. Elsewhere, on the street, for example, you'd have considered me for a madman (oh yes!), a sort of old slipper in a way. You'd have laughed and gone on your way. But here, in my own surroundings, you might as well admit, you can see what I am. I have two other rooms like these," he went on, pointing to a door half hidden by a potted fern, "but that's the setting for my private life, if you allow. So you can see that I'm rich. I expect nothing from you – neither money, neither anything else. Only perhaps a little imagination. A spectacle of imagination."

"A spectacle of imagination?" Florent repeated.

His heart began to pound. A sort of pink sugary fog filled his head; he struggled vainly to dissipate it.

"I know you longer than you think," the old man continued with a smile. "In fact, I had the good fortune to meet an impulsive young man full of kind thoughts who didn't hesitate to make rescue of unfortunate pedestrian victim of post office."

"You were there?"

"And why not? I come, I go, I walk on two feet like every man. Also, I am knowing your plans. I can give you a connection, as you say in your modern language."

"What plans?"

"You like restaurants. You dream to own one. Isn't it?"

"How . . . did you know?" Florent stammered, flabbergasted. He glanced toward the door.

"Don't worry, I'm not a sorcerer. Sorcerers wear feathers on their heads, they concoct frightful brews, and always are making mistakes. I, however, wear hat, I like good food – and I rarely make mistakes. How do I do it? I have my sources who are very well informed, that's all."

Florent got to his feet. "What connection do you plan to plug me into?"

The old man smiled gleefully. His face was astonishing. The two little buttocks of his plump pink chin had a vaguely lecherous appearance that contrasted strangely with his very deep-set sooty eyes under bushy eyebrows, from which there issued an austere gaze as impersonal as a bronze inscription on a building. Egon Ratablavasky rose in turn and took Florent's arm with genial familiarity.

"Don't expect heaven and earth," he said. "In this life, opportunities are never as fine as we think. It's when they look good that you must be suspectful. They're only pretty mummies and some fine night they'll unwrap their – how do you say – Band Aids, they'll come up to you in your sleep and strangle you."

He's a total crackpot, Florent thought. And I had a two o'clock appointment at Bertrand . . .

As he spoke, Ratablavasky led his guest to a window looking down onto Place Jacques-Cartier. "Do you know a restaurant called The Beanery?" he asked softly.

"The one on Mont-Royal near St-Denis?"

"The very one. Well, it's for sale. For a song. You know the food there is excellent?"

"Of course. It's Québécois cuisine. The restaurant's a kind of neighborhood institution."

"Institution: that's the word! Thirty-six years of fine cuisine – now there's a priceless treasure no one can steal from you, isn't it? You have some savings – $11,780, if my memory is correct. . . ."

Florent looked up sharply.

"I know everything," the old man murmured, smiling wanly as he gazed absently down on Place Jacques-Cartier. "I love this country and I adore to learn what I can about it. My love feeds on information, though, not kisses. Very well, young friend: with a little capital and some goodwill, plus a smile from certain bankers – I can get you those smiles for the price of a chicken feather, as they say in my country – the restaurant is yours, if that's your pleasure. You'll take those thirty-six years of good cooking and gradually you'll increase them to thirty-seven, thirty-eight, thirty-nine, and so forth, as you please. Your wallet will grow a belly while you become a benefactor of humanity with feeding them delectable meals. What do you say to that, Monsieur Florent?"

"Why not buy it yourself if it's such a bargain?" he retorted suspiciously.

The old man's lips curved in an indulgent smile. He laid his hand on Florent's shoulder. "Come, come, I'm sure you didn't really mean that. Look at me: I sleep near my grave. Can you see me as such a galley slave? Up at five, in bed at two, not to mention fires in the oven, employees who steal, bloodsucking suppliers, inflation, and complaining customers? I'd be dead before I turned the slightest profit! Anyway, what do I need with profits? When you're my age, young friend, you'll know the only money that counts now is in St. Peter's till. I've been lucky enough to meet an impetuous young man, full of kind thoughts, who doesn't hesitate to bring rescue to pedestrian victim of the post office. . . . That day, before my eyes, chance opened the gates of your soul and I wanted to help you. Go, think it over," he said, showing Florent to the door. "I won't keep you any longer – you probably have much customers to call on. As for me, my siesta awaits. Don't delude yourself about my puny person," he added, after eyeing both ends of the corridor. "You're merely an instrument in my hands, which I'm using to make my own merits bear fruit before the All High." He grimaced. "I strongly urge you, go and see Monsieur Saint-Onge at The Beanery. He'll confirm what I've just said. Besides," he added with a honeyed smile, clutching Florent's sleeve, "you might well be thinking my brain is a little – how do you say – cracked. You have my permission. If it advantages you, why not take it?"

Florent slowly descended the stairs. He decided to have a beer in the bar, where he pondered what had just happened. Was he dreaming? Was his most cherished wish about to come true, as if by magic? To open a restaurant! To be done forever with the endless visits to record stores (handshakes, forced heartiness, feeble jokes, heavy lunches, bad coffee) and the stacks of orders he'd yawn his way through every night!

The waiter had no sooner served him than a short, fat, ruddy man came up to his table, smiling. "Captain Galarneau," he thundered. "Excuse my lack of ceremony, I'm a product of the army. May I sit?"

Florent studied him for a moment, shrugged imperceptibly and nodded.

"Same for me," the captain shouted to the waiter. "I won't take up much of your time – you're in a hurry. Me too, though I'm retired. Let me say right off that I know old Rat.

He told me about you. Yes, yes, news travels fast. This is the twentieth century after all, for cripes sake! Now then, listen to me and make the most of your chance. Egon's a bit gaga over the ladies – we all have our warts, haven't we? – but in his way he has a heart of gold. For months now he's been looking for a tough, ambitious fellow with real balls to give a nudge along the road to success and relive his own youth by proxy, as they say. He must have praised himself to the skies and what have you, but don't believe a bloody word he says. He'd kill the pope if he had to. No, Egon wishes he was still young; therefore, he needs a young man. Makes perfect sense, right? But don't expect big bucks from old Egon: he's as tight as the bark on a tree. On the other hand, he's got lots of connections. Doesn't cost him a penny to use them – and it pays off for you. Cheers, and good luck!"

With that he raised his beer, knocked it back, and for a moment his mouth seemed as wide as a river's.

On his way out of Bertrand's record store Florent called Elise to tell her about his adventure (she begged him to forget the whole thing) and back at Musipop he told Slipskin, who was fascinated. He bombarded Florent with questions, even asking about Ratablavasky's furniture. The intercom buzzed.

"Your father on line two," said Mademoiselle Relique, whose tone, exacerbated by the receiver, was as sharp as a staple.

"Hi," Florent began, "I'm buying a restaurant."

"Eh? What's that? What did you say?"

"You heard me, I'm buying a restaurant. The Beanery, on Mont-Royal."

"Are you serious? The Beanery? A fine spot, I grant you. I used to eat there during the war. But buy it? You can't be serious."

"I'll tell you all about it later. I'm in a bit of a rush. But listen, you know the business community – ever hear of a guy named Egon Ratablavasky?"

"Egon *who*? Hang on! Let me get a pencil, then say it again but slowly, son. I'll ask around," he added, after making a note. "Trust me – my nose is long and my arm goes on forever. Oh yes, before I forget – your mother wants to know if you're coming for Sunday dinner."

Florent made a face. "Uh – I don't know. I'll call you back." He hung up.

"Don't forget, you're leaving for Quebec City tomorrow morning at eight," Mademoiselle Relique nagged in her tiny, dry voice that sounded, this time, like the sand in an egg timer. She wore a mouse-gray coat and clutched a bus ticket in her black-gloved hand. "Sherman's are complaining they haven't seen you for two months. . . ."

"Old dustball," Florent muttered, watching her leave, while his friend Slipskin, a cigarette in his long freckled fingers, gazed upward, smiling dreamily.

Around six o'clock that evening, Gustave Saint-Onge, the owner of The Beanery, was feeling particularly offended at having to discuss something as momentous as the sale of his restaurant over the telephone and – even worse – with a kid who seemed still wet behind the ears.

He shook the dishwater from his left hand. "What I hear from your end, my friend," he said, "when certain subjects come up, is Chinese. Come over here if you want to talk. If not, a pox on you and bye-bye!"

"I seem to be collecting every weirdo in town," Florent grumbled, hanging up the phone.

"I can see what's coming," said Elise, "and I'm worried. Maybe they're weirdos, but you're playing right into their hands. I have a hunch you're about to blow all our savings. Even though," she added, pouting flirtatiously, "even though we promised to save them for somebody else."

And she passed her hand slowly in front of her belly, outlining an imaginary roundness. Florent seized her by the shoulders.

"Stop tormenting yourself, Mamma Squirrel. You'll have your nice-house-with-a-yard-and-trees-perfect-for-kids. Why do you think I want to make lots of money? For our twenty-three children!"

She shook her head, smiling scornfully. "Let's just start with one, lover boy."

"Hell!" Florent muttered as he left the house. "I didn't think it mattered that much to her. But when you stop and think, I suppose that's one of the reasons we went to the altar. After three years I guess nature's getting impatient."

And so, turning over these weighty thoughts, Florent walked the six blocks from his house to The Beanery.

It was a tiny place squeezed between two buildings that had left it only fifteen feet of frontage, forcing it to stretch like a railway car. A counter with stools ran almost its full length. At the back, on either side of a wash basin with a towel dispenser above it, they had managed to tuck in two booths. Behind them, in a small closed room, the cook carried out his activities. Every cubic inch had been judiciously used, after long reflection. The washrooms were in the basement: to get to them you had to walk behind the counter and down a stuffy staircase. Everything was spotless. The establishment had six employees divided into two teams, each working an eight-hour shift. There was room for only seventeen customers at a time, but they followed one another at a steady clip, for the restaurant was famous for its hearty country fare.

"So you're the lad who phoned me!" exclaimed a heavy, thick-set fellow in his sixties.

A broad inquisitive face appeared in the kitchen doorway. Gustave Saint-Onge curtly turned around and the face disappeared. He pointed to a stool.

"Pull up a seat so I can have a chat with the future restaurateur." Florent obeyed, disconcerted, for aside from a couple at the back murmuring sweet nothings over their beef stew, the place was uncharacteristically quite empty.

"Tea? Coffee? There's homemade apple pie fresh from the oven," Monsieur Saint-Onge offered, his sales pitch rather off-putting.

Without waiting for a response, he placed a wedge of pie in front of Florent. Its aroma seemed to justify his patter. The inquisitive face appeared again, then withdrew in a flash. The boss, though he was facing Florent, still had time to get a glimpse of him.

"Bertrand!" he barked. "Bring some forks, will you?"

A tall, lanky, limp-wristed man no longer in the first flower of youth approached them, a huge apron tied tightly around his waist. He looked so effeminate that Florent couldn't help smiling.

"Better thaw out the veal for tomorrow," he murmured to Saint-Onge, with a sidelong glance at Florent.

"Jimmy! You're right, I'd forgotten. Take out twenty pounds right away."

With his hands on his hips, he watched Florent eat. After a few mouthfuls, the young man pushed away his plate.

"Your pie would bring tears to my grandmother's eyes, Monsieur Saint-Onge, but I just had dinner and I'm ready to burst."

"I see. How about a cup of tea to ease the digestion?"

Florent didn't even have time to reply before the steam from the tea was rising to his face.

"Young fellow, you're a sight for sore eyes," Monsieur Saint-Onge began, running a rag over the counter. "Who sent you here?"

"Nobody."

The restaurant owner studied him, ran his hand across his upper lip, and said, "Okay, I might as well come clean, though you may think I change my mind with the breeze: to tell you the truth, I'm not interested in selling. Maybe in four or five years, but not now. Someone must be stringing you a line. As a matter of fact, you aren't the first one to show some interest. I get a kick out of seeing you all parade up to my front door, but my answer's the same. You're right – this place is a gold mine, so I'm hanging on to it."

Florent stared at the bald forehead that ended in a semicircle of gray hair far back on his skull. It was glistening with sweat now and seemed to be winking derisively.

"Disappointed, eh?" asked Monsieur Saint-Onge with a hint of commiseration in his voice.

"Well, a little. Especially after what Ratablavasky told me. You know him?"

At once, the expression on the coarse peasant face of Gustave Saint-Onge became respectful, almost fearful.

"Well, well. So Ratablavasky (he pronounced it Raltabasky) approached you. Why didn't you tell me right away? I don't like these little guessing games. . . . Of course that sheds a different light on things. He wouldn't send me just anybody. How old are you?"

"Twenty-six."

"Married?"

Florent nodded.

"That's good – as long as you don't run around. A married man that runs around is four times worse than a wild bachelor – take my word."

He pulled a handkerchief from his pocket and wiped his forehead.

"Of course the place is up for sale. Look at my face: it tells the whole story. I've had two heart attacks since June, which is quite enough for one year. Sell out or it'll kill you, the doctor told me. So I'm selling. But not to just anybody. I put thirty-six years of my life into this restaurant, and I don't want it turned into a greasy spoon the minute I'm out of the picture. A man's got his pride. But you understand that; otherwise you wouldn't be here. My mind's at rest on that score. Very well. Since I'm dealing with one of Raltabasky's protégés, I can afford to set easy terms, since money doesn't mean much to me anymore." Florent covered a smile with his hand. "I already wore myself out trying to put a few bucks together. You can have it for forty-five thousand – fifteen down, the balance in six months, at nine percent. How does that sound?"

"Hmmm – it's a lot of money. Do I have to let you know tonight?"

"Of course not. Ask around, take your time. I'm not worried: unless you're nuts you'll be back. But here, why not take a look at the merchandise?"

And he began to show Florent around the restaurant. Every corner was examined, the slightest flaw in construction or outfitting scrupulously pointed out. Florent tried to learn a little more about Ratablavasky, but Gustave Saint-Onge dodged his questions with an embarrassed look, and put an end to the conversation by showing Florent to the door after a second cup of tea.

What's happening to me? Florent wondered the next morning as he was driving to Quebec City. That guy's just given me the chance of a lifetime. Fifteen thousand cash, the balance in six months – plenty of time to negotiate a loan. The restaurant has a ready-made, steady clientele. It'll pay for itself and I'll be rich at thirty-five. Fantastic!

An hour later he parked outside the Fleur de Lys shopping center, and the energy he displayed when he walked into Sherman's record store doubled his sales. The little cashier was so bewitched by his enthusiasm that she went into the bathroom twice to touch up her makeup.

"Too bad you have to leave Quebec so soon," she said, smiling timidly as he was leaving.

He didn't follow through, however. Too many other thoughts were running through his mind, particularly supper with his friend Aurélien Picquot.

Picquot was a genuine character: now fifty-two, he'd come from France after the war, and he was currently in charge of the kitchens at the Château Frontenac Hotel. Florent had met him there two years earlier, during a convention. One night about eleven o'clock, long after hours, he'd turned up to find the dining room empty except for a man with energetic features accentuated by a long waxed mustache, black as the bowl of a pipe. A chef's hat sat on the table before him and he was quietly sipping a Pernod, obviously weary after the pandemonium of suppertime. When he saw Florent arriving so late he made a sardonic remark, to which the younger man replied in kind. And so it was through a polite exchange of insults that they came to size each other up, then to appreciate what they saw and finally to discover their shared passion for fine food and candor. Florent got dinner on the house that night, and the two men, despite the great difference in age, ended the evening together very agreeably at the hotel bar – still on the house.

"Do you come to Quebec every month?" the chef had asked in the small hours of the morning. "What would you say to our dining together when you're here? Unless, of course, you think I'm too old – or too odd."

Florent reassured him that neither was true, and thirty days later he kept their date. Since then, their monthly meal had become a ritual.

Several times, Florent had invited his friend to visit him in Montreal. Picquot shook his head. "Too much noise and grime! I'd rather stay here in the provinces."

"*Sacrebleu*! What's come over you?" Picquot exclaimed when a radiant Florent had taken his usual place opposite him at the table. "Have you found a Rembrandt in your basement?"

"Monsieur Picquot, I've some amazing news for you."

Sensing that their conversation was about to become confidential, the chef signalled to the waiter to keep a respectful distance. Florent recounted his adventure. Picquot pulled a face. "Bah! Peasants' fare. I thought your palate was more refined."

"It's as good as any. Besides, what you call peasant fare is all I can afford and, anyway, it'll be a challenge."

The chef tugged at his mustache, like a film version of a Saxon warrior. "Who fixes the grub?"

"I don't know."

"Ah, but you must find out, my friend, and *tout de suite*! Above all, you must know his plans. When a chef changes establishments he often takes the restaurant's prosperity with him. Even a humble scullion like myself: if I hung up my apron – and *entre nous* I've been thinking more and more about doing just that – well, take my word for it, profits would tumble!"

Florent promised to contact the cook at The Beanery as soon as he returned, to come to some arrangement with him, and also to find out what he could about Egon Ratablavasky, whose strange ways Monsieur Picquot found disturbing.

"It's probably a case of senility or inversion, or a bit of both. Nonetheless, you must always be wary of old fogeys: they're sometimes grade-A scoundrels in disguise."

It was late at night when they parted, their stomachs sumptuously awash in Prince de Polignac.

"Now don't forget. Call me within forty-eight hours," the chef said imperiously. "I want to keep a close eye on developments. It's not worth the trouble to encourage friendships if fate makes mincemeat of them as soon as one's back is turned."

Florent was leaving the hotel when one of the waiters clutched his sleeve and requested a few minutes of private conversation.

"You seem to be the only person my boss will listen to. We all like him, despite his, well, colorful personality, because, as you must know yourself, he's goodness personified. But I won't deny that he's made the past two months a nightmare here."

He had lowered his voice until it blended into the general murmur of the lobby. Florent had to lean so close that he grazed the young man's cheek, to the horror of an old American woman who was sitting in an easy chair to rest her swollen legs.

"I'm sorry to drag you into this painful business," whispered the waiter, "but I sense that Monsieur Picquot's been having personal problems, and it's affecting his mood and hampering his work. Just let me give you one example: today, among other dishes, we had on the menu a *filet de boeuf Richelieu* and a *chartreuse de perdreaux*. He showed up this morning, looking haggard, took the menu, glanced at it, then announced, 'No, definitely not, my mind's not on *filet* this morning. Or on a *chartreuse*. Especially not a *chartreuse*. Cross them off and replace them with an omelet.' It's the same thing almost every day. One time it's *caneton aux navets*, another it's *fricadelles de veau Smitane*, or the *tarte Bourdaloue* – and don't even think about a substitution! He'll fly into a terrible rage and he's quite capable of emptying a saucepan in your face. 'My reputation rests on this menu,' he'll say. 'And no one's going to tamper with it.' I'm telling you all this in confidence, so you can help him. I won't try to pretend that the management isn't well aware of all his good points, but they're getting fed up with these moods of his."

Then with profuse apologies for keeping Florent so long, the waiter wished him good night and left. Florent briefly considered going back to his old friend for more details, but decided that the time wasn't right. He got in his car and was back home on Marquette Street in the middle of the night. Elise had long been asleep. An unsealed envelope was waiting on the kitchen table. It contained a black-bordered card with a few words of thanks, from the widow of Médéric Duchêne.

TWO

When he got up next morning Florent had a spirited discussion with his wife. Elise was against his taking any steps toward purchasing The Beanery until he knew exactly why Ratablavasky wanted to let him in on such a fantastic deal.

"I'm telling you, he's just an old weirdo that got religion," insisted Florent. "There has to be a priest involved, dredging up old sins to scare him. Happens all the time. Anyway, I'm keeping my eyes open. I'm old enough to look out for myself, for Pete's sake!"

Still, Elise managed to extract a promise that he wouldn't make any decision before she'd met Ratablavasky herself. His very name terrified her. It made her think of a round ball bristling with pointed teeth. Florent was setting out for The Beanery, to meet the cook, when the doorbell rang.

"Greetings, gang," came a familiar voice.

Shuffling footsteps could be heard in the corridor, then a young man wearing jeans, a checked shirt, a leather jacket, and a nonchalant expression appeared.

"Where've you been hiding?" Florent asked in surprise. "We haven't seen you for months."

Ange-Albert smiled, flopped into a chair and stretched out his legs. He was an old school friend, nicknamed "Mattress" because of his fondness for sleep and the pleasures to be found between the sheets. Florent was about to repeat his question when the telephone rang. He went to answer it.

"Can't find out much about your Rata-whatever," Florent's father began. "One chap tells me he's just arrived, the next one says he's been around for twenty years. Anyway, he's rich and, so far at least, I haven't heard anything bad about him. Have you decided to buy the restaurant? Yes? Terrific! What about the bank loan? Oh, you've got company? Sorry. Right, call me back. Bye." He hung up. "Damn cabbage head," he muttered as his secretary looked on, bewildered. "I forgot to ask if he was coming for Sunday dinner!"

Ange-Albert had always been exceptionally straightforward with his friends. This quality, along with his unfailing good humor and phenomenal skill with the dice, constituted the bulk of his virtues. If he once possessed others, they'd dissolved in laziness. Oddly enough, though, no one seemed inclined to hold this against him. On the contrary: he attracted kind words and deeds the way a cat attracts caresses, a fact that struck him as quite normal. He worked six months of the year and was constantly changing jobs. His employers, unimpressed by his inertia but won over by his sweet nature, generally paid him off for two weeks' work after just a week on the job, and in a big city like Montreal he could live without too many financial concerns. He was much too bright to scrounge, and no one ever saw him borrow. Thus he spared his friends, who showed their gratitude by making life as pleasant for him as possible.

As it happens, Ange-Albert had just quit his job as a gas station attendant, after a two-week trial.

"The hours were too long," he sighed. "And the boss's wife was always on the make. Her husband nearly caught us a hundred times. I could smell trouble, so I split. Now we can get together whenever I want and the husband's out of the picture."

Florent looked at his watch, grimaced slightly and stood up.

"Listen, I'm glad as hell to see you again, but I have to run – I've got an appointment. Stay for supper. Something fantastic just happened. Elise'll tell you all about it."

Fifteen minutes later Florent walked into The Beanery. Gustave Saint-Onge was out, but he met the cook, a short, skinny, taciturn, potato-faced man who told him, without beating around the bush, that he knew exactly what was going on. He'd work for Florent if he was given a raise.

"How much?"

"Hadn't thought about that yet. Let you know tomorrow," he said, turning around so he could finish a huge shepherd's pie. Florent shrugged and left the restaurant.

"Only thing left now's the bank loan."

He decided to phone Ratablavasky and ask his advice. He reminded him of the offer he'd made two days earlier.

"My dear Monsieur Florent, good day to you," the muffled, singsong voice greeted him. "I was just sitting by one of my glorious ferns and wondering about you. Now let me guess for why you call: for money, isn't it? Ah! If only I had enough I'd give you some from my heart's bottom. But alas, you must go see a banker. I recommend the Royal Bank of Canada. Such a respectable name: their managers are sure to be cultivated men who would be sympathetic of your problems."

He went on in this vein for a while, then apologized and hung up. Florent hadn't said three words.

Is he a smartass? Or just plain nuts? Florent wondered. I can't figure him out . . . but I've got a hunch my plans aren't going far. . . .

The owner of the cigar store where he'd placed his call was watching him, intrigued. Florent left and walked along Mont-Royal, chewing his lips. Suddenly, across the street, at the corner of Papineau, he spotted the neo-classical facade of a branch of the Royal Bank.

"Hell," he muttered, "what can I lose?"

At the risk of being flattened by a line of trucks that were carting away the debris from a building being demolished, he ran across the street and into the bank. He had to wait for twenty minutes.

"Spufferbug's going to bitch," he thought. "But if this comes together, wow! He'll freak out when he hears the news."

"Monsieur Boissonneault?" cooed a curly-headed secretary (who sounded as if her voice wore ringlets, too).

Florent entered the office of Albert-N. Paquette, branch manager for twenty-eight years and three months, commander of the Knights of Columbus, churchwarden in the parish of Saint-Pierre-Claver, and a subscriber to the Montreal *Gazette* since August 1932. The interview got off to a very bad start. Florent didn't have a duly signed copy of the offer to purchase. His wallet, which contained all his papers, was in his car. In addition, from the look on Albert-N. Paquette's face, it would appear that his client possessed none of the facial characteristics of the good borrower, the chief one being that the sight of said borrower ought to arouse in Albert-N. Paquette thoughts both agreeable and optimistic.

"Where do you live?" he snarled.

"At 4830 Marquette."

"How long?"

"Fourteen months."

"Hmmm – that's not long. You rent?"

Florent nodded. Albert-N. Paquette couldn't suppress a discouraged pout. His pen scratched the paper at the same speed, but, it seemed, with less vigor. Florent wriggled his toes in his sweat-soaked socks.

"Married?"

"Uh-huh."

"What parish?"

"Civil ceremony."

Albert-N. Paquette struggled to hold back a sarcastic remark, sighed, and applied all the weight of his bad mood to the tip of his pen, which bent disturbingly. Now its scratching almost covered the chattering of the secretaries at their desks on the other side of the partition.

"Do you have any children?" the manager asked, in the same tone as if he'd been asking, "Have you paid all your debts?"

Florent shook his head. Albert-N. Paquette assumed an Olympian expression, spread his fingers, brought his hands together and slowly tipped back his chair.

"My dear friend," he said in a weighty, almost funereal tone, "you've no doubt read in the papers – if you read them at all – that our society is presently undergoing a period of great economic unrest."

That's it, Florent thought. I'm screwed. Okay, you old poop, let's get on with it!

"Inflation is wreaking havoc. The dollar's worth fifty-nine cents, and at the rate things are going we'll soon be using paper money to insulate our houses. Why all this inflation?

Because people are spending too much. They think only about enjoying themselves. Our parents, *your* parents, most likely, stayed at home, because someone had to bring up the children, correct? But now, *phfft*! No more kids! They've been replaced by pills. Result: demand exceeds supply, the dollar's tumbling and *so is the country's economic health*!" His index finger stabbed the air to punctuate his remarks.

Disgusted, Florent got to his feet. Albert-N. Paquette stopped, smarting a bit because his speech had been interrupted just as he was about to take flight. "I see you're in a hurry," Paquette said, "I won't keep you any longer."

But then a mischievous gleam lit up his eyes, which he screwed up nastily. "By the way, just for my records: Do you have any references at least?"

"I sure do," Florent replied, beginning to enjoy himself.

"So. A friend, I assume?"

"A very close friend. A man with a lot more money than you and me: Egon Ratablavasky. Recognize the name?"

Albert-N. Paquette's pen stopped dead above the paper and a wave of astonishment crossed his faded features, washing away the half smiles, mocking winks and disdainful pouts that had been their principal ornaments since the interview began. "I see. Egon Ratablavasky is a friend of yours. How much did you want to borrow?" he asked in a faint, submissive voice.

Two hours later, Spufferbug nearly had an attack. "For God's sake, Bwassanoo!" he exclaimed as he saw Florent come in. "What's going on here? Do you know what time it is? We've been waiting for you for hours! What do you think this is – a convalescent home?"

Florent silenced him with a gesture. "I'm leaving," he announced.

"What?"

"I'm clearing out. Find yourself another nigger."

"You mean you're . . ."

"I mean that ten minutes from now my office'll be as empty as the inside of your shiny skull. I'm leaving and on my terms. It's my turn to have people working for me. You like money? Me, too."

"Shut up and get out!" exclaimed Mademoiselle Relique, rushing toward her boss with a glass of water.

Florent shrugged and withdrew into his office. Slipskin found him clearing out his desk drawers. "What's going on?" he asked, smiling. "You hit your head, or what?"

"Me? I just got rid of a small surplus of bile, that's all."

"I haven't seen anything like it for years. Better not hang around: I wouldn't put it past him to hold back your vacation pay. . . . So it's on, the restaurant?"

"You said it. We sign the deed of sale day after tomorrow."

Slipskin's expression betrayed his frustration. "What about the money?"

"It'll be tight, but I'll manage. The bank's lending me $25,000 and I've got savings."

He walked past his former boss's office without so much as a glance. He felt like bursting into joyous song. The lemon-yellow color of his Pinto affected him like fireworks. He was about to start up when Slipskin ran outside, carrying a box and gesturing to him to wait. "The box is empty," he said breathlessly. "It's only an excuse. I wanted to say, if you need a partner . . . I've got some money in the bank, too. The more people in a business, the less the risk, right?"

Florent thanked him and promised to call that night, but he was only being polite.

Elise opened the door, a finger to her lips. "Quiet – he's asleep in the living room. I thought he'd burst at lunchtime: he packed away a *tourtière* and a half!"

"You'll be seeing plenty more *tourtières*, my friend: in two days the restaurant is ours!"

They shut themselves away in the kitchen, and Florent told her of the day's events. Elise listened, skeptical. "You don't waste any time," she sighed. "But where's it all going to end?"

She sat down, picked up a small glass jar and mechanically began filling it with dried grapefruit seeds. In one of the cupboards there was a row of similar jars, labeled Orange, Apple, Watermelon, Lemon, and so forth. Florent told her what his father had reported. She was somewhat reassured. "You're probably right." She sighed. "I'm the one who's afraid of thinking big."

He was so delighted with this confession that he decided to take Slipskin up on his offer, so as to share the risks. Then Ange-Albert appeared, cutting short their discussion.

"Hmmm!" he said, when Florent had described the happy turn of events. "Wonder what the chances might be of some little job for me."

"For you? I'll see. . . . Have to get back to work myself first, though," he said with a smile.

Then, to crown the day, he invited his wife and Ange-Albert to Old Montreal to celebrate their good luck. They did so joyously, coming home in the small hours of the morning, as happy as a convention of traveling salesmen.

About three o'clock, Florent, with his eyes shut and a smile on his lips, was drifting gently in a rosy haze of Vouvray, when a bell started ringing in the distance. It came closer and closer and then started assailing his eardrums. He found himself suddenly high in a steeple, lying under a great bell that swayed back and forth, making a tremendous racket. He groaned and opened his eyes. The telephone was shrilling in the dining room. He grabbed the receiver, dropped it twice, then finally managed to find his right ear. Slipskin was at the other end, in a state of excitement that turned his normal lisp into incomprehensible babbling. Eventually, Florent grasped that the other man had been waiting to hear from him all night.

"Well, I . . . I must have gone out," Florent stammered. "Tomorrow. . . . Come see me at The Beanery tomorrow . . . around eleven. Right." He hung up and grumbled, "What's got into him? Talk about ants in your pants . . ."

He dragged himself back to bed, yawning, and soon he was being carried away by the sumptuous party being held in his honor in a strange place that resembled both the château at Versailles and a McDonald's.

THREE

Smiling, Ratablavasky moved toward Florent and clasped him in his arms for a long time, while the younger man held his nose in disgust at the fetid odor that seemed to emanate from his benefactor's feet. "That bottle," the old man crooned, "proved that your heart contains not only blood, but splendid sentiments, as well."

"It's nothing," Florent murmured, feeling queasy. "You've been so generous to me that . . ." (Phew, he thought, I'm going to suffocate.)

"No, no, no!" he protested. "Don't belittle your kind act, which comes from a noble soul and nowhere else."

He released Florent, stepped back, and picked up the bottle. "You should know that for a lonely old man, cognac is like a flame in a cold fireplace."

"Listen to him with his lonely!" Captain Galarneau sniggered, nimbly picking up the bottle. "He talks as if I'm an old mattress or a motel ashtray. Jimbobbaree! Baron Otard *fine champagne*! You weren't raised on pig piss, my friend! I'd paint the Jacques-Cartier Bridge free of charge if somebody guaranteed me a lifetime supply of this little brew. Shall we sample it?" he asked, drawing the cork. Ratablavasky watched him with an indulgent smile, then left the room and came back with three snifters.

"Well, now," said Captain Galarneau, who was squirming in expectation. "At the risk of being considered a bumpkin, I take mine with ice. That's my law!"

He picked up the telephone and ordered ice and cigarettes. They sat around the table, and Galarneau started to pour. "Come, come, my friend," Ratablavasky protested. "Do you think we're getting ready to climb the North Pole by foot?"

Florent gazed at his glass in disbelief. It was full to the brim. Shreds of winy vapors were beginning to swim about in his stomach, already upset by the previous night's excesses, and he felt as if his eyes were sinking into their sockets.

"Stop complaining," Galarneau replied, raising his glass to peer at it. "This will slide down your throat smooth as baby Jesus's velvet pants. My goodness me!" he exclaimed, slowly turning the glass. "Look at that color! First time I tasted this little brew was in Marseilles, at the back of an old garage. I sang my lungs out for an hour while the Germans raised hell all around us. Bring on the ice!"

There was a knock at the door. "Come in," Ratablavasky warbled. "Ah! So happy to see you, Mademoiselle Rachel!" he exclaimed, rising with somewhat foolish gallantry. "Come in and have a drink with us, like friends."

A buxom young chambermaid entered the room, carrying a dish of ice. Florent was struck by her coquettish pink flesh, as graceful as a little parasol. "Oh, Monsieur Ratablavasky," she smiled and cooed, "I don't think I have time."

"Bah! Everything will be made up when the times are right," said Ratablavasky, guiding her to a chair with one hand behind her back. She complied with good grace. "Mademoiselle, let me introduce my most delightful friend, Monsieur Florent."

She held out her hand. "Pleased to meet you," she said gaily. "A drop, Captain, just a drop."

"Your health, mademoiselle!" Galarneau proclaimed, staring at his glass, which he had been gazing at for a moment now, with an almost desperate avidity.

He opened his mouth, shut his eyes, smacked his lips. All the muscles in his face relaxed, and a deep sigh escaped from his chest as the cognac made its fiery way down his throat.

"I didn't know you had a protégé, Monsieur Ratablavasky," Rachel said, glancing at Florent.

"I've been looking for one since months, mademoiselle, and now at last I find him."

"Monsieur Ratablavasky's like a father to me," Florent added, for something to say.

If the truth be known, he couldn't stop staring at the chambermaid. She had huge sparkling eyes, a mouth both wide and delicate and sharply drawn, teeth that were somewhat large and very white and perfectly placed, cheeks that were chubby without being fat. Everything about her suggested utter frivolity, nonchalance, an appetite for pleasure, a sort of animal abandon. You could tell she'd be comfortable anywhere, with anyone, in any situation. She was a girl who would scare off bad luck.

"Monsieur Ratablavasky," she began, looking admiringly at the old man, "is the nicest person in the world."

"Quite right!" yelped Captain Galarneau, who had just refilled his glass. "And if anyone denies it, I'll punch his face."

"I don't have the smallest merit," said Ratablavasky softly, putting his hand on Florent's shoulder. "It's this young man who has them all. Or, if you'll allow me, my only merit is to discover him. You'll see, mademoiselle, what a good restaurant he'll make."

"You've just bought a restaurant?" the chambermaid asked, delighted.

Captain Galarneau barked a satanic laugh, then, at a sign from Ratablavasky, stopped abruptly.

Florent chose his words carefully: the combined powers of the chambermaid's looks and the Baron Otard were taking their toll.

"What's your name?" he asked in a parched voice.

"Rachel Gourdin. Funny name, isn't it? Captain," she said, reaching out her arm, "I think you're drinking too much."

And she took his glass, which he'd just filled for the third time.

"I say . . . let me be," he stammered, waving his arms jerkily. His face was very red and his eyes were rather wild. Ratablavasky rose and gripped his shoulders.

"See here, my alcoholic friend," he said energetically, but with compassion, "a man your age should never fall into such ugly excess. You'll come with me and participate of some outdoor air."

They left the room. Florent turned his glass in his hand, staring at the table. He felt something like little electric shocks in his stomach and below. His penis had become intolerably sensitive. Sitting beside him, Rachel sipped her cognac and smiled. He looked up and was distressed to realize that he was absolutely incapable of sustaining a conversation. His head was filled with a confused buzzing and he felt barbarically drunk – uncontrollable impulses and all. "I like you," he said suddenly, letting the back of his hand glide onto Rachel's thigh; at the same time, his words and his deed filled him with boundless amazement. She laughed, as if he'd just told a good joke.

"I don't come here often," she said casually, "but I think the bedroom's next door."

Florent reacted as naturally and unconcerned as if he were enjoying some preposterous dream. He rose, embraced her tenderly, whispered something in her ear that made them both burst out laughing, then began kissing her ardently.

Ratablavasky and Captain Galarneau still weren't back when they left the apartment an hour later. "Twenty to twelve!" Rachel exclaimed with comic horror. "And my rooms aren't made up yet." She started to laugh. "The boss'll chew me out again. You're not bad yourself – take care now!"

She kissed him, then fled down the corridor. The old yoyo's done me too many favors, Florent thought on his way downstairs. I shouldn't have used his bed. What a bastard I am! Elise ought to throw me out.

And struggling against the blues that assailed him after each of his (rare) infidelities, he rushed off to The Beanery where Slipskin had probably been waiting for some time. "Holy mackerel!" he exclaimed, as Florent entered the restaurant. "Boissonneault, you'll be the death of me!"

He got up, clenching his fingers impatiently, and dragged Florent into the street. They collided with gawkers drawn by the sight of a crane that was smashing an old office building, which was gradually crumbling amid clouds of dust. "Your wife says you want me to come in on the business?"

Florent nodded. Slipskin looked at his watch. "Twelve-fifteen . . . Saint-Onge'll be here in an hour. We have time for a talk."

It was settled in twenty minutes flat. They decided to incorporate and buy shares in the restaurant. Slipskin would invest five thousand dollars, Florent twelve. Profits would be split accordingly, as would the proceeds if they sold the restaurant. Florent, who wanted to retain control of the business, insisted on taking out the loan himself. Slipskin would look after the books, while keeping his job at Musipop. Any administrative decisions would be made jointly. Florent advised his associate of his concerns about Berval, the cook at The Beanery. "If you ask me," said Slipskin, "we'll have to hire someone else. He's just trying to take advantage of the situation to get a raise."

They went back to The Beanery and discovered that their fears were justified. "What can I do?" asked Monsieur Saint-Onge, who had slicked down his hair for the occasion and sprinkled cologne on his handkerchief. "My cook isn't part of the equipment, he's a human being! I can't regulate him like my ovens. Once I'm out of the picture, it'll be up to you to make him toe the line."

"I have to think about my old age," the chef defended himself. "I'm no spring chicken, you know, and I haven't got the Queen of England for a cousin. . . . It's fifteen hundred a month plus my three meals, otherwise I go back to the logging camps. The pay may not be any better, but at least I'll be able to go hunting."

This scene was taking place in the cellar, amid bags of beans and potatoes. For this delicate discussion, Monsieur Saint-Onge had been sensitive enough to choose a discreet spot so as not to corrupt the rest of his employees, thereby jeopardizing the sale of The Beanery. At a sign from Slipskin, Florent decided to accept the cook's terms. Old jerk-off! The unspoken epithet was directed at Berval. Better enjoy it while it lasts. Your reign's nearly over.

They parted company after making an appointment with the notary for the afternoon two days later.

"Better start looking for another cook pronto."

"Don't worry," Florent replied, "I'll take care of that. A friend of mine can give me a bunch of names."

He gestured for Slipskin to wait for him and slipped into a phone booth. An operator at the Château Frontenac informed him that Aurélien Picquot had just quit his job. "What's that? When?"

"Yesterday. He's resting now."

"Resting? Is he sick?"

"I don't know. Do you want to talk to the head of personnel?"

The bureaucrat in question, who sounded as if he'd just slammed a drawer on his finger, snapped that personnel files were confidential, even after the employees had left. Florent said something appropriately rude and dialed Picquot's home number. The service had been suspended that very day. "I'm going to Quebec," he told Slipskin, sticking his head out of the phone booth. "I've just hit a snag."

He called his wife. "We don't see much of each other these days," she remarked. Then she lowered her voice and added, "And Ange-Albert's starting to get underfoot. Couldn't you take him along?"

Ange-Albert didn't need persuading; he even canceled his daily crap game. "I used to have a girlfriend in Quebec – worked for a guy that made calendars. We spent a nice winter together back in 1969. She might not mind seeing me again . . . even though I sort of ran out on her."

The road was wide and the driving was easy, and the countryside was vast, gray and monotonous, with a scattering of roadside restaurants famous for their lousy food. They began to philosophize, each in his own way. "What have you got in mind for yourself?" Florent asked his friend. "Here you are, twenty-six and no prospects. Doesn't that make you feel kind of empty?"

Ange-Albert listened, smiling, as he slumped in his seat, his head thrown back. "I've got all kinds of irons in the fire and I like it that way. It's all I want; in fact I'm kind of sorry for guys like you that go looking for trouble."

In six years this gallant lad had seen a good deal of action. He'd been a veterinarian's assistant in a small clinic in Rosemont. He'd sold beauty products door to door. With his pleasant smile, gentle manners, good looks and infallible intuition for amorous opportunities, he was a born charmer who'd been known to spend long hours with his customers. Next, he went to the North Shore, where he lived by his wits for three years, sometimes logging, sometimes working as a store clerk or truck driver, but most often as a "special guest" in hotels or boardinghouses, where he consoled passionate widows, insomniac old maids or disappointed wives – or simply lent the owner a sympathetic ear. He finally tired of small-town life and returned to Montreal, where the string of baroque jobs and short-lived liaisons had continued, while the weeks, months and years slipped by in silence.

"I can't understand why you work so hard," he told Florent. "After all, everybody ends up the same way: sitting in a little room, half deaf and blind, clutching a handful of pills and a hot-water bottle. So why waste your breath? I guess you're just made that way."

A long discussion followed. By the time they were crossing the bridge to Quebec they'd made such progress in their elaboration of the formula for perfect happiness that Florent was nearly flattened by a two-ton truck. "Where shall I drop you?" he asked his companion, his heart in his mouth.

"What do you mean? Aren't we having supper together?"

"No, I've got a date."

Florent left Ange-Albert at the Café Buade and five minutes later walked into the kitchen of the Château Frontenac. "Monsieur!" he was greeted by the tearful voice of the waiter he'd talked with in the lobby two days earlier.

Abandoning his duties, he took Florent aside and gazed at him sorrowfully.

"It's too late now. The evil's been done. Yesterday morning Monsieur Picquot arrived in a worse state than ever. He wanted to make nothing but *boeuf bourguignon* and omelets. Can you imagine! Omelets and *boeuf bourguignon*! The director came, they had a row . . . and suddenly Monsieur Picquot lost his head to the point that . . . to the point that" – the waiter looked away, and his eyes filled with tears – "that he threw a cup of melted butter right in the director's face."

"He melted his brains along with the butter! Where is he now?"

"At home. And he's going back to France."

The waiter tried to add something else, but his voice cracked like an ice cube. He raised his immaculate sleeve to wipe a small flood from his left eye, then finally managed to murmur, "Ah monsieur, what a man . . . ! What a man we're losing! He had such a way with snipe in aspic. . . ."

Florent became angry. "Enough! Let's see what's going on here!"

Ten minutes later he parked outside Picquot's apartment on Ste-Ursule Street and punched the doorbell with a martial thumb. Several moments passed. Nothing. He rang again, then began to gaze at the old olive-green door decorated with molding and small flower-shaped ornaments. Suddenly he had an ominous thought. "Oh no! What if he's . . ."

He ran at the door, pushed it with his shoulder, and it opened. A long hallway with dark wood paneling suddenly appeared before him. He sped along to the kitchen.

Aurélien Picquot was sitting in the middle of the room, leaning on a table that held two cases of beer – one of them nearly empty. "Hello, sonny," he said sorrowfully, showing no surprise at Florent's presence.

In the gray light that poured from the dirty window he looked like an old conquered general, watching his flags burn. "For the love of holy heaven!" Florent exclaimed. "What's got into you?"

"A brainstorm, you might say. A stupid brainstorm," Picquot murmured, despondent. "But I regret nothing. That bumpkin deserved a lesson."

"As far as that's concerned you can rest easy. But I didn't come here to criticize you. I . . ."

"Oh yes. Oh yes, you have. The whole world is reproaching me. I reproach myself, night and day. It's as if I have the Three Pyramids on my back."

Florent came over and put a hand on his shoulder. "What is it, Monsieur Picquot? I don't want to stick my nose in your private life but, after all, I'm your friend. Wouldn't you feel better if . . ."

"No, no. Later. I can't say anything. Trifles, mere trifles."

"Trifles? If you're throwing melted butter at people for mere trifles, I'd better start watching my step. . . . Aren't you being just a wee bit impulsive?"

"Poor child! You didn't know me in my youth! The years have thickened my blood. I'm far less hotheaded than I used to be. My wife left in '41. Shall I tell you the circumstances? I won't mince words: two days before Christmas I'd thrown myself on her, wanting to make love, even though she had a terrible toothache. When it was over, she got up and put on a dressing gown, a taxi came to fetch her, and I haven't seen her since."

Florent peered at his friend shrewdly. "Tell me now, could it be amatory problems that have been tearing your guts out for the past two months?"

"YES!" Picquot howled, pounding the table with his fist. "AND I FORBID YOU TO TALK ABOUT IT! I'm sorry," he went on, more gently, "love has puréed my senses. And as it happens, I'm quite pleased. I've been rescued. I was utterly fed up, you see. Why break your back over a pheasant Souvaroff that some boor from Connecticut will wash down with 7-Up? Talk about pearls before swine. . . . That's why I'm sick and tired of haute cuisine. I'm through with it. Nowadays all you see are lovers of packaged soup. In twenty years there'll be no one left on the earth but vulgar Yankees."

"And you're leaving Quebec? You're going back to France after thirty years? I don't believe that for a minute. This is your country now."

Aurélien Picquot remained silent. He ground a cigarette butt with his toe. Dozens of other butts were strewn on the floor.

"Listen," Florent began, "here's a suggestion. No, let me finish. And for the love of Brillat-Savarin, promise you'll control yourself! What would you say . . . What would you say about coming to work in my restaurant?"

Picquot heaved a long sigh and ran his hand over his face. His faded eyes were like globules of gelatin, and the

Molson's beer had made his cheeks resemble withered tomatoes. "*Hélas*, it's true, I've become quite accustomed to Quebec," he sighed, pointing to the two cases of beer. "And to crown it all," he added in a broken voice, "I don't feel I have the strength to leave."

He jerked his head up. The gelatin globules began to spit fire. "Listen, leave me alone – my head's splitting. I need time, do you understand? I'll give you my answer in two or three weeks, if you still need someone then."

Florent was about to ask if he could suggest anyone else, but his courage failed him. He got up, shook his friend's hand and stammered something between "I'm terribly sorry" and "Hope you're feeling better soon," then left the apartment.

He had arranged to meet Ange-Albert at two o'clock, at a restaurant called Aux Anciens Canadiens. At three-fifteen, having patiently ingested two beers, a cucumber salad and a dish of meatball stew, Florent saw his friend arrive accompanied by a buxom, attractive young woman. It was easy to imagine her kneading bread or handling cookie sheets. "Well?" she asked Ange-Albert, as if delivering an ultimatum.

He blushed slightly and approached Florent. "Umm . . . it's about that hundred dollars. Could you give me an advance . . . right now?"

"What hundred dollars? I don't have it on me, old buddy."

"So that's it," said the young woman. "I've walked twelve blocks just to hear that?"

She plunked herself down across from her companion, raised her hand and delivered a slap that silenced every conversation in the restaurant. "Good-bye," she said. "Pay your debts if you want to get into my bed."

Ange-Albert rubbed his cheek, then came and sat across from Florent. "First time I've borrowed money in ten years, and see what happens. . . ."

His smile was pathetic. "I was glad to see her. Too bad it didn't work. Are we going back to Montreal?"

When Florent reached his house, after dropping his friend at the Central Station (what the hell was he going to do there?), Elise stood before him, arms folded. "So it's all wrapped up. You sign the deed tomorrow?" she asked abruptly.

"Right – tomorrow afternoon. Why?"

"Because I've just decided something, too, if you don't mind: you're not signing anything till I've had a chance to see your Ratamaski or Batalanski or whatever. If you insist on taking risks you should have stayed single. When you've got a wife and child . . ."

"What child?"

"What child! The one we're trying to make, dummy!"

"All right, all right," he grumbled. "Don't burn the house down – you'll see the old guy tomorrow." He left the kitchen muttering, "What's wrong with women nowadays? At this rate we'll soon need their okay to take a leak."

FOUR

After an hour at the mirror Elise still wasn't satisfied with her makeup. "I want to look my best," she explained. "These old turkeys freak out at the sight of a good-looking girl. I didn't work two years as a waitress for nothing. . . ."

Florent waited for her in the kitchen, drinking cup after cup of coffee. Another fifteen minutes went by. The coffeepot had been squeezed dry. A quivering black energy was circulating through Florent, filling his body with spasms and submerging his mind in a flood of thoughts that he couldn't quite put together. "At last," he sighed, as Elise appeared, satisfied after one final touch-up.

"You're driving badly this morning," she observed mildly when they'd been on the road a few minutes. "Too much coffee."

They drove on to Place Jacques-Cartier. Elise began to examine the old hotel's facade. Terrific-looking place, the Nelson, she thought. "Have you ever stayed here?" she asked innocently as they entered the lobby.

Florent turned around abruptly. "Me? No. Why?"

They walked up to the reception desk. "Is Monsieur Ratablavasky in?" Florent asked, looking glum.

"M-m-m-onsieur R-r-atablavasky?" the fat clerk stammered. He rolled his eyes in alarm, as if someone had slipped up behind him and poured a bottle of castor oil down his shirt. "Monsieur Ratablavasky? He . . . I . . . well . . . Monsieur Ratablavasky . . . Are you his . . . son?"

"What? No."

"A relative?"

"I'm a hundred-percent Québécois, buddy. Can't you tell?"

"Bah!" said the clerk. "What difference does it make? They're burying him this morning," he announced with a dazzling smile. "He died day before yesterday. The chambermaid found him in the bathtub. Stroke."

Florent gazed at him, transfixed. "Do you want to sit down?" asked the clerk, alarmed. "Death affects me that way, too."

Elise dragged her husband to an easy chair. The fat desk clerk came, too. In his nervousness, he had taken out his comb, and was now running it jerkily through his hair. "The funeral's being held right now," he told them. "At Notre-Dame church, not far from here. For two days now the boss hasn't known which way to turn. It's complicated, burying a foreigner! The police, the embassy, all sorts of papers to sign . . . and the hotel has to keep running. . . . He was quite a guy. Just last week he gave me $12.25 in tips."

"The church," Florent murmured, with an effort. "We must go to the church."

He rushed out, because he was ashamed of his tears. They walked up Place Jacques-Cartier.

"Come on now," said Elise, "take it easy. He was a total stranger."

"If I'm rich," Florent whimpered, "it's . . . it's thanks to him."

Elise was more skeptical. "Let's wait a bit before we start counting our millions. This whole business is incredible."

They made their way up St-Paul Street, then along St-Sulpice, next to the church, and entered through a side door. "Say," Elise whispered, "isn't one of your cousins a vicar here?"

Florent didn't hear her. All his attention was focused on the catafalque that stood in the middle of the central aisle. Facing it, a priest made slow gestures with his arms, while an altar boy was mounting the steps with a haste better suited to the schoolyard than the church. The choir was dimly lit and the entire nave was plunged in a sad and solemn gloom, filled with the odors of incense and dust. Florent, gesturing to Elise to follow him, fell to his knees on a bench near the coffin. He gazed at it with sad astonishment. Elise shrugged and let her eyes wander. Aside from the priest, an organist and the altar boy, they were alone. "I don't understand," Florent murmured. "His friend Galarneau didn't even take the trouble to come. . . ."

The celebrant, carrying an aspergillum, descended the steps from the altar and walked down the aisle, followed by the altar boy. Suddenly the organ boomed. The church seemed colossal and frightening. "Amazing," Elise murmured, looking at her husband, whose shoulders were heaving. Despite her efforts, she felt her own eyes fill with tears.

Pallbearers appeared from between the confessionals. They were probably employees of the undertaker. With a vacant look, the priest murmured some more formulas, then the casket was lifted and carried through the transept toward a side door.

Elise and Florent followed it, uncertain what they should do. A hearse was parked at the foot of the stairs, its back doors already open. On the sidewalk across the street, a waitress from Stash's was cleaning the restaurant window. Elise stood on the landing. Florent descended the steps and walked up to the hearse just as the pallbearers, lunging like bowlers, slid the coffin inside. No one paid any attention to him. The driver got behind the wheel and started up the vehicle. Florent leaned over toward him. "Is the burial . . . Are you going . . . ?"

"Cremation, young man, cremation. Ceremony strictly private."

In perfect unison, the four passengers lit cigarettes and Monsieur Ratablavasky set out on his last earthly journey.

Elise was still waiting at the top of the steps. "They don't waste any time on small talk," she said, as Florent joined her. "Where are you going? Poor baby, there's nothing you can do here now."

Florent said nothing and went back into the church. The lights had been switched on in the nave, and now it looked more like a railway station. In a corner, two workmen were joking as they did something with electrical wires. An old lady with tight curls scurried along the altar with a feather duster. Vaguely disturbed, Elise followed her husband.

Florent, lost in thought, walked along a lateral aisle, head bowed. He stopped before an ornate funerary chapel, closed by an elaborate iron grille. A white marble bishop lay sleeping there, doggedly peaceful. "Monsignor Ignace Bourget," Elise read in a low voice. "Right, the famous Monsignor Bourget."

She peered at the Spartan face of the stubborn, authoritarian old bishop who at one time had controlled the destiny of an entire people. Florent, dreamily pinching his nose, was miles away from such historical considerations. They heard footsteps gliding behind them. He turned around. "My cousin," he murmured, irritated. "The last person I feel like seeing now."

Father Octavien Jeunehomme was walking down the aisle, holding a breviary, his thoughts, as usual, elsewhere. Heedless of changing customs, he still wore a soutane. With his clean-shaven face, his pale, smooth, yellowish skin, and large, weak, dreamy eyes, he looked like a tubercular adolescent. When he was ten feet from Florent, he suddenly noticed him; he stopped then and stretched his lips in a sickly smile. "Good morning, cousin. Am I witnessing a sudden conversion?"

The priest extended a limp hand, which Florent quickly clasped, and pointed to the chapel without seeming to have noticed Elise's presence. "I've just read a biography of our dear bishop. Take my word, he was a difficult man. It seems he had a very delicate palate and wouldn't tolerate the slightest lapse in the rules of fine cuisine. It's told that between 1866 and 1874 he changed cooks twelve times."

"You remember my wife?" Florent interrupted caustically.

Father Jeunehomme turned toward Elise, and his mind seemed filled with a considerable commotion. Red-faced, he stepped toward her and awkwardly clasped her hand. "Of course," he stammered, "I'd forgotten you were married. . . . I thought the lady was a visitor . . . How idiotic . . . You must excuse me . . . Delighted to meet you . . . You were married recently, I believe."

"Three years ago," Florent replied imperturbably. "You were at the wedding."

More and more flustered, Father Jeunehomme was scarlet now. "Quite so, quite so, I remember. What can I be thinking of? How time flies!"

He had a sudden inspiration. "Why not come to my room for tea. We can have a chat before dinner."

Florent looked questioningly at Elise. She nodded. "I want to see that room of his," she thought. "I've been hearing about it as long as I can remember!"

They crossed the nave, speaking softly, and went out a low door that opened onto a series of ill-lit corridors. The prevailing atmosphere was quite bizarre. The mingled odors of old wood and wax, the solemn silence that reigned throughout, the glints off the carefully polished dark wood paneling all combined to clear the mind of everyday preoccupations and plunge it into nostalgic reverie. "It's like being in a novel by Paul Féval," said Elise, smiling at the priest.

"It's true," he replied, eyes glowing with pleasure, "or by dear old Eugène Achard, or the Baroness Orczy. Do you know her work? She wrote *The Scarlet Pimpernel.* I adored it when I was young, and I still enjoy dipping into it."

They had come to the main body of the building. Father Jeunehomme hiked up his soutane and started up a monumental oak staircase. "My room is on the third floor, at the far end of the corridor," he said, already winded.

From the corner of her eye Elise was watching her husband, who was visibly making a great effort to wrench himself away from that morning's painful impressions. "You've been assigned to this parish for a while now, haven't you?" he asked, for something to say.

"Two years . . . no, three . . . I don't remember. Here we are. Do come in."

Elise was not disappointed. She'd never seen anything like it.

"I apologize for the clutter," said the priest uncomfortably (he had just spotted, on the table, a pair of socks that were somewhat too redolent of his intimate odors). "I'll fetch some chairs, then we can have a nice chat."

The room hardly seemed to exist. The walls were completely hidden by shelves of books that partially blocked the only window. Nor had the floor been spared, except to permit the most essential movements. It was necessary to keep one's elbows at one's sides to avoid setting off avalanches of books. Even the ceiling was in use: the priest had plastered it with photographs and prints of famous writers. A path snaked through the room to a black leather armchair, above which curved a splendid standing lamp. Between the chair and some bookshelves stood a table, a tiny refrigerator – and a cake stand. The table held a huge copper samovar, with an electric cord that got lost between two volumes of Flaubert's *Letters*. The device was purring softly; now and then a drop of boiling water fell from its spigot onto a morocco-bound edition of *The Alexandria Quartet*, which seemed to be standing up well to the ordeal. The cake stand was an odd little three-tiered piece of furniture with cabriole legs. On it the priest had arranged a number of plates laden with an amazing assortment of cellophane-covered pastries. *Madeleines*, cats' tongues, *mille-feuilles*, and ladyfingers sat next to *clafoutis*, *barquettes*, *petits fours*, *rum babas*, and *polonaises*.

Near the door there was another heap which might be a bed. The priest must have gotten enough daily exercise to stay in relatively good shape just from clearing off a place to sleep.

"Try to ignore the dust," he said, struggling to free a chair that was swamped by the complete works of George Sand. "My cleaning woman left last week. Claims she's too old . . . But I know the true reason for her defection. The true reason wears purple and runs this presbytery."

As he spoke, he tripped and brought his heel down on *Federalism and the French Canadians*, inflicting some damage to the pseudo-Amerindian face of the Right Honourable Pierre Elliott Trudeau who, like the good politician he was, continued to smile at his reader.

"Thank you," said Elise as she sat down. "I'll pour the tea, if you want. Where are the cups?"

The priest got flustered again. "Ah yes, the cups . . . I forgot . . . You see, I . . . I only have one. I'll bring some more from the kitchen," he said, his voice breaking like an adolescent's.

"Hey," Elise began when the door was closed, "does he really do nothing but read?"

"That's right. My parents don't talk about him much. The family's kind of ashamed of him. I mean, a priest who doesn't hear confession and forgets to say mass . . ."

"The parish priest doesn't seem to be his greatest fan."

"What do you expect? The archbishop put him here as a sort of retreat in disguise. He's been shipped from parish to parish ever since he was ordained. He gets on everybody's nerves, poor guy."

"Sssh, here he is."

From the priest's agitation it was obvious that he seldom had guests and that their visit was quite an event for him.

"Here are two cups – now we need only pour," he said, his cheeks flushed with emotion.

He dipped his lips in the infusion, appeared satisfied, and held out a cup to each guest. Florent didn't really know what to say. His thoughts were divided between Ratablavasky's death and the signing of the deed. Father Jeunehomme crossed his legs, coughed into his hand, and answered Elise's smile with an embarrassed little grimace.

"You've been a reader since you were a child, haven't you?" she asked, trying to sound relaxed and natural.

"My governess first began reading to me when I was five. I could listen to her for hours."

"You had a governess?"

"My parents really hadn't time to care for me."

"By the way," Florent broke in, "how is my aunt? Still enjoying Florida?"

"She's well," the priest replied laconically. "My family had a large bookstore in Quebec City," he went on, turning to Elise. "It's a demanding trade."

Florent laughed. "Lucrative, too, when you're as wily as my aunt."

"There was a time," the priest went on, "when I could pride myself on knowing almost the entire literature section in our store (for I'm interested only in literature). I used to read more than four hundred books a year. Now, I must restrain myself. My eyesight is failing. And people talk," he added with a derisive smile.

Suddenly he pointed to the cake stand. "I forgot to offer you a pastry! Come, take one, do!" he said, picking up a plate and removing its cellophane covering. "The Duc de Lorraine delivers them every other day. Tell me what you think of them."

With these words he sank his teeth into a *baba*, his eyes dark with pleasure. Then, gazing at each one in turn, he asked, "Did you know about my great good fortune? I'm flying to France in a month."

"Indeed," Elise replied. "Is it a pleasure trip?"

What next? Florent thought. Now my wife's talking like a nun.

"No, a study trip," the priest replied gravely. "I'm going there to carry out some research. You know Gogol, of course?"

Elise and Florent nodded, though the writer's name meant nothing to them.

"But of course," the priest continued. "Who doesn't know the greatest Russian writer of the nineteenth century? Well, then . . ." Enthusiasm had dissolved his shyness, and he leaned forward in his chair. "I'm going to France to attempt to track down one of his works that has disappeared. Fragments of it, at any rate. You know, the famous second part of *Dead Souls* that Gogol burned on the night of February 11, 1852, in a torment of religious anguish, just days before his death."

"That he *burned*?" Elise asked, astonished. (She nudged Florent, who was yawning.) "How do you expect to find it?"

Father Jeunehomme raised an emaciated finger. "Ah, there's the rub. Everything is still in the stove where he threw the manuscript."

"What?" Florent exclaimed, suddenly interested.

"Yes, yes, that's what I said," the priest continued, unable to control himself. "Gogol died in the home of Count Alexis Tolstoy, where he maintained an apartment, on February 22, 1852. Now the writer Pogodin, who obtained this information from eyewitnesses, maintains that the stove (which our compatriots would describe as 'potbellied') where Gogol carried out this frightful literary hecatomb, was never used again. You know the Russians and how terribly superstitious they can be. The Tolstoy family regarded that stove as both terrible and sacred. It had become the tomb of a masterpiece, an evil instrument that had first consumed the work, then brought about the death of the man. For Gogol never recovered from this rash act. He watched the last sheets of paper turn yellow, then lay down on a sofa and never got up again. Afterward, no one dared enter the room where the tragedy had occurred, and the stove was never used again. In 1854, the count had it sealed and put in an attic. It showed up in Paris, in 1921, with some Russian emigrés, distant relatives of Count Tolstoy who had been driven out by the Revolution. It is still sealed. Forty years later, it turned up again at Fontenay-les-Tours, in the possession of one Félix Farbe, who had bought it no one quite knows where. There was talk at the time of breaking the seals to examine the contents, but Farbe died suddenly and his property fell to his heirs. Since then, nothing. But I shall go to Fontenay-les-Tours, and I'll find my potbellied stove!" he concluded triumphantly.

Florent guffawed. "You're going across the Atlantic for a handful of ashes?"

"Careful, my friend," the priest replied gravely. "Paleography has made tremendous progress in the past twenty years. Scholars can now restore palimpsests. Or they may reassemble some dusty fragments and from them piece together a poem, a story, valuable historical information. Remember the Dead Sea Scrolls. X rays are used now, and fluoroscopy, and I don't know what else."

There was silence for a few moments. Father Jeunehomme used a handkerchief to wipe up some tea he'd spilled on his soutane during his passionate exposition.

"Tell me, though," said Elise, who was moved by his strange story, "why would he burn his manuscript if he died of grief ten days later?"

The priest sighed and let his hands fall on his knees. "It would take too long to explain," he murmured. His expression was despondent. A moment later he added, "He was a bit crazy, I think."

"Whew! Am I glad to be out of there!" Florent exclaimed as he stepped into the presbytery's small garden. "After all his weird stories, here it is one-thirty and my appointment with the notary's at two."

"*Your* appointment?" asked Elise sarcastically. "Am I allowed to come, too?"

"Come on, of course you can. Did you see that pile of pastries? I wonder how he survives. Apparently that's all he eats. They made me ravenous."

He went into a restaurant and came out with a big bag of roasted peanuts. He ripped it open with his teeth and, without breaking his stride, held it out to Elise.

A long caravan of trucks filled with construction debris appeared suddenly, making a deafening noise. Elise and Florent took shelter in the car and gulped down the rest of the peanuts. "Shit, there's plaster dust in my teeth," said Florent, disgusted, as he started the car.

The office of the notary, Philippe Pimparé, where the deed was to be signed, was located on Fleury Street, in the north end of town, just a minute away from La Barrique, a fairly good French restaurant where the notary ate lunch every day on the stroke of noon. He demanded that his meal be served the instant he set foot inside: tomato juice, filet of sole meunière, applesauce, and coffee alternated with tomato juice, minute steak, fruit salad, and coffee.

Florent drove down Papineau, weaving in and out of traffic and squeaking through the amber light. He looked at his watch, then said, "Well, in spite of Gogol and his potbellied stove, we'll be on time."

At the corner of Jarry, a wedding procession had been brought to a standstill by an accident. The bride stood in the middle of the street in her white gown and veil, next to a convertible whose left side had just been rammed by a van. She was weeping bitterly as blood trickled down her face, spreading a red stain on her gown. Her bridegroom, arms dangling, looked at her aghast, already overwhelmed by the demands of married life. Their families were bustling about, giving contradictory orders and looking for handkerchiefs while the bloodstain grew larger. There was a sudden scream of sirens, and two police cars came screeching up. Exclamations of relief were heard on all sides.

"Wow!" said Elise. "If I was superstitious I wouldn't sign any contract today!"

"I'll sign it," said Florent, "and I'll get rich, too!"

However, they'd lost a good five minutes gawking at the accident.

"Monsieur Boissonneault, I presume?" the notary asked as they entered his office. "It's about time. Messieurs Slipskin and Saint-Onge have been twiddling their thumbs for six minutes, and my secretary hasn't stopped piling files on my desk. Madame, my compliments. Kindly be seated while I read you the deed."

Fifteen minutes later he looked up. "There it is. Are there any questions?"

"Sounds fine to me," Saint-Onge mumbled.

Looking grave, he took out his pen, signed, then handed the document to Florent, who offered it to Slipskin. They shook hands silently and Pimparé, the notary, was soon alone again, with his secretary and his paperwork.

"Where did you dig up that notary, Monsieur Saint-Onge?" Florent asked, irritated.

"He's been looking after my business for twenty years. Competence is worth more than personality. Now then, let's have a little gin at my place – port for you, madame – then I'm off for the airport. No more beans! Florida, here I come!"

Two hours later, Elise, Slipskin and Florent arrived at The Beanery. It was the midafternoon slump, between noon hour and the five-thirty rush. There were just two customers at the counter. Gustave Bleau was chatting with one of them, while the other, a haggard little old man, was gazing into his cup of coffee so dejectedly that he seemed to want to jump in and put an end to it all.

Berval, the cook, had just left. In the kitchen, sixteen-year-old José Biondi, a cigarette stuck to his lips, was washing the dishes as he mentally performed a delicate repair on the carburetor of his sports car. Leaning against a wall, Bertrand (whom they had secretly nicknamed Bernadette), the receiver wedged between ear and shoulder, was whispering sweet nothings into the telephone, scraping carrots all the while.

The arrival of the new owners cast a pall of silence over the restaurant. Florent walked into the middle of the establishment, swinging his arms and looking rather smug.

"How's tricks, boss?" asked Gustave Bleau, only faintly sarcastic.

Florent smiled broadly in reply and turned to Elise and Slipskin. "Would you like a coffee?"

They nodded, somewhat uneasy under the employees' gaze. Bleau wanted to serve them, but Florent went behind the counter and intercepted him. "I work here, too," he said with a condescending little smile.

"Whatever you want," said the waiter, going into the kitchen.

Florent walked back and forth behind the counter, trying not to show how giddy he felt in his new role. "Goddamn it," Slipskin swore to himself, "you'd think I hadn't put a cent into this place. He's acting like my boss!"

He downed his coffee in two gulps, then went behind the counter, too; he was about to take a look in the kitchen but a bombardment of frosty stares forced him to retreat. He came back and sat beside Elise, who was looking everywhere, delighted at how clean it all was. Gustave Bleau came back with a pot of pork and beans glistening with fat, and set it in the warming oven.

"Well, Gustave," Florent began, aiming at a tone of jovial familiarity, "pretty busy at lunch today?"

"The usual, boss. Our problem isn't bringing in the customers, it's kicking them out at closing time."

The waiter's words delighted him. He spread his arms, placed his hands on the counter as if it were a ship's rail, and delightedly breathed in the odors of frying and coffee and Javex that wafted through the restaurant. "At last," he murmured, "I've got my restaurant."

José Biondi and Bertrand had approached him silently, and now they watched him with no expression. As for Slipskin, he was bent over his cup, which Bleau had just hastened to refill, blinking rapidly, his thin lips curved in an imperceptible smile.

"Look at that rat's face," Florent's father whispered to his wife, when he spotted Slipskin through the window around midnight.

Elise spotted them and rushed to open the door. "Hello, angel! Come give your father-in-law a hug while I can still talk to you – the future millionairess!" And he kissed her so effusively that Slipskin grimaced in surprise.

Florent's father was a perfect example of the happy invalid. A polio victim at fifteen, he had virtually lost the use of his left leg. ("But not the middle one," he would guffaw, while his wife lowered her gaze and sighed discreetly.) Despite his disability (or, who knows, perhaps because of it) he was filled with tireless good humor. His tactful ways with people and years of relentless hard work had enabled him to carve out an enviable place in the insurance business, and now he was comfortably well off.

A radiant Florent emerged from the kitchen, holding a rag. He introduced his parents to the staff, then showed them around. Monsieur and Madame Boissonneault, dressed in their Sunday best for the occasion, followed him, puffed with pride but still critical. "A bit small," his father observed, "but still, my boy, you've latched onto the goose that lays the golden egg."

He turned to his wife. "Just think, Rosalie, I used to sit at this counter before we were married! I knew Monsieur Lussier very well: now there was a man who knew how to make people happy! In thirty years, I don't think a single customer ever sent back his plate."

He gave his son a vigorous slap on the back that nearly threw him off balance. "You're a Boissonneault, my boy: show your stuff and you'll outdo him like an elephant's dong outdoes an alley cat's!"

Everyone burst out laughing except little José Biondi, who screwed up his eyes and looked blasé as he dragged on his cigarette. The visit ended in the cellar. Slipskin opened the doors, then stepped back and, with his hands behind his back, listened in, smiling courteously.

"I tell you, Rosalie, he's got a face like a rat," Florent's father repeated to his wife two hours later as he sat on the edge of his bed. Struggling, he pulled off his trousers and his withered left leg appeared. "I wouldn't let him use my wastebasket," he added contemptuously.

"Come to bed," sighed his wife. "After all, Florent's not a baby. It's been three years now, he must know what he's dealing with."

"A face like a rat," her husband muttered one last time, before he fell asleep.

FIVE

After some hesitation, The Beanery's clientele had decided to remain faithful to their restaurant, because the food was still just as good. Florent got up at five and went to bed late at night. Pale with fatigue, he was slowly learning his new trade – and getting thin. He was everywhere at once: the cash, the counter, the kitchen, on the phone with suppliers and meat wholesalers, trying to penetrate the secret that enabled you to know the difference between a piece of beef that was all gristle and one that would bring in a crowd of satisfied diners. His energy and capacity for work gradually won over the staff, who had scoffed when he'd first arrived on the scene.

Elise was one of his main assets. She worked at the counter from 7:00 A.M. until four o'clock. Unaffected and efficient, playful and decisive, in just two days she had transformed Gustave Bleau, the former truckdriver, into a faithful admirer who burned with the same disinterested zeal as Percival and Company in quest of the Holy Grail. The restaurant clients, surprised at first by this feminine presence that broke a long tradition, were soon won over by her cheerful personality and speedy service. The tips had even registered a slight increase. Only Monsieur Berval was dissatisfied, for he had the impression – well-founded – that Florent was trying to steal his secrets behind his back. He had tried to set José Biondi and the gentle Bertrand against their new boss, but Florent had quickly dropped him on a desert island in a sea of jealously by casually telling his co-workers about the raise he'd had to give Berval, and how the cook had forced Florent's hand.

Slipskin wasn't so lucky. The staff had unanimously decided to give him a hard time. He couldn't have cared less, though, since he only put in brief appearances at the restaurant, late in the evening and during the day on Saturday. He expended most of his energy in discothèques. Indeed, he was a virtuoso cruiser who spent the best part of his evenings persuading women he didn't know to put his virility to the test. There were times when alcohol had to come to the aid of his somewhat limited charms. He shamelessly offered it in quantity, with wallet open and fly aquiver, though he himself rarely indulged because of his health-food fetish. He adored Québécoises. "Those French-Canadian girls can really fuck," he would laugh, "if you handle them right."

On June 2, 1974, a month after they'd taken over The Beanery, Florent and Slipskin had a gross profit of $5,682.74, the bulk of which, it's true, went toward paying off their loan. Florent was able to withdraw a weekly salary of $250 for himself and $125 for Slipskin, and the reduced turnover both had feared for the first months hadn't occurred. Quite the contrary: The Beanery served an average of 250 meals a day. In one month, customers had devoured 500 gallons of soup, 122 loaves of bread, 80 dozen eggs, 400 pounds of beef stew, 77 veal hearts, 350 pounds of shepherd's pie and the same of meatball stew, 1,837 pounds of pork and beans, 168 *tourtières*,

150 sugar pies, 600 gallons of coffee and 28 pans of bread pudding. The restaurant's strength lay in the quality of its food, its speedy service and relatively moderate prices, all made possible by the low upkeep on a place so cramped that people wondered how it could accommodate such an avalanche of food. Short of a disaster, the restaurant should pay for itself sooner than anticipated.

Florent had only one regret: that he hadn't been able to embrace the kind Ratablavasky. As soon as his good deed was accomplished, it would seem, his benefactor had gone to Heaven to post it, and from there he was smiling down on his young protégé's career. Florent would talk about him at the drop of a hat, with a fervor that got on Elise's nerves.

"Stop turning him into a saint! Maybe death made a good Samaritan of him. Does anybody know what was going on in that Russian's head – or whatever he was?"

"Think what you please, I judge people by their actions. A month ago I was selling records for a son of a bitch who was on my back if I took three minutes for a pee. Today I'm running a restaurant, and in five or six years we'll have a big stone house with trees all around it like you've always dreamed of. And who do I owe that to? To Egon Ratablavasky. So I say to him: enjoy your stay in Heaven, Monsieur Ratablavasky, till I can come and shake your hand."

It was in this pleasant state of mind that, some days later, Florent received an unexpected visit. He had just persuaded a customer to sleep it off at home instead of in his plate when the door was flung open with such vigor that it left a permanent mark on the wall.

"*Bonjour*! Here I am!" exclaimed Aurélien Picquot. He headed straight for Florent and embraced him. "What a joy to see you again, my young friend! *Voilà*, I've done it – my mind's made up!" he whispered so enthusiastically that his remarks became dangerously audible. "Take me to the kitchens. This restaurant's already fine reputation is about to be transformed into fame!"

Florent gestured to Elise to replace him at the cash, then hurried his friend outside. "What on earth's going on?" the chef protested. "Do you usually entertain on the street?"

"Of course not," Florent replied, dragging him to a nearby delicatessen. "But I'd just as soon my cook found out about your plans a little more . . . gradually."

"Bah! Milk teeth and twaddle! Stove spatterers are of no importance! Most of his sort should be institutionalized for poisoning the public."

Florent opened the door for his friend, and they sat down in one of the booths. "Anyway, Monsieur Picquot, my place is just as good as this! Business is fine and I owe a lot of it to him."

"Meaning what?" Picquot retorted, rounding his eagle's eye. "Are you rejecting my services?"

"Hardly! What's got into you this morning? I want to be fair, that's all."

A platinum-haired waitress in hot pants came up to them with a jiggling of cellulite that pegged her past forty. "What'll it be?" she asked sulkily.

Picquot eyed her disdainfully and said, "Nothing." Florent, slightly uncomfortable, asked for a coffee.

She turned her back and muttered as she walked away, "Best place for a Frenchman's on a boat going home."

At a conciliating gesture from Florent, Picquot changed his mind and remained seated. He smoothed his mustache three times and then a radiant smile lit up the lower half of his face. "*Mon cher ami*, I have the pleasure of announcing that as of two days ago I have mastered your Québécois cuisine – absolutely!"

"How about that! Congratulations! Now you have two specialties."

"No," he replied dryly, "when I left the Château Frontenac I renounced *haute cuisine* forever. These times are no longer worthy of it. People salivate, but they taste nothing. I've been wasting my time trying to please such robots."

Florent smiled. "Isn't that a pretty bleak outlook?"

"Absolutely not! The proof: I've found another branch to perch on, a little lower down, it's true, but solid. Where do you think I've been the past little while?"

"Not at charm school, that's for sure," said the waitress, who had suddenly returned. She slammed a cup of coffee down in front of Florent, spattering him in the eye.

Picquot watched her walk away. "She doesn't miss a beat," he said, his voice softer now. "I like that. Must come back for a chat with her. *Alors*, let me ask you again: where do you think I've been?"

Florent shrugged his ignorance. "At Saint-Sauveur, young man! I've just spent two weeks in a chalet at Saint-Sauveur where I've acquired my new knowledge. I've collected all the traditional Québécois cookbooks that exist on heaven and earth and, in a manner of speaking, digested them. Let me recommend, *en passant*, that you contemplate a collection of recipes assembled in 1879 by the Reverend Mother Caron of the Sisters of Charity of the Providence. You'll see that a blend of the odor of sanctity and the aroma of fine cuisine can result in a most happy marriage. And if you're curious about the results of my research, go up to Saint-Sauveur and ask the good people about my *dégustations*. After a week of free samples of my fare they wanted me to run for town council."

Florent was amazed. "If Montrealers are anything like the folks in Saint-Sauveur, we'll all be millionaires in a year!"

"Now, *cher ami*, I must leave you," said Picquot, getting up from his seat. "I must get my baggage from the station. And when shall I take up my post?"

He did so that very day. Monsieur Berval, who kept his ears open, had drawn his conclusions and taken his leave. When Florent came back from the delicatessen he found the cook sitting by the stove, downing a bottle of gin at a speed that turned his cheeks to tomatoes. His apron was hanging in a kettle of vegetable soup. "I want two weeks' pay, young fellow: I've been on the phone and I make supper for four hundred in Chibougamau tomorrow."

A long discussion followed. Florent complained that the cook hadn't given him advance notice, but he finally relented and they went to the bank together, for his ex-employee wanted payment in cash.

"Get rid of that lout," Picquot grumbled, as Berval jostled him on his way out of the restaurant.

The chef bent down and started dragging a huge padded black leather trunk. Some customers turned and stared disdainfully. Picquot looked up and saw Elise. "Madame . . . Boissonneault?" he asked, growing flustered. What a woman! he thought. Why didn't I notice her before? My eyesight's failing.

"You're Aurélien Picquot?" Elise asked with a smile. "My husband's been singing your praises for ages. I'm glad to meet you. Here, let me help." She made a move to open the door.

"Never mind, madame, never mind." He gave the impression of standing on tiptoe to speak. "It's not the first threshold I've crossed."

He made a strenuous effort to lift the trunk. His spinal column made a cracking sound like an old beam and his glasses, a comb, and two boxes of mints fell to the sidewalk, but the trunk didn't budge.

"Let me give you a hand," said Gustave Bleau, emerging from the kitchen where the staff were splitting their sides in private.

His hands swooped down on the leather handles, a shudder ran along his huge arms and with a single thrust of the torso he lifted the trunk. "Where does it go?" he asked, panting.

Picquot pointed to the kitchen. What a splendid nose! he thought, peering at Elise. Just a shade too long – the touch of imperfection to prevent her beauty from being cold. And the eyes – so gentle, so carefully made up! Like Agnès, but fresher. He walked past Gustave Bleau and pushed open the kitchen door. "What in heaven's name do you expect me to do in this broom closet!"

José Biondi looked at him, deeply offended, but Picquot didn't even seem to notice him. "If you expect my art to soar you'll have to enlarge."

"You want your trunk in the cellar?" the waiter asked, placing his burden at Picquot's feet.

Laughing, Picquot held out a key. "Open it!"

Some curious customers approached. The key went into the lock and the cover was raised. For a moment, little José Biondi's face was stamped with something like amazement. Both Gustave and Bertrand exclaimed and stepped back, dazzled by the kettles, saucepans, frying pans, and casseroles that fitted into each other like pieces of a puzzle. "My lord," Elise murmured, "it looks like gold."

A burst of laughter from Picquot stopped three people on the street. "Come now, I'm not Cleopatra, frying eggs in twenty-four-carat gold! It's only copper. If you rub copper, it smiles at you! Take away that scrap," he ordered, pointing to a cupboard. "Bad saucepans make bad food."

After several days of anxiety and amazement, the staff of The Beanery came to the conclusion that Aurélien Picquot wasn't as disastrous as his behavior first led them to believe. If they worked like slaves and didn't ask too many questions, the days passed quickly enough. His extraordinary skill and capacity for work made up for the tremendous patience required to deal with his volatile personality.

As soon as he arrived he inspected the restaurant from top to bottom. At second glance, the kitchen still seemed tiny, but well laid out. He was satisfied with the storeroom in the cellar, but not with the state of cleanliness of the huge meat grinder that stood outside the washroom. "What's the meaning of this!" he exclaimed in horror at the sight of some packages of instant mashed potatoes. "Throw this American trash in the street: it's a dishonor to the profession!"

The same fate befell the powdered beef broth and a carton of Jell-O. He had them put in garbage bags, carefully sealed as if they contained dangerous substances – "Which they are! Those products cause more harm than arsenic." – and threw them in the trash can himself. When Len Slipskin learned of this a few hours later, he slipped outside discreetly and put them in his car as a gift for his mother.

But the changes didn't stop there. That same day Florent had to purchase an electric mixer. In the following week, Picquot bought three big pressure cookers. "That's the only way to prevent vegetables from being watery when they're cooked in large quantities. My spiritual master, Alexis Soyer, invented this process in the nineteenth century. I won't tolerate boiled potatoes that fall apart in your mouth like watermelon."

He had a broom closet demolished and the space gained was used for a warming table with adjustable temperature. "Another of Soyer's inventions, my friends. Remember that name: Soyer, a great cook and a genius of an inventor. Thanks to him a *tourtière* or a stew can still taste fresh hours after it's left the oven."

He improved the lighting, had a fan installed in the transom over the back door, and the kitchen painted white. Cracks, holes, and useless nooks and crannies disappeared. Pearl-gray linoleum, easy to maintain, covered the dreadful asphalt tiles with their motif of split peas. "A kitchen should look like an operating room," said Picquot. "The most tenacious germ should die in an hour, of melancholy."

He was very pleased with the ingenious menu holder over the counter, on which each dish was listed on a movable tab. He looked at it for a long time, then said, "Later, when I've got my hand in, I may add a *cipâte au lièvre*. But we mustn't upset tradition."

The food at The Beanery, previously excellent, was now unbeatable. Customers were quick to react. Tips were a little fatter. After two weeks, wonder of wonders, there were lineups at mealtime, just like at Da Giovanni! People waited, smiling, for the privilege of tasting the shepherd's pie or braised veal heart. The excellent food put them in such good spirits, they were quite philosophical about the verbal storms that sometimes erupted in the kitchen and even behind the counter.

Delighted with the turn of events, Len Slipskin started coming more often and, amazingly, no one complained, for they were short of manpower. Elise and Florent slept six hours a night and worked like the damned the rest of the time. Now and then they made a valiant attempt to restore their love life to what it had been before The Beanery, but their determination didn't measure up to their desire. "If we make a baby this way he'll be as dull as a chair," Elise sighed.

Florent wanted to take on another employee, but Picquot discouraged him. "Little capitulations to laziness pave the way to bankruptcy. Too many fixed assets, too many salaries, and bam! At the first sign of trouble the bailiff's at the door. Hold on a while longer – your nerves will get used to it. You don't get rich basking on the beach!"

If I knew where to find Ange-Albert, Florent thought, I'd ask him to give me a hand.

A telegram brought the answer the next day. "In Calgary with CNR. Traveling everywhere. Nothing but English! Back in Montreal soon. Love to Elise."

"We ought to expand," Slipskin suggested one night, after examining the contents of the till with glowing eyes.

"You'd be wrong," Picquot retorted. "That's an example of the American mania to turn good restaurants into factories. How can you control the quality of the food when there's hardly enough time to lift the lids of all your saucepans?"

Florent nodded agreement. "I like money, but I like a family life, too," he said, with a glance at Elise that brought an equivocal smile to the lips of Gustave Bleau.

"Did you know that Camilien Houde used to come here when he was mayor?" an old taxi driver asked one day. "If you keep feeding people like this the old glutton'll come back to life."

Picquot emerged from the kitchen, cheeks burning and eyes filled with tears, and shook his hand. "For a cook like me, the greatest solace comes from ordinary people."

SIX

The inevitable finally happened. After being constantly badgered by accounts of the success of the rejuvenated restaurant that were making the rounds of Plateau Mont-Royal, Joseph Latour decided that a portion of The Beanery's new prosperity should make its way to his wallet. Latour was the owner, editor-in-chief and proofreader of *Le Clairon du Plateau*, a modest tabloid that came out every Tuesday – unless the printer was on a bender, in which case publication was put off until the following day.

That morning, as Latour was thinking about The Beanery, he was suffused by a wave of optimism that gave him the bizarre sensation of somebody licking his joints. (He'd mentioned the phenomenon to his doctor, which led to some teasing in questionable taste.) So far, his frequent attempts to obtain an advertising contract from the restaurant had left a strong taste of castor oil in his mouth. On his fourth visit, the former owner, Monsieur Saint-Onge, had leaned on the counter and told him in front of fourteen customers: "Look here, Latour, you seem hard of hearing so read my lips: if business was bad, I'd try to improve things, maybe slip you the odd ten bucks to get my picture in your rag. But more people know my restaurant than your *Clairon*, so what do I do? Pay good money to give *you* publicity? You're the one who should be paying *me*."

Latour left with his blood pressure at an all-time high, swearing never again to set foot in The Beanery. Certain little vicious remarks had been appearing in his paper for some weeks, but since they infringed on the ads, he'd resigned himself to suppressing them, especially since their effectiveness seemed very limited.

But now The Beanery had changed hands. For a while, Latour considered starting again, but he had his own professional honor. In his place, he delegated Rosario Gladu, his chief, in fact his only ad-man and reporter.

One morning around eleven, Florent was serving a little boy who wanted "A pint of pork and beans to go and my mom'll pay you tomorrow," when he found himself facing a thick-lipped man in his thirties, with curly blond hair, a blotchy face, over-ripe cheeks, and a smile that exuded energy. "Monsieur Boissonneault?" he asked, extending his hand.

"That's me."

"Congratulations on your fine restaurant. Very nice atmosphere. You know, an uncle of mine, Onésime Ledoux, he's got bladder cancer, but he drags himself here twice a week for your famous *tourtière*. Let me introduce myself: Rosario Gladu, of *Le Clairon*."

"Yes, of course," Florent replied, vaguely embarrassed. He remembered seeing the name somewhere among the potato peels.

"I'll have a coffee, if I may."

The reporter sat by the little boy, who fixed him with a concentrated stare like a cat's, his hands in his pockets splitting the seams of his poorly mended pants. Soon the child jumped off his stool and sat at the end of the counter, near the door. "Does your wife still pull your hat over your face when you come home late at night?" he asked suddenly with a pitiless grin.

"What?" said Gladu, turning around. "What'd you say? Who are you, anyway?"

"You know me. I live near your house. Sometimes you send me to the corner store for beer."

Florent, with his hand over his mouth, pretended to be scratching his cheek and a deep silence had settled over the kitchen. "I know who you are!" Gladu exclaimed, half angry, half amused. "You're the little beggar that drains the bottles along the way! Go on, take your beans and screw off!"

He got up, wanting to cuff the child, but the boy was already on the sidewalk, making faces. "Little asshole," said Gladu, as the child disappeared. "What's the world coming to?" he asked, turning toward Florent. "Is it the TV or the radiation or what? There's no children anymore! Before they're out of diapers they smoke and drink and walk around with a pocketful of safes, if you'll pardon my French. Does that kid come here often?"

"Nearly every day for a week now," Elise replied, coming up from the cellar with a bunch of parsley.

"Let me introduce my wife."

"Delighted to meet you, madame. On behalf of *Le Clairon du Plateau*, greetings from the staff and my boss, Joseph Latour."

Monsieur Picquot rushed up, holding a ladle. "*Mon cher monsieur*, this Latour wouldn't be a native of Nantes by any chance?"

"Nantes? In France? Oh no. He's from Saint-Casimir-de-Portneuf. Only yesterday he was telling me that most of his brothers – he's got seventeen – still live there, and his mother, too, but she closed up the house a couple of years ago, because of her eyes. One day she was doing her laundry –"

"He's of no interest to me, then," Picquot interrupted, and went back to the kitchen.

For some time the door had been swinging non-stop and the counter was lined with diners. Elise was snowed under. Florent told Gladu, "You'll have to excuse me, but as you can see I've got my hands full just now. Did you want anything in particular?"

"Yes, yes, yes, I was just getting there," Gladu replied somewhat hoarsely. ("Okay, buddy," he told himself, "move it.") "I've got a ver-r-y interesting proposition for you."

With his elbows on the counter, he gazed deep into Florent's eyes and let a few seconds pass. "What would you say about becoming the most famous restaurant in Plateau Mont-Royal?"

Florent laughed. "I think we already are."

"Do you? Come, come now, you know what most people do after work? Hang around the house. Don't ask them to go out for a beer or Chinese food or good plate of beans like you make them. They're no more apt to move than the Jacques Cartier Bridge. And you can't go door to door to try and change their ways, can you? Now that's where the *Clairon* comes in. We've got people on our editorial staff who can move the pillars of a bridge as if they were cans of baby powder."

God almighty, Florent thought, if I don't buy an ad from this pain in the ass he'll be here all afternoon. "How are your rates?" he asked aloud. "If they're reasonable I'll put in an ad from time to time."

Rosario Gladu, almost choking with joy, named a ridiculously low figure that would have bankrupted the paper if it had been their usual rate. Florent asked him to come back later that evening when he wasn't so busy. "You like baseball?" asked Gladu, who had to make a superhuman effort not to throw himself at Florent and kiss his hands. "I've got tickets for the Expos-Pirates game tomorrow, but it's my little girl's first communion party . . ."

"Thanks anyway, but I'm tied up every night."

Gladu glanced at the kitchen to let Florent know he could have the privilege of bestowing the signal honor of a free ticket on the employee of his choice. But he'd scarcely had time to look back when a radiant Aurélien Picquot was standing before him. "Thank you, I'll take one. It's been an age since I've been able to follow Cromartie's development at the bat."

"Well, fuck a duck!" Gladu murmured, almost skipping along the sidewalk. "Tonight the beer's on the boss! Who said personality courses don't pay!"

Around nine o'clock he was back at The Beanery with one too many under his belt and a suitcase full of press clippings – his articles. Florent introduced his associate, and when Gladu heard Slipskin's name he began to stud his speech with English expressions, and the occasional complete sentence. His affected manner and grating accent brought a condescending smile to Slipskin's lips. "I thought about you all afternoon," said the reporter. "And when I start brainstorming I get results! First, I want you to see my accomplishments: here's an article from the front page of the *Clairon* last month that caused quite a stir."

He held up a paper and pointed to the headline: "BURNY HONORED AT MANOIR SAINTE-ROSE."

"You know, they even talked about my article in *Le Progrès de Valleyfield*? Another thing: I was one of the first five people in the province to talk about 'The Venice of Quebec.'

That's something, eh? I used it in one of my columns, 'The News of the Day.'"

He picked up a clipping and stuck it under Florent's nose.

> Fate gave me the great good fortune this past week of visiting the prosperous city of Valleyfield. We should note, incidentally, that ever since the city's system of aqueducts has been improved, thanks to the administrative initiative of Mayor P. O. Gingras (one of those men who, in his absence, no one could replace), the population has been pullulating with joy and purified water. In fact the entire city arouses the admiration of visitors because of all its urban progress. There are even those who are beginning to call it "The Venice of Quebec."

Florent continued to read while Gladu translated another of his articles for Slipskin. "You see? With me you're gonna hit the bull in the eye twice: for a start, I'll write your ads – and you'll see I've got a way with words. But besides, who's to stop me from mentioning your restaurant in my columns? I wouldn't do it for the guy that killed my kid sister – but for nice guys like you . . . the limit's the sky!"

Slipskin glanced questioningly at Florent, and the transaction was concluded. They agreed on a series of twelve ads, nine inches square, on page three, with a photo of the inside of the restaurant adorned with a logo Gladu would submit for their approval in two days. Each ad would be billed at twenty-five dollars, with the possibility of a twenty percent discount for a yearly contract.

The conversation now became very cordial. Gladu stopped talking business and launched into an account of his amorous conquests in the discos, bars, and clubs of Plateau

Mont-Royal. He and Slipskin discovered shared tastes, and the journalist was so delighted that he invited him on the spot for a beer at the Gogo Bar (Lucien Moffette, Prop.), an establishment two blocks from The Beanery, with a very colorful clientele. With a little luck, in less than an hour you'd find a divorcée, a wan secretary, or a homesick country girl who'd come to the Gogo Bar with the hope (sometimes unacknowledged) of finishing the evening in a motel. Slipskin accepted. They were soon at a table with a pair of twins who'd been forty for longer than they could remember. Gladu's jokes and Slipskin's English had such an effect that the evening ended in a vigorous and unpretentious orgy that forged indestructible links between the reporter and Florent's associate.

SEVEN

The following day was marked by an extraordinary event. "What is it now?" Florent asked, when he saw coming back for the third time, his pockets bulging with money, the child who, the day before, had cast certain doubts on Rosario Gladu's reputation.

"It's my mom. She wants to know if you got . . ."

"At the rate she's been eating, your mom's going to crash through the floor," said Florent, trying in vain to look severe.

Tight-lipped, the little boy bent his head and stared at the floor. "What does your mother want this time?" Elise asked gently.

"Two cans of sardines. Big ones."

Florent laughed. "You get those at the store, not here. You sure it's your mother that sent you?" he asked with an ironic smile.

Looking deeply offended, the little boy moved toward the door, then changed his mind and came back to the counter. "No, it's my cat," he said, peering coldly at Florent.

"Your cat? And the blood pudding you bought a while ago: was that for your cat too?"

The boy nodded, giving Elise and Florent the same rebellious look. From the kitchen, Picquot muttered, "I'd send that brat straight through the door."

José Biondi craned his neck and, at the sight of the boy, hid his face behind a contemptuous cloud of smoke. "What about the sausages?" Elise went on.

"For the cat. Are you gonna tell my mom on me?"

Florent looked helplessly at his wife. "She'll find out on her own, you poor kid. I suspect you've been into her purse. At least give her back what's left."

"She went away. She won't be back till after dark. She works in a nightclub."

"What about your father?"

"Him? He went to work in some other place."

It was clear from his expression that he'd answered this question before and that he found it particularly tiresome. "What people!" sighed Picquot. "What people!"

He turned toward Bertrand, who was peeling potatoes and reading a Harlequin romance. "Bandit seeds, that's what we're sowing. Watch out for the harvest!"

"Who's your sitter?" asked Elise, leaning over the counter.

"Don't need one. I'm old enough."

"And who gets your meals?"

"Nobody. I go to they fridge and I eat Mae Wests and peanut butter and all kinds of stuff," he told her, amazed at the question. Then he asked suddenly, "Wanna see my cat?"

He ran out and was back in five minutes, carrying a fat tiger-striped alley cat lying upside down in his arms. With his swollen belly and half-closed eyes, the cat seemed stuffed. Once he was inside the restaurant, though, he was revived by the smell of food. He started to look around inquisitively, licking his chops; then he escaped from his master's arms and ran under a table, the perfect spot to plan an expedition in tranquillity. "This is Breakfast," said the little boy, still winded from running. "He's been my cat for a long long long long time. He was my cat when I still wet my pants."

"And what's your name?" Elise asked, laughing.

"Emile. Emile Chouinard."

And that was when the extraordinary event occurred. "Now then, *Monsieur* Emile," said Picquot, going behind the counter, "will you be good enough to keep your feline out of my sight. Or I'll turn him into stew," he warned, with a threatening look.

Elise gestured to the cook to lower his voice, then turned toward the child, who was peering delightedly at Picquot. Something about the cook's words had touched a celestial chord in him. He approached the table just as his cat, after long and clever calculation, was about to shoot toward the kitchen, caught him by the tail and picked him up. Breakfast was transformed into a quivering mass of docility. "Here," he said, offering the animal to the cook, "you can borrow him for a while. But be real careful!" he added, wagging his finger.

Then, as the others looked on, bemused, he headed for the door, smiling, and ran out onto the street. "Your pickpocket's a bit cracked," exclaimed Picquot, slightly embarrassed at the laughter that rose up around him. "Now what am I supposed to do with this foul creature? What if an inspector were to come? There would be quite a scene, my friends! To the cellar with you, scruffy beast!" To Bertrand, who was having trouble holding back his laughter, he added, "Belt up and get back to your vegetables!"

The boy was back in half an hour. "Hi, Emile," said Florent. "Your cat's gone. An inspector just took him away."

The child had stopped dead in the middle of the restaurant, hands on his hips. "My name's not Emile," he said coldly.

"But that's what you just told us."

A look of haughty disdain spread over his features. He came up slowly, climbed on a stool, and bent over the counter until he was nose to nose with Florent. Everyone was watching him. "My name's *Monsieur* Emile," he said steadily. "I'm not a baby, y'know. I look after myself. And anybody that doesn't call me *monsieur* gets a kick in the goddamn shin, okay?" He turned back to Picquot and said, with his most charming smile: "Now gimme my cat. You had him long enough."

Aurélien Picquot had unintentionally set off a process of self-actualization in Emile that soon made him one of the restaurant's regulars. But contrary to what might have been feared, his constant presence turned out to be surprisingly tolerable. Being "monsieur" visibly forced him to behave like a grown-up, at least within the realms of possibility. He no longer picked his nose while he ate. The permanent storm that tangled his hair subsided in intensity, and more and more, his socks tended to match. Alas, only the pungent smell of urine indicated that despite his phenomenal maturity, it was still a bit hard for Monsieur Emile to get along without any maternal attention whatsoever. Picquot, who had never had children and didn't know much about them, found himself confronting a sizable problem. He couldn't bear the child's presence in the kitchen and thought he was out of place in the restaurant. But the robust camaraderie Monsieur Emile had instigated between himself and the cook, like an army engineer throwing a bridge above a precipice, was able to reach some untouched fibers in the old marriage victim until he'd become grumpily dependent on his young friend. Elise's presence helped ease the tensions in this strange conflict. She lavished her unused maternal gifts, making Florent smile and reducing Monsieur Emile to a state of bliss.

The child's mother continued to fulfill her obligations as a barmaid until late at night. Her own sense of responsibility was so demanding that she was often obliged to entertain strangers in her room; at such times her son gradually got used to eating three square meals a day. His clothes would start to look more respectable. Various stains still stood out against their faded colors, but the edible products (egg yolk, peanut butter, and so forth) that were the main components gave way to more noble compounds: ink, watercolor, mercurochrome. Aware of how frail his privileges were, Monsieur Emile never tried to abuse them. He spaced his visits, making them frequent but short, and tried as much as his temperament allowed to be calm and obedient, his only real shortcoming being an exaggerated propensity to ask for Coke and to treat customers with rather contemptuous familiarity. His privileged status made him the envy of the neighborhood kids. Some wanted to copy him and carve out a little place beside him. Monsieur Emile would take them, one at a time, into a backyard, where a series of solid kicks in the belly would put an end to such disloyal competition.

Elise gazed at him, sighing lovingly. Every period left her depressed for a week. "I'd love to have six children," she sighed one day, "but I'll die without ever being a mother."

"*Six* now!" exclaimed Florent. "Holy horseradish! You add another one every month. How would we support them? I'll have to discover some trick for doing without sleep!"

"No, no, no, my friend, not at all," said Picquot. "I'm going to make your fortune. Just think of it: yesterday, when I was going to bed, I had a flash of inspiration. Our restaurant will be famous all over Montreal. And we'll do it with an old recipe from Savoie that will be all the rage: we're going to make *crics*!"

"*Crics*! What's a *cric*?"

"A simple little dish that's quite marvelous. Grated potato, egg, salt, pepper, and milk, all combined to make little pancakes, which are then fried. I'll prepare some right now, and you'll tell me what you think."

He led them into the kitchen and five minutes later he put on each plate a sizzling little pancake, creamy smooth, that everybody thought was delicious. "These *crics* will be our trademark, the signature of The Beanery. We'll serve them with everything: stew, *tourtière*, cold meat, roasts, or even by themselves, instead of an omelet."

"*Cric* sounds . . . foreign," Slipskin observed. "We need another name."

Silence ensued while everyone pondered. "How about *grands-mères*?" Florent suggested hesitantly.

Picquot, galvanized, held out his arm. "A stroke of genius!" he declared. "We have the name: now let's shake the skillet."

Two days later, Rosario Gladu turned out a dithyrambic article about an old Québécois recipe just rescued from undeserved oblivion by The Beanery. Slipskin suggested offering them free for a week, as a side dish. The succulent potato pancakes were greeted first with surprise, then affection, and finally Picquot's discovery became rather fashionable. Fame came soon after, thanks to a long article by Maurice Côté, the famous gossip columnist of *Le Journal de Montréal*, who went to the restaurant himself to sample half a dozen *grands-mères* while the cameras rolled.

The same evening, Monsieur Emile celebrated the *grand-mères*' success with a spectacular attack of indigestion.

His mother's maternal instincts were aroused, and Madame Chouinard arrived at the restaurant in apple-green hot pants, support hose that tried vainly to slim her thighs, and frizzed hair, her face made incandescent by three simultaneous cosmetic procedures. "Would you mind telling me for the love of all that's holy just what you fed my little boy tonight?" she exploded, slamming the door against the wall.

"You come to pay the bill?" asked Gustave Bleau, unruffled. "I just added it up – thirty-six meals this past month, not to mention the first two weeks, when he ate here at least twice a day."

This brief account instantly mollified the barmaid. She approached the counter, pulling up her stockings. "I didn't say that to shock you," she simpered. "But honestly, I'm *so* worried! He's been throwing up yellow for an hour, the poor little tyke. It's the first time since our vacation on Cape Cod when we ate some fish that had gone off. Is that you, Elise?" she exclaimed, turning away from Gustave, who was listening to her with a quizzical gaze. "My little boy's told me *so* much about you! He simply *adores* you!"

"Really?" Elise asked, touched.

"Does he! He's always singing your praises. My Lord!" she exclaimed, looking at her watch. "Eight-thirty already! I should've been at the club half an hour ago. Must run. Thank you *so* much for everything you've done, but *please*, don't feed him whenever he asks – it's like trying to fill the subway tunnel."

"Who's looking after him tonight?" Elise ventured.

"My neighbor, Madame Duquette. Heart of gold. She promised to look in on him now and then. Of course I had to put him to bed. Poor child couldn't even stand up."

"Can I . . . do you mind if I look in on him, too?" asked Elise, blushing.

"Of course not, I'd be thrilled. I live at 756 Gilford, corner of Resther. The door's not locked. Help yourself to a beer or a soft drink if you're thirsty – the fridge is full."

She waved good-bye, then scampered off as fast as her high, laced boots would take her.

Gustave Bleau ran his rag over the counter for a moment, then turned to Elise with a compassionate smile. "Well, Madame Boissonneault, time you were off to see the family . . ."

At nine o'clock Elise arrived at Madame Chouinard's apartment and climbed the rickety front steps with no handrail, which were strewn with the remains of newspapers. She pushed open the door to a dark vestibule filled with the strong aroma of fried sausages. A few feet ahead of her were two facing doors; at the back, you could make out a staircase. She went up to the door on the left and stuck her nose against a little card in a brass frame, where she read:

Floretta Chouinard
Variety Artist

She hesitated for a moment, intimidated, then knocked gently. Behind her, someone coughed and the other door opened. "She's out," announced an amazingly wrinkled old woman who stared at Elise with big piercing eyes.

She brought an exceedingly long gold-tipped cigarette to her lips. "I . . . I came about her little boy," said Elise, taken aback.

The old lady's face registered surprise. "Why you must be the wife of the new owner of The Beanery!"

"That's right."

"I'm so glad to meet you!" she exclaimed, coming up to

Elise as if to embrace her. "I'm Madame Duquette. I look after the kid now and then, as a favor to Floretta."

She sniggered. "Now and then . . . meaning I practically raise the little beggar. So you came to see him? That's nice. He really likes you, you know – he's crazy about you!"

Her expression changed abruptly and her tone turned glum. "He was sick again today."

"I know. His mother just told me."

"His mother, his mother," the old lady grumbled, as if to herself. "Okay, let's go, since that's what you're here for."

She turned the doorknob and walked down a narrow hall. The movement of her long bony legs fluttered her outrageously flowered skirt. Breakfast appeared in the kitchen door and walked resolutely toward her, his ears against his skull. "Get out of my way, you damn cat!" she cried, her foot swiping at the air. "I'd like to wring his neck," she muttered, shutting the door to the kitchen, where the cat had just retreated.

Elise looked around, appalled at the dirt and the mess. A pair of nylons hung from the shade of a hideous cheap scarlet vase made into a lamp. Three apple cores were drying on a radiator. Elise stole a glance at the kitchen, where a box of cornflakes floated in a sinkful of greasy water.

The old woman stopped, brought her finger to her lips, and gestured to Elise. There, under a heap of blankets, Monsieur Emile lay sleeping, his mouth agape. The smell of urine caught in her nose. Lips creased with disgust and pity, Elise watched the child and made a move toward him. "Let him sleep," whispered Madame Duquette, pulling on her arm, "otherwise I'll be stuck with him till all hours of the morning."

She led Elise into the kitchen, kicked out the cat and plopped into a chair after sweeping away a pile of *TV Guides*. "Have a seat, you pretty child. Guess you wanted to talk to him, eh? I doubt if we'll be able to wake him up," she said with a knowing look.

"What do you mean?"

The old woman stared at her wide-eyed. "Come on don't tell me you didn't know . . ."

She stared silently at Elise for a moment. Finally she said, "He drinks."

"Excuse me?"

"He drinks," the old lady repeated.

And to illustrate her remark, she brought her thumb to her mouth, like the neck of a bottle. "It's the honest truth," she sighed. "And God must be heartless, letting a helpless kid get off to such a bad start. . . . Barely out of diapers and he's into the bottle. . . . Oh, the world's a miserable place."

She got to her feet as Elise looked on, incredulous, and opened the refrigerator. "How about a soft drink?"

Elise shook her head.

"Yes, my dear, if you ask me it's criminal, passing on a vice like that to a child."

She uncapped a bottle, flopped into her chair with her knees slightly spread and took a long swig. "I've tried everything," she said, when she'd got her breath back. "But he drinks. And like they say, once a drunk, always a drunk. You can't fight a mother."

"A mother?" Elise repeated, stunned.

"What do you expect?" the old woman burst out. "She's a cold fish. I could tell you things about her but I know my place! You can't imagine! She used to put beer in his bottle at night, to put him to sleep before she went to work. And he'd be dead to the world, let me tell you! But when he bawled with the gas or colic, I'm the one that looked after him. You could tell her a thousand times it was no way to raise a child – might as well talk to the doorknob!"

She leaned forward, with her eyes wide and a nasty smile. "She's *rather fond* of the bottle herself. . . . If you could see her some nights . . . But worst of all, and you won't believe this, she lets the kid have two beers a day! Did you ever hear the like? And if you ask me, he's been cheating for the past few months, the little monkey! The other day my neighbor, Madame Poupart, brought him to me in quite a state, let me tell you!"

She slumped back, arms dangling, mimicking someone out cold. "So what do you expect, my dear? Some people are born to drag around misery, like a horse drags a cart."

Thanks to the *grands-mères*, The Beanery's already large clientele grew even larger. Slipskin racked his brains to find some way to make room for more customers. They decided to advance closing time to 2:00 A.M. Extra staff had to be taken on. Gustave Bleau suggested his friend Gisèle. Under the grim gaze of a former longshoreman who'd washed up in the restaurant business, she'd been working for four years at The Bus Stop Coffee Shop, a greasy spoon in the southeast part of town, trying valiantly to pass off dishwater as vegetable soup.

Florent saw her: he liked her straightforward manner. As for Slipskin, he couldn't resist any woman who was the least bit attractive. Gisèle's muscular thighs and generous, upthrust bosom sent his sense of economy into the stratosphere. The next day, she was working at the counter.

She was a nervous little woman with a snappy comeback, who had kept the good humor of her native Gaspé even after six years in Montreal. From the first, the customers liked her. Her gaping bodice was a balm for tired eyes. She even managed to draw a smile from the taciturn José Biondi, who paid her the signal honor of letting her bum the odd cigarette. Often, after a long look at her thighs or her cleavage, he'd go down to the bathroom for a brief and solitary meditation, emerging quite cheerful and breathing hard.

For the moment, though, it was Gustave Bleau who enjoyed the favors of the splendid creature. The frequency with which they happened to be in the cellar together whenever Picquot asked for potatoes or ground meat led to suspicions that he was even enjoying them on the job.

Gisèle's presence, added to Elise's, was less agreeable to Bertrand. "Sweet Jesus," he sighed to himself, "a little more and I'll be in a convent."

Ange-Albert's arrival a few days later put Bertrand in quite a state. Florent had just come back from a supplier's when Bertrand rushed up, all agog. "Boss, a friend of yours just got here. Good-looking fellow, and nice, too. Poor thing – he looked so tired I sent him to the cellar for a snooze while he was waiting. And I took the liberty of giving him some soup and apple pie."

He'll never change, Florent thought, he's got himself fired again.

Ange-Albert was asleep on the floor, his head on his rolled-up coat. Unshaven, with his complexion the color of mud, he looked like a hangover with feet. At Florent's approach he slowly opened his eyes, propped himself on his elbow and stuck out his hand. "Hi. Nice place. Business is good, I hear?"

Florent gave a brief satisfied smile. "Not bad, not bad at all. How about you?"

"Just fine."

"Still working for Canadian National?"

He nodded. "Just got in from Vancouver. We partied all night on the train. The boss bought the gin. I've got him in my pocket, let me tell you. I visit empty stations, scribble reports, sleep in hotels – *la dolce vita* all the way."

"Empty stations?" Florent asked, surprised. "Why empty ones?"

"Because of some law, the National Emergency Act Governing Means of Transportation. The railway companies have to maintain their stations and other buildings even after they're closed down. So to cut maintenance costs they try to rent them. I visit the stations that haven't been rented and file my reports. I'm still being trained, but I'll be traveling solo in a month. And you better believe, I can't wait!"

The burst of enthusiasm that had just taken hold of him proved to be more than he could take. His features contorted and he cradled his forehead in his hand. "Wow! The gin's kicking back."

Florent smiled. "I'll bring the lush an aspirin," he said, and went upstairs.

"Want me to get him some Fermentol from the drugstore?" Bertrand asked, all compassion.

After a two-hour nap, Ange-Albert was at the counter, grinning and looking rested. Several cups of scalding tea had put him back in shape. While Florent worked, his friend talked about his new career. Renting disused railway stations was an odd-sounding business, about as profitable as manufacturing toilet tanks, but it enabled a dozen civil servants to collect Canadian landscapes under pleasant conditions. "I saw a station you'd love," said Ange-Albert, tucking into a plate of stew. "A little place just outside Sainte-Romanie, in the Eastern Townships. You could rent it for fifty dollars a month, with a nice apartment upstairs where the stationmaster and his family used to live. If I ever wanted a rest cure in the country, I can't think of a better place."

He pushed his plate away and asked if Florent could put him up for a few days, while he looked for an apartment. "I have to find the right place," he smiled, "now that I'm in the service of Her Majesty."

Florent couldn't refuse him this favor, though it pained him. His work was eating him up. He came home at night, drained as a drunkard's bottle. Though Elise worked only twenty hours a week, she wasn't much better off, because all the housework was left to her. At the end of the day they were both drawn, heavy-headed and sometimes sharp-tongued. For some time their bed had been nothing but a piece of furniture designed to facilitate sleep. Sadly, Elise saw motherhood receding into an increasingly vague future.

Slipskin, on the other hand, had never been in finer form even though, since meeting Gladu, half his nights were devoted to the various Venus-à-gogo on Mont-Royal Street. Every night around six he could be seen at the cash register, rings around his eyes but his color bright, chatting amiably as he watched the comings and goings of customers whose money fell onto this fingertips, making him shudder with well-being. He even tolerated fairly well the presence of Monsieur Emile and his cat, though it was obvious that he considered a child the equal of the cat and neither one worth very much. Florent saw him angry only once, and that was with Gladu.

Slipskin and the journalist had taken leave of each other that morning at dawn. Gladu, unsuccessful, had gone home to his wife's abuse, while Slipskin would round off the night in the arms of a demolition contractor's daughter, a charming person of 185 pounds, who between the ages of seven and ten had studied the electric guitar. Slipskin had succeeded in winning her favor after a goodly number of gin gimlets, followed by a copious but vile Chinese meal at the Mandarin Palace (thumbing his nose at his health-food principles). Once the supreme moment arrived when he was to savor the fruits of his efforts, Slipskin turned first pale, then red; gasping for breath, he ran from the bed while his evening's companion looked on stunned. He tore into the bathroom, bent double by an excruciating pain that reduced his virility to dust. Cold compresses brought some relief, but the pain continued most of the night. The girl didn't last nearly as long: she left an hour later, sneering disdainfully.

Terrified, Slipskin went to the hospital. After a hideous three-hour wait, a urologist examined him and told him he was as healthy as a kitten full of fish.

The next night Gladu called for him at The Beanery as usual. Generally, Slipskin wasn't one to confide secrets, but he was so obsessed with his misadventure that he recounted it in detail, as Florent, Gustave Bleau and little José Biondi listened. As his tale proceeded, Gladu grew increasingly agitated: he bent his head, bit his lips, blinked, breathed deeply. Then suddenly he was overcome by an attack of giggles that would rattle the shoulders of a dinosaur. His limbs seemed about to scatter to the four corners of the restaurant. They sat him down, pounded his back, undid his collar. One customer, who thought he was choking on a fishbone, felt ill and asked for a glass of water, which she never received.

Finally, with trembling hands and body shaken by hysterical gurgles, the journalist gestured to Slipskin and the others to gather round and cut off indiscreet gazes. Then he took a small bottle of hot pepper sauce from his pocket and poured three drops into a condom. Slipskin watched for a moment, aghast, then an angry howl poured from his mouth while Gladu, succumbing to giggles again, flung himself back in his chair. "You goddamn son of a bitch, you'll pay for this!" Slipskin threatened, contorted with rage.

He grabbed the bottle, threw it at the wall and left.

For two weeks, he refused to have anything to do with his companion in debauchery. Every day, Gladu came to the restaurant and complained to Florent about his friend's thin skin. "He's got the sense of humor of a turd! They pulled that one on me twice, when I was in training at the Valcartier military base, and I had a good laugh once the swelling was gone. If he thinks he's going to get my sympathy by whining he's in for a long wait!"

Meanwhile, customers were still crowding into The Beanery. Kettles of soup, beans, and stew were emptied as soon as they were filled, sizzling *tourtières* redolent of savory and bay flew onto plates, while Florent bustled around, pale, thin and pleased with his success, almost worried at the extent of it. His parents complained that they never saw him. The once sacred Sunday dinner with the family was now a thing of the past.

One Saturday morning his mother called and made him promise he and Elise would come the next evening, without fail. "Your father tries to hide it, but I know he's fretting," she confided. "He spends a fortune on gossip sheets, trying to keep up with every scrap of news about your restaurant."

Florent listened, smiling contritely. He made a formal promise to come the next night, and was about to make a further commitment when the restaurant door opened wide and he thought for a moment he would die of fright.

"Greetings, young friend," began Egon Ratablavasky, smiling protectively. "I see your business runs like a house on fire."

He laid an emaciated hand on Florent's forearm. It was a very ugly hand. Under masses of red hair that went to the base of his fingers like some unhealthy growth, you could make out the bulging tendons, and the swollen bluish veins that crisscrossed cunningly under the pale, flaccid skin strewn with liver spots.

EIGHT

"You heard I was dead? Bellhops' foolishness! I've never in my life been in such health. Though the same can't be said of my beloved brother, alas, whose remains I've just placed in the earth. I've been in Czechoslovakia, dear friend; he died there in his villa near Brno, of a frightful abdominal fever."

Florent, still badly shaken, was skeptical. "What about the funeral at Notre-Dame? Was that your brother's, too?"

"Of course. It was really his! Yes, yes, it would be in your interest to do some traveling, my young friend. You'd see many instructive customs. Yes, that's how it's done in my country. If we can't close a relative's eyes, we hold a . . . symbolic funeral, so as to comfort his soul, which has departed without our help."

"And the coffin, you burn that symbolically, too?"

"No, I rented the coffin – empty, of course – from an undertaker who kept it for afterward reusing."

"But when I asked the driver of the hearse, he said he was going to the crematorium."

"What else could he say?" Ratablavasky asked shrewdly.

"But let's drop this sad subject if you permit. I came here to – how do you say – measure the health of your business. Outside my door I almost stepped on a letter about you from the Royal Bank that had been put under my door because I have the – how do you say – moral responsibility for your debt. And so, here I am."

It was almost noon and the restaurant was starting to fill up. Gustave Bleau, with more work than he could handle, was sweating like a seal on a furnace and darting furious looks at his boss. Florent had to excuse himself and help out. "Can you give me half an hour?"

"I'd gladly take a cup of tea," Ratablavasky answered with a smile. Then, for no apparent reason, he began to blink, a sort of nervous tic.

I don't know, Florent thought as he stacked dirty plates, but I think he's putting me on. What's in that bank letter, anyway? They probably want information on the business. But why go through him? He wished Slipskin were there to help size up his benefactor.

"Who's that smirking old wreck?" Picquot whispered. Florent, who had gone into the kitchen, put a finger to his lips, then slipped out the back door and ran to a pay phone. Slipskin couldn't be found. Back at the restaurant, Florent caught sight of Picquot behind the counter, pretending to wipe it down as he directed at Ratablavasky a series of glances as subtle as a sledgehammer.

Gustave Bleau came up to Florent. "If you've got things to talk about, boss, I can manage on my own. Gisèle should be here any minute."

Florent went to find his benefactor and suggested they grab a bite at the corner restaurant. "I've just now finished lunch, dear young friend. Besides, you have much things to do. No, no, two words on the sidewalk – that's all I require."

They walked to the corner, then stopped. Across the street, workmen were using power saws to fell a maple tree. Ratablavasky put one hand over his ear and half closed his eyes while Florent gave his report. "Well, well, what excellent news!" he exclaimed, pinching Florent's chin. "My old nose didn't fool me. I predict you'll soon be very rich, my friend. What fun!"

He threw himself in the younger man's arms, to the amazement of a truck driver who ran a red light, grazed a baby carriage occupied by sleeping twins, then came to a stop only to be given a ticket.

Florent and his benefactor chatted awhile longer, then Ratablavasky pinched his chin again and left. Florent watched him go, with his black cape giving him a turn-of-the-century air, and a gray fedora pushed rakishly back on his long white hair, "artist-style." I have to get to the bottom of this symbolic funeral business, Florent thought.

Suddenly, Monsieur Emile came screeching up and hurled himself at his legs. Florent swore and nearly lost his footing, to the great delight of his young friend, while Breakfast looked on, blinking. "I want some shepherd's pie!" the child shouted. "My cat ate all the cereal this morning!"

Florent looked closely at him. "Your eyes are glassy. And you reek of beer, you little bum!"

Monsieur Emile spun around, shot into the restaurant followed by his cat, and reappeared outside the back door with enough shepherd's pie to feed him on a trek across Tibet.

All down the counter you could see nothing but heads bending, forks moving, jaws working, tilted cups being drained. The customers didn't talk much, though some were acquainted. They were absorbed in the pleasures of the table. Near the till an old taxi driver, his cap pushed back, had just dug into a serving of beef stew full of juicy chunks of meat, while discussing with Gisèle the respective advantages of the single state and married bliss. Gustave Bleau walked past Florent with a tray laden with cups, and whispered into his ear, "The old guy isn't stingy: he left a dollar tip! And did you get a look at his flowered tie? Worth more than my suit!"

Ten minutes later Elise arrived. "You couldn't have come at a better time, sweetie," Florent told her, while Aurélien Picquot, with lips pursed and beads of sweat standing out on his forehead, manipulated three frying pans at once. "I've never seen it like this at lunchtime. Seems like half the city decided to come here today."

She dropped a furtive kiss on his cheek, then clutched his arm. "Did you tell Monsieur Emile he could sit on the floor of the restaurant?"

Florent glanced over the counter and saw the child squatting in the corner. "Holy horseradish! He's fallen asleep! He was reeking of booze," he whispered to Elise, who blanched.

Customers noticed the little boy and nudged one another. Florent picked him up and carried him down to the cellar. Monsieur Emile woke up. "You know," he murmured, his voice slightly husky, "I was hiding behind a post and I could hear the two of you just now. The old guy's as ugly as pus. If he comes back I'll kick his goddamn shins."

"You will? What for?"

Monsieur Emile said nothing, but swung his leg threateningly. Florent laid him down on an old coat that Elise had spread on the floor, and the child immediately fell asleep again. "Poor little thing," murmured Elise on the stairs. "We have to get him away from that house."

"How can we? He's his mother's child; it's up to her to bring him up."

And he rushed into the kitchen, his eyes stinging with emotion. As he pushed the swinging door he let out an exclamation. Ange-Albert, wearing his inspector's uniform, was helping Bertrand, who was all atwitter, wash the dishes. "Back from Ontario so soon?" Florent asked. "Weren't you supposed to be gone a week?"

"My boss hurt his back playing golf. I leave for Prince Edward Island in three days."

Watch it, buddy, Florent thought, my house isn't a hotel.

Ange-Albert leaned over and whispered, "Monsieur Picquot told me about your little . . . protégé." He mimed drinking from a bottle. "Is it true?"

Florent nodded sadly.

"Can I go and see him?"

Ange-Albert made several visits to the cellar that afternoon. Back upstairs, he observed with a look of concern, "Beer doesn't make you sleep like that. He must have drunk something else."

Slipskin arrived around ten o'clock. He gasped at the news of Ratablavasky's visit. "A real spook story," he said, scratching his chin. "What'd he want?"

Florent recounted their conversation. His associate's lips became thin and white as string, and his gaze hardened. "You're crazy!" he shrieked in a falsetto voice. "It's none of his goddamn business! What got into you?"

Gladu's arrival cut short his outburst. The two cronies had had a reconciliation a few days earlier, for Slipskin soon missed the journalist's hunting skills and his encyclopedic knowledge of Plateau Mont-Royal. Gladu came over and put a hand on their shoulders. "Quit the squabbling, boys: I just had a fan-goddamn-tastic idea." He stared at them in silence for a moment. "Friends, you're going to advance me a bit of money and we're going into business . . . safes! That's right: it's like a license to print money. I've got the figures. I even picked the brand name: Seventh Heaven Safes. What do you think about that?"

Around two o'clock in the morning Florent was on the verge of sleep when he heard furious pounding at his door; the glasses rattled in the china cupboard. Ange-Albert, who was sleeping in the living room, pulled aside the curtain and saw Aurélien Picquot, wearing sky-blue pajamas under a gabardine overcoat. Florent ran to open the door. "For the love of holy heaven, Monsieur Picquot, what the hell's going on?"

"Give me a cognac, then I'll tell you."

He gulped it down while his friends, sitting around the kitchen table, looked on with concern. The bastard's going to tell me he's quitting, Florent thought, his toes stiff in his slippers.

"*Voilà,*" said the cook with a sigh that sent shivers through the hair on his forearms, "I feel somewhat better now. I couldn't sleep. I kept thinking about that incident this morning, the false ghost. I was thinking and tossing and turning and thinking and tossing and turning some more. And then, without a second thought, I decided to come and talk to you. Tomorrow, I wouldn't have had the courage. I de-*test,*" he shouted, spattering the tablecloth, "sticking my nose in other people's affairs. But this time I can't help it."

"Come on, come on," Florent urged him, "get it off your chest. We all got up to come and hear you."

"That old man," Picquot enunciated slowly, his hand on Florent's arm, "fills me with horror. I was in the war for three years, I crossed the Atlantic six times, when every wave might conceal a German submarine. In a word, I've seen a lot, much of it dreadful. So it takes a great deal to make this old carcass tremble." After a long pause, when he seemed almost prostrate, he went on. "That man this morning made me tremble like an old woman."

"And you came and woke up the whole household just to tell us that?" asked Florent acidly.

Picquot looked at him, astonished, then brought his right index finger to his temple. "For heaven's sake, you don't realize, you don't realize a thing. He's much too ambitious for a man his age. He's a high-powered schemer. You can tell from his looks, from the way he talks, even his neckties! Rather than solemnly preparing for death like most old men – whose number I'll soon join – he snoops around, tries to be witty, and cooks up all sorts of tricks. You must avoid people like that, Florent – there's no telling what he might do."

"Could be, but still . . . the man did do me a fantastic favor," Florent replied, not letting his friend's anxiety sway him. "I mean, I can't kick the shit out of the old bugger and send him packing."

"If *I* were in your place," Picquot replied with an inspired look, "I would take my gratitude, stuff it in his . . . pocket, and then, if I may borrow your elegant phrase, I'd kick the shit out of the man *and* his favor – which should guarantee he won't be around for a while. In fact I'd even sell my business if need be, and establish myself somewhere else on a clear and solid footing. My friend, that man carries the *bubonic* plague ("Careful of the neighbors," Florent whispered.) while you" – and he turned to Elise and gave her a look full of affectionate pity – "you were meant for a life of peace and quiet with three fine children."

Florent got to his feet, somewhat exasperated. "Thanks for the advice, Monsieur Picquot. I promise I'll give it some serious thought."

Aurélien Picquot shook hands vigorously with everyone and went back home, where he slept the sleep of the just, his soul at peace, his duty fulfilled.

Elise pulled the covers up to her chin and huddled against her husband, shivering. "I just hope nothing happens to us," she murmured anxiously. "You should have listened to me and told the old lunatic to get lost. When I was listening to Monsieur Picquot I had chills up my spine."

"Come on, come on, go back to sleep," Florent responded. "Have you ever met a Frenchman that doesn't take himself for a character in a detective novel at least one hour every day?"

NINE

It was some time before Egon Ratablavasky turned up again. His unexpected reappearance and, even more, Picquot's reaction, had upset Florent. Without really admitting it to himself, he hoped the old man would simply forget him. One day at noon, though, he spotted the gray fedora above the curtains at the window. A grayish hand pushed the door open, and the Czech (if that's what he was) greeted Florent with an indulgent smile and gestured to him to go on with his work. He walked slowly to the back of the restaurant and sat in a booth. Florent, up to his ears in orders, could feel the black eyes focused on him, devouring him. Finally, he couldn't take it any more and went over to the old man. "Did you want something, Monsieur Ratablavasky?"

"Just a cup of tea, my friend," he said softly.

The door didn't stop banging. Customers kept filing in. Gisèle shrieked when she cut her thumb slicing bread. Egon Ratablavasky, his hands joined on the table, watched all the comings and goings with a delighted smile. Florent brought his tea. "Are you well?" he asked with forced friendliness.

"Extremely. I thank you kindly."

Florent stood beside him for a moment while the old man filled his cup, his lips frozen in a blissful expression that gave him the look of a character in a wax museum. The fetid odor Florent knew well rose from under the table, making a vile mixture with the smells from the kitchen. Reluctantly, Florent asked, "Did you want to talk to me?"

Ratablavasky looked up, astonished. "Not at all. I just thought to rest my old legs in a friendly surrounding . . . with your permission, of course!"

"Make yourself at home," said Florent, relieved. "And let me know if you need anything."

He turned to go but the sound of smacking lips stopped him. Ratablavasky was staring at him, smiling mischievously and gesturing at him with a gnarled gray finger. Florent came back and sat down. "The other day I told you incorrectly," the old man began in his odd lilting voice. "My brother is in the best of health – may it continue for ages. I paid the hotel manager to say I was dead. And I paid for my funeral, too. Yes, yes, yes!" he said, laughing at Florent's stupefied expression.

Ratablavasky's face suddenly became grave, almost fierce. "And why? Because I wanted to know with my own eyes if you had a little gratefulness for a poor old fellow . . . and your reaction filled my heart with much delight," he added, taking Florent's hand.

Florent stammered a few words, then rose and went back to his customers. Ratablavasky slowly drank the rest of his tea, then asked for another pot. Gisèle, fascinated by his foreign ways, couldn't take her eyes off him. From time to time Picquot stuck his head out of the kitchen, for a signal to let him know if he old man was still there.

Then Monsieur Emile burst in, followed by his cat and a quantity of greasy mud that he tracked across the floor.

"Flo-o-o-orent," he wheeled, "can I have fifteen cents for a bag of ch –"

At the sight of Ratablavasky he stopped dead and so did Breakfast, his ears flattened and his whiskers pointing back. Florent had his back turned. He was buttering toast, lost in thought. Monsieur Emile smiled strangely and minced over to Ratablavasky, who gave him a benevolent sort of grimace. Breakfast stayed put, his eyes dilated. "You want money, little boy? For buying what?"

"Beer," said the child insolently. "To get pissed."

He eyed Ratablavasky at length, then focused on his trousers, made of a soft, silky, flecked material. "But I don't want any money from you," he added, looking up.

The hum of conversations suddenly dropped. Gisèle and Florent looked on, nonplussed. Ratablavasky guffawed, then took out his wallet and put it down in front of him. "And why doesn't the little puppy want my money?"

Monsieur Emile's cheeks contracted vigorously. He swallowed and took a step forward. "'Cause you're mean!"

He let fly a tremendous kick, then took off like a shot while Ratablavasky, bent double, rubbed his shin and muttered imprecations. "Besides, you stink!" he yelled at the top of his lungs, then slammed the door.

Breakfast, caught by surprise, had taken refuge at the far end of the counter, between a customer's legs. "Jesus Murphy!" exclaimed a wide-eyed deliveryman, his mouth full of *grand-mère*, "if that's the kind of kids they're making nowadays I'm getting a vas-tectomy!"

Florent had rushed over to the old man and was trying to clean the mud off his trousers with a rag. "Who is that disagreeable child?" Ratablavasky spluttered.

He tried to make a joke of it, but his efforts didn't fool

anyone. His livid face furrowed with swollen veins presented a frightening expression of contained rage. He drained his cup, limped up to the cash register, bade Florent good-bye and put his hand on the doorknob.

"Good riddance, and may the earth swallow you up," Picquot muttered between his teeth.

"Oh! I forgot to pay!" Ratablavasky exclaimed with a tight smile. "Here," he said, placing a bill on the counter, "give some change to that – how can I call him – deliriant child. He needs it. Good-bye, then, and if you allow, I'll see you soon."

Monsieur Emile was waiting for him, for no sooner was the old man gone than the child's triumphant face was pressed against the glass door. Aurélien Picquot gestured him in and led him to the kitchen, while Florent gave him a lecture in front of everybody. "Here, you little bum," he said, offering him a slice of sugar pie still hot from the oven. "You've earned this, you've got more guts than the rest of us."

"I want some hard stuff on it!"

"Hard stuff? What's hard stuff?" asked the cook.

"You know: liquor."

"Did you hear that? There's no liquor here, you premature imbiber!"

"Liar! You hide it in the drawer by the fridge. I've seen it." And with a flourish he brought out a bottle of cognac.

"In the heat of my labors I sometimes need a little pick-me-up," Picquot explained to Florent, who had to bite his lip to keep from laughing. "All right, you wretched ragamuffin, one drop and no more: alcohol's bad for children; it softens the brain."

Monsieur Emile sat on the counter, swinging his legs and laughing delightedly. Florent took a long look at him, then murmured, "I think we haven't seen the last of your surprises."

Around six o'clock, when Slipskin found out what had happened, he wrinkled his nose till his nostrils were vertical, giving him a vaguely porcine look that was a sign of tremendous anger. Gesturing imperiously, he ordered Florent down to the cellar and there, safe from indiscreet ears, he let fly a string of remarks that stupefied his friend, whom he called a brainless collector of thugs, and threatened to leave him and his restaurant if such a scene ever occurred again. "And get that brat out of here or I'll break every bone in his body!"

"Come off it, Len – you're carrying on as if I'd run down your old man with a tractor. Keep your insults for your dog!"

Slipskin tried to explain, but Florent gestured him to silence. "Go and work at the counter for a while – that'll cool you down. Anyway, I have to go. I promised I'd have supper at my parents and I'm already late. We'll talk about all this later."

Just then Elise arrived. She took one look at Florent and asked, "What happened? You look mad."

"Tell you later."

Rosario Gladu was sitting at the counter, apparently absorbed in *Le Journal de Montréal*, but in fact listening intently. Florent slipped on his jacket and walked past Gladu. "You leaving, boss?" He clutched Florent's sleeve and drew him into a corner. "I wanted to show you my latest find. . . . Friends owe each other little favors, right?"

Holding up a large rubber doughnut, he gave Florent a ribald smile. "Here's a mind-blowing gadget. Helped me keep it up for four hours last night. Takes you back to the days you could ram like a rabbit. On the other hand, you gotta go easy: I don't know why, but it turns the liver to marmalade. My side ached all night."

Florent turned away, frowning. "Christabel!" Gladu muttered, watching him leave with Elise, "he looks like he swallowed a wad of pins. Better keep an eye on him: money's turning him pigheaded."

"No little belly yet?" Florent's father teased Elise on the front doorstep, patting her stomach.

"Not yet," she sighed.

"Look here, son, I'll have to give you private lessons. Some fine old traditions are disappearing."

"Leave them alone," his wife protested, blushing. "As if things like that could be taught. . . ."

Her husband guffawed, then gestured to his son and daughter-in-law to follow him into the basement. After showing off his latest progress on a huge yacht he'd been building for four years, he gave a brief maritime discourse, complaining about the high cost of materials, then he painfully climbed the stairs and hobbled off in search of beer. "Go sit in the living room" he told them. "We'll have a drink while your mother makes supper."

"Philippe," his wife whispered, "remember what the doctor told you."

Two weeks earlier, disaster had struck: Philippe's doctor had told him he was severely diabetic and sentenced him – with his robust appetite for food and drink – to a Spartan regimen.

He entered the living room carrying a tray laden with glasses and bottles that shook in an alarming dance. "Normally I wouldn't have a beer till Sunday, the only day the doctor lets me, but there's company tonight, so caution be damned!"

Elise took the tray from him, and he dropped into an armchair with a sigh of relief. "Now tell me, son, how's business?"

Ever since Florent had bought The Beanery, his father, despite his air of detachment, had been puffed with pride. The older man, who had devoted his life to getting his hands on as much folding money as possible, considered his son's success to be a sort of personal consecration. That didn't stop him from lavishing advice on Florent as Howard Johnson might have done to a ten-year-old. He had firm ideas about the menu, the padding in the stools, how to deal with suppliers, advertising and the best disinfectants for the washrooms.

Florent's mother appeared in the doorway without a sound. "Dinner's ready," she announced in a voice as smooth and pure as an altar cloth.

Elise exclaimed when she saw the table, dominated by a splendid *jardinière* in aspic, surrounded by a ring of mushrooms stuffed with crabmeat. "You come here so seldom" Madame Boissonneault smiled, "I have to use whatever tricks I can to bring you back."

"Don't listen to her," said her husband, giving her a slap on the rear. "In our bedroom, I tell you, she still has a full repertory!"

"Listen to him!" And she immediately began assigning places around the table.

The meal was very lively. Monsieur Boissonneault's verve was inexhaustible, aided somewhat by the tot of gin he'd downed before his soup. The suave, creamy aroma of a chicken prepared in the style of the Ile d'Orléans filled the dining room with optimism and well-being. Under the influence of wine and banter and fine cuisine, colors had taken on soft, inviting tints and, as they ate, everyone was filled with a sense of all-encompassing love that extended even to houseflies.

"Your cousin Octavien came to see us last week," said Florent's mother.

"Oh yes, the banquet man," her husband murmured, laughing behind his napkin.

"His cousin the priest?" asked Elise.

Her mother-in-law nodded. "You just saw him, too, didn't you?"

Florent nodded. "Why did you call him 'the banquet man'?"

"Oh, I'll let him tell you about that. It's his new obsession. I hope you'll get an invitation."

"He's really a charming boy," his wife sighed tenderly. "A dreamer, maybe, but so sensitive – and such a way with words! He'd just heard from his mother."

Elise looked at her, surprised.

"Surely you knew she's been living in Florida for years now. She and I've been writing every month since . . . my Lord, ever since I was married."

"And she never writes to her son?" Elise asked thoughtlessly.

Madame Boissonneault brushed aside the question with a wave of her right hand that could have meant either "I don't know" or "Would you like another cup of coffee?"

"Why, you little monkey!" Florent's father exclaimed with his mouth full. "You mean Florent never told you about his Aunt Bernadette! She's been such a hot topic of conversation in the family that maybe we're burned out!"

"She's a character," Madame Boissonneault explained, with a warning glance at her husband.

"I'll say she's a character! After her husband died she sold the three bookstores in Quebec City, then she buzzed off to Key West, of all places – some hole at the far end of Florida. I asked her, 'Why run so far, Bernadette? Have we all got the plague?' And she says, 'I'm too rich. I don't want all my nieces and cousins lining up at my door, asking how I am and telling me their troubles. God preserve me from that! If I want them,

I'll call them.' One day she stopped writing to her son: the poor kid was boring her with his literature and his words as long as your arm. Instead, every now and then she'd send him a plane ticket, round trip, so he could spend forty-eight hours with her and not a minute more, because Aunt Bernadette's a very busy lady. She's always claimed that absence makes the heart grow fonder, and I think I agree!"

Madame Boissonneault pretended to be shocked. "Is that how you encourage the children to come and see us?"

"I was speaking in general terms. Particular cases are something else. Mind you, in her case that principle's paid off." He turned to Elise. "She and her husband lived for twenty-seven years in two facing apartments, and they got along like Romeo and Juliet. Maybe we should've done the same thing, eh, Rosalie? With my appetites and my pigheadedness I've put you through a lot since our honeymoon!" He guffawed and pounded the table, making the silverware clatter.

"In her last letter," his wife began, discreetly trying to guide the conversation into more respectable waters, "she invited the two of you to come and visit her hotel in Key West."

"She runs a hotel, at her age?" Florent asked, surprised.

"Soon there'll be a casino, too," said his father.

"Thank her for me, but I don't know where I'd find the time to go to Florida. Why'd she ask us, anyway? I hardly know her."

"I told her about your restaurant," replied his mother. "I think she's pleased to know you're in business."

Her husband gently pinched her forearm. "I suspect the youngsters might crave something sweet. Could you rustle up a little dessert?"

She left the table and came back with a raspberry pie, still steaming, and a peach for her husband. "None of this hair-shirt nonsense tonight," he said, pushing aside the fruit. "I'll have some pie, if you please."

His wife served Elise. "Take the rest home with you. He won't listen to reason."

There was a lull in the conversation as there always is when the pleasures of the table are exceptionally intense. They had their coffee in the living room. Though he was pleased to have Florent and Elise there, Monsieur Boissonneault couldn't understand why he kept yawning. Around half-past nine, Florent looked questioningly at his wife and stood up. "Another rough day tomorrow. . . . We'd better get some sleep."

"Patience, my boy," said his father protectively. "Slug it out for another four or five years and your capital will be doing the work."

When Elise opened their door she found an envelope at her feet.

> Arrived in town this afternoon and I've just rented a terrific seven-room apartment near the old Manoir Dorion on St-Denis. My boss didn't like my hotel bills, so he suggested I look for another job. Drop over tomorrow night – 1811 Emery.

It was from Ange-Albert.

"I'm glad he's got a place of his own," Elise smiled. "Now our chesterfield can get some rest."

Ten minutes later they were in bed. The warmth soon restored their energy, which they proceeded to expend very sensibly. "What if it happened tonight?" Elise murmured languidly. She slipped her arm around Florent's neck and soon was asleep. Through the window, he watched an alley cat sauntering over the roof of a garage. I do believe that's Breakfast, he thought. Same size, same fur.

Suddenly his stomach contracted painfully, as if he'd just heard some bad news. He remembered Slipskin's anger. "I'd give my right eye," he muttered, "to know what put him in such a state."

He kept watching the cat, who walked tirelessly back and forth along the edge of the roof. Suddenly there was a strange transformation: two paws appeared in the middle of its belly, then two more. And then Florent flew out the window to have a closer look at this strange phenomenon.

TEN

The next morning, the following item appeared in Rosario Gladu's column "Today's News":

> Among the eating spots where I like to entertain the inner man, there's one peerless place with no match anywhere in town. That's The Beanery on Mont-Royal, run by the *mucho simpatico* Florent Boissonneault. In recent weeks, out of sheer decency, he has befriended a five-year-old youngster named Monsieur Emile, who dines at The Beanery at absolutely no cost to himself. "Not everybody has rich parents," was Boissonneault's humble explanation. "It's my small contribution to a just society."
>
> All this to tell you that The Beanery is a genuine gourmet gastric delight that's easy on the pocketbook, too.

By ten o'clock every household had received its *Clairon*, rolled up with a stout rubber band, one of many free services from the Quebec Liberal Party. At ten-thirty, Madame

Chouinard, with her hair in rollers, burst into the restaurant holding a copy of the tabloid. Seventeen heads turned, and in certain eyes there was a roguish gleam as risqué episodes were recalled.

Florent had just read the item. He was coming out of the kitchen with a bowl of pork and beans. Fearing a scene, he set down the dish, walked briskly up to Emile's mother, and led her into a corner. "It's not my fault, I swear," he said in a low voice, "it's that idiot reporter."

"But I don't mind in the *least*," she cooed, fluttering her eyelids as if she were chasing flies. "I thought it was absolutely *sweet*! A widow's life isn't easy, you know. My neighbors and family will tell you I do what I can. But those bastards, they'd let a baby starve to death on their doorstep if they had to move their fat asses. . . ."

Elise was watching, wide-eyed, from behind the counter.

The other woman went on, her voice gurgling like a bottle of pop. "If I hadn't read that little article I'd never had the nerve to come and ask you a *tremendous* favor."

She stopped for a quick breath, tilted her head to one side, and looked Florent in the eye. "I've got a fan*tastic* chance for two weeks in Palm Beach with my uncle, who's just had an operation on his lungs," she whispered. "He leaves tonight. Doctor's orders – he had to get his strength back. But the poor old man's too weak to look after himself. So – can you imagine – he asked me to go with him – all expenses paid!"

She brought her hands together. "Dear friend, would you have the kindness to look after the boy while I'm gone? You're the *only* person I'd trust with him. The neighbors are out of the question – your wife saw for herself the other day," she said, turning toward Elise, "what kind of neighborhood I live in. Fights on the front steps, furniture flying out the windows, the lanes full of perverts that walk around with everything hanging out. I'd have moved ages ago if I could afford it. . . ."

Bewildered, Florent looked at her, then at his wife. Elise was beaming and nodding. "Did you say Palm Beach?"

"Yes, my uncle reserved two rooms at the Skyline Hotel, a thousand feet from the beach, out of this *world* – wall-to-wall carpet, a little colored boy on every floor – everything you could ask for! Of course I'll pay for his board."

"Oh, we'll manage," Elise protested. "When do you leave?"

"Tonight at seven. You're an angel," she added, bending over the counter to kiss her. "I don't know *how* to thank you."

She kissed Florent on the mouth, then took a notebook from her pocket. "Give me your address so I can send postcards."

The customers kept eating as though nothing had happened, but there was an ambivalent smile on many lips.

"I'll send the boy over with his suitcase right away. Thanks again!"

Elise and Florent watched her leave, astounded at her gall. Her tact was less impressive: as she stepped outside a huge black appeared from behind the door and held her around the waist. They walked off together, roaring with laughter. Gisèle shrugged and heaved an exasperated sigh.

"She's a cunt," said José Biondi. "My brother laid her a hundred times."

Monsieur Emile arrived ten minutes later, dragging a suitcase and followed by his cat. He had a rather stunned smile, like a little boy who's just been given his first bicycle. Elise smoothed back his hair. "I hope you'll be as good as you usually are. You'll sleep in the living room tonight, and I'll make you French toast for breakfast tomorrow. Do you like that?"

The boy nodded enthusiastically, then looked around anxiously until he found Breakfast crouching under a bench. "Oh, there you are!"

He bent down, clutched the cat in the middle of its body and held tight. The cat took advantage of his position to sniff a customer's back, which gave off an interesting aroma of stale sweat. "Will you get a sandbox so my cat can shit?" he asked anxiously.

Laughter erupted in the restaurant. "Come here, sonny," Picquot ordered. "I'll show you how to make a *cipâte au lièvre.*"

"Oh no," sighed José Biondi. "Is that little bum going to be underfoot for two weeks?"

Monsieur Emile raced into the kitchen and sat docilely at one end of the counter, staring hard at Picquot. For a heroic thirty minutes he made no more noise than his cat, causing the chef both anxiety and amazement. From time to time the child would glance at an open cupboard where, the night before, Picquot – thinking himself undetected – had hidden a flask of cognac.

About half-past eleven there was such a mob that Picquot thought it prudent to cook more potatoes. Behind the counter, Gisèle, Elise, and Florent were sweating like a chain gang. "I'd give anything for a half-hour nap," the young man sighed, wiping his face on his apron. No sooner had he spoken than the door opened on Len Slipskin. It was unusual to see him at this hour.

"Great timing!" Florent exclaimed. "We need reinforcements."

Slipskin took off his jacket and went behind the counter. He looked glum – and agitated. "What's wrong?" Florent asked.

"What? Oh . . . nothing. I didn't sleep very well. My mother gave me salami for supper. Yuck! That chemical shit they put in the meat could kill you!"

He stood at the cash register, tight-lipped, all through lunch hour. By one o'clock it was quiet enough for Florent to sit down and grab a bite.

"Monsieur Picquot," Slipskin called out cheerfully, "leave the kitchen and have some lunch. I'll serve. You, too," he told José Biondi, with a friendly tap.

"You don't have to coax me!" said Picquot gratefully, putting Monsieur Emile on the floor. "My legs are as limp as noodles."

"What can I offer you?" Slipskin asked in a voice dripping honey. He brought out a tray laden with steaming bowls of soup, but miscalculated and spilled one.

"Our Anglo friend seems nervous today," snapped Picquot, whose trousers had just been spattered.

Slipskin, red-faced, apologized profusely. Gisèle offered to help, but he insisted on cleaning up himself, refusing any assistance from his "customers." He's weird today, Florent thought, watching Slipskin bustle about, all smiles and concern. But who knows what goes on inside their square heads. . .

Monsieur Emile had slipped out, unnoticed. Twenty minutes later he was standing in the kitchen doorway with cheeks flushed and gaze syrupy. In the midst of a series of peculiar leaps, his feet got tangled up and he fell on his face. "What's going on, little fellow?" asked Gisèle, setting him on his feet. "Good grief, he's as soft as putty!"

Monsieur Emile smiled seraphically, seemingly oblivious to what she was saying. Florent swore, then picked up the child and rushed him into the kitchen, because three customers had just come in. "Call a taxi and take him home," he told Elise, who had come after him, distraught.

Picquot shifted from one foot to the other as he looked on, embarrassed. Florent turned to him. "No, no, don't say it. I know! From now on I'll keep my cognac at home." In the toilet tank, that is, he added to himself.

"The taxi's here," announced José Biondi, looking at Monsieur Emile with a mixture of surprise and admiration.

Elise concealed her discomfiture as well as she could, took the child in her arms and rushed out of the restaurant. A wizened little old lady in black coat and hat was dipping chunks of toast in her tea. She'd seen it all. "If that was a child of mine," she squawked, "I'd've thrown him under a streetcar."

Florent was in the cellar, slumped on a chair. "What's wrong with me?" he murmured. "I've never been so tired in my life." He felt as if his heart had been pushed way down in his chest and was palpitating somewhere near his navel. He brought his hands to his face and rubbed it for a long time. "My cheeks feel like lead. . . ."

He got up unsteadily and went upstairs. "Jesus, boss," exclaimed Gustave Bleau, "you look like you spent the night in a vat of gin and then rolled your face in icing sugar."

"He's right," Slipskin added. "You look worn out. What's wrong?"

"I don't know," Florent leaned on the counter. I'd better get a grip on myself, he thought, or I won't make it through the day.

He straightened up, drank three coffees and dashed cold water on his face, but by eight o'clock Gisèle had to take over.

Monsieur Emile spotted him through the window and went to let him in. At the end of the hallway, Elise gestured not to make any reference to the incident that afternoon.

Florent whistled admiringly. "Crackerjack! You look as good as a rock star, my boy!"

"Elise bought it for me," he said. Blushing happily, he threw back his shoulders to show off a red T-shirt with a magnificent steam engine on the front.

"What's wrong?" Elise asked Florent. "Don't you feel well?"

"I'm wiped out, baby. Think I'll take a shower and hit the sack."

"What about Ange-Albert? We were supposed to drop in on him tonight."

He went to the bathroom without replying. Monsieur Emile watched him, puzzled.

Elise spoke to Florent as he was getting into bed. "What will we do with the child? We can't just leave him . . ."

"Tomorrow, Elise, tomorrow," he sighed, gesturing feebly. "My mind's turned off." Two minutes later he was asleep.

The next morning he felt quite refreshed. Aurélien Picquot found him at his usual place behind the counter, making toast and serving coffee. Around eight o'clock Slipskin came in.

"What are you doing here?" Florent asked in surprise.

"I've come to work."

"To work? It's hardly worth the trouble: you have to be at Musipop at eight-thirty," he said, rushing into the kitchen.

Slipskin tied an apron around his waist, picked up a tray and started loading it with dirty dishes. Florent came up with two plates in each hand. Beaming, Slipskin announced, "I've quit! No more Musipop."

Florent looked at him, astonished.

"I should be pulling my weight, right? Before you work yourself sick."

About eleven o'clock Picquot seized Florent's shoulders and looked deep into his eyes. "Do me a favor, my friend, and get out of my sight. I've been watching you: you look as if you left your blood at home!"

"He's right, boss," added Bertrand. "You're so pale it gives me shivers."

At two o'clock Florent finally had to surrender to his fatigue. He called Elise to come in and replace him, then took a taxi home. "I can't figure out what's wrong with me," he murmured in agony, as he ascended the stairs to their apartment with quaking knees, drooping head, foggy mind, and one obsession: the desire to sleep, to sleep until the end of time.

Elise had already left, and the empty apartment seemed lugubrious. Shivering, he slipped under the covers and was about to doze off when the telephone rang, filling him with dread. He staggered out of bed, picked up the receiver, dropped it, picked it up again, then had to sit down. It was Elise. "I want you to stay in bed till tomorrow, understand? And out of the kitchen! Slipskin will bring you your meals. And before I have to sign up for the Widows' Club, I've decided we're taking a vacation – next week! If you can afford the time to be sick, you can afford the time to get better."

He hung up and stared into the dining room. The oak table seemed appallingly heavy, as if it would sink through the floor. He imagined the racket it would make and started to tremble. "A hot bath," he murmured. "That should straighten me out."

The bathroom filled with steam. Standing at the window with a towel around his waist, Florent watched the house next door slowly disappear in a pink haze. The sound of running water gradually calmed him. Grimacing with pleasure, he stepped into the tub. His legs turned the color of brick. He took two or three deep breaths, rested his back against the glazed enamel and amused himself watching the water rise to his stomach. Suddenly he felt overwhelmed by the warm, spongy atmosphere. He was filled with sickening, gelatinous sorrow, and the bit of courage he'd just gathered fell apart. He gazed at his penis shriveled up in the warm water. Poor thing! it looked panic-stricken, ridiculous, as if it were trying to hide under his stomach to escape some threat. "That's right," Florent muttered, "hide. Can't even make a baby. . . ."

On his way out of the bathroom he shrieked, and his legs nearly gave way. Ange-Albert was sitting at the kitchen table, smiling. "Wha . . . what're you doing here?"

"Elise told me you were sick. I rang three times but nobody answered. What's wrong? Tired?"

Florent slumped into a chair, and his eyes filled with tears. "Shit, I don't even recognize myself. . . . I feel like an empty sack. . . . I'm scared of everything. . . . I work for three minutes and my head starts to spin, my thoughts are all muddled. . . . That goddamn restaurant's ruined my health. . . . I've gotta sleep. . . . I'm sure I just need to rest." He got up, suddenly comforted by the presence of his friend.

"Right! Go to sleep, pal, and don't worry about me. I just came to watch TV."

In ten minutes Florent was snoring. His drawn, rather thin features made his chin look unpleasantly pointed.

Ange-Albert was patiently watching a long movie about the American Civil War, in which the tenacious son of a ruined plantation owner managed to restore the family fortune, sustained by his love for a young Northern woman who had nursed him back to health after he had been wounded by a cannonball. When the birth of their first son was announced, Ange-Albert went to make himself a huge cheese sandwich. Florent was still asleep. His friend gazed at him pensively as he wolfed down his snack, then silently left the house.

At six o'clock Slipskin rang the bell. He had brought a meal prepared by Aurélien Picquot. Florent yawned and looked at him glumly, with sleep-swollen eyes. "I'm not hungry and I'm not in the mood to see anybody."

Slipskin smiled. "I understand. Same thing happened to my father when he opened the antique store. But my mother put him to bed for ten days, and he's been working ever since."

"What's new at the restaurant?"

"Everything's fine. Monsieur Emile's cat fell into a kettle of pea soup but I think he'll survive. The kid rubbed him with ice cubes all morning and he seems better now. Oh! I forgot. Ratablavasky stopped in at two o'clock: he wanted to see you."

"Tell him to fuck himself. I've had enough of him. Sorry, I'm dead tired. I'm going to bed."

"Try to eat something," Slipskin urged, as he closed the door.

"Sure, sure," replied Florent impatiently. Then he went to the kitchen, sat down at the table and proceeded to eat with amazing appetite. I must be coming out of it, he thought, wiping his lips.

He was asleep when Elise came home and didn't wake up until late the next morning when Breakfast, whom they'd decided to keep in the apartment, and who was trying to tell Florent he was hungry, started licking him.

And so several days passed. Madame Chouinard's vacation seemed to be stretching into a sabbatical. One morning they received a rose-scented postcard from Palm Beach.

> Hello, my loves! Must stay another week or two. I sprained my foot and can't move. Would you be angels and take care of my boy a bit longer? I hope the little squirrel's okay and not causing too much trouble. The weather's fine, the palm trees are gorgeous, and I'm as black as a Negress. Yours, Floretta

Florent was gaining weight, but he didn't seem to be regaining his strength. Instead, his lassitude was growing. Twice he forced himself to go to the restaurant, but had to come home after an hour, his head spinning and ears ringing from the sound of the dishes. "That business has done me in," he sighed.

One morning Monsieur Emile walked into Florent's room, as serious as a judge. "I have to tell you something," he said in a tone that made his friend smile. He came closer and put his hands on the blanket. "You're sick on account of me, right?" he asked defiantly.

Florent frowned, surprised.

"It's 'cause I got up on the kitchen table the other night," the child went on without pausing for breath. "And 'cause I run in the restaurant and I play the TV too loud and my feet make too much noise when I get up at night to pee, right?"

His voice was quavering. A little more and tears would flow. Florent clutched his arm. "Will you tell me where you got those nutty ideas?" he laughed. "I'm sick from working too hard, that's all. And I'm glad you're here, even if sometimes I'd like to warm your backside."

The little boy's face grew less anxious, but his gaze remained defiant. "My mother . . . my mother says some people can't stand kids . . . because they're too much work."

Florent laughed again and rumpled the child's hair. "It's true – some people are like that. But we like you a lot and as far as we're concerned you're staying. Besides, I'm better now, can't you tell? Day after tomorrow I'll be back at the restaurant."

Monsieur Emile couldn't bear any more. He ran out and worked off his excess emotion by banging on a garbage can with an old typewriter carriage.

Despite all his good resolutions, Florent spent days in bed, racked by drowsiness, incapable of concentrating. Just a few minutes of television threw him into a state of unbearable confusion. Rock music, which he consumed in great quantities and which usually affected him when he was tired like a cup of strong black coffee, now grated on his nerves. One day he forced himself to listen to a Pink Floyd record; by the end, he was trembling and drenched in sweat and felt, Good God! as if the walls of the room were slowly coming together. He rushed into the shower.

In the past, showers worked wonders. The comforting warmth would enclose him like a womb, transforming rage into philosophy and irritation into multicolored balls.

Today, though, nothing worked. The curls of steam seemed like shrouds, threatening to stifle him; the murmuring water reached out like an endless corridor, swelling with echoes, then winding down into lugubrious reverberations. Florent could vaguely make out the walls of the corridor that extended as far as the eye could see, the cracked and dirty floor, the wan lights. Into what sinister room was he being pushed? He could already see his rigid body covered with hoarfrost shut away in a drawer, his icy eyes emitting desperate appeals.

He rushed out of the bathroom, terrified. His foot slipped. He gripped the washbasin but landed, dripping wet, on the floor, his buttocks bruised.

"Get on with it, get a grip on yourself. It's all in your head. Your imagination's running wild."

A newfound calm relaxed him somewhat, but the rigid brick and plaster of the bathroom walls seemed threatening. They represented his fate. He had become the creature of misfortune. He was no more than a prop in the bathroom, within four inflexible, indestructible walls. Farewell, fine ambitions! Farewell, Elise, who would leave him soon to offer her pretty body to a man who could make her a baby. If the shower pipe were strong enough he'd hang himself and bring his insignificant life to a speedy end.

When Elise came home that night she took one look at him and went straight to the phone. "Enough of this nonsense. I'm calling a doctor. You're as pale as iceberg lettuce."

She had told Florent's parents about his health the day before, and Monsieur Boissonneault insisted on taking him to the doctor himself. "Though I don't know why we're bothering! I know exactly what he'll say: get some rest and curb your ambitions. Do it, my boy! Be a house cat for a couple of months, and deal with the ambitions later. And here's some advice from your old man: if you're down in the dumps, a good hot gin toddy with lots of honey and cloves will dissolve those dark thoughts – instead of just chasing them away like pills. I know what I'm taking about," he added self-importantly. "I've been an expert on sickness since I was fifteen." And he proudly showed his useless leg, as Elise tried not to smile.

The examination went as expected. The doctor listened to Florent's heart, then asked him about work, his family, his marriage. "No problems," he replied, "nothing major, anyway. Everything's fine."

Rubbing his chin, the doctor looked like a crossword addict trying to remember the name of a queen of France who'd died of diabetes; he shrugged and scrawled a prescription for Valium, with three weeks' rest and a warning about overwork, "which is as hard on a young colt as an old horse," he said with a fatherly smile.

"I'm well on the way," Florent muttered as they went home.

"Throw out that prescription," his father ordered. "I'll make you a toddy that'll curl the hair on your legs."

At noon the next day, just a few minutes after Slipskin had brought him his lunch, Florent was surprised to see the fleshy face of Rosario Gladu at the kitchen window. The excited reporter gestured to him to approach. Florent half opened the door, and Gladu stuck his head in. "Is he gone?"

"Who?"

"Slipskin, for crap's sake!"

"Just left."

"Can you spare me five minutes? I sprinted over to see how goes the health," he said, amiably forcing his way in.

He stopped in the middle of the kitchen and looked around. "Holy hell, what a setup! Modern as a week from Monday – with a Maytag dishwasher, no less!"

He slumped into a chair. "Christmas, you look half asleep! You could use a shot of alarm clock. You starting to pull out of it?"

"It's slow," Florent sighed, and tears welled in his eyes as he realized he was in for a good ten minutes of tiresome babble.

"Take as long as you need, my friend," Gladu recommended with a medical air. "Why rush back to work if you'll be farting ice three days later? My old granny used to say, 'Without his health, a guy isn't worth sparrow poop. All he can do is sit on the porch, watch the boats go by and knit.' Take my brother Antoine: didn't give a hoot for his health. At eighteen, he was burning all his candles at both ends. But still . . ." He waggled his forefinger, his eyes dilated, and lips stretched in a bitter grimace. "But still, *he had a delicate stomach*. Yes, my friend, like tissue paper! Got it from Ma. We warned him, but he didn't give a shit: ate what he pleased, day or night, and the amount! Eight eggs for breakfast was just an appetizer . . ."

He stopped again and sighed. His cheeks drooped like pancakes, and his eyes darkened. "One night," he said, his voice different now, "round about midnight, he got a craving for a jumbo rigatoni with mambo pepperoni or something of the sort. I told him, 'Watch out, little brother, your guts won't thank you!' But he just says, 'Mind your own business.' So the rigatoni arrives and, Christ on a cracker! The delivery boy isn't even down the steps and his plate's clean! Plus a family-size Coke that he downs in three swigs. And then zip, off to bed."

Gladu stopped. His voice was very thin. "Poor little bugger. He'd just got between his last sheets. . . . Around 3:00 A.M. his belly starts puffing up like a balloon, his eyes roll back, and by the time the ambulance arrives he doesn't recognize a soul. . . . Two hours later he croaked."

Gladu wiped his lips with his hand and smiled. "But I didn't come to talk about my kid brother," he said briskly. Now he smiled toothily, his features fixed in packaged friendliness. "Slipskin's been talking about you at the restaurant, practically nonstop . . . when your wife's not around, needless to say, and the old fellow's messing around with his saucepans."

"What's he saying?"

"He says . . . he says, my friend, you aren't cut out for business, that's what he says."

Maybe he's right, Florent thought morosely. But why won't this fat clown screw off so I can get some sleep?

"You want the truth?" Gladu asked a moment later.

"If you've got it," Florent said carefully, struggling to keep his eyes open.

"He lied. It's as simple as that. You are cut out for business – but not for restaurants."

He rose and started talking very fast, glancing at the door now and then as if a thousand urgent matters might summon him at any moment. "I've got an idea for you – two, in fact. Think it over before you say no. . . . Sell your shares. The restaurant business is tough. Takes a galley slave to make a go of it. You'll bust your balls, my friend: up from morning till night, night till morning, suck up to this one, give shit to that one, always wear a smile even if you've got a toothache, add, subtract, clean up messes, juggle pots: the St. Lawrence River stops more often than you do! Sell off your shares, old man. There's a better way to get your money to work for you. Two, in fact. Now listen, before you say anything. Afterward you can tell me to go jump in the lake. Wednesday night on TV I discovered a *psy-chi-a-tric* way to make money. By selling cloth! Nothing to it – but somebody had to get the idea. We'd have a slogan: 'Suitaman.' Get it? Men's suits. Every time a customer heard 'Suitaman,' without realizing it he'd think 'new wardrobe.' Say it often enough and our fabrics would push everything else off the market, they'd be the best ones, the *only* ones. And it's all scientific as shit, straight from Dr. Fred himself, glasses, couch, the works. And I'm not the only one that uses psychiatry. You know why the people that make Cherry Blossoms stick a fat juicy cherry inside their chocolates? Because they've read Fred. They know that without actually *saying* it, you can make people think about it, and if you tickle a customer's crotch – discreetly – you stand a hell of a chance of making him open his wallet."

A triumphant Gladu gazed at Florent, whose astonished look exceeded his wildest expectations. In it, Gladu saw recognition of his own genius.

He pointed his forefinger with a look of inspiration and predicted, "No risk, big profits. And it's a cinch. Two or three phone calls a day, the odd handshake, and the rest of the time you can be screwing or sunbathing. All we need is the bread. I know at least three Jews on St. Lawrence sneezing their lungs out behind piles of old cloth; they'd give anything for some fresh stock. We'd just have to . . ."

Florent shook his head. "What's your other project?" he asked with an effort.

Tight-lipped, Gladu screwed up his eyes and gazed at the ceiling, as if the project had just appeared there. "More money, more risks. Yesterday my brother-in-law introduced me to a guy, wants to start a demolition company. It's good business in Montreal these days – seems they're running out of room for new buildings. I think the Arabs are gonna demolish Rosemont and put up fifty buildings thirty stories high. That'll get rid of the old shacks and put us in the wake of progress, as they say. This guy's got piles of contacts at city hall. Even lent the mayor his car for two months, back in the mayor's student days."

The journalist stared, his nostrils flared. "Trouble is, that sort of thing needs a fair amount of cash. We wouldn't be the only ones. And the more people, the more problems."

He patted Florent's shoulder. "Take your time, chew it over, I'll be back in two or three days. Not a word to Slipskin, though, or I'll tear your guts out. I came here as a friend – treat me like one."

The door closed. His footsteps rang out in the lane. Florent collapsed on his bed, exhausted. "Sell my shares," he murmured, as in a dream. "The business is killing me. . . . Sell my shares . . ."

He felt as if the clinging sheets were about to suffocate him.

ELEVEN

Florent dragged himself to The Beanery a few times, but the smell of pork and beans made him sick to his stomach. Whenever he went near the cash register, he made a mistake. The smallest complaint upset him, he dropped plates, spilled coffee, served veal to a customer who'd ordered beef, while the beef cooled off in a corner. He worked for two hours, then collapsed on a chair, dazed, his legs like jelly, eyes burning, his face dry and aching. He was surrounded – and irritated – by solicitude, and felt as if he was being pushed around in a wheelchair. Monsieur Emile took the prize: he watched Florent constantly, trying to anticipate his gaffes, and tolerated, saint-like, all his whims and moods.

For some days he'd been struggling to overcome the awkward propriety that was a legacy of life in the back lanes and yards, even venturing little signs of affection when he was alone with the boss or if no one was watching them. One afternoon, snuggling up to Florent, he whispered, "I don't wanna go back to my mother. I wanna stay with you and my cat."

He reflected for a moment, then added gravely, "I'll sell my cat if he bugs you too much, but I won't live with my mother. She's always on my back."

He pretended to pick a crumb off the floor so Florent couldn't see his face, then blurted out, "I love you guys, not her."

Florent smiled and reached out to hug him, but the child had already run to the kitchen. His arrival was particularly spectacular as Gustave Bleau was coming the other way with a trayful of soup. When the floor was mopped up and Gustave had changed his clothes, Elise laid her hand on Florent's shoulder. "Poor darling, you're asleep on your feet. Why not go home to bed and come back tonight."

He snapped his head up and shot her a furious look. "Why not just bury me? I'm like a dead man."

"Sshh," she said, glancing at some customers at the counter who had turned to look at them.

"Fuck the customers!" he shouted. "They eat us alive, but I have to give them a smile as wide as the Jacques Cartier Bridge. And look at you, for Christ's sake! You're so pale it's scary. You've aged ten years in two months. My health's shot and soon I won't have a wife – all because of this goddamn greasy spoon that has us on the go twenty-four hours a day, stuffing a bunch of pigs! Well, screw 'em! I've had it!"

Jerkily, he paced the restaurant, followed by his devastated wife, who tried to coax him down to the cellar. Monsieur Emile stared at him all agog and Bertrand looked on with bulging eyes, chewing on the corner of his apron.

Picquot came out of the kitchen, gestured to Gustave Bleau to give him a hand, then grabbed one of Florent's arms and raced downstairs with him, holding him as steady as a post. Florent's head was bowed and his face was awash in tears. "Enough!" the chef commanded, showing no emotion.

"You're not going to destroy the business just because your brain's overheated." To Elise he said, "He must be taken to a *qualified* doctor. Another scene like that and we'll *all* be out on the street!"

"Florent, we have to sell," Elise whispered, stroking his face. "This is no life for you. Let's take a holiday. You'll see, in a month things will be different."

"The restaurant's empty," Gisèle announced, and with no warning started to sob.

"There, there, girl, save your tears for your wedding," Picquot told her, "and bring me the cognac. Your boss needs a drop."

Slipskin, delayed at a supplier's, hadn't witnessed the scene. Gisèle described the events later that night – embroidered somewhat by her vivid menstrual imagination. He rang Florent's bell around ten the next morning, and found him sitting in the kitchen, where he'd been staring for ten minutes at a can of asparagus soup, debating whether to open it now or later. He dragged himself to the door and at the sight of Slipskin couldn't suppress a grimace.

"What time is it? Where's my lunch?"

"Later for that," Slipskin replied, smiling. "I wanted to see how you are."

Wearily, Florent waved him inside. Slipskin, breathing hard, observed his wobbly gait, and bit his lip. They went to the kitchen, and Florent slumped onto a chair. "Coffee? I don't drink it anymore – gets me too wound up."

Slipskin declined, grabbed the end of Breakfast's tail and started to stroke the cat, chatting aimlessly. Florent was intent on the cat's frantic meows and beseeching looks. Then Slipskin launched into a detailed description of his businessman's woes. Florent nodded in halfhearted agreement, glad of the company but anxious for him to be gone, his mind floating in a tasteless soup, each thought joined to an equally powerful contradictory one. Then Slipskin relaxed a little, dropped the cat and, while leaving out a few details, got to the point: the restaurant. He proposed that he buy back Florent's initial outlay. "But I couldn't give you much more than fifty percent of its value," he added quickly, embarrassed. "I'm doing it as a favor. I haven't got much money and – don't take this too hard, but the customers aren't coming like they used to. Ask Picquot. The other day he had to throw out ten pounds of hamburger. But hopefully, hard work'll get us back on the track."

"Which means you'd give me six thousand dollars?" Florent asked.

Slipskin nodded.

"That's ridiculous! It's robbery! Maybe business is down, but it'll pick up in a month! You know as well as I do, that restaurant's a gold mine. I won't sell for less than ten thousand."

Slipskin wouldn't budge. Florent came down to ninety-five hundred, then to nine thousand. The other man rose and, smiling stiffly, extended his hand. "Six thousand, two hundred and fifty. My final offer. Sleep on it and let me know tomorrow."

Florent stared at him, then blurted out, "Okay, take the goddamn restaurant – and good riddance! Just the thought of all those animals chewing makes me sick. Elise'll be overjoyed . . . and we're going to Florida for a holiday." Suddenly he was sobbing. "Sorry. You're right, it's high time I sold. That restaurant's turned me into an old woman."

Slipskin stood up. He was pale, and he rested his hands on the chair back to conceal their trembling. "I'll bring a certified check with your lunch and a paper for you to sign.

Now I'd better get back to work. . . . And for God's sake, stop crying."

Florent wiped his eyes on his sleeve and showed Slipskin to the door. "At last," he murmured, his voice breaking, "I'll be able to breathe." Then he stopped suddenly and clutched Slipskin's arm. "What about the loan?"

"The loan?"

"Come off it – the twenty thousand I borrowed from the Royal Bank."

"Don't worry, I'll take care of it. What do you want for lunch?"

When the door had closed behind him, Slipskin stood on the front step, heaved a great sigh and wiped his forehead. His gaze fell to his trousers, which were covered with cat hairs; with a look of disgust he started brushing them off. He heard scratching and turned his head. Inside, Breakfast had jumped up on the windowsill and, with both paws against the glass, was fiercely and contemptuously spitting.

When Elise found out what happened, she wept with relief, then hurried home to embrace her husband. Florent had just closed their suitcases and was about to make reservations for Miami. Elise persuaded him to postpone it. "Why not go to the Laurentians? You'll get as good a rest, and it's cheaper. You're unemployed now, remember. There might not be much in the bank when you go back to work."

Monsieur Picquot offered them his place in Saint-Sauveur. When Florent mentioned rent, the chef was furious. "Listen to the child! Just two days ago he was at death's door and now he thinks he should pay for favors! Keep your money – it stinks. In any case," he whispered in Florent's ear, "I may be joining you in a few weeks. I'm not keen on working with that reprobate. I have a little hunch that the minute your back is turned he'll turn the restaurant upside down. In my humble opinion he cares more about cash than gastronomy."

The next day Florent decided to visit Ange-Albert's new apartment on Emery Street. It was huge – seven rooms on the first floor of an old house. The adjoining building, with its boarded-up windows, seemed doomed to demolition. The apartment, furnished as lavishly as a monk's cell, was in pitiful condition. The windows wobbled in their casements, the floors chanted litanies with every footstep, the walls were furrowed with cracks big enough to put your thumb in. In the entrance hall stood an ancient gas furnace. The day he moved in, Ange-Albert had lit it to see if it worked. The resulting uproar in its rusty entrails persuaded him to suspend the operation.

Elise wandered pensively from room to room, contemplating several generations' accumulation of dust and soot. "All this for sixty dollars a month," said Ange-Albert, gesturing broadly. "Of course it needs a bit of fixing up, but with a couple of friends it shouldn't take more than a day or two."

Florent was unconvinced. They went to the kitchen, where the taps wept an endless lament. Ange-Albert opened the refrigerator. It had been packed so ingeniously with beer that there wasn't room for a leaf of lettuce. "Don't you ever eat at home?" Elise asked.

"Yes, but I just buy what I need, and I often go to the restaurant across the street. The boss gives me credit and his daughter's going to do even better."

Bottle caps dropped to the table and, beer in hand, they started the housewarming. Three hours later, Elise asked Florent, "You sure you can find your way home?"

"Sweetheart, I'm back on the road to happiness!" he exclaimed, slamming down his bottle. "My friends, you can't imagine what the past month's been like. Sitting here over a beer with you, I feel every sip like a rock's being taken out of my stomach. Now that my trouble's over, I can tell you, two days ago I was sure I was heading for the asylum – I even imagined you were making eyes at Slipskin," he said, running his hand through Elise's hair. "It was despair – the real thing. I felt as if I was being pushed into a furnace headfirst."

By 1:00 A.M. he was completely blotto. Elise rummaged in his pockets and offered the car keys to Ange-Albert. Slumped on the seat, leaning alternately against his friend or his wife, Florent kept repeating some incomprehensible story about holidays, orangeade and a man who owed him ten dollars. It was monotonous, but they laughed because the shadow that had hovered over him for so many weeks had started to move off.

The next day, Florent tended his head for a while, then decided to go to Saint-Sauveur. Slipskin called to say that he'd found a new waitress – Gisèle's sister – so Elise was free to leave. What would they do with Monsieur Emile? There was still no sign of his mother, who was likely being held hostage to the Florida sun by another sprained ankle.

"He can stay with me," Picquot offered, his friendship verging on the heroic, for he knew nothing at all about children. "My neighbor does nothing but watch television: for a few dollars I'm sure she'll look after our young friend when I'm not there."

Monsieur Emile was sitting on the edge of the counter, frantically swinging his legs, his eyes brimming and lips tight, sensing that silence was his best ally. Elise turned to Florent, not daring to speak, tormented at the prospect of leaving the child behind, but afraid his presence would spoil Florent's convalescence. "What the hell," Florent decided, "let's take him! I need cheerful people around me."

Monsieur Emile almost threw himself in Florent's arms but, overcome by decorum, merely shouted, "Holy shit, I got lucky!" then ran out to buy potato chips and offered everybody a handful.

They reached Saint-Sauveur in late afternoon. Picquot hadn't skimped when he selected the site for his gastronomic retraining. The chalet, made of peeled and varnished logs, had six rooms and all the comforts of a house in town. It stood off by itself, on a point facing Lake Duhamel, half hidden by the yellowing foliage of a clump of trees. There was a huge fieldstone fireplace in the living room, and an old shed behind the house held the venerable carcass of a 1920s Cadillac. Monsieur Emile left it only to eat, after half a dozen ultimatums. After supper they went for a walk. It was late October. The place, deserted by vacationers for two months, was nothing but solitary roads and boarded-up cottages. A sad setting, Elise thought. Let's hope it doesn't bring back his black thoughts.

She looked at Florent, who was breathing the chilly air, a blissful expression on his face.

The next morning he was out in the yard splitting wood at seven o'clock. A few days passed. His strength was coming back quickly. He rose with the sun, ate a hearty breakfast and spent the day puttering or strolling in the countryside, going on long walks with Elise and Monsieur Emile and returning to the chalet at nightfall. By nine o'clock he was asleep by the fire, digesting a logger's supper.

Early in November there was an unexpected change. Florent started showing interest in The Beanery again. At first it horrified him and he fought against what he considered to be a dangerous invasion, but his obsession proved more cunning than he was, and it took on all sorts of disguises. The most tenacious was concern about money. "Our savings are disappearing, winter's coming, and it'll be hard to find work," he said one day. "I'll have to go back to Montreal soon to look for a job. I could work half days at the restaurant while I check out the possibilities."

Elise tried to talk him out of it, fearing a relapse, but her heart really wasn't in it. She knew that his sickness had been a great humiliation for Florent. It had sapped his confidence and undermined his self-assurance. The tamest project seemed uncertain, dangerous. He saw himself condemned to a perennially low salary, and the thought sickened him. He craved a return match. And wouldn't the most impressive victory be won on the very site of his defeat?

Country life began to pall. "I feel like a patient in a sanatorium," he would grumble. "I don't want to spend my life watching the clouds go by."

Suddenly, splitting firewood was unbearable drudgery. The village grocery store ran out of everything. The butcher sold them shoe leather. The isolation of the chalet, originally a blessing, now seemed disastrous. "If this goes on I'll turn into a bear; I'll be useless in business."

"I liked you better when you were sick," Monsieur Emile told him at dinner one day.

Florent looked at him, startled, then turned to Elise. "Okay, get ready to leave tomorrow. If I stay here much longer you'll throw me out the window."

The next day, as soon as he was back in Montreal, he went to see Slipskin. "Have you hired anybody to replace me?"

"Not yet."

"I've got a favor to ask you. I'm all better now. Let me work here half days while I look for a job. It's easier to ask for work if your wallet's full."

Slipskin's face crumpled like a lettuce leaf. He forced a smile and muttered something, nodding assent, then ran down to the cellar. "What's wrong with that animal? You'd think I had the plague! My friends have short memories!"

Picquot stepped out of the kitchen and took him aside. "I'm glad to see you. You're our saviour. The restaurant hasn't been the same since you left. Your Anglo skimps on everything: margarine instead of butter, tap water instead of milk. I cheat where I can, but the customers are starting to notice, and I've had about all I can take."

"You're right, of course," added Bertrand, sneaking up silently. "Business is rotten. . . ."

"Who asked you?" Picquot interrupted, skewering him with his gaze. "While you babble the gravy's turning to glue. Out of my sight! Scat!" He took Florent by the arm. "Shall I tell you something?" he asked in an undertone. "As long as your bank loan's still outstanding, you're responsible, aren't you? You haven't changed that yet?"

Florent shook his head. "*Alors* . . . it's as if you still had a stake in the business, no? Think about it, my friend. If God has restored your health, you'd be a fool not to take advantage of it." And with that he returned to his saucepans.

TWELVE

When Florent had been back at The Beanery for three days, he fell once more into a gloomy indolence that was alarmingly reminiscent of his illness. Elise pleaded desperately with him to find a job as quickly as possible, even offering to take care of the household expenses alone. Slipskin, who seemed tortured by Florent's presence, proposed an interest-free loan so he wouldn't have to work and could "recycle" himself full-time. Florent, puzzled by Slipskin's behavior, refused indignantly. "Is he afraid of me? Does he think I've freaked out? Or does *he* freak out at anything that brings back the old days?"

Florent's father, still unaware of the deal with Slipskin, showered him with judicious advice. "Go easy at first, son. . . . It took your mother nine months to give you the gift of health, and we added lots of porridge to maintain it. It's not as simple as just waking up fresh as a daisy, like a necktie back from the cleaners."

If I had a necktie, I'd hang myself with it, Florent thought.

Pondering these and other gloomy notions, Florent started his part-time job at the restaurant. One evening he was leaning on the counter, listlessly waiting for a customer, whose arrival would force him to move his numb limbs and engage in a semblance of conversation. Slipskin had an appointment – a remarkably frequent occurrence since Florent's return.

"Those lousy dizzy spells are back!" he sighed. "You'd think the air in Montreal was poisoned."

"What are you up to, Monsieur Emile?" asked Picquot, opening the back door. "Leave that jalopy alone. If our friend Slipskin catches you he'll fry your bottom!"

The child must have responded with his usual lack of courtesy, for the chef slammed the door furiously and went back to work. "Miserable brat," he grumbled. "He needs *discipline*."

Utterly unconcerned, Monsieur Emile continued to play in Slipskin's car; earlier in the day, its rear tires had been mysteriously deflated. Armed with a pocket knife, the tip of his tongue showing between his teeth, he was struggling to open the glove compartment.

Three customers had just sat down at the counter. The first two ordered coffee. The third put his hands on his hips and looked Florent straight in the eye. "How're you fixed for pigs' feet stew?"

"Fine."

"Have you got what I'd call lots?"

Florent nodded.

"See, I've got six White Fathers just back from Kenya coming over tonight. They want a taste of home. There's a taxi at the door and his meter's running, if you get the picture."

Florent motioned to Gisèle to take over behind the counter and sped into the kitchen. "*Zut alors*!" Picquot exclaimed. "Wild beasts that ingest swill and disgorge curses! A raid like that won't leave enough for supper!"

Florent was busily filling containers with stew when the back door slammed and Monsieur Emile's voice pierced his eardrums. "Hey, Florent! Look what I found!"

Florent cried out in amazement as the child, proud as a rooster, came in twirling a revolver. The chef sprang at him and snatched it away. "Damnation! First alcohol, now firearms! I swear, we've sown the seeds of vice!"

Florent took a step, his face contorted with rage. "Where did you get that?"

"Slipskin's car."

"Where's my stew?" asked the customer. "Are you waiting for my taxi to put down roots?"

Florent kicked the kitchen door, disappeared briefly, then came back with four large containers, which he set on the counter. "That's thirty dollars," he said, giving the customer a look that singed his eyebrows. "And if you find anything better, don't hesitate to change restaurants."

The customer paid and left, slamming the door so hard that the paint on one panel flaked off, revealing, to everyone's amazement, a crude drawing of the Sacred Heart.

Monsieur Emile was weeping bitterly at Picquot's harsh words. Florent gripped his shoulder. "You're going to come with me and put that gun back where you got it, you miserable little troublemaker!"

Gisèle stuck her head in the doorway and asked, "What's going on?"

"Nothing, nothing," replied the chef with his most affable smile. "I'll call when I need you."

Florent and the boy went outside and headed for the car. "Why has he got a gun there?" Florent asked himself.

Monsieur Emile pointed to the still-open glove compartment. "That's where I found it," he whimpered.

"Was it open?"

"Yes," he replied with an admirably straight face.

"You're sure?" He's a careless idiot then, Florent thought. Looking reproachfully at the boy, he said, "You should have left it where it was. You could have killed somebody. Besides, who said you could play in the car?"

He slipped his hand into the glove compartment to put back the revolver. As he withdrew it, something fell out. Monsieur Emile stuck his hand inside and brought out a plastic tube full of pills. Florent took it and glanced mechanically at the label; the shock stopped his digestion. "There's another one," said the child.

He rummaged through the assorted objects in the glove compartment and held out a second vial, nearly empty. Florent left the car without a word and headed for the kitchen, followed by Monsieur Emile. "The look on your face!" Picquot exclaimed. "Did you find a corpse?"

Florent showed him the tube. "What's this gibberish?" asked the chef. "'One cap. A.M. and bedt. Egon Ratab . . .' Ratablavasky!"

He looked at Florent, thunderstruck. "By St. George's cross! This is very odd," he muttered, then turned to the child. "When did you find these pills?"

"Just now – with the gun."

The boy was lying, as anyone but a saint would have done. The day before, while he was investigating the yard, he'd spotted – half hidden under an empty tin can – a magnificent, rain-soaked two-dollar bill. He'd bent down, slipped it in his pocket, then hidden behind a garage to admire his find, safe from indiscreet gazes. His face had lit up in triumph and a troubled gleam had filled his eyes. He'd run to a store on Mont-Royal Street where he was sure nobody knew him, and come back a few minutes later with a bag holding six lovely bottles of beer and a package of Sen-Sen, those mints that are so effective at camouflaging inappropriate odors on one's breath.

Then he just had to choose a good spot for his binge, not too far from the restaurant, where his absence would quickly be noticed. He went back to the yard, hid his bag under the back steps, made a brief diplomatic appearance in the kitchen to let people know he was around, then went out again. His gullet was burning.

Slipskin's car was some distance from the kitchen, by a ratty looking fence. The doors were locked but one window was open a crack. That was all Monsieur Emile needed: in two minutes he'd snared the lock with a bit of wire and was comfortably settled on the back seat, a bottle between his knees. To avoid surprises, he locked the door and hid his bag under the front seat. After the second bottle, he had a strong urge to pee. He relieved himself near the fence and came back to the car. Now he was drowsy. Prudently, he slipped a pinch of Sen Sen in his mouth, stretched out on the seat, then changed his mind and got down on the floor. It was less comfortable, but safe from prying eyes.

When he woke up, the car was heading down St-Denis Street. Above him he could see Slipskin's carrot-colored hair. The pleasant aroma of beef stew filled the air. His stomach was growling and there was a bitter taste in his mouth. He considered signalling his presence with Frankenstein's celebrated yell (it would be fun to make the creep sweat a little), but he was afraid that even with the Sen Sen, his breath would betray him and Slipskin would search the car.

It was around noon, so Slipskin must be delivering lunch to Florent, who was working nights at the restaurant now, spending his days job hunting. It was best to stay hidden behind the seat: Carrot top would go straight back to The Beanery and he could easily slip out of the car, with no one the wiser. Then he'd just have to invent some little story to account for his absence.

The car drove off St-Denis and into a battered laneway. Monsieur Emile was surprised – Florent never took this route home. Suddenly, he almost smashed his nose against the back of the seat. Slipskin had slammed on the brakes. An odd series of events followed: first, the boy heard a crumpling sound, as if someone had reached into a paper bag and snapped a lid. The aroma of stew was so strong that the child's lips glistened with saliva. Then he heard a click, followed by fumbling in the glove compartment. Curious, he slowly raised his head, then lowered it immediately, stunned: Slipskin had just taken out a revolver – a real one! – and put it on the seat beside him. So he wanted to kill someone. Florent? Monsieur Emile huddled in a corner, shuddering. He wasn't really surprised. He'd always thought Slipskin was a rotten bastard. A polite one, of course. There were always one or two in the gangster movies on TV. They were the worst, the ones you had to shoot down first, or they'd shoot you in the back – and grin as they did it.

There more weird noises, then the car shot off again. Eyes shut, Monsieur Emile tried to think of how to thwart the smiling gangster's plans.

While Slipskin was going up to Florent's, the boy rushed over to a variety store that gave him a view of the apartment. Slipskin stayed only three minutes, then raced down the stairs and started his car. He had barely turned the corner when the child rang Florent's bell.

"What are you doing here!" Florent exclaimed with his mouth full. "Did Slipskin bring you?"

"No, I walked," the child lied, relieved to see his friend alive.

He decided then and there to keep his adventure to himself and do his own investigating. Especially because he had to get back those four bottles of beer.

Florent held out his hand. "Give me the pills, Monsieur Picquot. I'll try to find out about them."

"Excellent idea. Where?"

"The Charleroi Pharmacy. They filled the prescription."

Picquot joined Florent on the steps. "Shall I go with you, my friend?" he asked hesitantly, almost fearfully.

Florent drove away, apparently without hearing him. "What's got into him?" asked Gisèle, bursting into the kitchen. "He nearly ran down Madame Dubuc!"

Picquot shrugged, and as soon as Gisèle had gone, enjoined Monsieur Emile. "Not a word to a soul, little man, all right? Otherwise something dreadful might happen to us."

"Course not," he grunted, annoyed not to be credited with better judgment.

Slipskin arrived just then and blurted out, "Where's Florent?"

"At home, sick, as usual," Picquot replied in a funereal tone.

"Poor guy. I wonder how much longer I'll be able to keep him."

Two hours later Elise heard something that astounded her. "Phenobarbital!" she exclaimed, taking the pill from Florent. (He'd been careful to put both tubes back in the glove compartment.) "What's that?"

Breakfast, who was sitting on the table, reached out his head to sniff the tablet, then recoiled in disgust. "The pharmacist wouldn't say much, so I went to the library and looked in a medical encyclopedia. I was in a cold sweat. Phenobarbital, my pet, is a tranquillizer – a strong one. For serious cases. Russian doctors use it in psychiatric prisons, to bring hotheads into line. See what's happening? In Montreal, I'm obsessed with death, I can't hold a fork, the restaurant smells make me sick. Then we go to Saint-Sauveur and I take ten-mile walks, I putter around, eat like a bear – but back in Montreal, it starts all over again."

Elise gripped his hands, her eyes filled with tears. "I don't believe it. My God, I don't believe it! So you *weren't* sick!"

Breakfast watched her sobbing in Florent's arms, then he jumped off the table to look for a quiet spot where he could dream in peace.

"Why did he do it? Why?" she asked over and over, wiping her eyes.

"You mean *they*. There were two of them. The old man helped. The old man supplied the drug, and Slipskin put it in my soup. Why? To force me to sell out, cheap. I sold my share for a dog's turd. Now I realize what swine they are! When I came back from Saint-Sauveur, Slipskin was afraid I'd want to hang on to the restaurant, so he started the treatment again."

"Are you positive?"

"Well, I've got a plan that should clear this up once and for all. Tomorrow, you get him out of the restaurant for a couple of hours. While he's gone, I'll fill the capsules with this." And he took from his pocket a flask labeled:

DR. DORION'S

GENUINE PURGATIVE POWDER

PATENTED FORMULA

Elise smiled. "Are you serious?"

He poured a bit of powder onto the table, broke open a capsule and compared the two substances. "Perfect," he said with a satisfied smile. "They look identical."

He wet his fingertip, touched the purgative and brought it to his tongue. "Even better! It's revolting! I'll know right away if they're drugging me, without having to wait for the effects."

Elise watched him, shuddering; she was overcome, terrified, transported with delight. "My Lord! And I was sure . . . I was going to call a psychiatrist. . . ."

Breakfast returned to the kitchen and watched them with astonished eyes, laboring to make the connection between the dreadful capsule and the passionate kisses he was witnessing. But he soon lost interest and ambled into the living room, summoned by the warmth of the radiator.

Florent's final doubts were soon dissipated. Slipskin, undoubtedly stricken with remorse, was stepping up the doses to get his former associate out of the picture as fast as possible, appalled as he was at his victim's sighs and crumpled face and staggering gait. Florent, who felt he'd earned a little fun, continued to have his lunch delivered. Sometimes it was the soup that was drugged, at other times the coffee, the mashed potatoes – or all three. His morale had climbed several notches, and his rancor, too. He'd been had – royally. How could he get back The Beanery? By denouncing Slipskin to the police, as Elise had been begging him to do for two days now. Picquot, though, didn't agree.

Florent invited him over one night to talk things over. The chef arrived around ten, unbelievably agitated, and looked out the window for ten minutes until he was sure his taxi hadn't been followed. When he'd calmed down a little, Elise showed him into the kitchen and immediately began to argue that the most sensible thing to do was go to the police the next morning, and file a complaint against Slipskin and Ratablavasky.

"If you don't mind!" the chef interrupted. "We've reached a decisive point. Your entire future depends on this conversation. It's important for me to collect my thoughts, and that requires solitude and silence."

Florent couldn't help smiling. "Go in the living room, Monsieur Picquot, make yourself comfortable. We'll try to be quiet."

Half an hour later the chef reappeared, holding a big black notebook in which he'd carefully listed his arguments. He bowed to Elise. "You first, child."

"I've said all I have to say."

"Well, then," he began, tugging at his mustache. "I beg you to give me your full attention. Now, you know I can't claim objectivity in this matter: no one's more partial than I where the police are concerned. I loathe them all. They're responsible for three-quarters of the crime on earth. To quote a humorist I hold in great esteem, a police inspector makes twenty-five thousand a year – plus his salary. And if they're not underhanded, their incompetence, stupidity, laziness . . ."

He sighed. ". . . would drive a man to suicide. Think of it: last year the rate of crimes solved in Montreal rose – to a dazzling thirteen percent! But I don't want you to accept those arguments. Perhaps I'm blinded by hatred. After all, there may be some sensible, hard-working, helpful inspector somewhere. I've heard of such things. But consider this: Slipskin's skill may well have let him poison you without your knowledge, I grant you, but . . . but how can you establish a clear, irrefutable link between the poisoned food and the fact that five weeks earlier you sold him your shares for a song? In other words, what evidence do you have that on a given date you were under the influence of a drug, and that because of that drug you'd made a bad deal? There's an assumption, granted – but is it enough to convince a judge?"

Florent raised his hand. "I . . . I'm not finished. Now ask yourself the following question: what's more important? Sending Slipskin to jail (supposing you can do it) or getting back your restaurant? If you notify the police you lose control of the matter, it falls into the hands (and what hands!) of justice. You lose your bargaining power to a flock of simpletons. But you also lose a powerful weapon: threat! Yes, indeed! Let's suppose that you act by yourselves. You squeeze the rascal. You wave the proof of his ignominy under his nose. You demand he release the restaurant forthwith, or else. The police, oh yes, the dread police – dreadful in theory, in point of fact laughable. I know that scoundrel. He's such a coward he'll have trouble staying on his feet. He'll sign whatever you want. As for the money he's already given you to buy back your initial outlay, he'd never dare ask for it, take my word. The thief will get his comeuppance and you'll have a double revenge!"

Picquot wiped his brow and sat down. His notebook was a formless mass in his palm.

"And if all else fails," he concluded, "there's nothing to stop you from going to the police!"

Elise and Florent, impressed by his speech, looked at him in silence, then Florent murmured, "You're right."

They decided on a move that would stun Slipskin, forcing him to release his claim before it occurred to him to seek out his old accomplice. Ratablavasky had undoubtedly seen it all before and wouldn't lose his head so quickly. Florent could use Picquot, whose volcanic rages had always been very effective.

Three days had already gone by. Now it was Friday and Florent had decided to wait for the restaurant to close, then lure his enemy into the kitchen where they could work him over at their leisure. All day, he struggled to appear at his worst. During supper, he feigned a fainting spell while carrying a bowl of pork and beans, spilling half the contents on Slipskin, who had to go to the cellar and change. He then advised Florent to go home and rest until the next day, but Florent refused, insisting he was completely recovered and feeling better than ever, though his haggard look, staggering gait and countless slips belied his claims. Their scheme was beginning to bear fruit. Slipskin – a crook but no sadist – couldn't bear to look at Florent. His hands shook, he dropped plates and yelled at everybody. He went to the kitchen and offered Florent two months' paid holiday to look for work. He refused, saying, "I want to earn my living like anyone else. You've helped me too much already."

A sickly grimace twisted Slipskin's face. He sighed and slumped out of the kitchen. "Tee hee, you bastard!" muttered Picquot, as José Biondi, suspecting something was up, looked puzzled. "I'd swear you'd been into the capsules, too!"

Nine o'clock came, the usual time for Florent to go home. Slipskin waited for this moment, as eager as Tantalus. "I'll stay here," said Florent. "Elise is visiting friends and I don't like being alone in the house."

And then, to keep Slipskin from leaving, Florent made so many blunders that the other man had to do the work of two. Around eleven o'clock the swindler's nerves were in the same state as those of the *Titanic*'s captain when the Atlantic Ocean was licking at his chin. Business was petering out. Once the door opened and two rubbies staggered in. Slipskin got rid of them. "Holy mackerel!" he sighed. "I've had it!" Turning to Florent, he announced, "Closing time!"

Heart pounding, Florent turned the key in the lock. Then he went to the till, where Slipskin was fiddling with the day's receipts, the tip of his avid tongue in the corner of his mouth.

"Okay," he said harshly, "let's talk. Go to the kitchen."

Slipskin looked up, surprised, and Florent's expression made him squirm. "What's up? Something wrong?"

He followed Florent, who pushed the door and waved him inside. When he saw Slipskin, Picquot untied his apron, chuckling with hateful joy. The purring of the refrigerator seemed very loud. "Well, what is it?" Slipskin repeated, louder now, an evil glint in his eye. "What're the two of you up to?"

"I made a little discovery three days ago," Florent replied, showing him the pill bottles. "Interesting, eh?"

The chef, whistling, had taken two huge butcher knives from a drawer and placed them on the buffet beside him.

"What's that?" Slipskin stammered, his lips growing whiter and thinner. "Medicine?"

"Don't play innocent, you son of a bitch – you know very well what it is," Florent said, gradually overcome by savage rage. "It was in your glove compartment."

"Scum!" shouted Picquot, crimson. "Filthy trash! You deserve to fry! If I didn't have such self-control, I'd slit your throat like a pig!"

He picked up a knife and moved toward Slipskin, whose shoulders had sunk. Florent gestured to the chef to post himself at the kitchen door, then locked the back door and returned to his enemy. "You know what I did three days ago, you bastard? I emptied your capsules and filled them with some powder of my own. It's the strangest thing: ever since, life's been looking very different. I'm not tired anymore, my depression's gone, and if I had to sell my share again, the price would shoot up like you wouldn't believe!"

"I don't understand what you're talking about," Slipskin said weakly. "Let me go or I'll call the police."

Picquot roared, brandished the knife. "Don't!" the poor devil yelped and bounded into the next room.

There was a snap and the chef came back holding the telephone. "*Voila*! This should simplify matters," he announced, and threw it in the sink.

Florent made a move toward Slipskin. Their faces were almost touching. His jaw muscles were so tense that he had trouble talking. "Now listen here, you Anglo asshole. I'm not a prick like you've been for the past two months. I could put a knife through your eye just to teach you a lesson. You're alone. There'd be two of us to describe the accident. And quit smiling!" he shouted, with a ringing slap.

"*Voila*! At last! Bravo!" exclaimed the chef.

Slipskin made a run for the dining room door, but Picquot got there first. A copper saucepan flew at his legs. It threw him off balance, and he landed on the floor. Florent grabbed him and pulled him to his feet. "Now, my friend, you're going to take a piece of paper and make me a nice donation: the restaurant for the sum of one dollar."

"A dollar?" Slipskin moaned. "That'll ruin me!"

"Could be. But as a consolation prize, you can keep your eye. Next time, open it a little wider before you start fucking around."

"Please let me explain. I didn't have a choice. It's not my fault, Florent."

"Monsieur Picquot, will you keep an eye on him while I go out and call the police?"

"Okay, okay," said Slipskin hastily. "What am I supposed to write?"

Picquot brought pen and paper. Slipskin bent over the buffet and wrote as Florent dictated.

Suddenly there was staccato rapping at the door. Someone was knocking so hard that the thorns on the Sacred Heart were multiplying alarmingly. Florent looked into the other room and exclaimed, "Crap! It's Monsieur Emile's mother! What lousy timing."

"Great gods! She's as drunk as a Polish regiment!" Picquot exclaimed as the pounding intensified. "Shall we let her in? What a racket! *I'll* have a word with that painted strumpet!"

"No, Monsieur Picquot. Be polite and show her in. And you," he said to Slipskin, who was putting on his jacket, "stay in your corner and keep quiet. You aren't leaving till we've settled our little business matter."

Madame Chouinard burst into the restaurant, squealing, "Where are you sweetheart? Mummy's come to take you home and show you all your presents."

"Calm yourself, madame, your child's not here," said Picquot, gawking in spite of himself at the two immense tanned breasts blossoming in a bodice covered with midnight-blue sequins.

Florent appeared in the kitchen doorway. "Evening, Madame Chouinard," he said with forced cordiality. "As you might imagine at this time of night, your boy's been asleep for ages. Go and get him if you want, though. I'll tell my wife. How's the ankle?"

"A little better, thanks," replied Madame Chouinard, with an extraordinary effort to give her lips their usual elasticity. "I still limp a bit, but only on stairs." Then she pounced on him and planted a long wet kiss on his mouth. "Thank you *very, very* much for everything you've done for my little boy," she cried, as Florent discreetly wiped his lips. "You're a pet, and so's your lady."

She tried to step back, but her feet got tangled and she had to clutch the counter. "Sorry, I had a bit too much to drink on the plane," she smiled. "I was so homesick I was in a fog, and when that happens I have to drown my sorrows or I turn vicious. I hope my little lamb wasn't too much trouble."

Then, before he could reply, she unbuttoned her coat and started to take it off. Picquot clutched the collar and briskly pulled it up. "Shall I call a taxi or would you rather make your own way home?"

Madame Chouinard shot him a furious look. "What's with you, Frenchy? You seen enough of my face? This here's a public place and I've got the right to be served."

She turned to Florent. "You wouldn't have a drop of left-over coffee?" she simpered. "That would put some strength in my legs. I wouldn't want Madame Boissonneault getting the wrong idea about me."

Florent had no coffee. And even less desire to continue the conversation. Though she was drunk she could feel it, like a stinging sensation in her diaphragm. She did what she could to look offended, then headed for the door. "You know my address?" asked Florent.

"I should – I sent you postcards."

"Can I go now?" Slipskin asked when the door was shut.

Florent read what he'd written and showed it to Picquot. At the chef's nod, he opened the back door. "To be on the safe side, we'll see the notary tomorrow morning. I'll pick you up at eight. And don't try any tricks: with the evidence I've got you could be in the slammer for a good long stay."

Slipskin grimaced, shrugged and disappeared into the

night. Five minutes later, Florent had reconnected the telephone. At home, Elise picked up the phone almost before it rang. "God, you've been ages!" she exclaimed. "I've been trying to call for half an hour."

"Sweetie, we've got our restaurant back. Tomorrow morning we see the notary and everything's settled. Happy?"

"Listen to him," Picquot grumbled. "Sounding the trumpets of victory, though we've scarcely won a skirmish."

He went on in the same accusing tone but Florent, wild with joy, didn't hear him. He hung up, turned to Picquot, and held out the keys he'd taken from Slipskin. "Do you mind locking up? I want to go home to my wife."

Elise was very happy, despite the call she'd just received from Madame Chouinard announcing her plans to pick up her son the next day. "We have to celebrate my victory!" Florent decreed. "I'll open a bottle."

Elise, who was superstitious, objected that everything wasn't settled, that it was tempting fate to scoff at danger before they were sure they'd escaped it. But the cork popped, anyway, and by midnight Elise was sure that happy times had returned.

Their happiness ended when the doorbell rang at seven o'clock the next morning. Florent opened it and recoiled, white as whey at the sight of Slipskin and Egon Ratablavasky, as solemn as a cathedral. The old man smiled, took off his fedora and tossed his long white hair. "May we, dear young man, have a three-part conversation? I have a pleasant news for you and your delightable wife."

Without waiting for an invitation, he sat down at the dining room table. His air of distinction and respectability gave the intrusion the semblance of a friendly visit, as if he were some wealthy, debonair relative. Slipskin, very cold, stood in a corner and stared at the floor. Ratablavasky took a wad of papers from his pocket and slowly began to spread them on the table. "Let us commence," he said apologetically, "with a disagreeable prelude."

Florent, rooted to the spot, watched him in silence, fascinated by his sparkling teeth, which seemed at times to produce a sort of luminous halo around his mouth. He must spend hours polishing them, Florent reflected.

A familiar odor began to spread through the room, blending sickeningly with a powerfully scented perfume. "Now then," Ratablavasky smiled, looking down, "I bring these papers together before my eyes and what do I discover? My compliments, madame," he said, rising as Elise came in, shuddering, her face puffy. "Do, I pray, excuse this early morning visit."

He sat down again. "I bring together these papers, then, and what do I discover? That for some time now I have been the owner of the delicious restaurant called The Beanery."

"What!" Florent exclaimed, seizing the document.

"Ho ho! Hee hee! Such emotion, dear fellow, such emotion! Very well, here's the story. You sell your shares to Mister Slipskin, here present. The same Slipskin repeats the action, thus becoming my agent, in a manner of speaking. Correct?" he asked, turning around.

Slipskin nodded. "Verify, verify," Ratablavasky urged, pushing the papers toward Florent. "The notary guided, the law was totally respected." He waited a moment, then spoke again: "Now, as to the unfortunate consequen –"

"Skip the speech," Florent interrupted, "I get the picture. Good for you. Now screw off!"

Elise covered her face with her hands and sobbed.

"Come, come, let's show some courage," said Ratablavasky, extending a hand, which Florent pushed away disgustedly. "We've swallowed the bad news, now let's relish the good. You have obligations, isn't it, in respect to the Royal Bank . . ."

"What do you mean, *obligations*?" Florent pointed to Slipskin who was sitting with his legs crossed, taking everything in, squinting with glee. "That bastard took over my debt when I sold him my shares!"

Then he stopped, a resigned smile on his lips. "Yes, that's true . . . a verbal agreement. . . . It was just a verbal agreement. . . . You've got me by the short ones. . . . Screwing people's obviously nothing new to you. . . . Okay, get on with it. I want to air out the room. . . ."

The old man started and his face turned red, but he said nothing. "Well?" asked Florent.

"Very well, dear young friend, here are my proposals: if you show wisdom and don't try to make trouble for those who are protected by the power of the law, yes, of course, we'll be happy to sign an agreement, *on paper*, to repay the bank ourselves. After all, you still owe $12,780 and a few cents, isn't it?" He paused, then continued. "On the other hand, if you persist . . ."

He raised his hand, extended his forefinger and traced a dizzying fall. Florent was silent for a moment and then, his face grim but his voice calm, said, "Get out. You make me puke. I'll think about your generous offer. . . . As for you," he told Slipskin, "I'm glad you're taking over. Saves me the trouble of getting even. Before long your skin won't be worth any more than mine."

At the same moment Picquot was making a majestic entrance at The Beanery, his speech and complexion florid, his soul magnanimous. He was busy giving orders when Slipskin and Ratablavasky appeared, all smiles. The chef's jaw dropped, and he felt as if a lead weight had fallen on his shoulders, taking his breath away. "What . . . what are you doing here?" he stammered. "Ah, I see," he murmured, after Ratablavasky, with charming good grace, had informed him of the latest developments.

He took a deep breath, ran his hand over his forehead, shook his leg. His strength seemed to come back. "Far be it from me to question your legendary honesty," he said at length, "but I would be grateful if you'd permit me to confirm your statement."

"Go ahead, go ahead," Ratablavasky smiled, pointing to the telephone.

The chef hung up almost immediately, utterly distraught. "I understand how you feel," the old man said gently, "but there are sometimes situations, you see . . ."

Picquot looked at him, seeming not to hear, then said, "If you'll allow me, I'd like to take my saucepans."

Slipskin nodded.

Picquot slipped out. There was a certain commotion, then Picquot's voice grew louder, ringing out like the trumpets of Judgment Day. "Menu for today, November 16, 1974. To begin, cabbage coup *à la* watch-it-run!"

There was a deafening cash, and fifteen gallons of soup spilled onto the floor with a sound like a furious sea.

"Secondly," Picquot continued, while Slipskin, who had raced to the kitchen, took a direct hit that sent him to the floor, "meatball stew Anglo-style."

Picking up a huge cauldron, he poured the contents over Slipskin, who landed on his back again, gagging on the cold gravy, slipping and rolling among the meatballs. "Thirdly," continued the chef, his voice constantly rising (two curious passersby pushed open the restaurant door and stood in the doorway, aghast), "we are honored to present to our faithful clientele this airborne blueberry pie."

He hadn't finished his sentence when a baking dish flew from the kitchen to the cash register, landing in a bluish haze. The two gawkers vanished. "As for you, you mass of clogged arteries," he shouted at Ratablavasky, who was watching everything with a condescending smile, "I advise you and your vile acolyte to behave yourselves. It will take me half an hour to gather up my kettles, then I'll leave this brigands' nest forever."

Slipskin, wild with rage, wanted to strike him, but Ratablavasky stopped him with a gesture. "Leave him, my friend. . . . Let our gentle chef terminate his departure. . . ."

Meanwhile, as soon as the two men had gone, Florent called the police to lodge a complaint. An officer turned up early that afternoon and took down his statement. "An investigator will be in touch with you shortly," he promised.

He said good-bye and left. Two days passed with no sign of an investigator. Florent called headquarters on Bonsecours Street. He was referred to the commercial fraud department. No one had heard of his case: the report had likely gone astray. But they promised an inspector would be at his house within the hour. Florent waited all morning. The inspector was still taking his time. Furious, he called headquarters and asked who was in charge of his dossier.

"Monsieur Drouin, Oscar Drouin," a secretary replied.

"Let me talk to him."

"I'm sorry, he's in a meeting. Do you want to talk to his assistant?"

The assistant listened to his story, then admitted he could do nothing, as such matters weren't within his jurisdiction.

"Who should I speak to then?"

"Inspector Blouin. He'll be here in an hour. Give me your number and –"

"Never mind, I'm on my way."

Twenty minutes later he marched into police headquarters. An amazed reception clerk told him she didn't know Inspector Blouin. "Ask on the second floor. I've only been here six months. Maybe they know him."

He went upstairs and asked for the inspector. He had to wait twenty minutes, then a fat man with sleepy features gestured to him from a doorway. "I'd like to speak with Inspector Blouin," said Florent.

A look of annoyance appeared on the policeman's face. "Who gave you that name?"

"Inspector Drouin's assistant."

"Inspector Drouin retired two years ago and this is the first I've heard about any assistant. Besides, there's no Inspector Blouin here and never has been. As you can see that damn inspector's become a curse for us. Not a day goes by that we don't get a call for him. Just what do you want?"

"To file a complaint against two individuals who stole my restaurant."

The policeman looked at him closely, went to his office, picked up the telephone and spoke for several minutes. "Go up one flight," he said, reappearing in the doorway, "and ask for Inspector Gouin."

Incredulous, Florent asked, "Inspector who?"

"Gouin, Gouin, Oscar Gouin," he repeated impatiently, shutting the door.

Florent was on his way when he heard hurried steps behind him. "Monsieur! Monsieur!" shouted a tall blond young man, all out of breath. Florent stopped. "Excuse me, but I couldn't help hearing your conversation just now. I know Inspector Blouin."

"You do?"

"I mean, his name was Thouin, Gérard Thouin, but everybody called him Blouin – I don't know why. Probably a joke."

Florent stared at the stranger. He began to feel vaguely giddy. The other man smiled innocently as a lock of blond hair fell over his left eye.

"Did you say Thouin – or Drouin?" Florent asked, his voice quavering.

"Thouin, Thouin," the other man repeated confidently. "But he was known as Blouin."

"And where is he?"

"He drowned in Miami in 1970. It was always considered to be a suicide."

Florent leaned on the banister. The other man put his hand on his arm. "Listen, don't tell anybody I mentioned him, okay? It could mean trouble. Good luck." He winked and went back downstairs.

A moment later Florent resumed his climb. On the next floor he entered a large room where a secretary was typing at the back. He hesitated, then said, "I'd like to speak to Sergeant . . . Gouin."

"You mean the inspector?"

"Right."

"I'm sorry, he's out."

"I'd like to speak to his assistant."

"He doesn't have one. Come back at the end of the day."

Florent turned and disappeared into the stairs. The secretary shouted after him. "You could speak to Sergeant Drouin."

He went down to the ground floor. As he was crossing the vestibule on his way to the exit, he felt a hand on his shoulder. "The director wants to talk to you," said a policeman. He seemed to be making extraordinary efforts not to laugh, focusing his gaze on Florent's shoulder, where his hand was still resting. Florent followed him through the lobby, then down a corridor to a large glass door, with a shadow moving behind it. The policeman knocked. "Come in," snarled a voice.

The policeman opened the door, stepped aside, then disappeared.

The director was standing in the middle of the room. He greeted Florent with an affected heartiness that made his voice especially disagreeable. "Come in, come in and sit down." He went behind his desk, settled himself in his chair, and looked at Florent with an odd smile. He was a stocky, broad-shouldered man with coarse features and a sharp, intelligent gaze that roamed the room unpredictably.

"You're Florent Boissonneault, right?"

Florent nodded, no longer capable of being surprised.

"I used to know your father well. Is he still alive? Give him my regards. He used to be quite a fellow." And he launched into a series of anecdotes about himself and Florent's father in their youth, some of them rather titillating.

Florent listened, smiling politely, waiting for him to get to the point. He had a long wait. Suddenly the director looked at his watch, started, and got to his feet, extending his hand. "I nearly forgot my meeting. I must go. Now don't forget, tell your father to drop in and see me. I've got some fine old cognac."

He showed Florent to the door. The younger man was walking like a robot, his mind more and more muddled. He turned to the director, stared at him for a moment, and tried to tell him he'd just lost his restaurant and had never in his life felt so bewildered.

The director immediately guessed what was in his mind and, without giving him time to open his mouth, told him, with an artificial smile, "Look, my friend, I've heard your story. I've known Ratablavasky a long time and I assure you, there's no more honest man on the face of the earth. Think carefully about what you're going to do. I'm sure you've been misled. Appearances are one thing, you know, reality's something else. Besides, I've discussed your case with Inspector Thouin, so he could help you see things a little more clearly. He promised to call you tomorrow."

He patted Florent's shoulder and opened the door. "Don't forget to tell your father you saw me, okay?"

The next day Florent received a letter from the Royal Bank advising him that after a recent profitability study of his business, the bank wished to repossess all its capital, as provided by the law governing call loans. He had three days to settle his debt.

Florent equivocated for half a day. He thought (mistakenly) that if he repaid his debt he would still have rights to the restaurant. He could then demand that it be placed under trusteeship until the courts had untangled the mess and, once his enemies had been proved guilty, force them to sell back their shares. But where could he get the money? He decided not to ask his parents. Elise suggested Father Jeunehomme, and after much hesitation he went to the Sulpician Seminary.

An old nun with a white mustache and crinkled, laughing eyes opened the door. "Father Jeunehomme can't see you, young man – he's convalescing."

"I'm his cousin."

"Are you? What a pity he's away! He's always complaining he never has visitors. . . . He went to Saint-Gabriel yesterday afternoon. He's at his mother's chalet."

Florent phoned immediately. Father Jeunehomme seemed delighted to hear his voice and issued an invitation on the spot. Florent took advantage of it to tell his cousin of his problems. "If you could lend me a little money I'm sure I could hold off the bank. I'd be able to hire a lawyer who'd uncover their dirty tricks."

The priest agreed, adding some remarks that were so disjointed it was obvious he hadn't understood a word. Florent hung up and, turning to Elise, said, "Change your duds, kiddo, we're going to the country!"

Elise had pulled herself together after the visit from Slipskin and Ratablavasky. On the road, she struggled to appear happy and optimistic, relieved at her husband's reaction to the latest events, in contrast to the melancholy paralysis that had poisoned him for two months. They arrived at Saint-Gabriel in midafternoon.

Father Jeunehomme, pale, his brow furrowed by a deep crease, greeted them in robe and slippers. "Excuse my appearance – I'm a little under the weather."

Awkwardly, he took Elise's coat, stepping on her toes, dropping the hanger, the coat and her handbag. "I've fixed you a little snack," he said, showing them into the dining room. (His mother's chalet was a rather opulent country house.)

On the table were several tins of biscuits, some cakes, a camembert, bread, and a bottle of wine. "When I thought about what you told me, it upset me so much I developed a migraine – which happens at the slightest upset. Will you allow me a half hour in my room?"

"Did you take anything for it?" Elise asked.

The priest smiled wanly. "You've obviously never had a migraine," he sighed. "It's a calamity for which there is no remedy. Make yourselves comfortable now," he added. "Eat, read, rest. I'll be with you shortly and we can discuss your problems at leisure."

Then he lay down in the dark, with a hot-water bottle on his head. Two hours passed. "He's certainly a nervous type," Florent observed.

Late that night he still hadn't emerged from his room. Elise and Florent put together some supper, took a walk and went to bed. At nine o'clock the next morning the priest's door was still shut. "I got up in the night," Elise said in a hushed voice, "and I saw a light in his room. He must have been reading. Go and knock."

Florent stuck his ear against the door and heard the rustling of paper. "Feeling better?"

"Uhh no . . . well, yes, a little . . ."

"Don't you want breakfast?"

"Umm . . . in a while . . . actually, I'm not feeling too well. . . . Eat without me. I'll join you shortly."

An hour later, Florent went to his bedroom and made him get up. "It's unforgivable, I know," the priest stammered, blushing. "Around eleven last night I couldn't get to sleep and I made the mistake of picking up *The Tenants of Silver House*, a novel by Dickens. It's the same whenever I start a good book: I couldn't put it down till I'd read the last page. Otherwise the story keeps going around in my head, and nine times out of ten it sets off a frightful migraine."

He sighed. "It's a real infirmity," he said with a guilty smile.

By midafternoon Elise and Florent had left, with a cheque for nine thousand dollars, repayable at their convenience, at four percent interest. "I'll be back in Montreal in a week or two," said the priest, holding out his long, translucent hand. "I'm planning a Zola banquet for the first of the month, and I'd be delighted if you could attend."

"What's a Zola banquet?"

"The title may be a little pretentious: in fact it's an intimate dinner for ten that I give in a restaurant to honor the memory of a great writer, followed by an informal discussion of one of his works, which each guest will have read in advance. Next month we celebrate Zola, and I've selected *Pot-Bouille*. I'll send you an invitation."

"Just what I need now – a banquet," Florent grumbled as he started the car.

He went to the bank that evening. Father Jeunehomme, he learned, hadn't had an account at that branch for several years. Dismayed, Florent phoned him. The priest apologized, all aflutter, and promised to send another check, special delivery, that very day. A week later nothing had arrived. Florent called Saint-Gabriel several times, but there was no answer. No one at the Sulpician Seminary knew where he was. As the Royal Bank was becoming more and more insistent, Florent gave in and called Ratablavasky. "Take over my debt," he told him. "I'm giving up everything."

"Splendid! I'll make my way to your house instantly. We'll sign a little paper and the dove of peace will nest in your spirit."

He arrived at Florent's twenty minutes later, with Slipskin. He presented a paper from the bank, discharging the loan, and asked for a receipt for $12,780. "Now then," said the old man, puzzled by Florent's icy silence, "everything's settled, heaven smiles on us and, as we say in my country, the little birds can fly away."

"Fly away," Florent repeated, snickering. "Not a bad idea. I'm cleaned out. I have no way of earning a living and you've taken all my savings, too. Why? Do you have the slightest idea yourself? Go ahead, you old crook, empty all the pockets you can. You'll still rot in the ground like everyone else."

Ratablavasky blinked and twisted his lips in a mocking grimace. "Young people have an agile tongue," he said, taking a wad of papers from his jacket pocket, "but their judgment still sleeps in the cradle. There, dear fellow, are the documents that prove I am owning the restaurant."

Then, moving jerkily, he tore up the papers. "And here's the new owner." He pointed to Slipskin, who blushed slightly.

Florent, appalled, said nothing. The old man was amused at his reaction. "I am obedient of the orders of life, dear fellow. Life demanded a more . . . adequate owner, and I am life's humble servant."

He took advantage of Florent's discomfiture to shake his hand. "My compliments to Monsieur Picquot," he said, heading for the door. "Tell him I've forgotten the soup."

Florent watched them go down the stairs and onto the street, laughing. He slumped into a chair and started to cry. Hearing footsteps, he looked up. Monsieur Emile was staring at him. He began asking questions, and Florent gave a brief account of the events of the past few days. The child listened very attentively, reflected for a moment, then slipped away.

An hour later firemen were speeding to The Beanery. The flames were quickly brought under control and damage was slight. But when Slipskin opened the cash register to clear it out, he saw he'd been relieved of the day's receipts.

When Madame Chouinard came home from work around midnight, her son lay, fully dressed and snoring, in the middle of his room. There was a strong smell of rum in the air, but her search didn't turn up a trace of a bottle. And even if she'd beaten him with a plank, Monsieur Emile wouldn't have told her.

"Where did he get the money for it?" she muttered.

The bottle of rum kept running through her head all night. She saw it now full, now empty. Her son snatched it from her just as she was bringing it to her lips, then he ran away laughing, his eyes rolled back.

At eight o'clock she knocked at Madame Duquette's door. "What can I tell you, my dear?" asked the neighbor. Her eyes were puffy with sleep and her pumpkin-colored baby-dolls showed off her bowed legs. "*I* don't know where he got the bottle. He's always in and out, in and out, running every which way: you'd have to nail his feet to the floor to keep him in one place. I've got my own house to run, and with what you pay me I certainly can't hire a security guard to keep an eye on him."

A colossal row ensued. Monsieur Emile took advantage of it to make his getaway to Florent's house. He found him slumped in front of the television set, holding a beer. "Here," said the boy, taking a rumpled Lipton's Soup package from his pocket, "it's a present."

"Where'd you get that?" he exclaimed, taking a thick wad of bills from the package. "Ten, twenty, forty – two hundred and ninety dollars! Monsieur Emile, first you're going to tell me where the hell this came from and then you're going to put it back. You've been in your mother's purse, haven't you!"

Monsieur Emile burst into tears. "No! I stole it from the restaurant and I won't take it back. Never never never! Fucking bastards!"

Moved, Florent stroked the child's hair. Elise took over when Monsieur Emile's sorrow grew noisier. Florent fiddled with the money for a while.

"If I had the guts," he muttered cynically, "I'd buy a gun and clean up Mont-Royal Street."

Inspector Thouin never got in touch with Florent and neither did any of his colleagues. Florent, almost relieved, made sure they forgot all about them.

THIRTEEN

At ten o'clock on the morning of November 30, 1974, the bells of St-Pierre-Claver church on St-Joseph Boulevard start to ring as usual, but more than one passerby turns around, puzzled by their tone, which is somehow different. The notes sound dry and choked, and they drop like balls of lead, leaving no echo. Confused and vaguely unpleasant memories are aroused. People try for a moment to identify them, until the flow of daily thoughts resumes its course.

The sky today is one solid cloud. It bulges weightily over the city and you would look in vain for the sun, which it seems to have swallowed. Some light sifts down from it, gray and powdery. It hardens the outlines of every object and comes crashing down onto surfaces. The air stings your eyes, numbs fingertips and forces legs to move quickly. The mood is one of anxious waiting. Strangers on the sidewalk catch themselves staring at one another, not knowing what to say. And suddenly, a minuscule event occurs. A snowflake appears from the void, swirls through the air and begins a cautious descent broken by pauses, as if it were afraid of shattering its complex, fragile form, before coming to rest on the ground and disappearing.

Winter has arrived. Metal doorknobs turn to ice. More snowflakes appear, discrete, almost foolish amid so much space, but their number keeps growing, and soon the color of the streets has softened.

Tonight, those laggards left unprepared by early autumn's perfidious mildness must bow to the inevitable. Grumpily, they will put up storm windows, weatherstrip the frames, dig out the scarves and lined gloves and coats and heavy as armor consigned earlier to disdainful neglect. A rugged boundary will be established between outside their houses and inside. Inside, warmth and life will prevail, with soppy music on the radio and the aromas of coffee and toast. Outside, it will be enemy territory, filled with shadows by four in the afternoon; people with cheeks chewed by the cold will rush with bated breath to another oasis of warmth. For months the world outside will transmit, through carefully sealed windows, only cold and frozen images that night will fill with lunar sadness.

For ten days now Elise and Florent had been staying with Ange-Albert. He was out of work, and was only too happy to put them up because it allowed him to live off the twenty-eight hundred dollars Florent had got from selling his furniture and records. As for his car, it had broken down two days after they moved in with their friend and now was quietly rusting near the house.

Since the disaster of The Beanery he'd hardly even tried to find a job. He devoted his time to sleep, to love (with certain precautions by Elise, owing to their precarious situation) and to movies on television. In the evening they'd have a beer at the nearby Saint-Malo or the Faubourg St-Denis. From time to time they'd buy some grass and the evening would end on a long cosmic pause. Despite Elise's apprehensions, Florent's morale remained high, though he'd lost all ambition. "Why get your arteries all clogged up for the sake of money?" he would say. "Look at Ange-Albert: he's always taken life as it comes. Is he in any worse shape than me?"

Elise, well aware of the bitterness behind this self-styled philosophical detachment, pretended to agree with her husband, in the hope that time would do its work and restore his taste for success.

But on November 30 an unexpected arrival began to harass everyone in the apartment. The cold. After painstakingly examining the old gas furnace, Ange-Albert decided to light it. For half an hour everything went well, and the first hint of warmth encouraged them to unbutton their coats. Then suddenly the sheet metal framework started to tremble violently, and the chipped tiles began to jingle. There was a sort of scream, as if a singer had aimed at high C and missed, and with a dry clatter the fire went out. A strong smell of rotten cabbage was added to the stench of mildew that drifted through the apartment. Florent sprang at the furnace and turned the valve. "Holy horseradish! We'd better hustle our buns and get this fixed or we'll be blown to kingdom come!"

Ange-Albert raised his hand and slowly rubbed his thumb against the adjoining fingers in the classic distress sign of those whose wallets suffer from chronic anemia. "I know," said Florent testily, "but we aren't going to let ourselves go up in smoke just to save a buck."

"Why don't we call the fire department and ask for an inspector?" Elise suggested. "He'd tell us if the furnace can be fixed, and it won't cost a cent."

"Good idea," said Florent. "And maybe if we slip him five bucks he wouldn't mind dirtying his hands and working on the insides."

He picked up the phone book and two hours later, after he'd gone through three departments, two divisions, and six subsections, a little voice as round and hard as a billiard ball told him an inspector would come the next morning, at precisely ten o'clock.

"Be there," the voice added. "We ring three times and then move on – and don't chase after us. Too many houses to visit. The winter's short."

"We'll be there," Florent promised. "Weirdo," he murmured as he hung up.

They went to the kitchen and drank some hot coffee, rubbing their hands and stamping their feet, while wisps of vapor rose from their mouths to the flaking ceiling.

The next day Florent was lying on his bed, gazing drowsily at the old alarm clock that was hiccupping on the dresser, when he suddenly became aware of two facts:

(a) the clock showed two o'clock in the afternoon;

(b) no inspector had appeared.

Shivering, he pulled on his pants, went to the pompously named *salon*, a piss-green room furnished with a disemboweled sofa bed, and placed a call.

"Rosarien Roy," said the voice from the previous day.

Florent identified himself and asked why no one had come. "Why do you think?" asked Rosarien Roy.

Florent was taken aback. He hesitated, then confessed that he had no idea.

"We didn't come because we couldn't come. Period. Between you and me, you're no rocket scientist. Call back in two days. I'll see what I can do."

A buzzing sound indicated that the conversation was over. Florent left the room like a sleepwalker, unable to believe what he'd heard. He went to the kitchen and made a cheese omelet. It wasn't until he'd eaten it that he really blew up.

A few seconds later Rosarien Roy, who was sitting at his desk gazing suspiciously at a dog sauntering along the street, received a telephone call in which his personality was described in terms that left him drenched in sweat from his socks to his shirt collar. He tried several times to hold back the description, but the description won out and when Florent hung up, Rosarien Roy was filled with a tremendous choking rage, far too great for the modest dimensions of his soul, that made him choke. He worked it off during the rest of the day, storming at secretaries, pounding the desk with his fist at the drop of a hat. Toward the end of the afternoon his superior called him. "I've had some complaints about you. Fellow named Boissonneault, on Emery Street. What's going on? There's been bitching about you before."

"I'll take care of the young man myself," promised Rosarien Roy in a quavering voice.

He rang the bell at seven o'clock the next morning. Florent opened it in the throes of a coughing fit; he was waxen-faced and in a dreadful mood because Elise had just told him the pipes had frozen during the night.

"Rosarien Roy, fire department," said the visitor, stepping into the vestibule as if taking possession of the house.

He was a scrawny little man in his late forties, with a broad flat chin, an evil mouth, a hooked nose, perpetually prying eyes, and a face so withered that he looked as if he slept with his head in an oven.

"Let's have a look at that furnace," he said with a threatening smile.

He stopped in the middle of the corridor and peered at it for a moment, but almost immediately his attention was drawn to the floor, from which his toe drew long laments. "Mmm-hmm!" he said, delighted.

He began to visit the other rooms, running his hand over the walls, exploring cracks, shaking half-rotted windows, making sparks jump from the electric outlets, meditating before greenish damp spots spread across walls and ceilings. "Hmmm! Hmmm!"

He rocked back and forth on his heels and whistled as the others looked on in silence. "You're not spending much time on the furnace," Florent observed acidly.

"It's like this, big mouth," said Rosarien Roy, turning to face him. "There are two aspects to the problem of heating: the unit you heat and the unit you heat *with*. Let's say you've bought a magnificent house, solid as a continent. More legal than the law. And you furnish it with a heating device that's full of soot. Covered with cracks. Rust-eaten, too. Well, now, one fine day, *boom*! The whole thing blows up. Bye-bye comfort. You sleep on the lawn. BUT!" he exclaimed, raising his hand to prevent Florent from speaking, "let's say you bought a splendid *device*! Solid as a continent. Safer than all the cops in Quebec. And you install it in a hovel that's open to the winds. (This, by the way, is a hovel.) What happens? The device overheats, it deteriorates, and one fine day, *boom*! It blows up and they find your bones in Cartierville. I don't even want to examine your furnace. It doesn't interest me. Because you aren't going to use it. I forbid it. The only heating system I'll allow here is electricity. But watch it: I'm talking about 220. No portable heaters, understand? It'll require installation by accredited electricians. The wire will run under the baseboards. The rats inside the walls. Understood? That's all."

He slowly buttoned his coat and walked to the door, then wheeled around abruptly. "And also – don't try any tricks with me," he added. "I've got my eye on you. I'll drop in every day – big mouth!"

The door slammed. Florent rolled his furious eyes to the ceiling. "Holy sprouting horseradish! You know what it costs to rewire for 220? I wouldn't have a penny left in the bank."

An hour later an employee from Gaz Métropolitain came to take away the meter. "But our stove won't work!" Elise protested.

Ange-Albert gestured to her to cool down. "I can see," he told her when the man had gone, "you don't know a thing about bureaucrats. Just tough it out for a while. They rant and rave and threaten – and then fall asleep on their chairs. In two days everything will be settled. A guy I know worked fifteen years for the gas company. He talks big – but if I slip him a twenty and a good bottle of scotch, I can talk him into hooking up the gas . . . and fixing the furnace."

Elise went out on the back gallery and into a shed that adjoined the kitchen. They could hear her rummaging, then she came back with a hotplate. "Here. We can cook something on this and it'll give us a little heat."

"What in the world!" exclaimed Picquot when he arrived at the apartment a few hours later. "Are you in training for Siberia or what? A little more and your breath will fall on your heads. What's going on?"

Florent recounted their misadventure. "Very well, you'll come to my house!" the chef suggested. "I don't know what to do with my seven rooms. I spend my evenings walking back and forth and yawning. You'll give it a little life."

Obstinately, Florent shook his head. "I'll find a way. Even at the risk of being diddled again. After all, it's time I learned."

"Dear friend," said Picquot testily, setting a box of provisions on the table, "ever since the matter of the restaurant I find you're a bit quick to take offense. You helped me out when I took my leave of that wretched Château Frontenac? Very well, now it's my turn."

He walked through the kitchen, frowning, clapping his hands to warm them, appalled to find his friends in such conditions. "Here, child," he said to Elise, "take this saucepan and set it on the fire. I was wise to trust my intuition: last night I made you a Soyer Soup, the famous dish invented by Alexis Soyer during the Irish famine of 1840. Pork fat, garlic, onion, turnip, anchovy, pepper, and tomato. Simple, succulent, comforting: exactly what you need."

Soon they were all seated before steaming bowls of soup. Picquot kept trying to change Florent's mind. "There's nothing shameful about leaning on friends when times are difficult. Look, three days ago I was walking along Ste-Catherine Street, with no job, no plans, my spirits dragging their heels. At the corner of St-Laurent I stumbled on an old gentleman. 'Sebastien Laulerque!' I called out. It was indeed he. A rather unprepossessing individual who'd behaved somewhat foully way back when, but later, God knows why, befriended me. We started chatting. He asked about my work, and I told him about the treachery of that trash Slipskin and the loathsome old man. Well! Since yesterday, thanks to him, I have a job!"

Elise exclaimed her delight. "Wait, don't rejoice too quickly. It's an odd setup. I work for an advertising agency, in the food photography section. I'm charged with making tempting presentations of those vile industrial preparations that have been nourishing Americans for thirty years, under the impression they've been frequenting the summits of haute cuisine. I don't spare the food coloring or varnish or bits of wire and gelatin and cornstarch, and heavens! the results are passing fair. And the imbeciles pay me insane wages."

He went on in this vein for a while, arousing laughter around him, but the glacial cold finally won out and he invited everyone to a restaurant for coffee.

Ange-Albert insisted they go to Chez Bob Snack Bar, a grungy little restaurant just across the street. After much hesitation, Picquot finally agreed. Monsieur Clouette, the potbellied owner, smiled broadly when he saw Ange-Albert, who was a regular. "Your daughter's not working today?" the young man asked, taking a seat in a booth.

"Oh no!"

Monsieur Clouette came over to their table, ran his rag over it and distributed menus. Picquot took out his glasses, frowned, and mercilessly started reading.

"Will she be here tonight?" asked Ange-Albert.

"I'm not sure," the restaurateur replied evasively, then headed for no apparent reason for the cash register.

Elise and Florent smiled behind their menus, amused at his lack of enthusiasm for any conversation about his daughter.

"Four coffees," Picquot ordered in a martial tone, "and make it your best."

After one sip he got to his feet. "This stocking juice is undrinkable," he decreed, half gagging.

Florent managed to make him sit down again. "I beg you, for Ange-Albert's sake, be nice and stay with us. We'll leave in fifteen minutes, I promise."

"Nice for Ange-Albert, nice for Ange-Albert," muttered the chef. "What's the meaning of all this?"

Florent whispered in his ear as Ange-Albert blushed, and from behind the counter Monsieur Clouette gazed suspiciously at all these fine people. Picquot waited patiently for a few minutes, casting glances at his cup that would have made it burst with shame if it had any sense, then everyone got up and left.

"Brrr! What weather!" said the chef, huddling in his fur coat. "It's essential that we get you out of that icebox. A polar bear would catch pneumonia."

"While we're waiting, how about going to the Saint-Malo?" Florent suggested. "They make *café filtre.*"

"Splendid!" exclaimed Picquot. "When we French are abroad we always need a morsel of the motherland to comfort us if we're to feel at ease."

Florent opened the door, and abruptly recoiled. "Good day to you, big mouth," said Rosarien Roy, who was sitting in the glassed-in terrace. "As you see, I've taken a liking to the neighborhood. And believe me, it's going to last! I can see your door from here! Life is sweet!"

Florent glanced at him, furious, then turned and walked along the street.

In the next few days a fierce battle ensued between the inspector and the unfortunate tenants. At great expense, Florent bought electric heaters that operated on 110 volts and brought them to his lodgings at night, cautiously using the laneway. The next morning, they were confiscated. He appealed to the city's legal department, who promised an investigation, but warned it would take at least six months. Then Ange-Albert found in the shed one of those portable furnaces commonly known as a fireball. He spent a whole afternoon patching it, his fingers blue from contact with the metal, and managed to get it working. But a neighbor, no doubt bribed by the inspector, saw it through a window and soon it had joined the electric heaters.

Florent persisted, declaring that nothing would make him leave the apartment. Emergency measures were needed. They started putting pepper inside their socks. Ange-Albert, who had got the recipe from an old bum, insisted that pepper stimulates the circulation. Each in turn took baths heated further with hot-pepper sauce. A certain sense of well-being lingered for a while, sometimes followed by cruel inflammations. Ange-Albert went to a war surplus store and filched, God knows how, three sleeping bags. Before getting into them, they would place a hot brick wrapped in wool inside, and the night passed as well as could be expected, amid the sound of taps that had to be left on to keep the water from freezing in the pipes.

Time passed, and Rosarien Roy's demoniacal zeal showed no sign of exhaustion – unlike Florent's bank account. Their daily sessions at Chez Bob Snack Bar to warm up lasted longer and longer, but became less and less profitable for the owner, especially since Florent had got in the habit of stuffing his pockets with little packets of sugar. A cup of coffee now lasted an hour. A ham sandwich could easily take up half the afternoon. As for omelets, to Monsieur Clouette's despair they were endless. His kind heart – and his daughter – were all that kept him from throwing the cold-numbed group out on the street.

For some days now, Ange-Albert had managed to secure chaste rendezvous with young Mademoiselle Clouette, unknown to her father. They would meet on street corners, in front of a boutique, in the middle of a park stripped bare by winter. Then Ange-Albert would go home to the apartment shivering and ever more discouraged at the prospect of sharing his bed that night with only a hot brick wrapped in what used to be a woman's slip. Florent teased him for the slowness of his amorous progress. Ange-Albert had always been the envy of his friends for his success with the ladies, which piled up discreetly in his life like a stack of buckwheat pancakes on a farmer's plate. "Is it possible you're in love?" Elise teased him. "Look at him! Rosine makes him blush like a rose!"

The only misfortune that had befallen Mademoiselle Clouette to date was her given name. Her parents had, on the other hand, endowed her with pretty features and a delicate conformation that kept Ange-Albert on the alert, particularly because he was not insensitive to the practical advantages, during a lean period, of having a seventeen-year-old mistress whose father owned a restaurant. With astonishing patience, Ange-Albert had decided not to storm Rosine's virginity while she – despite her blushes and naïveté – had her eyes open and seemed well aware of the disadvantages of getting together with someone who couldn't afford to turn off the taps in his apartment during the winter. When his patience had really run dry, Ange-Albert would consult his little black book and spend a night away from home – never more than one, because fraternal solidarity required him to share his friends' fate as long as they stayed under his roof.

Elise, who could already see their savings running out, and didn't share her husband's blasé indifference to the guild of the miserable, started looking for a job. It might give him a better push than all my speeches, she thought.

An incident took care of that task a few days later, with unexpected results.

As they hadn't heard from Monsieur Emile for several days, Elise and Florent decided to pay him a visit. At the same time, they could thaw out their limbs beside a heater and – with a little luck – perhaps grab a bite to eat. They put on mitts and tuques and braved the cold. The wind poured over them like icy water, penetrating to their very bones. They walked along St-Denis Street, eyes filled with tears, their cheeks ablaze and stiff as cardboard. As they passed Le Jardin St-Denis, Florent glanced mechanically inside the restaurant, then clutched Elise's arm. She turned to him, surprised. He jerked his chin toward the window. She looked in and saw Rosarien Roy bending over a table and holding forth, wide-eyed, arms whirling, obviously trying hard to persuade the person he was addressing. The other man listened gravely, with his gray-gloved hands on the table.

"Ratablavasky," Elise murmured unsteadily.

They sped away; they hadn't been noticed. "I can't stand living like this!" Elise sobbed. "We have to go away, Florent, leave Montreal, do you hear?"

There was no answer at Monsieur Emile's. They returned to the apartment, colder than ever. Ange-Albert greeted them joyfully. "I just found an old vacuum cleaner in the garbage – and it works!"

"Big fucking deal!" Florent grumbled.

"Don't you get it?"

He plugged it in. First it sounded like the trumpeting of a herd of elephants, then it started clicking violently. The sound's intensity diminished somewhat, then rose higher and started to quaver, until it seemed they were on a battlefield, amid the whistling of a weird, sadistic bomb that would dash to the ground, then suspend its course for a few seconds before exploding and slowing rising to the sky where, tirelessly, it would all begin again. Florent assumed his friend was having them on.

"Give me your hand!" Ange-Albert shouted.

He placed it in front of the exhaust. "Well, well!" Florent murmured, smiling sardonically. "Heat!"

"Not much for the moment," Ange-Albert admitted, "but in five or six minutes it'll be blazing."

"And how long do you think we'll be able to put up with the racket?"

Elise shook her head, overwhelmed, left the room and got into bed. Ange-Albert began then to pad the vacuum cleaner with pillows, and was able to reduce the noise. In an hour, there was a semblance of warmth in the room, along with a strong scorched smell.

Meanwhile, Florent told his friend of the conversation he'd witnessed at the Jardin St-Denis. Ange-Albert had a long stretch, then gave Florent a determined look. "Okay, pal, time to act. They're getting ready to cut us in little pieces. But don't you worry, I'll take care of everything."

He slipped on his coat and went into the shed. For several minutes there was the sound of sawing, then he came back with half a dozen little wooden cubes.

"What's that?" Florent asked.

His friend smiled, sat at the table, sanded the cubes carefully, then took some ink and transformed them into dice. Florent snickered. "You think you can save us with shooting craps?"

"There's a few things about me you don't know," Ange-Albert replied, smiling quietly. "These little bits of wood have got me out of a fair number of tight spots."

He started shaking them and tossing them on the table, watching to see how they landed. Three hours passed. Florent went out to buy *La Presse* and looked through the help wanted ads. Ange-Albert was still shaking his dice tirelessly. Now a satisfied smile lit up his face. He looked at his watch, slipped on his coat, and went to join Rosine, who was waiting for him in a café on St-Denis.

FOURTEEN

The next day began with a frustration of major proportions. About nine o'clock the postman handed them an envelope containing an invitation printed on Imperial Japan and signed by Father Jeunehomme. The letter had been sent to Florent's old address, then returned to the post office and now, alas, had reached him three days late. Here are the contents:

> I am pleased to invite you to an intimate dinner to honor the memory of our great writer Emile Zola, who passed away on September 28, 1902, but who will lie forever in the hearts of all lovers of literature. We shall meet at the restaurant Chez Pierre, at 1263 de la rue Labelle, Montreal, at seven o'clock P.M. sharp. To prepare for this friendly and informal gathering, it is recommended that you reread Zola's masterpiece, *Pot-Bouille*, in which the dinner party at the Café Anglais, described in Chapter x, has served as guide for drawing up the following menu, which I am pleased to submit to you:

MENU

Potage crème d'asperges
Timbales à la Pompadour
Truite à la génevoise
Filet de boeuf à la Châteaubriand
Ortolans à la Lucullus
Salade d'écrevisses
Cimier de chevreuil
Fonds d'artichaut à la jardinière
Soufflé au chocolat
Sicilienne de fruits

VINS

Madère
Château Filhot 1958
Johannisberg
Château Pichon-Longueville
Château Lafite 1948
Sparkling Moselle
Roederer

Your host,
Rev. Octavien Jeunehomme
amans litterarum

R.S.V.P.

Florent gazed at the card, his stomach gurgling. Then he tore it into a thousand pieces and went to the kitchen to gorge himself on stale bread.

At noon, without prior arrangement, three people turned up in the apartment in quick succession, and great was the ensuing din. First came Monsieur Emile, frozen stiff, wearing neither coat nor mittens, lost in a hockey sweater that was worn thin by age, stiff with grime and torn at the elbows. He was accompanied by his cat, who had lost a bit of one ear in a backyard brawl.

"Where have you been?" Elise cried.

"I'm coming to live with you," he replied, completely untouched by the niceties of conventional conversation.

By exercising patience, Elise eventually learned that he'd just spent two weeks with another of his mother's "uncles" – an Arab, this one – where he'd been given nothing but pineapple pudding and packaged eggnog to eat, and his mother and uncle had left their bed only to carouse.

"I'm coming to live with you," he repeated.

Florent tried to explain that he'd need his mother's written permission. Monsieur Emile barely listened: for him, it was already settled.

"I saw Old Rat just now," he announced abruptly.

"Monsieur . . . Ratablavasky?"

"Yup. And I told him everything."

Florent felt as if the whole apartment had slammed him in the stomach. "Wh-what?" he choked. "What did you tell him?"

Monsieur Emile bent down, picked up his cat and, totally unconcerned, began to stroke it. "Everything. I told him about the pills and the fire and the money in the till. And then I told him I hated him and I wished he was dead."

"Oh Lord! That's all we needed!" Elise exclaimed. "What's going to happen now?"

"You should've kept your trap shut, kid," said Florent, irritated. "Did he say anything?"

Monsieur Emile shook his head.

"No, he smiled. Like that," he added, grimacing. "So then I got scared and I ran all the way here. Hey! it's cold," he said, shivering. "Isn't the heat on?"

Florent merely smiled, rubbing his hands together. Ange-Albert brought out his dice and made them dance in his hands. "Courage, my friends . . . in two or three days these little bits of wood will make us as warm as . . ."

He didn't have time to finish. The front door slammed, and footsteps clomped on the stairs. "Ratablavasky," Florent whispered.

"Go and hide," said Elise, grabbing hold of Monsieur Emile. She pushed him into a closet, where he nearly broke some bones on an old rocking horse left behind by the previous tenant. When she came back to the living room, Florent had just shown in Rosario Gladu, swathed in a huge coat of synthetic fur. The journalist was standing on the threshold, unnerved by the commotion his arrival had caused. He greeted Florent. "It's been a whale of a time since we got together, eh?"

Florent eyed him, saying nothing.

The journalist smiled woefully and looked around the room.

"I bet," Florent said, "that Old Rat sent you to see if I had anything left to steal."

"He's the one, all right," Gladu admitted unhesitatingly, "but his heart's in the right place."

"Is that so?" Florent snickered. "You mean he's near death and wants to leave me Place Ville-Marie?"

"Mind if I sit down?" spluttered Gladu, who seemed miserable. "I've got a bit of a cramp in my leg."

"Why not try the stairs?" replied Florent, opening the door. "They're terrific for cramps. By the way, I read your article on the new owner of The Beanery the other day. . . . Very good. . . . said some nice things about me . . ."

"Ah, so you read it," he sighed. "Look here, Florent, I want you to understand, it's the boss . .. the newspaper business, you know . . ."

Florent pushed him gently onto the landing. "Go on," he said, "cut the chitchat and go play in the snow, it'll put roses in your cheeks."

"See here . . . it was . . . it was Ratablavasky asked me to come and see . . . and see if you were really . . . destitute," he said, involuntarily bringing up his arm to protect himself.

Florent looked at him without faltering, a disdainful smile on his lips. The journalist regained his courage and went on: "The other day he found out you were being harassed by some turkey that works as an inspector for the city. It got him right in the heart. That's the truth! He went and met the guy . . . to try and persuade him to . . . And he'd like to see you," Gladu concluded in a slight falsetto.

Breakfast, who had been sitting there observing everything, let out a savage snarl and took a few steps toward the reporter, his claws like buskins. Florent waved Gladu out. "Before you tell him to piss off, Florent, think it over," said Gladu hastily. "He's a weird bird, you know. . . . You don't know the whole story about The Beanery. . . . He dropped a hint the other day. I didn't follow it all, but it seemed like –"

"Fuck off, sleaze!" Florent yelled. "You make me puke!"

Gladu pursed his lips, buttoned his coat and started downstairs, but the front door slammed again. "Is this the residence of Florent Boissonneault?" demanded the imperious voice of Aurélien Picquot, who seemed not to recognize Gladu.

He climbed up several steps, then there was silence. The men looked at one another. "You? Here?" Picquot asked, flabbergasted.

"Umm . . . well . . . I had an errand for Ratablavasky. . . . How's life, Chef? Still slinging hash?"

"I have *never* heard the like! It thinks it can make conversation! Cave dweller! Moldy crust! I'll cook *your* hash!"

He hurled himself at the journalist. "Leave him alone, Monsieur Picquot," Florent ordered.

"What's got into him, for crumb's sake?" Gladu yelped plaintively. "I didn't do anything!"

"Didn't do *anything*? Take *that*!" And raising his arm, he imprinted his fist on the journalist's face. "Now disappear, vermin – you're polluting the stairs!"

Gladu obeyed with utmost speed, but as he passed the chef he delivered a punch to his belly. A tuba-like sound escaped from Picquot's mouth. He grabbed the journalist by one shoulder and a frantic scrimmage ensued in the shadows. The walls creaked, the steps moaned, there was a sound of puffing, like seals. Florent rushed at them, but couldn't tear them apart. Suddenly Gladu rammed his fingers into Picquot's eyes, freed himself with a thrust of his knee, and ran down the stairs four at a time. His adversary lost his balance and tumbled heavily down the stairs, landing headfirst against the door, which the journalist had just slammed, yelling, "Frenchy asshole, go back where you came from!"

Picquot moaned and tried unsuccessfully to get to his feet. "I feel as if I'm at the opera," he murmured, shutting his left eye. "Where are all the voices coming from?"

Florent looked at him, aghast. His old friend's entire left side was trembling. He slowly closed his other eye and turned his head to the wall. "Don't move me," he whispered. "Call an ambulance. My condition's worsening . . . worsen . . ."

Florent raced back up the stairs while Elise brought a blanket and covered Picquot up to his chin. Monsieur Emile, petrified, observed the scene with mouth agape.

Ten minutes later the chef was being strapped to a stretcher. He seemed to be sleeping peacefully, but the trembling persisted. The siren's scream awakened him. "Ah, there you are," he said, grasping the hand of Florent, who was bending over him.

A few minutes passed. Again he opened his right eye and gestured Florent to come closer. "I had a call . . . from your . . . father," he said, with great difficulty. "He's been looking . . . everywhere for you . . . the poor man . . ."

His head sank into the pillow. "Vendetta . . . vendetta . . ." he murmured from time to time with a smile of satisfaction, as the ambulance ran through red lights and the driver and his sidekick traded juicy stories.

That night, despite the emotional upset of the day, Ange-Albert slipped the dice in his pocket, took Monsieur Emile to his mother's, then went to the Faubourg St-Denis. Lady Luck was smiling on him: Rosarien Roy was there, drinking coffee.

FIFTEEN

For the past two weeks, Monsieur Boissonneault had been worried sick. Florent, wanting to spare his parents his financial woes, hadn't been in touch with them since The Beanery had slipped through his fingers. "They'll see me on my feet or not at all," he had decreed.

Elise was given strict orders not to call them.

On the morning of November 16, just a few days after Florent's financial collapse, his father, who enjoyed checking out antique shops, turned up a splendid brass spittoon decorated – God knows why – with a sculpted full-length portrait of Queen Victoria, executed when the monarch was putting a severe strain on the palace furniture.

"What a spiffy present for the boy!" he exclaimed, picking up the gleaming object, which distorted his features until they resembled those of the august queen. "Just the ticket for the restaurant! Give it some atmosphere."

He bought it and decided to take it straight to The Beanery. "And I'll treat myself to a *tourtière* before I go back to the office."

Slipskin greeted him with a poisonous smile and brought him up to date so deftly that Florent's father left The Beanery without his spittoon, and was nearly run over by a bus as he was crossing the street. He rushed into a phone booth and called his son. The number had been disconnected. Panicking, he went to the apartment, where the landlord told him Elise and Florent had left without giving an address. Next, he went to the post office, but they could tell him nothing, either.

"All right, then, back to The Beanery!" he announced in a threatening voice. "And if I have to smash some plates, by Christ, I'll smash 'em!"

Slipskin, who hadn't yet digested the humiliation Florent had made him swallow, behaved boorishly, and only after Gustave Bleau's intercession did he return the spittoon. "You're one fine son of a bitch," Monsieur Boissonneault sputtered, "and that's being polite! I don't know what went on between you and my boy, but I know from the look on your face it was something smelly. That's right, laugh! Laugh your guts out! But we'll see how hard you laugh when I wrap your foot around your throat, goddamn Anglo shitface!"

He grabbed the spittoon and slammed the door so hard that the Sacred Heart on one of the panels gained eight new thorns and a pretty halo.

For four days, Monsieur Boissonneault carried out a frantic investigation, but his efforts yielded only sweat, pains, and headaches. His fingertips were black from going through the phone book. He'd never realized before how little he knew about his son's life. But the hardest thing was putting up a good front for his wife. Afraid she'd be worried to death, he told her their son had taken a surprise trip to Bermuda for his health. The proof? A postcard had come to the office, but his secretary had inadvertently filed it somewhere.

Meanwhile, he was calling on Florent's friends, garnering sympathy but no information. He finally thought of Aurélien Picquot. That gentleman's name was not in the telephone directory, however, as he had an unlisted number. After an unproductive shouting match with an information clerk, he stormed the offices of the telephone company, where an oratorical marathon worthy of Mirabeau or Réal Caouette finally yielded results. He got in a taxi and sped off to see the chef who, following Florent's instructions, refused to tell his father where he was. He did promise to let him know about the visit, and he'd just done so in the ambulance.

Elise and Florent were in their second hour in the Notre-Dame Hospital emergency ward. At their feet, lined up like onions, a half dozen coffee cups presented rims like gaping jaws, as if to proclaim their dismay at having to serve as containers for such a foul brew. Elise touched her husband's shoulder. "Call your parents. This is killing them. You don't have to give them our address, but for God's sake, set their minds at rest."

Florent was on his way to the telephone when a nurse beckoned and showed them into a tiny room.

Seated behind a desk buried in files, a fat man with a blotchy face was signing papers. His gray crew cut looked like a nylon. The nurse left without a word. The doctor, seemingly unaware of their presence, kept signing mechanically. Nudged by his elbow, two syringes filled with yellow liquid and armed with needles, rolled across the desk. On the back wall hung a calendar with a photograph of a huge green-and-black capsule floating in a pinkish intersidereal space. A caption read: "Besradine – when tranquillity is a must."

The doctor's head jerked up. He consulted a file, then looked Florent square in the eye. "Are you a relative of Aurélien Picquot?" he asked.

His face presented the same blank confusion as an open file seen from a distance. He adjusted his glasses and added, "I'm sorry, but Monsieur Picquot has died."

Elise burst into tears. "What are you talking about?" Florent exclaimed.

The doctor slowly turned over a sheet of paper. "Excuse me," he said, in the same neutral tone, "that was another patient. The pages got mixed up. We're keeping him under observation. Slight cerebral hemorrhage involving the frontal lobe. An operation may be necessary in a few weeks."

"Is he conscious?" stammered Florent, feeling a swarm of butterflies in his stomach.

"Monsieur . . . (the doctor consulted the file again) Picquot has an excellent chance of recovery. We've given him a sedative. Total rest till further notice."

"Could I –"

The telephone rang. The doctor picked up the receiver and pressed it to his ear. He nodded, emitting little approving grunts and tracing circles with a pen. Then he hung up gently, bowed his head and began signing again. The two syringes resumed their monotonous motion. "That's all I can tell you for the moment," he murmured rather wearily. "Call me in two or three days. Dr. Givrane. 876-2232."

"Sweet baby Jesus!" Florent's father exclaimed, his voice quavering with emotion. "Where are you, son? I've been looking for you for two weeks! Christmas! I was about to put the police on your trail!" He stopped, and his voice was replaced by hysterical chirping: his wife had just learned that her son's trip to Bermuda had been a scam to spare her delicate nerves. "Where are you?" Monsieur Boissonneault repeated. "Downtown? I'll pick you up in a jiffy. How're you feeling?"

"Just fine. And so's Elise."

"Good. At least that's cleared up. You're still together?"

"Leave him alone," his wife whispered.

Florent laughed. "Of course we are. Why?"

"I just asked, like that, you never know: life's so complicated nowadays . . ."

"Will you leave him alone!" his wife barked. "You're wearing him out with your questions."

"You're right. I'll shut up. But listen, while I think of it, that Slipskin's a swine if you ask me, with a filthy mouth on top of it! Bastard didn't show me any respect – even had the cheek to suggest I was a thief! A man of my age, if you please, who's been in the insurance business for thirty-five years! Anyway, let's forget it. You're having supper with us tonight. I want you to see the bit of black hair I still have – at the rate things are going I'll be totally gray in a week."

Reluctantly, Florent agreed, and arranged to meet his father in twenty minutes at the Select, a restaurant at the corner of Ste-Catherine and St-Denis. Monsieur Boissonneault showed up at the appointed time, clutching a crumpled speeding ticket.

Elise and Florent were sitting on stools with their backs against the counter, watching a huge crane that was demolishing the St-Jacques church. They were so thin and exhausted that Philippe Boissonneault's spirits sagged. He limped up to them, his arm outstretched.

"Hi, Dad," Florent murmured, smiling wearily.

Monsieur Boissonneault took Elise in his arms. "Poor little girl, you've been having more than your share of troubles," he whispered, his eyes stinging with emotion.

The news of Picquot's accident, though he'd condemned him to all the fires of hell, was the last straw. He felt they were being swept away by winds of misfortune. Thanks to Slipskin, he could now measure the full extent of Florent's plight. He mentioned it on the way home, but Florent responded dryly that the past didn't interest him.

With the help of breathing exercises and a swig of cognac, Madame Boissonneault had gathered a small stock of courage. She adjusted better than her husband, and could tell at a glance that her son was recovering from a cruel ordeal and that nothing would irritate him more than too much solicitude. Instead, she cheerfully ordered everyone to the table.

During dinner Florent made several unsuccessful attempts to reach Picquot's doctor. Eating his fill of familiar food in comfortable surroundings had turned him to jelly. To Elise's surprise, he decided to spend the night, and even ended up recounting his misadventure with Slipskin and Ratablavasky. His mother listened, in horror. His father picked up the telephone. "I'm calling my lawyer," he said, his face as red as if he'd been slapped. "He'll round up those animals and stick them in a cage – in the Bordeaux jail."

His son stopped him. "We can't do a thing, Dad – the law's on their side. All their papers are valid."

"Never mind, I've got more than one trick up my sleeve. Their papers may be valid, but you can't say the same about them."

Florent took a step toward him, his expression wild. "One word to your lawyer and I'll never set foot here again."

Bewildered, Monsieur Boissonneault put down the phone and slumped in a chair. "What's going on between your ears, for Pete's sake? Do you *like* being poor? The minute I try to give you a hand like any normal father you bite my head off!"

"Don't you see – I'm fed up with the whole show! They

won and that's that! Now I'd rather think about something else. Your lawyer can't turn water into wine. He can't wipe out a contract just by touching it. Do you really think a judge would believe all this about pills and plots without a shred of evidence? You know where all the evidence is now? In here," he said, tapping his temple.

Now his father became sullen. "All right, son, but I thought you had more gumption. I've hit a few snags in my career, too, but I've always made my way around them. You want my secret? I'm pigheaded. Go down to the cellar: you'll see a thirty-two-foot yacht that's two-thirds finished. I've been working on it for four years. At first when I talked about it, people looked away so they wouldn't laugh in my face. Now they ask for the date of the launching. That's the way to act: otherwise you'll end up selling pencils on the street."

Madame Boissonneault took her son by the arm. "Why don't you listen to your father for once? Tardif's the sharpest lawyer I've ever met: he might see something ordinary folks –"

"All right, if it'll make you feel better, phone him!"

Folding his arms, Florent sat at the end of the table. Elise smiled at him gratefully. Exasperated, he sprang to his feet. "Right. I'm going to bed. Good night."

His father made an appointment to see his lawyer at nine o'clock the next morning. The interview lasted a long time and the only positive result was that, by keeping a certain distance from the lawyer, Monsieur Boissonneault and Florent were able to tolerate his bad breath for a fairly extended period. Once they had left his office, though, both father and son looked somewhat vexed. "What'd I tell you?" Florent asked bitterly.

"Will you take some money, at least? It's not much, but I offer it gladly."

Florent shook his head. His father didn't want to force the issue. "Where shall I drop you?"

Florent smiled at the innocent ruse. "Don't worry about me, thanks. I have a few things to do."

Monsieur Boissonneault looked at him with eyes like a scolded spaniel's. "You really don't want me to know where you're living?"

Florent put his hand on his father's shoulder. "Try and understand me, Dad. I'll tell you when I'm in better shape and I can entertain you and Mother properly. I'm entitled to my pride too, right?"

Back at the apartment he was startled to find in the kitchen a ravishing seventeen-year-old preparing a ham omelet. With surprising zeal, Ange-Albert was scouring the countertop. Rosine turned to Florent and her pretty doll's lips bore a timid hint of a smile. Blushing, she said, "Hello."

With just a hint of smugness, Ange-Albert made the introductions. As they chatted, Florent examined Rosine with a connoisseur's eye. His voice was subtly different, sounding vaguely like a crooner's. He left the kitchen shortly and peeked casually into Ange-Albert's room. The single mattress on the floor had mysteriously doubled in width. A pair of panty hose hanging in the closet showed that his patience was beginning to bear succulent fruit. He was joined by an exhilarated Ange-Albert. "She's a dish, eh?" he asked in an undertone. "Sometimes it pays to fast." Then his face darkened. "How's Monsieur Picquot?"

"Not good. Cerebral hemorrhage. He should pull out of it, but it'll take time."

Suddenly Elise's footsteps could be heard on the stairs, then the door opened. "Good, you're home," she told Florent.

"Can you help me bring up a box? The taxi's waiting at the door. Your mother insisted on giving me some groceries. She practically cleaned out her pantry."

Rosine was so awed by Elise that she left almost at once, claiming her father wanted her at the restaurant. In fact the cold, as much as Elise, was driving her away. "I'll be back," she promised. "I'll try and bring another vacuum cleaner."

"Another one!" Florent grumbled when she'd left. "We aren't going to use vacuum cleaners for heat! Our eardrums will be shot in a week."

Ange-Albert gave him a knowing smile. "Listen, stop worrying. I'll look after the heat. I ran into our inspector yesterday, at the Faubourg St-Denis."

"Good luck, if you try to reason with him. I'd rather teach a brick to swim."

There was a slight click as Ange-Albert stuck his hand in his pocket. "For the moment he's still thumbing his nose at me, but if I keep shaking my dice I've a hunch my method's going to pay off."

"What method?" asked Elise. "Are your dice loaded?"

"No way," Ange-Albert laughed. "But my fingers are."

But the operation took time. And time cost money. Florent had nearly exhausted his savings. The last month's rent had reduced Ange-Albert's fortune to the distressing sum of two dollars and nineteen cents. Madame Boissonneault's provisions hadn't been on the shelves long enough to gather dust. Monsieur Emile, whose visits were more and more frequent, had devoured a fair amount. He invariably arrived famished, grubby, and clad in his perpetual steam engine T-shirt, which Elise took great pains to remove from time to time so she could wash it.

Now they had to start thinking about necessities. Ange-Albert and Florent set out on a serious job hunt. Florent soon had to sell his car, but it didn't bring much.

About the middle of December Elise got a job selling panty hose, but her hot-blooded boss – who wanted her to try the merchandise on herself so he could judge the effects of various colors on her legs – forced her back to the frigid apartment. Ange-Albert, who'd been there before, decided then it was time for his little "emergency ingenuity" as he called it.

The literary season was in full swing. He began watching out for book launchings. At first, he went alone: with his bedraggled briefcase, he looked like a young writer sniffing out grants. His smiling cockiness made it easy for him to slip into the crowds that such events attracted. He would make his way to the cold buffet where, with a glass in one hand and an hors d'oeuvre in the other, he would relieve his gastric distress as discreetly as possible amid the cultural chitchat, the hugging and kissing that marked these occasions. He persuaded Elise and Florent to come with him, but it meant at most one or two meals a week. Something else was needed.

On Mondays, some bakeries offered stale bread and pastries at cut prices. They compiled a list, divided up the nearby areas and then, first thing in the morning, they would all make the rounds. In the end, though, all the starch wrecked their stomachs. Once more, they needed something else.

Ange-Albert considered the breweries. All had reception rooms to which various groups and associations were invited to stuff their faces and get ripped – for nothing. But brewers were more eagle-eyed than publishers. They put on a more lavish spread, but it took a lot of talent to get anywhere near it. In the end, though, Messrs. Dow, Molson and company provided an average of one meal a week to the wretched tenants of Emery Street. But still their stomachs growled, and Florent was on increasingly intimate terms with humiliation.

One afternoon when Elise, weakened by ten hours without food and racked by a cough she hadn't been able to shake for two days, had had a hysterical crying fit and talked about going back to her aunt in the Gaspé, Florent, without a word, put on his coat and went to the social welfare office (the pogey, as Ange-Albert called it familiarly). He came home with two three-dollar meal tickets and took his wife to Rosine's father's restaurant for a shepherd's pie.

Not nearly as good as The Beanery's, he thought bitterly.

This thought made him suddenly realize how far he'd fallen. He felt giddy. That night, he borrowed some money from Rosine for a monumental bender. Elise had to help him to bed. "Go home to your aunt, baby," he crooned, smiling. "My good years are over."

Two minutes later he was snoring. Elise sat on the edge of the bed and took a long look at him. Sick with grief, she wondered, has the business with The Beanery really wrecked him?

Their daily visits to Chez Bob Snack Bar seemed more and more like a permanent stay. The owner's patience, however, was moving the other way. In spite of discreet attempts by Rosine – who had been very careful not to tell her father about her love life – Monsieur Clouette now refused to give them credit. His courtesy was shrinking, and Florent knew it wouldn't be long before it degenerated into outright rudeness.

One morning after a particularly cruel night, when Elise, Ange-Albert and Florent were warming their icy hands over a coffee, Clouette abruptly asked what they were doing in his restaurant.

"What're we doing?" Florent asked acidly. "Can't you see?"

"We're drinking a coffee and having a chat, Monsieur Clouette," Ange-Albert added, conciliatory.

"Monkey balls!" he exploded, red-faced. "You aren't drinking it, it's evaporating!" He scurried to the cash register and came back with a crumpled ten-dollar bill. "Screw off and go somewhere else for a while. My nerves need a break!"

Happily, the lean times eventually ended. Soon afterward, almost in spite of himself, Ange-Albert got a job with a manufacturer of religious statues, named Angelo Corni. Religion was on the skids, forcing Corni to shift targets, and now he produced erotic-religious statuary destined for private clubs in the U.S.A. Demand exceeded his means of production, and for a while he'd been getting supplies from the clergy, who unloaded old statues for ridiculously small sums. On the first day, Ange-Albert learned about grafting breasts, tongues and penises, about placing revealing rips in tunics, about puffy lips and the plumping of thighs and buttocks, all of which were then colored, with consummate art, by a grouchy, arthritic old painter. Corni, a gnarled little man with a huge waxy nose, followed the operations with a funereal air and drooping lip, muttering incomprehensibly as if he were saying his rosary.

On December 16, Florent was granted permission to visit Picquot. He and Elise went after supper, leaving Ange-Albert at the Faubourg St-Denis with his dice, his patient smile, and Rosarien Roy – who, incidentally, had dropped in that very day for an inspection.

"My dear friends," Picquot murmured when he saw them, "what an experience! To put it mildly, I've grown old overnight."

His voice was nearly inaudible, fragile as sea foam. Inside the room, Florent was appalled at his thinness and at his chalky pallor, which the half light couldn't conceal. Unable to speak, he took his old friend in his arms. Elise, who had more self-control, kissed his cheek and plumped up his pillow. "You're looking rested. How do you feel?"

"Like a wreck, dear child," said the chef, who shuddered constantly. "They drug me like a psychopath and won't let me get up. I have to relieve myself in ridiculous containers. But it's the food that's doing me in. Today, they allowed me a demitasse of coffee . . . and I confess, I couldn't swallow a drop. It tasted of rusty metal."

He stopped, stretched out his legs and smiled. Suddenly his face looked ten years younger. "Nonetheless, I'm delighted to see you," he said, clasping Elise's hand in his icy fingers. "You bring health. The doctor promised I'd be on my feet in a month – but I'd say two weeks. However, for a year or two I'll have to treat myself like a china vase. What about you youngsters? How are you? And I beg you, don't hide anything."

Florent started telling some dutiful lies. He had a job at a record store. He liked the work. Ratablavasky had left the country. As Florent spoke, Picquot grew more serene. The shudders diminished. The old intonations came back to his voice. Elise and Florent were touched to realize how much he'd been fretting about them.

"I won't try to hide it," he told them shortly, "my nerves fell apart whenever I thought about you. I was absolutely forbidden to phone! But I finally bribed a nurse, who promised to let me know if there was ever an emergency. I'll sleep easier now. What can I tell you? You're all I have. Oh, I had a cosy childhood, I grant you. Life was like a vast château with no end of doors for me to open. I had more friends than I knew what to do with, I went through women by the boatload. But good food made me flabby. Rich sauces spell the death of love. And my impossible *métier* gradually cut me off from all my friends – to say nothing of my character, which I know all too well. . . ."

His eyes grew heavy. "Go now," he murmured suddenly, "I'm about to drop. But come and see me often, if you can put up with me!"

Before they were three steps from the hospital, a stocky potbellied man positioned himself on the sidewalk in front of them. Florent started. "Evening, young fellow!" said Captain Galarneau, clutching Florent's hand and pumping it vigorously. "Out for a stroll with the little lady?"

With this, he bowed deeply to Elise, who took fright and tried to lead Florent away. The captain blocked their path. "Steady, now! I haven't eaten anybody yet!" And he burst out in a coarse guttural laugh.

The young couple's faces were engulfed in a blast of hot, fetid air that reeked of cognac and rotten teeth. Elise gazed in disgust at his big alcoholic's nose, at the cavernous hairy nostrils. "Come on, get on with it," said Florent contemptuously, "what do you want?"

"Personally, not a thing!" Galarneau replied vigorously. "Wishy-washy fellows like you are not my style. Grate on the ass, if you get my drift. But not everyone shares my views. Old friend Rata-tat-tat asked me to give you this."

He thrust his hand in his pocket and pulled out an envelope so violently that it almost tore in two. "Whoops! Sorry! Arm's too stiff. Read it right now, will you, so I can proclaim your reply from the rooftops."

Florent gave him a look, then took the letter and opened it. Galarneau clasped his hands behind his back and squared his shoulders. He gazed unsteadily at Elise, a derisive smile lifting the corners of his thick lips, edged with a thread of dried foam. He blinked and started to sing to himself, his face twitching in a way that suggested a grimace.

Florent slipped the letter in his pocket. "My answer's no. And tell him, once and for all, for God's sake, leave me in peace."

"Right, General!"

"As for Monsieur Picquot, I can't answer for him, but I'll certainly advise him to send you packing. Surprised?"

"Nothing surprises me, General, when pigheaded youngsters like you want to remake the world without reckoning with the lessons of their elders. Because we *did* give you a lesson, and a heck of a good one! Too bad for you if you didn't learn anything! I'm a Canadian," he went on, in a rather odd chain of associations, pounding his chest so hard that he swayed on his legs, "and I dragged my carcass all the way to Dieppe to defend my country. That's why I admire people like old Rata-tat-tat. They have a knack for breaking little diehards like you, that turn up their noses at everything and won't listen to their superiors. YOU SHOULD ALL BE CRUSHED LIKE VERMIN!" he exploded joyously, throwing up his arms like an orchestra conductor in mid-fortissimo. "Whoops! Sorry!" he said, bending down to retrieve the fur hat he'd just knocked off a young woman's head.

Florent snickered. "Old wino," the woman muttered, striding away, one hand straightening her hair.

"I entreat you, dear lady," he went on, with many bows, "to accept my fullest apologies for a period of two years and two months!"

He returned to Elise and Florent. "My pretty birds, I must leave you now. But remember this, and remember it well: The Old Man's head is a lot harder than yours. Har har! You'll bite your brow with your upper teeth before you're off his mind."

He gave them a military salute and moved off as quickly as his numerous libations permitted. "What's in the letter?" Elise asked.

Florent offered it to her.

My Dear Friend,

I have allowed myself to call upon the French-language services of the splendid Captain Galarneau to ensure that the essence of my thoughts will reach you intact. The distinguished journalist Gladu has told me of his visit to your home. I know that you fear me and even despise me. And from your point of view you may have good reason to do so. But I beg you to believe me when I ask that your present situation is torture to my fatherly heart. I ask you, then, to be so kind as to accept the honest assistance I am offering you. Even now I can see your young features twisted by a skeptical grin as you read these final words. Come and see me, with your wife. We'll chat. I'll explain my recent behavior in a way that I hope will set your minds at rest. In a word, I'll convince you and we shall crush any venomous obstacles along our way. Would it make you feel safer to know that in a few weeks I shall leave Quebec forever, so I can breathe my last in my ancestral land?

As a pledge of my sincerity, here are the arrangements I have made with respect to your unfortunate friend Picquot: despite his illness he will keep his job.

Through my influence, he is guaranteed a long convalescence safe from the cares of earning a living. Could you ask for better proof?

I await your presence.
Egon Ratablavasky

"Your benefactor's lost his marbles," Elise murmured, shivering. "Throw that letter away and let's go home. My toes are numb."

Despite the distance, they walked back to the apartment, to save the bus fare. They took long strides through the breathtaking cold, their minds numb. "Home at last!" Elise exclaimed, closing the door behind her.

But the temperature inside was cruelly like that on the street. Huddling under her coat, Elise burst out crying. "I can't take it anymore, Florent. We have to do something. . . . We're living like bums. . . . Sometimes I even think of going back to live with Aunt Emma."

Florent, upset, held her and tried to calm her. "In a week at the most," he promised, "I'll have a job, anything, even wiping asses in a nursing home, and we'll be in a heated apartment, with cupboards full of food. I swear it. Do you hear me, I swear it."

She raised her head and tried to smile. "It's okay. Never mind what I just said. . . . It was that old drunk . . . My nerves are shot."

She pressed against him with almost desperate ardor, as though to crush some obscure drive within her. "I'll never leave you . . . I married you and I'm staying with you, even if it means freezing my feet."

Florent smiled pensively.

They went to their bedroom and turned on a light. Monsieur Emile was asleep on the bed, mouth agape, grubby boots on the covers. A stained-glass panel depicting a vase of roses lay beside him, its wooden frame partly broken. Bewildered, Florent picked it up and looked at the child. "What's he doing here?"

Elise shook him, but in vain. Monsieur Emile muttered but didn't wake up. Florent bent down and smelled his breath. "The little bugger's drunk again!"

Grumbling, he left the room and headed for Ange-Albert's. The passionate sighs filtering through the door made him retrace his steps. "I don't have the heart to take him home in weather like this. We'll put him beside our bed."

"His mother will be looking everywhere for him," Elise observed.

"Well, shit, let her look! At least she'll have done *that* for him!"

They slipped the child into a sleeping bag and tore off their clothes: so began their first night as a household of five, while a raging cold swept over the city.

It was seven o'clock the next morning when a half-awake Spaniard tripped on a roll of electrical wire and smashed his nose against the staircase. A volley of Iberian oaths burst through the walls. Florent sprang out of bed. He opened the door and shouted, "Who's there?" using his left hand as a fig leaf.

"Thees ees seven-four-two Emery?" the Spaniard asked, rubbing his cheek.

"Yes, but nobody asked for any . . ."

A second Spaniard appeared at the bottom of the stairs, carrying an armful of space heaters. Ange-Albert emerged from his room. "I got our inspector to play last night," he announced, smiling modestly. "At nine o'clock, before witnesses, he owed me one thousand nine hundred dollars. I settled for getting the apartment heated."

A few hours later a gentle warmth was beginning to fill the rooms, awakening several families of cold-numbed cockroaches that renewed their lease with frenzied joy. Undisturbed by the pounding of hammers and drills, Monsieur Emile was still sleeping like whole cord of logs. The previous night Ange-Albert, busy celebrating his victory with Rosine, hadn't heard him come in. Now he gave him a long sad look, then went back to the kitchen where the Spaniards were gathering up their tools as Elise made breakfast.

"How'd you swing that?" Florent asked when they'd gone.

"Simple: I'd been working on him for a while and in the end he thought I was an okay guy. Last night I took out my dice, he got interested, he challenged me – and I took him on. He couldn't sneak away; he had to save face: there were fifty people watching."

"More than that," said Rosine, making her entrance draped modestly in a bathrobe.

She greeted Elise and Florent shyly and sat by Ange-Albert. Florent sneaked a peek at her slender, lusciously shapely legs.

"Honestly, Ange-Albert," said Elise, "I can't figure out how you do it. Show us."

He rummaged in his pocket, then sat down again. With hands slightly open, he shook the cubes, his fingers performing a sort of low rotation while his gaze was fixed on the dice. "This will be . . . eight," he murmured.

Immediately, his fingers stopped. The dice fell to the table without rolling, as if magnetized. Florent counted the points. Precisely eight. Ange-Albert picked up the dice, which started to roll with a slight clicking sound. He watched them with acute concentration that etched painful creases around his mouth. "Ten," he whispered.

His hand froze. The dice fell. Elise counted ten. He repeated the operation a dozen times. The dice almost always obeyed him. "Ange-Albert, your dice are loaded," Elise scolded affectionately.

"No way."

"I still don't get it!" Florent exclaimed.

"I do," said a child's voice. "It's magic. I saw a guy do it on TV the other day."

They all turned around. Standing in the doorway, with one sock drooping over his slipper, Monsieur Emile was following the scene with a knowing look, scratching his head all the while. Furious, Florent confronted the boy. "So you're finally awake, you little lush! You're going to do me a favor and get out of here as fast as your grubby little feet will take you, and go home before your mother gets the cops after us!"

Elise crouched in front of the boy and grasped his shoulders. "Why do you do it!" she asked, her voice completely changed. "You'll make yourself sick – you'll ruin your whole life."

Monsieur Emile looked at her impassively, saying nothing. "Do you want to end up an old drunk?" she went on. "Dirty and sick, with no money and no place to live, all alone, like a stray dog?"

Rosine watched the scene wide-eyed, uncomprehending. "He's likely following his father's footsteps," Florent snickered.

Monsieur Emile didn't care for this remark; he made a face and stomped off to the bedroom. "What did he do?" asked Rosine, leaning toward Ange-Albert.

"Got drunk."

Elise and Florent had followed their protégé, who was lying on the mattress on his stomach, pouting. "Where do you get all that booze?" Florent asked him for the third time. "From your mother?"

"No!" barked the child.

"Do you steal it? Make it? Answer me!"

Monsieur Emile turned over, tears streaming down his face, fists clenched. "Quit bugging me! It's none of your business!"

"Okay. Thanks for your kindness. It's really very nice of you. . . . And by the way . . . would you mind telling me where *this* came from?" he asked, indicating the stained glass.

"I didn't take it! Some men gave it to me! It was in an old house next door to our place! They smashed it all up with a tractor! And if you don't believe me, fuck you!"

With this he threw himself back on the mattress and began to sob even louder. Elise and Florent looked at each other, distraught. "Where on earth did he find that liquor?" Elise asked.

She glanced sadly at Monsieur Emile, who was in a rage, furiously biting the pillow. "Probably at home. . . . I wouldn't be surprised if his mother takes a nip between trips to the sack, and she likely leaves bottles lying around." Shrugging, he left the room.

SIXTEEN

Despite pressure from Florent, Ange-Albert refused to use his dice to pay their way. His new job brought in $110 a week, which he shared with his friends, and that was all he needed. "Gambling's too risky," he said. "I'd end up in the mob, and I'm not wild about winding up at the bottom of the St. Lawrence in cement boots."

And so Florent had to go job hunting again. As the apartment got warmer, his enthusiasm had cooled down. But luck didn't smile on him often.

On December 18 he landed a job as usher at the Cinéma Lumière in Longueuil. He showed up at seven o'clock, donned his uniform, and left five hours later, with seven dollars in his pocket and an unforgettable image of the brash and brilliant Marx Brothers.

The cold was bone chilling. The dagger that stabbed the lungs with every breath was a reminder that despite its blazing summers, Quebec wasn't far from the North Pole. Florent, optimistic because of his new job and Ange-Albert's triumph, considered the situation and decided to go home by taxi. The meter read $6.10. "Keep the change," he told the driver, smiling magnanimously. Then he climbed the stairs, delighted with his evening.

Next morning, the boss told him apologetically that he didn't need him anymore.

That day Elise and Florent had to borrow money from Rosine to buy Picquot some slippers. At the hospital, Florent squeezed his wife's arm and pointed to a passing taxi. On the back seat sat Father Jeunehomme in his Roman collar and soutane, leafing through a book. "Poor thing," said Elise. "All he knows about life is what he's read."

The chef was sitting by the window, a chess set on his lap, wearing a dressing gown on which scarlet dragons pursued one another across a background of green.

"Splendid!" he exclaimed. "You always remember your old Frenchman!"

He rose, waited until Elise was close enough, then kissed her awkwardly. He seemed rested and relaxed. "You know," he told Florent, "your father's becoming a bit of a nuisance. I don't know how he did it, but he tracked me down to my hospital bed. How he does carry on, the dear fellow! He tried to pump me for a good half hour, but you know me. . . . *Enfin*, I'll pass on his message, since he begged me: he'd like you to come to his house on Christmas Eve, for *réveillon*."

"Poor man," Elise murmured with a reproachful glance at her husband. "How is he?"

"If he's as healthy as his tongue, he'll live to be a hundred! It's amazing what I found out in just half an hour: I know more about you now than you do yourselves."

"When do you get out of the hospital?" Florent asked, to change the subject.

"Three long weeks from now, my friend," the chef replied with a frustrated look. "Alas, my Christmas celebrations will bear the scent of iodine. But enough of that! Take this chair, dear girl, and you, young man, sit at the foot of my bed. Ah yes! In three weeks I'll be breathing the air of Saint-Sauveur and chatting quietly with my friends at Le Petit Coin de France. The doctors can't get over it. I'm recovering like a babe in arms. Mind you, *I'm* not surprised. It's all in the constitution. My parents made me tough! Now in November 1944 I boarded the ship for Canada. The sea was a horror, rough enough to make a whale throw up. The passengers were green as lettuce. Whereas I, rather than suffering in my cabin, calmly ate my three meals a day and strolled the deck from morning to night, to enjoy the sea air. I saved their lives, in fact. In five days I spotted four submarines the radar hadn't picked up. Back up, take on speed, zigzag – we got off with a good scare, except once when a torpedo bashed in the end of the hull: people were asking my advice about everything. Sometimes when I'm daydreaming I tell myself that if I'd patrolled the ocean then, instead of disembarking at Quebec, Hitler might have given in a few months earlier and a lot of lives would have been saved."

He held forth for an hour, then asked the nurse for fruit juice all around.

"When I hear him string a line like that," Florent said as they left the hospital, "I feel as if the disease that'll do him in hasn't been invented yet."

Elise laughed, cheered up by the visit. "He's adorable, like a little boy in short pants. But I wasn't sorry to leave – he wears me out."

"I wish I had half his energy!" Florent sighed.

At the corner of St-Denis and Sherbrooke he suddenly announced, "I feel like taking a look at The Beanery."

"Why?"

"No reason. Just to look."

He hailed a cab. "And by taxi no less!" Elise said testily. "What's going on? I think you're about to do something you'll be sorry for."

"Now, listen . . ."

He stopped the cab at St-Denis and Mont-Royal. Ahead of them they could make out one corner of The Beanery's sign. Elise got out of the car, took a few steps, then stopped and stamped her foot. "Do as you please – I'm not going!" she announced, incensed. "If you're dumb enough to go chasing trouble when trouble's forgotten you, you can go by yourself!"

A man in a black coat, his shoulders covered with dandruff, turned around and looked at them. "Hee hee!" he snickered, scurrying away. "The little birds are squabbling!"

Florent defended himself. "I don't want to go in."

"Big deal! What difference does it make? I'm waiting here," she added, leaning against a wall.

He went on alone, across St-Denis, then continued more slowly along the sidewalk across from the restaurant. The window was steamed up, but he could distinguish Slipskin at the cash. The door burst open and Rosarien Roy appeared, withered and yellow as an old lemon. His fists were clenched, his hat was crooked, and he was furiously shouting and gesticulating. "You haven't heard the last of me! Next time we meet, by Christ, it'll be in court!"

He slammed the door and walked away without noticing Florent. Slipskin's red head didn't move. By peering hard, Florent could make out his former associate's long nose. Funny, he thought, I ought to hate him but it's as if I didn't have the strength.

He turned and went to rejoin Elise. "Now are you satisfied?" she asked.

His rage had died down. He shrugged, sighed and walked on in silence. Suddenly snowflakes appeared. When they came to the apartment the grayish-white sky had swooped down on the city. Little by little, all sound was muffled, swallowed by the snow, and traffic was moving more slowly.

Ange-Albert let them in, still wearing his coat. "They're predicting a big blizzard on the radio," he said with a smile. "We'll sleep tight tonight."

Elise went to the kitchen, and soon the smell of fried onions filled the apartment. Florent burst into the kitchen. "Stop everything, Rosine's brought supper."

Rosine was red from the cold, and snowflakes were clinging to her eyelashes. She carried a paper bag. "Everybody like hot dogs?" she asked, smiling shyly.

"And how!" Florent answered, helping her with her coat. He took advantage of his gesture to graze her neck, which was soft as a petal.

She shuddered. "What a wind! I didn't think I'd make it!"

They sat around the table, and there was silence except for the sounds of chewing. Suddenly Elise cried out and brought her hand to her mouth. All eyes were on her.

She couldn't talk for the pain. In a moment she spat out a piece of sausage that contained a bone fragment the size of a dime. She stuck her finger in her mouth and removed a piece of decayed tooth. Rosine rushed to her side, helpless and desolate. "Oh God, it's my fault – if only I'd known . . ."

"It's nothing," she said with a forced smile. "It'll pass."

She tried to eat but she'd lost her appetite. In a few minutes the pain forced her to lie down. Florent looked in the medicine cabinet but all he found was an old green-stained toothbrush and a greasy scrap of paper on which someone had scrawled, "Chicken for Matilda."

"I'll get some aspirin from the restaurant," Rosine offered.

She was back in ten minutes, her nose blue. "I nearly got hit by a shutter. The wind's tearing everything off. There are branches all over the street."

As if to prove the point, a pane of glass was suddenly blown out of the living room window. While Florent tried to stop up the opening with cardboard, Rosine went to Elise. "Good God, your cheek's all puffed up!"

She bent over Elise with a glass of water and some aspirin, but her hand shook so much that she spilled some. "My Lord!" she said, desolate, "what else can I do wrong?"

Stoically, Elise endured the pain, unable to get to sleep, twisting and turning in her bed. Ange-Albert gave her a cold compress, which brought some relief. Rosine had to leave shortly. Ange-Albert offered to take her home, while Florent got into bed with his wife.

About three o'clock he woke up and turned on a light. Elise was looking at him, moaning softly. The swelling had almost closed her left eye. "We're taking you to the hospital," he decided, pulling on his pants.

"How will we get there in weather like this?" she asked plaintively, her voice somewhat husky.

Florent helped her dress. "My head aches," she said suddenly.

He looked at her, horrified. Headache? Infectious meningitis, he thought. Dead within twelve hours. Like Monsieur Pinard, when he and Dad went fishing at Lake Mistassini. Aloud, he said, "It's only tension. It'll pass."

On the stairs, he offered her his arm. Ange-Albert, who hadn't heard a thing, was fast asleep.

When Florent opened the door the storm took their breath away. They couldn't see the street. "Wait here a second," said Florent, going back up the stairs four at a time. He returned with a wool scarf, which he wrapped around Elise's head, leaving only a narrow slit for her eyes. "Hold my hand tight," he said, opening the door again.

The blizzard swept the city as if it would wipe it off the map. The night had disappeared, leaving only a vast white confusion, punctuated here and there by gray spots that you could only guess to be houses. Occasionally, just for a moment, details stood out with surprising clarity: a wrought-iron balcony suddenly appeared in the middle of a housefront, the corner of a deserted lane revealed a pile of overturned garbage cans, a disheveled head, with puffy eyes and an anxious expression, peered out from behind curtains, then was hidden again by the storm.

"We'll go to the St-Luc Hospital!" Florent shouted. "It's the closest."

They made their way slowly onto the street, their eyes bombarded by snowflakes, stumbling through the snow that was piling up at a hallucinating rate, transforming abandoned cars into shapeless mounds. Despite the vast rumbling that filled the sky, from time to time they heard the distant clatter of a snowblower, the only sign that man had not completely surrendered to winter's fury.

At the corner of St-Denis, they had to stop to get their breath. Something resembling strange phantom trains went screaming down the street, then were suddenly scattered in gigantic collisions, from which new trains would presently emerge. On their right, the traffic light at the corner of

Ste-Catherine, stalled on red and enlarged by a sinister halo, looked like a Cyclops' eye contemplating the disintegration of the city.

Elise moaned. Florent leaned over her. "What's wrong?"

"My head hurts," she said, her voice thin and trembling. She seemed to falter.

"Just one more little push," he urged, pulling her as hard as he could. "We're nearly there."

He imagined Monsieur Pinard's face and heard his father's voice, glum and flat, recounting the tragedy. "I can't go on," said Elise, leaning on a store window. Then she slumped against the door and said, "My head feels frozen."

Florent gazed at her pain-racked face, made almost triangular by her hugely swollen cheek. "Let's move it, baby," he said in a tone of forced jocularity. "The stores don't open till nine."

"If I take one more step I'll drop." She brought her hand to her cheek and shut her eyes. "All right," she said suddenly, "one more little push."

He had to help her straighten up. Ten minutes later, when they'd gone three blocks, Florent realized that his wife had reached the limit of her strength. He felt neither fear nor sorrow, only rage. "Fucking country!" he howled at the storm. "You want to bury us alive, is that it?"

The rest of the street had been cleared, but the wind had soon undone the snowblowers' work. Gripping Elise's shoulders, Florent walked off the sidewalk. He felt as if his forehead would burst from the cold.

On the other side of Dorchester Boulevard, all bloated with snowbanks, an indistinct, shifting glow was the facade of the St-Luc Hospital. Elise made a supreme effort, and two minutes later they stumbled against a frost-coated glass door.

They were nearly engulfed by moist heat and the storm's rage was cut in half. The harshly lit entrance was almost deserted.

They walked to the back, went down a few stairs, and found themselves in a chair-lined corridor that opened onto a large room crowded with stretchers. A number of people were waiting there, melancholy and docile.

"Come on," he told Elise, "we have to sign in." He started involuntarily. There was a grayish shadow around her left eye, which was almost shut.

"I'm not a very pretty sight, eh?" she said painfully.

Nurses were bustling about, their voices high, moving nervously. Someone gestured Florent to a wicket where a fat blonde was waiting for them at a typewriter. She looked blankly at Elise, and her fingers began to fly across the keyboard. Elise leaned against the wicket and answered her questions, breathing spasmodically. "Take a seat," said the typist. "Someone will call you."

They went back to the corridor. Florent spotted two chairs in a corner. Elise leaned against him and bowed her head. "I feel so numb," she said a moment later, "as if my head's going to open up."

She took a deep breath. "Florent, tell them to hurry."

An old woman in a mauve turban, whose puffy yellow face looked like peanut shells, turned toward them abruptly. "You poor little girl!" she exclaimed in a broken voice. "You might better ask them to walk on the walls like flies!"

Florent had been eyeing the woman. She wore a muskrat coat that looked as if it had lodged several generations of moths and had a stack of *Reader's Digests* on her lap, endlessly turning from one to the next, unable to settle down. "Have you been here long?" he asked casually.

The old lady leaned toward him, her bloodshot eyes

staring. "Sir, I was a young girl," she whispered in a voice filled with mystery.

An hour later Elise was called. They found themselves facing a young intern who looked exhausted. He listened to Florent for a moment, his gaze focused on a fat man on a stretcher who kept emitting tremendous belches, then gestured to Elise to follow him. She was back in three minutes, holding a small envelope.

"Two-twenty-two's!" Florent exclaimed.

"There's no dentist on duty," she explained, exhausted. "I'm supposed to come back tomorrow morning."

Florent, his face on fire, was in an examination cubicle, screaming. With a melancholy look, the intern kept repeating, "It's all I can do. How can I get a dentist on a night like this?"

"What about antibiotics? You ever hear of antibiotics?"

"What for? A painkiller will do till tomorrow," he said mildly.

The intern clasped Florent's shoulder and showed him to the door. "Go to the Notre-Dame Hospital, if you want," he suggested, smiling amiably. "But I'd be very surprised if you found a dentist tonight."

Elise swallowed her pills and they went down the corridor, which reeked of disinfectant. "No way we'll get there," Florent muttered as they approached the frost-coated glass door.

He paced back and forth, hands in his pockets. Elise had flopped onto a chair, where she was dozing. Just then Florent looked out onto St-Denis Street and a miracle occurred. The wind had just bared a large sheet of ice on the street. A taxi appeared, proceeding south with great difficulty. The driver tried to avoid the ice, but a violent gust of wind pushed it to one side. The car skidded, spun, and landed in a snowbank. Florent rushed outside. A corner of his scarf hit him in the eye. He brought his hand to his face, lost his balance, and landed in the snow. "Give you a hand?" he shouted to the taxi driver, who had got out of his car and was trying to open the trunk. He didn't hear Florent, who approached him and tapped his shoulder.

"Thanks," he smiled.

He held out a shovel and got behind the wheel. Florent shoveled as energetically as a treasure hunter. In ten minutes the car had been freed. "Thanks again," said the driver, holding out a two-dollar bill.

Florent shook his head. "Take us to Notre-Dame Hospital instead. My wife's sick and they won't take care of her here."

A blast of snow swept inside his coat, taking his breath away. The driver shook his head sadly. "Can't be done! I don't think I can even make it to Ste-Catherine Street. I'll probably just stay here and spend the night in the hospital cafeteria."

Florent gripped his arm. "Please! She's very sick."

His teeth were chattering, his nose was as blue as if it had been squeezed in a vice, his thoughts muddled by fatigue. Shivering, the taxi driver turned up his collar, seeming to hesitate. Florent pointed to the glass door behind which Elise was standing. Thinking he was beckoning to her, she headed toward them. The driver looked at her briefly, then opened his door and got behind the wheel. "Go ahead, get in. We'll try and get there – but there's no guarantee!"

Slowly, the car started up. Elise, collapsed on the seat, seemed asleep. Florent shuddered at her leaden color. The driver, squinting, the tip of his tongue showing between his teeth, was trying to penetrate the ever-changing mass of snow that whirled before him, spinning his wheel as if he were playing roulette. "What's troubling the little lady?" he asked.

"Her face looks like it's been worked over with a baseball bat."

"She has an abscess," Florent responded dryly.

"Toothache, eh? The worst pain in the world."

He stepped on the accelerator and the car swerved. Suddenly the shaft of a lamppost loomed, threatening, on their left, then disappeared. For a few seconds the passengers felt they were crossing through a cloud of hail. The driver whistled happily and jerkily applied the brakes: he'd just driven through a snowbank two feet deep. "Toothache?" he repeated. "And they couldn't do anything at St-Luc?"

"Apparently not," said Florent. "They sent me to Notre-Dame."

"Hospitals!" grumbled the driver. "They laugh in your face! Playing cards while patients are spitting out their guts!"

Florent leaned over his wife. "Have the pills started to work?"

She shook her head. The motor growled, moaned, seemed about to give up the ghost. "Ste-Catherine's been ploughed!" the driver exclaimed. "We can head east now."

For a few seconds there was a breach in the storm, and the St-Jacques spire stood out, impressive amid the debris of the demolished church. Eusèbe Gratton, the taxi driver, was sweating bullets; his cap, askew, revealed a damp skull that only a few black curls saved from total baldness. He barely missed another car, grazed a mailbox and finally straightened out in the middle of the street.

"Well, that's the worst of it. Just another fifteen minutes and we can knock off."

The meter showed four dollars. Florent wondered how he'd pay it. I don't even have fifty cents, he thought.

One of the back windows was stuck, and the snow was coming in a narrow opening. Florent, dazed, was peering at the snow as it piled up in a corner, forming an icy white pyramid. Suddenly, the taxi hit a big yellow dog that was tearing across the street, and without really wanting to, Eusèbe Gratton found himself on St. Christopher Street. Things went fairly well until the hill going up to Sherbrooke Street. The wind had partially cleared the right side of the street and the taxi, half on the sidewalk, managed to go five or six hundred feet. At the bottom of the hill, though, was a mass of snow they couldn't get through. "Well, youngsters, the honeymoon ends here," the driver announced. "Can't go another inch."

Turning off the ignition, he said, "Listen, I've got an idea. Come to my house. It's just two steps away, near Ontario. Maybe the hospitals don't have anything for toothache, but I do. You'll see! And we can keep warm inside while the storm blows itself out and they clear the main streets."

Florent turned to Elise. She shook her head. "I don't want to go out again," she murmured feebly, "I'm too tired. Let me sleep in the car for a bit. . . . My tooth doesn't hurt so much now."

Eusèbe Gratton looked Florent in the eye and shook his head vigorously. They got out, picked up Elise, and started walking.

After only three steps they couldn't breathe. They were wrapped in a vast, bluish swirl of snow that lashed out at their eyes in particular, so it was almost impossible to keep them open. They turned a corner. Gratton didn't know where he was. "That's the limit!" he muttered. "Imagine getting lost on St. Christopher Street!"

He stumbled and nearly fell against a garbage can the wind had driven onto the street. He picked it up and was just about to hurl it into the storm when he realized it was his. Through an opening in the blizzard to his left, he could see the corner of his front stoop. "Great! Let's go in while we can still see the door."

Entering a tiny kitchen, they were greeted by a large portrait of Pope John XXIII. The pope was smiling cheerfully, like a lover of good food who'd just polished off an excellent apple pie.

"Have a seat, young lady – don't wear out your legs," said the taxi driver, pulling out an old chrome chair.

There was a slight odor of heating oil in the kitchen and the rustling of wings in a chintz-covered cage above the sink. "Is that you, Eusèbe?" asked a worried voice.

"Hang on a minute, I'm going to see the wife."

Elbows resting on the table, Elise wept silently. Her lips were so distorted by the swelling that she had trouble holding back her saliva. Florent looked at her, his chest pounding. He patted her shoulder, saying, "Poor kitten, if I could only take your place for a while. . . . Be brave, in twenty minutes we'll be at the doctor's."

From the bedroom, Madame Gratton exclaimed: "What!"

The bedsprings creaked reprovingly, and a scrawny little woman with a prematurely wrinkled face burst into the kitchen, her thinning hair half hidden by a regiment of pink rollers. "Eusèbe, are you out of your mind!" she exclaimed when she saw Elise. "Get her to a doctor – fast! I don't want any trouble!"

"Not till she's taken my herbal syrup."

"Tsk, tsk. Poor child," his wife murmured, shuffling fearfully over to Elise. "You must be in agony. Who put you in a state like this?"

"She has a toothache," said Florent.

"That's what my husband said. . . . He's a great talker. . . . Such fuss! And why, I ask you?"

She went to the window and pulled aside the curtain. "What a storm! Next thing we'll be seeing churches fly through the air!" She looked up suspiciously, nostrils quivering. "What's that funny smell?"

"Don't worry, Ma," said her husband, coming into the kitchen with a small bottle. "I just spilled a bit of syrup. Bring a soup spoon, will you?"

An odd smell of savory, cloves, and raw onion had crept into the room. "Here, child," he said, setting the bottle on the table in front of Elise. "Take a good spoonful and swig it around and hold it against your sore gum. But careful not to swallow it or you'll singe your windpipe!"

As Elise brought the syrup to her mouth her right eye dilated. "Hang on, girly, it's your abscess fighting back. Your pain will soon be gone."

Madame Gratton looked on with folded arms, shivering in her old rose flannelette housecoat. "Poor child, her face hardly looks human. . . . Take her away, Eusèbe, I don't want to look at her."

"Go back to bed, then," he shouted, incensed.

Elise's face was scarlet now. She let out an almighty moan. Florent gripped her hand and led her into the bathroom, which was visible through a half-open door. She spat noisily into the sink, breathless now, feeling as if her mouth was full of live coals.

"Water," she pleaded.

Florent gave her a glass. The fumes from the medicine stung his eyes. Monsieur Gratton had come in and was watching them, smiling contentedly. "Be patient, girly. When the fire leaves your mouth the pain'll go with it."

"While you're yacking," his wife grumbled as she got back into bed, "the germs aren't standing still!"

Twenty minutes later Elise was asleep on the sofa. Eusèbe told Florent, "Look here, my friend, I don't want to stick my nose in your business, but if you don't trust hospitals I know a doctor on Stanley Street you can call on any time, day or night. Dr. Brosseau. Henri Brosseau. I can take you there as soon as the storm lets up a bit."

Florent smiled pitifully. "As a matter of fact . . . I wanted to tell you . . . I haven't got a cent to pay you."

"Pay me tomorrow – it won't kill me. But I'll take your address, young fellow. I want my fare – fine thoughts don't put food on the table."

He went to the window and lifted the curtain. "Heavenly days, the wind's died down. Another half hour and we can go."

He sounded like those people you see walking in the park in springtime, happily pointing out the progress of the vegetation.

Elise sighed and sat up on the sofa. Florent joined her. "We've found a doctor, lovey. Your trouble's nearly over."

"And how's the little lady?" asked the taxi driver, taking her hand.

To Florent's amazement, a wan smile appeared on her swollen lips. "A little better."

"What'd I tell you? Eh? That's fantastic syrup. It's my cousin Pamphile Sabourin's recipe and he got it from Brother Marie-Victorin himself."

As Florent got in the taxi he glanced at the meter. "Eight dollars and fifty cents," he muttered, horrified.

"Bah, don't worry about it," said Gratton, "it's just a machine – you can't expect it to take account of circumstances." He paused, then added: "Let's say the whole trip, including Stanley Street, for five bucks. How does that sound?"

Half an hour later he'd left his passengers at the Berri-DeMontigny metro station, as his car couldn't go any farther. It was a quarter to six, and the metro had just opened. Florent gave the driver a scrap of paper with his address and thanked him effusively. "Poor little thing, last night nearly did her in," the taxi driver murmured, suddenly overwhelmed with fatigue himself, as he watched Elise disappear down the stairs, sagging against her husband.

That morning, Florent was very grateful for Dr. Brosseau's business acumen, for his office was right downtown, just two steps from the Peel metro station. When he'd rung the bell twice, a buzzer sounded and a gruff, cordial voice said over the intercom: "Come in, I'll be right with you."

They entered a large waiting room furnished with carved high-backed chairs. In the center of the room a Cupid was ceremoniously pissing into a little pink marble fountain held up by two naiads.

Dr. Brosseau appeared, wearing a three-piece suit and tie, looking tired but smiling. He had a square, red face, a gray brush cut and a broad mouth. "Morning, folks. Aha! I believe I see an abscess. It's nothing, dear, we'll have it fixed in no time. Open wide. . . ."

He examined her briefly, clicked his tongue in satisfaction, then asked, "Do you have your Medicare card?"

Elise rummaged in her bag and gave it to him. "Some storm, eh? The bears must have snow in their ears. All right, let's look you over."

"Can I come with her?" asked Florent.

"A jealous husband," said the doctor, gesturing to Elise to get up on the examining table. "Why not, young fellow, if you like the sight of pus. There's nothing to be scared of, dear, I haven't tortured anybody yet. I'm too fond of collecting fees."

He peered and probed, then picked up a little flashlight. "Open wide again."

Taking out a tongue depressor, he began to stretch her mouth in every direction. Elise moaned. "Patience, lamb, just hang on for a second and a quarter. I'm going to put a drop of maple syrup on your gum and you'll forget all about your pain, Brosseau's word."

He opened a drawer, nimbly removed a nickel-plated instrument and stuck it in Elise's mouth. She braced herself on the table, shouted hoarsely and fell back limp as a rag. "That's it. Press on your cheek now, and spit into this compress. Your pain will fly away like a ditty. Hold on to her," he told Florent, "while I look in my medicine cabinet."

He came back with two vials of pills. "Antibiotics," he said, his index finger on one of them. "Two every hour till you see the dentist." He touched the other tube. "Percodan, in case the pain comes back. One every hour – no more."

Elise tried to smile. "The pain's almost gone."

"That's only the beginning!" the doctor said delightedly, going back into this office. "The best is yet to come!"

He put the Medicare card in the imprinter and they heard a familiar click. Florent helped Elise to stand up, and they started for the waiting room. "Oh no, not so fast!" exclaimed the doctor, retracing his steps, "I'm not finished yet."

They looked at him, surprised. "Yes indeed, little girl, you may not know, but you came close to slipping over to the Other Side. I can tell you now that everything's under control. But we can't just dampen the fire, we have to put it out. That means antibiotics first of all – starting now."

He gave her a glass of water. "Now I want you to lie on your tummy and show me your pretty behind so I can give you a shot of penicillin."

Docile, Elise tried to get up on the table, but she wasn't strong enough. Florent helped her. The doctor briskly pulled up her skirt, pulled down her pants and then, with his eyes half-closed, let his gaze wander between her buttocks to the tuft of pubic hair. "Take a deep breath now," he said, jabbing the needle into her pink flesh.

He turned to Florent. "You can pull up her panties; the College of Physicians doesn't mind."

Elise was no sooner sitting up than he held out two flasks: "Now I need a urine sample, to see how far the infection spread."

He went back to his office and the well-known click was heard again. "Now some blood," he told Elise when she handed him the flasks. "Pull up your sleeve."

"Are you sure all these tests are necessary?" Florent asked.

With a look of mock severity the doctor said, "That depends on you, my friend. Are you thinking of remarrying?" And another needle sank into Elise's flesh.

"Can I sit down?" she asked unsteadily.

"Of course! Of course! Is that any better? No? Your pretty color's disappearing into my syringe, is that it? Give her another glass of water," he told Florent.

He stood still for a moment to take her pulse. "Well, your heart rate's up where it should be. Better now?"

Elise nodded vaguely. The doctor went to the back of the room and opened a door. "Make yourself comfortable while I do my tests. I'll be twenty minutes or so."

The door closed with a thud. Once more they heard the click of the imprinter. Florent snickered. "Sweetie, I think your toothache's turned into a gold mine!"

Elise collapsed on a chair and dozed off. Now and then she would sigh and feebly smile. The pain had finally gone.

Florent, looking glum, paced the waiting room. Then he sat down and fell asleep almost at once.

The vigorous sound of throat-clearing made him start. Brosseau was standing in front of them, looking like a butcher in a blood-stained coverall. "Your blood's just dandy, dear, and your urine's even better: no staphylococcus, not a trace of albumin or sugar – everything's coming up roses. And you're pregnant. Or did you already know?"

Elise stared at him, stunned. Her stupefaction, plus her swollen face, made her look idiotic. Scratching his cheek, Florent had trouble taking in what he'd heard. Suddenly his eyes felt very dry and rather sore. He got up, the vague sound of organ music in his ears, took Elise in his arms, and held very tight.

"Pregnant?" she sobbed.

Later that morning, around ten o'clock, Elise had a molar extracted at the Notre-Dame Hospital. Fifteen minutes afterward, she glided voluptuously into bed. "I'm sleeping for you, my love," she said, stroking her belly and smiling gently.

SEVENTEEN

Before Ange-Albert was even inside the door he learned that the province of Quebec would soon be richer by one citizen. Elise and Florent's joy astounded him. How could they be so thrilled about an event that would make their financial situation even worse – if possible? But his good mood was soon restored. "That's something to celebrate! I'll get the champagne."

He tore down the stairs, heading for the liquor store, then suddenly remembered that his own fortune consisted of the modest sum of two dollars and twenty-five cents (his next infusion of cash was two days away). He stopped, crestfallen. "So much for a party."

The liquor store at 1246 St-Denis had been turned into a self-serve. He strolled up and down the sawdust-strewn aisles for a while, somewhat bewildered, trying to think of a substitute for his champagne. The store had just reopened: the shelves weren't all filled yet, and there were dozens of piles of bottle-filled boxes at the back. Smiling mischievously, he looked over the boxes, then knocked on the manager's door. A long, angular face with a worried and rather silly expression appeared in the half-open door. "Yes, *Sir*! What can we do for you?"

"I need some empty boxes," Ange-Albert said, loud enough to be heard at the cash register. "I'm moving."

"Ten cents a box," said the manager, somewhat taken aback by the young man's behavior. "How many do you want?"

"Oh, just one for now."

The manager stuck out his hand, waited for Ange-Albert to hand over his dime, then gestured to a clerk. "Bring this man a box from the cellar."

Then he shut the door. Ange-Albert waited until he was alone, then nonchalantly strolled over to a carton of Veuve Cliquot, lifted it on his shoulder and quickly walked to the cash. "Too bad it's not full, eh?" the cashier smiled.

"Oh, it's full, all right," he replied with a wink.

The clerk laughed and opened the door. Ange-Albert darted down the lane with his precious burden.

Late that night, as the manager and his subordinates were still trying to figure out what had become of the Widow Cliquot's twelve little daughters, there was a joyous celebration of Elise's pregnancy. She sat in the place of honor, on the battered living room sofa, blissfully happy but hardly drinking because of her delicate condition.

When she woke up the next morning she realized there had been a profound change in Florent. Taking both her hands, he told her, "I've messed up my career but our child's going to be a success. I don't want you to live in misery anymore. I'm going to start looking for a job right away, and I won't stop till I find one, even if it means walking poodles."

Elise laughed. "Maybe your father can suggest something better."

Florent frowned. "That reminds me – we're supposed to spend Christmas Eve with them, and it's only three days away. I get a headache just thinking about a whole evening talking about my career."

The three days passed. On the third, Rosine pulled off a tremendous coup: Ange-Albert would celebrate Christmas Eve with her family. But first she made him buy new shoes and a suit, which he'd done amid the greatest secrecy.

The cold had lessened somewhat since the previous day. Now and then there was a brief, sparse snowfall that filled everyone with poetry and the joy of Christmas, to the greater profit of the storekeepers.

"At last you're here!" exclaimed Florent's father, opening the door. "Come in, come in, leave the cold outside and get warm. You mother's upstairs making herself beautiful. Let me have your coats."

He limped to the bedroom and tossed their coats on the bed. "His limp seems to be getting worse," Florent observed sadly.

"Beer? Gin? Scotch?" his father offered. "For you, my lovely, I have a sweet little wine that'll be velvet in your mouth." He gave Elise a friendly pat on the rear, then suddenly stared at her. "Am I imagining, or are you putting on weight?"

Her eyes glimmered mischievously, and two dimples appeared in her cheeks flushed with cold. "Not from overeating," she said softly.

Florent glared at her. He'd made her promise not to talk about her pregnancy until their situation had improved. Monsieur Boissonneault blanched. "Did I hear what I think I heard?"

He dragged himself to a chair, which creaked in welcome. "Say that again, nice and slow, so I can be sure I heard right."

Elise stared at the floor, disconcerted and torn between her pleasure at announcing the good news and fear of displeasing Florent. He spoke first. "It's true, you heard right. Elise is one month pregnant. We wanted to keep the surprise for later."

"Mother!" Monsieur Boissonneault squealed, racing toward the stairs, as agile as a young man, "Get down here fast, you're a grandma!"

"What did you say?" she exclaimed from the top of the stairs, her face contorted, a powderpuff in her hand.

"I said, Elise is pregnant! Don't stand there like a stuffed goose, come and give her a kiss!"

"Lord, oh Lord! I don't believe it!"

She sped down the stairs, leaving a wake of face powder. Her husband, his cheeks streaming wet, had planted two loud kisses on Elise's cheeks. Now he had gripped his son's hand, and was busy dislocating his shoulder.

"No tears now, old lady," he sobbed. "This is good news, for Pete's sake, it's no reason for howling! It's the finest Christmas present we could ask for."

Florent tried to free himself. "Calm down, both of you! There's three babies born every second. Ours will be part of the gang, that's all." To himself, he said, "I am *not* going to join in the tears! Enough soap opera!"

Monsieur Boissonneault had run down to the cellar, at the risk of breaking every bone in his body. He announced breathlessly, "Here, I have my little secrets, too. A good dog always finds his bone."

He went to the dining room, brandishing a bottle of champagne all covered in dust. "I bought this the day you were born, my boy! And there's another one I'm keeping – for the christening! I'm a man who speaks his mind, but I know about good taste."

His wife brought glasses and the cork flew to the ceiling, leaving a mark he refused to remove. "To the baby's health!" he proclaimed in a lyrical tone they'd never heard before.

Glasses clinked, champagne spilled on the tablecloth. "The mother's health! A happy pregnancy and a nice fat tummy, to give him lots of room to play!"

Their glasses touched again, chipping a rim. "And you, my boy – good health. Your luck changes today, I'm sure of it. . . ."

He couldn't go on. His hand trembled, and he drowned the start of a sob in champagne.

Eventually they calmed down, and the conversation drifted to other topics. Gin had followed the champagne and at the third drink, Monsieur Boissonneault perceived the future of Quebec, of his family, and of the universe at large in such glowing colors that he resorted to one of his ribald limericks to express his exhilaration (an old habit that drove his wife to despair).

Winking at Elise, he asked, "Rosalie, do you know this one?"

There once was a young man from Denver
Who wanted a tan on his member
On the first of July
He zipped down his fly
And his glans was nut-brown by September.

Then, without further ado, he took Florent downstairs to show him the progress on his yacht. "I know I won't beat any records," he said gravely, "but it's not because of my leg." He tapped his forehead. "It's my head. Before I act, I think. That's saved me a lot of grief. You see, my boy, my philosophy's simple: perfection or nothing. And that's how I've made my place in the sun." He patted the hull. "When your son's big enough I'll teach him to navigate this little brig."

Florent walked around the yacht, preoccupied. "You sure you can get it out of the cellar?"

"No problem. Once the frame's off, she'll slip through the door like a cat swallowing a sardine."

Upstairs, Elise and her mother-in-law were seeing to the final details for the *réveillon*, while engaging in what is generally known as "women's talk."

Monsieur Boissonneault burst into the kitchen, slightly tipsy. "Let's move it, my little chickadees. I don't want to be hearing Midnight Mass at Easter! It's eleven-thirty. Hurry now, grab your hats and galoshes. I'll warm up the car."

He tripped on the doorstep and spilled gin all over his jacket. "You never think of other people," his wife scolded, running up with a rag. "The church will reek of gin! And look at you! Your face is going off in every direction! You know the priest doesn't miss a thing. He'll probably mention it in his sermon."

The priest in question, despite a lisp and a pronounced tendency to repeat things five times, delivered a fairly acceptable sermon, with no references to temperance, but the gin fumes clouded Monsieur Boissonneault's idea of it. Despite repeated prods from his wife, he dozed through the service, though that didn't prevent him from sounding off at length, on the way home, on the merits of a panic-stricken tenor who had bellowed "O Holy Night" to cover the organist's false notes. Soon they were all gathered round the Christmas tree in the living room. "This year," said Madame Boissonneault, blushing at her fib, "we really ran out of ideas. Your father and I couldn't think what to get you, so . . ."

She offered a little box to Elise and another to Florent. Each contained two hundred dollars, in twenties. "This is so extravagant," Elise stammered. "And we came empty-handed!"

"But you came! The finest gift you could give us!" said Florent's father, jubilant.

Florent, tight-lipped, kissed his mother, shook his father's hand, and sat down, irritated at such obvious charity. But his good humor won out. His father served drinks, forcing his wife to taste a specially concocted martini, which brought out red blotches on her face. They gathered around the table with sparkling eyes and lively tongues, hopping from one subject to another and laughing at everything.

"We just heard from your Aunt Jeunehomme," Florent's father announced. "I think age agrees with her. Or maybe the Florida sun's softening her hide. She mentioned you," he told his son. "Rosalie, show him the letter."

She opened a drawer in the china cupboard and handed her son an envelope. The letter began with the usual good wishes, went on to a brief account of the writer's health – which had improved remarkably, thank God, thanks to a strict diet of fish and tropical fruit. Then Aunt Jeunehomme announced point-blank that despite certain distressing financial reverses, she was optimistic about the New Year. She was about to open a casino in Key West that should be a gold mine. "In spite of my advanced age," she went on, "I'm not fool enough to want to hoard my money when I know my life's nearly over. So this is an invitation to my nephew Florent and his young wife, whom I haven't had the pleasure of meeting yet. My house in Key West is open to them for as long as it's mutually enjoyable. After the hard times they've had, the sun will do them good, and perhaps my fruit-based diet, too, if they wanted to give it a try."

Florent looked up at Elise, who had been watching him with an expectant smile. (She'd undoubtedly been forewarned by her mother-in-law.) "How about a taste of the good life in Key West?" he asked.

Elise let out a whoop of joy. "So it's settled?" asked Florent's father, delighted to see that his maneuvers had been successful. He'd let it be known that his son wasn't fully recovered and needed a long vacation to get back on his feet.

"You're doing the right thing," his mother rejoiced. "The sun will take your mind off things so you can just relax – sleep, eat what you feel like – and come home fit as a fiddle!"

And just as lazy, Elise thought, with a sorrowful look at her husband.

Florent smirked, thinking, so that's it – it was all worked out in advance. The parents thought I needed some deluxe convalescence to get me back in the saddle and ready to chase the big bucks.

Their *réveillon* celebrations ended at dawn. "I have a hunch that, as of today, things are going to improve," Monsieur Boissonneault declared. He was expressing the feelings of each of them. To everyone's surprise, Florent let his father drive them home, thereby revealing their address.

When they got to Emery Street the sun was struggling to rise in the humid, glacial sky, spreading a grayish light that accentuated the sickly appearance of the houses and pointed up the colors in the dirty snow. Monsieur Boissonneault had a lump in his throat when Elise showed him where they were staying. "Do you manage to keep warm?"

"No problem," Florent replied smugly.

Elise peered at the door that opened onto the inside staircase (the lock had been gone for ten years). "I think I see someone behind the glass."

"Likely Ange-Albert home from his party. Probably he forgot his key."

Elise kissed her father-in-law and got out of the car, while the older man clasped his son's shoulder and launched into one last anecdote about Aunt Jeunehomme's strange personality. "Monsieur Emile!" Elise exclaimed as she opened the door. "What're you doing here?"

Florent started and, cutting short his father's monologue, shook his hand and left. "Who on earth is Monsieur Emile?" he muttered as he started the car. (He'd forgotten the name of the child.) "Some underworld character? She seemed pretty friendly with him."

He went through a red light, put on the brakes and then, seeing the street was deserted, roared off again, absorbed in his worries. The evening's gaiety had flown into the stratosphere.

Meanwhile Florent, with folded arms, was looking at Monsieur Emile, who sat on the staircase. The child's teeth were chattering, and he was hugging his cat. "Why did you run away from your mother?"

"Because."

"Because *why*? Answer me, dammit! If you think I want to play detective on Christmas Day . . ."

Frightened by his voice, Breakfast meowed plaintively, trying to make a getaway. That was the last straw. Monsieur Emile burst into tears. "It's 'cause my mother wanted to kill my kitty 'cause he caught his paw in the wringer when she was doing the washing."

"The wringer!" Elise bent down to pick up the cat, who started to spit.

"And now he can't walk." Monsieur Emile sobbed even louder. "My mother wanted to kill him and when I was asleep her boyfriend put him in a box and he made a hole in the box so he could fill it up with smoke from his car." He stopped, sniffed noisily, and went on: "But then I woke up and I put on my clothes and waited till they were in the living room and then I took my cat and left and I don't want to go back there. Never never NEVER!"

Florent picked the cat up by the scruff of his neck while Elise took the child in her arms. "What a life!" he grumbled, ascending the stairs. "Spending Christmas nursing an alley cat!"

They entered the apartment, turned on a light and began to examine the animal as Monsieur Emile looked on in agony.

Breakfast appeared docile but he was in a very bad way, with dull eyes, bristling fur and stiff whiskers. He was breathing fitfully and licking his swollen front paw, which dangled pitifully. "Hmmm – your cat looks as if he's had it."

Elise gestured to him to choose his words carefully. "Is he going to die?" the child whimpered.

"I'm not a vet but I think he's got some smashed bones."

"Why don't we take him to a vet?" Elise suggested.

"And how would we pay for it?"

His gaze met Monsieur Emile's. "All right, all right," he grumbled. "I'll take care of it."

He put Breakfast on the floor. The cat struggled on three paws, then flopped in a corner. He raised his head and gave Florent a calm, innocent look as if he sensed that his fate had just taken a turn for the better.

Monsieur Emile was sitting on Elise's lap. She stroked his hair and told him, "Now you go straight home or your mother won't let you come here again."

"I don't wanna go to my mother's," he said fearfully, "I wanna stay with you. I don't like my mother. . . . She never takes care of me. . . . All she does is screw!"

"Monsieur Emile!" exclaimed Elise, scandalized. "Where did you learn to talk like that?"

Florent's face contorted to hide his laughter. "She said it the other day – she said she likes screwing!" Monsieur Emile protested vehemently. "She said even if she didn't get a cent, she'd do it, anyway."

Elise glanced at her husband. "Oh no!" he exclaimed. "The cat, okay, but not the kid!"

"Maybe she'd let him come with us to . . ."

"Elise, don't let your heart run your brain: we can't even pay for our own tickets, I have to look after a cat that's about to bite the dust, and you want us to take on a kid!"

The stairs creaked and they could hear someone singing "Adeste Fideles." Florent went to the door. "Merry Christmas Ange-Albert. Hey, what an outfit! Just get married?"

"Merry Christmas," his friend replied, shaking his hand. He noticed Monsieur Emile, still on Elise's lap. "What're you doing here? Merry Christmas," he said, bending down to kiss them.

Elise laughed. "A new suit! A new tie! Polished shoes! What's going on?"

"Brrr! It's freezing out!" Ange-Albert exclaimed, looking elated. "Must be twenty below."

He took off his coat and started humming again. Florent gave him a mocking smile. "Well, what's up?"

"Nothing, not a thing. I spent a very nice evening, that's all. Rosine's mother's a honey. I just have to work on the old man a little, and things'll fall into place. By the way," he added, brushing off his collar with a look of unconcern, "here's a good one. Listen: just as I was leaving for Rosine's there was a knock at the door. I open it and who do you think I see? Our grim inspector, Rosarien Roy, pissed to the gills – and sloppy sentimental. If I hadn't kicked him out he'd still be here, telling me the story of his life. Know what he said? That he never meant to play dice with me but old Ratablavasky made him do it, promising to make up for his losses. It was his way of helping out without our knowing, according to Rosarien. Trouble was, when it came time for the refund, Ratablavasky draws a blank! Now Rosarien's spitting fire, says he'll take him to court, drag him through the mud, get him deported, the works."

Elise and Florent were appalled. Ange-Albert, who didn't seem to realize the gravity of his news, grinned as if it was all a joke.

A moment later Florent murmured, "I must have a word with that inspector." Elise patted his arm. Monsieur Emile was fast asleep in her lap. The phone rang, and Florent picked it up, sighing.

"I knew he was with you, dear," Madame Chouinard giggled. "Keep him overnight? Why certainly! If you want to, who'm I to complain? But I want him home at noon for my turkey dinner: I only do it once a year – and it's just for him!"

EIGHTEEN

To Breakfast's great despair, his paw was put in a cast and he had to spend a week in one of Dr. Journet's cages. When he arrived he was sprayed with a disinfectant that smelled like the detergent Madame Chouinard used whenever her kitchen floor started to look like the garbage can. At those times, Breakfast stayed away from the house for days.

As the ravages of this olfactory intrusion penetrated to the depths of his fur, he went on a hunger strike and meowed for eighteen hours a day; alas, this brought about no improvement in his condition.

Early every afternoon, a girl went to visit him in the basement. She could have been pleasant company if she'd shown him any compassion. On the contrary, though, after checking that his cast was intact, she would deliver an endless lecture on a variety of subjects that had nothing to do with his problems. Then she would open the cage, grasp his muzzle and shove a huge pill into his mouth, pushing it to the back of his throat with a tongue depressor. It left him feeling nauseated for the rest of the afternoon.

That week was marked by just one pleasant interlude. Toward the end of the fifth day, just as he was preparing for a brief nap in order to rest his vocal cords, there was a deafening sound of galloping. "Breakfast! Breakfast! Where are you?" hollered Monsieur Emile as he tore down the stairs, followed by the girl.

He zigzagged across the cellar, looking everywhere, then stopped short and the girl stumbled against him. "There he is, there's my kitty cat," he sighed tearfully.

Surprised, Breakfast listened as Monsieur Emile murmured all sorts of strange and gentle words the cat had never heard before. He thought it was the boy's way to ask forgiveness for putting him in prison. Despite the strange pleasure aroused by the words, Breakfast still felt mortally wounded by his master's behavior; he curled up in a ball, facing the back of the cage, and shut his eyes. "All right, you found your cat," the girl snapped. "Now run along, I have work to do."

Hopelessly, the child left the clinic and, for the tenth time, went to Florent's to try to retrieve his cat. Florent, who was in the dining room with the telephone wedged between his ear and shoulder, hardly looked at him. "You say he's taking his vacation plus his Christmas break? Not before January 17? Can you give me his home number? Right, regulations . . . sure, I forgot. . . . Regulations are useful when you don't want to take your hands out of your pockets. Thanks a lot."

He hung up. "Well?" asked Elise, coming out of the kitchen. "Monsieur Emile, take off your boots, I've told you a hundred times."

"A thousand."

"No way to get in touch with the goddamn inspector till mid-January," Florent grumbled.

Sulking, he chewed the inside of his cheek. "I feel like dropping everything and leaving for Florida. Maybe Old Rat'll forget us . . . or croak."

"I wanna go to Florida, too," Monsieur Emile whined.

"Poor kid – it's not that we don't want to take you, it's the money . . ."

By tonight, Florent murmured to himself, that little problem may be solved.

Elise drew the child to her and pulled off his coat. "Let me have your T-shirt so I can wash it. It's filthy."

Docile, Monsieur Emile obeyed. "Careful you don't wreck it. Bob Forget ripped it here, under the smoke, when we were fighting the other day."

Elise smiled. "Is Bob Forget a friend of yours?"

"He's a bum!"

Ange-Albert and Rosine had promised to be at the apartment at six on the button, and they kept their word. They ate rapidly, almost wordlessly. "What's going on?" Elise asked, surprised at how tense and serious everyone was. "You'd think you were planning an assassination."

Florent patted her arm. "My dearest wife, I'm delighted to announce that Ange-Albert has promised to make us rich this very night, so we can live it up in Florida."

"Which reminds me, how much do you need?"

"Let's see: two plane tickets, plus contingencies – let's say seven or eight hundred."

"With a bit of luck you'll have that and then some!"

They slipped on their coats. "Look!" exclaimed Rosine, "They're working on the building next door."

The sheet of plywood barring the entrance to the next building had been removed. Workmen were going in and out, carrying paneling, glass doors, banisters, chandeliers. "I have a hunch our house is about to lose its little sister," Ange-Albert speculated.

Soon they were outside the Saint-Malo, a café on St-Denis Street. "Hardly anyone there," Rosine noted as she peered in the tiny glassed-in terrace below the dining room, where twelve tables were squeezed together.

"Let's stalk our big game," said Ange-Albert, pushing the door. They took a table on the terrace and ordered beer and coffee.

Near the door, a fortyish man who looked like a wrestler or a bouncer was slumped in a chair, gazing tenderly at his bottle of beer. Ange-Albert, with legs outstretched and hands in his pocket, whistled absentmindedly.

The café gradually filled up. There were scraps of conversation, smoke floated in the air, glasses clinked. The waitress, carrying a tray in one hand, rummaged in her apron pocket for change with the other, and answered her customers' eternal jokes with a friendly, resigned smile. Ange-Albert had taken out his dice and now he was rolling them on the table, mumbling numbers.

Suddenly the door was flung open. A man appeared, wearing a pelisse and fur cap. His feverish eyes, goatee and finely drawn lips gave him the look of a world-weary nobleman. With a wink, Ange-Albert said, "There's my man."

He smiled broadly. The other man, who didn't move, looked like a Roman emperor coming home from an orgy, attempting to gather his thoughts before he harangued the populace.

He took a few hesitant steps, then stopped, increasingly perplexed. Ange-Albert got up, made his way through the tables and approached the other man with outstretched hand. Bewildered, he listened for a moment, then graciously bowed his head and followed Ange-Albert to the table, where he was given a place between Rosine and Florent. "Armand de la Durantaye," he said, extending his hand to the women and then to Florent, who gazed at him in awe. With a wan smile, he asked Ange-Albert, "Would it be indiscreet to ask why you've so kindly invited me to join you?"

"We enjoy good company and you didn't seem to know anybody."

"I see," said the man with another faint smile.

Despite the cigarette smoke, a sweet perfume emanated from his person and gradually spread around the table. It was composed of the fragrance of rare soaps, of pure breezes traversing great family estates, of the lush smell of wood paneling rubbed with beeswax, and the heady aroma of healthy flesh, nourished carefully for generations. "I was to meet my father here at seven o'clock," said Armand de la Durantaye, "to discuss the purchase of this establishment, but I was delayed."

Inwardly, Ange-Albert addressed himself to St. Joseph, promising him a candle six feet high, If you treat me right!

"I'm really very late," said the newcomer, consulting his watch. "He must have left. Please excuse me for a moment."

He rose, gravely ascended the steps to the dining room and walked to the back. He returned to the table a few moments later. "As I thought: he didn't wait for me. The sale is through, the place belongs to me . . . unofficially, of course, since the deed hasn't been signed yet."

The manager rushed up after him, all servile bows, insisting it would be an honor to offer him and his young friends a drink. "If you insist, Perrier with a twist," he consented, seemingly unaware of his new employee's emotion.

Considering the circumstances, Florent and others demonstrated impressive restraint, settling for a beer. Armand de la Durantaye gazed at them with a melancholy and protective air. "You strike me as very pleasant people. Do you often come here?"

Ange-Albert decided it was time to strike. Florent looked on, stunned at the change in his friend. His smiling, lethargic nonchalance had been replaced by bubbling vivacity. He was able to capture the interest of their noble guest and two or three times even made him laugh – something that didn't seem particularly easy.

Armand de la Durantaye was a member of that rather demanding fraternity, a young-man-with-family-money. For want of anything better to do, he studied architecture, traveled the world, and casually indulged his lust, but the greater part of his energy was devoted to learning how to administer his father's fortune, for that dread day when it would descend upon his weary shoulders. "You enjoy dice?" he asked, his gaze resting on Ange-Albert's left hand, which had been casually shaking the pieces even as they spoke.

Rosine coughed nervously. Ange-Albert blinked, and an ingenuous smile revealed that teeth were even, small and white as milk. "How about a game of yum?"

"What's yum?"

Ange-Albert took out pencil and notebook and explained the rules of the game. "It sounds simple," the other man remarked. "Only takes common sense."

A spark of childish curiosity lit up his languid gaze. They started to play. The newcomer very quickly reached a level of excitement out of all proportion to what was taking place. Elise and Rosine watched, aghast, smiling tensely. Ange-Albert forced himself to lose. Victory made Armand de la Durantaye queerly euphoric. He slowly ran his fingers through his thick, silky hair until he looked like the young Alfred de Musset.

"Friends, I suspect fate is about to have a word with me. Let's play again."

Good God! thought Ange-Albert, he's easier to string along than a rubby with a case of beer. Time to step things up.

They began a second match, and the young man won again, though it was harder this time. "Shall we go up to the dining room?" he suggested, more and more excited. "It would be quieter. And make yourselves at home: eat, drink – you're my guests. Come now, please don't hesitate," he added, seeing that they were too timid to order.

He turned his head and was about to raise his hand, but a waiter was already at his side, bent double in his desire to please. Two bottles of Rosinet-Chambelles 1961 appeared on the table and a third game got under way.

Twenty minutes later he won again. His nostrils tightened, his heart was gripped by a childlike transport, and he suddenly felt that he'd become a demigod. Rosine watched him sip, his throat as rigid as a steel pipe. He turned to Florent and said with a defiant smile, "Now it's your turn."

Florent won. Armand de la Durantaye took his victory as a personal affront. He ordered two more bottles, drained his glass in one gulp, and demanded a return match. Florent demurred. "One game a night is my limit, or I don't get to sleep till dawn. It's a sickness."

Armand de la Durantaye insisted. To no avail. He was highly annoyed. "Let's go on then, you and I," he said to Ange-Albert, "since he's too afraid to move."

"Whatever you want."

Judging that his victim was done to a turn, he decided the moment had come to enjoy him. "This time, though, let's raise the ante. Ten dollars a point."

Armand de la Durantaye thought this was a splendid idea, and once more drained his glass. His eyes glittered softly, his lips took on a soft and sensual curve, and suddenly he looked exactly like Alfred de Musset on a binge. Florent offered to keep score. "Let's give it all we've got!" exclaimed the young-man-with-family-money, slamming down his glass.

To put his opponent at ease, Ange-Albert began by arranging to lose once more. Rosine kept her gaze fixed on his hands. Moving slowly, his fingers slightly parted, he shook the dice, smiling, his eyes half shut. He examined the diabolical dance to which he was applying all his skill. Twenty minutes later, Armand de la Durantaye had lost eight hundred and eighty dollars. He asked for a return match. His debt rose to two thousand, four hundred and forty. Still he played, tight-lipped, an almost imperceptible tremor crossing his face. Now and then he reached into his pocket, opened a small silver box and swallowed a pill. Elise asked hesitantly what they were.

He gave her a peculiar look. For a moment he seemed to be slowly moving away from her, like a passenger on the deck of a ship leaving harbor. "Surmontil. To raise my morale. Nothing better."

At ten o'clock he owed eight thousand, eight hundred dollars, but still insisted on playing. Fine droplets stood out on his forehead as he murmured with morbid satisfaction. "Tonight, Fate is speaking to me." Despite Florent's powerful kicks, Ange-Albert was taking pleasure in slowly demolishing his opponent.

At eleven o'clock, he'd won two adjoining houses on St-Denis Street. Trembling, his shirt wet with sweat, Armand de la Durantaye rose and took out his wallet. One by one, eight smooth and crisp hundred-dollar bills dropped onto the table in front of Ange-Albert, who smiled uneasily, stunned by his exploit.

"Thank you," his opponent gasped, scrawling an IOU for sixty-seven thousand, six hundred and eighty dollars. "Thanks a million. Because of you I've spent a highly instructive evening that's helped to show me the way." He added his card to his the bills and offered them to Ange-Albert. "Come to my house tomorrow. We'll settle up."

He buttoned his cloak to the chin, nodded to his companions, left the restaurant and was immediately struck down by a car zooming down St-Denis. The restaurant emptied. "I saw him!" shrieked a hysterical little woman. "He threw himself right at the car! I saw him!"

Standing silent, their arms at their sides, crowds of onlookers watched as Armand de la Durantaye struggled to give up the ghost. Legs grew weak and stomachs gurgled. An aging playwright in high leather boots turned and rushed back into the restaurant, ordered a black coffee and sipped it with embarrassed sighs. An ambulance screeched to a stop, then drove off immediately, but the soul of Armand de la Durantaye was already traveling under its own steam.

After a brief interrogation, the police let Ange-Albert and the others go. Elise, her face distorted, accused him of pushing the other man to suicide. "Don't be ridiculous," said Florent. "He was drunk as a skunk when he left. He didn't see the car. It could jut as well have hit me."

Ange-Albert gave him five hundred dollars. "Here, go forget your troubles in Florida. I'd like to give you more, but I'm keeping the rest so I can afford the luxury of changing jobs."

Florent didn't need urging. An hour later their bags were ready and he had reserved two tickets for the next day's flight from Montreal to Miami. The next morning at ten o'clock, they went to Aurélien Picquot's room to say good-bye.

The chef took the news philosophically. "You're only young once," he said with emotion. "I'm not so petty as to ask you to spoil your youth keeping an old wreck company. Go now, enjoy yourselves and long live the sun!"

NINETEEN

All at once they were enveloped in humid heat. They walked down a covered passage, jostled by happy passengers. The heat seeped into their clothes, penetrated their hair to the roots, slid to the back of their throats. It was as powerful and invincible as the sun itself.

They entered a long glassed-in corridor and came to two carousels on which piles of luggage were turning. A large box, held together with string and endowed with the faculty of barking, was causing a certain stir.

Florent spotted an employee pushing a hand truck and asked him to take their suitcases to the exit. Shortly after, they walked out onto a platform. A bus stood there, purring and exuding suffocating smoke.

Elise dropped wearily onto a seat and shut her eyes, while Florent hoisted their suitcases onto the luggage rack. They waited a moment.

Across the aisle, a Chinese man who looked to be about forty had taken a thick sheaf of postcards from his jacket and now, with a peculiar smile, he was peering at a photograph of the Hotel Nelson.

Suddenly the driver threw his head back and a phenomenal quantity of Coke gushed into his stomach. Then he wiped his forehead, let in the clutch, and the bus was off.

They drove onto a freeway lined with dusty bushes. Outsized warehouses, grimy garages and fast-foot outlets that seemed to have been thrown together in half an hour stood here and there, surrounded by asphalt and cement. Elise and Florent smiled when they saw clusters of palm trees standing amid stacks of barrels, piles of old planks, and patches of scorched grass. A zillion postcards had made the poor trees look ridiculous, and the industrial setting only made things worse.

The air conditioning had broken down. Elise kept shifting her legs, which were sticking to the leather seat. Sighing, Florent raised his arm; there was an acid smell from his armpits.

In the distance they could see a large bluish mass bristling with towers: the city of Miami, which stands behind its worldly little sister, Miami Beach, on its sandy strip. The bus kept taking on speed, cutting in and out of automobiles that looked like big, bright, panic-stricken insects, then it drove onto a long causeway across Biscayne Bay, and into the area of the luxury hotel zone. Built in the antiseptic style of the 1950s and somewhat faded now, they bear such exotic names as Four Freedoms House, The Golden Gate, Rainbow Inn, Eden Roc. The streets are full of straw-hatted old men and extravagantly dressed old ladies, their heads wrapped in pastel-colored tulle, mincing under the dazzling sky, who smile bravely as they try to forget about coronary problems or trouble with joints and pancreas. The bus kept stooping to let out a handful of travelers, then came to a halt outside a tiny terminus.

"Next bus for Key West? Nine-thirty, sir," said the checkroom attendant. "Better get here early, though, if you want to be sure of a seat."

Made sluggish by orange juice and ice cream, they wandered the streets, relaxed, their skin covered with fine sweat; smiling, they bowed to the friendly dictatorship of the heat that rules Miami like a film goddess in a studio. Colors take on a sensual glimmer at its touch. The ugliness of things is toned down, dissolves in the shimmering air. Anger becomes a real exploit. Only the most pressing concerns can survive such torpor.

"How about a swim?" Elise suggested.

A bikini-clad old lady, the skin of her thighs drooping to her knees, was standing by a rock, stroking cream on her dry, brown face. She watched them as they made their way, hand in hand, into the giant waves. Some melancholy thought tried to creep into her brain, her lips quivered briefly, seeking a word, but her impulse was quickly extinguished. Her hand moved toward the rock and took a cigarette, then a thick cloud of smoke spread into her lungs, and her parched eyelids wrinkled with pleasure.

For a while they amused themselves, letting the avalanches of warm water that crashed tirelessly onto the sand sweep over them. Florent tried to dive in, but the powerfully throbbing water kept throwing him back to the surface. He raised his head and caught a glimpse of the old woman smoking, still watching them; she stood there, utterly unembarrassed, it seemed, by the extraordinary ruin of her body. Gesturing to Elise, Florent opened his mouth. Salty water gushed into his throat, setting off trumpets that the old woman repeated joyously. Her shoulders danced and the flattened globes on her chest, which housed a phenomenal quantity of fat, began to jump about.

Florent lurched onto the beach, held up by Elise, who thumped his back. "God Almighty, sonny!" the woman exclaimed, clutching his arm. "You just about drowned. Wanna cigarette? It'll dry you out."

A muffled growl rose from the entrails of the bus, and its entire carcass began to tremble. Elise, standing on the sidewalk with a suitcase in her hand, glanced anxiously inside the restaurant where her husband was wolfing down a hot chicken sandwich. They ran across the street and flopped into their seats. The bus clattered to a start.

Night had just fallen. Neon signs bathed the city in an unreal, shimmering light that made the sky look as black as tar.

Florent sighed and made himself as comfortable as he could. His hot chicken sandwich seemed to have sprouted a beak and claws that were taking cruel strolls in his stomach.

Now the bus was moving through the suburbs. White stucco walls, flat roofs, ornamental iron fences that held back an abundant extravagance of vegetation sped past. Then billboards, vacant lots and warehouses appeared with greater frequency between increasingly wretched houses. Florent briefly caught sight of a truck, laden with oranges, parked by the side of the road; at running-board level, he spotted the glow of a cigarette. Liberating gas rose to his lips. His chicken's beak had lost its edge. He rested his head on Elise's shoulder, and he joined her in sleep.

A low rumble awakened him. The bus had just driven onto a bridge that joined the mainland to a wooded islet. On either side, Florent could make out sandbanks sinking into the opaque black sea. Wisps of fog swayed here and there, swallowing clumps of trees. A tiny motel stood out at a turn in the road. In front of it, a black man was bathed in rosy glimmers from a neon sign. Another bridge appeared. Elise stretched, opened her eyes. "Where are we?"

"Go back to sleep. There's still a long way to go."

Bridges followed one another at an ever faster rhythm. The driver was going flat out, as if he'd vowed to reach the last islet as soon as possible, and then drive the bus into the sea. The fog grew denser, making the windows sweat. The dampness seeped into the bus. Their skin became moist and sticky, and the air was heavy with sea smells. Florent was daydreaming, eyes wide open, his mind filled with enigmatic warnings. Suddenly, with amazing accuracy, he summoned from the depths of his memory the sugary, singsong voice of Egon Ratablavasky. With a slightly ironic twang it said, "So, dear young man, we take flight of our friends?"

Agitated and suddenly avid for conversation, he awakened Elise.

TWENTY

The last passengers had filed off the bus. With a huge yawn, the ticket seller put out the lights and locked the doors, while the passengers went their various ways. In two minutes the station was as deserted as an ice floe. Elise and Florent stood in the dimly lit parking area, staring, bewildered, at the empty taxis lined up along one wall. "Dammit," said Florent, "I forgot to buy a city map. All I know is, she lives on Jordan Street, near the ocean."

"Let's walk," Elise suggested. "We're bound to run into somebody."

To say the city was quiet would be an understatement. Quiet seemed to be the very matter of which it was composed. Vegetation nourished by the heavy moist heat muffled any sounds. The air was filled with the rich and penetrating smell of pepper, mixed with a sugary fragrance. The vaguely Spanish colonial houses, with their closed doors and darkened windows, seemed to have been asleep forever, half buried by the vegetation.

Florent stopped. A rubbery flapping sound was approaching them. They turned, straining their eyes, but saw nothing.

Then, a moment later, a squat fat man, his head dropping to his chest, appeared at the corner, leaning on a cane. He waddled in a way that made his legs seem joined at the knees. Vacant-eyed and breathing noisily, he came up to them. A benevolent smile lit up his wrinkled face.

"Evening, folks. Looking for something? Take your time, now, don't wear yourselves out. It's a long way."

An hour later Elise and Florent, their shoulders racked by the burden of their suitcases, stopped before a monumental ironwork fence. Through the bars they could vaguely distinguish a great white mass at the end of a formal garden. They heard the constant murmur of the nearby sea. Silently and rather anxiously, they waited. Suddenly the lock buzzed loudly. Florent pushed the gate, and they entered an avenue lined with poincianas. The warm wet air was redolent of lilac and wet grass. As they approached, the white mass became clearer, took on volume, and stretched out its wings, revealing gables, arches, rows of dormer windows, looping gingerbread trim. "Holy horseradish!" Florent exclaimed. "What kind of weird castle is this?"

Suddenly a light appeared in a window at the top of the stairs leading to a high-columned veranda. A slender, motionless shadow appeared. "Who's there?" asked a worried voice.

"Elise and Florent Boissonneault."

There was a muffled exclamation and the shadow glided quickly down the stairs. "So you're here!" the voice declared happily.

A slight woman with her graying hair in a chignon stopped and took Elise's suitcases. "Come, follow me. Madame's been expecting you for several days. Of course she's unable to greet you herself," she explained, bouncing up the stairs. "She went to bed at ten o'clock, as is her custom.

Perhaps you'd like something to eat? Shall I have someone . . ."

"Don't bother, thanks," said Elise, blinking at the bright light in the foyer. "We ate on the way."

"Very well," she replied, turning toward them a thin, pale face, its exceedingly fine and somewhat quaint features marred by a small mole at the corner of the lips.

"Kindly follow me. My name is Lydie, Mademoiselle Lydie. I've been in your aunt's service for some years now."

Good grief, Florent thought, where'd they dig her up? France? Snooty accent . . .

"I come from just outside Paris," the woman volunteered, as if she'd been reading his mind, "but I've been in the United States for a long time now. It leaves its mark."

They crossed the foyer and another dimly lit room, then climbed the stairs and went down a long, dark-carpeted corridor that smelled of dust and lemon oil. Mademoiselle Lydie stopped at a door and took out a bunch of keys. "Here's your room," she whispered.

She pointed to the next door, which was slightly ajar. "Your aunt is in the next room. I'm sure she'll regret not welcoming you herself, but sleep is so important at her age. . . . I didn't dare waken her."

From behind the door came a vigorous, rather hoarse voice.

"Too late, my dear – thanks to that wretched tomcat the cook took in last night. Good evening, nephew."

"G-g-good evening."

"Is your wife with you?"

"Yes, I'm here. Please excuse us for arriving so late."

"Makes no difference, dear child. Go now, you must need your sleep. I'd come out and give you a kiss, but I'm really not presentable. Old ladies have their vanity, too, you know. Good night, now. Mademoiselle Lydie, be a dear and ask the cook to catch that cat and stick him in the cellar."

The next morning, Madame Jeunehomme greeted Elise and Florent in the kitchen. "Good morning, young lovebirds!" She put down her steaming cup of black coffee and embraced them. "I wasn't expecting you on New Year's Day!"

They exchange greetings, then for a moment looked at one another silently. "I wouldn't have recognized you," said the older woman, gripping her nephew's arm. "But I see you take after your father and grandfather: they liked pretty brunettes, too. Your mother was stunning at thirty-five, and to judge from her picture, she's still a beautiful woman."

Elise smiled, rather confused. Somewhat at a loss for words, Florent observed, "What a huge house!"

"And I eat in the kitchen, though the dining room is big enough to drive a train through. This used to be a hotel; it went bankrupt, so I got it for a song. I'm going to turn it into a casino. A proper pastime for an old biddy, don't you think?"

She rang a bell; a big, chubby-faced man with vaguely Spanish looks and an exceedingly hirsute upper lip came in, dragging his feet and staring at the newcomers with a child-like smile. "These young people would like breakfast," said Florent's aunt, motioning them to the table. "I understand you've had some difficulties recently."

Blushing, Florent nodded.

"A pity, but what can you expect? Happens to us all. Better when you're young and strong than later when the old carcass starts to give out."

She questioned him at length about his parents, about Quebec, which she'd left nine years ago, about all the changes back home. Then came Elise's turn. The older woman's bony face was wreathed in satisfaction when she learned that her niece came from the Gaspé. "There's no better stock in all Quebec. You can trust them with your life, if they haven't been ground down by poverty."

Then she rose, abruptly but in a lopsided way that suggested moving was difficult, and took a last sip of coffee. "Now I must leave you – there's a foreman waiting for me. But I wanted us to have breakfast together. We'll see one another at lunch. Mademoiselle Lydie will show you where you're to stay: it's a sort of cottage at the back of the property, quite pretty as you'll see."

Elise didn't conceal her surprise. Aunt Jeunehomme grinned. "It's best, I think. Young couples need to be alone. Besides, you'll be spared the unpredictable temper of an old lady who doesn't always watch her tongue. In any case, we can see each other a thousand times a day if the spirit moves us. 'Bye for now."

She walked away, her arms swaying strangely, as if to conceal her lopsided walk, and shortly afterward they heard her hoarse voice in the corridor, probably addressing the foreman. Elise and Florent looked at each other, speechless. Their aunt's welcome had left them dazed. Smiling quizzically, Elise stirred her coffee. "How long do you feel like hanging around, dear?"

Mademoiselle Lydie's arrival cut short Florent's reply. "You've finished breakfast?" she asked. "Splendid, everything's proceeding as it should. Now we'll go to your cottage and you'll tell me how you like it."

They went out the main door and crossed the grounds. Mademoiselle Lydie smiled at their exclamations of surprise, which were entirely appropriate: Madame Jeunehomme's hotel was an immense wooden structure of hysterically

Victorian design. It could have been the work of an American Ludwig of Bavaria at the peak of his megalomania. "Madame expressly forebade me to show you anything," she told them, anticipating their request. "She wants to give you the grand tour herself."

The very imposing main body stood five stories high, extended on three sides by a profusion of very curious wings, all bristling with finely worked weathervanes, studded with gothic windows, edged with extravagantly decorated cornices and topped with bulb-shaped cupolas and openwork towers, some as much as thirty meters high. On the far left, a small round pavilion, joined to the rest of the building by a long arcade, was – amazingly – monastically austere. The only truly bizarre note was struck by a sickly long and narrow chimney crowned by a massive, highly ornamented dripstone. Through such a bizarre chimney the tormented soul of Edgar Allan Poe must have departed for the Other World.

"It's quite an attractive building, and well constructed," Mademoiselle Lydie observed with unconcealed pride, "but it was abandoned for ten years. The roof leaks . . . but thank God everything will be fixed in a few weeks."

And as if to corroborate her remarks, two workmen appeared on the roof of the main cupola. They slowly made their way to a chimney and began examining it, gesturing broadly. "Until the late forties," their guide continued, "this was a very fashionable resort, known all over the southern States."

"Who built it?" asked Elise.

"It had a hundred and eight-seven rooms," the other woman continued, as if she hadn't heard the question. "After it's refurbished there'll be only a hundred and sixty. But magnificent! There won't be any more attic rooms for servants, which only make work for firemen." Then she turned to Elise and said, "John Ruse. Between 1882 and 1887. Imagine what it must have been like. Everything had to be brought in by boat: stone, bricks, wood, tools. The bridges connecting the islands to the mainland came much later, in 1937."

They climbed a broad staircase, lined with lamp standards, that straddled a ground-floor wing like a bridge over a river. An abandoned garden that had almost reverted to forest covered several acres behind the hotel. The sound of the sea became increasingly distinct, but the trees hid it from sight. The rear surface of the main building was covered with scaffolding. A load of beams swayed slowly in the air, and a chute projecting from a fourth-floor window spat chunks of plaster. Elise lifted her hair off her sweat-soaked neck. "I advise you not to venture into town before four o'clock," said their guide. "You'd find the sun quite intolerable."

There was a rather steep slope ahead of them. "One last little effort," Mademoiselle Lydie urged, wiping her brow with a batiste handkerchief.

They hurried up the hill and suddenly the sea appeared, rimmed with a dazzling beach, on which stood a crumbling Chinese pagoda. "A week from now you won't have to look at that horror. Now follow me, it's to the left."

They walked into the undergrowth, took a path covered with crushed seashells and walked for several minutes. Suddenly Elise cried out in delight.

"Do you like it?" Mademoiselle Lydie asked.

"And how!" Florent exclaimed.

Before them was a small clearing that led directly to the beach. All around, strips of bright green turf, freshly laid, glistened under three automatic sprinklers. In the shade of a cluster of poincianas, at the end of a gravel path, stood a pretty little gabled house surrounded by a broad portico with turned columns, their capitals joined by ornate wooden lacework. There were four rooms on the ground floor, and two bedrooms under the mansard roof, all spacious and well furnished. Mademoiselle Lydie opened the refrigerator, which was overflowing with supplies: "If you have any special cravings, call the cook. He goes to market every day. In any case, we'll be taking most of our meals together, unless your aunt has a change of heart."

She made a final inspection, occasionally flicking away some dust with her fingertip. At last she said, "I'll let you settle now. Your baggage will be here any minute."

They watched her move slowly away through the undergrowth, head high, her gait precise but nonchalant. Florent hugged Elise. "Kiddo, I'd say our bad times are over." When they'd put their things away, he suggested a swim.

"Know what?" asked Elise. "I feel like making love."

A workman named Waldos Sjinkovic, sent by Mademoiselle Lydie to replace the gasket around the refrigerator door, was unaware of this development. After a perfunctory knock he pushed open the screen door. What was happening on the floor caused him to execute an odd combination of attention and about-face. Then he went slowly back to the hotel, suddenly filled with feverish energy that his wife's absence (she lived in Valparaiso) forced him to devote to a used cigarette butt.

Later, they walked along the beach, sniffing with childlike enthusiasm the odor of seaweed. Then, after they'd been swimming for some time, Florent looked at his watch. "Oh oh! Better put on some clothes. It's nearly noon, and I don't want to keep my aunt waiting."

The phone was ringing when they got back to the cottage. "Did it occur to Lydie to provide you with any food?" asked his aunt.

"The fridge is crammed," Elise told her, "thank –"

"Don't mention it. You'll have lunch at home today – I haven't a second to spare. But I'll expect you in the dining room tonight on the stroke of seven. Dress as you please – you're on vacation and I couldn't care less what you wear."

Lunch was a cheese omelet and a slice of melon, then they went walking in the formal garden. The paths, overrun with ferns and high grass, were deep in rotted twigs, making them treacherous for the ankles. The place hadn't seen a gardener for a good twenty years. It cast Elise into a sort of ecstasy she hadn't known since she'd read *Le Grand Meaulnes* and *Paul et Virginie* in the convent at Rimouski, when she was seventeen. Soon, though, the heat of the day was too much for them, and they went back to the cottage for a nap. The phone wakened them. It was their aunt. "Well, then. Did you eat enough for three days at lunchtime? I've been waiting for you."

Madame Jeunehomme had, perhaps, exaggerated slightly when she'd said that a train could drive through the dining room; but you could have test-driven a Jeep without endangering a single piece of furniture. When the door was opened, the frozen torrent of garnet velvet draperies, the high ceiling, the dark paneling heavy with carved festoons all gave the impression that one was walking into an Orson Welles film. In the center of the room stood six huge oak tables. Around each one were three dozen massive, high-backed chairs where it was easy to picture a cardinal or a head of state. The dust-cover had been removed from one of the tables. Madame Jeunehomme reigned at the head of it, a smile on her lips, Mademoiselle Lydie on her right. "Ridiculous, eh? I don't often eat here: these huge empty rooms are depressing. I thought it would be an amusing way to honor your arrival. Take the seat on Lydie's right, dear child; Florent, sit across from your wife."

The cook entered, bearing a steaming tureen. Mademoiselle Lydie shot him a disdainful look. "It's *soupe aux gourganes* that I've been saving for you children. Pass me your plates."

Mademoiselle Lydie slowly drew her spoon through the soup, producing a pretty tinkle, then, with pinched lips and a vague expression, she turned to Florent. "Are you pleased with your little cottage?"

That woman doesn't like us, Elise thought to herself.

"Come, come, my dear," said their aunt. "Give them time to get acclimatized. Their heads are still full of snow."

"It's very pretty and very comfortable," Florent hastened to reply. "Auntie, you're going to a lot of trouble."

"Don't mention it. . . . And stay as long as you want. It used to be the gardener's house, but it's been gathering dust for twenty years. Someone might as well use it – it keeps the mice away. And if you want to give birth here, dear child," she said, gripping Elise's hand, "you're more than welcome. We don't lack for good doctors."

The cook returned. Glaring angrily, Mademoiselle Lydie gestured to him to change his sauce-stained apron. Sheepishly, he obeyed, then came back with a platter bearing a sizzling *tourtière*. "Here's my cure for homesickness! Put it here," she told the cook, "I'll serve."

"If your doctor could see you now!" exclaimed Mademoiselle Lydie, scandalized.

"For the moment, he can't, and when he can, he's more apt to be looking at my purse, like everyone else."

Florent smiled. "Wouldn't an occasional trip back home do more than a *tourtière*?"

She plunked her elbows on the table. "It wouldn't be worth sparrow shit, my boy. Because I have too much money.

Which is why I left! All those relatives fluttering around waiting for me to have a coronary give me the heaves. Here, I have peace. Mademoiselle Lydie – whom I pay handsomely – is well aware that she won't get a penny aside from her salary. As for the others, if I want to see them, I call them. And if they're a little bit fond of me, they come. Besides, I make the occasional visit back home. But I don't advertise them, so I can see whoever I want, or no one, depending on my mood. I paid a visit to Montreal three years ago. Ugh! What a city! Completely topsy-turvy. Are they still tearing everything down? Soon I won't recognize a thing. I'd rather live here – at least my memories are intact."

She struck the rim of a plate with her fork and muttered, "Why doesn't that creature bring the rest of the meal?"

At this, mademoiselle rose and left the room. "Go ahead," said their aunt, "eat while it's hot." Then suddenly, with a look at Florent, she said, "You really got taken for a ride, didn't you? I've heard what happened."

Florent turned red and Elise, startled, put her hand on his arm. "I can assure you," he told his aunt, "it'll never happen again."

"What do you mean?"

"I won't play any more games like that."

"What on earth are you talking about? You sound like a patient in a rest home! I could give you a hand, you know."

Florent shook his head. "I don't need any help. Elise and I are managing just fine."

His aunt burst out laughing with her mouth full. "Not a bad answer, my boy, not bad at all! I don't think much of people who accept help from others right off the bat. In any case, I just said whatever came into my head. After all, I hardly know you."

Her remarks offended Elise. "All we want is a few days' rest, madame," she said with a chilly smile, "then we'll go back to work like everybody else."

A sorrowful expression softened the old lady's face. "I see that I've hurt your feelings. You youngsters mustn't let yourselves be bothered by what I say or the way I say it. What can I tell you? My tongue's like a whetstone – it puts an edge on my words before they're out of my mouth."

Mademoiselle Lydie silently brought in a little jar of pickles, followed by the cook carrying a dish piled high with mashed potatoes in a ring of buttered carrots. The room was filled with the aromas of fresh-ground pepper, chives, and melted butter. Madame Jeunehomme picked up her fork. "About time! We've nearly finished the *tourtière*. Put the dish here and I'll serve – it'll be faster."

"Please to forgive, madame. The pepper grinder, she fall in the wegetables."

"With some help from the cat," added Mademoiselle Lydie. Her remark slipped into the air like a thin sheet of ice.

The older woman shot the poor man a look, and he tried to sink into the floor. "I thought that matter had been settled. We'll discuss it later, my friend."

Then with no further ado and a hungry look, she began to serve the vegetables. "So, Florent, you wanted to get rich, but now you're finding poverty attractive?"

"I just want to live modestly."

"For a while," Elise corrected him.

"For a hundred years."

Mademoiselle Lydie bowed her head over her plate and bit her cheeks to keep from laughing. "There aren't all that many ways to make a fortune," Florent's aunt declared, voluptuously sinking her fork into the creamy potatoes that covered a third of her plate. "You have to cheat."

All eyes were on her. "That's right. Why deny it? I didn't collect my fortune with a beggar's bowl. Come now, Lydie, don't be such a prude; you know it as well as I do. My husband used to say that to prosper in business you had to commit at least two robberies a day. But not everyone can be a thief. It takes talent – and perseverance. As you know, I used to own the biggest bookstore in Quebec City. Do you think I got rich on Racine's plays or Diderot's novels? Fluff! Expecting to make a living off cultivated people is like keeping a cow that just grazes on roses. I had other means. For instance, I used to sell Larousse encyclopedias to the school boards, and it was the strangest thing, but the next year the mice had been at them and they'd need a whole new set. I don't know how the good Lord will react when I show up, but I'll throw myself on his mercy and keep working. After all, he's the one who gave me my taste for money, so let him deal with the consequences."

The door creaked and the cook made a triumphant entrance, his gloved hands holding a steaming raspberry pie. With her long skinny fingers, Mademoiselle Lydie pushed a trivet to the center of the table. "You've redeemed yourself!" exclaimed Madame Jeunehomme, gazing at the golden crust and the ruby-colored syrup bubbling all around.

Elise, Florent and their aunt polished off two servings, while Mademoiselle Lydie picked at her plate, an expression of polite disdain on her face. Then Madame Jeunehomme dropped her fork and briskly got to her feet. "Let's have coffee on the terrace. After stowing away all that food we need some oxygen."

She went out through a French door. A table under a parasol, surrounded by wicker chairs, was rusting peacefully in the middle of a flagstoned terrace overgrown with grass. The view was broken by a row of potted shrubs. Madame Jeunehomme downed her coffee in two gulps. "Well, I won't keep you any longer. Why not go into town – I know you're dying to. As for you, Lydie, I'd like you to tidy up the papers in my office. My accountant comes tomorrow."

The sky was growing dark. A damp, sweetish breeze, lush with the smell of growing things, began to blow. Elise and Florent strolled along Duval Street, with its distinguished old houses. So much peaceful luxury induced a numbness from which they were stirred from time to time by the blaze of poinciana. But soon the setting changed. The streets came alive. The houses, with their pastel stucco walls, were somewhat dilapidated now, and looked vaguely Spanish. They stopped in amazement. A cactus stood before a facade, higher than the crest of the roof, its branches, fitted one into the other, giving an impression of unstable equilibrium.

A little farther along, the business section began. A dense crowd undulated lazily past large gray frame houses. On the ground floors were minute boutiques, greasy-looking restaurants, and dark grocery stores, still open despite the lateness of the hour, all flooding the street with Latin-American music. Slouched on the counters, children read comics amid family squabbles. Onlookers eyed pedestrians with expert, ironic gazes. In a deserted pool hall, a black man slept on a table with his legs apart. This mass of humanity gave off a satisfied hum, bathed in the gentle heat of the night. And yet every time they met a black man, Elise and Florent felt an impenetrable gaze, heavy as lead, slip over them. The atmosphere became somewhat sinister in the bluish half light, filled with activity and the smells of cooking fat and exhaust fumes.

They continued for another dozen blocks, when their surroundings became more familiar. The walls were cured of their dermatitis now. There were neon signs on the facades. The sidewalks were wider and cleaner. Suddenly there were more whites. You could see inside bars that were sparkling with lights. There was a splendid Southern mansion, complete with pillars, that was now a restaurant. Black-jacketed waiters plied the terrace amid the discreet clinking of crockery.

They retraced their steps and entered a cross street under a green arch of foliage. On the one corner stood a minuscule used bookstore. Through a window filled with dusty tomes they saw a corpulent black man sitting behind a counter, reading a newspaper. They went inside. A strong aroma of rum suggested that reading wasn't the bookseller's only pastime. "Yes, sir!" he greeted them delightedly.

Florent smiled vaguely and began rummaging about the shelves.

"Dirty books!" Elise sniffed.

The bookseller flung down his paper, and his eyes lit up as if he'd just been plugged into a high-tension line. "French Canadian?"

Elise nodded. "Terrific! I got a couple of books for you, in French!"

From under the counter he removed a cardboard box and, staggering slightly, dragged it to the middle of the store. "Take a look."

They squatted down. Leaning on a pile of books, he told them, "Uncle of mine used to live in Montreal."

Elise dropped a biography of Robert Bourassa that looked as if it had spent a long time in tomato juice.

"Used cars – he sold used cars." With a deep breath and a visible effort to control the giggles that had been threatening to get the better of him, he went on: "Hell of a slippery customer, my uncle – wouldn't've bought a spark plug from him myself. He used to say, 'When I got an old rattletrap with just a couple of miles left in her, I deal with the Frenchies. They're sweet as maple syrup.'" Florent gave him a glacial stare. "Hey, don't get mad, I was only kidding!" He plunged his hand in the carton. "Here take this, it's a present!"

He shoved a thick book at Florent and patted his shoulder, smiling amiably. "Come again!" he said, waving good-bye.

"*The Chemistry of Cosmetics*?" he said with a disgusted look, dusting off the cover. "What the hell am I supposed to do with that?"

There was a garbage can at the corner. He tossed the book inside. "*I* may be interested," Elise protested, retrieving the book from a heap of oily rags.

Florent smiled and kept walking. Elise wiped off the book with a handkerchief and put it in her handbag.

There were no lights in the hotel windows, and the garden was utterly dark. "It's like a graveyard," Elise said, shuddering.

They went through the iron fence and soon they had strayed from the path, walking around the terrace. All they could hear was the sound of the sea. Then Elise cried out and fell in the grass. "I tripped on a branch," she sighed, as Florent helped her up.

Just then a spoon clinked against a cup, remarkably loud. "You should have stayed on the path instead of risking your bones in that abandoned garden," said a hoarse voice on the other side of the shrubs.

"Is – is that you, Auntie?"

"It's me, all right. Who else would it be? Lydie goes to bed with the chickens. Come on, let's have a chat before we go to sleep. And whatever's happened to you, my dear? Your hair's a mess! A bit of hanky-panky? And they say that marriage kills romance. . . ."

"I – I fell."

"Florent, get two glasses from the table. There's some lemonade left. You must be parched, in this heat. Now then," she said, tilting the pitcher, "drink up."

They obeyed, then looked at the cloud-heavy sky, barely pierced by moonlight. A night bird flew tirelessly around the hotel, making plaintive cries. The silence lasted a minute or so. "I had a telephone call tonight," Madame Jeunehomme said at length, her voice different now. "My son is coming for a visit next month."

They stared at her, not daring to speak. The old lady sighed and started drumming her spoon against the edge of the table. "You see him from time to time, don't you?" she asked her nephew wearily.

"Now and then. Last fall, he invited us to his chalet in Saint-Gabriel."

The old lady scowled and the drumming grew faster. "What do you want?" she asked, her voice filled with irritation. "It was God's punishment. I didn't listen to my husband but paid more attention to my business than my child. I made a fortune from books but they poisoned my life. I don't have a son now, I've a bookworm. I spent a fortune on that lazy loafer, and what do I have to show for it? He stays in his room like an invalid and devours books by the truckload, instead of seeing to his ministry or some other useful occupation. If by chance he goes anywhere, you can be sure there's a book at the end of the road. You must know about his search for a manuscript by some Russian or other. . . ."

Florent yawned behind his hand. "You mean Gogol?"

"That's the one. It makes you wonder if . . . You know, a person can become addicted to anything, even reading. It may be the worst, in fact: it eats up so much time your whole life can pass you by. Drink is better, from many points of view. Well," she said, getting up, "that's enough. Let's go to bed. Another crew of workmen arrives tomorrow."

They watched her walk away, arms swaying in that peculiar manner. She opened the French door and turned to them. "If you like, I'll show you around the hotel tomorrow. And you," – she pointed imperiously at Elise – "don't forget to sleep as late as you need to. The more you pamper that baby of yours, the more beautiful he'll be."

TWENTY-ONE

About six o'clock the next morning, a squirrel tumbled though the bougainvillea outside the bedroom window, rustling its branches. Florent woke up fresh as a daisy, as if he'd been asleep since the Earthly Paradise closed down. He murmured to Elise, "Go ahead, love, sleep as long as you like."

Then he silently rose and went to the kitchen to make coffee. *The Chemistry of Cosmetics* lay on the table. He patted it absentmindedly, then opened it. "Hmm – eight hundred and fifty-two pages – all you ever wanted to know. The drawings look pretty good."

Two hours later his aunt found him still absorbed in the book. "God preserve me! You're turning out like my son! Are you ready to see the hotel?"

Her hoarse voice awakened Elise, who dressed, wolfed down some breakfast and followed them, her head still full of dreams. The foreman was waiting in the foyer. He was a red-headed giant with deep-set, gleaming eyes. He reeked of sweat from twenty feet away, and the workmen seemed to fear him like a life sentence. The inspection tour lasted all morning. The foreman listened to Madame Jeunehomme very attentively and respectfully, making notes on the numerous instructions that she issued in appalling English.

Everywhere there were canvas sheets covered with debris, torn sacks of plaster, whistling workmen whose zeal increased as the others came into sight. The ground floor of the central part of the building had been restored to its original splendor. On the upper floors the air smelled of mildew and mothballs, of recently disturbed dust. Madame Jeunehomme went from room to room, poking her nose everywhere. She didn't miss a thing. She ran her fingers over the paneling, checking the varnish, she hunted down cracks, peered at plaster moldings, probed walls and floors, and made the workers redo anything that didn't satisfy her. If her own eye or hand wouldn't do, she sent Florent up a ladder or crawling into cobwebby nooks and crannies. The foreman responded to her reprimands with drooping head and silence. Elise and Florent walked, wide-eyed, through immense once-splendid suites, their ceilings disappearing into the shadows. There were rooms and more rooms, all full of creaking sounds and faded odors, lit by dusty chandeliers and table lamps with moth-eaten shades. Bland neoclassical statues stood in niches along endless corridors with threadbare carpeting. At either end of the wing, an open-shaft elevator, decorated with bronze wreaths and garlands, glided silently down through the center of a marble spiral staircase.

The work force was concentrated in what was called the ballroom wing, where the walls had been knocked down to make room for the casino, bar, and restaurant. The restaurant opened onto a terrace where bulldozers were at work. Madame Jeunehomme turned to her young guests. "All the redecoration is being done in period style, though personally

I think it stinks. But I'd be crazy not to, now that Victorian's fashionable again!"

They lingered on the top floor, the one that had suffered most because of the damaged roof. Since it contained the cheaper rooms and servants' quarters, the furniture, which wasn't worth much, had virtually been thrown out the window. Their inspection was nearly over when the old lady suddenly brought her hand to her bosom and muttered something, furious. Elise and Florent stared at her. The foreman, to whom the incident seemed familiar, pretended to peer at the ceiling, while trying to hold back a smile. Madame Jeunehomme, suddenly pale, went up to him, inquiring, "Bathroom?"

He pointed to a door across the room. She went inside. Five minutes passed. No one dared to speak. The foreman wandered through the room, whistling, more concerned than he appeared. Elise was about to knock when her aunt emerged. "Always the same story," she grumbled. "Just a drop too much coffee and the palpitations start. Oh, children! If only we could keep from getting old!"

"Have you seen a doctor?" Florent asked.

"What for? They're for sick people. I just take some warm water and everything's back to normal. I've a tough old hide, my boy, thank God!"

They went down to the dining room. Madame Jeunehomme, satisfied with the progress of the work, appeared particularly playful. She amused herself for a while teasing Elise about her belly, claiming it was already rounding out. Then, turning to Florent, she offered him the use of her old limousine. "It's a Cadillac my husband kept under blankets. Not a scratch on it. It was his mascot – reminded him of the days when we were first rich. I never use it; Lydie's a terrible driver. I'd rather run around in my old Ford."

At two o'clock she rose, embraced them, and withdrew to her office. They looked at each other in silence, surprised by their aunt's good mood.

Over the following week, though, they saw her only once. Mademoiselle Lydie reassured them: "Madame is in splendid form and talks about you every day, but to tell you the truth, we're overwhelmed with work. Just think: the hotel opens in two months!"

"I could lend a hand," Florent suggested.

"You mustn't *dream* of it – she'd be terribly hurt! It would seem she had an ulterior motive for inviting you, and you're here for a rest! Have a good time," she concluded in English, "and leave the rest to us."

One afternoon, Elise said, "I wonder who the old guy is who's been pulling up in a blue limousine every evening."

Florent shrugged. "Probably some business associate, or her lover; I wouldn't be surprised if she has one."

They began faithfully following Mademoiselle Lydie's instructions. It was easy for Elise. Being pregnant made her sleep ten hours every day. A walk left her exhausted, with an aching back. Florent had to do all the housekeeping and shopping. They swam, slept, ate, and gently honed and polished the legitimate joys of marriage. Elise was intrigued by her husband's progress with *The Chemistry of Cosmetics*. "How can you enjoy all that gobbledygook? In this climate I can't even read a thriller."

"It takes me back to school. I was nuts about chemistry. Nothing I liked better than an afternoon in the lab."

And, smiling, he went on with his reading. Elise watched him, shaking her head. Lord in Heaven, she thought, is he regressing?

Eventually their aunt returned, more impetuous than ever, and once again they took their evening meal in the vast dining room with its freshly varnished paneling.

One night they were sitting around the table on the terrace, sipping liqueurs. Madame Jeunehomme, restored to dazzling form by two strong cups of coffee, was regaling them with her techniques for unloading unreadable novels on religious communities. Smiling, Florent leaned back on his chair and absentmindedly rubbed the glossy leaves of a potted shrub near the table. "My – my fingers smell of grapefruit!"

"No mystery there," said his aunt. "You've been torturing my grapefruit tree for the past half hour!"

Florent put his hands on the table and continued to listen. But he kept sniffing his fingers, his mind obviously wandering. A little later he asked, "Do they grow many of those trees around here?"

"Oranges and grapefruit provide a living for many people in Florida," replied his aunt, who was given to sententious pronouncements. "In fact, ten days ago I bought an orchard of five hundred orange trees and three hundred and fifty-two grapefruits."

When they were back in their cottage, Florent announced, "Thanks to you, kiddo, I've just had an idea!"

Elise looked puzzled. "I just might go into the cosmetics business. Don't look at me like that – I've given it careful thought. It doesn't need much capital, or scientific knowledge, and if it takes off, we'll need a shovel for the money!"

They went into the cottage. Feverishly, Florent leafed through *The Chemistry of Cosmetics*. "You know the main ingredient in all those creams and lotions and milks you buy?

Water! Look at this table: all those fancy 'moisturizing' creams are just oil-and-water emulsions – five percent oil and ninety-five percent water! The other ingredients don't cost much: talc, borate, glycerol, silicone, a bit of perfume."

"Yes, but good perfumes are expensive," Elise observed skeptically.

"My aunt will take care of that. Don't you see? I'm going to make my own cosmetics – out of plain old grapefruit leaves. Everybody's, into 'natural' products, so why not cash in on it? Some ground-up grapefruit leaves, a little oil, some fatty acid, lots of water, and there's your beauty cream. The nostrils of every female in Quebec will be quivering, and they'll all be slathering their faces with my wrinkle cream, but the smoothest hide of all will be on my wallet. Of course we'll have to go easy: start with one product, then extend the range, and handle the publicity side just right. I've already got the brand name: Gladu gave it to me one day: Seventh Heaven. Seventh Heaven Cosmetics. Doesn't it give you a funny feeling inside your belly?"

He gripped Elise's hands. "Don't you see, I have to bury The Beanery disaster once and for all. I'd kind of forgotten it, but for the past week it's been bugging me again. As soon as I start feeling better, there it is, gnawing at my guts. Hey, what's wrong? Where are you going?"

"It's nothing," Elise gasped, "I'll be right back." And trembling with joy she disappeared into the bathroom, to shed her tears in private.

"What is it?" Florent asked again from the other side of the door.

"Just a . . . a cramp. Don't . . . don't worry, it'll pass." God in Heaven, is this really happening? she asked herself. Has Florida cured him?

Florent grumbled, "What a woman! Tell her about a project and she gets a stomach ache!"

She dashed cold water on her face. Come on, dummy, she told herself, don't be a fool. Go back to him; he's bragging but he still needs you. First you have to calm him down.

Florent was strolling along the portico, hands behind his back, in marvelous spirits. Catching sight of Elise, he was aware of her feelings but carefully said nothing. Taking her hand, he led her on a walk that lasted into the night. Elise, eyes stinging with exhaustion, hounded him with questions, went over his calculations, made some objections, went into ecstasies. At three in the morning they were eating hamburgers under the dazzling lights in a fast-food outlet. They agreed to say nothing until they'd sounded out their aunt. "She likes her nephew well enough, but she's even more fond of money. If she gets off on my idea, she could even turn me down and use the grapefruit leaf idea herself."

They decided to visit the plantation the next morning, on the pretext of an excursion. "Let's go to bed now," Florent suggested, "so we can get an early start."

She hadn't seen him like this for so long. He drew her to him and kissed her cheek. "I'm glad you like my idea. Maybe it won't get off the ground, but it feels so good to have something in the works."

He dreamed all night, worrying first about how to manage his vast fortune, then about losing everything down to his toothbrush. He rose at dawn and shook Elise. Leaving the cottage, they caught sight of Mademoiselle Lydie walking away through the trees. "What's she up to, anyway?" Florent asked suspiciously.

Elise bent down and took a letter from the doorstep. "It's from Picquot!" She read:

Dear Youngsters,

Save your tears to salt your soup – I'm feeling better than ever. My doctor assured me that with proper diet, plenty of rest and a firm lease on my emotions, I could live to a crow's age! Today fate has truly blessed me: after a ten-year search, I've finally turned up the rarest of books, the illustrated biography of my spiritual master, the great chef Alexis Soyer, published by Field & Keaton in London, in 1859.

I've gone back to work at the wretched agency, where I was greeted – Heaven knows why – with open arms. Two weeks ago I had the notion of taking the sun for a time, in your company, but airplanes are off-limits for a year. And automobiles are tolerable only for short distances. The monotony of superhighways and the consequences to my spinal column of thirty years of cooking (I never refer to it, to avoid boring people) make the briefest jaunt a torment.

And now I'm writing you, despite my aversion to the pen, for I have important news. It would seem the appalling Old Rat has had a falling-out with Master Slipskin. One evening, in fact, while mulling over your pitiful fate, I felt an urge to stop in at The Beanery and tell that Anglo trash a thing or two. And so I go in. I look around. He's not there. From the back of the kitchen Bertrand catches sight of me, and gestures me in. "Go down to the bathroom," says he. "I've something to tell you." I was a trifle reluctant, given his proclivities, but down I went. The filth in the cellar! I'm sorry to say that hygiene left the restaurant along with us. Five minutes later Bertrand had joined me. Handshakes, embraces, exclamations – it was like bringing fresh salmon to a starving cat. Then he informs me, "Things are bad between Ratablavasky and the boss. They had a fight and Old Rat hasn't been around for three weeks." "What about business?" I asked. "Oh, it's pretty fair, but the boss is in a bad way." "What happened?" "You figure it out – if I even hint at it, the square-head threatens to send me packing. He has the manners of a pig, treats people like cattle. Day before yesterday I nearly burst into tears in front of customers. Have you found a job?"

When I told him, he said, "Remember me if you ever need an assistant. Eight hours a day, I'm wound up tight as a spring. If this keeps up I'll be covered with pimples."

Conclusion: If our enemies are in trouble, things are looking up for us. If this letter brings back too many bad memories, throw it away and forget it. But there's an old sauce stirrer in Montreal who wouldn't object to shaking your paw one day soon.

Picquot

P.S. I had a call the other day from dear Monsieur Emile who was, in the delicate local parlance, pissed to the gills. Young rapscallion! Tried to hit me up for five dollars. He asked me to meet him in a phone booth at some street corner or other. I tore over and rushed him off to Rosine's, who put him to bed on the spot. Since then, not a word.

Florent folded the letter, slipped it in his pocket and stood there musing for a moment. Then he exploded, "To hell with the goddamn restaurant. I'm not going to rub my belly with sandpaper for the rest of my life!"

They set off for the hotel. Their hostess was probably eating breakfast in the kitchen. As they entered the foyer they spotted Mademoiselle Lydie, giving instructions to the housekeepers. "No question of seeing madame before ten o'clock," she told Elise dryly. "She's in conference with her architect."

On their way back to the cottage, Florent stopped. "A good book on horticulture could come in handy before we visit the plantation. Let's look for one in town."

"Why not?" said Elise sardonically. "There's a book for everything nowadays."

They went back to the bookseller on Petronia Street who'd so kindly given them *The Chemistry of Cosmetics*. He was closed. In a manner of speaking, it's true: two days earlier a burglar had put the lock out of commission, and the owner had simply blocked the door with the complete works of Sinclair Lewis, topped by three sacks of potatoes. A passerby told them of another bookstore at the corner of Truman and Duval. They found nothing worthwhile, but as they were leaving the shop they happened on a peculiar spectacle.

There was a traffic jam on Duval Street. In the middle of the pavement a small, rust-colored mongrel, short-haired, squat and oddly shaped, had just been mounted by a quivering, dust-colored bulldog, while another dozen dogs of all breeds and qualities looked on, eyes shining and tongues hanging out, panting with desire. Car drivers made the best of it, waiting patiently for Nature to do her work, and laughing at the poor stoic bitch, whose luscious rear end had provoked a canine revolution in Key West. Florent gazed at her tearful, bulging eyes, her scarred flanks, and something in him snapped. He walked onto the street and whistled. Elise clapped her hand over his mouth. "You're out of your mind! We'll have all those dogs on our heels!"

The bitch had joyously perked up her head. She bounded over to Florent, dragging along her dusty lover who managed to free himself and hide behind a lamppost, stunned by his misfortune. "You're crazy! Can you see us going through town with this pack of horny mutts?"

Florent was crouching before the animal. "Poor girl, love can be rough, eh? But why are you out on the street, anyway? You're no model of virtue!"

The bitch, delivered from her horde of Don Juans, was fixing him with eyes moist with gratitude. Elise shook his shoulder. "I get the picture. Come off it, Florent! She's ugly as a stump, she smells like garbage, and I don't want her in my house!"

They started walking, the procession at their heels. Elise continued to remonstrate, while Florent used pebbles and twigs to scatter the canine suitors. As their ranks thinned out, Elise's annoyance diminished. When they were down to three she even agreed that Virtue – as Florent persisted in calling the bitch – had "an intelligent face." They were outside the hotel. The dog, ears flattened, belly to the ground, went inside the iron fence with fearful haste, then discreetly lay under a bush. Elise frowned, but said nothing. When they reached the cottage, she even ventured to stroke the animal, her lips pursed in disgust. "For heaven's sake," she pleaded, "give her a bath before you let her in or we'll be invaded by fleas."

Virtue didn't put up too much resistance to a good scrubbing. Now and then she would lift one paw and look fearfully at her master, then slowly put it back in the water. "Okay," Florent told her finally, "torture's over."

The dog sprang out of the tub, shook herself vigorously and completed her toilet with a long roll in the grass. Then she stood up and barked joyously: her coat, cooled by the bath, hinted at all sorts of good things to come. "All right," Elise told her, "you can come in now."

Virtue scampered into the kitchen and found a shady spot under a bench. Curled up in a ball with her muzzle resting on her paws and eyes wary, she made herself as small as possible to keep from drawing attention, sensing it was the best way to gain certain favors. Florent offered her some ground beef but she was too afraid to eat. Finally, out of politeness, she consented to lap a little water, then lay down again and tried to sleep, her ears quivering, as she kept looking around to see that things were under control. Then Florent called her and they went into the garden. Virtue was torn by contradictory urges. She would frisk about gaily, running rings around her masters, then trot beside them like a well-trained pet, even renouncing sniffing at inviting clumps of weeds or interestingly twisted roots.

"Her teats are almost dragging on the ground," Madame Jeunehomme observed. "She must have had dozens of litters, poor thing."

Florent's aunt was pale and drawn and short of breath. I wonder if she's sick and not telling us, Florent mused.

The old lady closed her account book and dropped it on the desk. "I don't like dogs. Especially bitches. They're too much like us poor French Canadians, always behaving ourselves and sneaking into our corner to eat. They're too naive. And too fond of serving others. I prefer cats. They aren't so flabby."

Then she opened a drawer, took out a bunch of keys and handed it to Florent with a smile. "Of course I've no objection. Here, take the limousine and go and visit my plantation. It'll help you learn more about Florida. You haven't seen much yet – you've been living like groundhogs. When you get to Sunland Gardens near Fort Pierce, ask for Keith Spider's house. He's my manager. If he's out, insist that his wife take you there. That'll get the kinks out of her legs: all she does is sit in a chaise longue, drying in the sun like a codfish."

She gave them instructions, opened her account book and went back to work. "Your aunt's as gentle as Javex," Elise laughed as they were descending the main staircase. "But did you notice how pale and thin she is? I'm sure she's sick and isn't telling us."

They walked to the left of the hotel, then around the rotunda-shaped pavilion until they arrived at the outbuildings, preceded by Virtue, who had her nose in the grass and was darting in every direction. At the sight of them, a group of workmen lazing about on the grass sprang to their feet and disappeared in the scaffolding. Florent walked up to the garage and played with the lock till the door slowly rose. A 1930s limousine gleamed in the half light. They gazed in awe. It seemed that at any moment Greta Garbo, in all her youthful splendor, might step out of the automobile.

Before Elise had the door open, Virtue was lying inside, silent and still, trying to make herself invisible. Florent started up the car. The sound of well-oiled humming filled the car. Slowing and solemnly, the automobile made its way along the path. All the workers on the scaffolding were motionless and heads appeared in all the windows. Elise smiled at her husband. "You should see the look on your face! Like a Rockefeller! Where are you going?"

"Back to the cottage, to get *The Chemistry of Cosmetics*. Be a sweetheart and read me the chapter on citrus fruits."

He laughed, and his laughter was coarse, almost vulgar. "I *feel* like a Rockefeller. And I love it! Like silk underwear!"

Around two o'clock they succumbed to hunger. At a fast-food stand they ordered coffee and key lime pie, whose crust had an odd aftertaste of smoked ham. Virtue waited, panting, in the closed limousine, her front paws on the book, staring at the restaurant window and watching her masters grimace as they ate.

They reached Sunland Gardens in midafternoon. Mr. Spider, an eager, cordial little man, offered them tall glasses of lemonade, then took then to Madame Jeunehomme's orchards, which extended to the shores of the Indian River. Then he left them, after sending his regards to the boss. They walked down rows of gnarled and rather stunted trees laden with small, gleaming green fruit. "I expected something more exotic," Elise complained.

Florent wanted to bring back some grapefruit leaves so he could start his experiments. They filled a big canvas bag and then, overcome by the heat, flopped onto the grass. A delicate lemony aroma drifted among the trees as leaves rustled softly overhead and time seemed frozen.

Yawning, Florent peered up at the sky. The heat had drained its color, emptied it of birds and clouds, so that it looked like a sheet of paper. He turned to Elise and gently started kissing the back of her neck. "Wonder where the dog is?" she asked, looking around uneasily.

"How romantic!" Florent laughed. "You could turn on a hundred-year-old priest!"

They heard barking nearby. "Hear that? Now don't worry, she knows when she's on to a good thing – she won't want to make trouble."

Elise sighed contentedly and snuggled up to her husband. A sensation of airy stillness, which didn't lead to sleep but merely blunted their awareness of things, slowly swelled the hidden urges coursing through their bodies. They exchanged knowing smiles. The trees seemed somehow closer now, bent over their heads to form that delightful shelter that lovers can erect almost anywhere to cut themselves off from the world. Lost amid the rustling leaves, they abandoned themselves, and a familiar harmonious sensation, like the force that impels the growth of plants, gently overtook them. Elise moaned.

Florent opened one eye. His gaze fell on Virtue, sitting a few steps away. The dog was trembling all over, gaze fixed on the hillock that stood to their right. He swung around. Elise cried out and pulled down her clothes. She caught a glimpse of a face shining in the bushes halfway down the hill. Branches cracked. "Thousand pardons, friends," said Captain Galarneau, slowly getting to his feet, his mug redder than usual. "I coughed three times to warn you to get your wits back, but passion's louder than a blaring horn, as the lieutenant-gen . . ." Squeamish, he didn't complete his remark. Without a word, Florent picked up the dog, gestured to Elise to bring the canvas bag, and they strode away.

Egon Ratablavasky was waiting on the roadside, near the car. "Please to excuse," he said genially. "But I was wanting badly to speak to you . . ."

Cutting through the orchard, Captain Galarneau had put on a remarkable burst of speed, which his corpulence rendered scarcely believable, and now he had just dashed inside the limousine. "Aha!" he exclaimed. "Very goddamn interesting!"

He emerged sweating, holding *The Chemistry of Cosmetics*.

Florent snatched it away and gave him a push. "Get the fuck out of here, you reptile!"

"What's that? A man of my age, who fought for Canada!" exclaimed the captain, his face twisted.

He raised his fist. "Friends, friends," said Egon Ratablavasky, interposing himself, "respect civilized customs, I beg you. Why such behaving? Why?"

Elise had locked herself inside the car and was pounding her fists on the window, trying to make Florent get in. He was leaning against a door, arms folded, staring at Egon Ratablavasky, eyes dilated with hate and fear.

"Have you sworn an oath to make the rest of my life miserable?" he muttered.

Captain Galarneau snickered and hummed a jig under his breath, winking comically at Elise.

Gradually, the smell of stale socks filled the air. Florent grimaced in disgust. "Stinking old alley cat," he said, choking. "Instead of preparing for death he wastes his final days poisoning people's lives! What did I ever do to you? Why do you keep tormenting me? Weren't you satisfied with taking away my restaurant? What more do you want?"

Looking pained, Ratablavasky shook his head. "That's just it," he said in a staid and gentle voice. "I must make explaining . . . I've been duped – insidiously duped. . . . It's most unfortunate . . ." He picked a blade of grass from his trousers. "I came here, my friend, not for tormenting but to discuss with you an advantageous deal! A *very* –"

"Who told you we were here?" Florent broke in, ignoring Elise pounding on his back through the window.

The old man smiled (it was more like a grimace) and turned to Captain Galarneau, who thundered, "I made an investigation and *boom*! Straight to the point! Here we are right on target!"

The car door swung open. "Please, Florent, get in," said Elise faintly.

The tip of a muzzle emerged from under the car and there was Virtue, swaying fearfully on her big paws. Ratablavasky stared at the dog, repelled. Florent grasped her by the scruff of the neck and tossed her back in the car. "About that advantageous deal," he said, getting behind the wheel, "you can take it and shove it up your ass. And don't hang around waiting to be called the names you deserve!"

Without a word, Ratablavasky bowed while Florent noisily started the car. Elise was trembling and excruciating cramps wrenched her abdomen; she kept turning around to see if they were being followed. A sickening smell of urine filled the car: realizing she was safe and sound, Virtue had pissed with relief.

When they returned, they found the hotel in an uproar. Father Jeunehomme, who had advanced his journey, was getting out of a taxi. In the semitropical surroundings his rumpled soutane looked odder than ever, like a coffin at a wedding. Madame Jeunehomme, tense with emotion she used gruffness to conceal, kissed him quickly, then asked a workman who was walking through the yard to bring her son's bags inside. "There you are!" she exclaimed, catching sight of Florent and Elise. "You certainly don't need introductions!"

At the sight of his cousin, Father Jeunehomme appeared upset, nervously cramming his hands in his pockets. "I believe," he stammered, blushing, "that I didn't behave very properly with you the other day."

"Don't give it a second thought," Florent replied. "As it's worked out, you did the right thing. After all, here we are, with your mother treating us like royalty."

Virtue had been observing Father Jeunehomme. Deciding he was harmless, she moved closer and started sniffing his shoes. "No, no," the priest insisted, "I behaved very badly. I wronged you by omission. I hope my mother will be able to make up for my negligence."

Madame Jeunehomme had been fanning herself with a newspaper. Now she glanced suspiciously at her son.

"Why don't we go in?" suggested Mademoiselle Lydie, who couldn't tolerate the sun.

"I've told you about the potbellied stove, haven't I?" the priest said, as he slowly climbed the steps. "The one where Gogol threw his manuscript in the flames?"

"Oh yes, you mentioned it," Florent replied with chilly courtesy.

"Well, the day you and your wife came to see me, I got a telegram informing me it had been found. It's in a little village in the south of France. The seals protecting it seem intact. I'm negotiating buying it."

His knife-blade nose with its nearly transparent nostrils quivered slightly.

"Octavien, that can wait," said his mother, irritated. "Did you have a pleasant outing?" she asked Florent.

"Yes, but an unpleasant meeting."

"What happened?"

They were now in the foyer. Madame Jeunehomme sank onto a sofa and slipped her hand under her left armpit. She was struggling to assume a jaunty air, but it was hard. They all knew that anyone imprudent enough to ask how she was feeling would be made to swallow his question. "And who did you children run into?"

"Our greatest enemy," replied Elise gravely, "the man who ruined us: Egon Ratablavasky. He came all this way to harass us. I was so scared I thought I'd die."

The priest started, considered leaving, then thought

better of it. His mother's bony chin jerked up, as if she was having trouble breathing. "Is he a fairly elderly man who talks as if he had a marble in his mouth?"

Florent nodded, surprised. "He called here this afternoon. Wanted to be sure you were staying here. I think he talked to Lydie, too. Isn't that right?"

Mademoiselle Lydie nodded. "And you told him we were visiting the plantation?" Elise asked her aunt's companion.

"He – he said he was a friend of yours. I didn't think . . ."

"He sounded very distinguished on the telephone," declared their aunt. "But I'd throw him out the door if he came here to bother you."

Elise, filled with trepidation, nearly burst into tears. Madame Jeunehomme patted her hand. "There, there, child, relax. I've met a good many poisonous creatures in my time. I know what has to be done."

She rose. "Now, let's have supper. My guts are singing."

On the way to the dining room, Father Jeunehomme asked Florent, "What was that gentleman's name again?"

"Egon Ratablavasky. D'you know him?"

The priest gestured vaguely. During the meal he seemed lost in thought, but that surprised neither his mother nor Mademoiselle Lydie. They had nearly finished dessert. Madame Jeunehomme snapped her fingers and said, "Come down from your cloud, son, and look at the present I've bought to celebrate your visit."

The chef made an entrance, carrying a tray bearing a superb white china coffeepot on a burner, with a tangle of flourishes that spelled out the monogram HB. The priest gasped and turned pale. "Balzac's coffeepot!"

"A copy, needless to say, just a copy," his mother corrected him. "Do you think I've started robbing museums?"

The priest got to his feet, overcome by emotion, and embraced his mother with surprising ardor. "Come come, what's got into you? Heavens above, do you want everyone to see me cry! Let's have coffee in the sitting room," she added, freeing herself.

Filtered light from shades of Tiffany glass and painted silk created an agreeably warm atmosphere in the vast room. For a time, Father Jeunehomme, still in a dither over his gift, struggled valiantly to take part in the conversation, telling anecdotes about his childhood that touched his mother and brought a smile to her lips. But soon the conversation turned to Quebec and politics. After two or three confused and irrelevant questions, which they struggled to answer charitably, he lapsed once more into dreamy silence. His mother, a sentimental, somewhat paranoid old nationalist, fervently defended the Canadian cause, accusing Lévesque and his mob (as she called them) of being in the pay of the Soviets, who were trying to break up one of the finest countries in the world on their way to conquering the rest of North America. The priest quietly approached Florent. "Can we have a word in private?"

"Of course."

"Now?"

Florent said to his aunt, "If you'll excuse us, we'd like to take a little walk in the garden."

"Go ahead – come back and join us later on the terrace."

When they were alone Father Jeunehomme said, "I think I know your Ratabla . . . vasky."

"Do you?"

The priest smiled. "Not personally. I don't associate with many people. But I think I've read about him. My memory's vague, but it wouldn't be hard to pin down. About how old is he, do you think?"

"Probably past seventy, but he's still got all his marbles, the fucker. Sorry."

"Such trifles don't disturb me," the priest replied, gesturing nonchalantly. "Give me a couple of hours to go to my room and check my summaries of what I've been reading. I should have more to tell you later tonight." With this, he left Florent, who returned to the hotel, bemused.

Two hours later, Madame Jeunehomme exclaimed, "Baby Jesus' tiny tummy! Will you tell me what that son of mine is up to? I just turn my head and he's disappeared!"

"He's doing some research, I think."

His mother shrugged and ordered more coffee. Elise bent over Florent's ear. "Research on Ratablavasky?" He nodded.

At ten o'clock, with a cavernous yawn, his aunt turned to her companion. "Be an angel and run me a hot bath. Time I packed my old carcass away for the night."

Elise, who had been suffering from stomach pains since early evening, also expressed a wish to retire. Soon the terrace was deserted. "You were right," Florent told Elise on their way home, "he's researching the old alley cat."

They went into the cottage. Elise began to inspect each room to be certain they were alone. Suddenly, she clutched her husband's hand. "Let's leave, Florent. I can't stand knowing he's so near."

"Where can we go? If he could track us this far, he'll find us anywhere. There'll be a settling of accounts some day soon, take my word."

They were on their way to bed when there was a knock at the door. "I found it," announced Father Jeunehomme, winded, his soutane half unbuttoned. "Or at least I *think* I did! I found an exceedingly rare volume in Mother's library."

He rummaged in his pocket and brought out a dog-eared little book bound in blue morocco. "Here it is. It's called *Racy Tales of the Church in France*, published by Hatier in 1939. Its by one Tristan de la Boissière – actually, Paul Chantaine – who was archivist at the Bibliothèque Nationale, a man with a scathing wit but an orderly mind, loaded with prejudices against us, but a meticulous researcher and generally quite reliable."

"Come in the kitchen," said Florent. "Would you like a coffee?"

The priest nodded, his excitement growing, and as he walked past his host, he accidentally stumbled into the bedroom. Elise, naked, slipped on a dressing gown. He closed the door as if nothing had happened and sat down at the kitchen table, feverishly turning the pages of the *Racy Tales*. "Here, here it is, page 72."

Florent was sitting opposite him, his heart pounding. The priest began to read, his voice thin and high-pitched. He scarcely stopped to greet Elise when she came in, her face flushed prettily. The reading lasted a good fifteen minutes, and presented some startling information.

"On April 6, 1931, a fifty-year-old named Egon Radablavasky (note the slight difference in spelling) came to the Cistercian Abbey at Gasquart-les-Moulineaux and expressed a desire to take holy orders. He maintained he was of Polish descent and had come from Germany, where he had worked for some years for a bookbinder, specializing in missals. Like so many others, he was terrified by the rising wave of Naziism. Seeing in it the hand of God, he had fled to France, wishing to dedicate his life to prayer and penitence, in an attempt to ward off the calamity that was threatening to afflict the civilized world. At first he wasn't taken seriously, but he persisted. In a week's time he had managed to obtain an interview with the Father Prior, who was as impressed by the newcomer's theological knowledge as by his fervor. Egon Radablavasky became a novice. Four years later, he cut all ties with the temporal world. His piety, common sense, modesty, and phenomenal erudition had won him the respect of his fellows. In 1937, he became treasurer. Under his influence the abbey, which was famous throughout the region for its cheese and confections, enjoyed a remarkable but short-lived prosperity, for one August night in 1939 he disappeared without a word, taking with him a sum that Paul Chantaine described as 'colossal,' though he was unable to be more precise. The agonies of war and the community's concern to avoid scandal guaranteed him impunity. After his departure, the good Fathers realized that he had defrauded not only the Community, but also some of his suppliers, all with consummate skill.

"Toward the end of the war, word began to get around that Egon Radablavasky, after carrying out various important missions for the Germans, had taken a new name and gone to America.

"To conclude, one racy detail," to use one of Paul Chantaine's favorite adjectives. "A curious functional anomaly somewhat reduced the ingenious malefactor's undeniable charm. I refer to a bizarre sudatory phenomenon affecting mainly the extremity of the lower limbs, which, it would appear, gave off a particularly disagreeable odor. Apparently this dermal affliction greatly humiliated the soutaned rogue, but he endured it like a martyr."

Florent was impressed. "Sounds a lot like our man. But there's one weird thing: this guy Chantaine says he was fifty in 1931. That'd make him almost a hundred today."

"Oh, you know – he could have seemed fifty, even if he was younger. And there *are* cases of extreme longevity. Just think of Verdi, who gave us *Falstaff* at eighty, or Claudel, still active at eighty-six – or Fontenelle, who died at a hundred with a joke on his lips."

"Another thing I can't figure out," Florent continued. "Why would he keep his real name, or just about?"

"The certitude of impunity," the priest murmured sententiously.

"God!" Elise exclaimed. "What next?"

She started to cry. Father Jeunehomme looked at her, desolate. Florent tried to comfort her, but his heart wasn't in it. The priest got up and headed for the door. "I'll walk part way with you," Florent offered.

"Me, too. I'm not staying here alone."

They walked beneath the somber mass of trees. In the nighttime calm, the sea boomed like a gigantic monster's breathing. The priest stopped to listen. Very softly he murmured, "Yseult, I hear the call of thy love, ever unsatisfied."

Elise and Florent maintained a polite silence. The priest said suddenly, "I was very sorry you weren't able to attend my Zola banquet. It was an unforgettable evening, a feast for the mind as well as the palate. Monsieur Cloutier, our former ambassador to France, kindly read us an extremely interesting paper on a visit Zola made in 1881 (the year he wrote *Pot-Bouille*) to Chambesle-la-Gassière, a castle he'd just bought."

"It's not that we didn't want to," Florent explained, "but your invitation arrived too late."

"What a pity! But never mind, in a few months I'm organizing a Gogol banquet. I'll keep you informed. You recall the famous passage from the beginning of *Dead Souls*, when Chichikov drives up? I've committed Nabokov's noble translation to memory: 'Sitting in the *britzka* was a gentleman whose countenance could not be termed handsome, yet neither was he ill-favored: he was not too stout, nor was he too thin; you could not call him old, just as you could not say that he was still youthful. His arrival produced no stir whatever in the town and was not accompanied by anything unusual; alone two Russian *muzhiks* who were standing at the door of a dram-shop opposite the inn made certain remarks which however referred more to the carriage than to the person seated therein. "Look at that wheel there," said one. "Now what do you think – would that wheel hold out as far as Moscow if need be, or would it not?" "It would," replied the other. "And what about Kazan – I think it would not last that far?" "It would not," answered the other.'"

He interrupted himself, as if suddenly gripped by a thought, and brought his hand to his brow, rubbing it with a circular motion, while his hesitant gaze moved from Elise to Florent. A moment passed. Florent wanted to resume their walk. All at once the priest asked, "What do you think about my mother?"

They looked at him, perplexed. "She's very . . . pleasant, very . . . nice," said Elise.

"That's not what I mean. What do you think about her . . . health?"

"She's amazingly vigorous for her age," Florent replied, "but I must admit that for a while now she's seemed a little tired."

"She was very sick recently," the priest interjected.

He was silent for a moment, hesitating whether or not to continue, then went on, despondent. "Three weeks ago she had an angina attack. Mademoiselle Lydie wrote me, but insisted I keep it secret. My mother refuses to talk about her illness. She thinks that disclosing it would mean the end. As she often says, 'Our death begins in other people's minds.'"

Florent clutched Elise's arm. "Now I understand – that limousine we used to see every night . . ."

"Her doctor," said the priest.

"And what does he say?"

"That medicine can help sensible people, but it would take another science to do anything for my mother. In a word, they can't do much. We must let her do as she wishes, while discreetly encouraging her to spare herself – which is absolutely impossible. Good night."

He left them and disappeared into the shadows. Florent and Elise slowly headed back to the cottage. Suddenly, at a bend in the path, they stopped, utterly shattered.

Seated on a small folding chair, Egon Ratablavasky was quietly waiting for them, his chin resting on his fist, his legs crossed. He seemed to be alone. He greeted them heartily: "Good evening, young friends! I was making a walk on the beach. It's very splendid there in the night, and I even left my friend Galarneau in a bar to be sure of having calm. I was wanting, you see, to talk with you."

He gazed at Elise, who seemed about to faint. "I know I'm not convenient, but if your ears will treat me kindly, this will be the last and final time."

Florent took his wife's hand. "You'll leave *now* or I'll call the police," he said, stepping forward so he could walk around the intruder.

Ratablavasky reached out to intercept him, but Florent jerked to one side, and the old man was knocked over. He sprang to his feet and slipped his right hand in his pocket. They heard a click. Somewhat breathlessly he said, "So sorry to call on the help of force, but duty requires. It is of utmost emergency that you listen."

Her lips quivering, Elise stared at him, aghast. "You son of a bitch!" Florent shouted, beside himself. "You know everything else so you must know my wife's pregnant: why do you have to torment her?"

In the moonlight the old man's cheeks suddenly turned lemon yellow. He gestured gracefully with his right hand. "Send her away," he said softly.

"I'm staying right here."

Florent folded his arms. "Okay, out with it. Let's get this over with."

"Most gladly, I thank you," said Ratablavasky, bowing his head. "My words will be small. You allow?"

He bent down, picked up the folding chair and, with a brief moan, sat down. Then, with his right hand still in his jacket pocket, he stretched his legs and smiled. In unison, Florent and Elise turned up their noses and stepped back in search of fresh air. In a muffled voice, the old man began, "Let us advance backward, into the past. You will recall, dear young friend, that I first made notice of you on the street, almost a year ago, when was happening an accident to the unfortunate Duchêne that there and then showed me the jewels that dazzled in your soul."

Florent scowled. More energetically now, the old man continued: "Oh yes yes yes, I know the price of men and your price is a very big one, very big, yes, for I've seen much happenings in my life, I've traveled to everywhere, talked to people, many of them! So to myself I said, 'Egon, the days of your youth have melted like butter on toast. You have no sons, alas, so your road must now be taken by another!'"

He leaned forward and pointed a long gnarled finger at Florent. "And so, dear young friend, I have choose *you*. And I will not chose no other man."

Florent felt his scalp shudder. "Some favor!" he sneered. "Thanks to you I lost my restaurant and ended up on the street. And now you're chasing us all over the continent, tormenting us with your cock-and-bull stories. Stinking alley cat! Go offer your love to some other nerd: I've done my share."

Abruptly, Ratablavasky lost his temper. "The restaurant, exactly. I'm here to talk about, but you don't listen! I was cheated! Odiously cheated by Slipskin. His soul is made of garbage and filth, if you want to know what's truth!"

Disgusted, he spat on the ground. "I'll be forever sorry of that. Only his appetite for money is ever working. He did you large wrongs and caused me many sorrows."

Ratablavasky was silent for a moment, lost in thought. "However," he continued, more serene now, "thanks to him you've passed every trial, with high-flying colors. And this is I think magnificent. Without wanting, he gave you the nicest present of all."

What a lunatic, though Florent. I've got it, that's just what he is: a megalomaniac and a sadist. "Okay," he said aloud, "get to the point – we're tired. What exactly do you want from me?"

"I am wanting *for* you, your complete happiness. . . . I want, dear young friend, that you own your restaurant once more and forever. . . . When my humble life is over I want for you to have much much money."

"Not interested. Find some other patsy."

"No, I beg you . . . Think it over carefully. . . . What else remains of a sorry fellow if he can't bequeath . . . Anyway, the plan you're making –"

Florent started. "What plan?"

A sardonic smile came to the old man's lips, making his face almost hideous: "Yes, yes – this afternoon at Sunland Gardens (a delicious name, yes?) I saw the leaves of grapefruit and the plump volume relating, how do you say, cosmic products? Isn't it? So, the guessing is not difficult. . . ."

Stunned, Florent gaped at him, then a wave of vulgar insults came to his lips, and his eyes filled with tears. "Tut, tut," said Ratablavasky, in his element now, "if you allow tempest to enter your mind, decent thoughts will be shipwrecked."

Elise was sobbing. "Go away," she pleaded, "for the love of God, go away."

For a moment, Florent couldn't think. He felt as if he were sinking into the ground. His mouth was filled with the taste of mud, torrents of black mud were raining down all around him, and only the desperate pressure of Elise's hand on his arm kept him from succumbing to unreasonable terror. Ratablavasky, his hands folded on his knees, observed them with his modest, smiling countenance. Florent gradually emerged from his hallucination, but still felt as if his heart was trying to bury itself in his lungs. Then a simple word entered his mind, and he tried desperately to attach it to something. Elise was chilly and shuddering, and he put his arm around her shoulder. "If you ask me, Father (not bad, he thought – my voice is hardly trembling), your immoral behavior is scandalous!"

"What!" said Ratablavasky, starting. "What did you say?"

"I said *Father*," Florent repeated with a venomous smile. "While you've been pursuing your investigations, I've been doing some of my own. Absolutely normal, wouldn't you say? (Thank you, Cousin Octavien, for saving me from Hell.) In fact I've learned a fair amount . . . and repeated some of it to certain people, in the strictest confidence. Of course if anything happened to me, if I were to die, for example, they might feel like saying something . . . or, who knows, paying a visit to Gasquart-les-Moulineaux?"

Ratablavasky, stock-still, had been listening with a look of fascination – or was it fear? The half light made it impossible to see his features clearly.

Florent went on, "To inquire about your piety. And at the same time (go on, try a little bluff), to check into certain, shall we say, *political* matters. You know what I'm talking about, I assume?"

Ratablavasky laughed nervously. "What are these nonsense?"

"Lucky for you if that's all it is. You'll just have to prove it."

While he was talking, Florent had switched on his flashlight. Suddenly he aimed it at Ratablavasky, who was leaning back in his chair with a cocky smile. His clenched hands belied his apparent relaxation, and Florent thought he discerned an attempt to throw him off the track. His chest swelling with fierce joy, he spoke again, his voice trembling, "If an investigation was carried out on *you*, then, as some of my friends have suggested, you'd come out of it smelling like roses. Correct?"

Ratablavasky slowly got to his feet. "Leave the chitter-chatter right here," he said calmly and steadily. "Madame is suffering bigger and bigger uncomfort. But do, I pray, consider carefully my propositions. Today, your hatred for me bubbles like soup, but tomorrow, ah yes, tomorrow it could turn to sweetest love, isn't it? I am not to be fearful. In my life, gentleness has always been my guide! In fact I am humbly sorry I had to take force to make you listen to me . . ." He took his hand from his pocket. ". . . using this cigarette lighter borrowed of a friend. Do please, forgive me!"

There was a cracking sound. Ratablavasky brought his hand to his cheek. "Prick!" Florent shouted, running to catch up with Elise, "that'll teach you to give decent people a hard time!"

"Tee hee! In my youth I acted the same," said the old man playfully, "but the years have corrected me! Good night! Take all the necessary time to rethink things over – and you'll see me again."

When they were back at the cottage, Florent called his aunt and asked her to alert the police. "Cripes!" he muttered, as he hung up. "She's as friendly as a rattlesnake tonight. . . . What's going on? I wonder if the Old Man got to her?"

TWENTY-TWO

After a night's reflection, Florent decided to let his aunt in on his plan to start manufacturing cosmetics. The old lady swore up and down that she'd never met Ratablavasky, and immediately hired two security guards to patrol her property day and night. But she didn't seem very interested in her nephew's project. During the next few days Elise and Florent thought they detected some slight changes in her. She showed them the same gruff cordiality, but her behavior was sometimes marked by a sort of ironic detachment when certain subjects – especially money – were broached. Florent tried several times to bring up his idea for a grapefruit face cream, but Madame Jeunehomme only responded with an enigmatic quip that ended the conversation.

"Old Rat must have got her thinking we're after her money," Florent grumbled. "If only she'd tell me off, I could set her straight."

But his aunt, a sensible businesswoman, avoided what she considered idle chatter so she could devote all her time to her fortune. Florent concluded that they were becoming a nuisance, but when he mentioned going home it angered his aunt, who perhaps saw her doubts confirmed.

"What's got into you? Aren't you enjoying yourselves? And what about Elise? Do you want her to give birth in some vacant lot?"

In fact, Madame Jeunehomme was torn between unhealthy suspicions and the maternal instincts revived by Elise's pregnancy. She wrenched a promise out of Florent to stay in Florida until the delivery. Holding back a sigh, he tucked *The Chemistry of Cosmetics* away in a suitcase and, with a disenchanted air, began to cultivate idleness. The latest defeat had made old wounds flare up: he started dreaming about The Beanery almost every night, awakening Elise with his cries. And whether it was the fatigue of her pregnancy or the horror of their meeting with Ratablavasky, Elise lost her appetite, becoming nervous and irritable and sickly pale.

"Dear child," her aunt said at length, "I don't want to hurt your feelings, but you seem to be fading away before my very eyes. I think you should see a doctor."

"I've been telling her for three days," said Florent, "but I've been wasting my breath."

Madame Jeunehomme turned to Mademoiselle Lydie. "Be a dear and make an appointment for this afternoon with the best obstetrician in Miami. Get cracking – I want to know today what's wrong with this young lady. You see, dear child," she said, pinching Elise's cheek, "I don't like opening the door to grief – it has enough keys without any help from us."

Elise took an immediate liking to Dr. Fingerton, a tall, elderly and fatherly man who looked a bit like Samuel de Champlain – with jaws kept in motion by a huge wad of chlorophyll gum. He examined Elise thoroughly, but could find nothing. He was surprised at her irritability. When she told him about the harassment she and Florent had been enduring, the doctor reassured her as well as he could, recommended plenty of rest, and prescribed a mild tranquilizer. At Madame Jeunehomme's insistence, Elise promised to see the doctor every week.

Shortly after supper one February night, Elise suddenly complained about nausea and sharp abdominal pains.

"I warned you not to eat fruit salad," her aunt scolded. "It took me six months to get used to tropical fruit."

"I should have taken your advice, too," Florent admitted.

He took his wife back to the cottage, helped her to bed, and returned to the hotel for coffee.

"I'd call the doctor if I were you," Mademoiselle Lydie advised.

"Oh, it's just diarrhea. I gave her something. She'll be fine tomorrow."

Then, at Father Jeunehomme's request, Florent spent two deadly hours filing index cards. When he went back to the cottage, the bed was empty. He looked in the living room and the kitchen. Then from the bathroom came a gasping sound. He opened to door and recoiled in horror. Sagged against the wall, a bath towel between her legs, Elise was standing in a pool of blood strewn with dark clots and fragments of pink flesh. She seemed not to see or hear him.

At the Key West hospital, Dr. Fingerton kept repeating, "I can't understand it, I really can't." And after Elise, an intravenous tube in her arm, fell into a bottomless sleep, he grilled Florent, pacing and shaking his head in dismay.

He listened to Florent's account of their run-in with Ratablavasky, delivered in something vaguely resembling

English. The next day, at their aunt's request, Elise was moved to the Dada Hospital Center in Miami, where for three days she was under constant observation. The blood tests showed traces of lead, but no definite conclusion could be drawn. After Madame Jeunehomme nagged the forensic branch of the Miami police for three days, two experts spent an afternoon at the hotel and returned empty-handed. Florent didn't dare tell anyone of his suspicions. Elise would have been terrified. Shortly afterward, she returned to the hotel for her convalescence. The nurse who was waiting for her had been ordered to watch over her day and night. A week later, to everyone's relief, her health seemed to have been restored.

"Now we just have to start another baby," she said, smiling bravely.

Florent touched her shoulder. "If you don't mind me saying so, sweetie, let's wait for the doctor's okay."

The calm at the hotel was short-lived. The opening of the casino, delayed by Madame Jeunehomme's illness, almost didn't take place. One evening in mid-February, Elise and Florent were walking under the arcade between the little pavilion and the main building when a familiar limousine swooshed past. Madame Jeunehomme had had another attack, a serious one. The doctor stayed until dawn, trying vainly to persuade her to go to the hospital, but she agreed only to a nurse. "And make sure she keeps her distance," the old lady insisted feebly. "The less I see of her, the better I'll feel."

Two days later her condition was improving, and she called for Florent. "Don't do anything to upset her," Mademoiselle Lydie whispered as she showed him into her room. "Just having you in the house creates tension."

"Old cow," he muttered, turning the doorknob, "I know you can't stand me."

His aunt was waiting for him in a wheelchair, made up and in her Sunday best; but her hollow cheeks and the shadows around her eyes betrayed her extreme fatigue. "Come in and sit down. I want to talk to you."

It was painful to listen to her faltering, increasingly hoarse voice. On the television in front of her a medical team was about to operate. She pointed to the screen. "I'm learning things," she said, smiling ironically, "and believe me, I have no choice."

She pressed a remote control, and the screen went dark. Florent felt as if something were lodged in his throat. All his rancor against the old lady had dissolved. Sitting very straight, she gave him a defiant look. "Well, now, you must be thinking, the old lady is starting to eye St. Peter. I can't be long now. . . . Let's hope there are no unpleasant surprises in her will."

"No," said Florent. "I like money as much as the next guy, but I don't go hunting inheritances. That's for people who are better than me at that game," he added with a bitter smile.

"Fine. Let's say no more about it. I was joking. I assume you know what's wrong with me?"

Hedging, he said, "Not exactly. Something like your heart or your arteries, I suppose."

"I have angina pectoris, my boy. It's nothing new. But if I don't act" – she paused to catch her breath – "right away, it won't be long before I'm what the doctors call terminal."

She pointed to the wall where the huge volumes of medical encyclopedia stood out. "I went to a lot of trouble to understand exactly what was happening. Doctors are as secretive as old maids." She paused, shutting her eyes, then went on. "I even had a cardiology resident come in to explain certain passages. I understand everything now. I can speak to them as an equal and they know it." Her bloodless lips turned up in a smile of childlike satisfaction. "Do you know what angina pectoris is?"

Shrugging, Florent indicated his total ignorance.

"Very well," she replied, struggling to conceal her growing shortness of breath, "it's the direct and painful expression of paroxysmal myocardial anoxia due to coronary insufficiency. Or, to drop the jargon, it means that one of the arteries that supplies my heart is blocked, and if I make the slightest effort or exert myself, the pain cuts through me like a knife."

Florent struggled against a surge of emotion that filled his throat and nasal cavities with moisture and activated his tear ducts alarmingly.

"And to make matters worse," his aunt continued, "my medical advice has been coming from a bunch of apprentice veterinarians. First they prescribed nitroglycerin, little pills you put under your tongue when the pain starts. The pain went away, but the disease was still there!"

She stopped suddenly, threw back her head, and grimaced. "Shall I go?" Florent asked.

"No," she said impatiently, "stay. Where was I? Two years ago, the little pills weren't enough. They prescribed rest. The disease got worse. For a woman of my disposition, a chaise longue is one step from the grave. So then the drugs began: Vialibran, Persantine, Vastarel, Glyo 5, Sursum, Marsilid, and finally, Cordoxene."

Florent listened, amazed at the list of medications that tripped off her tongue as nonchalantly as the names of perfumes. "As my condition, unfortunately, continued to deteriorate slowly, and I was becoming a walking pharmacy, I decided to take matters into my own hands."

She stopped and took several breaths, exhausted by her monologue. "In a way," she gasped, "I went back to school . . .

to get a better understanding of what was happening to my old carcass. Among other things, I learned that the average survival rate for angina victims was 9.7 years. Mine was diagnosed eleven years ago. You can imagine what that means."

She smiled at him, feeling more and more suffocated but pleased with the effect of her words. Florent held her gaze for a moment, then looked away. "Is it possible to . . . to operate?" he stammered.

"It is. In fact that's my only chance. Myocardial revascularization through implantation in the left ventricle of internal mammary arteries. Sounds pretty, doesn't it? I'll spare you the translation. Straighten my cushion, will you?"

Florent wedged the cushion in behind her back and sat down again.

"Last night, I decided to have the operation no matter what, even though they think I'm too old. That's why I wanted to see you."

She stopped again, growing more exhausted by the minute. Florent, perspiring heavily, was fidgeting.

"As soon as I feel better, I'm going to Cleveland. Apparently Professor Favaloro's team there works miracles. I'll be gone for a few weeks." She shut her eyes and for a long moment didn't speak. Florent grew alarmed.

"Do you need anything, Auntie?"

She smiled, her eyes still shut. "You scare too easily, my boy. Relax – and let me think."

He gazed at her, filled with shy admiration.

"Very well," she said, looking at him with eyes dulled by pain. "If I'd been lucky enough to have a son instead of a reference library, I wouldn't be bothering you. But as it is . . . I'd like you to help Lydie while I'm away. The work must go on. It won't be easy, because, as you're aware, she's none too fond of you, and I'm not sure she even knows how to hold a hammer. She learns quickly, though, and she's been devoted to me for years. If she sees that you're looking after my interests, you won't regret working with her."

Florent got up and patted his aunt's arm. "You can count on me. I'm no contractor, either, but I'll do whatever I can. You've been so kind to . . ."

She covered his mouth with her hand and smiled ironically. "It's not kindness, it's the way things are. . . . A whim, if you will. . . . I'm glad you've said yes. . . . Who knows, it may help me forget your . . . little mysteries."

She raised her forefinger. "I've made no promises, mark you – none at all. And will you *please* sit down. You get on my nerves, standing there like a post."

They chatted for a few minutes, until she asked, more gently, "Would you like some lemonade?"

Florent didn't dare refuse. She rang the bell for the nurse. After Florent had drained his glass, his aunt indicated that the conversation was over. He bent down to kiss her. Offering her cheek, she told him, "There's an old Spanish proverb my father used to say: 'Death is a courteous lady who always knocks before she comes in.' I've heard her knock four times now. . . ." She straightened up. "And I'm going to beat the old girl black and blue to keep her outside that door."

Madame Jeunehomme recovered fairly quickly. After a week, if she was very careful, she could start tending to business. Headstrong as she was, though, her mood didn't change with the return of her strength. The workmen weren't called back immediately. She spent three days in her room with Mademoiselle Lydie, drawing up a detailed plan of what had to be done before the hotel could open. Then she called for Florent.

"I'm leaving tomorrow. Later you'll go over this notebook with Lydie. Everything's spelled out. Lydie has a list of all my suppliers. You'll contact them as necessary. At first they'll try to rob you, which is perfectly normal. Then we'll see if there's any Jeunehomme blood in your veins. Do your best. And meanwhile, I'll be trying to get an extension on my old age."

Next she called Elise, kissed her, and told her she was leaving. "I forbid you to lift a finger for Florent! Rest, be happy, and get ready for another baby, since you want one – which is as things should be."

Florent spent part of the day going over the work schedule with Mademoiselle Lydie. With eyes half-closed in a disdainful expression, she answered his questions with laconic precision, sipping a cup of jasmine tea. Madame Jeunehomme had left nothing to chance. The tasks had been carefully defined to avoid squabbling between her nephew and her assistant. The estimates were attached to notes on the progress of the work and the direction it should take. A long list of tricks used by workers and foremen to steal time or materials appeared as an appendix. Catalogs were crammed with information on the use and durability of materials. At first Florent felt overwhelmed, then he was gradually overtaken by a feverish euphoria. When he took his place at the supper table, a brand new hotel-manager's soul was taking root within him.

Accompanied by her nurse, his aunt left for Cleveland at eight o'clock the next morning. They were driving, as she had been forbidden to fly, in a rented air-conditioned, chauffeur-driven limousine. Though they'd been expressly forbidden to do so, Elise and Florent went to the hotel to see her off. Madame Jeunehomme, standing in the lobby amid a sea of black suitcases, frowned when she saw them. "You young scamps! You know how I hate good-byes! Go on now, give me a kiss and get out of my sight! Where's my son?"

"I looked in his room," said Mademoiselle Lydie huskily, "but he wasn't there."

"Hmmm! He must be saying Mass, thinking I don't leave till tomorrow." She called Florent back and whispered in his ear. "Last night as I was falling asleep I got an idea. I may have an offer for you when I come back. Don't rack your brains trying to guess what it is – it has nothing to do with the hotel. I'm too fond of you to make you my employee."

She went to the door and braved the long flight of stairs while the cook carried out the last of her baggage.

"I hope she finds what she's looking for," Elise murmured as the limousine drove away.

Mademoiselle Lydie stood behind her, dabbing her eyes with her handkerchief.

What kind of offer was she talking about? Florent wondered, playing with the large bunch of keys his aunt had entrusted to him, every clink proclaiming his new authority.

Two hours later the contractor arrived, his mind made up to put her to the test. When he learned that the formidable old lady had been replaced by a tenderfoot, he put in a call to a real estate agent and bought a nice little lot in the Keys, sure that with a few smart moves he'd be able to build a villa there for less than the price of a postcard. Florent started discussing the next phase of the work. An appalling jumble of beams, plaster moldings, diagrams, barrels of nails, and rotating shifts spun in his head. He ended the conversation by telling the man, to Lydie's stupefaction, "Come back in three days. My wife's sick and I have to look after her."

The man looked stunned as he left. Mademoiselle Lydie was fuming. "What's got into you? Do you think you have all the time in the world?"

Florent eyed her scornfully. "You're coming with me, and we're going to check out this goddamn hotel from top to bottom. I like to know what I'm talking about when I give orders."

He took the plans to his aunt's office and spent the rest of the day and part of the night inspecting the hotel, taking notes and measurements, making an inventory of materials, climbing on scaffolding, inspecting ceilings, checking plumbing and trying to pick up the rudiments of the trade with a determination that won even Mademoiselle Lydie's respect. He brought in an old carpenter recommended by his aunt as experienced and honest. He besieged him with questions for ten hours, while plying him with cigars and cold beer.

At the end of the third day, he went to the cottage and told Elise, "Okay, I think I'm ready."

Father Jeunehomme was paying a call. He was on the veranda drinking lemonade and petting Virtue, who was curled up on his lap. "I've some more information about our good friend Ratablavasky. This afternoon I called one of my old professors at Louvain. It was he who gave me the little book I remembered the other day. Unfortunately, I've nothing vital to pass on. Dom Périgord is getting on, and his memory's not what it once was. He vaguely recalled meeting Ratablavasky around 1930. He couldn't quite say why, but he didn't find him especially likeable. But Ratablavasky tried to strike up a friendship and started a correspondence. Dom Périgord still has one of his letters, which he's going to send me. Ratablavasky asked his opinion of a collection of meditations he'd just published. It had an odd title: *A Christian Father Faces the Dawn.*"

"Where could I get a copy?"

"It's been unobtainable for years."

"Let's wait for the letter, then, and we'll see what we can see. I hope you'll excuse me, but I'm ready to drop. I'm going to have a bite and hit the sack."

Embarrassed, the priest got up and extended a long, moist hand. "I'm sorry . . . I should have . . . I . . . I want you to know I appreciate everything you're doing for my mother. You're filling my place. Books have devoured me almost completely, and God has taken what's left."

He said good-bye and strode off through the garden. Florent smiled compassionately after him and then went inside. Elise was already in the cottage, setting the table. "I've made *boeuf à la mode*. It's been simmering since eleven o'clock this morning." She set a plate in front of him and said in a quavering voice, "Please promise you won't wear yourself out with the hotel. I'm so afraid you'll get sick again."

Florent grimaced. "Don't waste your energy worrying about me, sweetheart. I'm in fantastic shape – never felt better in my life."

Having said that he cleaned off his plate in three gulps. The beef hit him as hard as the slaughterhouse club that had readied it for the saucepan. Florent began to nod off and he went to bed, where he was soon sleeping the sleep of the righteous.

The next morning Ladronito, the contractor, was confronted by a remarkably well-informed young man with very precise ideas about how the work was to proceed, who was letting him know with a half smile that he had an intimate knowledge of the inventory of materials and that he'd be checking on how they were being used. The contractor hid his frustration with a respectful smile, swearing to himself that he'd get a villa out of this woebegone building if he had to pull it out one nail at a time.

A work crew arrived at noon. Florent split them up, one group assigned to the top floor of the main tower, the other to the casino, where work had scarcely begun. Two days later, work was proceeding at a good clip, and Ladronito's villa was slowly evaporating in a mist of disenchantment. Florent was losing two pounds a week, but he kept up his good humor. He got up at six, went to bed at midnight, ate on the run, covered ten miles of corridors a day, checking everything, haranguing, shouting, fixing mistakes, and spending most of his evenings going through account books with Elise and Mademoiselle Lydie. Ladronito soon received instructions to hire a second crew, to make up the lost time during Madame Jeunehomme's illness. For sixteen hours a day the hotel rang with hammering, sawing, and the rolling of wheels. Every week a postcard bearing three or four laconic sentences came from his aunt. She invariably told them she was well but, surprisingly, didn't ask once about the work. From this, Mademoiselle Lydie drew bleak conclusions.

Fifty-three people were working on the hotel now. Twenty had to be housed on site, because Ladronito had recruited workmen from as far away as Miami. Florent set up a dormitory on the fifth floor of the main building and hired an assistant cook and two guards.

The workmen's frequent drinking bouts, their habit of using the hotel as one huge ashtray, and the efficiency of the Key West fire department, renowned for its poker parties, caused some concern. A fire extinguisher was installed in every room, and an alarm system in the dormitory. Mademoiselle Lydie threw up her arms at the cost. "Stop whining," Florent said. "I want to show my aunt a brand-new hotel, not a pile of rubble."

One evening toward the end of March, and old plasterer was staggering up the stairs to the dormitory when his attention was caught by a huge palmetto bug on the landing. The insect fixed him with an insolent stare and was all set to attack when it changed its mind and disappeared into a crack. The plasterer frowned, shrugged, pondered, and valiantly resumed his climb, sustained by the rum that had been his sole nourishment for two days. In the dormitory he heaved a sigh of relief and dropped onto his bed, only to get up almost immediately. His ablutions. He'd forgotten his ablutions. Without ablutions, sleep was worthless: he'd have a splitting headache the next morning.

He went to the bathroom, wet a washcloth and stood there, horrified. A stream of palmetto bugs came gushing out of the drain in the sink just ten paces from him. In a second, the insects had overrun the bathroom. The walls were covered with a shuddering mass that emitted a startling sound like thousands of diabolical little ditties. Shaken, but without losing his cool (he'd picked up a fair amount of entomological experience over the years), the plasterer went downstairs and came back with a bottle of kerosene. He poured it down the sink, struck a match, and threw it in.

Moments later, a barefoot Florent was running up the stairs. The fire had spread to the floor below. But a dozen workmen, torn from sleep by the plasterer's screams, were containing it, armed with axes, extinguishers, and wet blankets. In half an hour the fire was under control. Damage, though heavy, was not widespread. Florent made the contractor pay half and promise that the original completion date would be respected.

Three days later, the walls and ceiling in the main hall of the casino had blistered from poor quality paint. The same day, by sheer coincidence, Mademoiselle Lydie discovered a small network of discreet thieves who had been gradually stripping the hotel of its furnishings. Soon afterward, the interior decorator Madame Jeunehomme had hired to supervise the work was poisoned by restaurant seafood.

Florent took the paint supplier into the casino for a private chat that showed off his Jeunehomme blood in all its glory. Two days later the main hall had been restored to its original brilliance. Mademoiselle Lydie and Florent called together all the workmen. After describing the fate of certain period knickknacks and small pieces of furniture, he fired twelve people on the spot. Five were innocent and their rage had an impressive effect on the five guilty ones who hadn't been fingered. Sensing that Florent knew more than they did, they decided to keep their hands to themselves. As for the architect, after an outburst of self-pity, he was replaced by a better one, who, Florent discovered, was willing to work for less.

Some time earlier Madame Jeunehomme had hired a chef and a man to run the casino, who in turn had recruited the croupiers. Mademoiselle Lydie found the rest of the staff. On the evening of April 20, Florent went into her office. She smiled at him over a cup of tea. "I've just hired the last waiter," she announced. "We have all our staff now, and the advertising campaign's set to begin. Now I can stop and catch my breath."

"Only thing missing is the big boss. The decorators have finished, and all the furniture will be in place by noon tomorrow."

He eyed the telephone. Mademoiselle Lydie waggled her forefinger. "You know you aren't allowed to call her. She's working harder than any of us, and she needs to be left in peace."

Madame Jeunehomme arrived home at suppertime two weeks later, lost in the vast limousine. She was pale and very thin, and her skin seemed powdery, but there was a quavery smile of victory on her lips. As Elise and Florent were helping her up the front steps, she murmured, "How did everything work out?"

"I think you'll be proud of Florent," Elise replied. "He even lost some weight."

"It's true, you look exhausted," said his aunt severely. "You should have asked for help. Wasn't Lydie enough?"

"She was an enormous help and we hardly even fought!"

Madame Jeunehomme looked up abruptly. "If it isn't my son, come to meet me! Who dragged you away from your books?"

Father Jeunehomme was awkwardly descending the steps. "I saw you through the window." He kissed her on both cheeks and picked up a suitcase.

"How are you?" he asked fearfully.

"As well as can be expected. For the first time in my life I had excellent, conscientious medical care. The doctors answered all my questions, no one strung me a line, and they looked after me as if the fate of the earth depended on it. I've a fifteen-inch scar on my chest and enough tubes behind my ribs to water the lawns. As for the results . . ."

She waved her hand dubiously. "We have to wait. . . . For the moment, the motor's ticking over. . . . It's all I can ask. . . . Lydie, dear," she said, taking the hands of her assistant, who flushed with pleasure, "I'd like some clear broth and a small tuna salad with plenty of parsley and tomatoes brought up to my room. I'd rather eat alone tonight."

She glanced around. "What am I thinking? You were all eating – go back to the table. Your food's getting cold. I'll rest for a while and then join you in the living room."

She appeared on the stroke of nine, carefully coiffed, wearing an old-rose gown trimmed with lace that, at her age, was rather gaudy. Mademoiselle Lydie served coffee, which they drank in thoughtful silence. The soul of the hotel was back – for a long time, everyone hoped. Madame Jeunehomme, delighted by the affectionate deference being shown her, talked at length about her trip to Cleveland, but was remarkably silent on her stay at the clinic. Her manner was carefree, almost frivolous, as if she wanted to forget the time she'd spent rubbing shoulders with death. Surprisingly, she didn't ask a single question about work on the hotel and wouldn't let the others even mention it. At ten o'clock, visibly exhausted, she got up and took her leave. "My doctor made me promise to go to bed early, because of the journey. I'll see you tomorrow morning. Come to my room for breakfast at eight."

With that, she left the room, wrapped in gazes filled with emotion.

Greeting them the next morning, she said, "Today I don't mind looking in the mirror."

They stood on the threshold, surprised at her good cheer. She seemed to have been rejuvenated overnight. "Stop staring at me like a miracle cure," she said heartily. "Your omelets are ready."

Mademoiselle Lydie was setting a pedestal table by the window. The sun beat down on the white percale cloth, which simmered in the dazzling light. "I can't wait to show you the hotel," Florent said after they'd eaten.

"First the figures," replied his aunt. "You can't expect me to appreciate what you've done till I know the cost."

After they'd spent two hours in her office, the impeccably kept books and Florent's rigid control over the voracious suppliers produced the rarest of gifts, a radiant smile on

Madame Jeunehomme's lips. "Now you can show me the hotel, but don't walk too fast. Lydie, dear, be an angel and ask the cook to hold lunch for a while."

Taking Florent's arm, she set out on her inspection tour, her glasses perched on her nose, ferreting about and bombarding her nephew with trick questions, which he struggled to answer as well as he could, surprised and almost offended by her lack of confidence. Now and then, impassive, she would pat his arm in a sign of pleasure. Suddenly, after silently striding through the huge casino, she said, "You've done a good job, my boy, I won't deny it. Even better than I'd hoped. My architect outdid himself."

"I had to help him a bit: he died three weeks before he was to finish his plans."

"What? How did that happen?"

"Poisoned shellfish. They took him to the hospital, but it was too late."

Madame Jeunehomme rolled her eyes, indignant. "Can you imagine! Shellfish at this time of year! Poor idiot – he wasn't even forty! Life meant nothing to him. . . . He deserved what he got."

She continued her inspection in the restaurant. Through a row of large, high windows, harsh light poured onto the solemn, stuffy Victorian decor. Her brow was furrowed in vexation. "When are you putting up the drapes? It looks like a railway station."

"Tomorrow afternoon. I had a hell of a time finding them."

She stroked the claw-footed mahogany tables, gave a satisfied nod at the carved chairs upholstered in crimson velvet. ("With furniture like that I can ask two dollars for pickles," she snickered to herself.) They went into the kitchen.

"Very nice," she said, impressed by the layout. "I didn't think it was so big. You didn't skimp a bit on the plans, did you?"

"Absolutely not, Auntie. I did take the liberty of stepping up the air-conditioning. My friend Picquot drilled into me that heat is the worst enemy of fine food . . . not to mention . . ."

"Don't wear out your vocal cords, dear boy. I'm so pleased with you that you could persuade me a gaffe was a stroke of genius." She squeezed his arm and said, "This is going to be one of my best summers. My old bones and this pile of stones will get back in shape together. And to crown it all, I've found I have a nephew I can trust."

Here it comes, thought Florent. Payoff time.

"What are your plans? Do you intend to stay on much longer? For heaven's sake, don't look at me like that! I'm not sending you away, you know that. I just want to know how you see your future."

Florent shrugged, his face darkening. "I don't know . . . I haven't really thought . . ."

"I repeat: don't expect me to make you my manager. It wouldn't be doing you a favor. At your age you'd be bored silly in a place like this. Drink would become a problem or you'd start scheming to take away my property, which isn't much better. Oh yes! I've been around, you know, and one thing I've learned – there's nothing more unfair than treating ordinary mortals like angels."

Tired from speaking, she looked for a chair. Finding none, she went into the dining room. In a somewhat muffled voice she said, "Any idiot knows not to mix business and family. It's asking for trouble. At least that's how I see it. I'd rather hire strangers. If they don't work out, I show them the door and that's the end of it."

She stood up and pinched his chin, smiling. "Disappointed?"

"Not in the least," said Florent, half sincerely. "I really enjoyed working on your hotel but I don't see myself spending my life yelling at waiters. And I can't pretend I'd want to spend the rest of my life in Florida. I'd actually miss winter."

Mademoiselle Lydie appeared in the arched doorway between the restaurant and the casino and gestured to Florent. "The drapery supplier wants to talk to you."

As he walked away, his aunt mused, "I have a hunch he'll soon be wanting to get his fingers wrapped around a suitcase handle."

She called him back. "I wouldn't want you to get the wrong idea about me. I can give out rewards when they're deserved. Spend the summer here. The hotel doesn't open till September. I'd be crazy to go to a lot of fuss in the off-season. You have your wits about you, you and Elise. You can give me some ideas for the grand opening."

For a few days, Florent hesitated, then let himself be talked into staying, partly out of inertia, partly in the hope that by taking very good care of his aunt, he'd win her over, for he was still trying to launch his cosmetics project. But he was quickly disappointed.

About mid-August he had Virtue vaccinated in preparation for leaving, since Elise wouldn't dream of parting with the dog. They cast furtive glances at the suitcases stashed away in the closet. Elise bought gifts for friends and family. Florent was itching for his reward, but his aunt seemed to have given it no more thought than Sir George Etienne Cartier's rompers. The priest, seeing his mother's relatively good health, mentioned going back to Montreal. He missed his library. His mother offered to have part of it shipped to Key West. He shook his head awkwardly, twiddling his fingers. It was obvious to everyone but his mother that what he really missed was the solitude of his own small room. All that was keeping him in Key West was the imminent arrival of Ratablavasky's letter to Dom Périgord. The mystery surrounding the old crook was tormenting him almost as much as poor Gogol's last works.

While Dom Périgord, crippled with arthritis, sneezed his way through dusty piles of paper in search of the letter, Aurélien Picquot was making decisions. Toward the end of August he wrote to Florent, announcing that he would be visiting them soon. The letter went on:

> So much for the good news. I'm weary of having two thousand miles between us. At such a distance friendship's not worth cat shit. I wish I would have been there to comfort poor Elise during her frightful ordeal. You say your aunt's hotel's about to open. I'll take a room, and she can treat me like just another guest.
>
> And now that I've given you some pleasant news, on to sorrier matters. Our common enemy is prospering. The Beanery has been enlarged. Horror of horrors, the menu's bilingual! And to top it all off, on September 15 our Anglo is taking a bride. Or so I read in *Le Clairon du Plateau*. As for the old alley cat, thank heaven he hasn't shown his muzzle for months. I'll tell you shortly when I will be coming.

"Nothing about Monsieur Emile?" Elise asked.

Florent shook his head and stood there pensively. Then he said, "Too bad about Dom Périgord's letter, but we're clearing out day after tomorrow. I'll tell Picquot to stay put. It's time to go home. I've had ants in my pants for a week now."

Elise gave him a look full of questions and concern.

"Don't worry. I haven't the slightest urge for a fight with Slipskin. All I want is peace. If only my aunt would give us a little something for our two months' work, I would look for a job and not have to worry where our next meal's coming from."

Don't complain, Elise told herself. She's the one who pulled you out of the doldrums.

He announced their departure during supper, hoping to stir up his aunt's generosity. But her wallet stayed shut as she observed, "Pity you're leaving so soon. You'll miss the grand opening. The hotel will be full of artists and bigwigs. I've even snaffled the governor of Florida. Well, they say there's no cure for homesickness. I'll have a crate made for Virtue, something to remind her of her doghouse, if she ever had one."

She looked at the animal lying by the table. Virtue's good manners and goodwill had finally won over the old lady, whose stay at Professor Favaloro's clinic seemed to have opened hidden floodgates. It was no small victory to have won access to the dining room at mealtime. Virtue knew it, and didn't abuse the privilege, snapping up any food that people were good enough to drop for her, but careful not to beg.

Father Jeunehomme, enthusiastic at his mother's idea of a doghouse, offered to supervise the work and, on the eve of their departure, decided that a great contribution to the peace of mind of the poor animal, who would be terrified by the sound of the plane, would be a photograph of Marcel Proust. This he tacked inside, next to the window. It showed the writer, in his forties, slumped in a wicker chair on a sun-drenched portico, his hands on a walking stick. Lying at his feet, wide-eyed, muzzle between his paws, was a dog that looked like a carbon copy of Virtue. "In their own way," said the priest, "animals can think. I'm sure that in an hour or two she'll grasp the significance of the scene, and it will fortify her in a way we humans can't imagine."

Madame Jeunehomme gave her son a worried look, asking herself if he had lost his mind altogether.

Later that evening, she called Elise and Florent to her office. "I've a favor to ask you. My son will be going back to Montreal soon. I'd like you to visit him now and then. I know he's not the life of the party, but you might be able to tear him away from his daydreams for a while. I've been watching the poor boy; he's completely losing touch with reality, and there's nothing I can do."

She touched Elise's arm. "Your husband's head is full of plans, I know. Perhaps it will slip his mind, so I'd like you to look after my son. I'm sure you understand these things." Elise, very moved, gave her word. "Excellent. That's one thing settled. Let's say no more about it."

Madame Jeunehomme opened her desk drawer and took out an envelope. "This is for your airfare, and a little something to show my gratitude."

A hungry light gleamed in Florent's eyes as he took the envelope. "I have a thousand things to do tomorrow," his aunt went on, "but I'll take you to the airport – if you like."

Florent walked down the hallway holding the open envelope. "Tightwad! Seven hundred dollars! Seven hundred dollars for working my guts out for two months! If I'd known, I'd never have busted my ass."

The plane was due to take off at four o'clock. They spent the morning preparing to leave. At half-past ten, Father Jeunehomme went to the cottage to take down their Montreal address. "I'll be leaving soon, too. We can study Dom Périgord's letter together, when it finally arrives."

About one o'clock Madame Jeunehomme's old limousine pulled up in front of the door, the cook at the wheel, happy as a child with a bag of candy. Everyone got in. Virtue, all aquiver with foreboding, kept padding back and forth on the back seat. Florent did his best to conceal his disappointment, but his attempts at politeness didn't fool anyone. From time to time his aunt gave him a furtive glance and a bantering smile.

On the way to Miami they had a flat. Madame Jeunehomme raged at the cook, putting him in such a state that Florent had to change the tire, and they got to the airport fifteen minutes before takeoff. Florent rushed up to the wicket. "But your tickets are paid for," said the clerk, pushing away the money Florent offered him.

"Paid for? Who did that?"

He turned to his aunt, who was looking on in amazement. The clerk leafed through a register. Florent was growing impatient. "Come on, there must be a mistake! Hurry up. Our plane's about to leave."

The clerk looked up, turned the register around, and pointed to the middle of a page.

"Egon Ratablavasky," said Florent, stunned.

Elise brought her hands to her mouth to stifle a cry. "Screw him and his fucking tickets!" Florent yelled.

The clerk stared at him, aghast.

"Calm down," said Madame Jeunehomme, drawing them aside. "You children have been my guardian angels and there'll always be a place in my house for you, in good times or bad. Seven hundred dollars isn't much for all you did, I agree. No, Florent, don't deny it, you know I detest hypocrisy. . . . But that was just a token. I've another gift that I'm happy to give you, even though I know it'll cause you trouble."

He gave her a suspicious look. "I'm talking about my citrus plantation," she went on with a mischievous smile. "You've been dreaming about it for months – don't think I haven't noticed. I'm giving it to you, but on one condition . . ."

She stopped, obviously enjoying keeping him in suspense. "On condition that you get your restaurant back. On your own. That's the catch. Understand? If not, forget it."

Virtue, trembling all over, huddled in one corner of her doghouse, stunned by the roaring of the plane. In the half light she looked miserably at the photograph Father Jeunehomme had pinned on the wall. The face of the frail sickly man in the picture seemed to be shuddering as he sat in the blazing sun; at any moment he would throw his cane in the air and howl in terror.

TWENTY-THREE

From the surly sky a dismal rain pissed down on Montreal. The door to the baggage compartment clattered open, and Virtue and her box were flung onto a cart that reeked of fresh paint. A sudden gust of humid air engulfed her. She yelped plaintively and shuddered. Trying to understand what was happening to her had made her nauseated.

Twenty minutes later she got into a taxi and jumped onto Elise's lap. During the drive she sat with her muzzle against the window, gazing stupefied at this strange city bereft of sun and palm trees, where all the dogs seemed to be in a hurry, as if they had serious problems to solve.

In the apartment on Emery Street, Rosine had just put a chicken in the oven for supper, while Ange-Albert was in the shower, producing amazing variations on a Gilles Vigneault song. It wasn't long before the chicken reacted in a very interesting way to its contact with the heat. A many-layered aroma that moved from paprika through the exquisite scent of basil blossomed in its flesh, caressing Rosine's sense of smell and even gliding into the bathroom. Ange-Albert pulled on his pants and rushed out, nostrils aquiver.

Meanwhile Elise and Florent were on the sidewalk, gaping at the huge wooden struts holding up the left side of their apartment building. Where the adjoining building had once stood was now a vacant lot.

Ange-Albert opened the oven door. "I think it's done."

Rosine laughed. "Hands off! It'll be another hour."

Neither suspected they'd hardly get a taste of the precious bird, one of shy Rosine's first culinary successes, but the front door suddenly clattered and voices rang out on the stairs. "It's Florent!"

Ange-Albert ran to let them in. A haggard Virtue streaked between his legs and hid under a bed. The front room was filled with joyous exclamations. Little wet smacks were exchanged. Florent smiled at Rosine. "You're prettier than ever," he said, looking her over like a budding matinée idol.

Ange-Albert showed them around the apartment, which, under Rosine's influence, was beginning to look quite stylish. Rosine went back to her cooking, but in her excitement she'd sprouted ten thumbs. Elise helped make a salad and peeled some extra potatoes. Then they all gathered round the table where the chicken disappeared as if by magic, almost before it touched their plates.

Ange-Albert had left the manufacturer of religio-erotic statues, whose queer ways had become intolerable: suffering from some odd remorse, he forced his employees to hear Mass every morning – at his church so he could check attendance. After a few weeks of unemployment Ange-Albert had got a sales job at Draperies Georgette, a yard goods shop at the Plaza St-Hubert. As for Rosine, through prayers and subterfuge she'd managed to leave home with her parents' partial blessing. She worked for her father three nights a week and was taking courses at the CEGEP du Vieux-Montréal.

"What about Monsieur Emile?" Elise asked. "Any word from him?"

Rosine smiled wearily. "And how! He comes over the minute his mother leaves for the club. He should arrive any moment."

"Madame Chouinard's paying for a baby-sitter now," said Ange-Albert. "For the past two months. Ever since the night we had to take the kid to the hospital."

"The hospital!" Elise exclaimed. "What happened?" Ange-Albert stretched his legs and yawned. "Who knows."

"He gets mad if we dig," Rosine added.

"Of course we all have a pretty good idea. Hey, here he is."

An elephantine gallop shook the walls, reducing the life expectancy of the staircase. The door hit the wall and Monsieur Emile roared in, all smiles; his hands were grubby and his jeans were ripped, but his steam engine T-shirt was surprisingly clean. He came to a dead halt on the doorstep, gaping at Elise and Florent. "Holy shit! You're back! You sure were gone a long time!"

Elise held out her arms. He flung himself at her and fiercely clung to her thighs. "You were gone so long!" he repeated, his voice slightly weepy but under control. "You didn't even send me any postcards." Then suddenly freeing himself, he asked, "Where's my present?"

Florent guffawed. "You don't waste time on preliminaries, do you?"

Elise led the child by the hand into the bedroom. She crouched in front of a suitcase, then held out a cardboard box. "A suit to wear under*neath* the water!" the child exclaimed ecstatically.

"No. Just the flippers, mask and snorkel. You'll get the suit when you're bigger."

Monsieur Emile wanted to test it right away in the bathtub, but Florent managed to talk him out of that by promising to take him to the municipal swimming pool the next day. For now, he was satisfied to walk around in his underwear with his new gear, giving everyone a chance to note that Madame Chouinard paid more attention to her clients than to her son's intimate apparel. Elise judged the moment was right to try to shed some light on what was happening to their young protégé. "Does your mother let you come here every night, Monsieur Emile?"

"Sure."

"Your mother – or your baby-sitter?"

Monsieur Emile stopped parading around and looked at Elise in frustration. "Oh sure, my baby-sitter. She doesn't give a shit about me. She's too busy necking!" He burst out laughing and ran crazily around the apartment as Elise and Florent exchanged signals.

There was a surprised exclamation from the bedroom. Virtue, who had just decided to come out of hiding, was making her way toward Monsieur Emile.

"Hey, is that your dog? Where'd you get it?" He took a few steps, slapping his flippers on the floor as hard as he could. "What a weird-looking mutt."

Virtue stood hanging her head, a pleading look in her eyes as she tried to mollify this strange creature. The voice sounded human but the huge shiny feet, the single eye at the top of the face, and that odd threatening horn rising above the head. . . . Fear won out over her desire to please and a little puddle spread across the floor. Virtue gazed at it, terribly embarrassed. Monsieur Emile ran to the kitchen and came back with a rag and a hunk of raw beef. Immediately, the dog forgot her passing weakness. Flippers, goggles and snorkel seemed quite harmless, and she even allowed herself an irritable yelp when the child tired of his game and stopped parading between bedroom and fridge.

"What's her name?" he asked Florent. "Virtue? That's a dumb name for a dog. Here," he said enthusiastically, picking up the dog by her paws. "Come and meet my cat. He'll claw your stupid face!"

Ange-Albert had phoned Picquot to tell him his friends were back. "Don't move, I'll be there in a jiffy!" said the chef in a shaky voice. Five minutes later he knocked at the door. "My friend!" he exclaimed, flinging open his arms, and Florent felt the air sucked out of his lungs as if he'd been sitting under a bell jar. Then the chef looked delightedly at Elise. "Sweet girl – the Florida sun did wonders for you!" Then all his volcanic impulsiveness poured into a gallant kiss of Elise's hand that briefly brought back seventeenth-century France.

The spell was broken by Virtue's arrival. Picquot frowned. "What *is* this horror?"

"This horror," Elise said, annoyed, "is our dog, Virtue."

"Which is her front? Which is her behind? This animal is utterly incomprehensible. Only in America could such a mongrel be created. She seems to have an extra paw."

Florent picked up the dog and stroked her. "Whatever you say, Monsieur Picquot, my friend. But she's an exquisite creature, sly as an imp, and I hope you'll make us happy by loving her just a little."

"Why not?" the chef muttered, gazing at the animal with distaste. He leaned over and whispered a few words in Ange-Albert's ear that sent him down the stairs four at a time. He returned bearing a cardboard box, which he set on the kitchen table. From it Picquot took two magnums of champagne and an immense Paris-Brest. "Hee hee!" he giggled, delighted at the expressions of wonder all around him. "Old Picquot may be a miserable so-and-so, but he's not afraid to show his feelings." To Rosine he said, "Be an angel and fix me a cup of my vile herbal tea."

Elise took his hands. "You can't . . ."

"No, kitten," Picquot replied, slightly inebriated by the presence of two pretty women, "my doctor forbids any alcohol whatsoever for another eight months and seventeen days, on pain of medical excommunication."

Florent held out a magnum. "Do us the honor, at least, of popping the first cork."

At once a pontifical expression spread across the face of the chef, who slowly reached for the Veuve Cliquot. A few seconds later the downstairs neighbor rushed to his fuse box, positive the electricity in his apartment had just been blown to kingdom come, while Virtue took refuge in a soup kettle at the back of a cupboard. "*Voilà*. Now let's fill your glasses. Champagne stimulates the mind and makes for noble thoughts."

As Ange-Albert, slumped in an old armchair purchased from the Salvation Army a few weeks before, was beginning his third piece of Paris-Brest, Florent asked, "When did they demolish next door?"

"Last week."

"I had a look at the left side of the building: it's about had it! Don't you feel like getting out?"

Angle-Albert had a long stretch and let a belch slip into his clenched fist. "For one or two little cracks? No big deal." He drained his glass in one gulp. As intoxication crept over him, his eyelashes seemed to grow longer, and his face assumed an Oriental look.

Picquot finally accepted a glass. "All right, just this once – but only a drop. After all, it's not every day we celebrate such a reunion."

A few minutes later he popped the second cork. This time the downstairs neighbor, thinking there'd been an assassination attempt on the street, stood guard at his window, wide-eyed and sweating.

The conversation in the front room had turned to Slipskin and Ratablavasky. A livid Picquot, who had just heard about the strange incident with the airplane tickets, brandished a fist. "If I had my Browning or even a Mauser, I'd get rid of that white-haired trash! Do you know what I think, Florent?"

He faced his young friend, eyes wild, shirt half out of his trousers. "I think we're dealing with a *madman*, who should be treated accordingly. Slipskin must be aware of it, too, which accounts for his strength. He got rid of Old Rat, wasn't impressed by his threats – and now look at him! He runs the restaurant, pockets the profits, cuddles his sweet wife – and soon we'll have six more little Slipskins, all as crooked as their father, each with a restaurant and well-lined pockets. And yet, with just a bit of courage, those Slipskins could be replaced by Boissonneaults. Don't you agree?"

Florent grimaced and left the room. Perhaps I went too far, thought the chef. The wound's still raw. Hold your tongue, you blazing idiot, your brain is turning to mush.

He found Florent at the kitchen window, arms folded, seemingly lost in melancholy thought. "The champagne betrayed me," Picquot told him. "This time I went too far."

Florent turned around, furious. "No you didn't! What you said was true, goddamn it! Now don't back down!"

"How will this end?" Picquot murmured pensively, huddled in the back seat of a taxi, as Elise and Rosine cleaned up and Ange-Albert drained the second magnum while he and his friend Florent had a serious talk.

All night, Messrs. Pinchbrain and Butwrench wreaked havoc throughout the apartment, taking delight in multiplying sinister dreams filled with suffocating vapors. At 756 Gilford Street, Monsieur Emile smiled and snored in his grimy little bed under the watchful eye of his cat. On the stroke of eight the next morning, he knocked at Florent's door. Rosine let him in. "Gee, you look ugly!" he reproached her. "Tie one on last night?"

"Ssshh – you'll wake everybody up. What do you want?"

"Florent's taking me swimming," he replied, surprised at the question. "He promised yesterday."

After trying unsuccessfully to make the child come back later, she put him in the kitchen where a deal was struck: one hour of total silence in exchange for permission to fix his own breakfast, whatever and as much as he wanted. As he was tearing into his eighth slice of toast and maple butter (somewhat more of the latter than the former), Monsieur Emile noticed Virtue watching him suspiciously. "Here, doggie," he whispered, smiling slyly.

Virtue wagged her tail but held out for a guarantee. A slice of toast did the trick. She came up to her benefactor and put a paw on his knee. Monsieur Emile petted her, while racking his brain for some mean trick that wouldn't make her bark. He jumped off his chair, went to the fridge, then to the pantry, and came back with a piece of raw beef sprinkled with cayenne. Puzzled, Virtue gazed at the meat. The combined smells of pepper and beef presented a dilemma worthy of Corneille. Finally she plucked up her courage, opened her mouth, and snapped up the meat. Then she started trotting around so frenetically that in three minutes the entire household was awake. When Florent came into the kitchen he found Monsieur Emile innocently cutting out pictures of cars from an old newspaper. Yawning, Florent said, "Just let me have a coffee, and we'll go to the pool."

The building on Ontario Street struck Florent as a miniature man-made Florida: the heat, the steam, the easygoing atmosphere. A huge polyethylene palm tree in one corner completed the effect. The forebodings that had overpowered him since his return to Montreal condensed into three droplets in the middle of his forehead. Florent shook them off and ground them under his heel.

Half an hour later, after swallowing gallons of water, Monsieur Emile was looking up delightedly at a dozen hairy legs splashing above his head. As soon as they were outside he begged Florent to bring him back that afternoon. "No way. I have to drop in on my parents – I haven't seen them for months."

An extraordinarily clear image of a scoop of ice cream accompanied by chocolate cookies and a glass of 7-Up lit up in Monsieur Emile's mind. "Take me with you," he whined. "Please, Florent!"

"Philippe!" Madame Boissonneault shrieked, as if the stove had just sunk through the floor. "Elise and Florent are coming down the street – with a little boy!"

Her husband sprang up from his nap, almost knocking over a chair on his way out of the bedroom. "Adoption?" he muttered, his thoughts in a muddle. "They could have told us. As long as it's not a little nigger."

Monsieur Emile endured being kissed, questioned, teased about this and that, lifted up, weighed, complimented on his steam engine T-shirt. He politely answered Monsieur Boissonneault's boring questions, stoically endured his dumb jokes, and even deigned to say a few words about his cat. Then and only then did he let it be known that his stomach felt somewhat empty.

As Florent's mother was preparing a snack, his father took him aside. "I've got a suggestion for you," he said gravely. "I don't suppose you have a job?"

Unable to hide his irritation, Florent shook his head.

"Well, as it happens, I just heard – there'll be a good opening at the Prudential next week, in the –"

"Look, Dad, you know I can't stand office work. Why keep pushing it?"

Monsieur Boissonneault blushed violently, and his face looked bloated. "All right, all right. I just thought, while you were waiting . . . You don't have to tell them . . ."

Florent kept shaking his head. "Okay, have it your way," said his father. "After all, I'm not in your shoes, you have your own life to live, and I'll mind my own business." Inwardly he thought, Calm down, Philippe, calm down.

He turned on his left leg, snapped his suspenders and, with a wan smile, went over to Elise. "How's my girl? Did you toast your lovely bottom in the sun?"

Elise and Florent gave a detailed account of their vacation, carefully omitting the Ratablavasky episode, answering the many questions about their aunt.

"I may pay her a visit when the yacht's finished."

"How's it coming?" Florent asked.

Slightly embarrassed, his father cleared his throat and replied that the work was nearly done, but the size of the boat would necessitate certain minor adjustments. "I may have to widen the cellar door a little to get her out," he said, pretending not to notice his wife's pained expressions. "Just half a day's work."

Monsieur Emile tore downstairs to the cellar, followed by Florent, who grew pensive when he saw the size of the yacht. He went back to the kitchen, chatted for a few minutes, then looked at his watch and said, "We have to go now."

"Come for supper next Sunday," said his mother as she helped Elise into her coat. "We hardly had a chance to talk."

When Florent's parents were alone, his father grumbled, "We can be glad we've just got one son. Must've had rusty nuts when I made that one!"

That one? his wife wondered as she rinsed the dishes. Are there others?

Florent and Monsieur Emile got into the habit of going to the swimming pool every day. On the way home they sometimes stopped to look in the window of an antique store that had enough bricabrac to stun an auctioneer. One day, amid a jumble of knickknacks, umbrella stands, and old telephones, Monsieur Emile spotted an honest-to-goodness velocipede. Then and there, he developed an irresistible need to be enlightened on the development of the bicycle over the years. They went inside. The shop seemed deserted. There was a faint peppery smell in the air. Florent smiled knowingly. Monsieur Emile, eyes wide with amazement, hovered around the strange object, upsetting things as he passed, and even tried to mount it, despite Florent's orders. Then a voice behind them said, "Try it if you want."

Florent turned. A young man was smiling at them. His café-au-lait complexion and long black mustache that drooped on either side of a bony chin gave him the look of an Assyrian high priest. Returning his smile, Florent said, "No thanks – we're just looking."

"Come on, come on," said the antique dealer, his voice remarkably soft and sweet. "I don't give a damn if you buy it or not. . . . Is he your kid?" he added, pointing at Monsieur Emile, who was eyeing him derisively.

"No, he's my friend."

"That's good, very good," said the antique dealer, as if to himself. "Everyone should be friends."

Florent's gaze fell on a yellowing photograph of a farmer in his Sunday best, gaze fixed, chin out, who sat on a cane-bottomed chair with a missal on his knees. The antique dealer's face contracted in an expression of intense love as he stroked the photograph with his fingertips.

Holy horseradish! Florent thought. What the hell's a guy like this doing in the system?

"I could let you have a good price on it," said the dealer, pointing to the velocipede. "I think we paid less than five bucks."

"Five bucks!"

"Mm-hmm – last month my friend Robert found a *remarkable* place . . ."

The word *remarkable* stretched through the air like a piece of rubber. The antique dealer was silent for a moment, eyes half shut, a gentle smile on his lips, probably meditating on the remarkable qualities of his friend Robert – or on the beauty of the adjective itself.

"Hey, Florent, c'mon," whined Monsieur Emile, who was getting bored.

The antique dealer continued. "The people treat you fine, as long as you're decent to them. Money?" His right hand traced a slow curve, that sent this ridiculous question to the edge of infinity. "They aren't interested. They live close to nature . . . know what's important."

"Hey, Florent, c'mon," Monsieur Emile repeated a half-tone higher.

"Too bad it's so far away. Our truck just packed it in. Transmission's shot."

"Where is this place?"

"Eastern Townships – around Sainte-Romanie."

"Come *on*!" the child exploded, pulling Florent's hand. Florent casually asked two or three more questions, eyes riveted on the photograph of the farmer, which he seemed to admire intensely. In the end he actually bought it, said good-bye to the dealer, then looked around for Monsieur Emile, who'd developed a sudden interest in a collection of shaving brushes that had belonged in the nineteenth century to an American senator.

Back at the apartment, they found Elise going through the Help Wanted ads. She looked at Florent and said, "You look weird."

"Really?"

"It's 'cause he swallowed some water in the swimming pool," declared Monsieur Emile.

"Go get your cat. I want to see him. You promised to bring him this morning."

Monsieur Emile dashed to the door. Elise sighed. "Lord, that staircase isn't long for this world."

Ten minutes later, Monsieur Emile burst in on his mother, who was enjoying her midday breakfast. "Where d'you think you're going?" she asked, fumbling in her negligée for a flask of rum to fortify her coffee.

Meanwhile, on Emery Street, Elise was confronting her husband. "I'm positive you're keeping something from me. Did you run into Ratablavasky?"

"For Christ's sake, stop nagging!"

"All right, fine." She left the kitchen. Florent found her on the bed, crying. He tried to apologize but the effect was ten times worse than his outburst. He stood there, arms dangling, watching her shaken by sobs, her head buried in the pillow.

She gradually calmed down and said, "I'm sorry, but I feel as if I'm losing my mind. Since we've been back I'm a nervous wreck. I keep thinking he'll show up at any minute and –"

The door slammed into the wall and Monsieur Emile shouted, breathless, "Elise! Where are you? Come and see – I got him!"

"Hang on," Florent grumbled, "we're coming." He shut the bedroom door. Vexed, Monsieur Emile made a face and dropped his cat on the floor with a resounding plunk. In the kitchen, Virtue rose and perked up her ears.

"Cheer up, old girl," Florent murmured. "We'll soon have those bastards out of our hair, I promise." He smoothed her hair. "I'm working on something."

Elise's tears dried up instantly. "I thought so," she said, with a victorious smile.

A howl of pain followed by a peal of laughter sent him out of the bedroom. "She wanted to lick him," Monsieur Emile explained, "but Breakfast can't stand that. So tough luck!"

Breakfast, back arched, whiskers stiff, was shooting looks of loathing at the quivering dog huddled in a corner, torn between urges to bark, play, bite, and flee.

Elise picked up the cat. "Where's your manners? You'd think you were raised in a garbage can."

The doorbell rang. "I'll get it!" said Monsieur Emile. He

went to the landing and pulled the cord that unlocked the front door.

At the foot of the stairs a man asked, "Is your father there?" The child turned to Florent, an indefinable look on his face. Footsteps started slowly up the stairs. Elise turned pale and set the cat down at her feet.

"Telegram," announced a pudgy man. He took a deep breath, smiled ingenuously and added, "For Florent Boissonneault. Sign here please."

It was from Father Jeunehomme.

ARRIVE MONTREAL TOMORROW. IMPORTANT REVELATIONS ON CERTAIN PERSON. REQUEST SMALL FAVOR: PURCHASE RECENT EDITION UNPUBLISHED CORRESPONDENCE TURGENEV-VIARDOT. LIKELY AVAILABLE CHAMPIGNY OR LEMEAC. WILL REIMBURSE ON ARRIVAL. KINDEST REGARDS TO YOUR WIFE.

Florent was delighted. "Terrific! I'll put the squeeze on the old bugger yet!" He paced the room, folding and unfolding the telegram, then called, "Monsieur Emile, I want you to do something for me."

The child felt as if his whole body had been stroked by a velvet glove. Flushed with pleasure he asked, "What is it?"

"Does your mother get *Le Clairon du Plateau*?" The child gaped in surprise. "You know, the paper where Monsieur Gladu works."

"You mean the guy that his wife hits him over the head 'cause he runs after other women?"

"That's the one!" said Florent, laughing. "Okay, ask your mother if I can borrow the last issue, if she's got it, and bring it here this afternoon."

"I can bring you all you want – we got piles of them."

"Florent, what you are cooking up?" Elise asked urgently when they were alone. "Come on, tell me. Your secrets are getting on my nerves."

Reluctantly, he said, "I may have a plan."

"Like what?"

"I've got a hunch, and if my hunch is right there's money in it – lots of money. If I move fast."

Thank God, she thought, at least he wants to work again. She clutched his hand. "What is it? Stop talking in riddles."

"There's nothing definite yet. I wanted to keep it a surprise till tomorrow. But – oh hell! I've said too much already. I'm thinking . . ." He paused, then with an air of self-importance, continued. "I'm thinking of going into the antique business."

On Elise's face a dark O opened, from which no sound emerged.

"Don't look at me like that," Florent snarled. "I may have discovered a gold mine. In the Eastern Townships, in the middle of nowhere, and the dealers don't know about it. But I'll have to check it out. Seems hard to believe."

"But where does Rosario Gladu fit in?"

Florent planted himself in front of her, arms folded. "That's the second phase of my plan. I don't want what happened to my restaurant and my cosmetics project to happen again. So I've decided to put an end to this business with Old Rat. Gladu may have some dope on him – and on his fight with Slipskin. Besides, I have the feeling that since Slipskin got married he doesn't hang around with Gladu so much. They may have had a falling-out, too – all the more reason for a word with him."

"Where does *Le Clairon* come into it?"

"How should I know? But if they've had a fight it may show up between the lines. Those rags are all the same." Florent went to the kitchen, opened a can of beer, and drained it in two gulps. "Now I'm going to try and find that book for my dear cousin."

"I'll come, too. I don't want to stay here alone."

While they were on the bus, discussing sideboards and diamond-point armoires, Breakfast and his unwilling companion arranged a truce: the dog was allowed to remain ten feet away, as long as she kept perfectly still.

TWENTY-FOUR

Monsieur Emile's inspection of the apartment yielded eighteen issues of *Le Clairon*, seven *La Voix de Rosemont*, a dozen assorted circulars, twenty Molson bottle caps, several dusty Kleenexes, and – the best surprise of all – a box of paper clips and two boxes of rubber bands. In a flash of inspiration he took a pair of pliers and split some paper clips into a quantity of sharp-tipped U's. Then, armed with a rubber band, he performed a test on a wall of the vestibule. Six of the fourteen U's shattered the plaster, and two sank surprisingly deep into the wall. He ran to his bedroom and pushed the window up a few inches, carefully opening as little as possible the grayish cretonne curtains that guaranteed him total privacy. The window looked onto the street. A few minutes passed. Monsieur Emile was shaking with impatience. Suddenly Gugusse Tremblay appeared on the sidewalk, hands on his hips, making caustic remarks to a little girl on the other side of the street, remarks that mostly had to do with the size and state of cleanliness of her ass.

Since the previous Wednesday, Gugusse had been ranked among Monsieur Emile's mortal enemies. That day he had been playing in a block of abandoned houses with Gugusse and little Linda Bibeault. About three o'clock, after they'd shattered thirty windows and kicked down several doors, Monsieur Emile felt the awakening of a passionate interest in biology. He took Linda into a bathroom, dropped his pants and politely asked her to pull down her panties. Moreover, at his invitation the little girl performed some simple touching, the effect of which filled her with wondrous stupefaction and certain envy. Monsieur Emile had been in the process of repaying her good deed when Gugusse opened the door. "You can drop your pants, too," Monsieur Emile told him in a burst of generous camaraderie.

With an idiotic snicker, Gugusse ran and denounced his friends to Madame Bibeault. When Monsieur Emile's mother came home that night, she picked her son up bodily and gave him a stunning thrashing, the first real one he'd ever had.

For some days, Monsieur Emile had to avoid the neighborhood, for when they saw him all the children on the street would chant: "Pig! Dirty pig! Pull down your pants! Show your dink!" while curtains stirred at the windows, revealing big angry faces.

Monsieur Emile screwed up his eyes. The rubber band was stretched until it became translucent, then suddenly relaxed. Now Gugusse Tremblay was attacking the little girl's father, who, he claimed, came home at night with greasy hands. (Gugusse had a highly personal explanation for these stains.) The little girl stuck out her tongue and stood stock-still. Her gesture had a disproportionate effect, touching Gugusse in a particularly sensitive spot, namely his upper left thigh. He doubled over in pain. A small red spot spread over his pants. His second cry was even more piercing, as he brought his hand to the nape of his neck.

In two seconds the street was deserted. Satisfied, Monsieur Emile went to the kitchen and, taking advantage of his mother's absence (she was doing errands God knows where, and the sitter didn't come till five), he rummaged through the cupboards for a bottle of beer, but with no success. He gulped down three huge glasses of Nestlé's Quik, gathered up newspapers, paper clips, and rubber bands, and went back to Florent's – where he came up against a locked door.

He sat on the stairs in a rotten mood. "Shit," he muttered, "I have to pee." As the Nestlé's Quik was distending his bladder drop by drop until it felt as if a cigarette lighter was burning inside him, Elise was dozing on the bus, slumped against her husband who was leafing through the *Unpublished Correspondence* of Turgenev and Viardot, puzzled by its references to Imperial censorship, the discomfort of Russian hotels, society life in Paris, and Gogol's strange passion for shoes.

Perched on the windowsill that kept upstart Virtue at a distance, Breakfast was the first to spot Elise and Florent at the corner. He half closed his eyes with contentment, curled up in a ball in a sunny corner, and fell asleep.

"About time!" Monsieur Emile exploded on the stairs. "I just about peed my pants!"

"Here, give me those," said Florent, grabbing the newspapers and tearing up the stairs. "I was right!" he exclaimed triumphantly. "Not one ad for The Beanery for at least ten weeks! I was sure they were on the outs."

"I found one in *La Voix de Rosemont*," said Elise, "and look, here's another. Almost half a page."

"That clinches it. Slipskin's changed papers – they're on the outs. Okay, Rosario, you're ripe for a little grilling."

Suddenly there was a dreadful scream and a yellowish mass shot through the apartment, overturning everything in its path. Elise and Florent tore into the kitchen. It was empty. On the table gleamed a little heap of divided paper clips, next to a box of rubber bands. "Monsieur Emile!" Elise called. "Where are you?"

A trail of drops of blood led to the bedroom. It took Florent a good ten minutes to extract the piece of metal from his dog's leg. Under the bed where she'd taken refuge, she bared her teeth when anyone came near her. Elise found Monsieur Emile in the broom closet and sent him packing. "I didn't do it on *purpose*," wailed the child. "I wasn't *aiming* at her!" Indeed, the door to the broom closet bore eloquent witness to his sincerity.

Ange-Albert hadn't even got in the door when Florent was beside him, eyes feverish. "I've got a favor to ask you. When do you start work tomorrow?"

"Let's see-Thursday – 11:00 A.M."

"Could you be at *La Clairon du Plateau* at ten to place an ad?"

"For what?"

"I don't know. Whatever. A car for sale."

Ange-Albert stared, then smiled. "Let's talk about it over a beer. I don't know what you're talking about."

"It's simple," said Florent, setting two bottles on the kitchen table. "I want you to go see Gladu, that's all. Like it's business. And don't bring me into it."

Ange-Albert sat wide-eyed until Florent explained how he and Elise had checked out the newspapers. "If my guess is right *he*'ll talk about me and you won't have to lift your little finger. Then we'll know where we stand. I'm dying to find out what went on between Slipskin and Old Rat."

"Okay," his friend yawned, "if it'll help you out. Just be sure you wake me up in time!"

Florent turned to Elise. "I've a favor to ask you, too. I'd like you to drop in on my peace-and-love antique dealer and find out what you can about his gold mine in the Townships. I'm afraid if I go myself he might get suspicious." A few hours later, as he slipped into bed beside his wife, he said, "I haven't felt this good for ten years!"

"Let's hope it lasts!" she sighed.

Florent had been snoring for an hour when Elise finally fell asleep. Perhaps – who knows? – it was the result of a pious thought by Father Jeunehomme who, two thousand miles away, had just finished his bedtime prayer. He took off his slippers and put one leg under the covers, but changed his mind, and opened his suitcase, all ready for the next day's departure. He raised the lid of a tin of raspberry wafers and touched a small parcel tied up with a string. A vague smile fluttered across his lips. He shut the suitcase, took the key and slipped it under his pillow.

About the same time, Rosario Gladu was digging into a pepperoni, olive, and anchovy pizza at the Maple Leaf Restaurant on Mont-Royal, where he'd been going for the past two weeks in the hope of seducing the new waitress, Rose-Rita, whose husband had just gone up to James Bay. Head bowed, he chewed on a tough hunk of crust and made a melancholy assessment of his amorous efforts. After so many meals, drinks, chitchat, and fat tips, he was hardly any further ahead than the first day. He didn't even know her address. Although Rose-Rita was fond of dirty jokes, she guarded her charms jealously, leaping like a carp as soon as Gladu's hand turned bold, eluding his invitations and clearing the table from the wrong side when he became too forward.

As soon as he'd downed the last mouthful, the pizza started gyrating painfully in his stomach. Gladu sighed and went to the cash register. "Leaving so soon, Monsieur Gladu?" asked Rose-Rita, interrupting a hushed conversation behind the counter with Ben, the cook.

"Gotta go, honey." With forced gusto he dropped a fifty-cent piece in her hand and said, "Buy yourself a little nylon something to cover your you-know-what. The thinner the better." Outside, he muttered, "What a waste of time – the stupid cunt." He glanced at Rose-Rita, who was working on an elaborate sundae; behind her, Ben seemed to be working on their next night together.

Gladu headed home, rubbing his stomach, his chest filled with sighs, feet burning as if there were hot coals in his shoes. "Where were you?" asked a shapeless heap of blankets when he entered the conjugal bedroom.

"At *Le Clairon.*"

"I phoned at eleven. The cat answered. We'll talk about it tomorrow. Come to bed."

With a sigh, Rosario undressed. Suddenly, unable to contain himself, he slipped into the living room. He opened a desk drawer, removed a wad of papers covered with notes and drawings, and gazed at them lovingly. At the top of the first sheet the following appeared in capital letters:

DETAILED DESCRIPTION OF NAZEL (sic) FILLER
ORIGINAL INVENSHUN (sic again)

"Rosario-o-o!" the heap of blankets called. "Come to bed, you stubborn ox! You'll wake up the children!"

Rosario promptly obeyed, more miserable and gassier than ever. All night long, the harpy who was his wretched choice as life's companion, good days and bad (his marriage to date consisting exclusively of the latter), tossed in her sleep, her knees attacking him hard enough to disable a tank. He was filled to nausea with muddy melancholy, which mingled with the shreds of anxious dreams that had him walking naked past a crowd doubled up with laughter, his head covered with wet towels. For hours he reflected upon himself with horror: pitiful husband of a potbellied shrew who reeked of hair dye and cheap perfume; third-rate journalist who specialized in local gossip and the opening of snack bars; obscure inventor whose discoveries were doomed for the municipal incinerator.

At eight o'clock the alarm clock went into its usual state of controlled dislocation. Glassy-eyed and scowling, Gladu raised his head and pounded the clock. Madame Gladu emitted two or three grunts but didn't wake up.

Rosario silently gathered up his clothes, went to the kitchen, and made himself a cup of instant coffee with saccharine (his dieting wife had banned sugar from the house months before). Then he slipped out of the house, his tie scarcely knotted, happy to postpone until evening that day's inevitable domestic spat.

Outside he noticed an old copy of *La Voix de Rosemont* fluttering in the wind beside a trash can. One page blew away altogether, and Gladu's gaze fell on the ad Slipskin had been running for three moths. He made a face and the pizza, which had been still all night, began turning in his stomach again. "Life's a load of crap!" he sighed.

And so when Ange-Albert turned up in his office at ten, Rosario felt a dam burst inside him. He was filled with such an irrepressible need for affection that he would have kissed a dog.

"Greetings, greetings!" he shouted in a tidal wave of cordiality.

Ange-Albert stood on the threshold, taken aback. Gladu

was coming toward him, hand out, a shred of fingernail dangling from his teeth. "Come in, come in, sit yourself down! Haven't seen you in a dog's age!"

He offered his visitor a seat and went back to his sorry-looking swivel chair. "How's life been treating you? You look pretty as a titty! What can I do for you?"

"I want to place an ad."

"Fine, great. My secretary isn't here yet, but I'll take it down myself."

He opened a drawer and rummaged through a mess of papers, pens, and gumdrops. Ange-Albert looked around the room. Oddly, Gladu's desk was placed next to a yellowing refrigerator that looked as if someone had unsuccessfully tried to freshen up the paint. To the left of the door sat two more desks covered with scratches and, for the moment, unoccupied. On the opposite wall, above a disused fireplace, hung a large portrait of Pope Paul VI surrounded by an impressive show of bills and memos.

A gold-edged calendar hung across from the Pope. It sported a Mexican girl with overflowing breasts, who was about to bite into a banana with somewhat questionable avidity. Her presence seemed to give the pontiff a roguish look.

"What is it you want to sell, my boy?" Gladu asked, spitting out the fingernail. "Sleigh bells? Air locks? Peanut shells?"

An hour later, Florent exclaimed: "At last! What did he say?"

Ange-Albert, grinning from ear to ear, went to the kitchen and opened a beer. "I didn't have to lift my little finger: he's dying to see you. Apparently he's got something to tell you – wanted to call you then and there. I said it was maybe better if I had a word with you first, since he didn't come out of the deal smelling of roses."

"Perfect!" said Florent, rubbing his hands. "If we work him over first, it'll be easier to grill him." He helped himself to a beer. Virtue heard a second wet little click, and a metal strip landed in front of her nose. She craned her neck to sniff it, but quickly drew back her muzzle in disgust. Soon Florent's voice, piercing and spasmodic, got on the dog's nerves, and she stretched out in the middle of the dining room, where she could keep an eye on things. She managed to doze for a few minutes, eyes half closed, until suddenly a door slammed and something hollered:

"Vroom vroom vrrrrroooommm!"

Monsieur Emile had arrived!

Virtue broke out in a sweat from muzzle to tail, leaped up, and slid under the bed. A dreadful din filled the apartment and, worst of all, the telephone started ringing off the wall. Monsieur Emile called out, "Here, doggie, nice doggie – don't be scared!"

Virtue crouched in the shadows, panting, eyes wide with terror. Strangely, she felt those sharp pains in her left leg again. Then the inevitable happened: the quilt rose and Monsieur Emile's head appeared. He exclaimed triumphantly, "Gotcha!"

A hand came forward and grabbed her paw. A few seconds later she was struggling in the arms of her young torturer. He went to a sofa, set her down on a cushion, and petted her. Then he got the idea of exploring her ears with a popsicle stick. Florent, absorbed in a telephone conversation, was oblivious.

Once again steps could be heard on the stairs. A gentle, elastic, slightly muffled sound: Elise! Florent hung up, the door opened and there was his wife, all smiles and holding a parcel. Virtue took advantage of the moment to utter a plaintive cry (although Monsieur Emile was exploring his ear very gently). Elise turned around: "For the love of God, what are you doing to that dog?"

She dashed to the sofa and picked up Virtue. Florent came over to her. "Well?"

"He was very nice. I got three excellent books for next to nothing."

She put down the dog and began to unwrap her parcel. "There's Palardy's book on French-Canadian furniture, the *Encyclopedia* by Lessard and Marquis, and a brand-new book by Stéphane Moisan, *Discovering Quebec Antiques.*"

"I've got some good news, too. I'm seeing Gladu this afternoon. And Father Jeunehomme just called to say he'll be here about five with an astonishing revelation."

Monsieur Emile, sitting on the sofa, knees together, was following their conversation and picking his nose. Virtue lay at his feet, gazing at him attentively. The earlier calamitous visions he'd provoked in her were growing dim.

TWENTY-FIVE

The day that had started decked out in shining colors ended in disappointment. Rosario Gladu, his voice quavering with emotion, offered to meet Florent at home, but he refused, saying he'd rather go to the newspaper, and showed up about two o'clock.

A tall, bony woman with bulging eyes waved him into a chair by the door. "Please have a seat. Monsieur Gladu is in the little boys' room."

Florent sat down and immediately assessed the chair. He stroked the rungs, examined the legs, turned around to feel the back. A Windsor chair, he thought. Strip it down and patch it up a bit and it'd bring a good price.

Florent's visit had put Gladu in a terrible state. At five to two he felt an urge to go to the bathroom and run a comb through his hair; then he thought he should gargle, since nervousness gave him bad breath. It also affected his epiglottis, which went into spasms. A swig of mouthwash cleared his larynx; as it made its disinfecting way to his bronchial tubes Gladu emitted sounds like a speech of Hitler's speeded up. Florent turned to the secretary, who heaved a weary sigh, spun around on her chair, and started typing a letter, her hands limp, back bent, shoulders hunched.

A door slammed and Gladu appeared, his eyes still watery. "Holy Bob, if it isn't young Boissonneault! How was Florida? What's going on? You're white as a sink! Did you sunbathe in the cellar?" There followed a flurry of handshakes.

Florent wasn't taken in by this exaggerated friendliness, covering profound discomfort. His lips were pursed sardonically. "I was working," he hissed. "Trying to get back on my feet."

Gladu was upset; he blinked as if sand had been thrown in his face. The secretary looked at them in surprise, but then her face hardened in an expression of bitter disapproval. She had just been assured that the good-for-nothing she'd been tolerating, alas! all these years, had just been joined by another one – younger but as despicable as the rest of the male sex.

A spring squealed as Gladu lowered himself into his armchair.

"Sit down," he told Florent.

Glancing at the secretary out of the corner of his eye, Florent murmured, "Not here."

"Madame Bourassa," Gladu said promptly, getting up, "tell Monsieur Latour I'm at the Café Capitol. I have to go there, in any case, for my article."

She sighed. "As you wish."

Cautiously, Gladu stuck his lips in the foam, then drained his glass, eyes bugging slightly. When he'd got his breath back he said, "All right, now, let's talk like a couple of grown-ups."

He stretched his arm across the table and clutched Florent's hand, causing him to suppress a slight grimace. "Now I've had my eyes opened by bad luck, I can tell you, you were right. There's no doubt about it: Slipskin's a son of a bitch!"

"Is that so?" said Florent, withdrawing his hand.

"Yes, my friend. Just listen to this: I had this eighteen-year-old pussy, a little candy angel with hair down to here, boobs to burn a hole in your hand, and a voice – what a voice! When she talked I could hear violins!"

He stopped, choked with emotion, a tragic expression trying unsuccessfully to harden his fleshy face. "Anyhow – one Monday night about seven o'clock I introduce my little friend to that fucking square-head asshole. By midnight, he has me drunk as a pig. By two, she's in bed with him. Next morning at eight, he calls me to say he's pulling out of his advertising contract and that he has so much work he doesn't have much time for me. And two weeks later, he marries Josette in the Protestant church. I couldn't even raise a stink: he said if I did, he'd have some juicy tales for the wife."

Florent gazed at him impassively. "Did you bring me here to tell me about your love life?"

"No, no, I don't expect you to lose any sleep over it. I just wanted you to know, if you want his hide, you can count on me."

Florent shuddered and broke out in gooseflesh. He hunched over the table, an avid look in his eyes. "Why don't you just tell me everything you know about him? That'd be more useful than your bitching and moaning. Is it true he doesn't see Ratablavasky anymore?"

Gladu nodded.

"Why?"

"You tell me and we'll both know. One night last December, the three of us were at the restaurant having a quiet chat. I was drinking tea with Old Rat while Slipskin did the cash. All of a sudden, the old man stops in mid-sentence and gives Slipskin a look that'd curl your hair. A minute goes by. I act as if nothing's happening. Needless to say, it wasn't the first time I'd seen him go off the rails. Then he starts laughing out loud, pointing at Slipskin, and talking some gibberish that sounded like – get this! – that sounded like 'his soul was disappointed.' His *soul*! Anyhow Slipskin looks up and asks him to say it again – he didn't get it."

Gladu paused, his expression tragic. "Old Rat just got up, took his hat – and hasn't been seen since."

"Slipskin must've been happy."

"At first, sure, he was dancing on the ceiling. But two or three weeks later he was singing a different tune. Old Rat was plotting things behind his back."

"What kind of things?"

Gladu puffed out his cheeks, opened his eyes wider, and shook his head with an expression of profound ignorance, while a long noise like a fart passed his lips. "Haven't the faintest idea, my friend."

Florent bombarded him with questions, but Gladu's answer was always the same. Florent got up and said, "Look, if that's how it is, I have to go – things to do. Give me your number – if I need anything I'll call you. Hurry up, I haven't got all day."

"Don't get your nerves in a knot," Gladu grumbled.

Florent walked away muttering, "Pigheaded jerk. You could steal his soup bowl while he was eating out of it. Hope I'll have better luck with the priest."

He was disappointed. When he got back to the apartment Elise told him, "I sent Monsieur Emile out to buy pastries for your cousin."

"What? Is that brat still here? Let his mother take him for a change!" He collapsed in an armchair and told Elise about his conversation with Gladu.

"You should be happy. They're diddling each other for once, instead of ganging up on you."

Just then Breakfast made a slow, majestic entrance and, as a signal favor, came purring to Florent's knees. He smiled and stroked the cat, who rolled onto his side, shut his eyes, and began a series of voluptuous contortions, digging his claws in everywhere. Suddenly, he curled up in a ball, flattened his ears, and grew still. Resting his head against the back of the chair, Florent shut his eyes, as well.

Monsieur Emile, carrying a big cardboard cake box, burst into the apartment shouting at the top of his lungs, "Can I have one?"

"Ask Elise," Florent muttered sleepily. He pointed to the kitchen where his wife was making supper.

"Honestly! The least he could do is help out," Elise sighed a few minutes later as she saw her husband drowsily make his way to the bedroom.

Virtue was sprawled on the bed waiting, determined to defend her territory from her whiskered rival. Florent curled up bedside her and soon was in another world. Half an hour passed. Rosine arrived, followed shortly by Ange-Albert. Monsieur Emile talked them into a game of hide-and-seek. Florent muttered in his sleep and turned over. But sleep gallantly swallowed the uproar and transformed it into baroque dreams.

Rosine and Ange-Albert soon tired of crawling under the furniture and joined Elise in the kitchen. Left to himself, Monsieur Emile wandered around the apartment until, seeing that everyone was busy, he took a rubber band and a handful of paper clips from his pocket and amused himself puncturing a box of Oxydol, trying to make a picture of Elise. Twenty-two pieces of metal thudded into the cardboard and gradually

Elise's head took shape – like a squashed tomato. The twenty-third projectile, which was to mark the position of an eye, strayed from its course and, cunningly crossing the dining room, came to rest in the neck of the model herself, drawing blood. In two minutes flat Monsieur Emile had been picked up, spanked, and sent home to his mother. His howls, added to the furious kicks he gave the walls as Ange-Albert lugged him down the stairs, brought out the downstairs neighbor, who favored him with a few choice epithets that Monsieur Emile returned in kind. Florent remained stubbornly asleep, fists clenched, brow furrowed, and it was Father Jeunehomme's muffled voice that finally wakened him. He leaped out of bed and stood in the doorway, rubbing his eyes.

"Von Strohm – Captain Von Strohm," the priest was murmuring, as if it were some graceful compliment.

Rosine and Ange-Albert, side by side on the sofa, were listening politely, bored to tears. Florent went up to his cousin with outstretched hand.

Rising, the priest said, "Greetings, dear cousin, I was just sharing a piquant point with your friends that may interest you, as well."

"What is it?"

"Your wife was kind enough to invite me for supper," the priest went on, as if he hadn't heard Florent's question, "for I took the liberty of arriving somewhat early. I confess I was dying to get my hands on the Turgenev-Viardot correspondence – and of course I was eager, as well, to bring you a copy of your friend Egon Ratablavasky's book, which Dom Périgord finally tracked down, in Paris at the Librairie des Deux Mondes."

Florent brought him the eagerly awaited correspondence. "And now," he said with a mocking smile, "what about my book?"

Elise appeared in the kitchen doorway. "Good, you're up. Supper's ready. Sit down, everybody."

"After supper, then?" the priest whispered to Florent.

"At least tell me what you found out."

"It's all in the book," said the priest mysteriously.

He put his book on the windowsill and sat down. All through supper his gaze kept darting over the others' heads and lighting on his precious acquisition. Turgenev was winking seductively, anxious to have his letters read after nearly a hundred years of oblivion.

"Is your mother well?" asked Elise.

"Hmmm? Oh yes, very well, very well. The hotel opening was a great success. She's been hard at work. Customers have been pouring in – and money, too; at least I think so. The only thing that's bothering her is the grounds – she wants to enlarge them, put in riding trails. But her neighbor won't sell. She goes into terrible rages – in other words, she's happy!"

Florent was wolfing his food, trembling with impatience. Finally, unable to wait any longer, he asked his cousin to show him Ratablavasky's book. "Right now. Dessert can wait."

"I'll make the coffee," Rosine murmured, slipping away as the others went into the living room.

The priest opened a small black bag stamped in gold with his initials, surmounted by a cross. "Here you are." He held up a dusty, yellowing, dog-eared book, printed on cheap paper.

"*A Christian Father Faces the Dawn*?" said Ange-Albert, raising his eyebrows. "Weird title!"

The priest was handling the book with surgical dexterity. Elise and Florent leaned over his shoulder. In a voice filled with emotion, the priest said, "We know the name of the previous owner of this book." He slipped his index finger between the flyleaf and the cover, lifting it slowly. "'25 Dezember 1942. *Kapitan Kurt von Strohm. Afrikakorps dritte Divizion*,'" Elise read. "'*Als Andenken von meinen Freund Ernest Robichaud*.'"

The priest translated: "'Captain Kurt von Strohm, Afrikakorps, Third Division. Souvenir of my friend Ernest Robichaud.' The Afrikakorps was the name of the army Hitler sent to Libya in February 1941. It had four divisions under General Rommel, the Desert Fox. They were based in Tripoli and surrendered on May 12, 1943."

"Who's this captain?" Florent asked impatiently.

The priest shrugged. "Unfortunately we don't know much about him. Dom Périgord moved heaven and earth, but all he could find out was that after being sentenced at the Nuremberg trials to five years in prison, Kurt von Strohm lived an ordinary life as a civil servant until his death in the early sixties."

Rosine overcame her timidity to ask, "What about Ernest Robichaud? Who's he?"

The priest sighed. "We know even less about him! It would seem he gave the book to von Strohm. Unless it's a false name – Egon Ratablavasky, Ernest Robichaud. The same initials. Perhaps that's a clue. . . ." He picked up the book and pressed it against his chin. "In any case, I'm absolutely convinced this book has some very interesting facts to reveal to the person who knows how to read it."

These words were greeted with profound silence. Virtue, delighted at the unexpected pause, thumped her tail on the floor. "Let me borrow it," said Florent. "I'll dig out its secrets."

"Gladly," said the priest. "But I promised to return it as soon as possible. Take good care of it."

Eyes gleaming, he took his precious *Correspondence* from the windowsill and put it in his black bag.

He's like a child with a toy, Elise thought, touched. She offered him coffee but he declined, claiming he had important business. He offered his pale, moist hand all around, then silently glided down the stairs, hailed a taxi, and disappeared into the life of Turgenev.

Florent was engrossed in the other book. Leafing through it, he found it consisted of a series of brief meditations, couched in forbidding mystical jargon. It was illustrated with engravings depicting turn-of-the-century scenes of family life. Oddly, they had no religious content, but were vaguely reminiscent of Tarot cards.

"There must be a code," Florent muttered. "I'll need some help deciphering it."

Ange-Albert tapped his shoulder. "You still thinking of going to Sainte-Romanie?"

"As soon as I've settled my accounts with Old Rat."

"What would you say to seven rooms for sixty bucks a month?"

Incredulous, Florent spun around. "That's right," said his friend, "sixty bucks! Remember when I was working for Canadian National? There's an abandoned train station they've been trying to rent for ages. It's still empty."

"Have you seen it?"

"Yup. Quite livable. Just outside the village, with woods and fields across the way."

Elise approached them, looking worried. "Florent, do you realize we'll need a truck?"

"And lots of money," Rosine added quietly.

"I'll buy a used truck. As for the money . . . yeah . . . that's dicey, of course. But we still have twelve hundred dollars."

"A thousand and eighty," Elise corrected him.

"It's a start, anyway. We'll just go slow and sell off our loot as fast as we can."

"I hope so. But you're forgetting one small detail: you don't know a thing about antiques."

"And what's this?" Florent asked, punching the Palardy with his fist. "A box of suppositories? I know how to read, I'll read. While I read I'll learn. Besides, there's nothing to stop me hanging around the stores! Unless I'm a total idiot I'll pick up a few tricks."

The telephone rang. It was Picquot. "*Eh bien*, have you forgotten me? I've been pacing my room for three days now, wondering if I should move to an old folks' home."

"It's just –"

"Enough. I know all there is to know about man's ingratitude. Will you be home for a while?"

"Yes, of course."

"I'll be right over."

Twenty minutes later the chef arrived and announced he was leaving the advertising agency. "The very sight of my face in the mirror makes me sick. It's a fact: I'm no longer a cook, I'm a prostitute! I'm helping the Americans spread those vile concoctions of theirs around the world. It's the beginning of the end. Frankly, I'd rather beg. Yesterday I turned up a sample, just in from the U.S.A.: almonds, if you can imagine, *barbecue flavored*! That's right, almonds, the princesses of confectionery in the words of Brillat-Savarin, who devoted sublime pages to them. It took me a day to recover."

"Did you taste them?" asked Florent, deadpan.

Picquot looked at him stony-faced. "Don't be tiresome. Now let's go out for a drink – you're my guests."

They went to the Faubourg St. Denis. Picquot began his libations with a cup of very weak tea; then, the demands of medicine having been satisfied, he ordered a half bottle of Prince Noir and a foie gras sandwich. Florent drank his beer in silence, looking preoccupied. Suddenly Picquot asked, "Young man, what are you stewing about?"

"Nothing, not a thing," he replied evasively. "I was daydreaming, that's all."

"Daydreaming? You should practice your lying. I wasn't born yesterday, after all. What's going on?" And he began to plague his friend with questions.

Florent had vowed to keep his concerns to himself so he wouldn't worry his old friend needlessly, but he ended up telling him everything: his decision to have done with Ratablavasky, his meeting with Gladu, his plan to move to Sainte-Romanie.

"See here, young man, where's your common sense? Once you've paid for the truck you won't have enough to buy a beat-up chair. What are friends for? To stand around at parties?"

Florent felt cornered: he must either accept a four-thousand-dollar loan at four percent interest, repayable in one year, or never speak to Picquot again. He capitulated.

"Waiter!" the chef demanded, his eyes brimming. "A bottle! We'll drink to your success. Fate owes you that much."

About ten o'clock the next morning an interesting transaction took place at Draperies Georgette, amid tall stacks of curtain material and printed cotton. Ange-Albert's employer, the widow Georgette Lamérise, who had been in business on St. Hubert Street for seventeen years, agreed to sell to Florent for eight hundred dollars, a tomato-red 1964 Ford truck that was as good as new and spent the winter in a garage, on blocks. This bargain was explained in large measure by the motherly and somewhat sentimental affection Madame Lamérise felt for her employee, who was, as it happened, a very good salesman.

In the life of Madame Lamérise, a chubby creature with frizzy red hair, there was but a single passion: sleep. She'd have given yards of handwoven fabric for an hour's sound sleep. Alas, for years now, business worries and light-fingered staff had doomed her to insomnia. All signs seemed to indicate that if her soul was to find rest, she would require a second husband, one with daring and good business sense. But her blotchy skin, her little snub nose that dripped allergically all year round, her gray eyes filled with naive sorrow and perpetual amazement, combined to prevent her from finding one, even among the widowers of the Golden Age Club. Then one fine day the reassuring and efficient presence of Ange-Albert, who managed her business as if it were his own, while showing an extraordinary disregard for making money, brought back her youthful nights. And greatest luxury of all, on Monday and Tuesday, which were always slow, she could even grab a short afternoon nap in her little room at the back of the store. The nervous tic in her left nostril gradually subsided, and her stomach pains died down.

While she twittered away, praising the merits of the truck, Florent glanced into her room, which was separated from the store by a thin partition, concealed by a curtain with a pattern of mauve violins and green roses. A narrow iron bed, a waxed wooden table holding a hot plate and a tiny refrigerator, two chairs, a cupboard, and a sewing machine described with sad eloquence her chaste and mournful existence.

"I'd love to hear more," said Florent suddenly, his eyes stinging from the dye fumes, "but I have a million things to do, and my wife's expecting me home for lunch."

He held out a cheque. Madame Lamérise pushed it away. "Drive around first, then make up your mind. You can pay me this afternoon if you're still interested. I'm not worried; you're Monsieur Doucet's friend and that's good enough for me."

Twenty minutes later, sitting tall, looking jubilant, Florent parked the truck in front of the apartment. Elise spotted him from the window and went down to meet him. The tomato red color had a considerable effect on Virtue, who chased around the vehicle, barking.

Elise nodded, sighing pensively. "What's wrong?" asked Florent, slipping his arm around her waist.

"I hope . . . I hope it's going to bring us happiness," she replied, her voice quavering slightly.

Florent laughed and pinched her cheek. "Buck up, kiddo! In three weeks I'll know more about antiques than anyone in Montreal! And after that – we start hunting!"

The word seemed to awaken obscure memories for Virtue, who pricked up her ears, sniffed, and stared down the street.

In the front room Florent noticed the copy of *A Christian Father*, and his good mood vanished. He picked up the book and started leafing through it, then he threw it on the sofa in frustration. The telephone rang. "It's your cousin," said Elise, "and he sounds weirder than ever!"

"I've just received Gogol's stove!" Father Jeunehomme announced. His voice, breaking with emotion, was hardly more than a squeak. "The seals seem intact. I'd like to ask you a favor. I don't dare leave the rectory, because the workmen should arrive any minute to take the stove to my study. Would you do me a service and buy me three or four pairs of pliers, various sizes, and the most powerful flashlight you can find?"

"Right away."

He shrugged and hung up. "Very strange business," he said, going to the kitchen for a bite, since it was nearly noon.

"I'm going out, too," said Elise. "I have things to do."

They hadn't gone three steps when Monsieur Emile appeared at the corner street. When he saw them he stopped abruptly, slipped something in his pocket, and shifted from one foot to the other. "Where are you going?"

"Out to do errands."

"Can I come?" he whined.

"Some other time. We're in a hurry."

"Can I watch TV at your place, then?"

Florent laughed. "All by yourself? No way! We wouldn't have a stick of furniture left in one piece."

"Goddammit!" Monsieur Emile howled, stamping his foot.

He watched them move off, hands on his hips, pouting, then went and sat on the stairs.

"How about a drink?" Florent suggested when he'd made his purchases.

"What about your cousin?"

He shrugged and ushered Elise into a brasserie, where he downed three beers in a row. Elise, who was shivering, had a hot toddy. "Are you following Monsieur Emile down the road to drink?" she teased Florent when they were back outside.

Before he could reply he stopped, gaping. Elise cried out. Standing in front of them was Egon Ratablavasky, smiling good-naturedly. "Greetings, my friends," he crooned. "I am hoping of all my heart that your traveling was agreeable."

Florent first grabbed Elise's arm and pushed her out of the way. Then he took a few steps, turned, and jeered, "So our benefactor's being extravagant now, is he? Imagine – paying for plane tickets! Are we allowed to know what crazy scheme that was in aid of?"

"It was quite cleanly and purely an act of friendship!"

Ratablavasky approached and began a confused discourse in which the word "friendship" kept recurring. His voice enfolded them like a silky wing gradually blunting their awareness of things. Holy horseradish! Florent thought. What's wrong with me? My head's spinning as if I'd drunk a bottle of gin.

A car pulled up beside them. "If it isn't the young lovebirds, passing the time of day with my pal Rata!" exclaimed Captain Galarneau, opening the door. "Jimbobbaree! What a stroke of luck!" He got out and jauntily made his way toward them, drunker than ever, his cap askew. Elise, horrified, tried to drag away her husband, who gazed numbly at Ratablavasky and his acolyte while the old man kept up his strange monologue.

The next series of events occurred so rapidly that Elise and Florent had only a confused recollection of them. Captain Galarneau flung open a door and pushed Elise onto the back seat of the car. Florent sprang at his throat, but two powerful hands lifted him by the shoulders and threw him inside, next to his wife. A moment later the locked car was swerving violently, buffeting Elise and Florent back and forth in the dark.

"The sons of bitches!" Florent muttered. He was drumming his fingers against a metal shield that separated the front of the car from the back. There were blinds at the windows also. Their tumultuous journey was over in five minutes. The brakes were slammed on, hurling the couple to the floor.

The door opened. Ratablavasky stood before them in the light. "Be so good to get out," he said, his voice guttural and almost menacing.

Dazed, they stepped out. The car started up with a roar and disappeared behind a fence.

They were in the middle of a scrubby lot surrounded by a high wooden fence, behind which rose blocks of houses with boarded-up windows, probably doomed to demolition. In the distance they could make out Place Ville-Marie, but Florent couldn't pin down their location more precisely. The dry, stony earth was scattered with daisies shriveled by the cold.

"Pretty, yes?" asked the old man. "I drag my feet many times to this place to think about things. Please forgive my means to transport you."

Elise crouched on the ground behind Florent, her head between her knees, shuddering silently. Florent gradually got his wits back and gazed at the old man, trying to determine whether he was carrying a concealed weapon.

"What . . . suspiciousness!" Ratablavasky exclaimed, as if he had read Florent's mind. "For one last time I am offering you a friendly proposition, and my hope is large that you'll accept. I am asking perhaps more than the time before, but, tee hee! also am I giving more! If you want I am bequeathing you now and here my whole fortune, which is vast, I assure you, very vast. . . . And in return, nothing – or almost. Dust. . . . The pleasure of sharing some few moments in your private company, but of course honoring and respecting your privacy, keeping my eyes shut, if I may say so."

Florent, still staring, helped Elise to her feet. She slumped against him and buried her face in his shoulder. "I've had enough of your crap!" Florent shouted, choked with rage. "I don't know what the hell you're up to, but I warn you, next time we meet I'll have a gun and I'll blow your fucking brains out! So leave us alone! You've caused enough trouble."

Ratablavasky blinked as if he'd just heard a good joke and let out a long guttural laugh. Florent then felt something like a fiery needle rise from the pit of his stomach to his head. Mocking sparks glowed all around him. He pushed Elise away and advanced on the old man, fists clenched. "Laugh! Laugh your guts out, *Father*!" he raged. "But I've got something that'll have you laughing out of the other side of your face, you fucking Nazi! What gall, trying to pass off books of prayers!"

"How is dear Father Jeunehomme?" Ratablavasky asked, pretending not to understand.

Florent snickered hatefully and continued: "*A Christian Father Faces the Dawn*! Such an edifying book! I read a page every morning, and every morning I come at least a hundred feet closer to God!"

The old man's expression became grave. He was on the verge of speaking, but changed his mind. "And it's not just *any* religious book," Florent continued in a joyous frenzy. "So lofty it's stratospheric! And not intended for just any readers – it's aimed at the elite, if you please! The cream of the crop!"

Ratablavasky was staring strangely, rather frighteningly, as if trying to see deep inside Florent's thoughts. "The finest cream – like Captain Von Strohm, a man of exemplary piety."

For a moment, all was silent. Then the old man said calmly, "Give me that book. It has . . . sentimental value."

Florent was utterly calm. "Never," he replied firmly.

He turned and smiled at Elise, a few steps behind them, watching with a look of fearful disbelief. "And above all, don't bother nosing around our house for it. It's somewhere safe."

Ratablavasky took a deep breath, slipped one hand inside

the other and cracked his knuckles. Then, in a light, almost mocking tone, he said, "I would be disposed, in order to regain possession of certain trifles, to offer a certain amount of money. For you, this book has no value absolutely, less than a fly. For me, it has precious memories, believe me. The days of my youth. . . . I am offering ten thousand dollars."

Florent shook his head, turned, and followed Elise, who was heading for a pile of old planks, behind which there was an opening in the fence. Ratablavasky watched them.

Alone, he paced back and forth, decapitating daisies with his cane. Now and then he looked up, to be sure no one was watching. Night was falling slowly. Suddenly the place was deserted, and there was no way of knowing where the old man had gone.

After wandering for half an hour through a labyrinth of garbage-filled lanes, Elise and Florent suddenly found themselves on Prince Arthur Street, near a restaurant called Le Bateleur. Florent looked around, confused. "I don't understand. I really don't understand."

He hailed a taxi, which took them to the Sulpician Seminary. Elise, still trembling, refused to get out. "Relax," Florent told her. "Can't you see I've got him by the short hairs? Don't ask me why, but that's how it is."

He went inside, whistling, and asked for his cousin. "Father Jeunehomme has just gone up to his room," the porter told him.

Florent found him in a state of extreme agitation, sweating, with half the buttons of his soutane undone. "Here's your flashlight and your pliers," Florent told him, holding out the package.

"Thank you, thank you. The good Lord knows how helpful you've been. I'll make it up to you, believe me."

Florent smiled. "You won't have long to wait, if you mean that. I've read every page of *A Christian Father Faces the Dawn*, but I don't understand a thing. Mysticism and theology, you know. . . . Anyway, I'd like you to have a look at it. I'm sure you could find a pile of clues."

"Gladly. But not today, if you don't mind. This is such an intense time for me. . . . Call me in three days."

Florent had considered telling him of his latest meeting with Ratablavasky, but changed his mind and went back to Elise.

In ten minutes they were at their apartment. Elise could hardly stand up. "Good grief!" Florent exclaimed as he helped her up the stairs. "You'd think you were about to give birth!"

She shot him a furious look and stammered, "You! If you only knew what I've . . . I've just . . ." Sobbing, unable to continue, she flung open the door and threw herself on the bed. Virtue joined her and ran a sympathetic tongue over her. Florent was trying to console her when he heard the door open, and the sound of footsteps in the living room.

When he left the bedroom there was a furious exclamation. Egon Ratablavasky was waiting placidly at the front door, hands behind his back and smiling. "Good day, dear friend. I am here for two different intentions. First, to tell you that much future time will pass before our next encounter, for after thinking things over I want to give you the time to make your own success by your own strength so that self-confidence will fill your soul once more. And then your ear might be more welcome to my modest proposing. Isn't it?"

Elise appeared in the doorway, her mouth twisted in rage. "Get out of here, you filthy man! Go away! Go away!" She advanced on him, hands waving, eyes wild. Florent grasped her waist and roughly pushed her aside. Ratablavasky smiled and sat on the sofa, elegantly crossing his legs. There was a curious look on his face. Hugging her master's legs, Virtue stared at the old man, terrified, her nose quivering. The usual smell of unwashed feet, acrid and penetrating, filled the room.

"My second intention," Ratablavasky went on in his sing-song voice, "is to offer you a little more for that book in your possessing. Since it's a souvenir of very precious proportions, I might be predisposed to offer you as many as twenty thousand dollars if I could persuade you to –"

There was a click. Ratablavasky cried out and brought his hand to his right eye, which filled with blood. Florent, aghast, hesitated briefly, and then dashed to the old man, grabbed him by the shoulders, and pushed him toward the door, while Monsieur Emile, fearful and triumphant, came into the living room, an elastic dangling from his finger. Virtue started barking hysterically and shot under the bed, sick with fear.

Ratablavasky broke away from Florent's grasp and leaned against the door. "Very well," he murmured feebly, "I am bidding you good-bye."

For a moment, the pain kept him from going on. Big drops of blood fell to the collar of his shirt. He turned the doorknob and walked onto the landing. "Fear not, we'll see one another when the timing is right."

Florent watched him go down the stairs, very erect, his fedora set carefully on his head.

Monsieur Emile, somewhat shaken by his exploit, had gone to the bathroom, where he was throwing up the beer he'd snitched from the refrigerator while his friends were out.

TWENTY-SIX

Three days later, Florent returned to the Sulpician Seminary with the precious volume of meditations. Father Jeunehomme spent the entire night reading and rereading it, trying to sniff out a code, some subtle allusion or biographical detail, but to no avail. Either the meaning of the book escaped him or he was on the wrong track. All he read were interminably edifying observations, written in a vague, bombastic, exasperating style. "Leave the book with me," said the priest. "I'd like to show it to a friend, a remarkable exegete. In his time he's even been interested in deciphering codes."

In a few days, the priest returned the book. "I'm terribly sorry but it's hopeless. It's an empty shell."

Florent shrugged and considered the matter closed. "Whatever happens now, the main thing is, I have the book and he's afraid of me. Now let's concentrate on getting rich."

He spat in this hands and whipped through the books by Palardy, Lessard, and Moisan, which were joined by works on restoration and maintenance by Robert Le Corré and H.S. Plenderleith. He snickered. "Yesterday cosmetics, today antiques. Another few years and I'll be a walking encyclopedia!"

He befriended Jean-Denis Beaumont, a young antique dealer who sold odds and ends out of a shop at the corner of St-Denis and Laurier, fleecing ordinary mortals and keeping his real finds for a handful of connoisseurs for whom he had a respect that verged on the pathological. Florent spent many afternoons listening to him talk about china and old furniture. His cheerful cunning delighted Florent, who tried to steep himself in it, for he realized that this quality and flair were the mainstays of the business.

On the night of October 27, he stood before Elise, arms akimbo, looking smug. "This is it, sweetheart – I'm ready. We're packing our bags and heading for Sainte-Romanie. I'm itching to get my hands on those diamond-point armoires." Turning to Ange-Albert, who had been listening with a skeptical smile, he asked, "Who should I see about renting that station?"

The next morning Florent went to the offices of the Canadian Pacific Railway on the second floor of a gloomy old building near the St-Luc marshaling yards. V.D. Veedson, a little old man with wrinkled gray skin and two tufts of steel wool for eyebrows, was leaning on the counter reading his newspaper when Florent opened the door.

V.D. Veedson's mood harmonized especially well with that of the building. Half an hour earlier, on Metropolitan Boulevard, a transport truck carrying seventeen tonnes of canned beans had dropped a case on the hood of his car, which promptly assumed the look of crumpled cardboard. For a moment Veedson's heart considered stopping permanently. "Sorry, I don't speak French," he said, giving Florent a look that would have made the public relations department squirm.

Florent frowned and looked around for assistance.

"Robert!" barked Veedson, his mood worsening by the second.

Robert was in the bathroom, so the negotiations limped along between V.D. and Florent. After showing every piece of identification and explaining his intentions for the third time, Florent realized that renting the Sainte-Romanie station was the last thing on the mind of V.D. Veedson, who just wanted to get rid of him so he could be alone with his bad mood.

Robert crept up behind his boss and gestured to Florent. Then, jerking his chin toward the clock, he crossed his index fingers. He wants to see me at ten-thirty, Florent thought. Nodding, he gathered up his papers and left without a word. Twenty minutes later he was back, heart pounding. Robert rushed up to him with a handful of forms. "Here, quick! Sign these! Take this receipt and pick up the keys on the third floor. So long and good luck!"

Florent swept into the apartment and showed Elise the keys. "I did it, sweetie. That station's ours. We leave tomorrow."

"We do?" She was uncomfortably playing with her hair.

"Is that all you've got to say?"

"I was just . . . I was thinking about Monsieur Emile."

Florent exploded. "Out of the question! First of all his mother'd never let us take him. And besides – for God's sake – we've got other things to do than bring up someone else's kids."

At these words his voice lost its conviction, and he looked away. "You don't believe that," she told him. "You love that child and it kills you to see him turning into a delinquent, but you won't admit it because it might interfere with your plans."

Muttering, Florent went into the kitchen. Elise found him standing at the refrigerator, a bottle in hand. "Drowning your sorrows?"

He glared at her and took two or three swallows. "We have to see Picquot before we leave," he said shortly. "After all, it's thanks to him that . . ."

Elise just stared at him, her gaze fiercely ironic. Suddenly he blushed, set his bottle on the table, and went into the living room, slamming the door after him. Elise heard the telephone being dialed. Afraid of ruining her triumph, she didn't dare move. From the next room she could hear Florent's voice, jerky and high-pitched. "Idiot," she muttered, "change your tone or you'll ruin everything."

Florent stuck his head in the doorway. "Come here. We're paying old lady Chouinard a visit. But hurry – she's going to the hairdresser."

Their timing was bad. That morning, when she was making Monsieur Emile's bed, Floretta had found certain stains that couldn't be explained by her son's still distant puberty. "That goddamn bitch," she'd muttered, pulling off the sheet, "I pay her good money to look after my kid and there she is, heels in the air in his bed and with any bum from the neighborhood. That poor kid must have some tales to tell!" After a long hibernation, her maternal instincts were awakening. "Emile!" she screamed. "Get in here!"

He took one suspicious look at her expression and locked himself in the bathroom, where he could negotiate. Pounding on the door, she shouted, "Come out of there, you little idiot – I'm not pissed off at *you*!"

The doorbell interrupted her.

"What the hell do those two want?"

At the sight of his friends Monsieur Emile tore down the hall and threw himself at Elise, crying happily, "Hey, how come you're here?"

His transports exacerbated his mother's rotten mood. To Florent's suggestion she retorted, "Not on your life! What kind of heartless mother do you think I am?"

Her question was punctuated by a muffled explosion, followed by a long crumpling sound. Elise and Florent stared wide-eyed. At the end of the corridor it was suddenly light. The wall that used to keep it dark had just collapsed in a cloud of dust around a swaying iron ball.

"Use your heads," Madame Chouinard went on. "If I send my kid two hundred and forty miles away I might as well give him to you for good – with his mitts and his boots thrown in!"

Florent bowed like a reed, smiled as sweetly as he knew how, tried a thousand twists and turns in a voice as smooth and sweet as whipped cream: nothing doing. Elise took over, but couldn't go on. Madame Chouinard, enraged by her son's tearful supplications, waved her arms and, in a strident voice, was beginning to seriously bend the rules of common courtesy.

Florent slammed the car door and turned on the ignition. Glowering at Elise he asked, "Now are you satisfied?"

She was huddled in the corner, silently wiping her eyes.

At six o'clock they arrived at Picquot's, where they'd been invited, with Rosine and Ange-Albert, for a farewell supper. "Stop tormenting yourselves," the chef told them, "I'll look after the little nipper."

"So will I," added Rosine.

"Come now, Elise," said Picquot, patting her hand, "wipe those tears from your pretty eyes. This is a celebration. God knows when we'll be together again."

He stopped, for his voice was becoming ridiculously quavery. He went to the kitchen and came out bearing an elaborate strawberry cake that brought a blissful smile to Ange-Albert's face. Florent whistled in admiration. "Your departure caught me off guard," the chef apologized with comical false modesty, "but I'll prepare something truly special when I visit you in Sainte-Romanie."

"Imagine the look on Monsieur Emile's face if he was here," Rosine smiled.

"Don't talk about him, okay?" Elise said irritably. "I have to get used to having just my dog for company."

Poor Virtue slept very badly that night. As she lay at her masters' feet, the restless tossing of Elise and Florent, who were already on the way to Sainte-Romanie, kept her awake and even elicited a few growls.

The apartment was filling with a doughy gray light. The dog jumped off the bed and padded from room to room, shuddering and sullen, her bladder painfully swollen, but afraid to awaken anyone. She sat on a window ledge and peered sadly out at Emery Street, which looked more wretched than usual in the cold light of dawn.

Suddenly she shuddered violently. Eyes wide, teeth bared, she pasted her muzzle against the icy window and peered out at a man standing by the steps. He raised his head and waved hesitantly. The dog barked furiously. Jumping off the windowsill she tore into the bedroom. "Shut up!" Florent yelled.

She trotted around the room, moaning, her claws clattering like castanets. Florent opened one eye, waited for her to come up to the bed and, flinging one arm out from under the covers, gave her a slap that sent her, quivering, under the kitchen table. Elise sighed deeply, cleared her throat, picked up the alarm clock and looked hazily at the dial.

"What time is it?" Florent asked.

"Twenty past six."

He grumbled some vague threats and turned over heavily, determined to sleep for another hour. But a light had just flashed on in his head and the road to Sainte-Romanie unfurled before him as if he were behind the wheel of his truck. "Goddamn pain in the ass!" he exclaimed, jumping out of bed. "Why can't you piss the same time as everybody else?" He opened the door but Virtue refused to go downstairs, huddled trembling on the doormat. Elise said, "Stop yelling at her. She'll pee on the floor."

Florent returned to the bedroom without a word, dressed, and went to the kitchen, cheerful as a millionaire after the 1929 crash. The prospect of a bacon omelet awash in maple syrup brightened him up a little. When his plate was clean he said, "Okay, we just load up the truck, then bye-bye Montreal!"

On his way upstairs for the last suitcase he came face-to-face with Rosine. "We're on our way, baby!" He opened his arms and gave her a kiss that Elise's presence would surely have reduced by half.

Freeing herself, she said, "I'll go tell Ange-Albert," and sped to the bedroom, blushing.

Florent stood for a moment, dreamily rubbing his nose, then went to the kitchen. The sound of clinking bottles made him turn. The front door slowly opened on Monsieur Emile in dirty pants and a mustard-stained pajama top, with a shopping bag full of empty bottles in each hand. "Hi," he grinned, "I'm coming, too. I ran away."

One of the bags started moving. Breakfast poked out his head, looked around, and jumped out.

"But . . . but Monsieur Emile," Florent said uncertainly, "you can't. . . . Your mother doesn't want . . ."

"I don't give a shit!" howled the child. "I hate it at my mother's!"

Elise and Rosine tried to calm him down. The child stamped his feet, shouted insults, slapped Rosine, and then, suddenly calm, picked up his shopping bags and tore down the stairs.

Disconcerted, Rosine, Elise, and Florent just looked at one another. Suddenly, from the street, came a tremendous racket mixed with barking. "That's Virtue!" Florent exclaimed.

He took the stairs four at a time and came upon an incredible sight: Monsieur Emile, his face convulsed in rage, was throwing empty bottles at the truck, while the dog raced around him hysterically. Florent darted out to stop him, but the child spun around and threw a 7-Up bottle, which grazed his cheek before smashing against a wall. "If you don't take me with you I'll bust your goddamn truck!"

Suddenly Virtue howled and sat in the broken glass, licking her paw.

Thirty seconds later, Monsieur Emile started sobbing. They learned, first, that he'd sworn never to set foot in his mother's house again, since she didn't give a damn about him and fed him nothing but macaroni and cheese; second, realizing it would be hard for Elise and Florent to provide for him, he'd brought a supply of empty bottles they could cash in for five cents each in any grocery store; third, that he was sure he could bring in at least ten dollars a week collecting empties, an activity at which he'd long excelled; and fourth, that everybody including his cat could go to hell.

Over his words there drifted a disturbing smell of beer, which spoke eloquently of Monsieur Emile's morale since Elise and Florent's visit to his mother.

Elise looked at him, pale and speechless. "Come on now," murmured Florent, concealing his emotion with difficulty. "You aren't a baby, are you? We'd take you if we could, but we can't. The police would look for you and they'd put us in jail. Is that what you want? Anyway, we won't be gone forever. You'll see us soon, maybe in a week, and if you behave yourself your mother'll change her mind – I'm sure of it."

Rosine rushed down the stairs, a coat around her shoulders. Monsieur Emile huddled against her, silent, his face wooden. When Elise tried to kiss him she was rewarded with a kick. Rosine brought a finger to her lips and gestured for them to go.

Florent picked up Virtue and took her to the truck. Big drops of blood spattered the dust on the street. "Next stop Sainte-Romanie!" he grunted, stepping on the gas.

Elise turned her head and saw Monsieur Emile going slowly up the stairs, holding Rosine's hand. She wiped her eyes and turned her attention to Virtue, who was moaning softly in the corner.

Florent, his lip twitching, was in no mood to console anybody. He had a sudden image of Madame Chouinard waving her arms, half made up, her bosom covered with breadcrumbs. "Old douche bag," he muttered between his teeth. "Fucking foreign shit hole," he added abruptly, turning his thoughts to Egon Ratablavasky, who was probably fast asleep at this hour, his face lit up by a noble smile. "Two-faced Anglo trash," he went on, now aiming his guns at the happy owner of The Beanery, who was probably sipping his morning coffee in the company of his sweet wife. "I'll have your hide, you son of a bitch! Just wait till I get my hands on a couple of good armoires and you'll see who you're messing with."

Florent's rage then descended from his head to his right foot on the accelerator. Drivers crossing the Jacques Cartier Bridge that morning were witness to some very old maneuvers.

With Virtue on her lap, Elise was dozing, unaware of her husband's exploits.

The ashen morning light gradually turned blue, and the sun decided to contribute its portion of light. The landscape slowly opened up. A chain of wooded mountains appeared, its outlines broad and vigorous. Florent felt an agreeable sense of space. Breathing more easily, he gazed tenderly at Elise, who was still asleep. He wanted to drink some excellent coffee, to make love, to run through the fields, and to earn a vast fortune, all at once as the mountains became less undulating, more harmonious. The highway traced great gentle curves around them, so the truck seemed to be flying.

SAINTE-ROMANIE, 4 km, announced a road sign hanging by a thread. (Two days earlier it had been struck by the body of a sleeping man flying out an improperly closed door.) "Already?" Florent murmured, almost disappointed.

Virtue raised her head, yawned, and stretched on Elise's lap, waking her up.

"We're nearly there," Florent announced.

The dog slowly turned, moaning softly, for the cut in her paw was very painful. Summoning all her courage, she pushed herself up to rest her front paws just under the windows. A moment later, apparently satisfied with the lay of the land, she limped back to the middle of the seat, curled up in a ball, and went back to sleep. "It must be so pleasant to live here," Elise murmured. "The air smells so good. I'd forgotten how beautiful the country is."

"Provided nobody comes and messes up the landscape," Florent cackled.

They were driving along a secondary road that wound its way through a bumpy valley, between yellow fields interspersed with groves of trees. There were hardly any houses to be seen. Suddenly, at a turn in the road, the railway appeared on their right, puny and modest, as if knowing it was no match for the landscape. Then there were more and more houses, mostly brick, with gables, and with that somewhat starchy elegance you find in New England villages.

Two minutes later, they were in Sainte-Romanie, a village clustered around a trim brick church on a large hillock. Sitting on the front steps of the Boulangerie Marcel Berthiaume, a little boy was biting into a strawberry turnover still hot from the oven. Florent stopped and rolled down the window. "Hey, kid, can you tell me where the station is?"

Startled, the little boy looked up and a thread of jam trickled down his chin. He licked it and diligently swallowed. "There isn't one. They shut it down."

"I know. We're here to open it up."

With a sudden rush of emotion, the boy got to his feet, a look of fear mingled with respect spreading over his face, as if he were talking to the inventor of the railway. "Do . . . do you want me to show you the way?"

"I hope you don't mind dogs," said Elise, opening the door.

He shook his head and climbed inside. He'd sit beside a dog with rabies for the honor of guiding the "station people" (as he would call them from now on, looking mysterious). He sat beside Elise, stiff as a poker, his right hand on his knee to hide a jam stain. The truck started up.

"Well, where's the station?" asked Florent.

"Go straight till you get to the general store, down by the gas pump, then turn and go over the culvert with the broken board (not too fast), and after that you'll see a brick house with no front steps. That's Madame Larose's place. There's a road alongside it. . . . Watch out for the culvert!"

Florent applied the brakes, but too late. The window on the driver's side was swallowed up by the door. "Holy horseradish!" Florent muttered. "I just knocked ten years off my truck!"

Who are the strangers with the Lemieux boy? Madame Larose wondered, hanging out her kitchen window.

"Now you turn right," the child added, still stunned by the shock. "Not too fast here, either," he added importantly. "The road's all chewed up. After the second turn you'll see the station. There it is," he said, pointing.

Elise slipped him a quarter.

"Thanks a lot." He pushed open the door and jumped onto the platform. "Are the trains *really* coming back, like they used to?"

Florent laughed. "Why not?"

"Gee, my dad'll be glad!" he exclaimed, and he was off like a shot.

Elise watched him go, then turned to Florent. "Why would you string him such a line? In five minutes the whole village will know. You can't pull trains out of a hat!"

Florent shrugged and walked along the platform overrun with weeds, whistling. "Good-looking station, eh? Give me the keys."

It was a rather small building, a full ground floor and a second floor with a mansard roof. The exterior was painted the traditional dusty wine red, with faded lemon-yellow trim at the corners. Florent ran his fingernail over a plank. "Fresh paint. That's a good sign."

With its curved roof and gables and huge cornices supported by quarter-round corbels, it looked oddly like a Chinese pagoda.

"Two or three broken windows," Florent observed, continuing his inspection, "but the frames seem to be in good shape."

Elise exclaimed, "Look at the old porcelain stove in the waiting room! A real museum piece! Just a few pieces of furniture and we'll have a gorgeous living room!"

Florent made a face, but kept his thoughts to himself.

Around three sides of the station ran a grove of birch and alder through which you could just make out a bit of wall or the tip of a gable. Behind the station, the bush was moving back in on a small yard littered with rotting ties. At the far end stood a small shed, painted like the station and, surprisingly, scrupulously cared for. Across from it, beyond the railway, the land sloped down to fenced fields, edged by a distant line of trees. "Well, baby," Florent murmured after he'd walked up and down the platform for a while, "if it's peace we want, we're in the right place!"

Elise threw herself in his arms. "I'm happy! I'm so happy!"

She snatched the key from him and, after a struggle, managed to open the huge padlock on the front door.

Hearts pounding, eyes intent, they slowly walked through the waiting room, which emitted solemn creaking sounds. Virtue zigzagged ahead of them, nose to the ground, sneezing every meter. "They haven't even cleaned out the stationmaster's office," Florent observed. He stopped, startled at the unexpected fullness of his voice.

The wicket door sighed a long sleepy lament, then suddenly slammed behind them. Almost fearfully, Elise pointed: "Look, the telegraph . . ."

Barely discernible under cobwebs and dust, it was sleeping like a pharaoh in his sarcophagus.

Florent went back and forth, moving chairs, opening doors, jiggling drawers to chase away the strange aura that was slowly surrounding them. "Let's check out our abode!" he suggested with forced enthusiasm.

They stumbled up the dusty little staircase hemmed in by varnished walls where distressing scurrying sounds could be heard. The key turned easily in the lock, as if it had just been oiled. The stationmaster's apartment consisted of seven rooms, rather small but well lit, furnished in 1930s style.

As they were taking possession of their "abode," the Lemieux boy, his mouth full of mashed potatoes, was announcing to his family that the age of the steam engine was about to return to Sainte-Romanie, a village its M.P. had forgotten.

"I'll have a talk with the mayor after bowling tonight," muttered Monsieur Lemieux half an hour later, on his way back to his garage. "It'll be a treat to see the look on his face – the goddamn secretive crook."

"Quick!" Florent exclaimed, dropping into a chair. "Kraft Dinner, canned sausage, anything – I'm famished!"

A cloud of dust settled over his features, which screwed up in a coughing fit.

"If your guts are complaining, for God's sake come and give me a hand!" said Elise. She went to the kitchen, opened a cupboard, then another and another. "Florent, come and look! Dishes, canned food, jars of pickles – a package of diapers! It's as if somebody was expecting us!" Suddenly pale, she turned to her husband. "Did you by any chance . . ."

Briefly startled, Florent looked at her, then dashed to the refrigerator, but all he found was a hunk of fossilized bacon. "Whew, you had me scared! Now come on, calm down, for the love of God! The cans belonged to the old stationmaster and his wife made too many pickles, that's all!"

Elise looked over the shelves again, then turned to him, relieved. "Forget what I said and get some ground beef from the grocery store. Meanwhile, I'll rinse off the dishes."

"So you're the new stationmaster!" exclaimed Hamel, the grocer, delighted to be the first citizen of Sainte-Romanie to hold an official conversation with the newcomer. "Welcome to our neck of the woods! And my compliments to your good wife. No, sir, it won't hurt to have the train back. You can't believe how bad the road is here. Whenever there's a snowstorm it's blocked for three days, then when spring comes we lose our shocks in the potholes!"

"I'm not . . . not exactly the stationmaster," Florent stammered, thinking Holy horseradish! What can I invent? "They've named me . . . appointed me as an . . . an investigator. Yes, to find out if the station was shut down by mistake, since the road service here is as bad as you maintain."

"Holy crow! I don't just *maintain*! Now listen here, young fella: I bring three hundred tonnes of merchandise into this village every year, not an ounce less! Well, now, for four years transport rates have been sky high and climbing, and I don't know a Christian soul that can stop them. So every fall, the village practically turns into a canning factory. People aren't fools: they put up what they grow, and to hell with store-bought food! What can I do? I have to keep hiking my prices to keep transport costs from eating up my profits. Good thing I don't sell just groceries or, let me tell you, I'd have locked up a long time ago. If the train came back, though, everything would change, you know as well as I do: after all, it's our taxes that support the train; it's what they call a public service – the rates are the same for us all, as long as everybody does their bit." In a final outburst, he said, "Young fella, I hope you'll be on Sainte-Romanie's side. We're all counting on you."

On his way home, Florent thought, Suddenly I'm a VIP. God knows how I'll get out of it.

Elise heard him out, laughing. "Now stop complaining! For once you've got luck on your side, with everybody dying to please. Just drop a hint about how much you love antiques, and the furniture will pile up while you watch."

"An inspector!" exclaimed Mayor Meloche, stopping short on the sidewalk, his armpits still steaming from four games of bowling. "That's a load of . . . First I've heard about it, Hector! And may the sparrows dump on my head if I'm lying! Who told you, anyway?"

Hector Lemieux's eyelids crinkled in a way that warned you not to mistake him for the man who invented the left-handed monkey wrench. He snickered and rocked on his heels.

"Christ on a muffin!" the mayor exploded. "Fourteen years I've been mayor, and this is the first important piece of news to hit town without going through my good ear!"

"My boy showed him to the station this morning," said Lemieux sarcastically. "Then about noon he went to Hamel's for groceries. My Marcel tried to worm a little information out of him. And besides, about three this afternoon he went back to the store with his wife, and they left with an eighty-eight-dollar order. Meaning they aren't leaving town tomorrow morning."

Mayor Meloche seemed perplexed. He pondered a moment and said, "Uh-huh – I been thinking, I took the M.P. duck hunting last fall; maybe it's paying off."

"If you want to know what's going on, phone the Canadian National office."

"Anything but that! An-y-thing! When the government makes a decision, you don't ask questions! Least said, soonest mended. They're still in a state of shock, you might say; that could be enough to screw us altogether!"

He pulled on his parka collar to allow the excess heat generated by the conversation to escape, then started walking again. Suddenly he asked, "How old is he?"

"A kid. Twenty-five at the most. Hamel says his wife's quite a dish."

"A university kid, I suppose. They're smooth, all right. Have to know how to rub them the right way."

About nine o'clock the next morning, Jean-Marie Meloche, with an ingratiating smile and prying eyes, entered the waiting room. Florent spotted him from the window. "Here we go! Now that the village has started to gab, I'd better give them something to talk about," he said, going downstairs.

The meeting between the mayor of Sainte-Romanie and the railway investigator took place amid the greatest cordiality. "Everything's working – power, water, heat?" the mayor inquired, peering blandly at the newcomer.

Florent assured him that all was well. "You heat with wood, don't you?"

"Yes, why?"

"Oh, just wondering."

The mayor took a hesitant few steps, hands in his pockets. "You're doing an investigation, I hear?"

Florent felt a chill on his neck and a slight giddiness. "That's right. To decide if we should restore regular train service to your village. In fact I was going to come and see you about it this morning. What's your opinion?"

The mayor shrugged. "I've given lots of people my opinion. Lavigne, our M.P. – I have the great honor of counting him among my friends – he's likely told you about it. I've even written to him on the subject. But I wouldn't want to try and influence you: it wouldn't be doing either of us a favor."

With these words Mayor Meloche launched into a long plea on behalf of his village, in which the effects of closing down the station sounded very like those of a tidal wave or a volcano. Florent suspected that the principal ravages of the closing were electoral: the telegrapher, three railwaymen and a warehouseman, finding themselves out of work, blamed their misfortune on the incompetence of the mayor, against whom they'd been plotting ever since. Florent, increasingly horrified by the scope of his lie, promised to conduct his investigation with all necessary objectivity. "They've given me as long as I need for my report," he said. "Five months, six if necessary. I'll leave no stone unturned."

"Can't ask for more than that," the mayor smiled. "The truth will out." Damn civil servants! he thought. They're all the same. Six months to investigate a village station!

After shaking Florent's hand, he headed for the door. "By the way, while I think of it," he said, a hand on the doorknob, "have you had a look at your wood supply? It must be rotten by now. Just asking – the municipality's always provided heat for the station. It's a courtesy that goes back to my grandfather's time."

"There isn't all that much wood left," Florent admitted.

"Good! Glad you told me! I'll have twenty cords delivered this afternoon."

"Twenty!" said Florent, startled.

"Right, my friend. These old stoves have a hell of an appetite." He patted the huge Victorian stove in the waiting room.

"In any case, it's a fine-looking piece," observed Florent, who had just spotted a promising vein in the mayor's remarks. "She must be sixty years old."

"If my memory's right, it was Marcel Hamel's father – Marcel runs the general store – who put it in. That goes back to the turn of the century."

"A fine piece," Florent repeated, stroking it. "I'm quite interested in antiques. Do some collecting in my spare time."

"You might make some interesting finds around here."

"He's in my pocket!" said the jubilant mayor on his way home. He went up to the attic to unearth a few old-fashioned things, but came back empty-handed. "I bet he's going to prowl all around the county in his truck. Better warn my people to go easy on the prices."

Florent went up to their apartment. Elise had just got the same idea as Mayor Meloche. A ladder stood in the middle of the living room under a half-open trapdoor. "Well? No trestle beds in sight?" Florent asked, sticking his head in the opening. She was crouching in front of a box of books in the grayish light of a bull's-eye window that hadn't seen a duster since the death of Sir Wilfrid Laurier.

"Read this," she said, offering him a thick cardboard-bound volume.

"*A Few Flowers*? Weird title for an eight-hundred-page book!" His gaze fell on a poem entitled "The Ballad of the Patriarchs":

Under the auspices
Of our hospices
Folks grow old
Like gold.

We aren't aloof
And here's the proof
Even if you have no roof

You can hang your hat
At our place.

Pain in the head?
Legs like lead?
Stretch out on a bed
There's books to be read!

"Ah yes, Platt the poet. . . . He won't be writing anymore. . . ."

They rummaged in the box for a few minutes before going downstairs.

TWENTY-SEVEN

Florent trembled at the thought that people in high places might be making inquiries about him. To put them off the track he made a few trips around the village with a pencil and an important air, pretending to take notes.

A visit to the priest was essential. Father Adelard Bournival, a big, bald, energetic man with thick, slightly fossilized features greeted Florent with a glass of port and jokes that were rather spicy for a man of his calling, and showed great interest in any tittle-tattle about him that might be making the rounds of the parish. Florent left after an hour with the priest, his stomach lined with a piece of the molasses cake that was the glory of the priest's housekeeper, Madame Laflamme. "It's been good to chat with you, my son," said the priest, who was not unaware of Elise's charms. "Come for dinner next Sunday. And bring your wife. Father Comeau from Saint-Thrasinien will be here. The conversation won't be dull, I promise."

Florent was permitted a visit of the church and the sacristy, but he'd been unable to fulfill his wish to go down to the cellar, as Madame Laflamme had mislaid the key. "You aren't missing much," said the priest. "It's a rat hole full of useless old junk."

I'll see what's down there, Florent promised himself, if I have to dig a tunnel.

He gradually visited all the local farmers, under the pretext of asking what use they would make of the train if it were brought back. After a few words on the subject, he would smoothly turn the conversation to his "addiction to old-fashioned things." "I might buy the odd piece to round out my collection. Are there things that are just in your way? I could have a look if you want."

Because of his pleasant, straightforward manner, people were happy to show him around the house and outbuildings.

For several days his research bore little fruit. Elise was growing concerned. "I'm not going to fill up the station with commodes and old sewing machines," Florent said. "If I buy just any old stuff it would keep pouring in and they'd soon figure out that I'm a dealer, not an investigator. No, better to hold out for the real thing and take the poor jerk that wants to sell it for a ride."

Two days later, at Omer Lagacé's farm, he found the real thing. "Folks tell me you're interested in old stuff," said the farmer, finishing off the can of meatball stew that constituted his dinner. (He'd lost his wife eight years earlier and lived alone, eating whatever came to hand and leaving the care of the house to his late wife.)

Florent gave a slightly detached smile. "That depends."

"How about old sleighs? I got one out in the barn. Been thinking about chopping it up for firewood. My granddad bought it around the turn of the century. If you're interested, I'll give you a good price, harness and all. If not, no hard feelings."

Florent shook his head. "It's furniture I'm interested in."

"Take a look, anyway, it doesn't tie you to anything. She's just over here."

They walked across an icy field at the end of which stood a somewhat shaky barn. "Got anything else for sale?" Florent asked.

"Nothing special. Could've had a couple of wardrobes, if you go for that sort of thing, but I chopped them up last spring."

Idiot, Florent thought, favoring the farmer with his most jovial smile.

"Give me a hand, young fellow," he said at the door.

Florent lifted one of the sides of the double door, which was attached just by the upper hinge, and pulled. The daylight revealed a sundry assortment of dusty objects atop an inverted sleigh. "She's a fine piece," said the farmer, "real fine."

He began to dig for it. "When we were youngsters, what we loved to do, come winter, was pile into that sleigh, all bundled up in our bearskins, and take off across the countryside with a little flask between the legs and a pretty girl beside us. Yup! There was plenty of billing and cooing and maybe some other things, too! Must be why it took her so long to show her age."

As the jumble of planks and old tools and crippled furniture thinned out, the sleigh's terminal decrepitude became increasingly obvious. Florent assumed a look of irritation. "Listen, I don't want to waste your time. I don't think I'm interested in your sleigh. Haven't you anything else to show me?"

Peering at the back of the barn, he saw, half hidden under a heap of dusty planks, something that looked like a tin-covered icebox. The crudely applied sheets were spotted with rust, and half the paint had peeled off. "What's that?"

The farmer guffawed. "That? Uncle Florimond's icebox. Which reminds me, I should junk that thing first chance I get: come summer, it's so full of wasps you can't go near it."

"Your uncle made it himself?" asked Florent.

He drew nearer, driven by a strange intuition. The farmer went on freeing the sleigh. "Say, have a look at these wood appliqués! All handmade! No machine work here. Just replace the missing pieces and you'd have a hell of a good-looking piece. Course the wood's a bit rotten in spots, but we could work out a good price."

Florent wasn't listening; he was examining the icebox, which was nearly a meter taller than he was. "It's an old converted armoire," he murmured, opening one of the doors. The inside was also lined in tin, but under a loose sheet he could see a pegged joint. He shut the door and examined the outside again. On the left side, near the crossbars, he noticed that one corner of the tin was loose.

The farmer was concentrating on righting the sleigh and wasn't paying Florent the slightest attention.

Florent slipped his finger under the tin and pulled as hard as he could. Three nails gave way and wood appeared. His hand was bleeding.

A tremendous din suddenly filled the garage, and the farmer, straining like an ox pulling a mountain, heaved a satisfied cry: the sleigh had just landed on its runners.

"Linen-fold decoration," murmured Florent, pale with excitement. He quickly put back the tin and went over to the farmer.

"Look here – she's a beauty, eh?" he said, running his hand over the rough wood, ignoring the holes and cracks.

"It's missing a door," Florent observed, "and half the bottom's shot."

The farmer gritted his teeth. "Look here, sonny. If you were expecting to find the manufacturer's label on this sleigh, you'll be going home disappointed. Anyhow, that's all I got to show you." And he pretended to walk away.

Florent clutched his sleeve. "I'll take it. How much?"

The old man's eyes flickered with delight. "Thirty bucks. And considering how old she is, that's cheap."

"I'll come and tow it away in a couple of days. How much for that icebox thing in the corner?"

"Pile it in the sleigh and the good Lord'll bless you! You can pay me when you want," he added, peering covetously at Florent's billfold.

"Give me a hand," he said, handing the farmer his money, "and I'll get rid of your wasps right away."

"Elise!" Florent exclaimed, rushing into the station. "Come see what I found!"

Sweating and puffing, they moved the icebox into the shed behind the station. "Are you really sure this is one of the marvels of the New World?" Elise asked skeptically, rubbing her chafed arms.

"Depends if the doors are original. If they are and if the nails haven't chewed up the frame too much, this armoire will bring us a small fortune!"

He took a hammer to remove the tin covering, but stopped. "I need tools. I'll go get some pliers in the village."

"I wouldn't if I were you."

"Why not?"

"People will talk. And if your farmer finds out his icebox is worth three times as much as his barn, that's the end of your bargains. Get your pliers in Victoriaville."

Two hours later Florent was back with a tool chest. "Now let's get to work!"

The shed filled with a mixture of curses, creaking tin, and sighs of satisfaction. Elise helped in the delicate operations and made sandwiches and coffee. Night had long since fallen when they stopped, arms aching with fatigue.

What Florent had unearthed was a superb larder from the French régime, with two fretwork doors, the upper part of their linen-fold side panels decorated with a flower carved in the round and composed of six hearts joined at the points. The fretwork, carved from a single piece, was the work of an unusually skilled craftsman. Unfortunately, the top of one section of fretwork had been badly damaged by a nail. Other nails had left marks over most of the surface, but these could be easily camouflaged. The bottom and part of the back had rotted away.

"Poor thing's had a rough life," Florent sighed. "But if we don't screw up, we're looking at ten thousand dollars. I'll never make another find like this."

In three days the larder had been stripped, waxed, and polished, and all trace of nail holes had disappeared. But it would take an expert to repair the fretwork, and Florent needed some old pine to replace the rotten parts. "I'll go see Jean-Denis Beaumont in Montreal. He should be able to help me."

They carried the piece to the truck. Florent tied it down firmly, covered it with canvas, and got behind the wheel.

"Our investigator isn't investigating much these days," Mayor Meloche observed as the truck drove down Main Street. He got out of his chair and stuck his nose against the window of the general store.

"You expect him to announce his findings from the rooftop?" asked Monsieur Hamel. "Open your eyes, Jean-Marie: when you don't see them, that's when they're sticking their noses everywhere."

"Lord in heaven, what's he waiting for?" grumbled Omer Lagacé, gazing at his sleigh. "A team of horses? If he doesn't show up by Monday, she goes in the garbage."

"Ten thousand smackers," Florent kept repeating, zipping down the highway as if the devil was at his heels. "Maybe even twelve! Slipskin, you fucker, you're going to find out who I am!"

He arrived at Jean-Denis Beaumont's shop around noon, and found him with a tourist from Ontario. The two men were having an animated discussion over a curly wig that had come from a school in Joliette with a lot of old theater costumes. He was trying to convince his customer that the wig had belonged to Frontenac or, at the very least, to one of his natural sons. He turned to Florent with a knowing smile. "Give me ten minutes and I'll buy you a good lunch."

Soon the tourist was on his way, smugly bearing his relic of the French régime. "Now," said Jean-Denis, "let's eat."

Florent clutched his arm. "Ill show you something that's worth a lot more than your old wigs."

He led him outside and lifted the canvas. Beaumont whistled. "Holy Christ! Where'd you find that baby! First one I've ever seen. Three thousand dollars: I'll give you three thousand cash, in freshly ironed hundreds."

Florent laughed. "That's a good one! Your fingers are turning to hooks, you old pirate. Trying to pull the wig number on me, eh? Save your spit – I won't let this go for a penny under ten thousand."

The antique dealer smiled disarmingly. "I'd go as high as twelve or thirteen myself."

He got in the truck and examined the piece. "You need a mortise wedge for the fretwork on the left. We'll go see old man Morin. Give him fifty bucks and sweet-talk him a bit and he'll get to work on it right away; he likes beautiful things."

He ran loving fingers over the wood. "It really is a hell of a fine piece," he kept repeating. "Plenty of nail holes, but they hardly show. Where'd you find it?"

I could smell that one coming, Florent said inwardly. He winked. "In Scratch-My-Back County, not far from St. Rear End."

Beaumont didn't bat an eyelid. "This is something to celebrate. It's an event in the history of Quebec furniture. Champagne's on me."

"Old man Morin first, okay? I'd like to get this settled today."

They went to see the cabinet maker, who lived a few houses away. The door was opened by an old lady in silver-rimmed glasses, whose sunken features seemed to be held in place by the scarf tied under her chin. "He's at the chiropractor!" she shouted. "On account of his neck. But I'll let you in the shop. That's a fine piece," she said when the canvas had been removed. "Come back around two."

They went to Berri Street, across from the Laurier Métro station, where a restaurant called La Truite had just opened. "I forbid you to pay a penny," said Jean-Denis. "You've just turned up a piece from before the Conquest. There aren't three of them in all Quebec. You deserve a lot of credit."

"Talk like that can turn a guy's head," said Florent, smiling slyly. "And in that state he might make bad business deals."

"What a nasty thought! As far as I'm concerned, you're my brother. Keep your paranoia for others."

They ordered an apéritif, then a second. "We're celebrating like widowers!" Beaumont exclaimed suddenly. "It's unnatural!"

Florent looked at him, uncomprehendingly. Beaumont leaned across the table. "I met a couple of cute chicks in a bar last week. They share a place and they're both out of work. Why don't I give them a call?"

"What about my larder?" Florent asked weakly.

"Don't get so worked up. I'll take care of your larder."

Florent watched Beaumont lean on the bar with feigned nonchalance, his eyes half shut, mouth very close to the receiver, as if it too had a mouth, filled with intoxicating fragrance. "I made myself a promise," Florent murmured. "Come on!" he said, growing tense. "You're here on business – now stick to it!"

Jean-Denis came back to the table smiling smugly. "They're on their way," he announced, sitting down. "I move fast."

A bottle of Beaujolais appeared on the table. "I wanted to keep the good news for dessert, but I can't hold it in," said Beaumont. "I'm almost a hundred percent sure I've got a buyer for you. And I don't want any commission. You hear me? Not a cent."

"What *do* you want?"

"Nothing. Just tell me where you found it."

Florent settled back in his chair with a smile. "I'll gladly sell you my apples, my friend, but not the apple tree. Not after two or three or even six bottles of Beaujolais. Is that clear?"

"Okay, all right, let's drop it," said Beaumont with a frustrated grimace. "Business turns me into a bastard. I can't help myself."

"Here they come," said Florent.

He stood up on rather rubbery legs, while Jean-Denis went to meet the girls. Both were fairly pretty, one with dark curly hair, the other a bleached blonde, slightly vulgar but tastefully made up, the typical secretaries who spend their vacations in Nassau with the boss, but alert and nobody's fools despite their smiles. The wine quickly loosened their tongues. The blonde, Anne-Marie, leaned toward Florent to ask, "What do you do?"

He had always detested singles bar openers and gave a witty but vague answer that managed to make her laugh. Her friend suddenly seemed appealing. A bit flabby, but good color, he thought, discreetly looking her over.

Not as great looking as some guys, she was thinking, but he seems nice enough – and he's funny.

In the middle of the soup, Florent slipped his hand under the table, where it received a warm welcome. At that very moment, though, an image of Elise, or of the larder, interfered with his urges. With dessert, Jean-Denis ordered a bottle of Riesling, which, on top of the three of Beaujolais, lifted them up like a helicopter, smoothly and affectionately. Florent was floating above sunny French vineyards while his hand traveled slowly, almost indifferently, along the thigh of his companion, who communicated her pleasure with quick but remarkably effective caresses.

Alas, the larder was haunting him. Elise hovered over it, smiling sweetly. Suddenly Florent felt hot and queasy. He kept on joking, but Anne-Marie's blond flesh began to seem unreal as Elise's smile cruelly stabbed him between the ribs. Am I getting old? he wondered with a sort of melancholy relief. Fidelity's winning out.

He ordered a coffee. My lover's caught a chill, thought Anne-Marie, mildly exasperated because her fluttering eyelashes were having less and less effect.

Watching his friend with a puzzled smile, Jean-Denis Beaumont murmured, "First the larder." Then, swigging his cognac, he said, "Okay, girls, you'll have to excuse us, but business calls. Shall I drive you home?"

Anne-Marie staggered into her kitchen full of dirty dishes. "Weird guy, that Florent. Still, he asked for my number."

It was half-past four when they set out for Morin's workshop. My head's spinning, my stomach's full of rocks, and I'm going to talk business! Florent moaned inwardly. Idiot! You deserve to get screwed.

But as he stepped onto the sidewalk just outside the workshop, he took a somersault, landed flat on his stomach, got a bloody nose, and sobered up immediately.

"It's a fine piece! A hell of a fine piece!" said old man Morin, offering him a handkerchief. "I started on it right after dinner. Now all it needs is a bit of beeswax."

Florent looked at the fretwork. The broken section had been replaced by a beautifully carved little mortise wedge. He turned to the cabinet maker. "Congratulations! I'll be back with more work for you."

The old man gave him a wry smile. "Don't make too many plans for me, my boy! My bones are all coming out of their sockets. For a year now, work's been a real calvary. If it wasn't for my daughter and grandsons I'd've hung up my skates long ago."

He took a rag and rubbed the mortise wedge with much sighing and spitting. Soon the wood took on a fine luminous blond color that gradually blended with the rest of the piece. "Anybody who knows what he's looking at can always see the difference," he said, running his hand over the fretwork, "but this way it's more honest. That'll be fifty bucks and I don't give invoices."

He rubbed his neck as he watched them lift the larder, lavished advice on how to fasten down the canvas, then dragged himself back to his workshop.

"Now," Florent asked, "where's your customer?"

Jean-Denis went into the workshop to phone and came out all excited. "He's jumping around like a doughnut in boiling oil. Ask for twelve thousand and stick to it."

Florent felt his face getting hot, and little pink and blue lights danced before his eyes. "Where are we going?"

"Davaar Street in Outremont."

"I think I've been here before," he murmured as they stopped outside a big brick house dripping desiccated ivy.

A curtain stirred at a window; then the garage door opened, and a fat man gestured them in.

"It . . . it's Spufferbug, my old boss!" Florent exclaimed. "Fourteen thousand, you prick," he muttered with a rancorous smile. "Fourteen thousand or I keep it."

"Bwassonnoo! For God's sake! Don't tell me you're in the antique business!" he exclaimed, trying to hide his vexation. "Well, that's good news!"

Florent allowed Spufferbug to pat his back as if he were a good child, answering his questions in monosyllables. Then, with Jean-Denis's help, he undid the canvas. The larder appeared in all its glory. There was a deep silence. Spufferbug climbed up in the truck and walked around the piece, his eyes glowing maniacally.

"Fourteen thousand!" exclaimed Jean-Denis on the way home. "That's not a sale, it's revenge! I never thought he'd pay it. Good for you! Come to my place – that calls for a drink!"

"Here's your commission," said Florent, proffering a cheque.

Beaumont pocketed it without batting an eye.

They stopped at his place on Prince Arthur Street, where a Courvoisier bottle filled with cheap brandy awaited, the real stuff having been set aside for the host's personal use. "Promise to let me know when you get more pieces. I've got good customers, you know. They'll pay the price if the piece is worth it."

"I promise, on the head of my future son," said Florent. He drained his glass and left. As he got in the truck he thought, Why don't I drop in on Picquot? Poor man must be bored to death. And I can settle my debt.

Surprisingly, considering how late it was, the chef was out. Florent slipped a cheque in his mailbox, along with a thank-you note. Two hours later, Elise opened the door, her features ravaged by insomnia. "God Almighty!" she exclaimed, when she saw Spufferbug's cheque. "And I was expecting five hundred! Are we really going to be rich?"

Helped by the good news, she dropped her nightgown to the floor, where it was joined by a little mound of clothing. Meanwhile, back in Montreal, his guts tormented by a meal that his purchase had turned to cement, Spufferbug sighed and tossed in bed at the side of his weighty wife.

TWENTY-EIGHT

Luck is a tight-cheeked lady who rarely smiles at the same person twice. Florent didn't expect to find another Louis XIII larder the next day – and he didn't. In the days that followed he found so little of interest (a four-poster cradle and two pewter spoons bearing the hallmark of Etienne Labrècque) that he had to lower his standards, contenting himself with some pretty mediocre objects he could easily sell to the ignorant without arousing suspicion about what he was really up to.

He thought he was on to something interesting when he and Elise went to Farther Bournival's after High Mass on Sunday, November 23. The housekeeper, Madame Laflamme, had just showed them into a large, solemn sitting room where the priest, with his loud voice and easy laugh, was talking with a fat, timid-looking ecclesiastic who looked half asleep. Standing to greet them, the priest exclaimed, "If it isn't our investigating antiquarian and his charming wife!"

"What do you mean?" Florent spluttered.

Guffawing, the priest shook hands, his breath giving off a piercing odor of communion wine and tobacco. "Come in, come in and meet my friend Father Comeau, a well-read man if ever there was one, though he'd deny it out of humility. . . . He's a specialist in Greek and Latin literature – and in mathematics, too, I'll have you know."

Father Comeau got up, smiling painfully, as if his viscera had come undone and the slightest movement threatened to throw them into dreadful turmoil. He said almost inaudibly, "Now, now, now, don't exaggerate. That may have been so when I was a youngster, but now . . ." He extended his hand. "Delighted, madame. Delighted, sir."

Shortly afterward, when they were seated at the dining room table, Florent asked, "What did you mean, calling me an investigating antiquarian?"

"What did I mean?" The priest started chewing fiercely on a piece of bread, thinking, Good gravy, my stomach's been empty since this morning – except for the good Lord. I think He needs company. Aloud, he repeated, "What did I mean? Nothing. It was a turn of phrase. What exactly *do* you do?" he asked with a penetrating gaze.

"Why he's a trainee investigator," Elise replied with feigned surprise. "Didn't you know?"

Madame Laflamme, a small redhead with dry blotchy skin and a vaguely froglike mouth, turned to Florent as she set a steaming tureen in the middle of the table. "Don't let Father's questions get to you," she simpered. "He's always prying – and he loves to tease his guests."

With an indefinable smile the priest resumed his questioning. "And how does an investigator trainee spend his time?"

Florent had recovered his aplomb and launched into a brilliant improvisation on his activities, citing figures from the *Canada Year Book*, which he'd had the happy idea of consulting in preparation for this official meal. He concluded by saying, "Sainte-Romanie's a borderline case. I'm fighting as hard as I can for you, but don't be surprised if it takes time."

"Nothing's easy here," sighed Father Comeau, contemplating his soup with a meditative air.

Father Bournival was hunched over his plate, slurping it in as if he were alone in the world. "What soup!" he exclaimed with his mouth full. "My housekeeper has outdone herself! I should have guests every day." Then, with a sly look at Florent, he asked, "And what do antiques have to do with your investigations?"

"They're just a pastime."

"You certainly have time to pass!" the priest laughed.

"What can I do? Old furniture's my passion . . . so I'm taking advantage of my stay here. I've no other distractions."

Staring into space, Father Comeau slowly picked up his spoon. All the others looked at him. "Without passion," he murmured in a distant, muffled voice, "life would be unlivable. If I hadn't had mathematics years ago, I'm not sure what would have become of me."

Father Bournival pushed away his empty plate. "Well, my boy, collect to your heart's content. It's an honest occupation, after all, and I'm sure you'll learn from it." Then he turned to the other priest and launched into a long discussion about certain hanky-panky involving a young crop-insurance adjuster in Saint-Thrasinien. His guests tried to keep their eyes from glazing over. Did I really convince him? Florent wondered.

Just then, Madame Laflamme set before him a plate of roast beef and roast potatoes. "I gave you a bit extra," she said, "to feed your young appetite. Don't be shy about asking for seconds."

Elise watched, smiling. Their host reached across the table and touched her hand. "And what do you think of our village?" he asked point-blank, his gaze lingering for just a moment on her modest V-cut neckline.

"I'd love to live here forever," she replied, blushing slightly.

With his mouth full, he began probing into her past, his solicitude sometimes bordering on the gallant. He looked sad to learn that she'd been orphaned at four and had spent her childhood in a convent in Rimouski, put there by an old semi-invalid aunt, who took her in during the summer.

Meanwhile, Florent and Father Comeau, who had discovered a shared interest in Quebec folklore, were passionately discussing the old songs and fiddlers. It was almost four o'clock when they left, slightly wobbly from eau-de-vie. Madame Laflamme rushed to the vestibule to help Florent on with his coat.

"Did you find the key to the church basement?" he asked.

"Gracious, I haven't had time to look. But come back in a couple of days – I'm sure it will turn up."

"Anytime, Madame Laflamme," he replied with a twinkle, "night or day!"

Outside, Elise laughed. "I'd better keep an eye on you. I think you'd hop into her bed for a sideboard!"

Two weeks later Madame Laflamme still hadn't found her key. Florent drove to Montreal through a rather exciting snowstorm, his truck filled with priceless treasures: tottery prie-dieux, battered kettles, laryngitic radios, sprung armchairs – and an amazing collection of 1920s postcards depicting couples faint with love, gazing goofily into each other's eyes. He came back early that evening, in a foul mood, with a cheque for a miserable hundred and sixty-five dollars. "At this rate," he grumbled, "I'll need two canes to walk into my new restaurant."

Elise laughed. "Did you really think you'd find a rare antique every day the good Lord gives you? Go take a hot bath and wash away your black thoughts."

She found him fast asleep in the cooling water. Virtue lay on a chair beside him, watching him anxiously.

About three in the morning they were suddenly awakened by a whistle. After a few moments, the whistle sounded again, closer now. "Good grief!" said Elise, sitting up. "It's a train!"

A muffled growl slowly crossed the frozen ground and rose into the walls. Florent ran to the window. You couldn't see ten feet ahead. Without warning, winter's scythe had slashed open all the clouds. Tons of snow were falling gently, enfolding the countryside in solemn mystery. The growling grew louder, and was suddenly transformed into thunder. The windows jingled and Virtue, desperate, howled lugubriously. Elise was overcome by sudden, illogical fear. She called to Florent, but he didn't hear: possessed by all the fury of hell, a deafening black mass was roaring past the station.

In the other beds of Sainte-Romanie, throats were cleared, lamps turned on, and Florent's name was uttered sleepily. He stood at the window, chin resting on his fists, his expression glum. Elise put her hand on his shoulder. "The concession roads will be snowed in for three days," he grumbled without turning around, "and I haven't got even one old chair to strip."

"Will you stop griping!" snapped Elise. "Did you think you'd make a million in two weeks? Get a job as a night watchman if you're so anxious!"

Grasping her shoulders, Florent smiled. "Is my better half giving me ox-blood injections to boost my morale?"

"Could be," she pouted.

He slapped her rear. "You Gaspé girls! Maybe you're right. I want to dance faster than the fiddle. Let's have coffee. I'm not the least bit sleepy."

Let's hope he isn't heading for another depression, Elise thought, wiping a cup, as her husband scribbled figures on a slip of paper. He put down his pencil. "Okay. To go into business this spring, we need forty thousand – minimum."

Elise smiled skeptically. "That's a small fortune."

"It's dumb to start before you're financially sound. I want to open up across from The Beanery and ruin the bastards."

Elise spun around, and the saucer she'd been holding slid onto the stove, slipped to the floor, and came to rest in a thousand pieces. Virtue, intrigued, jumped off Florent's lap and cautiously sniffed at the debris. "No more, no less," Florent continued imperturbably. "Till I get that bugger by the short hairs, there'll be a weight in my guts."

"You sure as hell don't beat around the bush!" Elise exclaimed. "And I was worried that you were going into another depression! It's more like delusions of grandeur. Forty thousand dollars! Do you expect to lay your hands on Frontenac's bedroom set here in Sainte-Romanie? And even if all the angels in heaven got together and brought it to you, would you be crazy enough to bet your fortune against a guy who almost broke you?"

"Yes, I would!" Florent yelled, pounding his fist on the table.

Virtue scurried off and hid at the back of a closet.

Florent dressed and went outside. The snow was falling harder than ever. When he returned the apartment was dark, and Elise was in bed. He lay beside her, somewhat ashamed of his outburst. "I know you aren't asleep," he said, thinking,

My voice sounds ridiculous! "I can tell by your breathing." He stroked her cheek.

"Good night," she said softly. Then, slipping her foot under his in their private gesture of reconciliation, she fell fast asleep.

Curled up in the warm bed, Florent pondered as the snow lashed the window and the trees swayed and moaned above the station. The train . . . maybe I could use the train. . . . I'll ask some questions at the grocery store tomorrow, try to find out if the odd train goes through even though the station's shut down.

He was spared the trouble. At eight o'clock the next morning, Mayor Meloche appeared, hands in the pockets of his parka. His left hand was caressing a half dozen Revolucion Especial Cuban cigars he'd got from Hamel, the grocer, during a lengthy strategy session. Florent saw him from the window. So the train doesn't come often, he thought, dashing down the stairs.

Florent invited the mayor up for coffee. Meloche apologized repeatedly for visiting so early and offered to come back later, assuring Florent he just happened to be in the neighborhood and decided to drop in and so forth. He chattered and smiled and told jokes, trying to make the conversation seem ordinary and casual. "Well, like I was telling the wife, looks like we're in for a real bad winter. It's just December." Elise came into the kitchen just then, and he interrupted himself to ask how she was, then resumed. "Just December, like I said, and the water main's already giving us problems, always the same place, on Bordeleau Lane." He took the cup of coffee Florent offered him. "Thanks. Yes, a little sugar, please. And cream, if you've got it. Yup, sometimes it looks like we'll have to dig to China to keep the damn pipes from freezing. No problems with the water here?"

"None at all," said Elise.

"Apart from it not being easy to heat the station," Florent added, "everything's fine."

Meloche laughed heartily. "If the trains stopped more often out front, they'd cut the wind, don't you think?"

"For the time being, they're just passing through" was Florent's sibylline reply.

"They don't pass through often, that's for sure."

Elise picked up a rag and left the kitchen. She couldn't hide her nervousness any longer.

"That could get worked out," said Florent. "I was in Montreal a couple of weeks ago."

"With a load of old furniture – yeah, I saw you."

"You did? I don't know what's got into me this past month: I buy whatever I see, then when business takes me to Montreal I cart it along and store it in my in-laws' basement. I belong to a collectors' club, you see, which means I can make trades."

"Next thing you'll be going into business," the mayor joked. "In town, I hear, old junk's really in style."

"It's a risky business: if three guys open antique stores, two will be broke in six months. Anyway, I like my job too much to give it up. Monsieur Meloche, you can't imagine how hard I've gone to bat for you."

"What for?"

"The train – what do you think? My bosses aren't easily convinced, you know."

"You mean . . ."

". . . that I've come to the conclusion the station should

be reopened? And how! Hamel was right: your roads here are pretty bad. In any case, with the coming gasoline shortage, the good old days of highway travel are coming to an end: in ten years, maybe less, we'll be using the railways again. It's *much* more economical. That's my opinion – which my bosses don't exactly share! But I'm hanging in. Whenever I can put in a word, I do. You must have realized that last night . . . unless you're a heavy sleeper."

"Not at all," Meloche replied, his heart pounding. "Takes nothing to wake me up."

"Well, a couple of weeks ago (Holy Joker, pray for me!) I managed to talk them into using the Montreal-Sainte-Romanie-Victoriaville-Quebec City line as a backup to prevent bottlenecks between Montreal and Quebec. They complain about maintenance costs. Keep telling me it isn't profitable. But tomorrow? Tomorrow, when gas costs two and a half bucks a gallon and the Sunday drive's a luxury for the rich, we have to be prepared for the thousands who'll be looking for cheaper means of transportation. Otherwise we'll be had by the bus companies again. Now's the time to start getting people used to the railway again: the profits will come later! And we *must* keep our lines in working order, make our schedules more flexible, fit them to the way people live today – like before the war – start advertising campaigns, bring our fares down as low as we can. And gradually, I guarantee it, the trains will be as full as in the past, and the railway companies will be the gold mines they once were."

Mayor Meloche crossed his legs, uncrossed them, then crossed them yet again, trying desperately to look knowing, as if Florent's words coincided exactly with his own recent reflections. In fact, he was almost choking with admiration.

"And you ain't seen nothing yet!" The look on Meloche's face made Florent staggeringly bold. "That train yesterday was just a beginning."

He stopped. "But before I say any more I must insist on the strictest secrecy. If my bosses found out what I'm going to tell you, we'd be up the creek. Loose tongues have sunk a lot of plans, you know."

"As mayor," Meloche stammered, "as mayor, I have a duty . . . the municipality . . ." The rest of his thought was swept away by a wave of emotion. "Trust me," he said, his hand on Florent's arm.

Florent looked the mayor straight in the eye. "All right, then," he began slowly, almost moved by the sound of his own voice. "I've been trying, as I said, to persuade the planning department to reopen the line that goes through your village, and the station too, of course. But there's more: I'm also fighting to have a warehouse built, to be used for freight in transit for eastern Quebec. (Holy crow! The tall tales you can invent if you really let the old imagination loose!) And I tell you, they're far from turning a deaf ear to my arguments."

"Will it . . . will it mean jobs for our parish?"

"We'll need a clerk and at least three warehouse workers. And I've told them to speak to the local contractor about the warehouse."

Criminy! thought Meloche, getting to his feet in a rush of emotion, what a sweet deal for my cousin Réjean! I may be able to run for Parliament.

"In my opinion," Florent went on, "that's the most economical way to proceed. But we have to be patient. And once again, Mayor Meloche, I advise you to bury what you've just heard in your back yard and cover it with a rock."

"I swear. Not even a word to the wife." A little later he was cursing himself. Damn fool! He let you in on all that and you didn't even offer him some firewood! You're losing your touch. Get moving! Do something! Ask him for supper next Sunday. No, people would talk. Say, how about finding some old furniture? No, I can't pull furniture out of the air. Hey, what about Aunt Ophélie? Forgot about her! Of course! Ophélie . . . get your ass to the old folks' home and have her sign a proxy. Tell her whatever comes to mind. I saw her last Sunday – since that last uremic attack she's been so out of it I could pass off as the priest.

"Florent!" Elise exclaimed, alarmed, "he's back! And in a state!"

"Now I've done it," Florent muttered, glancing out the window. "I told one lie too many – my goose is cooked."

"I was thinking about you at dinnertime," said the mayor breathlessly. "If you had an hour to spare, I've got some things to show you."

Florent slid into the passenger seat. "You see, my old aunt had to close up her house last year and go to an old folks' home. She knows her days are numbered so she asked me a couple of days ago to get rid of her belongings – and I thought of you."

"Did she live in the village?"

"No, Victoriaville. But when she was younger she had a sort of cottage built on the David concession road, eight miles outside the village. She was fairly well off then. Her father was a contractor and on very good terms with Premier Lomer Gouin, if you get my drift."

He drove off the highway onto a narrow, winding road hemmed in by tremendous snowbanks and covered with glare ice. The Chevvy started to swerve. Meloche, clutching the wheel, told Florent, with a gleam in his eye, "According to family rumor, she was Sir Wilfrid Laurier's mistress. . . . With a little luck you might find a cigar box full of juicy letters."

With a smile, Florent started to whistle, trying for a nonchalant look to conceal his impatience to see the elderly damsel's possessions. Holy horseradish! Is luck on my side again? he wondered. "As long as he doesn't try and screw me when it's time to set the price."

The road suddenly became a seemingly endless spiral drawing them to the center of the earth, to meet up with some Jules Verne hero. "We're nearly there," said the mayor, delighted at the success of a controlled skid that landed them in a snowbank.

He managed to extricate the car, turned and stopped in front of an old arbor. About time! Florent thought.

At the end of a short path lined with fir trees stood a one-story brick house with a gabled roof half caved-in under the snow. Most of the windowpanes had been broken. The mayor got out and strode into the snow. "Such a beautiful house," he sighed. "This happened last winter. The man who was looking after the place was killed in a snowmobile accident, and my aunt more or less forgot to replace him. What can you do? If you're lucky enough to reach a ripe old age, your brain's bound to go a bit fuzzy."

Florent looked glumly at the house. "Geez, all that water must have wrecked the furniture."

"It's not so bad. A good half of the roof's still solid, and I put polyethylene sheets over the worst spots. Shit!" he exclaimed indignantly. "Did I leave the keys in my Sunday suit?"

They heard a reassuring clink, and he inserted a big brass key in the lock. There was a musty smell. Somewhere in the room a shred of tin clattered in the wind. "Wonderful moldings," Florent murmured, gazing at the ceiling as he walked respectfully in the half light.

"Oh, the house is worth fixing up," the mayor declared, "but who'd want a place like this? No phone, no power, and the artesian well's full of mud."

"I might, if the price was right," Florent suggested, after he'd visited all the rooms. "But the furniture's pretty well worthless – water damage."

Three hours later he was back at the station, an offer to purchase in his pocket. He took the stairs four at a time before letting his joy explode. "Baby, I just pulled off the deal of the century! A fantastic summer house, full of gorgeous old furniture, for three thousand eight hundred dollars!"

"A house! What are we supposed to do with a house? Are you going into real estate?"

Florent shook his head. "The furniture alone's worth ten thousand. I'll hold on to the house. You'll understand when I take you there this afternoon."

Elise was twisting a lock of hair, a sign of growing irritation. "Florent, are you out of your mind? First a restaurant, now a country house! You're counting your chickens very prematurely, my friend. At this rate we'll soon be under the Lacombe Law."

"But I *will* be rich! Might as well get used to it now."

And in fact the list of Aunt Ophélie's belongings was enough to take your breath away. Once they'd thrown out the moth-eaten curtains, old bits of rope, tubes of crystallized unguents and other garbage, there remained:

1 Victorian-style coat stand with seat and mirror;
1 oil painting in very good condition depicting the 1856 fire in Trois-Rivières, signed David-Fleury Berlinguet;

1 Windsor chair with curved back in two sections, with comb;
2 brass beds;
1 Empire-style chaise longue;
1 Regency dining room set, including six chairs, one table (colossal), a buffet, and a sideboard;
1 four-poster spool bed;
1 Victorian horsehair sofa with a miniature bust of Louis-Joseph Papineau in the middle of the upper crosspiece;
1 lamp table;
1 Regency-style tea table;
4 kerosene lamps;
1 drop-leaf pigeonhole desk containing six bow-handled drawers, exceedingly well made;
3 chests of drawers, of no particular interest;
1 double buffet with incomplete diamond points, the doors attached with unusual butterfly-shaped pegs;
1 mid-eighteenth-century flintlock pistol, with powder horn and shot bag, but lacking trigger, the name L. J. Lousteau carved in the butt.

Florent was indebted to the dust, the damp, the cold – and to Jean-Marie Meloche's self-serving ignorance – for the incredibly good price. Of course, certain pieces would have to be relacquered or varnished. Veneer had lifted, joints had separated, mildew, age, and mice had wrecked once-splendid fabrics. Overall, though, it was still an impressive sight.

Florent quickly transported the furniture to Montreal. It took four trips, and Monsieur Morin, the cabinet maker who'd repaired his larder, called him in twice to check evidence justifying additional expenditures on certain restorations.

Up to his ears with work, Florent hadn't had time to see Ange-Albert or Picquot, from whom he'd had no news since leaving Montreal. Suddenly he missed them. And though he wouldn't acknowledge it, he was worried about Monsieur Emile.

One morning he and Elise decided to call on their friends. "Boissonneault! Of all people!" Picquot exclaimed. "*Nom de Dieu*! I should have hung up on you! Not a word for a month. How's Elise? Now then, I *demand* that you put in an appearance – promptly!"

Twenty minutes later they were at his apartment. The door was ajar. "Take off your coats and fix yourselves a martini!" he shouted from the kitchen. "I can't leave my stove. There's ice in the living room."

A moment later they saw a radiant Picquot, beads of sweat standing out on his forehead, arms wide. He looked remarkably good – slightly heavier and ten years younger. He swept first Elise, then Florent, into his arms. "Utter silence for a month. What's your excuse for such behavior? My good sense tells me to throw you out the door for such discourtesy! Well? How are you both?" He stared hard at Florent. "Have you made your fortune? I received your cheque, for which I thank you. But I don't need it, you know. If ever . . ."

"No, it's all right, things are coming along, honestly."

"Is that the truth," Picquot asked Elise, "or is it his pride talking?"

"It's true," Elise smiled. "We've saved nearly twenty thousand dollars."

"Splendid! Nothing could please me more. Success at last!"

His expression grew fierce. "Hold on to it, my boy! Give no quarter! Success is as fickle as calamity, believe me.

Be vigilant! And now, shall we eat? The veal kidney *aux trois moutardes* won't wait."

"You look marvelous," Elise observed as she took her place.

"Why, thank you, thank you very much."

His face turned so red that they were startled. "It's true," said Florent. "Should we congratulate your doctor – or someone else?"

"Please . . . if you don't mind . . . that is . . . thank you very much," Picquot stammered, increasingly agitated.

Elise looked at him, torn between curiosity and the fear of making a faux pas. Finally she said, "Are you annoyed because we think you look terrific?"

"It's not that," said Picquot brusquely. "It's that . . . it's that . . ." He stood up, fists on the table. "I've taken a mistress, *voilà*! You wanted to know – now you know. But this is an exceedingly private matter, and I won't tolerate the slightest indiscretion."

The meal continued in silence. Elise and Florent kept their eyes on their plates, struggling to keep from giggling. Finally, with a visible effort at calm, Picquot said, "*Bon*, let's just say that the person in question is a lady of a certain age, highly refined, mind you, and you'll meet her at the appropriate time and place, if you wish. And that's all for now. Has that blasted Czech come back to trouble you?"

Florent shook his head. "No, but if he ever does I'll be waiting. He's been following us like the tail on a dog. It's as if he's in cahoots with the devil."

"Please, don't even say it," said Elise, blanching.

"So I've committed another gaffe! Relax, child, relax. My brain just skipped a beat, that's all; as you know, it's not the first time. Let me put on some music to cheer things up."

"What time is it?" Florent asked suddenly. "Eight o'clock? And it's Thursday? Monsieur Picquot, why don't call Ange-Albert at Draperies Georgette and ask him and Rosine to join us?"

The chef's face took on a doleful expression. "I was hoping that particular friend of yours wouldn't show up; I've been racking my brains for some time now, trying to find something good to say about him. First of all, don't try to phone him; the store no longer exists. Arson, I believe. There's a lot of speculation apparently. So he's working elsewhere – *if* he's working – which I doubt."

"You sound so . . . For God's sake, what's going on?" asked Elise.

"What's going on is that your friend has gone back to his dice. Quite fanatically. And in the company of . . . shall I say, individuals known to police, back-alley thugs, corrupters of young girls . . . It's disgraceful!"

Florent squirmed as if he had both feet in boiling water. "What about Rosine?" he asked.

"And Monsieur Emile?" Elise broke in, her voice unsteady.

"Monsieur Emile! Don't mention him! Needless to say I've had to take over, to the extent I was able: after all, I'm not his maid! I take him to the cinema from time to time, or for walks, or he has a bite at my place now and then. Last Wednesday we went to the botanical garden: it was quite agreeable. In short, I try as much as possible to remove him from those smoky dives they've been frequenting. I must say, it's rather too easy for him there to indulge his inclination for a little nip, as you might imagine. Rosine does what she can to hold the fort, but it's no picnic for her, poor thing, and I wonder how long she'll put up with her young man's follies.

As for him, I don't much care what happens. But the child! Last Thursday he arrived here dead drunk, after being led a merry chase all over town by an unscrupulous taxi driver who had the gall to present me with his bill. Payment is, so to speak, pending, and I suspect that state to continue."

Eyes lowered, Florent was silently fiddling with the hem of the tablecloth. Elise was fighting tears. "My Lord," she murmured, her voice breaking, "we have to do something."

"I agree completely!" Picquot exclaimed. "No use denying it, that child belongs to *all* of us! And he's more wretched than any orphan. I went last week to see his mother. Whew! I wouldn't trust that washed-up tart with my pigs. If I hadn't put her in her place with a few well-chosen words she'd have invited me into her bed, I swear it. And did you know," he asked, more and more agitated, "that Monsieur Emile is not five years old, but *six and a half*!"

Elise and Florent were taken aback. "The little devil won't go to school! And his lady mother agrees. You may not believe me, but that slippery painted eel has got it into her head that every school in Montreal is the hub of a narcotics network, a precipice leading to eternal damnation. Not for her lad! To repeat her very words, he's got enough problems as it is. Listen to this: madame proposes to wait until she has sufficient funds to pay for private tutoring for the boy, if you please. In other words, instead of giving my cat leftovers, I'd starve him to death with promises of caviar. I spent a full half hour trying to get that nonsense out of her head, to no avail. The child will have no education unless we adopt him!"

"Why did you go to see her?" asked Florent.

"Well, I was going to write, but since you're here I'll tell you now."

He took a small breath and his gaze briefly suggested terror. Elise and Florent were intrigued. "I'm about to take a month's vacation," he said hesitantly. "And I'd decided, if you have no objections, to spend a few days with you in your charming railroad station and . . . and . . . to bring along Monsieur Emile for a little holiday. What do you think? You could keep him as long as you wanted. Needless to say, I would undertake responsibility for all his needs and even provide him a small allowance."

Florent's eyes were like saucers. "What about his mother? Did she give her permission?"

"I gave her, shall we say, a tidy sum for the custody of the child. Mind you, we're not talking about adoption, either official or unofficial, but rather a *loan*, as she put it. Nor is there any point in bringing the little scamp to the attention of the Social Assistance people – there would be dreadful reprisals. She was quite categorical on that score."

Elise pushed back her chair and threw herself in Picquot's arms. "Now, now, now," he said, crimson, "what's all this about? After all, I've only done my civic duty, I . . . Come now!" he pushed her away gently. "Enough sentimentality! I've a soufflé au Cointreau to prepare and I need to concentrate."

"I had no idea he was so fond of Monsieur Emile," Florent observed a few hours later, on the way back to Sainte-Romaine.

"What a marvelous man," said Elise, filled with emotion. "And being ill only seems to have improved him."

Florent laughed smugly. "Sickness matured him, and the mistress took off the rough edges. He's ready to sign on for my new restaurant."

Elise peered out at the snow-covered fields that disappeared into the night, punctuated here and there by a bare and solitary tree. For several minutes now she'd been radiating barely contained tension, sighing, biting her nails, trying to get comfortable. Florent turned to her. "What's wrong? You're wriggling like a cabbage worm. Worried about something?"

She shook her head, smiled, shut her eyes for a moment, then said, struggling to remain calm, "Don't hit the roof but . . . I think I'm pregnant again."

The truck swerved onto the shoulder and came to a stop, a tiny glow in the cold expanse of night.

"Are you glad? Really glad?" Elise murmured under Florent's frenzied caresses. "I was afraid it might interfere with your projects."

"Are you kidding? What a way to end a day!" he exclaimed, elated. He took his wife's face in his hands, gazed at her for a moment, then covered it once more with kisses. "How far along is it? How long have you known?"

"About a week . . . but I'm not absolutely sure," she added quickly, overwhelmed by emotion at Florent's reaction. "My breasts are swelling and my nipples have been sore for two days now, like the other time."

Florent began counting on his fingers. "It's December 30 – that means late August, early September. Poor kid, you're in for a rough summer," he said, taking her in his arms again.

It took a tremendous effort to dissuade him from turning back. He wanted her to see a gynecologist the very next day. "Relax. First thing is to have a pregnancy test. It's silly to sound the alarm if there's no fire."

"You're right," Florent grumbled, continuing on to Sainte-Romanie. "A fine start. It was just a paternal instinct."

"I'll see that some of your paternal instincts are directed at Monsieur Emile," said Elise, smiling slyly. "With such a generous supply, you should have at least two children."

They arrived at the station in the middle of the night and found Virtue in a state of extreme agitation. "What's going on here?" asked Florent. "Someone make you drink a pot of coffee?"

Drawing Virtue to her, Elise cried out: on the animal's flank was a large wound covered with half-congealed blood. Florent examined her. "Looks like she's been beaten with a stick. . . . I don't get it."

"Please, God," Elise sighed, "don't let our troubles start again."

They went to bed in silence, not daring to express their forebodings. At dawn, a second train passed through the village, consolidating Florent's reputation in the most isolated farms. They listened to it rumble past, then went back to sleep. Florent dreamed a police cordon was being set up outside his restaurant to control the flood of customers.

TWENTY-NINE

The news of Elise's pregnancy caused a great stir in Florent's family. Arriving in their whale-sized luxury car, his parents drove her to a gynecologist in Montreal, maintaining that the trip on the bumpy road would be too hazardous by truck. In fact it was a pretext to see with their own eyes if their son's living arrangements were propitious and appropriate for offspring.

They found the station charming, quite comfortable and delightfully located, but made no bones about their concern for Elise, considering it highly desirable for her to return to Montreal because of the low standards of rural hospitals.

They all felt better after the visit to the gynecologist. Elise was in splendid condition and her earlier miscarriage didn't necessarily mean she was in danger of another. With proper care, and plenty of rest and calm, there was every chance of a perfectly normal pregnancy. If there was the slightest problem they could simply call the obstetrics department at Sainte-Justine Hospital, where Dr. Grojean practiced. Florent's father insisted on driving his daughter-in-law back to Sainte-Romanie, and his wife prepared dinner, making Elise lie down "to recover from the trip." They stayed until late that evening, refusing to leave until the young couple had promised to spend August in Montreal with them.

"On hot days we can swim in the backyard," Florent's father promised. "I've just bought a thirty-foot swimming pool from Faucher, and a huge sack of sea crystals – a fantastic invention. You throw a handful in the pool and it turns the water into genuine seawater. You can stay afloat without swimming!"

Three days later, Florent's bank account (he took the precaution of banking in Victoriaville instead of at the local credit union) passed thirty thousand dollars. One night as Mayor Meloche was slipping under the quilt, he confided to his wife, "I think young Boissonneault screwed me royally. I've never seen a house cleared out so fast – you'd have thought there was a fire."

"Stewing again," sighed his wife. "You won't be able to digest your supper."

"I'm just telling you what I see. The little bugger pulled a fast one, all right, plain as day. I ran into him yesterday across from the church. Looked like the cat that swallowed the canary. Kept expecting him to burst into song. Well, I hope he'll hustle now. I don't want to be six feet under when the trains come back."

Despite the sharp cold and the unploughed roads, Florent had started patrolling the region again with growing enthusiasm. Mayor Meloche had kept his thoughts to himself, but the locals were getting suspicious of Florent's passion for the old things they had lying around, and prices were soaring. Maple-sugar molds that once sold for fifty cents now couldn't be had for less than two dollars. He had to put fifty carefully counted dollars on the corner of a table before he could get his hands on a three-burner stove from the Forges Saint-Maurice. Armoires, on the other hand, were still to be had for ridiculous prices. Tottering with age, disfigured by layers of paint, and often mutilated, they appeared to be worthless. Florent would look down his nose at them, set a price, hoist them into his truck and then spend days stripping them. (Since Elise's pregnancy, she wasn't allowed to help because of the harmful fumes.)

"I never see you anymore," she sighed from time to time. "I eat alone, and we make love as often as if you were working up in Lac Saint-Jean."

Looking pained, Florent would attempt a show of contrition, but felt only a vague tickling. He asked for a little more time. "You know how important this restaurant is for me. I have to prove once and for all I've got it in me. Would you like it better if I was brooding all the time?"

Elise said nothing. Florent stroked her hair: "Just give me another two or three months, that's all. And when we have fifty thousand in our account, I promise we'll go away for a month's holiday, wherever you want."

Elise shrugged. "Fifty thousand! By then there'll be three of us!"

The next day, on a whim, winter decided to tighten its grip. About three o'clock in the morning a fierce cold wave struck Quebec, sinking thousands of sharp little teeth into everything within reach. Window frames rattled, the panes cracked, and the wound was promptly covered by a thick coating of frost. Houses contracted furiously to close up any fissures, and blankets reeking of mothballs were called into service, as the oil level in furnaces sank visibly.

Florent woke up feeling great, walked naked around the glacial apartment, glanced outside at the luminous stillness and enthusiastically welcomed the challenge of spending the day in the cold. He whistled as he dressed, while Elise watched drowsily, then impulsively tore off his clothes and returned to the summits of pleasure and warmth offered by the conjugal bed. "You should stay at home," Elise murmured, snuggling up to him. "Ten steps in this cold and your cheeks will crack."

"On my antiquarian's word, I'll be back early this afternoon. I've got a hunch luck's on my side today."

He could hardly have been more mistaken. Despite the succulent aroma of a bacon omelet that perfumed the kitchen, Virtue watched, not moving a hair, as her master ate his breakfast, unwilling to leave the comforting warmth of the heavy-breathing furnace.

Elise was sitting by the fire, leafing through a book. In the silent apartment, nails creaked now and then with an enigmatic, muffled sound. The windows were dazzling rectangles, the snow seemed ablaze. All sound had vanished. Trees and houses were so still they seemed eternal. The furnace going full blast barely managed to chase the cold from the kitchen, signalling its triumph with silly little clucks of pleasure. Elise was digesting her dinner, peaceful and contented. Suddenly, through the window, she saw the mailman stride from his car through the snow, his face red and stiff, gaze fixed, a cloud of vapor at the end of his nose. She threw on her coat and ran down the stairs. There were two letters at the door. One was addressed to her. The envelope made a dry grating sound, somehow threatening, then released a photograph. Seizing it, Elise turned white as a sheet. She turned it over and over, lips quivering. She felt as if her feet were spinning around her ankles, as if her thighs were filled with ice. Her belly contracted spasmodically, terrifying her. She ran back up to the apartment, crumpling the photograph, then collapsed in tears on a chair, while Virtue, whimpering, licked her fingers.

Florent, meanwhile, was in a barn, shivering, nose dripping. He was trying to bargain for a rickety medicine chest with fleur-de-lys appliqués, its inside sticky with a brownish substance that smelled of Castoria. After several minutes he said, "Nope, fifteen bucks is way more than I can spend. I'd better be going now. See you next time."

"Whatever you want," said the farmer peevishly, a sardonic smile on his lips.

"Spend the night with your sow," Florent muttered, rushing back to the truck. "Holy Christmas! If this keeps up I won't be able to afford a thimble!" Then, frantically jiggling the ignition key, he exploded. "Shit! Don't conk out on me today! Okay, I get the message. I'll go home and wait till the weather's fit for a man to go out in."

Stepping into the waiting room, he noticed a torn envelope in front of the door; another, intact, lay on a bench. Recognizing his mother's writing, he opened it.

> Dear Children,
>
> Your father came down with a terrible flu after his bowling last Tuesday and I had to keep him at home, which doesn't stop him from going down to the basement every minute to look at that boat of his that's given me so many headaches. Your cousin Bernadette came over last Sunday and parked little José with me. He hasn't wanted to play inside for a month now. I'm sure Elise . . .

Suddenly Florent looked up. An odd sound was coming from upstairs, a mixture of stifled sighs and sniffling. He bent down, picked up the open envelope and gazed at it, perplexed. Taking the stairs four at a time he called out, "Elise! What's going on?"

Virtue greeted him with a whimper and led him to the bedroom door, which was locked. "Elise! For God's sake, what's going on?"

Her answer was a series of sobs, and as Florent got more worked up they grew louder. "Open up! Say something! What did I do? For Christ's sake, open the door!"

Tired of shouting, he went to the kitchen. A crumpled piece of paper lay on the table. By the time he'd unfolded it, his face looked like an old sponge deformed by dishwater. He saw himself lying on his back, naked, legs apart, while a pretty, rather chubby girl with pear-shaped buttocks hungrily caressed him with her mouth. The scene was the Hotel Nelson, in Egon Ratablavasky's bedroom.

"The son of a bitch!" He fell onto a chair.

He felt as if his skull was swelling monstrously until it would fill the kitchen, while inside the vast sphere, his brain rolled like a marble, out of control.

"Okay, don't lose your cool." He took a deep breath and tried to summon the strength to get a big glass of ice-water. "If it was faked – but I'm such an asshole – I walked right into it . . . I can kiss my marriage good-bye. And Elise pregnant . . ."

Virtue chose this moment to lay her head on his knees, sighing like a consumptive actress. Florent gave her a smack that sent her running to the living room, eyes watering, pains shooting through her skull.

Florent went back to the bedroom door. "Elise, I saw the picture. Open the door so I can at least explain."

"Never! Go away! It's over! I'm taking the next bus to Montreal." And with this she opened the door, God knows why, and collapsed at Florent's feet in tears. He tried to pull her up but she gave his cheek a ringing slap. The edge of her ring broke his skin and blood welled up, then slowly dripped. Florent recoiled, brought his hand to his face and stared at his fingertips. Under the circumstances, the wound became his best advocate. "Listen to me!" he said, taking her head in both hands and dragging her to him. "I haven't had a chance to say a word. The picture came from Ratablavasky. Did you know that?"

"I don't give a damn where it came from!" she screamed, freeing herself. She tore to the bedroom closet, and empty suitcases tumbled down with a thunderous roar that would drain the blood from an artilleryman's face. Florent seized her by the waist. "You're going to listen to me!" he shouted. "Before you leave you'll at least listen to me!"

He dragged her forcibly into the kitchen, filled with gut-wrenching anxiety. His timing couldn't have been worse. He left the bedroom with an angry wife and came into the kitchen with a Fury. Elise's voice rose until it was unrecognizable. Her hands had sprouted ten claws that grew longer and sharper. The pointed toes of twenty shoes struck at Florent's legs, turning them from red to blue, from blue to purple. She had become eight-armed Shiva, avenging love betrayed. "Filthy bastard! Two-faced son of a bitch! You'll never see your child! Get yourself another whore, if that's what you like!"

Cupboard doors slammed and banged and dishes went flying, hitting walls and shattering with a pitiful sound. Florent wasn't deft enough to parry all her blows. Their best blue dishes, a wedding present from Elise's aunt, disappeared into the whirlwind, one piece at a time. Now it was the turn of the soup tureen lid, which bore the likeness of a smiling old fellow with a beard divided into seven braids, outstretched arms and a flower in each hand. It curved across the room and broke in two against the stove. The tureen followed shortly, heavier in its flight. It was saved in a most unexpected manner: the door opened and Monsieur Emile took it smack in his sternum; from there it landed at his feet, intact.

"By all the Olympian gods, what the hell's going on!" exclaimed Picquot, looming up behind the child.

Elise and Florent froze and stared silently at their visitors. They could hear Virtue next door, huddled, whimpering, in a wardrobe.

"*Ventredieu*!" said the chef. "I haven't witnessed such a calamity since the night my master, Arnaud de Baculard, had a temper tantrum in the Belles Gourmandes restaurant."

"Wh . . . what are you doing here?" Florent stammered, while Elise vanished into the bedroom.

"What am I doing? What am *I* doing? See here, my friend, your emotions are scrambling your memory! I told you we were coming two weeks ago: and here we are! I even went so far as to take up the automobile, which I've avoided for twenty years, to come and see you."

Monsieur Emile slowly rubbed his chest without a word, eyes like saucers. He suddenly raised his head to Picquot, gestured to him to bend down, and said in a scarcely audible voice, "Can I go and get my kitty?"

"Yes, yes, child, go, leave us alone for a minute. I've things to say to your friend Florent." When the door was shut he asked, "Now what's all this about?"

Florent went into the living room, collapsed in an armchair, and started to cry. "Ratablavasky. My life . . . my life's ruined," he stammered, "through my own stupid fault."

"And what does that mean? Explain yourself! Gallons of tears won't dissolve the cause of your sorrow."

With few words and many blushes, Florent told of his quickie with the chambermaid at the Hotel Nelson eighteen months earlier. "Now I understand that big grin. She was in cahoots with Old Rat. I'll never get out of this one!"

Picquot stood there thoughtfully. They could hear whispers in the waiting room, where Monsieur Emile was trying to cheer up his cat, disoriented after three hours in a cardboard box. The bedroom was utterly silent. Picquot crossed his legs, uncrossed them, tugged at his tie. "Mm-hmm . . . we'll have to see . . . and her being pregnant doesn't help matters. . . . Have you any cognac?"

Florent brought a bottle and two glasses that had survived the massacre and half filled them. The chef sniffed at his glass, warmed it in his hands. "It's perfectly obvious that you behaved like an idiot . . . but such idiocy is not unusual. . . . It can be explained . . . and forgiven."

He leaned over to Florent and, murmuring like a confessor, asked, "Was this the first time?"

Florent nodded. The first time she found out, he added to himself.

"All is not lost, then. Trust me."

He sipped some cognac, swirled it in his mouth, and breathed deeply, eyes half closed. "Elise, child!" he said suddenly, struggling to his feet. "Give me just one minute of your time. If I'm disturbing you, you can throw me out."

The bedroom door was slightly ajar. He went in. A few moments passed. Florent was hunched in his chair, biting his nails. The minutes dragged on like geological eras.

Virtue found the courage to emerge from her hiding place and crept up to Florent with a pleading look. He gestured her onto his knees and petted her. "What are they doing in there?" he asked huskily. "Why the hell didn't I keep my dick in my pants instead of playing stud with a chambermaid?"

He set the dog on the floor and stuck his ear against the wall. He heard an indistinct sound, then Picquot's voice rose. "Come come, child, what would that commit you to? Less than nothing! Now then . . ."

The bed creaked and two feet were set on the floor. Florent picked up Virtue and flung himself in the armchair. In the kitchen, Picquot was still pleading. "After all, you have to talk to him. You're not movie stars, to get divorced on a whim! It's different for them – anything for the box office, *n'est-ce pas*? They have to get themselves in the scandal sheets or no one will remember their names. But you! Come see the look on this poor ninny's face," he said, gently pushing her into the living room. "Like a slice of stale bread!"

Elise, her hair a mess, her face blotched with red, walked through the room ignoring him, then sat in a shadowy corner where, stubbornly and silently, she gazed out the window.

Shortly, a bewildered Picquot grunted and sat down, picking at a microscopic spot on his tie as he waited for Florent to speak. An avalanche of fists pounded the front door. "Now can I come in?" shouted Monsieur Emile.

"Not yet!" the chef replied. "Be patient! We'll call when we're ready."

"I'm hungry, goddammit!"

"Hold on, I'm coming," said Florent, glad of the distraction.

In the kitchen, he picked his way through the broken dishes to the refrigerator. Monsieur Emile was waiting in the open doorway, looking around curiously. Hands shaking,

Florent held out half a loaf of bread and a package of cheese slices.

"You two having a fight?" the child whispered.

Florent nodded.

"Sometimes my mother does, too. The other day she kicked the toilet bowl and all the water ran out on the floor 'cause her boyfriend was supposed to call for her at seven o'clock but he forgot to –"

"Tell me later," Florent interrupted. He went out, shutting the door behind him.

"Now, Boissonneault," said the chef. "Your wife won't wait till the snow melts."

"I'm a son of a bitch," Florent declared, going back to the living room, "and it serves me right if you leave me."

Excellent preamble, Picquot thought, getting up. "Children," he said, "I'm going now. If anyone can solve your problem it's certainly not this old sauce stirrer. Talk it over and use the common sense that nature's given you. You hold the happiness of both your lives in your hands, as any idiot can see. I'll take Monsieur Emile so you can have peace and quiet. We'll drop in on an old friend in Victoriaville, who runs the kitchens at the Manoir Victoria, and come back late tomorrow. If I see that we're still *de trop*, we'll be on our way to Montreal *tout de suite* and Madame Chouinard can take her son back. Dear Elise, remember what I told you: no matter what, Florent loves you. You have two pieces of evidence: the state of his face and, with all respect, the state of your womb. Only a moron or a psychopath would have the gall to make you pregnant with the notion of leaving you. Acknowledge that he's neither one nor the other. But remember, too, dear child – and believe me, I permit myself this observation with no intention of wounding you – one day you might be very pleased to have granted Florent your pardon, for as the priests tell us, we are all fallible, and I know hell's not populated exclusively by men. It's easier to ask for clemency when one has practiced it oneself. And after all, to be quite crude, it was just a poke. Now I've said far too much. Till tomorrow night around eight."

And while the chef dragged Monsieur Emile, screaming with rage, to the car, Florent spoke softly to Elise, not thinking, guided only by his heart, which inspired many blunders but also certain touchingly droll phrases that he wasn't even aware of. Elise raged once more, then started crying again, and Florent shed all self-respect and joined her.

It was long past supper time, and they couldn't ignore their hunger. But first they had to clear out the kitchen. Into a cardboard box went the broken dishes, including the good blue set, which was almost completely smashed. Fate had spared two saucers, three plates, one cup, a salad bowl, and the tureen, unintentionally saved by Monsieur Emile. Florent put together a cold meal, which was followed by a discussion in several chapters, marked by abrupt changes in tone with anger, tears and mockery in every imaginable order.

Between the curtains, the owl that perched on the roof of the shed every night caught a glimpse of the quarreling couple. He deigned to watch for a few minutes, then fell asleep. Eventually, fatigue overcame them. Elise withdrew to the bedroom, Florent to the living room. An hour later, he was granted permission to enter the chamber but not the bed, by God! Never! He had to be content with a sleeping bag, and spent the night listening to the house creak and the wind sighing in the trees.

At seven o'clock he rose silently, took a long contrite look at his wife, then went to the kitchen. Armed with a tube of glue he tried to resurrect the blue dishes.

Seeing him at work a few hours later, Elise smiled quizzically. He held out the milk jug. "Take a look at this."

Elise was flabbergasted: was this the same pitcher that had smashed against the stove yesterday? She had to squint to make out the web of cracks. It was marred only by a small nick in the base. Elise looked at the other pieces, silently praising Florent's skill. Penitent love had given him a surgeon's fingers. By late afternoon the dishes were restored almost to their former splendor. Florent, sick with fatigue, refused to finish repairing the sugar bowl, leaving it without one handle. He said theatrically, "Let it be a reminder to me."

He set it prominently on a shelf, then went to lie down. When he woke up several hours later, his wife was curled against his back. Turning around, he tried to speak, but Elise covered his mouth with her hand and shook her head. "Promise me," she said a moment later, "promise you'll never mention what happened yesterday."

He felt sickened by a sense of shame that was new to him, and with it came the utter certainty that he'd never find the appropriate words or attitude. Should I touch her, he wondered, or let her cry by herself – or make love to her . . .

Perplexed and tormented, he stared at the ceiling.

"Well?" Picquot asked when he and Monsieur Emile arrived at eight. "Shall I take him or leave him?"

"He can stay," said Elise, impassive. Then, pointing to a tiny bandage on his chin, she asked, "Did you cut yourself shaving?"

"Shaving! It was *this* little shaver, with his wretched paper clips," exclaimed Picquot, lightly cuffing Monsieur Emile. "He used our hotel room as a firing range, despite my threats. One of his projectiles ricocheted off a mirror and *voilà*! I came close to being a one-eyed chef!"

Monsieur Emile scowled silently at the ceiling. "Would you like supper?" Elise asked with the same lack of expression. "No? You've eaten? Where's your cat?"

With a gesture, Florent told Picquot the matter was closed, and Monsieur Emile sensed it would be greatly appreciated if he showed no interest in the previous day's events. "I'll get him!" he shouted, running down the stairs. Then he stopped, and turning to Elise, said almost insolently, "You're gonna have a baby, eh? He better not crap in my bed!"

Breakfast appeared shortly, fur standing on end, a threatening look in his eyes, indignant at all the carting around he'd had to endure during the past two days. He escaped from his master's arms and set off to inspect the apartment. "I've had supper," Picquot remarked, "but I'd be glad of a cup of coffee with a drop of cognac, if there's any left."

A howl came from the next room and everyone went running. "It's okay, it's okay," said Monsieur Emile, pointing to Virtue and Breakfast, who were cautiously sniffing each other.

After a momentary amnesia that had terrified the dog, Breakfast had recognized her old companion. "Come see your room," said Elise, taking the chef by the arm. "I think you'll like it. We've given you a beautiful brass bed."

"Brass or sterling silver, I won't be spending much time in it. I leave tomorrow."

"Tomorrow!"

Picquot winked mischievously. "Ah yes, such is life. The heart has its reasons and so forth."

They looked at one another briefly, saying nothing. "In that case," said Florent, "I'm coming, too."

Breakfast appeared in the doorway and looked him straight in the eye as if he'd just read Florent's innermost secrets.

"You're going, too?" asked Elise in a quavering voice.

"Mm-hmm. I've promised myself a little visit to my old friend Ratablavasky."

THIRTY

Monsieur Emile wasn't his usual lively self that night. Despite his usual shouts and threats, slaps, and all kinds of projectiles, he was very upset by what had happened the night before.

Elise was washing his face before putting him to bed when he asked suddenly; "Are you and Florent gonna fight like that all the time?" Elise was taken aback. "'Cause if you do, I know you'll give me away. Pierre Lemieux's parents, they fight every single night. Once his mother even fell downstairs, right onto the street, and she got a great big bump on her forehead. So last September they sent Pierre to stay with his grandmother and his father went to the States with a woman that had a disease."

"A disease?"

"A disease," said the child with tranquil self-assurance.

Elise picked up the washcloth again. A moment later, filled with emotion herself, she said, "Listen, do you really think we're so crazy we'd . . ."

"I like it here," he whimpered. "There's . . . there's lots more snow than in Montreal."

"So that's it," Elise smiled. "What you really care about is the snow!"

He nodded vigorously, but the mocking smile that blossomed on his lips showed he hadn't confided everything that was on his mind. Elise finished washing him and took him to his room. As she was bending over to tuck him in, he threw his arms around her and hugged her tight.

"Monsieur Emile, you're suffocating me!"

"I love you!" And he dived under the blankets, making little clucking sounds, and nothing could persuade him to reemerge.

Very moved, Elise went to the kitchen. Aurélien Picquot was launched on an endless speech about the evils of Ratablavasky. As he listened, Florent watched Elise out of the corner of his eye. She's nuts about that little bum, he thought. By God, we'll have to adopt him. Adopt him! And just yesterday we were talking about divorce!

"*Alors,*" said the chef, irritated at his friend's inattentiveness, "I now have the honor of asking you *for the second time*: what do you intend to do about the old alley cat?"

Florent started. "I . . . I haven't really decided. Anyway, I'm prepared for more pictures – faked pictures."

"Of course he'll do that," Picquot agreed. "He wants to poison your marriage and sap your strength so he can dominate you completely. That's his goal! I call it moral disarmament, and next will come all-out war!"

He got up and strode back and forth, livid with rage. He was like a passenger on the deck of a ship in distress because of the captain's stupidity. "I deduce that he's no longer frightened by Father Jeunehomme's revelations. He's likely cozied up to the police or even, who knows, some senior Justice officials . . . Why not, eh? Why not? By the way, where is that book that gave him such a fright?"

Florent shrugged. "For what I got out of it . . ."

Elise went to the bedroom. "Florent, come here!" she exclaimed, her voice tight with emotion. Utterly dismayed, she stood looking at an empty drawer. "The book's gone," she whispered.

"So he's been here," said Picquot, flabbergasted.

In the next room, Monsieur Emile was sitting up in bed, hearing every word. With a grimace of frustration, Florent headed for the kitchen. They sat down and finished their coffee in silence. Florent, increasingly glum, was drumming his fingers on a plate. His gaze fell on the dog lying in a corner and stopped on her flank: the wound had left a big scar. "If it's war he wants, he'll get it!" Florent exclaimed, pushing back his chair. "'Night everybody, I'm going to bed."

The next morning at breakfast he asked, "Monsieur Picquot, would you do me a tremendous favor and stay one more day: I have to go to Montreal and I don't want Elise to be alone here."

With a gratified smile, the chef twirled his mustache. "Precisely what I was going to offer, but I thought you should make the first move." He got up then, went to his room and returned with a leather holster from which he took a big Mauser that gave off an icy sheen. "Foresight is the goddess of cooks, but her advice isn't limited to our saucepans. I never travel unarmed. Colt, Mauser, Browning, Parabellum – I know them all. The war years made me a weapons expert. Let him come. I'll turn him into a sieve."

Elise said, "I think I saw a pistol in the stationmaster's office." She went downstairs, waited a moment, and called Florent.

He went downstairs.

"What is it?" he asked. "Can't you find it?"

"There's no pistol, I want to talk to you. Why are you going to Montreal?" she asked, her features tight with concern.

"I can't tell you right now. You'll have to trust . . . if you can," he added, blushing.

Picquot came downstairs. "You haven't found the pistol? So it's gone the way of the book . . . and other things as well, I'm certain! The crook! If I could get my hands on . . ."

Florent went upstairs and brought down his coat. "I'm leaving now, Monsieur Picquot," he said, holding out his hand. "Keep an eye on my wife. I'll be back first thing tomorrow."

"Call me tonight no matter what," Elise whispered as she kissed him, "and please, please promise . . ."

"Oh!" exclaimed Picquot. "I nearly forgot!" He approached Florent. "Could I ask you a favor?"

"Just say the word."

Monsieur Emile, in his pajamas, was leaning over the banister. "Where you going, Florent?"

"You, child, bring down my coat, will you?" asked the chef.

"Where you *going*?" he repeated, dragging the coat to Picquot's feet, relieving the floor of a considerable quantity of dust in the process.

"To Montreal on an errand," Florent told him.

"Take me, too," whined the child.

Blushing like a schoolgirl, the chef handed Florent a little box wrapped in pink silk. "Would you be so kind as to give this to the concierge at this address?"

Florent read: "Mademoiselle Emilienne Latouche. I see. I guess that's the lucky lady, eh?"

"Guess all you like – it's of no importance to me," Picquot retorted, racing upstairs.

Florent was driving his truck through the village. "Imagine that! He's really in love!" he murmured, smiling. "But he carried on as if I'd found out he was taking up ballet."

But reflections of another sort soon claimed all his attention. He patted the wallet in his inside pocket and stepped on the gas. An occasional unpleasant thought pulled down the corner of his mouth, and he spat on the floor in annoyance.

He reached Montreal about ten o'clock and went to *Le Clairon*. "Monsieur Gladu's working at home this morning," declared the tall, bony woman who acted as secretary, "and he's *not* to be disturbed." Her big bulging eyes peered meaningfully at the door.

"What a harpy," Florent muttered, going into a phone booth. "Like someone with a pickle up the butt."

"Boissonneault! Is that you yourself in person?" asked Gladu through a mouthful of porridge. "Speak of the devil – I've been wanting to see you. Get your butt over here."

He darted to his bedroom and, under the placid gaze of his daughter Yolande, a five-year-old who was blossoming into worrying obesity, divested himself of his pajamas and donned a red-and-brown checked suit. "Come in, come in!" he said, pulling on Florent's arm as he tried to wipe his boots on the mat. "My wife's in the hospital, so we can have a drink in peace. Say hello to the nice man, precious," he said to his daughter, who was slowly making her way over to them.

"Good morning," she said in a lilting little voice, staring drowsily at Florent.

"Sit yourself down!" Gladu insisted, petulant. "I just bought a fine bottle of Barbados rum. About time it lost its cherry!"

Little Yolande advanced a few steps and clutched Florent's index finger. "Want to come to my room and see my toys?" She spoke slowly, as if hypnotized.

"Go watch TV, precious," said her father, patting her back, "the nice man hasn't got time for Yolande. He's here to see Daddy and then he has to go far, far, far away."

She turned and walked down the hallway, lumbering heavily from foot to foot. "Man hasn't got time? Hasn't got time?" she said softly.

"I have to look after her for a few days," Gladu explained uneasily, ushering Florent into the living room. "The wife's in the hospital for her veins."

They entered a large tomato-red room with imitation Spanish-style furniture. On their right stood a television set of vaguely funereal appearance. Gladu, obviously proud of the decor, pointed to an armchair. "Take a load off your feet, I'll be right back with the fuel." He brought a forty-ounce bottle of rum, glasses, a bottle of Coke, and a bowl of ice cubes, which he set on the table. He filled Florent's glass almost half full, with a little bit more for himself. "Coke?" he asked. "Help yourself." He sat on a sofa. "So how's life been treating you, pal? We don't see much of you anymore."

Florent's face was impassive. "I don't live in Montreal now."

"You don't? Well, I'll be damned! I'll be damned," he repeated, waiting for more information, which wasn't forthcoming. "Would it . . . would it be indiscreet to ask where you've gone to?"

Florent gestured vaguely, then asked offhandedly, "Have you seen Slipskin or old Ratablavasky?"

"Those two? I'd rather slash my wrists than shake hands with that scum, both of them! More rum?"

Florent pointed to his drink, which he'd hardly touched. Gladu poured himself three fingers of rum, dropped in an ice cube, and flavored it with three drops of Coke. The conversation obviously disturbed him. Florent glanced at him with a mildly disdainful smile, sipped his drink, then set down his glass. "I wanted to see you about Old Rat," he said slowly.

Gladu gave him a look that contained an odd mixture of anxiety, guile, and the desire to make himself useful. "That so?"

"He's started harassing me again. Tried to wreck my marriage."

Gladu took a long look at his drink, then turned on Florent a gaze filled with sincere commiseration. "The old son of a . . . He's getting worse with age. You'd think the devil rammed the fires of hell up his ass."

Florent produced a wad of bills from his pocket and dropped it on the coffee table. "It's yours if you'll give me a hand."

Gladu looked up at him. A look of ingenuous lust crossed his face. "Holy crow! Sonny boy, you come a long way from that cockroach nest on Emery Street. Fancy cars, plenty of pussy, and mink coats, eh?"

Florent shook his head, his lips pinched smugly. "No time to play, my friend – I'm working. But Old Rat's busy, too. At throwing us out on the street."

Gladu sighed. "He's got more than one string in his bow, as they say."

"But we can take the bow away," said Florent.

"Sure, sure." Gladu eyed the money again. "Question is, how. He's a slippery bugger . . . And I don't feel like trying to saw through a plank full of nails, if you follow me. I got a family to support and –"

Florent interrupted. "There aren't really that many choices."

Gladu seemed not to understand.

"Do I have to draw you a picture? In your line of work you must have loads of contacts, right?"

"Could be," mumbled Gladu, abashed. "Depends what you mean . . ."

"I wasn't thinking of the archbishop."

"I . . . I got a lot of contacts in the Knights of Columbus and the Kiwanis," he said, his face gradually lighting up, "and the Golden Age Club . . . I'm on the board of my credit union . . . and I'm a close personal friend of the Liberal organizer in this riding – I often go hunting with him. During elections, I look after the telegraph, and I'll have you know, my friend, not many work it as good as me."

"That's child's play," said Florent disdainfully. He reached down and picked up the money. "Forgot everything I said. I came to the wrong address."

Gladu leaped to his feet and clutched Florent's arm. "Wait – not so fast! You want his legs broken or . . ." He pointed upward with his index finger. His knowing look worried Florent.

"I haven't decided yet. Find me somebody I can trust, then we'll see."

"Sit down a minute," said Gladu, dropping onto the sofa, which moaned like a wounded animal, "and let me think." Resting his elbows on his knees, he began kneading his face like plasticine. A few moments passed. Florent watched him, his expression both ironic and concerned.

"Yeah, yeah, yeah," Gladu muttered in a cavernous voice. "If I went through . . . I could ask . . . hmmm . . . his sister . . . and the number . . . right, okay."

Smiling broadly, he gave Florent a clear, bright look. "Call me first thing this afternoon, pal – I'll have word for you then."

Florent nodded. "Okay. But before I go, I'd like to dictate a little letter." He took some paper from his pocket and spread it on the table.

> Dear Florent,
>
> This is to say that as far as old Ratablavasky's concerned, I think I've got the perfect person to put a few dents in him so he'll leave you in peace once and for all. But it's going to cost more than expected, because I have to tell you that in the past three days I've got in over my head, so to speak, and the person in question tells me the operation's a lot riskier than we thought. And if you should want the individual to join his poor old mother, the cost will be at least double, not to mention expenses.
>
> Rosario Gladu
>
> N.B. I could have phoned, but with everything you read about electronic spying in *Le Journal de Montréal* I'd rather get word to you slower, but private.

Gladu looked up, highly annoyed. "I don't get it."

Smiling, Florent slapped his shoulder. "You know, Rosario, I've always trusted you, and now I want you to transcribe that little note so I can keep that trust, because it's as important to me as my own two eyes."

"I get it," he grumbled. "If we were friends . . ."

"But we *are* friends, Rosario, *sensible* friends – the best kind. But there's no two ways about it: either you write that note or I go."

A few minutes later Gladu handed him a sheet of paper. "Now are you happy?"

Florent skimmed the letter and slipped it into his pocket. "I'll call you at two. Work hard. And don't try and pass off some snot-nosed brat on me that doesn't know which end is up. I want somebody with a head on his shoulders, who does clean work. If you find him, my wallet will treat you kindly."

"Don't worry, pal, I've got more than one trick up my sleeve. You want proof?" he asked, pulling Florent into the bathroom. There he pointed to an odd red plastic device on the wall next to the toilet. "Believe it or not, I thought this one up myself."

Florent gaped. "This" consisted of a toilet-paper holder integrated into a transistor radio, the whole surmounted by an overflowing ashtray. Gladu turned a knob and a shrill voice spouted sports news.

"Well? Whadda you say? Good thinking, eh? With this baby you got a butt in your mouth – and your butt on the pot! The smoke hides the smell and the music hides the sound, and while you're cleaning out your body you can cultivate your mind, instead of gawking at the cracks in the ceiling. A Lebanese guy from Toronto bought this invention off me. Bad move, though, the bugger screwed me blind. But I'll get it back. I'm full of ideas!" he said, taking Florent into the kitchen. "And how, about that? Neat trick, eh?"

At the kitchen counter, he pointed to an electric can

opener surrounded by screws, springs, and oddly shaped pieces of metal. What was curious about the can opener was that it was mounted inside a chunk of cut glass that let you see the mechanism. "Say what you want, it's smart and it's easy to clean! It could even go in the living room! Just needs a couple of adjustments, then I can start marketing."

"Terrific," said Florent. "Now you'll have to excuse me. I'd better be going."

"Not till you see my antipollution plan."

He raced to the living room and came back with a big black notebook, which he opened on the table. Florent saw scrupulously drawn cross sections of noses, accompanied by numerous legends.

"That's right, the nasal filter! Simple as sin, but somebody had to think of it! Looks a lot like a cigarette filter, but instead of putting one between your lips, you stick two of them up your nose. Change 'em every three days. A gold mine! I can't figure out why it's so hard to sell. Governments are robbing us blind with all their antipollution projects, but this here invention could save millions. If every citizen made one small effort every three days . . ."

"Very interesting, Rosario, but really, I have to go, I've . . ."

"Hold on," he said, rummaging feverishly in a drawer. "I don't just work on serious things, I'm interested in pleasure, too, which probably won't come as a surprise. For instance, I've got this new gadget to make women come, no less. Look!" he exclaimed, pointing to a drawing of a rubber glove covered with thousands of little teats. "Love Glove! There's a fortune in those two little words!"

"You're right. We'll talk about it later," Florent promised, opening the door. "Two o'clock, right?"

Gripping his arm, Gladu gave him a pleading look. "You're up to your butt in money and I've got the ideas. When Old Rat goes belly-up maybe the two of us could . . ."

Florent freed himself. "Let's take care of him first, okay? As for the rest, there's a time for everything. . . ."

"What a pain in the brain!" he exclaimed, striding away. "He could've eaten up my whole day."

Now Florent had to kill time until two o'clock. He decided to call on Jean-Denis Beaumont, whom he hadn't seen for two weeks. "I'm sure he's sold a few pieces. Might as well pick up my share; I have a hunch I'll be needing some bread."

At the corner of St-Denis he stopped, open-mouthed, before the strangest sight. A huge gothic steeple was slowly being pulled along the street by a tow truck. A silent crowd was watching on the sidewalk. Florent rolled down his window to question a tall pimply teenager dragging on a butt. "That? It's the steeple of Ste-Madeleine church they demolished last week. Some guy from Connecticut bought it to put in a theme park. Those fuckin' Americans are something else, eh?" He whistled admiringly and continued on his way.

Jean-Denis had hung a sign in his window to tell his customers he'd gone to lunch (at eleven o'clock!). Florent grumbled, then suddenly realized he hadn't been near The Beanery for ages. Why don't I just take a look? It'd do me as much good as a coffee.

Slipskin was out doing errands, but Florent didn't have to see him to stimulate his hatred. Slipskin had seen to that very effectively. The restaurant had just taken over an adjoining shop. Its modest front, a neighborhood landmark for more than thirty years, had been totally disfigured. Florent was furious. The bugger's bought Lemieux's jewelry store! He's turning my Beanery into an American restaurant!

He paced up and down the sidewalk, biting his lips, totally unconcerned if he was visible from the restaurant. His gaze suddenly fell on a miserable yard goods store diagonally across from The Beanery. An awkwardly hand-lettered sign in the window indicated that the business was for sale "because of siknes." A moment later Florent was making his way through dusty piles of fabric, looking for the owner. "About sixteen feet by forty," he murmured, running an eye over the premises. "Room for thirty customers, maybe more."

He stopped at a showcase covered with crumpled paper bags, used wrapping paper, and a jumble of spools of thread that, with the years, had all taken on the same indefinable color. On the far wall was a large colored poster of models dressed in the styles of the forties. A small door behind the counter was open, but although Florent peered carefully he could distinguish nothing in the half light of the back room. He drummed his ring against the showcase, cleared his throat several times and then, as there was no sign of life, took a couple of steps toward the door. "Anybody there?"

There was a muffled grunt, then he heard a cord slip and a bell tinkle in a distant room. Almost at once, a door banged at the back of the store and he heard a young man's voice, both hoarse and clear, as if it were breaking. "I'm coming already!"

A redheaded teenager with thick glasses and two bright red pimples on his left nostril appeared. "Sorry, I was out back. So what can I do for you?"

"I saw the ad in the window. You're selling out?"

The boy looked at him furtively, then blinked in awe. With a look of alarm at the words "selling out," he brought his finger to his lips and gestured Florent to the front of the store. "It's not my business," he said in an undertone. "It's my uncle's."

As he listened, Florent took a quick look around, to evaluate the state of the shop. "He's sick, my uncle, but it's as if he didn't want to be sick, y'know what I mean?" said the boy, blushing as if he'd just uttered an obscenity. His gaze left Florent's shoulders and came to rest in the middle of his stomach.

"Does your uncle own the building?"

The boy nodded, ventured making eye contact with Florent, then dropped his gaze to his stomach again. Apologetically, he said, "The building's not for sale, though." Rubbing the tips of his shoes together, he added, "It's for rent."

There was a hoarse cry from the back of the store. The boy dashed into the darkened room. Florent tried to listen, but the creaking floor betrayed him, forcing him to stay put. Hurried whispers could be heard, interrupted from time to time by bad-tempered growls. The strange secret meeting was soon over, and the young man, blinking more than ever behind the thick glasses that made his eyes bulge like a frog's, came back to Florent. "It's my uncle back there," he explained with a confused smile. "Last year he lifted a package that was too heavy for him and he's been paralyzed ever since, y'know what I mean? He was scared just now because he thought I was trying to sell the building, but I only want to rent it."

"How much?"

"A hundred . . . a hundred and sixty-five a month?" he said fearfully.

As Florent didn't seem about to pounce on him, but merely gave him an uncertain smile, he ventured to add, "But . . . you'd have to buy the stock. *Everything*."

Florent glanced disdainfully at the merchandise. "How much?" he asked again.

"I'd have to ask my uncle." He was back almost at once. "Two thousand."

"One thousand four hundred and not one penny more," retorted Florent, striding authoritatively through the store, picking up a length of dusty cloth, tapping a wall, frowning for no particular reason. Let's sign the bloody lease before some other uncle comes into the picture and doubles the rent, he said to himself. I'll ask Jean-Denis to get rid of these rags.

He found the young man in a junk room littered with wobbly tables and mutilated store dummies, dimly lit by a grimy little window. "I'm ready to sign right now," said Florent. "But for five years minimum. And I can't give you one cent more for the merchandise; in fact, I'm only taking it as a favor to you, because I haven't got the slightest use for it. I want to turn this place into a restaurant."

This revelation caused the young man endless confusion. The blood rushed to his face again, concentrating in his nose, giving the pimples on his left nostril a paroxysm of well-being. "I'll . . . I'll talk to my uncle, but I don't know what he'll say."

Florent waited for a few minutes, peering at the pressed-tin ceiling with floral motifs. It'll look terrific once it's painted, he mused.

"My uncle's tired," said the young man. "He has to rest for a while. Can you come back at three o'clock?"

Florent walked the street, hands in his pockets, nervously jingling his loose change. He was still haunted by his mishap with The Beanery. He was afraid Slipskin's role might be played this time by an old storekeeper and his apparently shy young nephew. I need advice, he thought. I don't know where I'm heading.

He walked into a restaurant and looked for the pay phone. "He-e-e-llo," said his father at the other end, placing a soggy cigar butt between the fingers of his secretary, who disgustedly tossed it in the wastebasket. "That you, Florent? Jumpin' Jersey, where are you? In town? Come on over – we'll go and eat at . . . You can't?" His expression darkened, then immediately lit up. "You need advice? Another restaurant?"

He was very flattered by his son's confidence. Dismissing his secretary with an imperious wave, he began to question Florent. No, of course, for the location and size of the establishment the rent didn't seem excessive, far from it. Yes, of course it was risky to go into business across from The Beanery, but after all, he was acting like a real Boissonneault, and who could fault him for that? Sure, he could get information on the owner – no problem. The elder Boissonneault had a friend at city hall who'd look into it at once. If Florent called back at three he'd know everything, including the dimensions of the backside of the fellow's mistress, if he was interested. But for the love of heaven, not a word to your mother before everything's settled, okay? She's had enough trouble with her nerves as it is.

When Florent's father hung up, he sat there for a moment, dazed. Then, glancing at his watch, he asked for a taxi, slipped on his jacket, and went out.

While the investigation was proceeding, Florent was digging into a plate of shepherd's pie in a little restaurant on Mentana Street. "Ours at The Beanery was a hell of a lot better," he muttered, "and we charged twenty cents less."

Fifteen minutes later, he rang Gladu's bell. "I got him!" exclaimed the journalist, sounding like a zoologist who, after long years of research, found himself face-to-face with a very rare snake twenty meters long.

Nervousness made his flabby, rather vulgar features look vaguely muddy. "This pal of mine's absolutely trustworthy, and he'd bust a chesterfield over the Pope's neck if you asked him. Go wait in the car while I take my little dumpling to the neighbor's."

Shortly afterward, Gladu slipped behind the wheel of his car, breathing hard. "He's at the Pink Flamingo Motel in Ville d'Anjou." With no transition he added, "Little bitch – when she found out I was leaving her with Madame Courville for the afternoon she went bananas and shit her pants like a sausage machine. I had to give her a bath."

Florent touched his arm. "What's the guy's name?"

Gladu gave him a knowing look and snickered. "Around me, he likes to be called Georges-Etienne. With other people, I couldn't say."

Florent shuddered. "Are you serious? You don't know his name?"

"What difference would it make?" And Gladu launched into a long description of life on the shady side of the law, which took them to the Pink Flamingo. He parked outside room 27. It was nearly three o'clock. Gladu turned to Florent with a look of trepidation. "Listen, pal, watch out, okay? The most important thing is, don't ask a lot of questions. You could end up in a vacant lot with your mouth sewed up with wire. Promise me, okay, pal?"

While Gladu knocked on the door as delicately as a nun, Florent thought, I feel as if I'm trading an aching toe for an aching foot.

"Come in," said a pleasant young voice.

At the back of the room, sitting at a paper-strewn table, Florent saw a black-haired man in his thirties adding up figures in a notebook. Looking up, he asked Gladu, "Is this the man with the restaurant?"

Gladu nodded briskly.

"Come here."

They obeyed. The man gestured to them to sit on the bed. They were extremely uncomfortable, their knees level with their navels, because of the soft mattress. Georges-Etienne turned to them and crossed his legs. He was slim and well dressed, with a narrow, well-trimmed mustache and dreamy blue-gray eyes. He could have been an army man turned art dealer, or something of the sort. He leaned back, stifled a yawn, then suddenly seemed to be staring most attentively at Florent's hair. "Describe your problem, will you? I'm not sure I understood Rosario."

Florent was careful not to give too many details, presenting Egon Ratablavasky as an old gentleman with bizarre tendencies, who had a certain fortune and, it seemed, some influential connections. For two years he'd been inflicting every possible torment on Florent, who couldn't figure out what was motivating him and wanted an end to the harassment. He was prepared to pay whatever was necessary. He wanted it understood that for the moment he was thinking only of intimidation. However, if such means didn't bear fruit, he wouldn't hesitate to opt for a more radical solution.

At the name Ratablavasky, Georges-Etienne flinched imperceptibly, but said nothing. When Florent had finished, he merely asked for a detailed description, the old man's address, the names of some friends or acquaintances, any peculiar habits, and so forth. He spoke courteously, listened attentively, and didn't take notes. Still, it smelled a little too much of self-control for Florent's liking. Something about his expression, a certain severity in his voice, led one to suspect that not even the crudest vulgarity or brutality would frighten or even displease him.

Florent concealed his uneasiness as well as he could, but his skin was soaking and he wanted only one thing: to be outside. "Stop worrying," said Georges-Etienne affably. "As of now, your troubles are mine. Trust me. I always go softly – and by degrees." These last words were uttered with a smile that made Florent feel strangely disgusted.

"How much?"

"One thousand dollars, payable immediately, please."

Only after he was seated in the car did Florent become aware again of Gladu's presence. "I don't know if you're thinking what I'm thinking," said the journalist, "but I'd rather have somebody crush my fingers for two days and three nights than be on the wrong side of that one."

Florent smiled, saying nothing. He was imagining Georges-Etienne in a black velvet suit, at the wheel of a Porsche in some deserted spot in the country, fastidiously crushing the body of an undesirable lying bound hand and foot, and doing it as nonchalantly as Florent might walk through a pile of dead leaves.

I've *got* to get inside Old Rat's apartment before he does, he thought suddenly. Jesus, the negatives – God knows what he might do with them.

Gladu tapped his elbow. "Hey, I'm talking to you! How about a beer at the Au Coq Rapide Bar-B-Q? It'll give us a lift and I could introduce you to Ghislaine, this new chick. She's a barmaid there."

"Thanks, buddy, but I'd rather go home. I'm asleep on my feet. Could you take me back to my truck?" As he was turning the key, Florent murmured, "Let's hope Gladu doesn't try to follow me."

With a watchful eye and after several cautious detours, Florent parked the truck in a dark lane not far from Mont-Royal

Street, and returned to the yard goods store. The bolts of cloth in the dusty window suddenly reminded him of Les Draperies Georgette: "Hey, why not have supper with Ange-Albert?" he said aloud as he pushed the door. "That'd give me the push I need to go to the Hotel Nelson."

The young redhead was all smiles. His hair was combed and he was wearing his finest suit. "Afternoon. My uncle can talk to you now."

He's put on his fancy duds, Florent thought. That's good: it means they're going to sign.

The young man went behind the counter, then stepped aside to let Florent by. The room was fairly large and reeked of rubbing alcohol; it was lit by a night-light that filled the room with a bluish glow. There were piles of cardboard boxes everywhere.

A sudden hoarse sound made Florent start. In the corner, he saw a camp cot half buried in blankets. The boy gestured to a chair. "Sit there," he said, flipping a switch.

A bare bulb over their heads filled the room with glaring light. The face of an old Jewish man appeared amid the covers and Florent sat down, feeling profoundly uneasy.

"This is my Uncle Abie," said the young man with forced joviality. "What's your name?"

Florent introduced himself and tried to smile at the bald, oblong face, the eyes almost rolled back but peering at him with maniacal intensity. The nephew hesitated briefly, then timidly touched Florent's shoulder. "Move up, he can't see you too good."

Florent moved his chair, and the young man brought a small low table covered with papers. This is some day for emotions, he thought. All we need is a murder.

"See, this isn't his room," the young man felt constrained

to point out. "He just spends the day here to keep an eye on the business."

"Does he understand us?" asked Florent, controlling his feelings with difficulty.

A furious growl was his answer, and the old man blinked as he fidgeted in his bed. Bending over his uncle, the young man said a few words in Yiddish that immediately calmed him. Curiously, all his shyness seemed to vanish in the sick man's presence. He started shuffling papers: "Last month already, the doctor said sell, but he won't. This business is his life, y'know what I mean? So last month I put in a bed and I went to work for him. But just two days ago we got a better idea." He glanced affectionately at his uncle, who was looking at him and seemed to be drinking in his words. "We'll stay in business, but we'll work out of the house. When he's feeling better, we'll go into mail order: birthday cards, get-well cards, all kinds of cards. We'll make plenty of money without leaving home! Good idea, eh?" he said with a knowing look.

Florent nodded and shifted on his chair for the tenth time. "So," the young man began hesitantly, "we talked over the rent, my uncle and me, and . . ."

There was another growl. Florent turned around. Grimacing with the effort, the old man was imperceptibly shaking his head from left to right.

"My uncle wants a three-year lease, maximum, and the rent would be one seventy, on account of inflation, y'know what I mean? And about the merchandise – we can't go below . . . below seventeen hundred and . . . and it's cheap at the price," he added, his face once again shamefully flooded with red. "It's a nice place here, you know: it's clean, it's big –"

"And it's old," Florent interrupted, not daring to look at the sick man.

"Could be, but they don't build like this anymore. The walls are two feet thick; that's right, two feet. In the winter, the furnace runs four hours a day, maximum."

The old man was stirring again. His breathing was becoming more spasmodic.

Florent ran a hand over his face. "Okay for the rent. But your merchandise – I don't want to hurt your feelings, but I can't imagine what I'd do with it." (He shuddered, imagining the look in the old man's eyes.) "I can't pay more than sixteen hundred. And that's my final offer."

The young man turned to his Uncle Abie and talked to him at length. Florent ventured a quick look. The old man listened, impassive, then blinked three times and heaved a raucous sigh. The nephew turned to Florent, relieved. "So all right. For you, my uncle says, he'll do it. I'll get the papers ready. It won't take long."

"How long?"

"Maybe half an hour."

Florent got up. "Fine. I've got time for a bite next door."

The restaurant smells of Javex and vinegar that greeted him seemed like a celestial aroma. He slumped into a booth. "Whew! My nerves are in my galoshes!"

He stood up and went to the telephone. "Everything's in order," his father announced triumphantly. "The fellow seems honest, his titles are clear, taxes are paid up – but I'd still like to take a peek at his . . . You're signing a lease in ten minutes? I see. Well, good luck, and don't forget to come and see us." With a grimace of annoyance he hung up, staring at the ceiling as he rubbed his left leg, which had suddenly started to ache.

Florent waited for three-quarters of an hour, then returned to the store, revived by two bowls of soup. The nephew was placidly waiting, seated at the table. His uncle seemed to be asleep, but he opened his eyes as soon as they started talking. Florent read the contract quickly, asked for a minor change in a clause dealing with maintenance, then hurriedly affixed his signature. The young man was about to do the same when a horrible growling filled the room. The old man, propped on his elbows, purple faced and eyes bulging, seemed to be having a fit of apoplexy.

"*Vos iz mit dir, feter*?" the young man cried out. "What's wrong, Uncle?"

The old man was still sitting up, his gaze incandescent, in a state of anxiety that was dreadful to see. With an exclamation of joy, his nephew rushed over to the bed, clutching the papers. He spoke to his uncle in a halting voice, his eyes filled with tears. Florent watched, stupefied, as he put the pen in the sick man's stiff hand and helped to guide his movements. As the first attempt was unsuccessful, he put a piece of cardboard under the papers. "There you go!" he said triumphantly, handing Florent a copy of the lease. "He wanted to sign it himself. It's better that way, eh? So you can move in tomorrow night if you want."

"Thanks . . . all the same," Florent stammered, "but it'll be another couple of months." They shook hands and Florent slipped away, forgetting his scarf and gloves, which the young man ran out to give him.

No doubt it was this deep turmoil that prevented him, a few minutes later, from noticing his former friend Slipskin when their vehicles met at the corner of St-Denis and Mont-Royal. Slipskin didn't see him, either. He was daydreaming lugubriously, a cigarette butt clamped between his lips, which were stretched in a bitter grimace.

A month earlier, Ratablavasky had suddenly decided to open hostilities. It started with petty provocations, childish spitefulness. Slipskin had shrugged it off with a disdainful smirk. A week ago, though, Old Rat had stopped pulling his punches. Slipskin's wife suffered the same fate as Elise: one morning the postman handed her a thick envelope that smelled of musk. Inside she found an amazingly complete list of all her husband's conquests during his career as a womanizer, a career that overlapped alarmingly with the time they had been keeping company.

Though he racked his brains, Slipskin had no clear idea what his enemy was aiming at. He'd tried several times to meet with him, but Ratablavasky evaded him.

Bertrand stuck his head out the kitchen door. His boss had just entered the restaurant. Slipskin stood on the threshold, shivering, glum and foul mouthed, and glanced around the room. Bertrand snickered to himself. Poor boss, down in the dumps tonight, eh, son of a bitch? You'll never be down enough for me, no sir! I'd like to take shysters like you and serve 'em on toast to the pigs.

Slipskin sat at the counter. Leaving her customers, Betty, the young waitress he'd just hired, came rushing over. "Bring me a bowl of soup, will you?" he asked morosely.

Meanwhile, Florent was climbing the stairs to his old apartment on Emery Street, delighted to see light in the windows. The new carillon in the vestigial steeple of the church of St-Jacques had just sounded six o'clock. I'll invite him for supper at Chez Marmontel, Florent thought, ringing the bell, then maybe ask him to come to Ratablavasky's.

A luminous rectangle appeared on the landing, and a shadow came hobbling down the stairs. The outer door opened. Florent recoiled. In the harsh illumination of the streetlight, his friend Ange-Albert stared at him, stunned and sleepy-eyed. But he looked so different that Florent exclaimed, "Holy Christ, what happened to you?"

He gazed at Ange-Albert's swollen face, marked by several cuts that hadn't healed. Ange-Albert greeted him and shook his hand. "Christ, I'm glad to see you. Come have a coffee. Isn't Elise here?" As he spoke he dragged himself up the stairs, clutching the banister. He seemed to be pulling up the weight of the staircase with his shoes.

"What the hell's going on, Ange-Albert?" Florent asked. "Somebody beat you up? You can hardly stand up!"

"You said it. Last Friday I got my lesson." He stopped to catch his breath. "My first lesson. The second one came afterward when Rosine left me."

They went to the kitchen. Ange-Albert started rinsing out cups. The air was heavy with the smell of overripe garbage. The apartment seemed abandoned. A pair of pantyhose was draped over the back of a chair. Some old cosmetic jars had rolled into a corner, where they were gathering dust. Everything spoke of a sudden break, of depression, of solitary restaurant meals, of endless evenings in cafés with casual acquaintances, tanking up on beer and stale jokes. "Never mind the coffee," said Florent. "We're going out to eat. You could use a decent meal – you're a wreck. We'll celebrate Elise's pregnancy: we're hoping she'll make it this time."

Ange-Albert turned heavily. "She's got another one on the way?" He clasped Florent's hands. "Good luck . . . this time, buddy," he stammered, "and congratulations, and above all, be careful!"

There was silence. The two friends looked at each other, unsure what to say next. Then Ange-Albert muttered, "I'm hungry."

Florent guffawed. "Put on your coat, then. I'm taking you to Chez Marmontel."

"Marmontel! Hey, that's expensive."

"Yeah, but what food! Anyway, my morale needs a boost, too: you can't imagine the night I've got ahead of me." As he was helping his friend down the stairs, he asked, "What happened to you two anyway? Why did Rosine leave? Were you screwing around or what?"

"Dice," Ange-Albert grimaced. "Goddamn dice. I wanted to live off them, and the buggers nearly killed me."

Florent helped him into the truck and, while they were driving, got the details.

Three weeks after Elise and Florent left for Sainte-Romanie, he'd got tired of his job at Draperies Georgette. Remembering his triumphant craps game at the Saint-Malo, he told Rosine, "You know, a couple of games like that every month and we could live like kings."

Rosine objected but couldn't prevent him from quitting his job. Soon she had to resign herself to accompanying him to St-Denis Street cafés where, with a good-natured smile, he resumed his gambling.

In two weeks he'd become a local celebrity. Despite his winnings everyone liked him, for he didn't abuse his skill and was wise enough to fleece his opponents in moderation, with the occasional crushing defeat to avert charges of cheating. His circle of acquaintances began to grow. He was playing everywhere, sometimes in dubious establishments. "I have to enlarge my field," he'd explain to Rosine, "or I'll run out of pigeons."

From time to time losers would get angry, demanding other dice or even asking for their money back. Smiling calmly,

Ange-Albert always acquiesced. "I don't need the money," he would explain. "I play for the fun of it."

As the days went by, his wallet became a more and more pleasing sight. Rosine's warnings were even becoming less urgent. One evening when he'd just pulled a particularly spectacular number at the ultrachic Ciro's Bar in Côte St-Paul, one Marc Lalonde introduced himself to Ange-Albert, overcome with admiration, and suggested arranging meetings with certain handpicked opponents. This would enable him to make his astonishing virtuosity better known, at the same time increasing his income, of which Lalonde requested only a small percentage by way of commission. "You can judge by the results," he had told Ange-Albert. "If you aren't happy, we'll call it quits, and no hard feelings."

The meetings took place, and the money fell into Ange-Albert's pockets as promised; he was ecstatic and lost all perspective. "Better make hay while the sun shines," Lalonde advised paternally, "because pretty soon, you'll be too well known. No one will risk *barbotte* or Lucky Seven against you."

One night when Ange-Albert, urged on by his impresario, had in less than an hour won the splendid sum of $2,419, Lalonde apparently decided the good times were over. He made his usual offer to drive Ange-Albert home, and led him out the back door of the Barina Bar, where the game had been played, saying his car was parked out back. Outside, Ange-Albert realized that half a dozen rather sinister-looking friends of Lalonde's were waiting patiently by the car, despite the bitter cold, drinking Dutch gin. Waving them over, Lalonde handed Ange-Albert a chequebook. "It'll suit me fine if you write me a check for $8,247.66. If I remember correctly, that's about what you've got in the bank."

Ange-Albert looked around him, then handed the cheque to his impresario. "Now," Lalonde ordered, "empty your pockets. Little assholes like you need a lesson now and then. Thanks. Oh yeah – one last bit of advice: shut your trap if you want to stay healthy."

And to show him just how nasty an unhealthy state could be, he administered a beating that left Ange-Albert flat out in the snow for two hours.

The next day, Rosine, who had long since stopped accompanying him on his nocturnal peregrinations, packed her bags and left. "And that's about it," Ange-Albert sighed. "I've phoned her parents twenty times, but she's always out. And I'll have to eat another omelet tonight – my jaws still hurt."

"Poor bugger," said his friend, as he parked the truck near Place Jacques-Cartier. "I wish I could feel sorry for you, but you were asking for it! Keep your hands off those goddamn dice!"

"My hands? Just looking at them gives me stomach cramps."

They were walking slowly down St-François-Xavier Street when Ange-Albert's heel caught on an icy bump and he landed in Florent's arms. With a cry of vexation, he got his friend on his feet and they hurried along the street. Someone had recently had the bright idea of replacing the charming old graystone building that housed Chez Marmontel with a parking lot.

It was a few blocks farther, at La Petite Coquille, that Florent disclosed to his friend the latest damage wreaked by Ratablavasky and his own intention to get back the negatives. "You're going to his place?" asked Ange-Albert, startled. "Who do you think you are, Arsène Lupin?"

Florent continued his confidences and told him about

Georges-Etienne. His friend's amazement was unbounded. "And you've got the nerve to preach to me about three little pieces of wood in a shaker?"

"What else can I do?" asked Florent bleakly.

"Go to the cops."

"Screw that! With all his money, he's had them in his pocket for years. Besides, I have no evidence. None. Could you put your finger on a single clue? He never leaves one. It's his trademark. He's been torturing us for two years now. How far will he go? Nobody knows. Why did he pick us? Nobody knows that either. Nobody understands a goddamn thing that's going on, including him, most likely. But I've had enough. I'm even sorry I didn't arrange to have him rubbed out right away. A silencer smack in the forehead and our troubles would be over."

Ange-Albert nervously wiped his plate with a piece of bread, then looked up. "If I were you I'd go and see your cousin, Father Whatsit."

Florent glanced at him, then laughed so hard that, at a nearby table, a pudgy little man in patent-leather shoes pricked his throat with a fishbone and had to deposit the contents of his mouth in his handkerchief. "Thanks for the advice," said Florent, "but I don't see how a priest who's so out to lunch he has trouble finding his own shoes in his bedroom could help me untangle this spaghetti."

"Okay, okay, you know best."

He took a roll, broke it in half, buttered both pieces, then, with a contemplative look, dug into a garlic-laden salad.

Florent had put down his fork ten minutes earlier. He fidgeted on the edge of his chair, constantly looking at his watch. Finally, he couldn't take it any longer. "Hurry up, buddy. You can't believe how anxious I am to get this job done."

A few minutes later they were walking along St-Paul Street. "I'm coming with you," said Ange-Albert.

Florent shook his head. "Thanks, but everybody has to deal with their own problems. You don't know what you'd be in for. And you're in bad enough shape as it is."

"But what's to stop me from having a beer at the grill if I feel like it?" said Ange-Albert with a mocking smile.

They headed for a laneway that ran along the right side of the hotel and opened onto a courtyard that was used as a terrace in the summer. "His apartment's on this side," Florent murmured. He looked up. "See, it's on the top floor – the two middle windows. It's dark."

The hazy light that veiled Place Jacques-Cartier brought a soft glow to the glass in the two windows, accentuating their black opacity, which suggested the smooth surface of a coal vein. "How do you expect to get in?" asked Ange-Albert skeptically.

"I don't know. I'm thinking. Go ask at reception if Old Rat's in. They might recognize me."

Florent paced back and forth, shuddering. "He's been gone for two days!" Ange-Albert announced, rejoining him. "And they don't know where."

Florent looked at him, his lips compressed by mental effort, his gaze hard and abstracted. "We need a master key. I'll try and find a housekeeper."

"At this hour? They usually work mornings."

Gesturing vaguely, Florent went through the back courtyard to a tiny crêperie that was part of the hotel. They sat down and examined the menu. "Coffee?" Florent suggested.

"Umm . . . if you don't mind," said his friend rather awkwardly, "I'd rather have a crêpe with ice cream."

A waitress took their orders. Florent was slightly queasy, but a feeling of boldness and lightness won out, masking his stage fright and fed by it, too. His mood must have been written on his face, for Ange-Albert was watching him in surprise. The waitress came back with their order. With a good-natured grin, Florent said, "One of my aunts is a housekeeper here."

"Madame Labonté? Or Madame Paquette?"

"Madame Paquette. She never works nights, does she?"

The young girl smiled – in fact, if you looked closely, she wasn't all that young: bags under her eyes, dull skin, an oblong face, lips that were too broad and thick brown braids only pointed up her look of exhaustion and her declining freshness. "No, of course she doesn't."

"Too bad. I had a surprise for her."

At the word "surprise," Ange-Albert started slightly, for Florent's shoe had just lightly struck his shin. "I wanted to leave a present. Today's her birthday."

"Leave it at the desk, then. They'll give it to her tomorrow."

Florent shook his head. "No, I wanted it to be a *real* surprise. . . . You know what she's like: such a tease. . . ."

The waitress hesitated briefly, then agreed. "It's true, she likes a laugh, if her rheumatism isn't bothering her too much."

"I could . . . maybe I could leave my gift in her apron pocket. Her work clothes must be here in the hotel, aren't they?"

The waitress smiled. "Mm-hmm. I can fix that up."

"Thanks, that's very kind. I'll just go across the street to buy a little something and I'll be right back."

"What's up?" asked Ange-Albert as they strode across Place Jacques-Cartier, cheeks frozen by the wind. "Have you really got an aunt working here?"

"Sure, my half-ass cousin's grandma, jerk. Don't you get it? Only way I'll lay my hands on a master key is to get in her apron pocket. In the meantime you'll distract the waitress."

"And what if the key isn't there?"

Ten minutes later, Florent asked, "So, Doubting Thomas, what do you think of my instinct now?" He was walking through the courtyard, twirling a big bunch of keys. "Now all we have to do is go up to Old Rat's apartment without being noticed. You sit in the lobby, as if you were just killing time, and if you see anything that bothers you, call room 303 or run up and get me."

The lobby was filled with a great crush of long-haired young people in jeans, ponchos, leather jackets, and Indian smocks, moving amid laughter and cigarette smoke. The tall asthmatic desk clerk was sweating behind the counter, punching the cash register, making change, giving out keys, always three steps behind. The two friends agreed to meet in half an hour, and Florent managed to make his way unimpeded to the narrow winding staircase that led to the upper floors. At the first landing, he was already out of breath. "What's wrong with me?" he murmured. "Am I scared? Get it together, Boissonneault, this is no time to be shaking in your boots. Think about your wife and child! Think about your life!"

He spat on the wall with bravado and continued his climb. At the third floor he stopped, wiped his moist hands on his trousers, and pricked up his ears. Somewhere in a room a bottle of beer went "Pschtt!"

A woman's tender voice softly intoned a few words, then burst out laughing. Florent entered a corridor, walked its length, and turned left. A heavy oak door with a brass knocker glowed softly at the end. Florent stared at it. The wings of his nose were frozen, his fingers stiff, as if anesthetized. I'll knock first, he told himself. And if I hear anybody, I'll beat it.

An insidious little voice whispered, Why not take advantage of the situation and kill him?

Idiot, he replied. What with?

A knife, the voice replied, a bookend, a piece of wood, whatever.

He approached the door, picked up the knocker, and let it fall twice. There was only silence. Behind him, another bottle of beer went "Pschtt!"

He turned around briskly. The corridor was deserted. In fact he was no longer quite so sure he'd heard a sound. Suddenly he could hear feet dragging on the other side of the door, then an indistinct grumbling. He fell back. "Who's there?" asked an old woman's voice.

Through widened eyes, Florent checked the number on the door. "I'd like . . . I'd like to speak to Monsieur Ratablavasky."

The lock made a series of clicking sounds, then a small round head with gray braids and silver spectacles appeared. "For goodness' sake, will you stop bothering me with your Rata-whatever! I don't know the man from Adam – or Eve – and if I have one wish, it's that he never shows his face in front of me!"

"But . . . but . . ."

"But: I've been living here for four years and I'm going *deaf* with people asking for that diabolical-sounding name – as if I didn't deserve to be left in peace, at my age!"

The door slammed and her footsteps receded, accompanied by the same furious grumbling.

Florent slowly turned around, utterly confused. Am I going crazy? This is the same oak door, the same brass knocker. There isn't another one on the whole floor!

He walked past all the doors, then decided to inquire at the reception desk. As he started down the stairs, a strange sound made him raise his head. Leaning on the banister above him, Egon Ratablavasky was watching him, a handkerchief over his mouth, shoulders heaving in a fit of laughter that sounded more like snorts. Florent, rooted to the spot, looked at him, speechless; he felt as if his cheeks had turned to plaster and were coming away from his face. Several seconds passed. At length Ratablavasky managed to calm down a little. "Good day, dear young friend. It would appear (he brought the handkerchief to his mouth again) . . . it would appear that you are wanting to see me, isn't it? Please to forgive my breakout of laughing. My housekeeper is so . . . shall we say, so *excellent* a friend to me. Come up, come up! To you, I am opening with pleasure the door to my humble apartment."

Florent hesitated briefly, then shook his head. He had gradually recovered his sangfroid. "No, I changed my mind. It's okay. Good night."

He started back down the stairs, then stopped again and turned to the old man. His lips twisted in a sarcastic smile. "Oh yes, before I forget: my wife thanks you for the picture. And sorry to disappoint you, but we aren't getting a divorce. Despite our youth, we won't let a silly thing like that come between us. On the other hand, I was very upset the other day when I noticed I'd lost a book of meditations I've found very edifying lately. . . . My piety took one of those falls . . ."

Ratablavasky burst out laughing and dashed down the stairs with surprising agility. "I don't know what you are meaning about this book," he said, standing beside Florent, who held his nose and stepped back. "As for the photograph, rest assured that my aim was not what you are accusing. I just wanted to show you my, how shall I call it, *potency* . . . and I hoped you might give me a little visit. And I want you to know," he said with a mischievous wink, "I am highly honored to see you bring your friend." He tried to pat Florent's shoulder, but he was pushed away roughly.

"Keep your hands to yourself. We've got nothing in common, you and I."

"To the contrary, we have much! We are often thinking about each other, isn't it?"

With a shrug, Florent resumed his descent.

"No, no," the old man pleaded. "I have still much things to tell you."

Ange-Albert was sitting in a corner of the lobby, discreetly finishing a glass of beer (it was forbidden to drink alcoholic beverages outside the grill) when he saw Florent, followed by Ratablavasky, dashing toward the exit. Florent gestured to him to follow.

Place Jacques-Cartier was covered with a bumpy layer of ice, and the occasional pedestrians were crossing it cautiously. "Brrr!" said the old man, pulling up his collar. "This temperature is – how you say – not fitting for discussion."

"What discussion?" Florent retorted. "I've wasted enough time listening to your garbage! Get lost!"

Nodding sardonically to the old man, Ange-Albert walked away with his friend. "Stop!" exclaimed Ratablavasky, his face distorted. "I beg you, my friend, have the infinite goodness to give me one minute of your time!"

He rushed up to Florent and clutched his arm. Taken aback, the young man turned and stared at the unreadable features, the facial enigma, grotesquely vulgar with its buttocks-shaped chin, its oddly black and deep-sunk eyes, the childishly perfect nose and above all, the lips, lustful and gluttonous, blossoming with unbearable insolence, which Florent would gladly have sliced with a razor.

The old man's eyes watered, and he began to moan. "How tragic, oh, how tragic, when the heart no longer hears the words of the mouth! In this manner does fate begin to roar. How can I say – I made a mistake. Yes! I like too much joking without considering the consequences. I was wrong with you, but yet it was love that guided my hand, I beg you to believe me that! I wanted to teach you, like we teach little puppies, without appealing to your faculty of – how you say – understanding. Imbecile! Oh, what an imbecile am I! What can I say to you now?"

His voice suddenly dropped, became urgent, halting. "It is the universe, yes, the universe, that molds men's acts. Those laws are acting harder than you, than I, than all humanity – do you understand?"

Good Lord, he's gone off the rail altogether, Florent thought, with a knowing look at Ange-Albert, who stood slightly behind them.

Ratablavasky went on in the same muffled, breathless voice. "And what are these laws?" He raised his forefinger, then his middle finger. "All is good. All is bad. And when the good and the bad are united . . . then you have Perfection, for you have complete Life. But you don't understand," he sighed. "For pity's sake, only a few brief moments and my words will possess a meaning to your mind. And then perhaps you will love me. A tree: bring your mind to a tree. He grows, he makes shade, he makes fruits, he is totally useful, a tree. And then a man comes, he cuts down the tree and builds a house: that, too, is totally useful. Alive, it is useful, dead it is useful, too. Now let me talk about man, about you, your friends, everybody in the whole world. An honest man? Nothing better! A thief? Very well, he makes honest people cautious. Free? How marvelous! Unfree, perhaps even better, for it leads to love of freedom and the struggle to win it. And those are the laws of the universe. They cause struggles and struggles produce Perfection. Isn't it?"

He stopped to catch his breath. Ange-Albert was gazing at him with an astonished look that gave his face the smiling steadiness of the full moon. Ratablavasky seemed to have forgotten his presence. With a contrite and humble look at Florent, he said, "I was wanting to have some fun with your goals in this life, but for your good, only for your good. Please, I beg, you must believe what I say. For you, as for a son, a true son, I wanted Life's Perfection. A slave, and then free! For a freed slave is the freest of men, isn't it? And that is why the photograph was sent. . . . But you didn't understand," he sighed, "for I acted with too much hardness."

His shoulders slumped and he gave Florent a despondent look. However, the younger man thought he detected a tiny flame, a sort of roguish, implacable quivering that tried to disappear in the depths of the pupils. For a moment combined hatred and fear made him seem stupid. "Okay, let's go," he said at length, turning to Ange-Albert, "I can't take another minute of this crap. And you, crackpot, I've got a bottle of champagne at home to celebrate when you die."

Ratablavasky bowed in an attitude both deferential and ironic, pulled his collar up and slowly walked back to the hotel, head high, gait springy and nonchalant, as if the whole business hadn't the slightest interest for him.

"At last you're home!" Elise exclaimed a few hours later. Virtue, who had run out before her, was pawing at her master's thighs and whimpering with joy. "Are you all right? You're sure?" Trembling, she threw herself in his arms. Florent's eyes crinkled with contentment.

The photograph's been forgotten, he told himself. With a lump in his throat, he succumbed for a few moments to a joyous tangle of emotions.

"What a day I've had," sighed Elise. "I was worried to death – and I caught Monsieur Emile in the closet twice, drinking beer. And then this afternoon – the grocer got the weirdest call for you – he wrote down the message. . . . I had to fight with Monsieur Picquot to keep him from alerting the entire police force. Good thing he's asleep now, poor man. He's absolutely wiped out."

"Not *absolutely*," Picquot announced, emerging from his bedroom fully dressed, a revolver strapped to his chest.

At the sight of him, Florent turned pale. Good God! he exclaimed to himself. I forgot to deliver his package to Emilienne Latouche!

THIRTY-ONE

Taking advantage of his lengthy observations of his cat, Monsieur Emile decided on a typically feline procedure to awaken Florent next morning. He crouched by the bed and with stiffened fingers imitated Breakfast's morning promenades across his master's stomach. There were grunts and groans, some furious flailing of arms and a volley of abuse, then the sleeper opened his eyes and sat up. Clucking contentedly, Monsieur Emile got to his feet. "Hey, Florent, what'd you bring me?"

"Screw off, brat!"

Florent scratched his head, his features distorted by yawns; he peered groggily at his beat-up slippers, then headed for the kitchen. Monsieur Emile persisted. "Did you bring me a present?"

"Cool it, kid! Your present is, I'm keeping you here."

"Coffee?" asked Picquot from the living room doorway, as the unhappy child disappeared.

"What? You're up already?"

"What do you expect?" asked the chef grumpily. "After all, someone must sacrifice a certain amount of sleep if we're to maintain a modicum of order."

Florent flopped onto a chair, elbows on the table, as Picquot brought his coffee. In front of him was a sheet of Hamel's letterhead. Last night before going to bed, he'd read it over and over. In a large, careful hand the grocer had transcribed a telephone message he'd received for Florent, which even now must be making tongues wag all over the village. It read:

> Dear and affectionate friend,
>
> I learned with joy of the fabulous purchases you make in this so hospitable region. May old things make of you a new man. Eternally yours, E.

"The work of a lunatic," Picquot muttered with a threatening stare as he took his place. "And only another lunatic couldn't guess his identity!"

Florent touched his friend's arm. "Don't worry. I took care of him yesterday – for good."

The chef stood up, ashen. "By St. George's cross! Don't tell me you . . ."

Florent shook his head. "But it's in capable hands. It's as good as done. Now for God's sake, sit down. You look as if you're going to faint."

"I was so wise not to have children," Picquot murmured, sinking back in his chair. "Paternal love would have destroyed me. You haven't been incautious, at least?"

Monsieur Emile approached. "Oh please, can I sit on your lap?" He was irresistibly cuddly this morning, and Florent told him to climb up.

Picquot continued. "Give me some details, anyway. I'm not quite sure I follow."

"I know what happened," said the child very seriously. "He got him rubbed out, that's all!" Seeing Elise, he exclaimed,

"You're up! It's about time!" And he jumped down just as Florent was bringing his coffee to his lips. "Make me French toast like the other day, Elise!" he said, hugging her knees as Florent wiped off his nose.

Elise cuddled the child as the chef bombarded Florent with questions – without much success.

"Very well, I won't press the matter," said Picquot, rising. "I wouldn't want to overstep your confidence. In any case, to judge by the crumbs you've deigned to toss my way, your decision seems to me – and I choose my words carefully – like utter madness. Dear boy, you're liable to get the worst of this mess, take my word! And on that, I'll ask you to excuse me: I must pack my bags. I'm leaving shortly."

"Why all the secrecy?" Elise asked. "We haven't been able to get a word out of you since last night."

"I want my French toast!" shouted Monsieur Emile.

Picquot was back shortly, carrying his suitcase, a coat draped over his arm, his face as merry as a morgue.

"Stay for dinner," Elise suggested timidly.

"Impossible. I have obligations."

Monsieur Emile stamped his foot and screamed: "I want my French toast!"

Florent exploded. "Give him his goddamn French toast so he'll shut up! And you, put down that suitcase. I'll give you a blow-by-blow account of my day yesterday. I didn't want to upset you, but I can see you're dying to know."

Monsieur Emile poured a phenomenal quantity of maple syrup over his first slice of toast (he'd asked for six), and with eyes half closed with contentment, wolfed it down as Virtue, at his feet, looked on voraciously. Florent led Elise and Picquot by the arm to the living room, shut the door, and gave them a detailed account of his day.

A weighty silence filled the room. The chef cleared his throat repeatedly, ran his hand over his brow, pulled on his mustache. "What a mess! Will we ever see the end of it? *Tiens.*" Rummaging in his inside pocket, he took out his revolver and offered it to Florent. "You need this more than I do. Above all, don't hesitate to call if you suspect any trouble. I am at your *complete* disposal, understand? In any case, I've been planning to leave the advertising-poisoning agency so I'll have plenty of free time . . . until I start in your restaurant!"

He went to the kitchen. "Come, child, give me a kiss, I'm leaving now. Promise you'll behave yourself."

Monsieur Emile, self-conscious at Picquot's solemn tone, pressed his sticky lips to the rough cheek. Then the chef turned to Elise. "Try to avoid strong emotions, dear girl," he said in a different voice, embracing her. "In your condition it could be disastrous."

Then he clasped Florent's hand for a long time, while Breakfast, sprawled out in the middle of the room with one paw in the air, claws spread, meticulously licked his anus, utterly indifferent to their farewells.

As Picquot was getting in his car he saw Mayor Meloche approach. "*Tiens, tiens*, the vultures are looking for carrion."

"Nice day," said the mayor, smiling broadly. "Monsieur Boissonneault in?"

"You should know better than I," the chef retorted.

He slammed the door and drove away. "Poor children," he murmured as he drove out of the village. "I'd give my right hand and my forearm, too, for them to be left in peace."

And it was then that he decided to keep an eye on Ratablavasky personally.

After the mayor left, Florent told Elise, "Sweetheart, we have to roll up our sleeves. Another message like the one Old Rat just sent and nobody'll let us in the door. Let's hope it won't be long till somebody kicks the shit out of him."

Florent went to the presbytery at eight the next morning. "Madame Laflamme, I just had an urge to look around the church basement. Did you ever find that key?"

The housekeeper gazed at Florent in a state of rapture that had most of her faculties in suspense. God Almighty, he thought, the old bag's turned on! Why me?

The woman made some incomprehensible cooing sounds, minced out of the kitchen, and returned dangling a key as if it would open the gates of heaven. "I found it just day before yesterday," she chirped. "And guess where! In with Father's hunting gear! I can't imagine what it was doing there!

"Do you think Father would like to come with me?"

"No, no! I trust you completely. In any case, he's still at Mass."

Florent got back in the truck. He smiled smugly. Wow! An hour with her and I know all her secrets!

He parked beside the church, a few feet from a lateral door that opened onto the apse, and left the truck door open. This would make it almost impossible to see him from the street when he came up from the basement and got in the truck. "Providing Father doesn't come rooting around, if I find anything interesting, we can clear out tomorrow."

The door creaked and he was greeted by a blast of damp and chilly air. Worm-eaten stairs disappeared into the darkness. He groped along the wall until he found a switch. In the yellowish light that appeared eight feet below him, wooden crates, piled against the wall, appeared to shudder. The moldy staircase seemed to creak a little more at each step.

"I'll be damned!" he exclaimed, looking up at the bulb. It was fist sized and had a sort of pointed hood, like the ones made by Thomas Edison himself. "I'll take it later. Should be worth twenty bucks."

It was a vast basement with worrisome scurrying sounds, but apparently nothing of much interest. At the back, by a small window covered with cobwebs, two tall stacks of *La Semaine du Clergé* were piously moldering. Florent picked up one copy, then another, leafed through them, sneezed, and kicked the pile in frustration. He managed to hit an arthritic rat hiding in the papers. It stuck out its head and shot Florent a look of hatred, as he walked away dragging his heels. "I don't think I'll find Champlain's furniture down here."

He felt something brush against his leg and jumped aside. His foot caught on something hidden in the shadows that made a metallic sound. "What's this?" He shuddered, pointing his flashlight at a small wooden box. He broke open the lid and his eyes widened in delight. Six magnificent candlesticks lay side by side in a bed of dust. He picked one up, wiped it on his sleeve, and murmured, "Looks like silver."

He closed the box, picked it up and made a dash for the staircase. As he was setting his foot on the bottom step he heard a door shut, and Father Bournival's head appeared. "Find anything, my friend?" asked the priest's deep bass voice.

"Umm . . . yes . . . I was just going to show you these candlesticks I found in a corner."

The priest glanced at him slyly. "Excellent – I always knew you were an honest lad. . . . Bring them up and let me have a look."

Florent, hard put to conceal his frustration and shame, set the box on the ground and lifted the lid. The priest's expression became very grave. "Heavenly days, am I seeing things?"

He picked up a candlestick and examined it, wiping the dust with his fingertips. "If I'm not mistaken, these are the candlesticks from the old parish church that burned down in the twenties, in Father Beaucage's time. . . . Old Rouleau would know. . . . Everyone thought they'd been stolen."

He looked at Florent. "No question of selling these, my boy. . . . They're a precious relic of our parish. Besides, they're solid silver! Anything else?"

Florent shook his head, more and more hard-pressed to hide his disappointment. "Come," said the priest, "let's have a look, anyway. You've got me curious." He spent a long time looking at *La Semaine du Clergé*, moved a pile of planks, cursed the rats and the lack of light, then decided to go back upstairs. Under the staircase, he spotted a box that seemed filled with broken plaster statues. "What's that?"

He tried to bend over for a closer look, but the excess baggage deposited around his waist by thirty-two years in the priesthood made the operation so difficult that he straightened up. "You're young," he said, giving Florent a tap on the back. "Bring that up to your truck so I can see what's inside."

Florent squeezed under the steps and, with his face draped in cobwebs, painfully removed a small, half-rotten lidless chest that was obviously ending its career as a garbage container. The priest was outside, glancing furtively inside the truck. "Thank you, my son. The good Lord will repay you."

He rummaged in the debris for a time, under the sorrowful gaze of a Christ lacking both a chin and one ear, then straightened up with a sigh. "Push it over to the door. I'll have the beadle throw it out."

Sick at heart, Florent carried the candlesticks to the presbytery, politely refusing Father Bournival's offer of a coffee "to heat up your pipes."

"Not even with a drop of Hennessy Three Star?"

Florent shook his head, claiming an urgent errand. Watching him through the window, the priest told his housekeeper, "I don't think your sweetheart's intentions are altogether honorable. I caught him in the basement with half a dozen silver candlesticks – and a shifty look you don't expect from a good Christian."

Madame Laflamme shrugged, offended. "With all respect, Father, you're talking through your hat. As if I need a sweetheart at my age!"

Florent got in the truck, musing, I should have laid on the charm and got her to keep him upstairs.

He glanced at the chest, stuck his hand inside and felt something soft, like old rags, buried under the plaster. "What the hell, I've got nothing to lose," he said, hoisting it into the truck. "I'll take a look after supper."

And so it was that after a most disappointing day. Florent put his hands on several bundles of letters from the pen of one Magloire Blanchet, parish priest at Saint-Charles during the Rebellion of 1837, which shed some very interesting light on the uprising of the Patriotes. But it was the last time Luck would smile on him in Sainte-Romanie.

The next day, as he came home to eat after a long morning that had yielded nothing but transmission problems and a rocking chair studded with nuts and bolts, Elise handed him a telegram:

MUST SEE YOU MY PLACE TOMORROW 3 P.M. RE VERY DECISIVE MATTER. ROSARIO

He'd barely finished reading when Picquot's car roared up to the station, missing the waiting room stove by a hair. "What's he doing here!" Florent asked in astonishment.

He rushed to the stairs, followed by Monsieur Emile, who had decided this was not the most auspicious moment for putting on his shoes. "I've some ex . . . extr . . . extra*ordinary* news!" Picquot gulped.

Waving his arms in the air, he seemed to be trying to fill his lungs with all the air in the station.

The child looked at him in horror. Florent made him sit down until he felt able to climb the stairs. "Sit down and let me unbutton your coat," said Elise. "There's no reason to work yourself into such a state!"

With nodding head and half-closed eyes, Picquot offered no resistance. The bellows filling his skull with a curious din gradually diminished. He loosened his tie, sipped some water, and sighed, "Children, children, such news!"

Florent gripped his shoulders. "Is Ratablavasky dead?"

Picquot shook his head, smiling wearily. "If that were so I'd have brought a cartload of flowers. . . . He's still alive, alas . . . and more than ever!"

He took another sip, smiled at Monsieur Emile who sat cross-legged in a corner, his frightened eyes drinking in everything. Picquot continued, "I went to the Hotel Nelson about eight o'clock last night."

Three pairs of disapproving eyes were turned on him. "In a personal capacity, of course," he hastened to add, wagging his forefinger. "Anyone would have done the same, out of sheer curiosity! In any case, I would have been hard to recognize in my dark glasses, parka, and scarf."

"Just . . . just why did you go?" asked Florent.

"Well! I'd decided to spend the evening in enemy territory to test the waters, so to speak."

"And?"

He rose and took a few steps, obviously delighted with his performance, until a dizzy spell forced him back to his chair. "And . . . until eleven o'clock, not a thing. But after that, my friends, what an adventure!"

After three hours of "discreet surveillance" that took him from bar to grill, from grill to crêperie, and from the crêperie back to the bar, Picquot concluded that his clandestine mission was garnering more calories than clues. So he went to the reception desk and asked for Ratablavasky's room number. "He left on a trip two days ago," said the chubby-faced clerk, whose jaws were working a wad of gum that gave off a foul artificial cherry smell.

Picquot frowned. "Never mind. I need his room number. A personal matter." Armed with the information, Picquot left the hotel, re-entered through a side door, and took the stairs up to the rooms. Soon he was forced to stop, his face bathed in sweat. "Thunder and destruction!" he muttered, out of breath. "Am I about to lose my faculties when I need them most?"

He leaned against the wall, took two or three deep breaths, then continued his ascent more cautiously. At the third floor, he sneezed and advanced slowly to the intersection of three dimly lit corridors. It seemed surprisingly calm, as if the hotel were abandoned. Picquot looked around briefly, then took the corridor facing the stairs, turned left, and stopped again. Fifty feet ahead of him, wan light spilled from a half-open door. Suddenly, with surprising clarity, he heard a car horn. Someone's opened a window, he thought mechanically.

Cursing the myopia that prevented him from reading the number on the door, he advanced stealthily, afraid the floor would betray him. Then he made out the number: 303. Ratablavasky's. His own calm surprised him. It must be rage: the rage I feel at the thought of that . . . that obscenity.

He stood outside the door, not quite sure what to do, one hand in his coat pocket, fiddling with a box of mint drops given him the night before by Mademoiselle Emilienne. Suddenly he heard something creak, like footsteps on broken glass. The door opened slowly (now the sounds from Place Jacques-Cartier could be heard very clearly), and he saw in the doorway the back of a man deep in contemplation. Picquot almost cried out.

The room looked as if a tornado had hit it. The furniture had been overturned and smashed, the floor covered with broken glass, clumps of earth, torn books, chunks of wood. The man coughed, then recoiled slightly, still with his back to the chef. "Good evening, Monsieur Picquot," said Egon Ratablavasky. "You are in excellent health, I hope? Come, come," he said, finally turning around, bestowing on Picquot a smile marked by elegant sorrow. "See how miserably my enemies have been to me."

"I . . . I had nothing to do with it," Picquot stammered, "and I won't allow you . . ."

"Of course not! I know you to be an *exceptionable* friend, and I am much pleased to profit by your splendid presence. Come. I will show to you *everything*." Amicably, he took Picquot's arm and showed him all six rooms in his apartment. None had been spared. "Through there," said the old man, pointing to a window that gave onto a fire escape, "my enemies were making their escape when I arrived."

Picquot followed obediently, knees knocking, his heart in his mouth, but with a ready retort and curious gaze. If I get out of here alive, he was thinking, what a tale to tell!

"Don't forget a singular detail," said Ratablavasky happily, "so your young friend's joy will be complete."

"What's he got to do with this?" growled the chef, shaking his arm free.

Ratablavasky's clear and youthful laugh dismayed Picquot. "Let us continue our strolling. It will only make stronger our health," the old man proposed, taking the chef's elbow.

"Enough, you pompous ass!" roared Picquot, freeing himself again. "Do you take me for a . . ."

He escaped and headed for the hall, followed by his host who had obligingly opened the door. "Moldy crust!" the chef shouted from the corridor. "I won't rest till I know that you're roasting in hell – and to judge by the state of your carcass that should be soon!"

Ratablavasky listened in the doorway, arms crossed, eyes half closed, and smiling cynically. "I wish you to offer my deepest regards to Monsieur Florent," he said in his lilting voice. "To him and to you, my door stands always open. But alas, for two days now I am not living here, for the danger to me is large. And this very night I depart on a voyage to strengthen my health."

About to shut the door, he thought of something. He stopped, and his smile gave way to a grave expression. Bringing his hand to his pocket, he said, "Here is small present for your young friend."

Picquot hesitated but Ratablavasky gave him a haughty look. The chef, moved in spite of himself, took the proffered book and leafed through it suspiciously.

"No, no, if you please," said the old man, "it is pure present, with no hidden motif. Be so good and deliver it in his hands."

"And here's the book that caused so much fuss!" exclaimed Picquot, taking from his pocket a copy of *A Christian Father Faces the Dawn*. "I'm damned if I can figure him out! Do you know what he said to me next? That the twenty thousand dollars he'd offered for this book was just a ruse to help you out. And what's even odder – he seemed quite sincere!"

Florent examined the book. "It's the same copy, all right."

"I wanted to tell you as soon as I could," Picquot went on. "Our monster has taken a hit, but watch out for reprisals! If he's crouching in the shadows, he'll be hatching some new plot."

Florent got up. "Are you up to another drive? My truck's ready to pack it in and I have to meet Gladu in Montreal."

"Do you think *I'm* about to pack it in? Give me a sandwich, and some strong black coffee, and I'll take you to Los Angeles, if necessary."

"You don't meet Gladu till tomorrow," Elise reminded him.

"I'd rather go right away."

"Me, too," yelped Monsieur Emile, clutching Elise's arm.

"*Everyone's* going," Picquot decreed. "There's no question of anyone staying here alone. But watch out, you young scallywag! I don't want to catch you in my glove compartment. There's a bottle of cognac, but it's a gift for Mademoiselle Emilienne."

"Who we'll be meeting someday soon, I hope," Elise teased.

"Dear girl, I don't know where you find the strength to smile in the midst of all this."

Monsieur Emile made them stop twice so he could pee by the roadside, then at a restaurant because he had hunger pains. After that, his bodily needs wavered between these two poles, expressed through whimpering, stamping feet, kicking the back of the seat, and other such adorable acts. Elise, huddled in a corner nauseated (since she'd become pregnant, car rides were intolerable), wasn't strong enough to hold him down. Picquot said nothing, but sighed furiously in a more and more disturbing rhythm. Suddenly he slammed on the brakes and glared furiously at the child. "Do you want to go back to your mother? One more word and I'll drag you there by the ears – and so fast your feet won't touch the ground."

This frightened Monsieur Emile, who clammed up and cowered in a corner. Florent whispered to the chef, "I think he's feeling pretty much like all of us. Try to be understanding."

"What a mess!" Picquot groaned, "What a mess! Will we ever see the end of it? I'd give almost anything for one little piece of good news."

Rather than risk going back to the apartment on Emery Street, Florent took a room in a hotel on St-Hubert. Picquot decided to do the same, "To keep matters under control." As soon as Florent was in his room, he dialed Gladu's number.

Madame Gladu answered. "I don't know where he is," she snarled, "and for his sake, it's just as well."

Then he tried to contact Ange-Albert, with no more success. With a lump in her throat, Elise watched from the chair where she sat, holding Monsieur Emile, who'd become remarkably well behaved. Florent concluded sadly. "We'll have to tough it out till tomorrow."

In the next room Picquot was snoring, exhausted by his night of spying.

"My poppa's in the toilet," piped up the fat little girl in her monotonous voice. "You can go into the living room."

Florent paused before a blowup of a press clipping hung conspicuously in the vestibule. It showed a picture of Gladu, smiling triumphantly, above the following article:

> REPORTER ROSARIO GLADU BACK ON THE SCENE
>
> Rosario Gladu, star reporter on *Le Clairon du Plateau*, is making quite a name for himself. Along with a quick-fingered photographer, our valiant contributor produced stunning photo-journalism for the March 3 edition of *Le Journal de Montréal.*
>
> Rosario recorded the fatal fall of a 30-year-old suicide victim. The man had jumped from a 45-foot-high tree, and Rosario was quick as a flash to catch the various stages in his final journey.
>
> There's no doubt that Rosario's piece helped boost circulation of the morning daily.
>
> Congratulations, Rosario! And keep up the good work!

"That's something else, eh?" said the real-life Gladu, greeting Florent with a broad smile and outstretched hand. "Like I always say, if you roll your stones you'll pick up moss!" With no transition he said, "He's at The Caprice. That's where he's waiting."

Florent frowned. "The club on St-Denis? It's a hole. We won't be able to hear ourselves think."

"That's the spot, though. You don't think I picked it, do you?" Bending over to his daughter, who was silently listening, her nose in the air, he said, "Get your coat, precious – you're going for a drive with Daddy." To Florent he added, "Anyway, you'll be able to meet my new broad. Does a strip show Thursday afternoons." His eyes lit up. "You can tell me what you think of her . . . performance."

"I gather your wife's out," said Florent facetiously.

"Getting her hair done. Did you find your coat, precious?"

He's putting on a good front, Florent thought, but I bet he's pissing his pants.

Gladu came back and asked, "You know how I got together with the chick?"

"I can't imagine."

"With a tattoo, pal, a tattoo."

Gladu unfastened the top buttons of his shirt. An amazingly realistic drawing of a vulva appeared in the middle of his sternum, exploiting with unusual felicity the abundant hair on his chest. Florent looked on aghast, as Gladu choked with laughter and wrinkled and smoothed the skin for additional verisimilitude. Florent said curtly, "Let's go. It's nearly three o'clock." The child waddled up with her coat on. Jesus, she looks like she's sprouted another chin since the last time I saw her, Florent reflected.

Georges-Etienne was sitting at the back of the room, sipping a cognac. His slender fingers twirled the snifter without moving the liquid. The doorman who showed them to the table refused Gladu's tip. "It's on the boss." Georges-Etienne nodded to Florent, then turned to Gladu. "What's this?" he asked, indicating the dreamy-eyed child.

"My daughter, Yolande. I had to bring her – the wife's at the hairdresser."

With an imperceptible shrug, their host invited them to sit down.

After a waitress had taken their order the mobster brought his chair closer to Florent's and patted his hand, with a smile curiously warm in such an icy face. "Good news. Your investment paid off. I don't think Ratablavasky's going to meddle in your affairs anymore."

"Is that so?"

"A couple of days ago I dropped in with a few of my friends. After our little chat his apartment wasn't a very pretty sight. Neither was he, for that matter," he added, nodding in commiseration.

Florent could hear his heart speed up, while his mouth filled with bile. "Is that so?" he repeated.

Despite himself, his lips curved in an ironic smile. Gladu looked on impassively. Young Yolande, her hands flat on her knees, was watching a naked dancer perform on a platform. The woman was pulling a long mauve fur snake back and forth between her legs as a group of truckers looked on, blank-faced. "That's not the way I heard it," said Florent, while Gladu gave him a bewildered look.

He picked up his beer and slowly, out of bravado, drank a long draft, then went on. "A friend of mine ran into him yesterday, and he was hale and hearty."

"Maybe . . . maybe it was somebody else." Rosario fluttered, clutching the table with both hands.

"No way. They talked for a good fifteen minutes. What've you got to say to that?" he asked, struggling to overcome his fear. Sneering disdainfully, Georges-Etienne waved off Florent's criticism.

"Well, I think I've got an explanation," he continued. "You asked a few questions and figured the old guy was too big a fish for your rod. So instead of attacking him you trashed his apartment. But I asked for more than that. A thousand bucks is a hell of a lot for some broken furniture."

Gladu stood up, took his daughter by the waist, and bounded away. Holding his snifter in both hands, Georges-Etienne peered at Florent, still smiling. "I suppose you think I'd rub out something like that for a measly thousand bucks. I'm not running a charity." Leaning closer, he said, "If you really want us to get rid of him, my friend, you'll have to invest a little more. Of course there's nothing to stop you from going elsewhere."

"Which is precisely what I intend to do."

Still smiling, Georges-Etienne moved back slightly. There was a snapping sound and the cognac danced in his snifter. "I'd be the last one to hold it against you, but I advise the utmost discretion regarding our arrangements. It's extremely important to me. Discretion at all costs. And in case I haven't made that clear enough, here's one last argument."

His hand shot out toward Florent, who screamed: his arm was sliced open. He watched, stupefied, as the blood spread over his trousers and dripped on the floor, while Georges-Etienne, with growing delight, swirled his brandy snifter, which now lacked a base.

Florent had his wound bandaged in a drugstore. "Maybe I should just jump off a bridge," he muttered, furious.

Picquot was so discouraged that he nearly wept. "Children, I'm taking you to France. You won't get any peace as long as that creature's alive. We'll hide away somewhere quiet in the country and wait for death to deliver us from him. I've got enough money to provide for your needs – you and all the children that you'll have."

Smiling, Florent found the strength to make a joke. Elise's calm strengthened his resolve. When she saw him with his arm in a sling she thought it wise to send Monsieur Emile out for a paper, which he agreed to do for a fee. Soon he could be heard stomping down the corridor.

"Let's grab a bite," Florent suggested. "I haven't eaten a thing since breakfast."

"Me, too!" trumpeted Monsieur Emile, dropping the newspaper. "I want a strawberry sundae!"

And while a blend of powdered milk, gum arabic, and monoglycerides slipped down the throat of the child, who swung his legs contentedly, they tried, in carefully veiled terms, to list the possible ways they could get themselves out of the mess they were in. They came up with three: a lawyer, a detective – and plain and simple murder.

"Let's start with the lawyer," suggested Picquot. "I used to know an excellent one in Quebec who'd have solved this by crying fraud. But the poor man died under rather odd circumstances: he was squashed by a piano in Miami."

Florent went to a pay phone and returned twenty minutes later. "This afternoon at five," he announced. "I managed to get my hands on a lawyer."

The lawyer in question, Rodrigue Théorêt, whose office was at the corner of Saint-Denis and Sherbrooke, hadn't understood a thing Florent told him; he thought his would-be client might be a crank or – you never know – the perpetrator of a hoax. But alas, it had been a long time since he'd had the luxury of picking and choosing, and he had to be content with whatever turned up on his doorstep. Besides, he was a very honest man, his thinking clear but dull, and even a small measure of success would have overwhelmed him. He really excelled at such peaceable activities as puttering around the house, strolling philosophically in the woods, or – his favorite activity – fishing.

He listened politely to Florent's account, which was continually interrupted by Picquot's impenetrable clarifications. It sounded to him like a fabric of preposterous adventures that owed more to literary fantasy than reality, and he even wondered if the three people in his office were mildly unhinged members of some sect who didn't dare declare themselves. Still, he thought, I can try to put some sense in their heads. When Florent was finished, he said, "Friends, if I were you I'd start by calming down. You've got yourselves mixed up with a rather odd character, that I grant you, but he doesn't sound all that dangerous."

Picquot threw up his hands. "Not dangerous! He virtually tore them away from their restaurant! It was a genuine act of plunder!"

"Are you sure of that? Your friend had a rough time, and in desperation he sold his shares for peanuts: it happens every day. Doctors call it nervous depression. As for the business of the pills, a judge wouldn't be impressed."

He smiled at Florent. "You know, we all have our ups and downs. Even I . . ."

"With all due respect," said Picquot curtly, "we're talking not about you but about my young friend, about his wife, and about two years of utter *shit*!"

The lawyer's eyebrows shot up, and a tight smile gathered his lips in a lump of puckered flesh. He glanced furtively at his watch to confirm that the interview had gone on far too long. "To get back to the pills, you'd have needed an expert opinion to confirm you were being drugged by your associate."

"What about the picture?" Elise asked mildly.

"Well, that, yes, I have to admit that was a real stab in the back and I'm glad you had the maturity, Madame, to . . . But precisely how can you prove even that? You need solid evidence – which you've destroyed!" Seeing their looks of consternation, he added quickly, "Still, I think I can help you."

He suggested that Florent prepare an affidavit listing all the evil deeds perpetrated by Slipskin and Ratablavasky, to be signed by Ange-Albert, Elise, and Picquot, a declaration that could prove useful in the event that Ratablavasky and his henchmen decided to strike again – which the lawyer considered unlikely.

"Do you know what I really think" he asked finally. "Forget about this man. Like everybody else, he'll get over these whims of his."

"What a turnip!" Picquot fulminated outside the office. "I wouldn't have been surprised if he'd tried to put *us* in straitjackets! As for his notarized list, if you want to know what I think –"

"I intend to do it," Florent interrupted. "But first, I'm going to see a detective. If blood has to be spilled to get this settled, I want people to know I had no choice."

An hour later they were at the Denis P. Massue Agency, located in a gloomy old building on St-Antoine near Bleury. A fat jovial man showed them into a scantily furnished office that reeked of reheated coffee; folding his huge hands, he cracked his knuckles and settled in to listen to Florent.

It wasn't long before subtle changes appeared on his coarse and vigorous features. The impassive, blasé look typical of motel scroungers and people who hang around morgues gradually dissolved, to be replaced by attentive politeness. His once fixed and sleepy gaze began to roam, picking up speed and settling on each of the speakers in turn, examining their clothing, studying the expression on each face. The changes confused Florent. His speech became aggressive, and he started to parry imaginary blows. The detective's expression turned from interest to worry. This obscure, tangled story, in which verifiable facts evaporated as soon as they'd appeared, made him pensive. He was filled with gnawing fear at the prospect of getting involved in some weird business that might turn out to be more serious than he'd thought, that was opening before him like a shadowy tunnel writhing to infinity.

"Excuse the interruption, but you did say Ratablavasky? Egon Ratablavasky? A fairly elderly chap?"

He put his hand over his mouth, moved a sheet of paper on the desk and, with a forced smile, asked abruptly, "How much are you prepared to pay? You know, we work according to our clients' means."

"Well – as much as necessary."

With both arms resting on the desk, Picquot leaned over the detective. "My dear friend, please understand: money is *not* an issue. We're concerned about ridding the earth of this scum that's had us living in terror for two years."

"Umm, yes, I see, I see. . . . Mind you, our agency rarely deals with matters like this. . . . It's just that, well, you see, it could end up costing a fair amount – say ten thousand dollars or more!"

"So?" replied Picquot, almost threateningly. "I have the funds. I can provide guarantees."

"Fine. Perfect. Excellent. Excellent. But first, I must make a preliminary evaluation. House policy. By the way, too bad you don't have that picture. . . ."

He asked some questions, casually scribbling on a scrap of paper, then stood up. The interview was over. "I'll contact you as soon as possible." And with surprising speed he showed them to the door.

"Good grief," Picquot muttered, "you'd think we had the plague!"

Elise turned to Florent, her smile belying her distress. "We mustn't have any illusions: we'll never hear from him again."

They walked a short distance in silence. Then Elise exclaimed, "But we still have a couple of aces up our sleeve!"

Picquot and Florent shot her a questioning look. "Have you forgotten about Father Jeunehomme? Maybe he's heard from that other priest in France."

"You think so, do you?" asked Florent sarcastically.

At the presbytery, the portress told them, "Father Jeunehomme's not too well these days. Are you relatives?" she asked, absentmindedly pulling at her white whiskers. Then her crumpled face lit up at the sight of Monsieur Emile, who had just pushed open the door, followed by Elise. "What a dear little boy!" She went to the back of the room, returned with a box of chocolates, pushed open the wicket, and bent down to the child. "Would you like a candy, dear? And what's your name?"

Her brusque manner had vanished, and now she looked like any fat country grandmother. Florent waited a moment, then asked with a hint of impatience, "Excuse me, Sister, but I must see Father Jeunehomme on a very important matter. Is he too sick to. . . ."

With an enigmatic look born of discretion, she disappeared behind her wicket once again, then returned almost at once. "He'll see you now. You know the way? I'd like to have a visit with this little fellow. . . ."

Monsieur Emile, eyes glued to the chocolates, didn't need coaxing.

Father Jeunehomme, more waxen than ever, was at the top of the stairs, lost in a rumpled soutane that accentuated his thinness. Extending his chilly hand, he said, "I'm glad to see you." Elise introduced him to Picquot, and the priest gestured to them to follow him.

Heavens, the chef thought, that poor fellow's dying!

"I hope we didn't get you out of bed," said Elise.

"No – why do you say that?"

"They told us you were ill."

The priest shrugged and smiled ironically. "I'm not very popular down there."

He opened the door and let them in. Picquot exclaimed at the piles of dusty volumes in the room. "You haven't lost your appetite for books," Florent observed.

"Oh, it's as keen as ever – let me clear off this chair for you – but I'm somewhat discouraged."

"Why is that?" asked Picquot, with such exaggerated interest that Elise and Florent couldn't help smiling. "Have you been having problems?"

The priest sighed. "No, a great disappointment. May I offer you a cup of tea? I was about to have some myself."

He went to a small table, on which an electric samovar was purring, and bustled about with awkward, nervous gestures.

"If it's not indiscreet, what disappointment was that?" asked Florent.

"Quite frankly, I don't have the heart to talk about it. Instead, I'll selfishly take advantage of your company to get my mind off it. Dear me, I'd quite forgotten . . . your own trouble with that eccentric monster. . . . I trust it's all in the past."

Florent grimaced. "No such luck! In fact, that's why we came to see you. I was wondering if your professor in Louvain turned up anything more about Ratablavasky."

The priest, busy filling an exquisite blue china teapot, slowly looked up at the ceiling, and it seemed for a moment that his soul had gone soaring into the clouds until the end of time. At last he said, "No, I don't remember, I really don't remember."

"Are you sure?" Elise implored.

Picquot sprang from his chair as if it were electrified. "Father, allow me. . . . This is a matter of life and death, do you understand? These youngsters are at their wits' ends!"

Father Jeunehomme gave them an aggrieved look. "He's bothering you again?"

"His threats have increased more than ever," the chef replied.

"I'm sorry, dreadfully sorry. . . . I haven't heard from Dom Périgord since he sent me that odd book – what was the title again? Ah yes . . . *A Christian Father Faces the Dawn*, I think. What a curious title!"

He handed each of them in turn a china cup as translucent as a rose petal, then poured the tea. There followed a moment of silent contemplation that enabled them to appreciate the delicate Souchong aroma. Then Florent began to pace back and forth in the narrow space that was free of books. "I'd give my right eye to see him hauled into a paddy wagon, on his way to rot in jail! That filthy fucking bastard's driving me out of my mind!"

The priest coughed, and a red spot appeared on his pale, dull discourse on the relationship between a presumably modern turn of phrase and its actual origin in Balzac's 1846 work *Splendeurs et Misères des Courtisanes* – the beginning of the third part, to be precise – but, self-conscious at the stunned looks that greeted his explanation, he allowed the conversation to drift to more general topics of dubious interest. Everyone was searching for the felicitous phrase that would allow them to depart. Then Florent committed his faux pas.

"How's your research on – I forget his name – that Russian writer who threw one of his books in the fire?"

The priest's usually pale complexion became cadaverous. "You mean Gogol?" It took him a moment to gather his strength. His face and his entire body were so drawn that Elise moved to his side, thinking he was going to faint.

"I didn't want to bring it up," the priest began, "because I don't like bothering others with my personal problems. Indeed, it's my priestly duty to show compassion for others in distress. . . . But on the other hand . . . keeping it all locked up . . . it's so difficult. . . ." He looked at his guests, despondent. "Ah, dear friends, poor Gogol will be the death of me. . . . For so much effort to come to this. . . ."

"What on earth is it?" asked Picquot, in some irritation.

The priest hesitated briefly, then got to his feet. "Come with me."

They headed down a long winding corridor, then descended an oak staircase that creaked as if each step held the suffering soul of a former member of Father Jeunehomme's flock, condemned to purgatory in the presbytery. The priest, more and more worked up, took out a bunch of keys and opened a little door that led to a low-ceilinged basement. "Watch out for the beams," he said, moving forward into the gloom.

A rhythmical hissing indicated the presence of a nearby pump. Florent murmured, "We can't still be under the presbytery."

The priest said, "We're now in the basement of an old out-building that was razed in 1848."

Picquot punctuated this historical footnote with an impressive oath: his knee had just encountered a mass of metal the size of a fire hydrant. "I should have brought my flashlight," the priest apologized.

The floor rose slightly, and light from a minuscule window enabled them to see a door covered in sheet metal. "My laboratory," the priest explained, turning a key.

Narrowing their eyes against the flood of light, they entered a large, newly refurbished room that had been illuminated in the past through four small windows, now blocked. Against three walls stood long tables on which were set out devices that seemed intended for photography or related activities. The fourth wall, in which there was also a door, was lined with shelves of books.

"Astonishing!" exclaimed Picquot. "It's like something from a Gaston Leroux novel." He approached a curious little stove that stood in the middle of the room. "What's that?"

The priest cried out. "Don't touch it! That's the cause of all my troubles."

Turning to him, Elise murmured, "Gogol's stove?"

He nodded, his eyes moist. "The very one: the stove that became the tomb of a masterpiece."

He approached it, lifted a burner with infinite care, and gestured to the others to approach. A mass of paper, three-quarters charred, lay on a bed of ashes at the bottom.

"I don't understand," said Picquot. "What is this?"

The priest's face was marked by surprise and pain. "No one ever told you about the second part of *Dead Souls*, which Gogol, in a burst of religious mania, threw in the fire on February 12, 1852, nine days before his death?"

Picquot glanced inside again. The mass of paper suddenly seemed impressive and lugubrious.

"That is the fruit of three years' toil," the priest sighed, closing the lid. "I've spent vast sums, I've worked day and night, I've brought in dozens of experts. They all agreed that I was wasting my time trying to derive anything from these remains. Already the vibrations caused by moving the stove so often have reduced more than half the text to ashes. And it seems there's no way to handle what is left without destroying it altogether."

His listeners were moved and sorrowful, though none of them had read a word of Gogol. Elise approached the priest and gently drew him toward the door.

"Not a single scrap of text?" asked Picquot. "You couldn't save a thing?"

The priest's lips turned up in a bitter smile. "Oh yes. . . . After two months' work we managed to reconstitute a group of words with absolute certainty."

He took some paper from his pocket and handed it to Picquot. "Is that Greek?"

"No, these are Cyrillic characters," the priest replied and read: "*Boud'te lubezny, dorogoi kapitane, printesi mne banotchkou gortchitsy.*"

"And what does that mean?"

"'Kindly bring me a pot of mustard, dear Captain.' *Dead Souls* ended with a mustard pot. Sublime, isn't it?" asked the priest with a bitter grimace.

That evening Elise and Florent, along with Aurélien Picquot, Monsieur Emile, and Ange-Albert, whom they'd tracked down at home, went to have their affidavit witnessed by a notary.

Ange-Albert had unearthed a white shirt and tie for the occasion, to help mitigate the bad impression that the traces of his brief and stormy career as a professional gambler couldn't help but produce on the magistrate.

THIRTY-TWO

Winter eventually resigned itself to leaving Quebec, but marked its defeat with three unforgettable snowstorms that would enter meteorological history as the Three White Sisters. A fire devastated Saint-Hyacinthe because the fire trucks were stuck in snow in the middle of town. For two days Montreal was without bread or milk. Three people froze to death near Sherbrooke, four on the outskirts of Saint-Félicien, on their way home from fox hunting. A power failure hit all of eastern Quebec for a day, and the resulting lovemaking, encouraged by candlelight and the need to keep warm in bed, was marked by an extraordinary intensity that surely hastened the coming of spring. Aided by shoveling bees, plates of stew, and glasses of gin, Sainte-Romanie withstood the Three Sisters, but the general store ran out of snow shovels.

Elise, whose belly and breasts were now so monumental that she was self-conscious, had just emerged from what Florent called jokingly her "sleep tunnel," a rather gloomy period during which only the active presence of Monsieur Emile had kept her from sleeping sixteen hours a day. As for

Ratablavasky, he seemed to have vanished into thin air during the blizzard. Florent called the hotel repeatedly and was told each time that though they'd had no word, his suite was being held for him. Florent tried to erase him from his memory, but an incident on the morning of March 27 wiped out any hope of success.

He was looking through *La Presse* in a little restaurant in Arthabaska, waiting to call on an old doctor who was closing up his house, when his gaze fell on a photograph of Georges-Etienne above an article headed:

A PUZZLING DEATH

> The body of a 43-year-old man was discovered in bizarre circumstances yesterday at 4043 Rachel Street. The victim, businessman Georges-Etienne Cartier, was known to police. His body, burnt to a cinder, was still in his bed when a friend made the macabre discovery. Oddly, no other trace of combustion was found in the room, and even the bed linen was intact. Police have not yet determined where the death occurred, but it is assumed to involve a settling of accounts. Police are not yet certain of the motives for the murder. Sergeant Bourgie of the Homicide Squad is pursuing the investigation.

Florent carefully avoided telling Elise and tried to convince himself it was just another news item, perhaps more unusual than most, but he shuddered as he made the connection between this sinister death and the damage done to Ratablavasky's rooms at the Hotel Nelson.

Local opinion of him had done an about-face, and his

antique hunts were yielding virtually nothing. One afternoon early in April he ran into Mayor Meloche outside the church. "If it isn't Florent!" the mayor exclaimed with surprised familiarity. "Are you going in to pray to the patron saint of steam engines?"

Florent didn't know quite what to say. "You owe her a couple of candles, at least," the mayor went on impudently. "But my hunch is, she won't be granting many more favors." With a wink and chuckle, he walked away.

Back at the station, Florent announced, "Okay, kiddo, time to pack our bags. Looks like Meloche has been asking questions at Canadian Pacific. That's why I can't even get my hands on an old spittoon. I'm finished."

"Do we have to go?" asked Monsieur Emile, his hockey stick ready to knock the icicles off the station cornice.

"Yup, my boy, the whole family's going back to Montreal!"

Monsieur Emile made a face that augured badly for the hour to come. Two days earlier, Elise had told him with all the tact she could muster that his mother wanted him back. She'd started hearing the neighbors' malicious gossip, and Picquot's money was having no effect. She was being accused of nothing less than renting her child to a couple of young perverts.

"All the money in the world," she told the chef, "couldn't make up for my baby. It's been three months since I saw him and that's long enough. I want him back."

"I don't wanna go to my mother," the child whimpered, "I wanna stay with you."

Virtue, who had learned that Monsieur Emile's fits of temper often ended in kicks to her rear end, prudently left the scene. "Be reasonable," Elise said gently. "You're a big boy now. When we're in Montreal you can come and see us as much as you want, like before."

"I don't *wanna*!" he screamed. "I wanna stay with you! I don't like my mother. She never cooks things for me. All we ever eat is stuff out of goddamn cans!" Face contorted with rage, but dry-eyed, he stormed off to his room.

Elise whispered, "I think we've got a *big* problem."

Florent snickered. "We? You mean Picquot? He's the one that turned us into a drop-in center. God knows it's just what we needed," he said, pointing to Elise's belly.

She smiled. "The expectant father's trying to be tough, but it isn't working. You love that child as much as I do." She turned and called, "Monsieur Emile, come here. Florent will tell you all the things we're going to do in Montreal."

"No!" he barked, furious.

Monsieur Emile's anger lasted a good three-quarters of an hour, before it was unloaded on the cornice, which was stripped of icicles. One sailed through a window, which landed in pieces near the waiting room stove. After some token ranting and raving, Florent replaced the pane, with his protégé's help.

Meeting Meloche had been a relief in a way, for he had no choice now but to leave Sainte-Romanie. In any case, it would be a lighthearted departure: Father Blanchet's letters had yielded the tidy sum of six thousand four hundred dollars, bringing his savings up to thirty-six thousand, eight hundred. Florent had almost reached his goal.

By eight o'clock their suitcases were stacked in the living room. Monsieur Emile had quickly realized a long face wouldn't win him any sympathy, and he'd helped them pack with relative good grace. His unusual calm indicated, though, just how upset he was at the prospect of returning to Montreal.

About nine o'clock, Elise said, "Bedtime, little caribou. You can't keep your eyes open. Here, let me wash your face."

Florent touched her arm. "Go and rest, I'll take care of him. You can hardly stand up yourself." Taking the child's hand, he led him to the bathroom.

Screwing up his eyes to keep the soap out, he asked, "Will you tell me a story?"

"Of course."

With Breakfast at his feet, Monsieur Emile listened most attentively to Florent's story. Tonight's was about an old gentleman who owned a cauldron with the power of speech and – just as surprisingly – the ability to fill up every night with fresh sausages, potatoes, and turnips. When it was over, Monsieur Emile decided to repay the favor with a story of his own.

"Once there was a little kid that ran away from home with his cat 'cause he didn't like it there. And his cat had a tummy ache from eating too much canned meatballs. And his cat was crying and crying. And the kid had a tummy ache, too. And they walked a long, long ways and the cat got sore paws but not the kid, 'cause he had these big boots. Anyway, they stopped at a great big house where there was a man and a woman that weren't very old. And they told the kid, 'Take off your coat or you'll be too hot.' And they all lived together for a long, long time and everybody was happy and they never ate canned meatballs, just ice cream. And then some bad guys tried to hurt them, but the kid wiped them out. And then his cat had kittens and everybody was glad and that's the end of my story. Did you like it?"

When Florent went to the living room he had a lump in his throat and stinging eyes. "Sly little monkey, damn his hide." He told Elise the child's story.

She was very moved. "We've absolutely got to keep him. If he goes back to his mother, he's lost. For heaven's sake, open your eyes!"

Florent looked at her unhappily, then jerked his thumb as if opening a bottle. "Are you really prepared to take him on with *all* his problems? Think about it now, sweetheart – it's not just noble sentiments. The kid may already be a goner."

They went back to work, putting most of their belongings in the truck so they could make a silent, early-morning departure while Mayor Meloche was still snoring beside his wife.

The sun rose gloriously and at once made every icicle in the village shed tears. The crust of ice that had formed on the fields the week before was softening, and by late morning tiny depressions here and there announced that spring was once again making its way toward the lakes and rivers. At dawn Florent's truck had discreetly crossed town and disappeared into the countryside, planting a thousand troubled questions in the mind of Madame Laflamme, who had spotted it through the window as she cooked the priest's salt pork.

The day passed peacefully. Doors would open and people would step outside to sniff the mild breeze that was tenderly enfolding the village and driving great chunks of snow off the roofs. At a quarter after four, as the wind turned slightly raw, the bus from Montreal stopped in front of the general store to let off a passenger.

An hour later, the visitor went back to the store, utterly dejected. The grocer's wife was surprised to learn that Florent wasn't at the station. "Isn't his wife there, either?"

"He's likely gone to Montreal, my boy," said Monsieur Hamel, genuinely commiserating, but thrilled at the prospect of telling the whole village about the ill-timed visit. "He goes there a lot, you know – something to do with old furniture."

The grocer wracked his brains to find him a place to stay, for the bus wasn't due back until seven o'clock the next morning. Ange-Albert, wracked with hunger pangs, waited quietly in a corner, eating a chocolate bar.

In a small tobacco store at the corner of Mont-Royal and St-Hubert, where he'd gone to phone Picquot, Florent was eating an identical bar. "Stay where you are," his friend ordered. "I'll be right there. And I might as well tell you straightaway: when you see me I'll have just turned in my resignation to those unsavory jokers at Barnmeal, so I'll be ready to return to my saucepans."

He arrived shortly, overflowing with the sort of enthusiasm that made one concerned for his blood pressure; he shook Florent's hand, went into ecstasies at Elise's belly, then took Monsieur Emile in his arms and kissed him with extraordinary effusiveness. "Hey, your beard prickles!" the child protested, taking umbrage at so much sentimentality.

"And now," Picquot proclaimed, "let's examine your new quarters!" He shook his fist at The Beanery and shouted, "Foul profligates, your time will come!"

He approved of the store's dimensions. "Here's the ideal spot for my kitchen," he said, pointing to the back of the shop, "but we'll have to move this partition a few feet. I can't work well without my comforts. Alexis Soyer declared that the triumphs of haute cuisine depend on comfort and common sense."

Florent pointed to a bare camp cot with sagging springs. "That's where my landlord ended his business career."

Monsieur Emile was about to jump on it, just to check out the springs, but Picquot picked him up by one arm and set him down a few feet away. "Stay off that, child. We'll keep the bed," he told Florent. "I'll sleep here for a while in the beginning. Don't look at me like that! Opening a restaurant, you know, is like launching a ship. It's a delicate operation that requires constant vigilance. In the early stages, my boy, customers are as frail as newborns, and you must take very good care of them."

Soon he and Elise were standing behind some rolls of burlap. "Dear girl, I have a favor to ask you. I know how proud your husband is, and it does him great credit. But he lacks experience. We have a dreadful battle ahead of us, far more dreadful than he realizes. He'll need every cent he has to keep afloat. So I've decided to invest my first year's salary in the restaurant. He'll think it's charity, but I'm counting on you to convince him that it's not. He can pay me reasonable interest and that will be quite enough. With the little nest egg I've managed to accumulate, I've no need to work anymore. If I'm doing so now, it's because I want to."

Elise burst into tears and threw her arms around him. "Now, now, now," the chef muttered, his own eyes watery, "none of this whimpering."

They ate supper at the apartment on Emery Street. Florent looked at his watch: seven-fifteen. He was somewhat surprised at Ange-Albert's absence. "Has our lady's man found another nest?" he asked facetiously. "Not that it would be a bad idea. . . . Since I had Old Rat's apartment wrecked I'm not wild about staying here."

With a resigned gesture Elise said, "No matter where we are, he'll track us down."

"And that, dear girl, is why sooner or later there must be a direct confrontation," said the chef. "In my opinion, it can't happen too quickly. But let's talk instead, if you will, about setting up our restaurant. To begin with, what do you intend to call it?"

"Chez Florent," piped up Monsieur Emile.

Florent turned to Elise. "Why not?"

She smiled, with her eyes slightly narrowed, like a cat that's just spotted a prey. "While we're waiting for 'Florent's Beanery'?"

Meanwhile, in a tiny ice-cold room in the Sainte-Romanie presbytery, Ange-Albert was trying to adapt his spinal column to the uneven contours of an old bed that reeked of mothballs. Sadly, he recalled dazzling nights with Rosine in an equally uncomfortable bed, realizing to his horror that he – the casual Don Juan – was becoming as sentimental as an old maid in love.

Some ninety miles away, Elise and Florent were mulling over very different thoughts. Pens in hand, their heads full of numbers, they were preparing for battle under the Napoleonic guidance of Aurélien Picquot.

"We'll begin, youngsters, by outfitting our restaurant, and the rest will follow as sure as puppies follow dogs. Many bankruptcies are caused by excessive emotion. Instead of keeping a cool head, the new restaurateur becomes infatuated with his establishment-to-be: nothing's too good for him, he ties up an insane amount of capital in equipment, and when business is too slow – which is the case nine times out of ten – he hasn't enough cash left to tough it out, and his creditors get the business for a pittance. First, then: what sort of restaurant will it be? Have you thought about the menu? How many customers can we accommodate?"

"It'll be a little like The Beanery," Florent replied, "but better and bigger. Our place measures sixty feet by forty. I drew up some plans the day before yesterday: we can put in an L-shaped counter that will seat seventeen, with booths for another sixteen, for a total of thirty-three. Before they enlarged, The Beanery could seat twenty-two."

Elise looked skeptical. "You really want to make another Beanery? If you ask me, you haven't got a chance."

"Voilà!" exclaimed Picquot, pointing his forefinger. "My boy, this delightful child has just saved you from the abyss. *Every restaurant must have its own distinctive personality*; otherwise, it will stagnate and die. We must compete with Slipskin not only with our prices, *but with our style, as well.*"

A long discussion ensued, fueled by steaming coffee, punctuated by shouts, filled with comings and goings, the scraping of chairs, and nervous scribbling. Three hours later, Chez Florent was born. It was a small restaurant, not only because of the locale but also by choice, open from six in the morning until eleven at night. The new menu consisted for the most part of traditional Québécois cooking, but discreetly refined, with a muted complement of French or European specialties. Pancakes with maple syrup, *tourtière*, *cipâte*, home-style baked beans and shepherd's pie would be found side by side with *coq au vin* and *sauté de veau Marengo*, not to mention the famous *grands-mères* Picquot had introduced and made popular at The Beanery. But since they were appealing to a working-class clientele that was easily scared off, Elise suggested renaming the European dishes to make them seem home grown. Such dishes as *crème de brocoli*, *potage Crécy*, *potage Parmentier*, and *velouté Aurore* would be listed as plain old broccoli, carrot, potato, and tomato soups, along with the more familiar pea and cabbage. *Coq au vin* would be introduced as a *fricot de poulet à la mode du Bas-du-Fleuve*, and the veal dish named after Napoleon's victory over the Austrians would be rechristened *fricassée de veau de Saint-Félicien*. The menu would be rounded out with some quickly prepared dishes: fried pork and beef liver, chopped steak, sausages, and the indispensable sandwiches.

It was the desserts that would most clearly declare a joint allegiance to Quebec and France, for it's well known that a sweet tooth emboldens the most timid diners. The menu would include not only such well-loved local specialties as *tarte à la ferlouche* and maple syrup pie, doughnuts, and molasses cakes, but also *crème caramel*, mocha cakes, and even *diplomates*.

Picquot rounded off the evening with a lengthy diatribe against instant mashed potatoes, canned fruit, the systematic use of processed foods, and all the culinary disasters that had devastated the Western world since the Americans had decided to plant their flag in our plates. "Those pigs," he thundered, "are sapping our civilization and transforming all of France into a pitiful, shameful, base *supermarket*!" He stopped, scarlet and gasping, dull-eyed and uncertain where he was.

Holy Christopher! Florent thought. He looks as if he's going to have a stroke.

Elise brought him a glass of water. "Dear Monsieur Picquot, why don't you sleep here? It's after three."

They didn't have to twist his arm. He would sleep in Ange-Albert's room, where he lay down, fully clothed. "Friends," he said hoarsely, "tonight, I want you to know, I feel it's been a long time since I was twenty. Florent, child, bring me some more water . . . and those pills in my jacket pocket."

Elise curled up against her husband, who stretched his arm behind her neck in the position that had been their prelude to sleep since they had first started sleeping together. "If you want my advice," she whispered, "start looking for a replacement. Our friend's years in the kitchen are numbered, poor man."

About seven o'clock, a ray of sunlight pierced a rip in the window blind and landed on Picquot's forehead. With a deep sigh and a smile as delightful as it was unexpected, he opened his eyes. He gazed sleepily around the room, then smiled again. Aloud, he said, "Ah, it's good to wake up among friends."

He rose, smoothed his trousers as well as he could, straightened his tie in front of a dull shard of mirror, and went to the kitchen. Soon the kettle was boiling for coffee, and Virtue was lapping her breakfast. When Elise came into the living room she caught the chef cooing into the telephone, crooking his little finger and twirling his mustache like a cavalry captain making time with a pretty peasant girl. "Ah, you're up. I was talking to a supplier. What would you say to a cheese omelet?"

Half an hour later everyone sat down to breakfast. "How do I feel?" asked Picquot. "Like Alexander Graham Bell after he invented the telephone, that's how I feel."

"And how's Mademoiselle Emilienne?" teased Elise.

With his nose in his coffee cup, Picquot struggled in vain against a violent blush, then spoke to Florent. "While you were emptying Sainte-Romanie of its odds and ends, I wasn't twiddling my thumbs. I've been contacting restaurant suppliers to get some idea of prices." He beckoned them over, took some catalogs from a briefcase, and tossed them on the table. "First, a fundamental question: how much money do you have?"

"Thirty six thousand dollars."

"And how much is your rent?"

"A hundred and seventy a month, with a three-year lease."

Picquot began scribbling and muttering, his face taking on the paternal, concentrated look of an old family doctor. "Mm-hmm – you'll have to keep at least twenty thousand in reserve to get you over the rough spots, and God knows there'll be no lack of them. . . . Slipskin will stop at nothing to hang your scalp above his counter, and there's no reason to think Old Rat will stop his tricks and scheming. Consequently, youngsters, here's what I suggest: for the first year, I won't take a salary. I've saved quite enough to live on. What I'll do instead is ask for a share in the profits – let's say ten percent – starting with the second year, to a limit of twenty-eight thousand five hundred, which would represent a year's salary plus a bit of interest. No, no, and no! I do *not* want thanks. This is strictly business."

Florent, advised by Elise of the chef's intentions, had to be content with a simple handshake to express his gratitude, but waves of emotion made even that difficult.

There followed an endless procession of plates, sieves, pressure cookers, pie stands, deep fryers, double boilers, butcher knives, steam tables, and cake pans, all wrapped in clouds of figures that talked of liters, dollars, kilograms, and heat, which stretched out before them for four hours. Florent selected, Picquot corrected, Elise took notes and sided with one or the other when the discussion grew too heated. The price of the gas stove with two ovens, of the electric slicer, the refrigerator, and the sink added up to six thousand dollars. Cutlery, crockery (service for one hundred), and the various kettles and utensils would be over three thousand. "Too much," sighed Picquot. "It's too much."

"Couldn't we buy secondhand?" Elise suggested.

"No, dear girl, we'd just be buying other people's problems," he replied, shaking his head. He took back the list, and by striking off everything that could be considered superfluous, managed to recover eight hundred dollars. "Now," he said, wiping his brow, "let's eat. While we're at it, we can talk about decorating."

That question was settled in ten minutes. Florent had decided on an old-fashioned decor, making good use of the antiques he'd left on consignment with Jean-Denis Beaumont, who had been instructed a few weeks earlier to stop selling. He had also decided to save money by doing without a carpenter. With the help of Ange-Albert, who was very handy when he put his mind to it, Florent would build the partitions, the cupboards, the counter, and even the booths. All the work would be done amid the greatest secrecy. They would enter the premises only from the back lane. It was essential to delay as long as possible Slipskin's knowledge of his competition. The same was true for Ratablavasky, whose lengthy disappearance wasn't fooling anyone.

"I'm cooking up a little something for the pair of them," Florent confided to the chef, who had just hailed a taxi to take them to Bell et Rinfret, where they'd decided to buy building material. "But don't mention it to Elise. I want to work up to it slowly."

Elise had gone back to the apartment – her legs swollen, back aching – to get a few hours' rest and to be company for Virtue, who disliked being alone. At the bottom of the stairs she stopped to watch some workmen demolish an old Victorian building across the street. Suddenly she heard someone running and Monsieur Emile appeared, open galoshes flapping, revealing mismatched socks. Elise had persuaded him the previous day to pay a diplomatic visit to his mother to let her know they had no intention of undermining her maternal prerogatives.

"Hey!" he exploded. "I can stay with you guys all the time now! My mother said okay, if Monsieur Picquot gives her some more money."

"Are you *sure* that's what she said?"

The child stopped short and gave her a hurt look. "If you don't believe me, go and ask her. She told me when she was drying her hair." He followed her in silence up the stairs, entered the apartment and headed straight for the TV set, a ploy that combined the satisfaction of a good sulk with the fun of watching cartoons. Elise tried to tidy up, but her distended belly caused so much strain on her back muscles that she had to lie down. Monsieur Emile went silently into the bedroom. "I'm not mad, you know," she assured him tenderly.

He sat on the bed with his hand on her belly. "Does your tummy hurt bad?" he asked softly.

Lord, his manners are improving, she thought, tight-lipped. He's really becoming our child. Eyes filled with tears, she turned away, then smiled and cuddled him.

"Elise," he pleaded, more and more winningly, "ask Monsieur Picquot to go and see my mother. . . . Maybe she'll say yes if he gives her lots of money. . . . She never has enough."

"Okay, I'll talk to him tonight." To herself she said, I wonder if she told him to ask? "Now are you happy?"

He smiled delightedly and hopped off the bed. "Shut the door, will you – I'm going to try to get some sleep."

She fell into a troubled torpor, constantly interrupted by the baby's kicking. She was awakened by a creak. Someone was standing there in the half light. She sat bolt upright. "My God, you scared me!" she exclaimed, her voice choked. "I thought it was Ratablavasky."

She brought her hand to her throat to control her pounding heart. Ange-Albert looked at her, embarrassed. "I'm sorry, I should've knocked. I just got back from Sainte-Romanie. I went there to see you and ended up spending the night at the presbytery. You may not know it, but there's some weird stories going around the village about you. . . ."

They went to the kitchen, where Monsieur Emile had just filled a bowl with enough cereal for a week's breakfasts. With an unequivocal reference to his own empty stomach, Ange-Albert opened a beer and watched as Elise prepared him a chicken fricassee. "How's Florent?" he asked amiably.

Through his cereal, Monsieur Emile said, "He's building his restaurant. And when you eat there you'll have to pay. Won't he, Elise?"

Heavy footsteps announced Picquot's arrival. "Now then, dear girl," he said breathlessly, squeezing Elise's hand, "I'm proud to say I've helped your husband save an astonishing amount of money. Do you know what our equipment will cost? Seven thousand, two hundred and fifty dollars – for everything! I'm quite astonished."

With that, he had to sit down to distribute his astonishment equally throughout his whole body. Then Florent burst in, exhilarated. "Where the heck have you been?" he asked Ange-Albert. "Listen, I hope you aren't working. I'll need you for two or three weeks, to set up the restaurant."

Smiling ruefully, Ange-Albert admitted that for some time now he'd been utterly available.

What makes him think he can feel so sorry for himself? the chef wondered. I'd like to see him coping with *our* problems!

Florent bolted his supper, then went with Ange-Albert to Mont-Royal Street, where Jean-Denis Beaumont was waiting for them. For a percentage, he'd managed to find a buyer for the bolts of fabric. By ten o'clock, the place had been cleared out. They returned to the apartment to find Monsieur Emile purple in the face, screaming his lungs out, an upraised hand about to throw a teakettle out the window. Florent grabbed him by the waist and plunked his behind on a chair.

"Cool it, young fellow! You're going to bring the walls down! What's all the fuss about?"

"His mother just called to tell him to go home for the night," Elise explained. "Monsieur Picquot's trying to talk her out of it."

"You can sleep here, you miserable troublemaker," the chef told him twenty minutes later.

With a smug smirk, Monsieur Emile docilely let them wash his face, then slipped into bed as silently as a sparrow's feather.

"What happened?" Florent asked Picquot.

"Dear friend, you're invading my private life. Why not just be happy that we can continue to enjoy the company of that delightful pest for another few weeks."

Though Elise questioned him with all the subtlety at her command, he didn't reveal a thing. Later, in their bedroom, she said, "Florent, we have to do something. Let's face facts: she's renting out her child, and it's absolutely horrible! Monsieur Picquot must have had to raise his offer again but he won't talk about it, to spare our feelings."

Florent pulled the covers to his chin with an abruptness that didn't augur well. "Kiddo, it's a hell of a choice. So we start adoption procedures. . . . I'm getting ready to open a restaurant, and you're due in a few weeks. Is this the right time? And do you think the kid's going to leave off the bottle when he leaves his mother? We've got some fine years to look forward to!" He turned on his side and seemed on the verge of falling asleep.

Suddenly he heaved a sigh that could have pushed the Nina, the Pinta and the Santa Maria right across the Atlantic. He sat up, scratched his head, then his shoulder, and then his head again, and finally his left knee. "Okay, I'll call the

Social Assistance department tomorrow. But no question of adoption before I talk to a psychologist, understand? I'm no Mother Teresa."

He could say no more: Elise was smothering him with caresses.

THIRTY-THREE

As agreed, the lumber merchant made his delivery at nine o'clock in the morning, from the lane. With Picquot's help, Florent put the final touches on his plans and Ange-Albert threw himself into his work with surprising enthusiasm, as if he could already smell the delicious aromas that would fill the restaurant.

"Now," said Florent, "a little preventive medicine."

He went over to Gladu's and found Rosario standing on the doorstep. "Can you give me five minutes?"

"Okay – but no more. I'm late. I'm supposed to go to the home in Sainte-Sophie and write up a tombola." He showed Florent into the kitchen.

Smiling irreverently, Florent announced, "I'm opening another restaurant."

Gladu's lips opened as if to let out a belch, and for a moment his eyes resembled those of a dead fish. "Well, for . . . Unscrew my belly button and my ass'll drop off," he said, though it was impossible to determine the link between this remark and the situation at hand.

"Rosario! Shut the door, I'm trying to sleep!" a voice shouted furiously amid creaking bedsprings. Tiptoeing to the kitchen door, he gently shut it.

Florent continued. "Except for Elise, Monsieur Picquot, Ange-Albert, and myself, nobody knows about this. So if Slipskin gets wind of it, I'll know where it came from."

Grimacing, Gladu replied, "I'd as soon lick a dog's ass as say two words to that turd! Anyhow, I don't expect anything from him. I'm a squeezed lemon as far as he's concerned. . . . He doesn't even know I exist. . . . Where's your place?"

"Practically across the street from him."

Gladu recoiled, staring at Florent as if he'd just announced that he'd bought the Arc de Triomphe. "Across the street? Are you crazy? Off your rocker? Bananas? He'll wipe you out in less time than it takes to say it. You won't get to sell a single hot dog."

"We'll see about that. I'm cooking up a little surprise for him. That's why I wanted to see you. I wasn't too impressed with the way Georges-Etienne treated me a while back, but I don't hold you . . ."

"Speaking of Georges-Etienne, did you hear what happened? Can you figure it out? If you came here to ask me to work against Slipskin, no problem: I owe him one, the bastard – he really put me through the wringer. But I'm not getting involved with Old Rat. I warn you now, if his name even comes up, I'm packing it in. The bugger's made me superstitious. Next thing I'll be carrying around a flask of holy water."

Florent laughed. "Cool it, Rosario. I'll look after Old Rat. This is about Slipskin."

"Wanna tell me what you've got in mind?"

Florent looked around the kitchen, obviously wanting

a note of caution in his answer. Gladu waited, his thumb hooked over his belt, slowly scratching his stomach.

At length Florent asked, "You know anybody in the police?"

With a suspicious look, Gladu ran his tongue over his lips, then said, "I got a brother-in-law that works at Station 16, on Rachel Street. But I warn you," he added at once, "he won't want to get mixed up in any of your bright ideas. Aside from the TV, his lawn, and his beat, there's not a thing in life he gives a damn about. His wife got him into the Lacordaires two years ago, and it's as if he was six feet under. *Requiem aeternam.* Bye-bye."

"I haven't any bright ideas. I just want him to hear what I've got to say. I'll tell you more about it when the time comes."

With a self-satisfied look, he held out his hand, which contained a twenty-dollar bill. "Let's call this a down payment."

"Holy Mary!" Gladu murmured when Florent had gone. "He doesn't skimp on treats. . . . If this keeps up I'll have my air conditioner in time for the heat waves."

Two days later Len Slipskin's curiosity was aroused by the two newspaper-covered windows in the old yard goods store across the street. "Wonder who's moving in?"

"I ran into Picquot over on St-Denis," Bertrand told him later that afternoon. "The old frog hardly said hello. As soon as I passed him he shot into a lane as if the devil was on his tail. . . . Jesus, boss, he's aged! The embalmers must have an eye on him."

Slipskin heard him out with a smile, standing at the cash register. Dreamily whistling under his breath, he made change for some customers, then casually asked Bertrand which lane. On a brief nocturnal stroll he learned that the old yard goods store was being turned into a restaurant. The next morning he sped to the Municipal Tax Assessment Office, where he learned the name of the new occupant.

"Looking for trouble, eh, Boissonneault?" he muttered threateningly. "Hope he hasn't made friends with Old Rat again."

Three days later, he dropped his young Greek cook and his vaguely Québécois cuisine and hired an excellent chef from La Tuque. Florent, alerted by Picquot's account of his ill-timed meeting with Bertrand, sent Jean-Denis Beaumont to The Beanery to glean news and prices. Jean-Denis told him about the change of aprons. "That's it," Florent murmured, "he knows. Okay, my friends, the battle's begun."

"The *victory*," you mean, Picquot corrected him, rubbing his hands with frenzied joy. "My boy, it's now or never: either go at him with your claws out, or throw your dreams out the window and get a job sweeping floors in some hotel."

Refurbishing the restaurant was proceeding at a frantic pace. Ange-Albert and Florent were working sixteen hours a day, sleeping on the spot to deprive Slipskin of any opportunity for sabotage. As for Picquot, he slept at the apartment on Emery Street, brow knit, Mauser within reach, making the rounds every two hours despite entreaties from Elise, who was more and more worried about his health. During the day, between naps, he supervised the outfitting of the kitchen and took notes, as serious as a general preparing for an incursion into enemy territory.

Jean-Denis Beaumont, who was becoming a fast friend of Florent's, took a great interest in the interior decoration, letting some pieces go for prices that made one wonder whether he might not be dreaming of joining his friend in the restaurant business.

By May 7, all that remained was to hook up the gas and give the cupboards one last coat of paint. That morning, Ange-Albert was putting in a booth when his gaze suddenly fell on one of the windows. The sunlight on the newspaper over the window had transformed it into a golden rectangle against which a motionless, thickset shadow took shape. Ange-Albert gestured to Florent, who was bent over, installing a row of maple stools at the counter. He turned, briefly observed the silhouette, then silently went out the back door and ran down the lane to Mont-Royal. Leaning on a cane, his nose a deeper purple than ever, Captain Galarneau was peering at the front of the restaurant. Florent felt his knees buckle, and his face was suffused with heat that made his ears blaze.

Old Rat sent him as a scout, he thought. Best thing to do is meet him head-on. He strode up and greeted him derisively. "My compliments, Captain. You've come to inquire about my health?"

Captain Galarneau spun around, feigning utter amazement, and his throat released a booming laugh. "Jimbobbaree, if it isn't young Boissonneault! I'll be damned! I thought you and the little lady were still in Florida. How are you, anyway?"

His breath reeked of alcohol, as usual. "Never mind the sweet talk, just tell me what you want – or what your boss wants."

"See here, boy," the captain boomed, "to borrow an expression from my youth, has your tail been stung by a horsefly?"

Bending forward, he swayed slowly as the tip of his cane traced little circles. "I just happened to be in the neighborhood, I noticed this window, I stopped to reflect on certain aspects of the business world – and then I see you! How was Florida, Flo, boy? When did you get back?"

Florent grabbed his arm, pulling him off balance, and his cane fell to the sidewalk. "Screw off, you old still! And tell Old Rat I'm in tip top shape and ready to see him anytime."

Freeing himself, Galarneau spluttered, "I'll have you know sidewalks are public property."

Grunting, he bent down and picked up his cane. "Besides," he added, "I haven't seen friend Ratablavasky for months. And by the way, he took you in, all of you, with that 'Ratablavasky' and his DP accent. You know his real name? Ernest Robichaud, from Sainte-Anne-des-Plaines. Yes, sir! Takes the wind out of your sails, eh? He's as *Canayen* as you and me, with quite a life behind him, I might add. Maybe I'll tell you something about it someday, Flo, boy, if you improve your manners a little. But not everything!" He hobbled away, but after a dozen steps he turned around. "And you want to know why? BECAUSE I'M SCARED OF HIM!"

His laugh was so loud that a passerby turned and stared at him pounding the sidewalk with his cane, his jacket all awry, shoulders shaking convulsively. Ange-Albert had witnessed the conversation. "Not a word to Elise," Florent insisted. "She mustn't be upset, in her condition."

They walked into the lane. "Egon Ratablavasky . . . Ernest Robichaud . . . what a mess! I wonder if I'll ever get to the bottom of it."

As they were finishing supper, Elise placed her hand on Florent's. "Ratablavasky came to see you, didn't he?"

Despite his forceful denial, she said, "Don't put me on – I can see it in your eyes."

He went on denying it, but finally told her everything. "Don't worry, though – this time I know how to handle him."

Waving his fork, Monsieur Emile listened attentively.

"I just remembered," said Elise, "there's nothing for dessert. Be an angel, Monsieur Emile, and go get a pint of ice cream."

Florent handed him a two-dollar bill. "I'm sick of being a kid!" he grumbled as he left the room. "You never find out what other people are talking about."

When he'd slammed the door, Florent spoke again. "Here's what I think. There's a secondhand store on St-Antoine Street where the owner sells handguns under the table. I'll go and buy two revolvers."

Elise was appalled. "Revolvers? Are you going to *kill* him?"

"*Two* revolvers: one for Old Rat and one for me."

Picquot sprang to his feet, his hands on the table. "That's a ridiculous idea, son. People haven't fought duels for a hundred years. And they were absurd even then."

Ange-Albert had been looking skeptically at his friend. "Before you make up your minds, hear me out," said Florent, struggling to master his feelings. "Whether my plan works or not depends on you. We've all agreed, right, to drop the idea of taking him to court? Old Rat's too slippery for that. Only death will rid us of him. But at the rate things are going, he could torment us for years. So," he concluded, with a rueful smile, "we'll have to give nature a push. And here's how: when he comes to see me – which he'll be doing soon – I'll arrange to get him in a quiet corner with one of you," he said, addressing Picquot and Ange-Albert. "Then I'll mow him down, just like that. If we find that he's armed (which I doubt), so much the better. If not, I'll stick the other gun in his hand and call it justifiable self-defense."

"Brilliant," said the chef, shaking Florent's hand. "*Superior*, in fact. And I hope to be the one to watch him croak!"

This discussion was interrupted by the arrival of Monsieur Emile with three liters of ice cream, on which he'd left the two-dollar bill as down payment.

THIRTY-FOUR

Two days before the opening of Chez Florent, Slipskin knocked twenty percent off his prices, repainted the front of his restaurant, and ran big ads in the neighborhood papers to announce a supercontest for The Beanery's clientele. First prize: a two-week holiday for two, all expenses paid, at a luxury hotel in Miami. Meanwhile, Florent was looking for a part-time replacement for Elise, who was increasingly indisposed by her pregnancy. Florent's father suggested a splendid woman he'd met some years earlier at the Brasserie du Coin in Longueuil. Her husband had just signed up for two years at James Bay, leaving her alone at home with twins born early that winter. She accepted Florent's offer at once, saying, "Baby-sitters aren't cheap, but I need to get out and see people."

It was decided that Elise and Florent would work mornings, and chubby Madame Jobin from eleven to seven, with Florent closing, either alone or with Ange-Albert. If necessary, they would take on more staff.

To attract clientele, during the first week Florent decided to offer a daily special at $1.99, including soup, desert, and coffee. By keeping his profits to a minimum, he managed to match The Beanery's prices. Picquot was so indignant at Slipskin's tactic that his culinary skill, set ablaze and expanded by rage, assumed proportions approaching genius. At 4:00 A.M. on opening day, he was bustling around the kitchen making *tourtières* for the daily special, while Florent put the finishing touches on the decorating. A puffy-eyed Elise arrived at six, her heavy breasts swaying from side to side under the pretty embroidered blouse she'd made for the occasion.

At ten past six a retired bus driver who came in was given a free breakfast, and felt awkward at his good luck. "Now that was a meal," he said, getting up. "I'll tell my brother to come – and my sister-in-law, too."

By eleven o'clock they'd served nineteen breakfasts, and Florent had the pleasure of watching half a dozen pedestrians on their way to The Beanery stop outside his window, hesitate briefly, then come inside. Two complimented him on the home fries Picquot served with the eggs, and a third praised the coffee. Elise, with her affable manner and swollen belly, won everyone over on the spot: a young salesgirl from Woolworth's offered her a stroller that was gathering dust in her shed. From the kitchen door, Picquot would beckon to Florent. "Well? How's it going? Are they happy?" He would listen to Florent's optimistic remarks, then invariably add, "This is a *remarkable* beginning. There'll be a few more tomorrow, and twice as many the day after, you'll see. But the big payoff will come at dinnertime."

At noon, when Florent's father checked in, there were twelve diners. "Your mother-in-law didn't sleep a wink," he told Elise, "but I'll call and tell her to stop worrying. I think it's off to a *very* good start," he insisted, with a touching attempt to conceal his apprehension. "But you should go home and rest, your eyes are falling out of your head. You can trust Madame Jobin," he said, raising his voice. "She may spill the odd cup of coffee in a customer's lap, but she's one of the most capable people I know."

There was an amused clucking behind the counter. "Maybe I spill coffee on Monsieur Boissonneault's lap to take his mind off mine."

The customers enjoyed this exchange. Florent shut his eyes and sniffed the air delightedly, giddy at the atmosphere of prosperity he could already sense in his restaurant. Then his father tapped him on the shoulder and whispered, "I've got a little favor to ask you when things have settled down."

He seemed uncomfortable. "It's about your mother. I'd like you to try to calm her down. You see, when I was building the yacht my calculations were a little off. We'll have to tear out part of the sub-basement to get it out of the cellar. Whenever I mention it, she hits the roof."

At the end of a week, the gross at Chez Florent was $1,376.12. The break-even point was between twenty-five hundred and three thousand dollars.

The next two weeks were marked by steady though very slow progress, but they seemed unable to make it over the two-thousand-dollar mark. Customers of the two restaurants, delighted at the battle raging between Florent and Slipskin, were growing flushed and portly, but Picquot, in the toughest fight of his career, was losing weight, sleeping badly, and couldn't stand the slightest remark, even if it was flattering.

One afternoon Elise received a call from a lady of a certain age, who shyly introduced herself, in a warbling contralto, as a friend of Aurélien Picquot's. "You wouldn't be Emilienne Latouche?"

"He's mentioned me?" the woman asked delightedly.

"Often. We're all looking forward to meeting you."

At the other end of the line there was a sigh filled with tenderness and resignation. "I'd like nothing better. But you know Aurélien: he's so terribly afraid of anyone prying into his private life. . . . But I've learned to be patient. He'll make up his mind eventually." She went on to share her concern about his health and to ask if he could be relieved of part of his work – without telling him why, of course, because he'd object – and to ask Elise to keep a discreet eye on him to be sure he took his pills and didn't work too hard. Elise was touched, promising to move heaven and earth to persuade her husband to hire an assistant, and invited Mademoiselle Latouche to come for a visit as soon as possible.

For a good ten days now Slipskin had been in the habit of walking past Chez Florent every morning, his *Gazette* under his arm, a smile on his lips, smooth faced, a living symbol of blatant success. Early on the afternoon of June 8, Madame Jobin, taking advantage of a momentary lull, drew Florent aside. "That Slipskin is a filthy pig," she said by way of preamble. "Can you imagine, he phoned me at home this morning to ask me to come and work for him – and he offered me forty dollars a week more!"

Florent was appalled.

"Of course, I told him what he could do with his forty dollars! I'm not so foolish that I didn't know he just wanted to pick my brains to hurt your business, and once he'd got his information, bye-bye, Judith! Good luck getting on unemployment! But there's something even worse," she said into Florent's ear. "A customer just told me he's spreading a rumor that you serve bad meat: that's why you can keep your prices so low, even though your sales aren't half of his."

For the rest of the day Florent was so pensive that it

affected service, and two customers vowed never to darken his door again. When he came home he announced to Elise, "It's time for our counterattack." And he reported Madame Jobin's remarks. "So far I've been playing fair. My only weapon's been good food. But that's not enough anymore."

"Do whatever you have to," said Elise listlessly. "I won't criticize you. He's done too much harm already."

"First we have to undermine his morale. Then, when he's really low, I move in for the kill, like he did to me – but without the chemistry."

He phoned Gladu and asked him over. He came into the kitchen to see a bottle of rum on the table, with glasses and a pitcher of lemonade. Florent had opened the windows to let in a little fresh air, for it was stifling.

"I want to ask you a favor," he said, holding out a glass to the sweating Gladu, who drained it in a gulp. "Nothing fancy. I'd just like you to go see Bertrand – remember him, the assistant chef at The Beanery? – and draw him out a little, without telling him why, of course. I need to know how things stand right now between Slipskin and Old Rat. It's very important."

Grimacing in disgust. Gladu shook his head. "Can't do it. I can't talk to a queer. Turns my stomach. Like somebody putting grease in my pants. Anyway, you know Miss Bertrand's got a loose tongue. Five minutes after I left, Slipskin'd know everything. Old Rat, too, most likely. No, sorry. I really can't. Too much crud involved."

Florent, obviously put out, didn't push it, but questioned him about his escapades with Slipskin. That was how he learned that his enemy had moved shortly after taking over The Beanery and now had a swanky upper duplex in Nôtre-Dame-de-Grace.

"Have you been there?"

"Sure, many times. It's fancy as hell – wall-to-wall carpets, thermostats in every room, picture windows, the works."

"Get up, we're going."

"Hang on, boss! I like the money I get from you, but I'd just as soon it's me that spends it, not my heirs!"

"Come on, you're getting your nuts in a knot over nothing. At this time of day he'll be at The Beanery. Anyway, we won't go in. I just want an idea of what the place is like."

At a quarter past midnight they drove up to 2426 Moineau Street. Gladu parked a few yards away, turned off the motor and lights. There were lights on the second floor. The ground floor was dark, the blinds drawn. Florent gazed at the house for a moment. "Who lives downstairs?"

"The landlord."

"You know him?"

"Monsieur Chagnon? Sure. Nice guy, Hector Chagnon. Painting contractor. Nuts about pizza. Slipskin sent me to him on errands three or four times."

"His apartment looks closed up. As if he's gone on a trip."

Gladu shrugged and rubbed his belly: the word "pizza" had covered the wall of his stomach with gastric juices demanding to attack Hector Chagnon's favorite dish at once. "Why don't we go and grab a bite? I've just found a swell Italian place at the corner of Ontario and St-Andre, with two cute little waitresses. . . ."

"I'm going to bed, my friend, I'm wiped out. And you know I don't like to leave my wife alone."

He was pensive on the way home, scarcely responding to Gladu's chitchat. "Find out if Chagnon's away," he said, "and if so, for how long."

"Will do, boss. Anything to make you happy! I'll find out tomorrow morning."

The next day he called Florent. "He's taken the whole family to Barbados for five weeks. A neighbor told me."

Florent hung up and started pacing behind the counter, rubbing his hands. Elise looked at him, puzzled. "Good news?"

"Very good. The Chinese torture's about to begin." He went into the lane. "Come here, Monsieur Emile, I want to talk to you for a minute."

That night around two o'clock, Monsieur Emile, thrilled but quaking with fear, slipped between the bars of Monsieur Chagnon's basement window and turned up the thermostat in every room as high as it would go. The electric heaters immediately began to crackle and layers of heat wafted up to the ceiling, then began to seek a way out into Slipskin's apartment, where the scorching temperature was already uncomfortable. "Good night," Florent murmured. "Sleep tight."

He walked away silently with Monsieur Emile, who was drunk with pride but still jittery with fear. When they were back in the apartment on Emery Street where Elise was waiting, pale with anxiety, the child gestured to Florent to bend down, then said in his most wheedling tone, "Oh, Florent, I'm so thirsty. . . . Please, can I have just one little sip of beer, please, Florent?"

The next morning Monsieur Emile was given another, less dangerous, assignment. He went back to his mother's apartment, where he found her frolicking with a Swiss importer who had flooded the place with chocolates, and began loading cockroaches into tin boxes with little holes punched in them. As the operation turned out to be more difficult than anticipated, he had to appoint some friends as assistants, paying them one chocolate for every five healthy roaches. In the days that followed there was a veritable public health campaign in the neighborhood. A storekeeper, thrilled at the bargain, offered a bottle of pop for every dozen cockroaches taken from his shed, dead or alive. Monsieur Emile, who claimed to be working for an entomologist uncle, concluded a secret deal in which five bottles of pop were equivalent to a beer.

Meanwhile, Slipskin kept strutting past Florent's every morning, but his fine colors were somewhat faded by insomnia and the bad temper of his wife, who was made irritable by the heat. "And he's too tight to buy an air conditioner," Florent snickered behind his counter.

A few days later, four centimeters of cockroaches were rustling happily in a big screen-covered tin basin that Florent had put in the outside shed. Restaurant scraps had the creatures in an energetic state that delighted Monsieur Emile and turned Elise's stomach.

About six o'clock one morning Slipskin was awakened by the telephone. "Shit! I was just getting to sleep!"

He recognized Bertrand's voice but the poor fellow was in such a flap that he made no sense. After trying to interpret the flood of onomatopoeia, interjections, and sentence fragments that gushed from the assistant chef's mouth, Slipskin hung up, jumped in his car and raced to The Beanery. To his great surprise, despite the early hour, a group of onlookers had gathered outside the window, talking animatedly, guffawing, and nudging one another. Bertrand ran up, disheveled, his face a mess. "Boss, boss, this is *dread*ful!"

Slipskin made his way through the crowd and looked in the window, gagging. The tables, counter, and floor of The Beanery were covered with an easily identifiable brownish, wriggling mass. Cockroaches were talking on the ceiling, exploring cupboards, nibbling at breadcrumbs, drops of gravy, a single bean – lively, happy, everywhere. Three had landed in a sugar bowl at the end of the counter and, after a long struggle to escape from their prison, seemed to be holding a peaceful consultation as they munched on a grain of sugar.

The Beanery was closed for two days. Slipskin ran newspaper ads to reassure his clientele, declaring that the situation was under control and that he hadn't been the only victim – a whole row of houses had been invaded. At this point his wife, her nerves shot, decided to take a few weeks' holiday at her parents' place in Magog. "I'd better lay off for a while," Florent decided, "or he'll stop blaming bad luck and start looking this way."

One night while leafing through *The Chemistry of Cosmetics* – as he'd been doing frequently in recent days – Florent cried out in delight.

"What is it?" Elise asked.

"I just got another idea."

On page 1018, in a chapter entitled "Internal Additives for Feminine Beauty," was a long paragraph devoted to okaloa salt.

Okaloa *Georgium aubinensis* is a tropical plant, found principally in central Africa, that was used frequently in nineteenth-century medicine to treat various intestinal conditions. In a relatively simple procedure, one could obtain from the root of the plant a white crystalline powder, low in toxicity, that looked and tasted almost exactly like ordinary table salt. Taken in minute quantities, said the author, okaloa salt gently stimulated elimination and, after a few weeks, gave the complexion a marvelous glow and transparency. The reader was warned, however, that improper use of the substance could cause diarrhea, nausea, and vomiting, though without long-lasting effects.

After two days of research, Florent managed to come by a few ounces. One night, with the help of Monsieur Emile, he gained admission to The Beanery and put a good twenty pinches of okaloa in the cook's salt shaker.

Results didn't take long.

At one o'clock the following afternoon, an old lady left her dinner on the sidewalk outside the restaurant, followed a half hour later by two other customers. People began complaining to Slipskin about fainting spells and headaches. Late that afternoon a bank clerk called him a "goddamn poison-monger" and left without paying, clutching his stomach. The popularity lost by The Beanery's kitchen was won by the toilets. Slipskin and his cook, their guts wrenched by pitiless diarrhea, could hardly stand on their feet. By late evening, no employee would have dared to put a crumb of bread in his mouth. The cook underwent a Stalinesque interrogation that yielded no results, and he threatened to quit on the spot. Then Slipskin turned on the exterminator who had cleaned out the cockroaches, accusing him of contaminating the restaurant's food, but he could prove nothing. The next day, as the situation was becoming catastrophic, he called the municipal health department. Twelve hours later an inspector appeared. The discomforts afflicting The Beanery's clientele had disappeared. Slipskin heaved a sigh of relief, but his restaurant's palmy days had just gone over to the competition.

"Could it be that son of a bitch?" he asked himself a hundred times a day, craning his neck to try to see what was going on at Chez Florent.

But the health department's investigation turned up nothing.

"Don't you think that's enough?" asked Elise.

Obstinately, Florent shook his head. "Have you forgotten, beloved wife, all the shit he put us through? I won't be satisfied till I've got my heel on his neck. What we need is a bloodbath, a real bloodbath."

"Wow!" exclaimed Monsieur Emile, "A bloodbath!" He looked up and his gaze lit on two huge cans of tomato sauce on the pantry shelf. "A bloodbath," he repeated, smiling.

That night – it was a Saturday – shortly after closing, someone cut the electrical wire that supplied the restaurant, and on Monday morning Florent found himself with ten pounds of rotten meat. "Well, well, Slipskin's left his calling card. He smells something. We have to wrap this up."

After Florent had a long telephone conversation with Rosario Gladu they went to call on the journalist's brother-in-law, the policeman at Station 16. The discussion began, was drawn out, and several times was nearly interrupted. Each time, however, it slowly and painfully got under way again. Florent, his hair disheveled, face sweating, was advocating the most important cause of his life. The policeman listened, stubbornly shaking his head. Gladu, glass in hand, would get up and gesticulate at his brother-in-law or, lips stretched in a syrupy smile, bend over and whisper a few words in his ear, hands fluttering. About midnight, the policeman's previously hardened features relaxed slightly. Florent, leaning across the table, was jotting figures on a piece of paper; he scratched his head, began his calculations again, then finally turned to Gladu, took out his wallet, counted his money, and left a wad of bills on the table. Flustered, Gladu took a long swig of gin and, without further ado, reached across and pocketed the money.

"The bastard's bleeding me dry," Florent grumbled later, slumped in a chair across from his wife, "but I think this will be the last round."

The following morning Gladu went to see a friend who worked for the City of Montreal sanitation department. He stayed a good half hour and left with a pleased expression, on his way to a pet shop to buy a small metal cage.

Two days later, he received a call from the sewer worker. "I've got what you wanted. Three males and a female. Bring cash."

Gladu took delivery of his merchandise, then went home to put it in a shed. Florent was sitting on a pile of tires waiting for him. He examined the contents of the cage.

"Perfect. We move tonight."

That evening Slipskin stayed at The Beanery long after closing time doing the books, apparently snowed under. For a while it looked as if he was going to spend the night. With clenched fists, Florent chattered nervously as he paced behind the counter. They had put out all the lights in the restaurant. Elise stood behind the cash register, not saying a word. Suddenly the phone rang. She picked it up. At the other end, Picquot told her, "Our bird's just left his perch, and Gladu's tailing him. He seems to be heading home to Nôtre-Dame-de-Grace. Good luck, youngsters, and may God help you!"

Palms damp and breathing hard, Florent kissed his wife and dashed to the garage with Ange-Albert. Elise was to stay by the phone to take Gladu's call in case Slipskin decided to turn back. If that happened, she would send Monsieur Emile to warn them. The child wasn't thrilled with the role he'd been assigned. Lying in a corner, he wept in rage and pounded his heels on the floor. Elise, furious at the dangers to which Florent had exposed the child so far, had demanded that Monsieur Emile stay with her. "I'll go by myself," the child stormed. "Goddamn sonofabitches!"

Meanwhile, Florent's truck pulled up behind The Beanery. Florent hopped out, approached the basement window – and stopped, stunned. "He's put in an alarm system."

Ange-Albert switched on a flashlight and began to examine the window, then straightened up. "Can't do anything about it tonight."

Ange-Albert and Florent devoted the next two days to becoming familiar with Slipskin's alarm system, and Elise endured Monsieur Emile's tantrum. Finally, taking a last look at a diagram he'd completed after much trial and error, Ange-Albert said, "Okay, I think I've got it."

Florent picked up a box containing pliers, a screwdriver, bits of electrical wire, tape, and a soldering iron.

About 1:00 A.M. the truck pulled up once again behind The Beanery; ten minutes later Ange-Albert slipped through the basement window.

When Slipskin arrived at the restaurant next morning, he noted a certain suspicious agitation in the basement. As he was on his way down to investigate, two policemen from Station 16 appeared with a search warrant, followed promptly by an official from the Public Health department. The inspector went to the kitchen and took from the refrigerator twenty pounds of ground beef of dubious color. The police went down to the cellar where they observed, with a look of disgust, a huge sewer rat perched on a sack of potatoes, giving them an unkindly stare, while three of his cronies, equally large and repulsive (they'd cost Florent fifty dollars each), scurried around, squealing furiously.

Slipskin was advised that legal action would be taken against him. Early that afternoon, a municipal official called to say his restaurant permit was temporarily suspended. Sick at heart, he let his employees go.

When the last one had left he took a key from his pocket, padlocked the door, and stood for a long moment on the sidewalk, staring hard at the window of Chez Florent. Then he got in his car, went to see his lawyer, and finally drove to Magog to join his wife.

Florent had followed this scene from behind the red curtain that covered the lower half of his window. Gesturing Elise into the kitchen, he announced gravely, "The Beanery's just closed down."

Picquot slowly wiped his hands. They looked at one another in silence. Curiously, no one felt like celebrating. "Youngsters," Picquot said sententiously, "above all, don't confuse a truce with a victory."

Perched on a stool, Monsieur Emile was listening closely. Florent went back to the counter. A few minutes later Monsieur Emile came up to him: "Now can we bust it to pieces?"

"Hey? What're you talking about?"

"Over there." He pointed across the street.

"Are you nuts? The police would arrest us."

"No they wouldn't – nobody'd see us."

"Tut-tut. Calm your little head. The police learn lots of things when they put their minds to it. I forbid you to set foot in The Beanery, do you hear?"

Monsieur Emile narrowed his eyes, made a face, and went back to the kitchen. "I say," said Picquot, seeing him perched on the stool again, "aren't you afraid of turning into a parrot?"

The child looked up and his gaze fell once more on the two huge cans of tomato sauce on the shelf. Florent's voice rang out in his head: "What we need is a bloodbath, a real bloodbath."

Looking smug, Monsieur Emile rubs his feet together. He is at The Beanery, sitting in a pretty yellow rowboat. He must hunch down a little to avoid hitting his head on the ceiling, for he is floating on a sea of scarlet blood, thick as syrup, that fills the entire restaurant. A few feet from him, Slipskin is struggling desperately, unable to reach the boat. Soon he will sink. Good riddance! As for old Ratablavasky, he's already a goner. His gray fedora is adrift at the back of the restaurant, soaking up blood. In a few minutes it will have joined its owner. Yes! A bloodbath! he needs a bloodbath – or the closest facsimile.

Elise was the first to notice he was up to something. She mentioned it to Florent, who alerted Picquot, Ange-Albert, and Madame Jobin, and all five began to keep a discreet eye on him. Two days passed. On the afternoon of the third day, Elise phoned Florent to tell him Monsieur Emile had disappeared. Putting two and two together, Florent rushed across to The Beanery, taking the back lane, where he hid behind a pile of old tires and waited. "The little sneak," he muttered.

The child appeared at the end of the lane, advancing slowly, looking calm, though he kept glancing left and right.

"What did I tell you, you stubborn little mule?" Florent exploded, emerging from his hiding place.

"What'd I do?" Monsieur Emile whimpered. "What the hell did I do? Can't I even go for a walk?"

"Going for a walk, are you! Well, I'm hunting flies," he said, cuffing the child on the neck. "If I catch you here again . . . Do you want the police on my tail? Eh? Is that what you want?"

Monsieur Emile wasn't listening, gripped by a rage in which the shame of being caught was stronger than the pain of being slapped. Though he stamped his feet and wept, he had to stay in his room for the rest of the day, after it had been cleared of any objects that might be transformed into projectiles.

"You two are really old-fashioned," Ange-Albert teased them. "You have to *explain* to him. When he understands what's going on, there'll be no more problems."

"He's right," Elise admitted.

At dinner the next day they told him in great detail what frightful consequences might result from his exploits at The Beanery.

Monsieur Emile nodded, biting into a slice of toast thick with jam. His expression was sober and reasonable, and he seemed, at last, to understand.

"That settles that," Florent sighed.

It's true he understood, Elise thought, but has *he* changed his mind?

Another three days passed. The Beanery was still closed. An imperceptible layer of dust was beginning to dull the nickel finish of the cash register. Someone, probably a child, had written in chalk on the front of the restaurant: KOKROACH SERVED HERE. Another hand had added: AND SHIT.

Across the street, Chez Florent was slowly settling into prosperity. Plump Madame Jobin was very popular with the customers (more than she cared to be, in fact), she'd won over Monsieur Emile (which caused Elise a certain jealousy) and, rarest of all, she'd adapted very well to the cavalier behavior of Aurélien Picquot. Only the state of the chef's health kept Elise and Florent from savoring their victory to the fullest. Picquot had obviously been overtaxed by his own success. He complained of headaches, dizzy spells. His hands began to shake, and he was sometimes late in the morning. "If you hadn't had the splendid idea of installing an air conditioner in the kitchen," he told Florent, "I'd have given you back my apron long ago. As it is, I sometimes feel like turning in half of it." In short, he needed an assistant. And though the turnover at Chez Florent looked very promising, it still wasn't high enough to warrant hiring extra help. They would have had to let Madame Jobin go, and Elise's pregnancy made that impossible.

"I'll stick it out till your blessed event," the chef told Florent. "But after that you'll have to get some help for me . . . or find a younger cook."

Florent clasped his hands. "Come on, Monsieur Picquot, you know I couldn't manage without you."

On Thursday, July 15, about six o'clock in the morning, Florent awoke, dumbfounded, under a big armful of daisies. While he muttered and rubbed his eyes, Elise, in a pale blue negligée that her bulging stomach transformed into a tent, looked on, smiling. "What is it?"

She sat on the edge of the bed, gripped his shoulders, and looked him gravely in the eyes. "My darling husband, this morning I go into my seventh month."

Florent looked at her, speechless.

"Don't you understand? Our child is viable. I could give birth anytime. You're sure of being a father."

"What a face, Boissonneault!" Picquot exclaimed when he arrived at the restaurant. "Did Sophia Loren invite you into bed?"

Florent smiled all day. More precisely, until ten o'clock that night, when Monsieur Emile disappeared for the second time. It was Elise who discovered it, when she heard Breakfast meowing in his bedroom. His bed was empty, his pajamas on the floor, his clothes gone. Elise phoned Florent at once. "It could be one of two things: he's at The Beanery, or at his mother's, filching beer. He's been agitated for a few days now."

Florent flung his apron on the counter and went out, cursing the day he'd first laid eyes on Monsieur Emile. An inspection of the back of The Beanery turned up nothing. Angrier than ever, he got in his truck and headed for Gilford Street, where Madame Chouinard lived. He parked on the next street and went the rest of the way on foot, hoping to learn that Monsieur Emile was at his mother's without having to ring the bell and get involved in delicate explanations.

There were lights in the windows, which were wide open because of the heat. He heard the lengthy sound of a woman's laughter, followed by a dry smack that could have been a kiss or the tearing of a soup-mix envelope. Then a guttural voice, loud as a hippopotamus or an ox, boomed out. "Hey, baby, I like that – do it again."

Suddenly Florent's courage gave out and he returned to the restaurant, where Madame Jobin was valiantly trying to do the work of two. "No," Elise told him on the telephone, "he hasn't come back."

Sighing, Florent hung up, then stood unmoving behind the cash register, staring vacantly at an astonished customer who was waiting to pay his bill.

Madame Jobin whispered, "Go back to The Beanery. I'll bet my wedding dress you'll find him there."

Florent asked her not to let in any more customers, and soon he was in the dimly lit lane, lined with staved-in fences and dingy garages, and strewn with trash cans, slashed mattresses, garbage bags, and defunct television sets. He realized that Monsieur Emile was a natural product of this wretched setting, that he was like a fish in water here and thereby had a tremendous advantage over Florent.

"The little bugger," he muttered. "If I get my hands on him I'll burn his backside."

He approached the basement window, looked all around, then switched on his flashlight. He cried out in surprise: the window had been removed and was leaning against the wall. "The alarm didn't go off? I don't get it. . . ."

He pricked up his ears, then stuck his arm in the opening. He shone the flashlight slowly around the cellar, illuminating canned goods, the meat-grinder, sacks of beans and potatoes. He saw nothing suspicious, but the street noises prevented him from checking sounds from inside. He stuck his head in and tried to listen. He heard only the beating of his own heart, muffled, wild, unbearable. "No way the kid could have defused the system," he murmured. "Is this a trap?"

He tried to be logical. A waste of energy. His thoughts fluttered about like a cloud of butterflies. He leaned through the opening again, his flashlight still switched on. "Monsieur Emile," he whispered, "are you in there?"

Suddenly, at the end of the lane, a motorcycle backfired; the sound quickly moved closer. He put out his light and slipped inside the cellar. Oddly, his fear had taken flight. He headed for the staircase, eyes peeled, climbed a few steps, thought better of it, turned and pushed open the bathroom door.

No one.

At the sight of the can he had a dazzling thought, like an enigmatic warning. He spun around. His fear was lulled only for a moment. Now it gripped him again, harder than ever. Drawing back, he stumbled into the huge meat grinder in the middle of the cellar, and his face twisted in pain. A moment later he went up the stairs again, but stopped almost at once, intrigued.

A persistent, almost imperceptible, sound had just come in range of his ears. It was like light breathing, deep and even, or the hum of an electric fan.

"Fine evening, isn't it?" said a familiar voice behind him.

His knees buckled, he spun around, stumbled on the stairs, regained his balance, and shone the flashlight into the recess where the toilet was. Egon Ratablavasky stood in the shadows, smiling and watching him. Florent's brain went on full tilt. A trap. Of course. And Monsieur Emile? He's here, I'm sure he's here. Unless . . . And I'm unarmed. Idiot. The perfect chance to get rid of him. And Slipskin'd take the rap. I have to find a way. Is he armed? Doesn't seem to be.

"Has your mouth swallowed your tongue?" Ratablavasky asked sweetly.

Florent didn't budge. The old man cleared his throat, then said, "Be so good, dear friend, and reduce your light a little, my poor eyes . . ."

"What're you doing here?" Florent asked hoarsely, stepping over to the meat grinder.

Suddenly something clicked. Of its own accord, his arm wrenched the metal pestle from the mouth of the grinder, and he took a furious run at Ratablavasky, who stood stock-still, wedged against the wall. But then something tripped him: he didn't know what. With a deafening sound, the pestle struck the wall, and Florent's field of vision was filled with blinding sparks. His hand opened slowly, dropped the implement, and something crashed into his head. His numbed brain abruptly gave up.

An icy smile appeared on Ratablavasky's lips. He took a few steps, bent over Florent's inanimate body, then suddenly changed his mind. The stairs creaked. Monsieur Emile's head appeared in the dim light of Florent's flashlight, which was still burning, then immediately disappeared.

The series of incomprehensible events that had just begun continued at a staggering rate.

Ratablavasky shot onto the staircase, assuring himself with a glance that the restaurant door was shut. A chair sliding in the kitchen told him where the child was. He went up and opened the door. He was enclosed in a flood of heat. The four burners of the gas range were on high. The blue flames were licking at four huge cans that bulged menacingly. Crouched behind a table, Monsieur Emile stared at him with phosphorescent eyes. Ratablavasky gestured toward the stove knobs, but it was too late. A can exploded like a cannon shot. It was followed at once by a second, then a third. Gallons of tomato sauce spurted all over the steam-filled kitchen. The sauce-spattered old man backed toward the door, his hands in front of his face, while Monsieur Emile, one leg scalded, huddled under the table. The fourth can exploded. Was it made of thicker tin? Whatever the reason, this was the one that awakened the neighborhood (including Florent) and gave wings to a passerby who ran to a phone and called the police. Monsieur Emile crawled to the door and set it ajar. Ratablavasky was standing there, wiping his face with a handkerchief. His expression briefly froze the child with dread, then he sprang to his feet and sped to the door that opened onto the lane. It was padlocked. The time it took for him to break the glass and slip out the window was ample time for the old man to grab him by the collar.

Suddenly a siren's screams filled the street. The police were coming. Monsieur Emile gathered speed, kicked open the swinging door and slipped between the legs of the old man, who groaned furiously and rushed after him to the door to the cellar. But a patrol car had just stopped outside The Beanery, sweeping the walls with its revolving light. Ratablavasky retraced his steps and went to open the door, which threatened to give way under the policemen's pounding. "Officers," he said, switching on all the lights, "I've been expecting you. There's been a stupid accident."

The two policemen, aghast, gazed at him in silence. Smiling and looking quite proper despite the streaks of tomato sauce, he was like a Grand Guignol character after the massacre. They came in, exclaiming with astonishment. The kitchen had been transformed into a sort of huge bleeding wound giving off trails of steam. "Officers, I tell you from the outsetting: all took place because of my fault. I am at your disposal."

While they were trying to contact Slipskin the old man was taken to hospital by ambulance. An intern examined him at once. He had suffered only minor burns.

THIRTY-FIVE

At the sound of the fourth explosion Florent came to, flat on his face by the staircase. Two inches from his nose, a round object that had fallen to the ground glowed dimly in the half light. He had been peering hazily at it for a moment when the sound of Monsieur Emile tumbling down the stairs brought him to his feet. Mechanically, he picked up the object, grabbed the child by the seat of his pants, and threw him bodily out the basement window. Not until he was in the lane did he feel the throbbing of a hideous headache. An attack of nausea forced him to sit down behind a fence for a moment. Monsieur Emile, trembling, his pant leg pulled up to cool off his burns, gave him furtive glances but didn't say a word.

The next morning Florent was sipping his coffee, trying to shed some light on the events of the night before, when Elise came in holding a round, flat box about three inches in diameter, that seemed to be made of gold. "Where'd you get this?"

Florent gazed at it for a moment. "In the cellar of The Beanery."

The box was decorated on both sides with an odd combination of concentric circles and isosceles triangles. Florent opened it. It was empty but gave off an unpleasant odor that he recognized at once: the smell of dirty feet that accompanied Ratablavasky everywhere. Inside, carved with great skill, was an inscription in a foreign language.

Long after these events were over, someone finally translated it:

Laden with fresh corpses,
The tumbrel of Death
Grinds through the night
Amid the debris
Of the fallen sky.

Elise and Florent studied the box, perplexed. "It probably fell out of Old Rat's pocket."

Overcome, Elise flopped onto a chair. "What will happen to us now? Things were going too well."

"I can't figure out what he was up to at The Beanery last night. Dammit, if only I hadn't tripped, we'd be celebrating today!"

His face was twisted in despair. He turned toward Monsieur Emile's room and waved his fist. "And it's all because of that little garbage thief! If he dares to show his face around here . . ."

"Come on – you know very well, sooner or later . . . We're being watched day and night."

"Kiddo, I'm fed up. . . . In a week at the most we'll be rid of him, I swear."

Virtue wagged her tail in vigorous support of Florent's declaration. Elise took his hand. "Florent, for heaven's sake, don't be so stubborn. Go to the police. . . . You aren't up to . . ."

He merely shrugged and looked away.

Suddenly they heard footsteps racing up the stairs. "Florent!" a breathless voice exclaimed.

"It's Picquot," said Elise.

The chef burst into the room holding a newspaper, terrifying Breakfast, who lay in front of the door. "My friends, it's absolutely astounding! Read this!"

On page three of *Le Journal de Montréal* was a photograph of The Beanery's kitchen after the explosion, with a brief article. Egon Ratablavasky wasn't named, but there was a reference to an old man of foreign origin who admitted to having set the fire, for which he was offering generous compensation. "I acted for intimate reasons," he was quoted as saying. "You must forgive my old age."

The article ended with some vague insinuations about the harmful effects of certain passions on people of advanced age. Florent read it and reread it, mouth agape. "What in heaven's name is he hatching?" Elise murmured. "Lord, I'm fed up with all this." And she began to weep silently. Picquot looked on, dreadfully upset.

"If I weren't an atheist," he murmured, "I'd be cursing heaven."

From that day, events moved very fast. Florent tried several times to reach Ratablavasky at the Hotel Nelson, to invite him for a discussion at a little apartment on Rosemont Boulevard that he'd just rented under a false name. There, with no to-do, he'd simply shoot him and that would be the end of it. The murder would make headlines in the scandal sheets for a day or two. *Allô Police* would run an article with photographs. The police would go around in circles for a while, then dismiss the case as a settling of accounts. And Florent would finally be able to live in peace with his wife and child.

One little snag prevented him from realizing his dream: Ratablavasky was nowhere to be found, although he was still living at the Hotel Nelson. His apartment had been fixed up. The old man had been seen the previous day. He'd left just two minutes ago. . . . He was gone for the day. No, no message. Call back later this afternoon. "They're laughing at you, my poor friend," Picquot concluded, despondent.

Though he was needed at his restaurant, Florent spent several evenings drinking coffee at the Nelson with Ange-Albert, in the hope of seeing Ratablavasky. In vain. Only Picquot, by sheer chance, caught a glimpse of him one night in Phillips Square, but when the old man spotted him he vanished.

Florent was furious. How had Ratablavasky been able to come to an understanding with the police over The Beanery? They went to the police. No one knew anything. "You'd better resign yourself to waiting," Ange-Albert advised, "and when you see him, strike."

"Bad, very bad," grumbled Picquot. "The best defence is attack. I learned that from Lieutenant Alexis de Bellevoie, a close friend of General de Gaulle, on our way to New York in 1944, across an ocean infested with German submarines."

On the morning of July 25, thirteen days after the explosion, a poster in the window of The Beanery declared that it was up for sale or for rent. Florent hardly rejoiced: the shadow of Ratablavasky spoiled his victory.

His anger at Monsieur Emile was short-lived. Recently the child had been as quiet as a mouse. His usual exuberance had given way to a state of despondency that was beginning to worry Elise. In fact, Ratablavasky had terrified him. For a week, he had nightmares almost every night. His appetite waned. Previously, nothing but rain would keep him inside, but now he stuck close to Elise, refused to play outside, cried over nothing. He was more and more jealous of Elise's pregnancy, referring to her "big dirty belly," making fun of her penguin-like walk, assuring her the baby would be born with one eye and no arms and that he'd decided to throw it in the garbage, anyway. Oddly enough, it seemed to Elise that his bad mood was also affecting the cat. Except for his master, no one was allowed to pet him. He wouldn't tolerate Virtue, who had to leave the room when he came in. Although he wasn't actually getting thin, he looked miserable and unhappy, with haggard eyes, dull fur and bristling whiskers. "They're a fine pair," Florent observed sarcastically one morning when Monsieur Emile, with the cat on his knees, was muttering as he picked at his cereal.

Elise told the child, "You can leave the table if you want. But don't come back in ten minutes asking for something to eat. . . ."

As Monsieur Emile ran out, Florent whispered, "Keep your eyes peeled, kiddo. I think our young friend's ripe for a binge."

He had guessed right. Two days later the bottle of cognac Aurélien Picquot kept carefully hidden in the restaurant had disappeared. They found Monsieur Emile collapsed in a garage, the bottle of cognac between his legs, his steam engine T-shirt torn. Florent exploded. "Either he sees a psychologist or he goes back to his mother!"

Elise started looking through the phone book, and an hour later she'd made an appointment for the following week.

Monsieur Emile's hangover the next morning took an unexpected form: a vast, inconsolable sorrow at having torn his steam engine T-shirt, which he'd been taking amazingly good care of. This time the effects of his spree were irreparable: once the T-shirt was mended the steam engine looked as if it had been sawed in two, had half its boiler cut off, and then been more or less repaired.

"Tough luck!" Florent told him. "Maybe it'll teach you a lesson. If you don't stop drinking, you'll end up looking like that one day. Can you get that into your head once and for all?"

Elise spent the whole afternoon unsuccessfully looking for another T-shirt. It was Ange-Albert who found one two days later in Sainte-Agathe, where Rosine, vacationing with friends, had agreed to a date, the first since they'd split up (he was careful not to breathe a word of it).

But there was a far greater disaster in store for Monsieur Emile. One day he and Breakfast were walking down a lane when he suddenly noticed that – the cat was gone! He called him every way he knew how, scoured the neighborhood, tried to lure him with a can of salmon, but to no avail. Breakfast was nowhere to be found. Seeing how miserable he was, Elise joined the search. The only suspect thing she found was a small flask that had been tossed near a shed, filled with a brownish liquid she couldn't identify. "It's an infusion of valerian," said Picquot after he'd sniffed it. "But . . . *sacrebleu*! That's what crooks use in Paris to lure the cats they cut up and pass off to restaurants as rabbit. There's not a shadow of a doubt: that cat was ambushed."

Elise and Florent looked at each other, thinking Ratablavasky.

"That's right," said the chef as if he'd read their minds, "Ratablavasky! A thousand times Ratablavasky! It's his way of getting back at Monsieur Emile for the tomato sauce shower. My friends, this can't go on. Today it's the cat, tomorrow it will be the dog, a month from now, it may be Elise! That monster is trying little by little to grind us down, by stretching out the terror. War! That's what we need! Shoot him on sight, like a wild animal! There'll always be time to explain to the law."

Monsieur Emile's grief was virtually indescribable. For three days he wandered the neighborhood with a discreetly armed Florent or Ange-Albert, calling his cat in a heart-rending voice, ignoring the children who made fun of him. Breakfast did not reappear. Then a fever confined Monsieur Emile to bed for two days. He barely talked, hardly ate, and took an odd hatred to Virtue, as if she were responsible for the cat's disappearance. When the time came to see the psychologist he went into a terrible tantrum, threw a jar of honey against a wall and locked himself in the bathroom. Finally, after many promises, remonstrances and arguments, Elise managed to take him to the appointment. Monsieur Emile was about as talkative as the chair he was sitting on. Gaze lowered, grouchy, he only looked up to cast suspicious looks at the stranger in a necktie who was simpering around him, asking a bunch of questions about things that were none of his business. After fifteen minutes the psychologist decided to cut short the session.

"You must be patient," he told Elise. "He seems very disturbed. Something's threatening him. Above and beyond the permanent threat of going back to his mother. As far as adoption's concerned I can't advise you; that's a decision for you and your husband. As you probably suspect, he'll never be an easy child. On the other hand, it's obvious that he chose you to be his parents a long time ago."

"Why'd that doctor ask me all those questions?" Monsieur Emile wanted to know when they were outside.

"I told you before – to help you. He's like a sort of friend."

"He isn't *my* friend. I don't even know him. Anyway, he looks mean: he hasn't got a single hair on his head! If he wants to help me, let him find my cat."

When they returned to the house Ange-Albert was in the kitchen, writing a letter. Elise was somewhat taken aback (Ange-Albert wasn't exactly noted for his epistolary skills), and her surprise grew when she saw him blush like a schoolgirl and awkwardly slip the letter in his pocket. Oh oh! she thought. Something's up.

"Ange-Albert," the child pleaded, tugging on his hand, "help me look for my pussycat."

"Hold on a minute," said Elise. "He's been going up and down the lanes with you for three days now. He must be getting fed up."

"No, no, not at all," said Ange-Albert, following the child with a promptness that made Elise smile.

"He's in love again. I wonder who it is this time."

About six o'clock they returned, empty-handed as always. Monsieur Emile's supper was a glass of milk and three cookies, and as soon as he left the table he expressed a desire to continue the search. "I can't come tonight," said Ange-Albert. "Florent asked me to give him a hand at the restaurant."

"Well I'm going, anyway."

"Absolutely not," said Elise. "You aren't to go running around the streets at night by yourself."

Monsieur Emile said nothing, but wandered around the apartment for a while, hands in his pockets, then went and curled up in front of the television. Ten minutes later, seeing Elise busy in the kitchen, he sneaked down the stairs and into the lane behind the house.

He stopped abruptly, stunned, incredulous. Before him, leaning against a fence, sitting conspicuously on a section of rotten beam, was a lovely, gleaming bottle of rum! Monsieur Emile looked around, heart pounding. A creamy haze began to fill his head, and he felt as if long warm threads were stroking the insides of his veins, undulating gently through his body. It was supper time. The lanes were deserted. Through open windows came the sounds of cutlery, of cranky children refusing to eat, of a father's grave and threatening voice trying to direct the course of the meal, the discreet lament of a dog sitting near the table, awaiting a charitable gesture. Monsieur Emile, still on the lookout, moved toward the bottle, walked past it with a false air of indifference, then came back, grabbed it by the neck and ran under a front stoop half hidden by a pile of old planks.

On his fourth swig he heard Elise calling him. He shut his eyes and wedged himself against an old rug folded in four that was ending its wretched days amid mold and cobwebs. The half light surrounding him had taken on a pretty bluish color, and the dampness was gradually disappearing. His mind wandered aimlessly. Pleasant images formed and enfolded him in a delicate glimmer of colors.

Suddenly he is back in Sainte-Romanie. It is summer. Noon. The fields are flooded with sunlight as far as the eye can see. Monsieur Emile rests against a warm bale of hay, his cat on his knees, his head protected from the blazing sun by overhanging golden wheat. The sound of the wind in a nearby clump of trees is like a cascade of delicate glass spangles. His head nods. Breakfast's purring, dazed by warmth and comfort, mingles with the cascade, and he shudders with pleasure.

Suddenly the sky grows dark, as if God had flicked off a switch. Icy rain starts falling with demented fury. Monsieur Emile is alone against the bale of hay, dripping wet, teeth chattering, and very upset. Far away, his cat is meowing hopelessly, but no matter how hard he tries, Monsieur Emile can't get to his feet. The meowing goes on and on, louder, unbearable. "Breakfast! Breakfast! Where are you?" he screams suddenly, coming out under the gallery, his bottom muddy, face covered with cobwebs.

He staggered to his feet, head up, looking around, distraught. It wasn't a dream: it was *real* meowing. His cat!

Philippe Saint-Onge, the boy next door, came running up. "Hey, Boissonneault, c'm 'ere! They found your cat! Hey, what's wrong?" he asked, stopping to peer at Monsieur Emile. "Are you *drunk*?"

"Where is he?" Monsieur Emile asked thickly. He hurried after the other boy. The cat's meowing had strengthened his ankles. Not enough, however, to keep him from stumbling twice. The second time, he fell full length on the potholed pavement, but an old cardboard box with BUFFET CHARLOTTE: MARRIAGE AND OTHER RECEPTIONS printed on it, full of moldy sandwiches, cushioned his fall somewhat. They stayed in the lane until they came in sight of an old three-story house with a pointed gable that some months ago had been ravaged by a mysterious fire, as happens so often in Montreal. "There he is! Up there!" Philippe Saint-Onge shouted, pointing. "I found him!"

Perched on the crest of the roof, a cat is crying its heart out, walking back and forth. Monsieur Emile doesn't have to look. He'd recognize his cat out of ten thousand. He darts toward the house, jumps the caved-in fence, and disappears through the back door. "Hey, you'll kill yourself," Philippe shouts fearfully from the doorstep.

A strong smell of damp and burned wood comes from the door, which opens onto a large devastated room. "He's drunk as a skunk," Philippe explains smugly to two other boys who have just appeared.

As the staircases haven't been badly damaged by the fire, Monsieur Emile quickly reaches the third floor and rushes to a skylight in the middle of the roof, about ten meters from the peak. With great effort, he manages to open a window and stick his head outside. "Hold on, pussycat, I'm coming!" he shouts, his voice quavering.

The cat's meows become even shriller.

During the blaze, firemen cut holes in the roof to help the gases escape. There is one below the window. It's a simple matter to slip one foot outside, then grip the shingles, crawl to the peak of the roof, and catch the cat.

Philippe Saint-Onge left the lane and, with his friends, went running to the front of the burned-out house. He sees a leg slip out the window, then another, and then Monsieur Emile, clinging to the edge of the opening, searching for a foothold. "Holy shit!" Philippe exclaims with enthusiastic horror, "he's gonna kill himself!"

A couple crossing the street look up. At the sight of the child, the man rushes to the house, while the woman, after a moment's hesitation, runs to call the police. Philippe Saint-Onge has run to tell Elise. He finds her, very upset, outside her house. "Madame! Madame!"

He recounts Monsieur Emile's latest exploit.

Elise is white as a sheet. A confused eddy fills her head. She feels only one thing clearly: a tremendous fright that turns her legs to jelly. "Come quick!" the child insists.

She takes a few steps, then changes her mind and rushes to the stairs that go up to her apartment.

Florent is bent over a huge basin, preparing the filling for a *tourtière à la mode du lac Saint-Jean*. Madame Jobin storms into the kitchen. The swinging door hits a jar of pickles on the edge of a counter, and the jar falls to the floor with a dull crack. "Your wife's on the phone. She . . . she doesn't sound good at all."

Florent raises his head. From her expression he knows something very serious has happened. Without a word he runs to the cash and picks up the phone. "What? I don't get it . . . Monsieur Emile? I don't understand what you're saying. Hold on, I'll be right there."

Josaphat Duval joined the municipal police force nineteen years ago. Until recently, thanks be to God, he's never had to complain about his health. For a week now, though, the slightest thing fills his stomach with hot coals that cause him hours of pain, in spite of all the medicine suggested by wife, friends, and pharmacist. It keeps him from eating both fresh pork and spaghetti, his two favorite dishes, and that bugs him.

On the evening in question he is sitting in a patrol car with his colleague Frédéric Brunet (nicknamed Paunch-O from a hernia he suffered while lifting weights at the station). They are on duty in a lane from which they can discreetly survey St-Denis Street near Mont-Royal. They can be found there several times a week. Some nights they haul in any drivers doing more than forty-five miles an hour. Other nights, when they're feeling stricter, the limit drops to forty. With head bowed, Josaphat Duval is taking an antacid tablet from its cellophane envelope when Paunch-O Brunet elbows him. "Holy crow! Did you see that truck? He ran a red light at eighty!"

Josaphat turned on the ignition and the car shot onto St-Denis. Dammit, this guy's really pushing it! He's just run a second red light, and a third. Josaphat puts on the siren, barely misses an old guy with an armful of flowers, performs a skilful maneuver that lets him weave between a bus and two delivery trucks, thereby gaining some ground, while muttering, "I'll slap the son of a bitch with so many tickets he'll have to mortgage his inheritance."

The truck stops abruptly at the corner of Emery and St-Denis. A little boy opens the door and shouts to the driver, who rushes onto the sidewalk and disappears. Josaphat Duval hadn't expected this turn of events. He stops his car in the middle of the street and runs after the man, with Paunch-O behind him. Flames rise from his stomach to his throat, and his brain seethes with rage. All because some bastard is acting as if he doesn't give one sweet goddamn about the police!

A group has gathered at the end of the street. "Hurry, officers," says a tall, distinguished old man with a curious lilting voice. "Make haste!"

They swoop into the crowd, jostling the curious. Josaphat finally spots Florent, recognizing him by his white shirt and pants. He puts out his hand to grab his shoulders, then holds back. "Get an ambulance here on the double," he orders Paunch-O, then gets busy clearing some room.

Florent has come up to Monsieur Emile. Beside him stands Elise, mute and expressionless. The child is wedged part way into a dented old garbage can, legs dangling, one arm folded under him, his torso bent in a strange and horrible way. His forehead is sliced open and a thin stream of blood pours from it. His eyes are half closed, his vision hazy, and he breathes haltingly through his mouth. His cat, skinny, its fur standing on end, walks robot-like around the garbage can, meowing hoarsely. Florent bends down and asks, "Monsieur Emile, what did you do?"

The child opens his eyes ever so slightly and his gaze falls on Florent, then on Elise. But it is such a distant gaze and takes such a vast effort. "My T-shirt," whispers the child, slumping over the steam engine, which a bloodstain is covering bit by bit.

Stretcher bearers come up and, with infinite care, lift the child, who seems unaware of it.

"Poor little nipper," says an intern at Saint-Luc Hospital a few minutes later. "He's had it."

Madame Chouinard, in an orange dress and matching stiletto-heeled shoes, has collapsed in a corner of the emergency room, sobbing. She keeps repeating, "They killed him, they killed him."

Florent has just taken Elise back to the apartment, where Monsieur and Madame Boissonneault, who have come as quickly as they could, are putting her to bed. He paces the kitchen, trying to answer an inspector's questions, while Ange-Albert, sitting at the counter in the restaurant behind lowered blinds, is lettering a sign:

CLOSED DUE TO DEATH

THIRTY-SIX

Monsieur Emile was buried two days later, in dazzling sunshine, at the Côte-des-Neiges cemetery. With puffy eyes, a handkerchief in hand and a curse on her lips, Madame Chouinard had taken charge of everything, baring her teeth at the gentlest suggestion. When she wasn't at the undertaker's, the tombstone maker, the florist's or the seamstress's, she was searching for a lawyer willing to prosecute Elise and Florent for the death of her beloved son. She saw four in two days. They listened to her briefly, but each in turn declined to take her case, advising her to drop the charges.

Monsieur Emile's tomb cost almost two thousand dollars. The funeral parlor was an orgy of flowers. Elise and Florent weren't allowed to go, Madame Chouinard having threatened to tear their eyes out if they showed up. Florent attended the burial from a distance, hidden behind a tomb. Some twenty people were present. Two sinister-looking men in black Fortrel suits, with ruffled shirts and black velvet bow ties, acted as pallbearers. They were probably colleagues of Madame Chouinard's.

On his way out of the cemetery, after the others had left, Florent found himself face-to-face with Rosario Gladu. The journalist shook his hand. "He was a good little guy," he said, moist-eyed. "A real pain in the butt, but his heart was in the right place. He'd still be alive if he'd had you as parents instead of that fat cow."

The autopsy revealed a large quantity of alcohol in the child's blood. Elise swore by all that was holy that Monsieur Emile had gone out perfectly sober, for the simple reason that there wasn't a drop of alcohol in the house that night. Who, then, had provided him with drink? "Ratablavasky, who else?" Picquot roared. "Just as he kidnapped the cat and put it up on the roof to lure that poor child."

In three days the chef had aged ten years; the bags under his eyes had grown so big that they could each hold a nickel.

Inspector Dorion, in charge of the investigation, listened politely but skeptically to their explanations. First of all, where *was* this Ratablavasky? The Hotel Nelson hadn't seen him for ages, though his rent was paid up for several months. The hotel owner claimed he'd returned to his own country – though he didn't know what country that was! And then the business about the old man kidnapping a cat, getting a little boy drunk and using the cat to lure him up on a roof – it sounded like bad Rocambole.

With the help of young Philippe Saint-Onge, they found an open bottle of rum that someone had been into, bearing Monsieur Emile's fingerprints, but no one could determine where it had come from. In any case, it wouldn't have been the first time the child resorted to theft to quench his thirst. In the eyes of the police, the matter came down to a lost cat followed by an unfortunate accident, for which the pathological state of the child provided a full explanation.

Florent decided then to produce a note written by Ratablavasky, which he'd found in rather unusual circumstances.

Some hours after the death of Monsieur Emile, Florent had gone to the Hotel Nelson intending to kill his enemy.

He used the key he'd wangled from the housekeeper to let himself in, but found the apartment empty. However, Ratablavasky still seemed to be living there: clothing, furniture, books, knickknacks, and everyday objects all were there. The monstrous ferns that had made such an impression on his first visit were growing as vigorously as ever. Trembling with fear, Florent walked through the silent rooms that seemed filled with an invisible, evil presence. As he entered the kitchenette he saw an envelope on a table. And his name was on it! With trembling hand he tore it open and removed a sheet of paper. It bore only these few words:

> Dear Monsieur Florent,
>
> I am desolated not to be at the appointment. But I am sure that even alone, you will get along with perfection. In the pleasure of seeing you again one day soon,
>
> E.R.

He was choked with anxiety. He felt Ratablavasky's eye on him at that very moment. He had to leave right away, without conducting the search he'd promised himself.

He returned to the hotel the next day and tried unsuccessfully to bribe the fat desk clerk. He didn't want much: just to be told when the old man arrived. Eyes lowered, the clerk shook his head with a frightened little smile, taking cover behind childish excuses. Florent spat a curse and left. Now he was certain: taking the offensive would always escape him, no matter what he did.

With raised eyebrows, Inspector Dorion gazed at the note, unimpressed. "Very interesting," he said at length, "except for one small detail: this note is dated last year!"

"Is that so?" Florent murmured, grimacing in dismay.

He wouldn't even glance at it.

The restaurant reopened the day after the funeral. No one felt brave enough to remain idle any longer. Monsieur Emile's possessions were sealed in a box and stuck at the back of a closet; and despite all her demands, Madame Chouinard was never able to reclaim them.

At this point, Florent received a letter from Madame Jeunehomme. His aunt had learned that he'd finally been successful with the new restaurant and rejoiced at the news of Slipskin's collapse. "I have just one thing to say," she wrote. "In a few days my lawyer will be sending the papers that will make you owner of the plantation, as promised. I hope to have the pleasure of seeing all of you soon – you, your wife, and your bundle of joy. Until then, I'll take care of your property as well as I can. The profits will be deposited in the bank of your choosing."

Florent wrote a long letter of thanks and assured her that as soon as Elise's condition and his business permitted, they would come to visit her in Key West.

Something he didn't feel it necessary to add was that the end of Elise's pregnancy was especially difficult, aggravated by the prostration in which Monsieur Emile's death had left her. The first contractions began, harbingers of the labor that would soon leave her exhausted on the delivery table. Her stomach, squeezed by the fetus, produced only heartburn and gas. Her legs, with their varicose veins, caused her constant pain. An immense fatigue, aggravated by the summer heat, kept her in bed for long hours when she could only gasp for breath and ponder sad events.

One Sunday night, Aurélien Picquot dropped in – with Emilienne Latouche! She was a plump lady well into her fifties, with remarkably abundant blonde curls and a starlet's makeup. ("How old do you think I am?" she would ask as soon as she felt comfortable with people.) Mademoiselle Latouche was timid and gently playful, with a deep, melodious voice and slightly affected manners. Such a perfect contrast to Picquot provoked smiles and inclined people to be optimistic, as they recalled that when opposites attract they protect each other from their excesses.

"You poor dear thing, I took the liberty of bringing you a little something," cooed Mademoiselle Emilienne, handing Elise a box. "If I can help to dry your pretty eyes, nothing would make me happier."

Elise unwrapped the package and admired six finely embroidered batiste handkerchiefs.

"Very thoughtful, don't you think?" Picquot whispered to Florent. "And she's almost always like that. Without her, I'd have been a goner ages ago."

After Monsieur Emile's death, Breakfast stayed on at the apartment. Florent, grief stricken at the sight of the cat, talked about getting rid of him, but Elise was fiercely opposed. Do cats have a form of intelligence that humans, with all their naive egocentricity, underestimate? Whatever the case may be, Breakfast seemed as affected as the others by his master's death. He spent most of his time under Monsieur Emile's bed. Once or twice a day he would slip into the kitchen, pick at his food, and ask to be let out. He accepted caresses only from Elise, and that rarely. Virtue, despite her placid disposition and goodwill, couldn't come near him. The cat could be seen sometimes prowling in the lane, meowing. Was it a coincidence?

Ange-Albert saw him one day lying against a wall near the spot where the child had fallen. He was careful not to breathe a word to anyone. The atmosphere in the apartment was hard enough to bear as it was.

The restaurant continued to prosper, but Florent had to force himself to pay attention to his business. Bizarre ideas went through his mind. He found himself wondering, for example, if he were engaged in a struggle against the forces of another world.

"That's rubbish!" Picquot told him one day. "Come now! Only imbeciles take such twaddle seriously. What you need is a good dose of rationalism. Diderot, Voltaire, Renan – that's who you should be spending your time with! Listen to me: we've simply got mixed up with a supremely clever maniac, and our duty is to outsmart him."

A few days later – August 28, to be exact – someone made a brave attempt to fulfill that duty under rather odd circumstances.

About mid-morning, Ange-Albert, who had recently been spending a lot of time away from Montreal – for reasons he didn't divulge – came to the restaurant and drew Florent aside.

"Could you lend me your truck for a week?" he asked, blushing. "I want to take a trip down to the ocean."

Florent gave him a surprised look, then an ironic smile lit up his face. "Aha! A pleasure trip. Right?"

"Yes," said his friend, looking away, blushing a deeper red. "A very important pleasure trip."

"That's why I'm a little uncomfortable. I use the truck every day. When would you want to go?"

"Right away."

Florent peered at him, puzzled. "Well, well! Where's the old drag-ass I used to know? Okay, go ahead, take it. I'll work something out. But be sure you bring it back on Thursday morning. I have to see my produce supplier."

Ange-Albert thanked his friend with an effusiveness that was most surprising and went away, beaming.

An hour later, Picquot muttered, "I'm out of vanilla beans. And I must have some immediately or my cream will be spoiled."

Florent went to the corner grocery. Then to a second. And a third. Half an hour later, he had to face facts: the neighborhood was awash in vanilla extract, but there was not a single bean to be found. He wasn't up to suggesting that Picquot make do with extract. "It's going to be a long week," he muttered, looking for a taxi to take him to a fancy food store on Laurier Street.

It was nearly noon by the time he headed back to the restaurant. And that was when events took an unexpected turn. A voice on the radio receiver in the taxi said, "1226 Emery. And move it – sounds urgent."

"That's our place!" Florent exclaimed. "Hurry up!"

The driver, dozing behind dark glasses, wiped out by the heat and his three hundred pounds steaming on the seat, turned to Florent and asked, "Where's that?" his lips barely moving.

"Emery Street, 1226," said the voice on the radio, with a hint of laughter this time. "Sounds like there's a baby on the way."

The taxi made a U-turn up over the curb, then sped toward the apartment.

"And to think at his age I was just as frisky," the taxi-driver said to himself as he watched Florent bound up the stairs.

"Elise!" he yelled, flinging open the door.

Virtue greeted him with hysterical barks, running around and around. There were wet towels in the bathroom, another on the bed. "It's started," he murmured, heading for the door. "She's gone into labor."

He stops suddenly. Virtue sits on the landing, petrified.

Footsteps are ascending the stairs. Florent sticks his head out, then jerks it back, white as a sheet. He brings his hand to his pocket, takes out a revolver and waits, focusing on the dark rectangle of the door. "This morning, my friend," says Ratablavasky's singsong voice as he continues his slow climb, "I am allowing myself to examine the revolver in your jacket pocket, for I had the desire to talk with you in full comfort. You may pull the trigger," he says, standing in the doorway, a cardboard box in his hand, "but I am much fearing that, as the military say, the bullets have lost their wings. How are you, dear young friend?"

Florent stares, eyes dilated with hatred.

"Your wife, I trust, still enjoys the blessings of health?" the old man goes on, his voice unctuous and dripping gravity.

With clenched teeth, Florent looks around for something to replace the revolver.

From somewhere in the apartment comes a faint sound of scratching. Ratablavasky advances. A look of sickly sweet sorrow crosses his face, while the vile odor that follows him everywhere gradually fills the room. "I have learned that a frightful accident has struck down poor Monsieur Emile. I read in the newspapers."

On the table a few feet away, Florent has just spotted a pair of scissors half hidden under a piece of embroidery. "I come, in fact, to bring a small tribute – with much lateness, I agree – to be placed on his tomb."

He lifted the lid with his left hand, revealing a funeral wreath trimmed with a silver ribbon and gold lettering that read:

TO MONSIEUR EMILE

The joke was so grotesquely cynical that Florent couldn't help snickering. The old man was preparing to show him something else when Florent flung himself at the table, picked up the scissors, and threw them at the door with all his strength. The points sank into the frame two inches from Ratablavasky's head. Still smiling, Ratablavasky set his box on the floor, pulled out the scissors, and shut the door behind him. "I permit myself to sit," he said, going to the armchair. "Without the inconvenience, isn't it, of being struck in the eye by a paper clipping. You remember the last time?"

Florent recoils, eyes wild, looking for something else to throw. "I desire," Ratablavasky continues, slowly turning the scissors in his hands, "I desire to tell you a long story . . . that will perhaps make you a little afraid . . . but *it will leave your spirit in the greatest clarity*. Please to sit on this chair facing me."

Leaning against Monsieur Emile's bedroom door, Florent does not move. The faint scratching comes from the other side. It's Breakfast, wanting to be let out. The silence is filled with a grave, muffled hatred. Ratablavasky's voice has put into the cat's brain a very simple idea, opaque as a ball of lead, that slowly rolls and pushes the animal to the door.

Intrigued, the old man raises his head. "Ah yes, I recognize," he says at once. "The poor child's cat, isn't it?"

Florent shudders. He bites his lips, perplexed. After all, he thinks, what have I got to lose? It'll be a diversion.

And while Ratablavasky launches into a hazy preamble broken by sighs and cackles, Florent moves his hand around his back, feigning the utmost attention. His fingers tighten around the doorknob and a furry mass bursts into the room, hurling itself at the old man, who throws up his hands and screams.

Florent jerks forward, aghast, and stares at the whirling claws that swoop down at the face of his enemy, who howls in terror. The scissors fly through the air and land on the floor, while blood spurts all over. Ratablavasky attempts one last defence with his bare hands, which are promptly covered with gashes, then he falls backward, wheezing, his knees in the air, feet grotesquely pointing at each other.

In two leaps the cat is under the table, staring fiercely at his victim. Ratablavasky's face is a bleeding pulp. Leaning against the doorpost, Florent vomits, then goes to the kitchen for a big glass of water.

Strange gurgling sounds come from the old man's mouth as he slumps against the armchair. Florent approaches him, torn between horror and hateful glee. "That's Monsieur Emile's answer to your wreath."

"Help me," the old man murmurs in a dying voice.

Florent looks at him briefly, then his gaze falls on the scissors. He bends down, picks them up, moves toward the armchair. Then he stops, disgusted. The notion of cutting his enemy's throat is repugnant.

He goes back to the kitchen and opens the door to the back stairs to let the cat out. Then he leaves the apartment, utterly drained. He will never set foot in it again. He'll call the police from the hospital. The hospital? And what if Elise isn't there! Kidnap Elise: Ratablavasky's final revenge!

Florent starts running crazily toward the Saint-Luc Hospital three blocks away. He turns his head at a familiar clicking sound: it is Virtue, openmouthed, ears flat against her skull, following at his heels. Passersby laugh at the sight, probably thinking the dog is chasing him. Florent, though, is worried sick: Ratablavasky's arrival just a few moments after Elise's departure strikes him as an unlikely coincidence. Hideous images go through his mind. He jostles a passerby, pushes between two lovers and runs faster and faster, as if he were borne by the wind. The heavy traffic on Dorchester Boulevard, which he must cross to reach the hospital, has become a pure abstraction for him.

Ligoris Beaubois, aged twenty-six, a truck driver employed by the United Canada Company (specialty, barbed wire), slams on his brakes to avoid the young lunatic and his dog who act as if they're being pursued by a colony of killer bees. He briefly loses control of his vehicle and ravages the grassy boulevard that separates the two lanes of traffic.

"No way! Dogs aren't allowed in the hospital!" a security guard exclaims, making his way toward them.

Florent bends down, picks up Virtue, and heads breathlessly for the information desk. "Boissonneault . . . Elise Boissonneault . . . Maternity . . . Hurry."

The young girl looks at him, startled, then goes through her records. "Boissonneault, you say? Elise?"

"Yes. Hurry."

"No one here by that name." Then, seeing the expression on Florent's face, "Good heavens, what's wrong?"

"It's . . . it's my wife," he stammers, tears running down his face.

"When did she come to the hospital? Here, take this Kleenex."

"An hour ago . . . three-quarters of an hour . . . I don't know."

"Perhaps she went straight to Emergency. Wait, I'll call."

Florent cannot wait. He shouts to an orderly who tells him where the maternity ward is, and stumbles up the stairs.

A horrified nurse, warned by the admissions clerk, is waiting for him on the landing. "Monsieur Boissonneault? Relax, relax. . . . Your wife's up here – in the labor room. About time you got here – she's been waiting for you for an hour. Follow me. And for heaven's sake, calm down! You'll frighten her with that look on your face!"

Florent scrubs his hands, dons a sterile gown, and follows the nurse. Elise, pale and drawn, is lying on a bed in a nearly bare room dominated by a big wall clock. When she sees Florent she smiles, enormously relieved, and takes his hand. "Where were you? What's the matter? What's going on?"

"Nothing . . . nothing," Florent stammers.

He leans over and kisses her, his throat muscles dreadfully tense and sore from fighting back tears. "I went out . . . to buy vanilla beans. . . . I . . . I got lost."

A second wave of relief passes over Elise's face. She is utterly serene now – as serene as one can be during childbirth! A contraction makes her grimace. "Help me now," she says, panting. "I waited so long for you."

Two hours later she brings into the world a perfectly formed little girl weighing seven pounds, three ounces, who seems most unhappy about all the pushing and shoving she's just been subjected to. Dazed, Florent looks at her. A nurse lays the baby in his arms. He holds her for a moment, rather frightened, then places her on Elise's stomach. Tears are flowing again, but this time he doesn't try to hold them back. His male pride is safe: many fathers – even the toughest – weep at the first sight of their offspring. It's accepted practice.

People bustle around Elise, who feels as if she's been scattered to the four corners of the room like dandelion silk in the wind. She speaks softly with her husband, while little Florence, crimson-faced, nurses with feverish intensity as her parents look on in wonder.

Suddenly Florent feels an unpleasant pinching in his chest: he's completely forgotten to call the police. What a chore. His legs don't want to move. The delivery room, with all its forbidding equipment, seems like an oasis. If he could, he'd lie down in a corner by his wife and child and sleep for two solid days.

"All right," says the policeman on the phone, gnawing on an apple core, "we'll send someone right away. Are you there?"

"No, I'm at the Saint-Luc Hospital. My wife just gave birth to a girl," he adds, though he's not sure why. Then he returns to Elise. "I've got some great news."

Sparing her the harshest details, he tells her about his latest adventure with Ratablavasky. "It's over now. He'll never recover. I'm sure he's lost his sight."

Elise, in a feeble voice, says something quite remarkable for a new mother. "If I'd been you I'd have finished him off."

Florent looks at her and laughs nervously. "Good grief, you're even fiercer than Breakfast!"

"Where is he? I want to see him. Go get him."

Florent shakes his head, grimacing, then, seeing Elise's look, gives in. "Okay, I'll look in the lane. But I'm never setting foot in that apartment again. I'll hire movers to take our furniture out."

Oddly enough, it was four days before the police came looking for Florent. The interview took place at the restaurant one night after closing. Picquot had insisted on taking part, claiming he had revelations of the utmost importance. (They never heard a word of them.) Florent was amazed at the investigators' attitude. It was as if they'd come to see him only as a matter of form. Their uneasiness was as plain as the noses on their faces. From their vague, innocuous questions it was obvious they just wanted to close the file. Florent pointed out that Ratablavasky had been torturing him, his wife, and his friends for more than two years, that he'd killed a child and was probably responsible for much more damage, as well. The case warranted an in-depth investigation, and he offered his full cooperation.

"Come, gentlemen, let's show some spirit!" said Picquot. "The man is an imposter, a murderer, a crook, and no doubt a spy, as well. What else do you need?"

"Are you trying to tell me how to do my job?" replied Captain Barbin, cut to the quick.

"Have you seen him, at least?" asked Florent.

The captain nodded.

"How is he?"

"Pretty badly chewed up. If I were you I'd stop worrying about him. But have your cat put down!"

"Where is the cat, anyway?" asked Detective-Sergeant Blaireau.

Florent shrugged. "Disappeared."

The policemen exchanged a smile, sure he was lying. But neither of them was tempted to pick up that particular cat by the scruff of the neck.

Elise and Florent rented a lovely apartment on Sherbrooke Street near St-Denis (six rooms, stained-glass windows, fireplace) in an old stone building that stood three stories high, beside a five-hundred-foot-tall balconied mastodon completed three weeks earlier. There was another unpleasant surprise for them, too: from their bedroom window they could see the roof from which Monsieur Emile had fallen to his death. Immediately, Elise talked of moving.

"Be patient, kiddo," Florent told her. "We won't be here forever. We'll get through this winter, then I promise you our own nice little house on the South Shore."

Ange-Albert's week of holidays with Rosine paid off. One day he brought her to the restaurant to announce their decision to have another go at life together. Shortly after that, he got back his old job at Draperies Georgette, which had just reopened, and started taking night courses in cabinetmaking. In a word, he was settling down, which brought him a certain amount of teasing.

Father Jeunehomme was slowly recovering from his cruel disappointment at being unable to resurrect the second part of *Dead Souls*. In September, he had a marvelous idea to celebrate the memory of Philippe Aubert de Gaspé, author of *Canadians of Old*: a banquet in an eighteenth-century Québécois seigneurial setting to be restored for the occasion. For the menu, he drew from the sixth chapter: "Supper with a Canadian *Seigneur*." For a week everyone read the old novel so they could hold their own in conversation, then made their way to Jean-Denis Beaumont's boutique, transformed into a seigneurial dining room for the occasion. The antiquarian-decorator had worked wonders and drew warm congratulations. The chef from Le Quinquet had prepared an Easter pâté: turkey, chicken, partridge, hare, and pigeons, covered in fat pork, wrapped in a thick crust, and resting on a forcemeat seasoned with onions and delicate spices. The dish had people talking about its cook long afterward. The old-fashioned, fragrant charm of *Canadians of Old*, long sections of which were read during the meal, combined with the wine, fine fare and entertaining jokes to create a luminous atmosphere that took the priest to the heights of ecstasy. When the meal was over he raised his long thin hand to ask for silence.

"Friends, I invite you to another celebration next month, this time to honor Flaubert. We shall try to relive, through our minds and our palates, the wedding feast of Emma Bovary, which is described in the fourth chapter, if I recall correctly."

In early October Picquot had to go to the hospital because of overwork and high blood pressure. Mademoiselle Emilienne went to visit him every day, long enough to read him all of *The Count of Monte Cristo*, which the chef maintained was a veritable balm for his frazzled nerves. When he came back to the restaurant he had an assistant.

"To prove how much I need you," Florent told him. "You're the soul of this establishment."

Florent was increasingly taken up with his work. The cosmetics project had resurfaced. He had contacted a chemist and given him two hundred pounds of grapefruit leaves with which to perfect a beauty cream.

Slipskin, who had opened a restaurant in Toronto, made a brief reappearance on Mont-Royal Street, to see to the liquidation of his business. Florent allowed himself one last bit of mischief, going through an intermediary to purchase The Beanery's sign. The champagne toasts lasted all night.

Florent's trials had toughened him. Elise noted, not without sorrow, that his youthful candor had been replaced by dry, taut ambition. "I've acquired a taste for winning," he said, "even if it means getting my hands dirty. Besides, is there such a thing as happiness that's perfectly clean?"

Two days after leaving the hospital, Picquot ran into Captain Galarneau on the street. He looked him up and down with the utmost contempt. "My word, Captain, you're certainly dragging yourself around. You wouldn't by chance have fallen on hard times?"

"Of course not, you old stuffed shirt! I'm as gay as a bird."

"Be that as it may, there's one individual who has received his just desserts! In fact I wouldn't be surprised to learn that, even now, he's roasting over the eternal coals."

Captain Galarneau, who, uncharacteristically, was perfectly sober, approached the chef with a broad smile and clasped his shoulder in a gesture of familiarity that turned Picquot scarlet. "Sorry to disappoint you, old turkey trusser," he said in a ringing voice, "but Ratablavasky (or rather Monsieur Robichaud – hee, hee!) isn't in nearly as bad shape as you'd like. He's gone back to the Old Country to be taken care of. With his money, you can do amazing things. In fact, you might see him one of these days, back sniffing the fine air on Mont-Royal Street."

He pinched Picquot's chin in his gnarled fingers and walked away laughing, while the chef, beside himself, bombarded him with projectiles, striking the back of his head with a chunk of wood, which had the bizarre effect of increasing his hilarity.

Had Captain Galarneau told the truth, or was he just enjoying torturing Picquot – and, by extension, his friends – to avenge Ratablavasky's suffering, or even, who knows, his death? Florent engaged in lengthy research to find out what had become of the old man, but with no results.

Winter has returned. It is one o'clock in the morning. In the building where Elise and Florent live, a solemn half light prevails, filled with creaking sounds and dark areas that one approaches only with outstretched hands. Only the old rococo lobby, silent and empty, casts a dim light onto the street that gives a waxen color to the snow. The wind whips it into clouds that bring a grimace to a dejected passerby who has lost his way in the neighborhood. A heavily laden tow truck lumbers up a hill. The motor screams, as if its burning entrails are about to burst. Lying at the foot of little Florence's bed, Virtue opens one eye for a worried look around the room, sighs briefly, and rests her muzzle between her paws. Night has become, for her, something difficult and complicated that requires great patience to get through.

In the bedroom, where Elise and Florent are fast asleep, Breakfast is awake on the windowsill, staring into the distance. His green eyes with their fine streaks of gold, in which there gleam unfathomable black pupils, might make you think that certain memories still cause him pain.

AFTERWORD

BY KENNETH RADU

There is a moment towards the end of *The Alley Cat* when Yves Beauchemin offers a possible reading of his text to account for the seemingly random and picaresque surface of his savagely funny, often disturbing narrative. The beleaguered hero, Florent Boissonneault, consults a lawyer, Rodrigue Théorêt, to find a legal means to escape the clutches of the arch-manipulator, Egon Ratablavasky. To the unimaginative lawyer's ears, the account of Florent and his friends "sounded like a fabric of preposterous adventures that owed more to literary fantasy than reality, and he even wondered if the three people in his office were mildly unhinged."

Baldly summarized by an exasperated victim of byzantine machinations, the plot and colourful incidents of *The Alley Cat* may well sound incredible. Théorêt, however, unwittingly touches the mainspring of *The Alley Cat*. For a novel emerging out of that most subtle, complex, and paradoxical of Canadian cities, Montreal, fantasy may well be a perfectly reasonable means of literary expression.

Improbable incidents pile on top of one another at a near breathless pace until their very improbability suggests not only tensions and contradictions beneath the exuberant comedy, but also coherence and moral vision sustaining the narrative art. Perhaps fantasy, with its origins in myth and folklore, allows for the mixture of the miraculous and the mundane, the orderly and the chaotic in a way that realism generally avoids.

Combined with its energetic narrative voice so aptly and unobtrusively translated by the gifted Sheila Fischman, the rambunctious plot may partly explain the universal critical and popular acclaim which greeted the novel upon its first publication. From the opening scene where a pedestrian is hit on the head by a "bronze quotation mark," to the brilliant satire of the Florida chapters, to the shocking, memorable last scenes so incredible and yet, within the context of the novel, so convincing as to be "real," one is struck by the relentless action, the powerful pull of the story as story, and by the extraordinary range of somewhat eccentric characters who threaten to run riot over the pages.

A marvellous character inhabits these pages, one Father Jeunehomme, the quintessential bookworm who has made literature his God and who is in quest of Gogol's stove, where supposedly the strange Russian writer burned the second part of *Dead Souls*. Cousin to the distinctly unliterary and modern Florent, his own mother converting a Victorian mansion in Florida into a hotel, Father Jeunehomme contributes to Beauchemin's mordant satire of the Quebec clergy, as do the other priests in the novel, and reveals the author's Gogolian sense of surrealist humour and incident. He also embodies two of the basic moral positions of *The Alley Cat*: a passion for the past alienated from the demands of the present can quickly transform itself into pedantry or psychopathology;

and the individual separated from the vital, contemporary world of eros, food, friendship, community, and economics (all of which abound in *The Alley Cat*) is soon diminished, however endearing, to one-dimensional self-parody. This intense insistence on physicality in Beauchemin becomes noticeable in the novel's incisive descriptions of people and place and in the many references to smells and bodily functions.

If one recalls Gogol's short stories, "The Nose," for example, or "The Overcoat," one will recognize the tradition from which Beauchemin draws at least some of his inspiration. If his characterization is Dickensian to some degree wherein a complex state of mind is represented by a physical attribute and/or habit, and if his plot is as convoluted and sprawling as anything found in Dickens, his sense of the real and his instinct for the vagaries of plot are so intensified and accelerated that the real becomes transformed, like Montreal in a blizzard, into a world of ambiguity and miracle where, as in Gogol, unexpected things happen with no apparent logic.

In a novel about a young man, taken in hand by a seemingly kindly older, foreign gentleman, and encouraged to invest time and money (borrowed from the bank) in a restaurant to be called The Beanery, food necessarily plays a large role, not to mention matters of finance. It is thanks to Beauchemin's estimable skill as a storyteller, however, that the novel does not sink into a bog of economic and fiscal details.

Readers will remember that *The Alley Cat* was originally written and published during the efflorescence of national pride and cultural consciousness of contemporary Quebec. The Parti Québécois had won its first mandate just five years earlier, and the concept of *maîtres chez nous* had ceased to be an inspirational slogan and had, in fact, become the reality of the new Quebec. It is not surprising that Florent is no respecter of traditional authority: the church, the police, old bureaucracies. In an effort to raise sufficient money to regain his position in the economic battlefield, he is not above unscrupulous practices in rural Quebec, where he begins collecting old Quebec furniture for financial gain and not for its cultural significance.

Florent's spirit of entrepreneurship, encouraged at first and later sabotaged by the foreigner, surely represents the economic spirit and the francization of wealth. Whether Ratablavasky, consistently identified by the foul odour emitted by his feet, is truly foreign is not entirely clear (one character suggests that his real name is Ernest Robichaud). He is perceived to have originated outside the parish, as it were. During the course of the book, the wrenches Ratablavasky throws into the works, the dismay and havoc he causes poor Florent and his long-suffering, patient wife, Elise, who tries throughout the novel to get and to stay pregnant long enough to give birth, are fictional equivalents of the forces that cultural nationalism and, to some degree, parochialism must overcome to establish themselves firmly on their own terrain. For that reason Ratablavasky is more mythic than real, more a malevolent presence than a human being, despite his odoriferous extremities, a kind of fairy-tale evil magician who has the remarkable habit of appearing when least expected (in Florida, for example), and who delights in slapping the mouth that feeds from his hand.

Similarly, Beauchemin's less than complimentary portrayal of Len Slipskin, the anglo *tête carrée* and one-time partner of Florent who joins with the foreigner and conspires against The Beanery and his former associate, reflects Québécois anxiety about French survival in the modern business world dominated, as the convenient legend in Quebec goes, by somewhat demonized Anglo-Quebecers and English-speaking North Americans.

As with any picaresque hero, Florent meets a host of varied and interesting characters who impinge on his life and ambitions. Like Dickens, Beauchemin makes characters vivid through physical gesture, costume, or voice. In addition to Father Jeunehomme, there is the master chef Picquot, the amorous layabout Ange-Albert, who works for a while in a factory producing erotic-religious statuary, Florent's father, who is building a sailboat in his basement, Gladu the journalist, Aunt Jeunehomme and other Quebecers of Florida who are not spared Beauchemin's satirical pen in the superbly realized central portion of *The Alley Cat*, and, most notably, Monsieur Emile.

A child alcoholic of six, tragically neglected by his prostitute mother, an erratic, volatile boy who comes and goes at will, a haunter of alleyways with his own cat, the aptly named Breakfast, Emile is a brilliant creation who contributes much of the novel's rowdy humour and much of its pathos.

Virtually undomesticated like his cat, Emile is possibly the real alley cat of the novel, at least psychologically. In French *le matou* indeed means a common male cat, but specifically *un chat non châtré*, a cat not castrated. Feral, independent of spirit, howling, prowling, demanding affection, seeking a home, attached to none, Emile becomes intricately involved in Florent's and Elise's efforts to create a family in a decidedly haphazard, disruptive, and eruptive world.

Nothing appears to be settled or safe in Montreal or even in Florida, where Florent acquires managerial skills in the reconstruction of his aunt's mansion. Trucks appear suddenly and dangerously, threatening pedestrians; buildings are dilapidated or under construction; the best laid plans are demolished by either whim or calculation of the nefarious Ratablavasky. Apparent randomness and the improbability of incident become signs of unchannelled energies, frustrations, ambitions and dreams almost realized, of uneasy transformations in political and personal life.

For that reason food, which I mentioned earlier, with its connotations of hunger, desire, consumption, satisfaction, and realization, acts as a structural and symbolic device throughout the novel. If Picquot is a remarkable character in his own right, he is also the one most closely associated with the role of food in *The Alley Cat.* Nor is it merely coincidental that he takes a special interest in the hungriest character of the novel, the child Emile.

The overcoming of the forces arrayed against Florent and his friends is also, appropriately enough, associated with food. In the metaphoric blood-bath of the final chapters, Beauchemin produces a stunning scene which may well read as a piece of melodrama, but which, if one follows the novel's Gogolian, surrealist logic, releases and reconciles the underlying tensions of the novel. In these gripping chapters, undomesticated child, cat, food, the demolition and reconstruction of Montreal, cold economics and passionate emotion, good and evil, fantasy and reality converge and combust in a bravura piece of narrative inevitability and art.

BY YVES BEAUCHEMIN

AUTOBIOGRAPHY

Du sommet d'un arbre [From the Treetop] (1986)

FICTION

L'Enfirouapé [The Bamboozled] (1974)

Le Matou [The Alley Cat] (1981)

Cybèle [Cybèle] (1982)

Juliette Pomerleau [Juliette] (1989)

FICTION FOR YOUNG ADULTS

Une histoire à faire japper [The Dog That Could Write] (1991)

Antoine et Alfred [Antoine and Alfred] (1992)